Fetish Galore!

BarbarianSpy

BarbarianSpy
FOR LITERARY HEAT

Published by BarbarianSpy
Jindalee St
Toronto, NSW 2283
AUSTRALIA

Fetish Galore!

A Gay Fetish Anthology from

Habu

Table of Contents

Introduction

This monster value pack anthology of over 80 stories, many of which have never been published before, from the pen of premier anthologist habu, explores the concept of gay male sexual fetishes. Included are stories indexed to 40 fetishes that meet the broadest definition of fetish: obsession with the unusual in sexual gratification.

A survey of readers and practitioners has revealed almost as many separate understandings of what a fetish is as there were respondents, with some opining that "anything goes" and can be included beyond the missionary and others believing that only a limited number of practices can be considered unusual in this regard. A frequent mention of the latter was the requirement that a nonsexual object come into play in the process (which accords with one of the definitions in the Urban Dictionary).

When a list of what people thought was a gay male fetish started to build, however, there were far more than the 40 indexed in this anthology. When habu got to bacon, he decided to close the list and to deal with only the most frequently cited examples. However, he also decided to go with the broader definition rather than a narrow one, because, at the end of the day, a fetish is very personal. It's what arouses and becomes obsessive and services the gratification needs of the individual.

So, the 40 indexed fetishes (others beyond the indexed ones creep in, of course, and are included in the indexes at the back of the book) offered in the more than 80 stories of *Fetish Galore!* are more of a foundation and a beginning for gay male readers than a comprehensive "end all." Fetishes are faddish; ten years from now habu assumes he could put together an anthology of 80 more stories indexed to 40 fetishes and many of the fetishes would be different from these and some would be ones not now known, tried, or obsessed over. Like bacon, for instance.

For ease in locating your favorite fetishes, the stories of this anthology are arranged by primary story fetish alphabetically in the table of contents and also alphabetically by story title in one index at the back of the book and by fetish in another index. In these indexes all fetishes covered in the story are identified, not just the featured one represented in the table of contents.

The initial, uncategorized, signature "Fetish Galore" story is an unabashed tongue-in-cheek romp at including as many fetishes—over 40 in this case—in one story.

If your favorite gay male fetishes are not included in this anthology, it may well be time for you to take up pen and start writing fetish stories of your own. And don't hold the bacon.

Fetish Galore

I had been banished. My wife would be joining me in a couple of months, but I was sent ahead—banished from New York—for my transgressions. April's father had known I was bi before he bought me for her daughter—and he also knew how I made my living, because he had been paying April's bills. But I suppose he assumed I would put all of that behind me when we were married. Look as I could, though, I couldn't find that clause in the prenuptial agreement. And the prenup had been voluminous, I can tell you.

I think he was surprised that April still wanted me after what happened in New York. But I was better looking and smarter than she was, so I guess she still considered me something she wanted on her arm and pulling her chair from the table for her and carrying her handbag on command, and smiling dreamily at her whenever and forever when she wanted to impress someone. She also considered me the perfect fit. The small, forever-young couple. She was barely five foot, and I came in only at five-four, and just as she would forever look like a teenager, I was likely to look barely nineteen and not yet having my age spurt well into my thirties. We both must have been graced with Fountain of Youth genes. In my case, women and men were willing to pay extra for the sensation that they were plucking the baby from the cradle for the first time. And I was good at making it seem to be the first time.

April must have also liked the first-time sensation, as she wasn't willing to let me go no matter what her father had caught me doing. That being the case, there wasn't much else Fred could do but get us out of town for a while—mainly me. He couldn't make too big of a stink about it. The guy who was fucking me and had bought me that Jaguar was farther up the feeding chain at Vado U.S. Pharmaceuticals than Fred was.

The pharmaceutical company president had been sniffing around me even before I met April. Indeed, it was at a party of his that I had first met Fred's daughter. The company president liked to role play. He paid ahead and I was sent to perch on a seat in the bar of a fancy Manhattan hotel until he showed up and sat down the bar from me and acted like each time was the first time. He'd notice me—for the first time—and would start with sending a drink my way and then making eye contact when I looked around to see who my benefactor was. And then the dance of seduction, as he conveyed in his eyes what he wanted and I pretended not to understand at first and then to blush. Sometimes he took it so slow that I had to politely ward off another suitor before the Vado U.S. president got around to sliding into the seat beside me and whispering what he wanted in my ear and how much he was willing to pay—which was above what the escort service was charging him so there was always a generous tip in it for me.

I would pretend that I wasn't "that sort" of person, but he would wear me down with sweet talk. I'd tell him he was handsome—which he wasn't; he was ugly as sin and slightly overweight, but he had a cock to die for—a girth that even I could feel, because, although I was slight of stature—while being quite well-muscled proportionately—I had developed a hole and channel that could take a military missile upon demand. Few men singularly tested that hole, so I usually had to put on a good act while being taken. But with the pharmaceutical company president I didn't have to pretend my channel was being taxed.

When I had demurely given in to his seduction, he took me for a ride around the city in the back of his limousine. I would strip down to the red brassiere and sheer panties he had specified beforehand as soon as we entered the backseat and the limo door clicked shut—while he stripped off his trousers and briefs as well, and, as always, I gasped at the size of him and gave a low moan. I would have done this for the client anyway, but in his case each time it was a revelation.

He would lean over and wrap an arm around my shoulder to hold me tight and, with a tube of ruby-red lipstick, he'd generously slather my lips. Then I went down on my knees between his spread legs and left as much of the red from the lipstick covering his cock while, jaws unhinged, I gave him a languid blow job—to the point where he was ready to explode. And then he'd lift my small body up from the floor of the car, rip at the sheer panties until they gave way, and take me into his lap—always facing away from him—and slowly lower my channel on his blunderbuss of a dick. He would come almost immediately, but then he held me there, his hands covering my nipples underneath the cups of the bra, and I would rise and fall on his cock while he murmured the name of some woman in the small of my back until I brought him back to life for a second coming.

Sometime thereafter—when we had both readjusted our clothing, I was delivered back to the hotel where he had "met" me. Each encounter started at a different hotel.

As time went on and he got bored with this, he wanted to do it right there in the hotel bar lounges. I'd meet him at the bar and we'd go through the preliminary ritual but rather than going somewhere in his limousine, he'd guide me to an already-booked table back in the shadows of the lounge and I'd go under the table and suck him off while bar life went on around us. Then there were the nights he'd call me on the telephone and I had to make him get off just by talking to him over the telephone.

The first time I met April was at an office Christmas party the Vado U.S. president held in his lavish Manhattan penthouse. I had been hired for the little party he was having afterward for a few very select male friends. The earlier segment of the party was all noise and clinking glasses and women checking out what other women had worn, and talk of the Hamptons and Paris in the spring.

I had gone out to the terrace because I found the crowd oppressive, when a young woman, smaller than I was, which was a surprise, came up beside me where I was standing at the railing and looking down into the bustling world of the city.

"I can't take the crowd, either," she said. She bordered on pretty, but only because she had the best of help money could buy to make her so. Her body was in good shape, though.

"Excuse me?" I said.

"You came out because you found all of that oppressive. Bulky people towering over you and pushing you underfoot. Or did I misjudge?"

14

"No. That's right, I guess. Right on, actually."

"Same with me. I feel like I'm going to be swallowed up. It will improve within a half hour. Most of them just came to check in and mark off their presence. This is an office party. The room will thin out soon. Do you work for Vado U.S.?"

I honestly was able to say yes, as the Vado U.S. president had put me on the payroll. I had no idea which branch I supposedly worked in or what my job supposedly was there—but I did have an office. As far as I could tell, though, I only had an office to give the president a break in his day. It would start with either phone or cyber sex—him contacting me in my office. My job—my only job for the company as far as I could determine—was to get him so worked up over the phone or on the Internet that he'd either show up in my office for a fuck or summon me to his office.

"I don't," April said. "My dad does. Fred. Fred Tipton. He's one of the national vice presidents."

She could see that this made no impression on me, which actually seemed to please her.

"Say, I have an extra ticket for the theater after this and no one to go with. I don't remember the name of the play, but if—"

"Sorry. I'm booked tonight. And—"

"Booked?" she asked. "That's a rather strange way to talk about a date or appointment."

"I'm a male escort. I do it for the money. Booked is how we phrase it." She was a nice little piece, but I saw no reason to be coy about it.

"Oh, I see," she said in a halting voice. There were several moments of silence as we both watched the sun going down over the New York skyline and tuned our ears to the volume level of the party beginning to wind down inside. At length though, she asked in a small voice, "And what do you do as an escort?"

"Anything the client wants—as long as they have the money to pay for it," I said.

"Do you have a card you can give me?"

And thus it started with April.

Later, after all of the guests, including April, had gone other than a half dozen older, obviously well-heeled men, the Vado U.S. president suggested that it was time that we withdrew to the billiards room for some more serious partying. The room was a large interior one, with a huge skylight. There was a bar at one end of the room, complete with bartender, a blond hunk who gave me the eye as soon as we entered. The carpeting was some sort of wild paisley print, the walls were lined with low bookcases, with pool cue racks on the walls relieved by blown up and framed black and white Mapplethorpe art photographs of young nude men in various provocative poses. Two pool tables were well spaced in the center of the room. There were club chairs around a large, square coffee table off to one side, where the men first sat as cigars were offered around. I wasn't offered a cigar—and neither was the bartender.

The bartender was told to put some music on, and I was told to dance on the coffee table and slowly strip as the six men, all in tuxedos, and all with their flies open, their cocks out, and their hands busy, sat around and watched me slow dance and strip. The bra and panties I was wearing were black and lacey. When I was down

15

to those, the Vado U.S. president told me to lie on my back on the table in front of him and spread my black-silk-stocking clad legs. He leaned over into me and ripped the crotch of the black panties open and slowly fucked me with the moistened end of his cigar while, at his invitation, the two men on either side of him each slowly rolled the stockings off my legs and licked my feet and sucked on my toes.

When the pharmaceutical company president became bored with this—and sufficiently aroused—he lifted me off the table, turned me, and set me down on his cock. I fucked myself on his cock, rising and lowering my channel by leveraging the balls of my now-bare feet off the thick paisley carpet, as the other men sat, bug eyed and hands busy with their cigars and their own cocks, and watched the Vado U.S. president get off.

Shortly thereafter, the room now in a blue haze of cigar smoke, I found out that one of the pool tables was for me and the other ones was for those guests of the company president who took breaks between fucking me on the pool table to play billiards on the other table. To the titillation of his guests, the company president had initiated my gangbang taking on the pool table by mining my channel with the end of a pool cue.

I thought maybe the guys had overdone it with the smoke late in the evening when a door was flung open and a couple of burly firemen stormed it—but it turned out only to be the company president's idea of a perfect ending to the evening. The firemen did a strip of the president's guests and then serviced or were serviced at the guest's option as the company president sat and puffed on his cigar and grinned.

I went home that night with the blond hunk of a bartender—having said I'd be happy to give him a massage after his tough day when he complained about how tough bartending was. At his apartment he got his massage, but this worked its way in my earning all of the tip money he'd made that evening by accommodating his interest in mammoth cock dildos and a change of progressively larger butt balls. Like most before him, he was amazed and aroused by how much the channel of someone with such a small stature could take.

After that evening of fetish debauchery and meeting April, she engaged my services often. She got some great tickets to events and she turned out to be a pleasant, undemanding, straightforward fuck.

But I was more into what the Vado U.S. president devised and was willing to pay for. Our liaisons continued after April's father had bought me for her and we were married—and after I was given an actual job title in the pharmaceutical company office, but, thankfully, not with any additional job responsibilities to speak of—other than to have the right wardrobe in a lower desk drawer, to always be ready to perform on the telephone or Internet, to be prepared to work late evening on demand, and to know how to get to the back staircase up to the company president's office—except when he decided to slum and take me on the desk in my own office.

It was here one evening that Fred Tipton walked into the president's office unexpected and unannounced and found me in a silky slip, lying on my back on the company president's desk, with him standing between my legs and holding one stockinged leg up with a hand, while he was using the other one to help guide his dick deeper into my channel. Tipton hadn't said anything; he'd just turned and walked back out of the office. I don't think the company president even knew he'd been there. But I saw him. And I heard from him the next morning. But there wasn't much else he could do—other than arrange my transfer to the Puerto Rico office—which is what he did. And he wrote a large enough check, that I didn't balk. I have no idea when the Vado U.S. president heard I was no longer in the New York office—or if he made any attempt to learn where I had gone.

It would have been OK with me if April had dumped me. The prenup gave me a good bonus regardless. And the "bigger company president" was ready to take me in—or so he'd said. Of course, no one ever knows such things for sure until they are tested, does one? And he was bigger in every way that meant anything to me just then—a bigger bank account and a really big dick—and he knew what to do with both. I liked April well enough, though, so marriage to her had suited me fine too. I had said yes to April's proposal because I knew I only had a few more good years. A male escort in New York—one available to either sex—only had eight or nine good years. By the time we hit thirty, we're really only good for the women. And that's not my style. I'd already found out that it was men who liked the thought of taking a smaller, underage-looking man more than women did. That was where the big money was.

Getting banished to Puerto Rico was enough to give me second thoughts on the march of time and my future prospects and made me willing to consider going cold turkey on men altogether. If that's what it would take to be able to continue to live the comfortable lifestyle I had.

And that's why I found myself in San Juan as third vice president of the Vado U.S. office there.

* * * *

My banishment to Puerto Rico all happened so fast—too fast for the office branch in San Juan too. They didn't have any place to put me when I arrived from New York. And my position was so important that they refused to let me in the company branch until they had carved out a suitable office space.

So, the very day I arrived, the president of the Vado U.S. San Juan branch came to my hotel, all apologetic, and handed me a nice check and suggested that I disappear for a week and arrive all over again when they were prepared to give me a proper welcome.

There was no embarrassment over the check. I was used to being taken care of. There was slight embarrassment that he didn't seem to want any services for what he was giving. He was British, maybe in his late fifties, all tanned and lean and a full head of white hair. He'd come in his tennis togs and he moved around the room on the pads of his feet like a conditioned athletic. I found him attractive. I found older men more attractive than younger, as long as they were in good shape—powerful men both in presence and stamina. And experienced men. I liked to learn new tricks, to experience the unusual things that turned experienced men on—their fetishes. So, normally I wouldn't mind taking this man on for a couple of rounds—especially as he was handing out checks.

But he made no suggestions—didn't make a move. And I would have bet that he knew exactly why I had been sent down there so quick-quick. I was prepared to try out my new-found determination to save it all for April—or at least for a woman. But he didn't test my resolve. For some reason I felt deflated. I wouldn't have done it really. But I would have liked for it to be my choice not to have done it.

I cashed the check and consulted the concierge at the El San Juan Hotel on where someone could disappear on the island for a quiet, but pampered week of incognito. He suggested a small resort hotel high in the hills above the city, and within hours I was being taken in a hotel car up into the mountains.

The hotel car left me at the entrance of the Sao Paulo resort, and roared right off again, with the instruction to come back and pick me up in exactly a week. It had all happened so fast that I didn't even have any contact numbers with me down in the capital.

I was all alone—and out of sight and mind—for a week.

I did a three-sixty at the entrance, taking in both how beautiful it was, with its lush vegetation and its view, from the entrance down into San Juan and out into the surrounding Caribbean. Surprisingly the hotel seemed deserted. There wasn't a soul around—not even a porter to carry my bags in. So, I hefted them up myself and sauntered into the entrance and up to the reception desk.

The hotel was plush inside, but, as I had found outside, it was deserted. There was no one at the reception desk even. I put my suitcases down and did a circuit of the entry lounge. At the other side of a two-story open space, surrounded on three sides by a balcony, was a large expanse of glass overlooking one of those "disappearing pools," where the far rim of the pool was below the water level and spilled water down an escarpment into a recirculating basin, making the pool look like it was pouring its water on San Juan at the foot of the mountain.

As I passed by a stone-cold open fire pit in the center of the lounge, I heard the clinking of ice in a glass and looked under the balcony to my right to see that I wasn't really alone. A bar was tucked under the balcony and a lone man was perched on a bar stool and was nursing a glass of liquor. He was a near twin of the Vado U.S. branch president down in San Juan. Well-muscled and trim but white-haired and maybe in his fifties. Movie-star handsome and deeply tanned. He was in shorts and stripped to the waist. His chest and arms and legs were nearly matted with curly salt-and-pepper-colored hair. I liked a man with fur. The gray was only slowly working its way down his body, and I immediately found myself wondering what color his pubes were. And if he were cut or uncut. I preferred the feel of an uncut cock inside me. And I preferred bareback, which was often possible with the class of men I serviced. They regularly got checkups and expected medical verification of any male escort they were assigned.

I surmised he was a European by his bearing, but more French or Italian than English was my guess.

He smiled at me and tipped his glass in my direction, and I just nodded and moved on, although I felt myself becoming aroused. I hadn't been fucked by a man in almost two weeks and my resolve was beginning to crumble.

I went back to the desk, and after a minute or two, the man from the bar padded out and went behind the desk. He was very well muscled indeed. In great shape for his age.

"Yes, may I help you?" he asked. The smile he flashed me was all white teeth and interesting and it seemed interested. The accent was English. So much for my powers to discern one European from another. At least I had been able to gather that he wasn't American. Just too suave and self-assured for that.

"I'm checking in. The name is Cameron, Ty Cameron."

"I'm sorry, Mr. Cameron. The resort is closed. Renovations."

"Closed," I asked, in surprise. "But the concierge at the El San Juan Hotel down in the capital made reservations for me."

"Nevertheless we are closed. But this is Puerto Rico. We are laid back here. If you don't mind being the only guest and are satisfied with the bare minimum of services—"

"No, that would be fine. I was looking to be a recluse for a week."

"There are only the two of us here now—just Rollo and me. The workmen won't show up again for more than a week. They should be here now, but I was informed they would not be coming today or tomorrow or the next day—but would do so in a week's time. That is the way it is here in Puerto Rico. But we will be all right. Some of the rooms are finished with their refurbishing, and Rollo can do anything. Anything, really," he said, and the look he gave me seemed provocative for some reason. "And he's a great cook. Alas, I am only the lazy, worthless owner."

"No that's fine. It should be quite restful."

"In that case, if you will register, please, and hand over your passport—sorry we have to hold it for our guests. It's the law here—I will go find Rollo and he will show you to your room."

When I had finished signing my name, I turned, and standing there was a mountain of a many from the Caribbean islands. Coffee colored, smooth-skinned, dreadlocks, built like a champion body builder, and with a white-teethed smile that reviled the one the resort owner had flashed me. Like the other man, he was only wearing shorts—and flip flops. My guess was that he was a good ten years older than I was too. But he was a beautiful specimen of a man.

"I am Rollo. If you are ready, I will take you to your room now."

My internal response was that Rollo could take me anywhere, any way he wanted me. But then that resolve of mine to stay true to April entered my mind again, and I mentally said "down boy" to my hardening cock.

"And I am Paul. I named the resort after myself because I'm such a saint," the resort owner said—and he said it with a silly little grin on his face. "With only the three of us here, there is no reason not to be on intimate relations."

I supposed he didn't mean for that to sound as it did, but it gave me a lurch of arousal anyway.

As I followed Rollo up the stairs to the balcony, I watched his two bulbous butt cheeks roll and bounce against each other, and I was sure he wasn't wearing any briefs.

He took me to a fine room overlooking the pool and San Juan below, with a four-poster bed and all done in white muslin. The bathroom was marble and the tub had room for all three of us—or at least that was my first thought. I'd had no intention of going into heat like this, but my best of intentions had always been a bit fleeting.

When he had set my bags down, handling them effortlessly like they were feather pillows, and had done the usual bell hop's circumnavigation of the room opening curtains and showing me what worked what, he turned and smiled. "Is there anything else I can do for you . . . Ty . . . anything else at all?"

"No not now, thanks," I said—even though it wasn't what I wanted to say at all. I had noticed before that he was studded. He had a stud in his tongue I'd never seen before and I had no idea how he managed to eat with it. It was a small ball, but it was on a stem protruding from the center of his tongue—sticking out a half inch or more. And he had rings pierced at both of the nipples on his heavily muscled chest. I immediately found myself wondering if he had a cock stud or ring too—and, if so, how big—how well I could feel it if he fucked me.

I came back from the reverie in embarrassment and found that he was still standing there, expectant and smiling.

"Oh, sorry," I said, and I started rummaging around in the pocket of my trousers for a tip.

"No need for that, mon, thanks. We are on first-name basis here and the resort isn't open. You may find another way to show any appreciation you have for me, assuming you still want to after you've tasted my cooking."

Then he laughed and was gone.

It had been a long, dusty ride up the hill, so I immediately stripped and showered and then dried off with a giant-sized Egyptian-cotton towel and padded out to the king-sized four-poster bed and laid down. I went to sleep almost immediately. When I awoke, I was surprised to find I had been so tired I'd just laid down on the bed in the nude.

Then I realized that what had awakened me was the sound of sex. I rose from the bed and padded over to a set of the full-length French doors that served as the room's windows and looked down into the pool area.

Rollo was on his back on the diving board and Paul was straddling the board with his legs and fucking Rollo in long strokes with a cock that dug forever. Rollo was in full arousal too, and his cock rivaled Paul's. However, it was special, in that, in contrast to the milk chocolate of his body, his cock and balls were jet black. And, sure enough, there was an extra thick Prince Albert ring piercing the cock head.

I don't know how long Paul had been fucking Rollo, but it went on for an impressively long time even after I started watching. I found I couldn't pull my attention away from what was happening below my window, and it was only when Rollo looked up and surely smiled that I realized that I was in full view and was stroking myself. I withdrew in embarrassment of having been found playing the voyeur.

I remained in my room for the rest of the day—taking another nap after I had masturbated to the image of Paul fucking Rollo. Dinner was delicious that night. We ate by candlelight beside the pool, with Rollo joining Paul and me after he had cooked the meal. Both men were fully dressed now, but in light cotton that enhanced the sexiness of their bodies.

The conversation was pleasant, but neither alluded to what they had done that afternoon or what I had seen. Neither did either make any provocative moves toward me, which I found both disconcerting and arousing in itself. When I went back to my room that night, I stripped and, after my shower, laid on the bed. I assumed that either Paul or Rollo would visit me, and any resolve I might have had not to entertain either of them—or more provocatively—both at once, which was a fetish I myself enjoyed, was gone. And not just a threesome, but two cocks inside me at once, the three of us working as one for a shared orgasm. I didn't know that I could recall taking two huge cocks like these men had at once, but, despite all the planning I had done on learning from my mistakes in New York, I ached for a trial of it with these two men.

But no one came that night.

By the morning, I was ripe for the taking—to the eventual enhanced arousal of all.

I woke with a rap on the door—alone in my bed—and found a breakfast tray waiting for me just outside the door. There was a card on the tray which said, "It's a fine day; a great day for a visit to the pool." I had found a couple of fluffy pool towels under the breakfast tray.

After I'd eaten and showered and shaved, I rummaged around in my luggage for my Speedo and the novel I was reading, grabbed my sunglasses, slipped on the bathing suit, and descended the stairs into the empty lobby and walked out to the pool. Only one lounger was now beside the pool, up close to the diving board, so I opened one of the towels out on that and laid down.

Within minutes I saw Paul moving through the lobby and toward the pool. He was naked and he was magnificent. He came out onto the deck and climbed agilely onto the diving board, strode rapidly down the length of the board, and performed a perfect dive into the pool. He then proceeded to do laps at a fast pace.

I was watching him so closely that I barely noticed Rollo coming out to the pool as well. He too was naked, his ringed cock swaying rhythmically against his thighs as he strutted. He was holding a tray with a drink on it, which he set down on the small table beside my lounger. Then he stood over me, his cock swinging freely above my head.

"I saw you yesterday. In the window," he said matter-of-factly. "You fuck men, no?"

"Usually they fuck me," I answered.

"I may make love to you, yes?"

"Yes."

"I try to be careful," he assured me. "You're so small and I am so big. I'll try not to crush you and if you cannot take me when we get to that point, tell me. I do not want to split you."

"You'll be surprised," I answered. "I can take you and Paul both—at once."

His eyes lit up in arousal at that, and he licked his lips. And I could see his cock swelling even further too.

"Ah, you are like a boy. So small and delicate—but perfect just perfect," he murmured. "Are you sure—"

"Yes, I'm sure," I declared. And I could see him trembling with arousal and anticipation.

He moved to the bottom of the lounger and gently took my thighs in his beefy hands and pulled me down to where my butt was nearly even with the bottom ridge. Then he took the second towel I'd brought out, folded it to make it into a cushion, and laid it on the patio tiles at the base of the lounger and knelt on it. He reached up and pulled my Speedo down and off my legs with both hands. He cupped my buttocks and brought my hole to his mouth and started a long session of

21

rimming my hole that not only opened me up nicely but had me moaning and begging for him.

"You are so nice," he whispered. "Your body, it is small. But your cock. Such a nice size, and so long. Nice balls." He drew the latter into his mouth and started to hum and the resonation was driving me silly wild. He pulled away from them and his tongue went back to my rim.

"Please, please fuck me," I moaned. But he ignored me as if I hadn't asked for it.

"Ah, yes, I see, it blossoms like a cavern. Rose Cavern," he muttered. And then he laughed, a deep, hoarse laugh. I raised my pelvis and put it into a slow rolling motion as he inserted first one, and then two, and then three fingers. We both sucked in our breath and moaned as I felt the knuckles of his hands at my rim on all sides, and I relaxed my channel, preparing for feeling his wrist there and the spreading of my channel deeper inside by the rest of his hand. But his hand wasn't sufficiently greased and he was impatient for other pleasures, so he stopped with a grunt of "Later. Save for later."

He withdrew his hand and his lips and tongue went back to rimming me. He sighed as I opened even more.

I hadn't noticed when I'd laid down on the lounger, but now I saw, as he finished rimming me and looked up over my heaving belly with a smile that there were restraints at the four corners of the lounger.

Rollo pulled one of these up and showed it to me and said simply, "May I?"

"Whatever you want. As long as you fuck me," I said in a hoarse whisper. "I want to feel that thick cock ring of yours inside me."

"Oh, I will. In more than one way. You like this toy of mine?"

I sighed a yes, and he rubbed his cock tantalizing along my inner thighs, running the warm metal along tender skin. I moaned and reached for him, wanting to draw him inside me there and then. But he laughed and pushed my hands away and took my wrists in a firm grip and started guiding them above my head. He did, however, move his cock head into position at my hole and give me the feel of the ring rubbing in circles around my entrance.

"For now the restraints will be good," he said while I was hyperventilating at the feel of his cock at my entrance, wanting it to plunge inside me. "What I do now, it will be dangerous for you to move too wildly. And I think it will make you wild, yes."

I didn't know then what he meant. But I was melting at the prospect of whatever it was—and I soon found out.

He pulled my arms over my head until my wrists could be secured to the top corners of the lounger. And then he secured my ankles to the bottom corners.

I thought he would thrust that huge, ringed cock in my widened and pulsing hole then, but he didn't. I saw his smile come up between my legs and his hands to my cock. His mouth opened, and I once again saw that gold ball thrusting out of his tongue on its stem. And then, as he closed his lips over my cock head, I found out what the tongue piercing was for.

The small ball searched out my piss slit, and then it was entering me there, the stem allowing it to bury itself nearly an inch inside my urethra. And then he was fucking my cock with his tongue stud. Pushing it in and pulling it out of my piss slit and pushing it in and pulling it out. And I was crying out and writhing and straining at my bounds, all the while trying to keep my pelvis steady for him. And coming again and again and again, as he let me briefly rest but then piss slit fucked me again. Until I had no more cum to give.

While this was going on, I looked over at the diving board and Paul was sitting there, watching us and stroking his own cock.

Only after I was exhausted and whimpering did Rollo stand and laugh and then enter me with his fat cock and punish my walls delightfully with that thick cock ring. Sliding in and out, giving me waves and waves of pleasure of thick metal rubbing across channel walls. He muttered in surprise when he entered me and felt my channel taking him tight, which was yet another secret I had learned in my business. He took me bareback, and when he came, he gushed deep inside me. I enjoyed Rollo immensely—and in the main because of the dance of fucking he did between my legs complete with the view of the undulation of his beefy muscles and the rhythmic swaying and tinkling music produced by his beaded dreadlocks.

He left me and exchanged places with Paul. Paul released the bounds on my wrists and ankles—but only long enough to turn me over on my belly. I was too weak and satiated to even think of putting up a struggle. He bound me again and Rollo handed him a rolled up, thick towel to wedge under my belly. And then he straddled my thighs with his and thrust inside me, bareback, as Rollo had done, and fucked me. At first he kneaded the muscles of my back and arms and his cock took on the rhythm of the soft, rolling gait of the massage, but as his own heat deepened, he stopped massaging me and went to fucking me hard like a dog.

He moved a hand around my thigh and milked my cock until I was almost ready to come again, and then I felt his hands at my throat and his fingers digging into my flesh, seeking out my windpipe. He brought me to the edge of his ejaculation and my unconsciousness three times before he released his load deep inside me, while I simultaneously experienced that fullest release of my own that morning . . . and . . . blacked out.

* * * *

When I came back into consciousness, I was on my back again, free of bounds, but Paul was sitting on the lounger beside me and I became conscious of my own moans and that I felt incredibly stuffed. My pelvis was elevated again, and one of my legs was spread and lay across his lap. I could feel the pulsing hardness of his erection on my thigh. He was worrying my nipples with one hand and looking down at me with an expression that approached awe. I looked down the line of my body and saw that his hand was inside me up to his wrist. It was slowly rolling back and forth and my pelvis was rolling with its rhythm. Rollo knelt beside my hips. He brought a cloth to my nose that smelled sweet and immediately started to make me feel groggy. I watched then as he lowered his lips over my cock and the stemmed stud in his tongue found my piss slit once again. And then I just went with the flow again until I drifted off into blackness.

I woke up in my bed, bathed and powdered and feeling a little groggy. It was dark in the room, but when I struggled up and went and pulled away the drapes on the French windows, I saw that it was only late afternoon.

Paul and Rollo were sitting, clothed in formal wear, on cushioned seats next to a table covered with a white cloth and set for three. Lit candles were placed here and there around the pool area. The two men were drinking from martini glasses. A third, unoccupied chair was positioned between them. I found my tuxedo in the closet and dressed and went down to them.

There was no mention of the debauchery at the pool in the morning. If I hadn't been sore, I would have wondered if I had dreamed it all. The discussion was light—sports and action and adventure movies and a bit on current events and the business market in Puerto Rico. Rollo seemed quite able to keep up his end of the conversation. They also discussed the peculiar behavior of the workmen who had been working on the resort and just walked off the job—with the promise that they would be back. Paul said they almost were apologetic about it—and looked embarrassed when he pressed them for a reason. But they had avoided giving him one other than "national holiday." Paul had lived in Puerto Rico long enough to know that they could find a national holiday excuse for any day they didn't want to work.

"What's a little surprising in their nonappearance is that they clocked in well before this. And they were good workers—well most of them. And good for other purposes as well," Paul said. "You would like them, I think, Ty."

That's as close as he came to mentioning what had gone on between us earlier in the day until much later, after the sun had gone down, and we'd plowed through three courses of food, including broiled lobster with shrimp and scallop chasers, had had our coffee, and were finishing off with snifters of brandy, sitting three abreast on the lounger next to the underlit pool, me sandwiched between the other two and them working my body through openings in the tuxedo with their hands.

After each of us had said, as all of us are want to do, that we needed to leave for our separate demands of the evening but didn't actually budge from the comfort and ambiance of the moment—Rollo cleaning up, Paul updating the resort's books, and me continuing my review of what I was supposed to be doing for Vado Pharmaceuticals in Puerto Rico—I did approach the subject again.

"I never asked you what the fees are for room and board here," I said. "Not that I care what you charge, but my company is picking up the tab, and I should know what to tell them if and when they ask."

"As long as you continue pleasing me, there will be no bill," Paul said with a hoarse whisper. His hand was squeezing my cock rhythmically at that moment, so I had to assume I was pleasing him. But I asked anyway.

"And do I please you?" I asked.

"Very much so—and Rollo too," Paul answered in even a deeper and more hoarse voice.

"I am quite pleased with the accommodations," I answered. "And Rollo too," I added.

"You are so accommodating yourself," Paul said. "I don't want to go beyond bounds. Is there anything not—?"

"No," I interjected. "I'm sure that anything you enjoy I will find equally enjoyable. Both of you—together—even. I'm sure I could—"

"After this afternoon, I'm sure you could too," Paul said with a laugh. "You needn't bother to lock your door here at night," he then said as he rose. "We both have keys to all of the doors."

"I feel safe enough, I answered," as Rollo also rose to leave.

In the middle of the night, under a full moon that I let stream through the undraped French doors as I lay naked in the four-poster bed in my room, both Paul and Rollo quietly entered. They both were naked. They moved to either side of the bed and reached up into the corner of the canopies of the bed and brought down restraints on leather leads.

"Is it OK to—?" Paul whispered.

"Yes, yes, of course, if that's what you wish," I whispered back. Rollo stretched my right arm and left leg up and out, as Paul did the same with the left. Then, as Rollo wedged pillows under the small of my back, Paul knelt at the foot of the bed between my legs and docked our cocks—pressing one cock head against the other and stretching his uncut foreskin over the tip of my cock. He closed a fist over the docked cocks and stroked them to hard. Rollo kissed me on the lips and then pulled up a club chair close to the side of the bed and watched as Paul and I moaned and sighed in unison.

When I had reached the shuddering and writhing stage, Rollo started handing various forms of dildo to Paul that he had covered in lube and both watched intently as Paul played in my widening hole with them.

When I was sufficiently dilated, Paul worked his way under me on the bed in full stretch and entered me from behind with his cock. Rollo then stood and took up the kneeling position between my legs that Paul had previously occupied. He then too worked his cock inside me and they double fucked me. As we were close to coming, Paul took my throat in his hands as he'd done the first time he fucked me and I ejaculated, in profusion, at the point of blacking out.

When I awoke it was after dawn and I was unbound in my bed.

For two days after this, the routine was more or less the same. Wild cocking at the pool in the morning, sleeping the afternoon away under the influence of some sort of drug, a quiet dinner of pretense that nothing was going on between the three of us—and double penetration sex at night. During this period, both Paul and Rollo frequently whispered in awe that they had no idea that someone as small of stature and young looking as I was could perform sexually as I did.

Even when I told them I had successfully lived in New York as a male escort, they remained almost incredulous—even though I repeatedly managed all that they said they couldn't believe I would be able to.

* * * *

I was lying half on the lounger by the pool on my side and Paul was sitting on the one beside me facing me. My torso was half over his thigh and my arm wrapped around to his back, where I was playing the tufting of hair above his tailbone. Paul had interesting patterns of hair on his body that I liked to run my fingers through. My other hand was following the trail of hair up his belly and searching out his nipples in the matting there. I had his balls in my mouth, sucking

25

on them, having just licked them down good. Paul was gently moving his fingers around my lower belly.

Rollo was sitting on the lounger on the other side, hunched over me, my leg wrapped around his neck, his attention intently focused on feeding the largest of a graduated string of balls inside my channel. Both men were breathing heavily and were erect and hard as rocks, and I sensed it wasn't long before one—or both—of them would be fucking me. Rollo leaned farther over and took one of my nipples in his mouth and rolled it between his teeth and bit down on it. He grunted with pleasure as I cried out, releasing Paul's balls from my mouth, only to have him push his cock into my mouth with a hand. And then he was leaning over me as well and chewing on the other nipple. I writhed in pain pleasure—and gasped as Rollo started to pull the string of balls out of my ass.

I felt a smattering of raindrops, and both Paul and Rollo sat up.

As Rollo was pulling the last of the balls out of my channel, Paul said. "I think it best we go inside. You haven't seen my cellar playroom yet."

"You don't want me to make you come first?" I asked. "I think you're close."

"I think it will be much more enjoyable in the playroom."

We were in a stonewalled chamber straight out of a horror movie. Torches on the walls along with implements of torture. A sling, a bucking horse apparatus with a dildo protruding from the saddle, and another saddle-type machine the function of which I had no idea. And I couldn't put much effort into figuring it out, because I was already a bit beleaguered. I was hanging from the ceiling with restraints at my wrists and above my elbows and wishboned back, restraints at my ankles attached to leads running off in each direction away from my body that had my legs splayed apart. Paul was between my legs in back feeding my channel with a cock encased in an apparatus with studs all over that were giving my channel walls extra special attention, and Rollo was in front of me, sucking my cock and adding weights to the end of a leather rope wrapped around my balls, stretching them toward the floor.

Paul said he wanted to hear me scream, and I was doing a lot of that. After a bit, Paul released my ankles and I was vertical—but he only did this so that Rollo could grab my butt cheeks from the front and roll my hips up and spread my cheeks so that his cock could join Paul's in my channel. They rode me until all three of us had come.

Then Paul told Rollo to let me down and to set me up with what he called the "Big F." As he went up the stairs he said, "Let's start at twelve and three—we can go up from there."

The Big F turned out to be an ass drill, with Rollo setting it at twelve inches of penetration and three inches of thickness. It was the machine I hadn't identified earlier. I was lashed down, half way reclining, with my legs spread and elevated and my hips rolled up. And a dildo-shaped drill was set between my legs. I could see it approach slowly from more than a foot away, and then it relentlessly drilled into my ass in a two inches in, one inch back, two inches in motion at the set depth and then went through a series of churning maneuvers. Then out it drilled, only to repeat the process all over again. A penis sheath went over my penis and balls and squeezed my balls and milked my cock in rhythmic motion.

"We'll let him go twenty," Paul called out from the top of the stairs. I'll be down to watch the last five minutes and listen to his moaning.

No sooner had Rollo set the controls and the drill started moving toward me, though, than Paul was back at the top of the stairs. "Grab the guns and get up here, Rollo. We've got visitors. I half expected this."

I was well over the twenty minutes and pretty much passed out from too much of a good thing—in this case accompanied by the rat-tat-tat of automatic weapons fire overhead—when I opened my eyes at the sensation that the machine had stopped . . . and was looking up—and around—at a circle of local Hispanic militiamen, stripped to the waist, in jeans, with bandoliers of bullets crisscrossing their chests and smoking automatic rifles at their sides. They were all heavily muscled, glistened with sweat, and covered in tattoos.

They looked as shocked to see me here, like this, as I was to see them. Someone called down from the top of the staircase in hurried and panicked Spanish. The man who looked to be the leader of the group answered him back in leering but unhurried tones and then directed me to "Come with" as I was released from the machine. I was literally dragged off the machine and up the stairs and out the back of the lobby and into the scrub. Looking back as I was dragged, I could see a swarm of blue-uniformed men exploding into the lobby from the front.

I was half in shock—if for no other reason than the surprise of it all—as I was manhandled through the scrub to a road, where two flatbed trucks were parked. I was slammed down on the tailgate of one of the trucks while the armed men fanned out in a semicircle facing the resort, which no longer was in sight.

The leader of the group wasted no time in moving in between my legs while slapping them apart. He had one hand at my opening and the other jerking at my cock. He almost went into shock himself when I smiled up at him and raised my hands to his chest and began to trace the tattoos that flourished there. He was working his fist in me, no doubt expecting me to cry out in pain and violation— which may have been what gave him a thrill. But I found him arousing, especially the tattoos, and I reached down and tugged at the front of his jeans, opening snaps until he was overwhelmed with the moment as well.

He fucked me hard, as then did the rest of the band—or most of them, in succession. While the last guy was doing me—and I was enjoying the undulation of his tattoos on his chest and arm as he was working on me, four of the band jumped up onto the back of the truck and urinated on me.

I didn't like that much, but they seemed to.

But shortly, each band member not having taken more than four or five minutes to shoot their load in me as keyed up as they had been, someone whistled a warning, and I was shoved off onto the side of the road, and the men were jumping onto the trucks and hauling ass out of there.

When I looked up, a policeman in a blue uniform was standing over me, surprised—and aroused—at what he found.

I was no less aroused by the uniform and the tenting at his crotch and came up on my knees and unzipped his fly and relieved any anxiety he had. And he let me do so without the least embarrassment—as did the next policeman who showed up. I'm sure they thought I was acting in relief from having been saved from the armed band. But in reality the rough fucking and tattoos on the Hispanic militants still had me in high heat.

* * * *

"OK, give me an order for these colors," Paul said brightly early the next afternoon as he came out to me at the pool. "Red, blue, green, gold, and transparent."

"Transparent's not a color," I said, moving a bit gingerly in my chair. Paul and Rollo hadn't let the scare of the previous day interrupt their visit to me in the night.

What had transpired the previous day was that the resort had been "visited" by a band of bandits, one of many roaming the hills of Puerto Rico of late and terrorizing the tourist resorts. Such bands swept in and divested all of the well-heeled visitors, even those in the middle of a golf game, of whatever could be quickly grabbed and then ran for the hills again. This band had marked the Sao Paulo Resort for visitation, apparently not being aware that it was closed for renovation. The renovation workers had heard this was happening, though, so they were staying away.

"Why should I put an order to those colors?" I asked.

"Just humor me and do it."

"OK, anything to please you, oh lord and master. How about green, blue, transparent, gold, and red."

"So be it."

"So be what. Why'd you ask me to put them in order."

"Because the lads won't sort themselves out."

"Excuse me?"

"The renovation workers couldn't warn me of the raid or the raiders would visit their villages some night. But the boys doing the landscaping were good enough to keep an eye on the resort from a distance and summon the police up from San Juan the moment the bandits arrived. Rollo and I were forced back across the pool—so sorry for your little encounter with the bandits for the short time they were in the hotel—but the police arrived before any real damage was done. We shouldn't have to worry about them again now until after they've seen that the renovations are complete and the hotel has bookings again."

"I still don't understand what—" But then I followed Paul's line of sight, because he wasn't looking at me. And there, by the door into the hotel from the pool area were five hunky Hispanic young men, standing all in a row, with big smiles and completely naked except for condoms of an assortment of colors—red, green, blue, gold, and a transparent one—and they were all in various stages of erection already.

"I told them I'd reward them for saving our lives—all of our lives," Paul explained.

I spent the afternoon with my legs spread and my channel entertaining cocks crowned with condoms in a variety of colors. I can't say I didn't enjoy the Hispanic hunks who had perfected the sculpting of their bodies the natural way—by honest hard labor. And I decided to be a good sport about it, because their loyalty to the resort very likely did save our lives.

The next day, my week was up at the Sao Paulo Resort, and the driver was waiting to take me back down to San Juan, where presumably the Puerto Rican branch of the Vado pharmaceutical company was ready to receive me.

I hadn't exactly had the quiet, celibate week I had planned on, but I'd had some really interesting—and stretching—experiences. And I decided that my life of being a good boy could start now just as easily as a week ago. April wasn't arriving for another three months. There was plenty of time to get my act straightened up.

As I was leaving, Paul and Rollo were standing at the door. Rollo looked really sad to see me go; Paul just waved and smiled and said, "See you around," which I felt was a little strange. I thought that all I'd let him do for me—in exchange for room and board and some interesting company—was worth more than a flippant good-bye.

I had thought the driver would take me back to the El San Juan Hotel—or maybe, if the office had really gotten its act together, to the apartment overlooking the sea that they were supposed to lease for me. But instead it rolled up to the door of a high-rise luxurious condominium on a hillock between the mountains and the coast that surely had great view of both the Caribbean and down into old San Juan as well.

"Please take the elevator to the penthouse, sir," the driver said as he opened the door to the backseat of the limousine for me. "The security staff knows who you are and where you're going. I'll take your bags on to the hotel and will be back and waiting down here for you when you are ready."

"I don't know who I'm going to see," I said. "Tell me who? And why you aren't taking me straight to the hotel." I was a little piqued I was being kept in the dark.

He didn't answer my questions. He just looked a little pained and repeated, "Please take the elevator to the penthouse, sir."

I walked into the lobby, which was two stories, the far wall of which was all glass and had a magnificent view over the city and water. A liveried attendant was waiting at an elevator that was set by itself, away from the bank of other elevators. He was looking at me and gesturing with an outstretched arm at the open elevator, making it pretty obvious where I was supposed to go.

A butler met me at the elevator and ushered me into a plush lounge that took up one corner of the building and provided a sweeping view from ocean to city to mountains across the expanse of a wraparound terrace.

"Dr. Holt-Evans will call for you shortly, sir."

Ah, that explained it. Peter Holt-Evans was the company's branch manager—the suave, mature Englishman who had banished me for the week. I wonder what he'd have to say to the concierge at the El San Juan who had sent me into the jaws of just exactly what I'd been sent to Puerto Rico to avoid—most evidently to the full knowledge of their branch president.

I was kept waiting for only about ten minutes when the butler returned and said, "The doctor will see you now in the examining room."

I stood, perplexed, and followed the butler down a corridor into the bowels of the penthouse apartment that evidently took up the whole floor. "Examining room," I thought. "A different doctor than Holt-Evans? A shrink, maybe? I'm going to be grilled about what I've been doing for a week? Did Holt-Evans find out and I'm in hot water here already? What do I tell him?"

But the examining room I was led into was a medical examination room, and Dr. Holt-Evans was waiting there for me. He was wearing a white medical coat that came almost down to his ankles.

"Hello, Ty," he said in a jovial manner when I entered the room.

"Hello, Dr. Holt-Evans," I answered. "I don't understand—"

"Ah, I'm sorry. I neglected to tell you. I'm the company physician down here as well as the president. A mere formality, but we exam all employees as they come on board at the branch. We offer full, comprehensive medical benefits, you know, but I'm afraid that comes with some level of intrusion into your personal health. This is a mere formality. But could you take off your clothes down to your briefs, please, and hop up on this table and lay back."

He was patting the top of a padded examination table, complete with foot stirrups.

I was still confused, but I did what he asked. He took a stethoscope and started listening around on my body—my throat, my chest, and my belly. Asking me to cough and breath deeply for him.

I murmured a query when he lifted my legs, slipped off my briefs, and inserted my feet in the stirrups. He then wrapped restraints around my ankles and raised the stirrup mechanisms up and to the side. But he ignored me and had one of my arms raised above my head and the wrist restrained to the side of the table before I was able to become more vocal in my questions.

The other wrist tied down, he cheerily said, "Not to worry. We're just doing a prostate exam at this point."

"I don't understand. Wouldn't I stand and bend over for that exam?" As I asked that question, a bit heatedly, he was snapping latex surgical gloves on his hands. "And why the restraints?"

"Well, because I'm going to conduct the prostate exam with my dick, dear boy," he answered jollily. And as he said it, he was unbuttoning his medical coat to reveal he was naked underneath—and had a very respectable full erection, already crowned with a condom.

"And I'm going to help him," another voice sounded from the corridor, as Paul walked into the room, naked.

I gasped as Peter Holt-Evans moved in between my legs and started lathering up my hole with lubricant.

As he fucked me, in long, deep strokes, Paul provided the explanation.

"Peter and I are brothers. Sending you to my resort was rather a test. The office in New York wanted you to pass the test. After seeing you, Peter wanted you to fail—but was, and is, prepared to cover for you for continued services rendered. So, he bribed the concierge at the El San Juan Hotel to guide you to my empty resort—and, as requested, I did everything I could to make you fail the test, to seduce and use you to the ultimate degree. And I must say you failed with flying colors."

If I was going to fail—and especially because the brothers wanted me enough to help cover my tracks—this is just the way I wanted to do it. I told Peter he could release the restraints and I'd gladly join in the fuck. It was as good an answer to my addiction to fetish sex as I was going to find.

Peter said he'd release me in a while—that using restraints and the medical angle was a fetish of his. "And Paul here has told me you are quite accommodating to fetishes."

I soon found another fetish of his—which gave even more motive to the restraints. As Paul watched, licking his chops and taking time for kissing and some mouth-on-cock play with both me and his brother, Peter lathered up my torso and pits and legs and pubes with shaving cream and shaved me smooth. I'd never had this done before but I was game. I'm game for almost any fetish that doesn't kill me—and for which I get paid well somehow.

When I was released it was only to become the meat between the Peter and Paul bread of a fuck sandwich, as the two brothers took me between themselves in double penetration and then left me to shower and clean myself as, aroused to the heights, the two brothers went in search of a bed to resume their fuck without me.

All told San Juan was promising to be an ideal assignment for me.

Age Difference

To Die in Madeira

I closed my lips over Sir Guy's cock and pushed his foreskin down with them, my tongue going to opening and flicking down into his piss slit as my mouth slowly took more and more of him inside the moist warmth of my mouth cavity. He sighed contentedly and ran his fingers through my hair. He reached up and pulled my cock down to his lips and started returning the compliment.

We were half way through his massage, and I was on my knees and elbows straddled above him on the massage table in the sixty-nine position, careful not to burden his frail, tortured body with the weight of my hard-muscled 190 pounds. He was moaning softly and making feeble attempts to slowly pump his engorging cock up into the warmth of my mouth. I moved my forearms so that I could palm the flaps of his withered buttocks in my hands and both cushion his brittle skin from rubbing against the vinyl of the massage table top and help strengthen his attempts to pump up into me. I was careful not to thrust with my own cock, letting him do whatever he could with it with his teeth and lips. This wasn't for me; it was for him. I was just here to serve.

We continued in this position until he gave a little jerk and semen dribbled out of his cock at the back of my throat as he gave a gasp of a sigh and then settled down.

He thanked me in a faraway voice from some fantasy land or poignant remembrance of his past as I climbed back off the table and carefully turned him on his belly and resumed the regular part of the massage on his backside, ever so gently working what was left of his muscles and exercising his creaking joints.

"The ass, work the ass," he murmured. "And don't neglect the inside, please. Fuck me, please."

"Are you sure, Sir Guy?" I asked. "I fear I'm too big and heavy for you. I don't want to hurt you."

"You always say that," Sir Guy responded. "And you're always wrong. You're never too big for me. You're big, of course. But just right. Indulge me, please." And then he laughed. "I think my ass canal is the last youthful part of me. Still flexible after all these years. Still able to take the big boys."

"I don't know, Sir Guy. I don't know if it's wise." But I had already placed the pillow under his hips, raising his withered flanks, and I was gently massaging his buttocks in circles, ever widening circles that increasingly opened his crease, revealing a puckered hole. I let a thumb strum across the hole and leaned down and blew on it, and Sir Guy gave a little gasp and then a long sigh.

"What's wise?" Sir Guy asked "You afraid I'll die on your table? That you'll fuck me to death?"

"Umm, Something like that, I guess," I replied. It had taken several months for my massage appointments with Sir Guy to reach this point. He was living in one of England's most exclusive rest homes, tucked away riverside at Henley-on-Thames. I had signed on as a physical therapist there. I really fancied myself as a writer, but I couldn't see enough money in that for years to come, and the middle-aged men who picked me up in the men's bars for my main source of income and who I had gotten into a routine of massaging as foreplay remarked so favorably on the massages I gave—even what went before the massaging of their cocks—that I took a course of study in massage to add some legitimate income to my upkeep.

I had taken to the old folks homes, as the clients were of the gentle sort. But Sir Guy—I had no idea if he was really a knight, only that everyone called him Sir Guy, and I knew he must be loaded to be living where he was—had recognized what I was immediately. And he had slowly cajoled me into helping him be what he was. But I remained skittish of giving him what he always wanted, as he was so fragile and seemed close to a wasting-away death from the moment I met him.

"I'm not afraid of death," Sir guy murmured, as I continued massaging his buttocks in circles and running my thumbs over his opening hole as they passed by. I thumped the hole with the pad of a finger, and it blinked at me and puckered up. Sir Guy groaned a "Yes, like that," and I pressed a thumb into the opening, which yielded to me and clutched at the invading digit. "And there is a certain kind of death I welcome and that there's no use living without."

"Oh, what's that?" I asked. I extracted the thumb and thumped it against the hole again, rubbed it across the hole three, four times, and then pushed it back in. His rim grabbed my thumb and pulled it in to the knuckle, and he moved his ass in little circles and moaned deeply.

"*Le petite mort*," he murmured through his sighs.

"What was that?" I asked.

"*Le petite mort*, the little death. Did you not read John Rhy's *Wide Sargasso Sea*?" He asked in a little gaspy voice. Paraphrasing poets, he presented each ejaculation, each orgasm as the point of a little death. "A death to be welcomed, wouldn't you say, Keith? And did you not know that the word for 'orgasm' and 'death' is the same in Olde English? I prefer that form of death. And when I no longer can die in that way, I welcome the death of the other kind; the final death. And you are helping me in maintaining the edge of life in these little deaths, Keith. Never forget that. Never think you are bringing harm to me in our massage sessions."

"Yes, sir," I answered. For indeed there seemed nothing else I could answer. I had grown fond of Sir Guy—to the point of becoming detached when I was wedged between the spread thighs of those middle-aged men from the bars and listening to them grunting and groaning as I split them with my thick cock and wondering if Sir Guy would still be there for our next massage session, if he had survived the week. But so far he always had been there.

"Now the ultimate kiss, if you please, Keith, with plenty of tongue. I grow weary but I must finish. I must have my little death again and pull one from you as well."

I lowered my face to his crease and blew on his hole again, which puckered nicely for me. I brushed his rim with my lips and he sighed and trembled for me. As I invaded him with my tongue, he gasped and cried out weakly in passion. His hole spread wide. He started to squirm and his knees scrabbled against the surface of the massage table, but I held him firm with my hands on his hips, not wanting him to rub his thin-skinned knees raw.

"Deeper, deeper," he cried out, and then "Ahh, yes, yes, yes," as I pushed my tongue far inside him and moved it about. I could feel him opening up more. I feared what came next, but he seemed to be opening enough to take me.

"Now, now," He cried out. "Fuck me."

We'd been here before. There was no talking him out of it. I mounted the table and then crouched down over him from behind on the balls of my feet, suspending my pelvis over his hips. He was scrabbling back at my dick with his long, thin, age-mottled fingers, managing only to grab onto my ball sack and squeezing, which brought forth a long, low moan of my own.

I placed the bulb of my cock at his hole and let his rim muscles pull that inside.

Weak as he was, he was able to arch his back and gasp his appreciation of being invaded. I fisted the root of my cock and moved the bulb around in circles just inside his hole, which opened even more. His fingernails were now scrabbling at my thighs, and he was yipping his little "yes, yes, yeses" and begging me to get on with the fuck.

I let my cock sinking in about four inches, and I started a shallow, slow pumping, which I hoped would satisfy him. But, as always, it didn't. He urged me on.

I got a hand under his belly and fisted his cock, putting a thumb over his piss slit, so I'd know when he came again. He'd never let me stop until he came again.

And then, as slowly and gently as I possibly could, I sank my thick seven-and-a-half inches inside him, being as careful as I could not to put any weight on his body. When I bottomed, he jerked, and I felt the wetness of his ejaculation burbling around my thumb.

"Now you," he murmured through a gasp and a groan, and he took my balls his fingers and squeezed and pulled on them, as I started a pumping action in as slow and controlled a manner as I could. Again, he insisted on long, deep strokes. I lost control, as I always did, however, much to his delight, and he cried out for me to ride him hard and deep, as I started doing just that, ejaculating strongly up into him in three spoutings just before my leg muscles gave out and I had to roll off of the table and onto the floor.

"Thank you," he murmured. "I live yet again."

I returned to gently messaging his muscles and working his joints, which had now become knotted again at the limited, but unusual exercise they had gotten during the fuck.

"It wouldn't bother me, of course, to die on this table with your cock churning inside me," Sir guy murmured as I worked his muscles. His eyes were closing, and I could feel his thin body relaxing, and I knew he was close to the restful sleep that concluded all of our sessions and that, alone, justified what we had done.

"But where I would really like to die would be to die in Madeira. Ah, to die in Madeira," he whispered, nearly gone now. "Would you like to see Madeira, Keith? You know, that lovely island in the Atlantic off Portugal?" he asked in his last waking breath. He was asleep and didn't hear my "yes."

* * * *

I had assumed it was just the ruminations of an old and wasting-away man, but, much to my surprise, Sir Guy actually did own a villa high on a hill overlooking a yacht harbor in Madeira, just to the west of Funchal. And when he asked me if I would take him there and stay with him and massage and otherwise service him until the end came, I didn't think very long and hard before saying yes.

I'd grown weary of making a living of fucking middle-aged businessmen sneaking down from London, Sir Guy had offered me more than that and the sporadic physical therapy appointments combined, and I could do my writing in Madeira as well as anywhere else—perhaps better, as new experiences would be all around me. Who wanted to read about pounding between the thighs of middle-aged men in the rooms above a Reading gay bar anyway? In any event, I didn't think Sir Guy would be long for this world now, and I was fond of him and thought he deserved to go where he wanted to go to die. It wouldn't be much of a demand on my time.

It turned out to be a bit more demanding of my time and of my hard cock than I had thought it would be. The breezes wafting through Sir Guy's open-walled villa hovering above the Atlantic restored his stamina considerably. I did think in the first week or two that this was just one of those fake flame-ups of vitality that often happened just before someone died, but it went on for months rather than weeks.

We were isolated up in the villa, just Sir Guy and me, other than the servants, who were not often seen and who spoke little English even when I encountered them. They all seem to glance down and away toward the marble-tiled floors whenever we passed in the hall. They surely knew why I was there and what I was to Sir Guy, but they chose to act as if I wasn't present at all. I began to feel stifled and trapped, but Sir Guy, sensing that I had become tense, alleviated my fears by giving me a tidy enough sum to return to England on my own any time I wished and to reestablish myself.

I did find more time to write than I had in Reading, but Sir Guy's sexual demands on me increased. As frail as he was, he always wanted me to take him hard and deep at the finish. Each time we enacted that little death he increasingly sought. And he always managed to maneuver me so that I gave him what he wanted. We normally had two massage and suck and fuck sessions a day on the terrace overlooking the small yacht basin, and after the first couple of nights, he also insisted on taking me into his bed at night and wouldn't release me until I had side-split him deep until he had achieved that little rejuvenating ejaculation of his and had felt me cream his insides. Then he would sleep the sleep of the dead. But, miraculously, each morning he would be alive—feeble and thin and living the on-the-edge life of translucent skin and bruising wherever I had gripped him harder than I should in the depths of our passionate fucking—but very much alive.

And each morning over breakfast on the terrace, I would suggest that perhaps we should take a day of abstinence, that the rest would do him good, and each morning he would demur and point to the massage table and say, "That . . . that and your magnificent hard cock, of course . . . are what keep me alive. When you deny me that, I will surely shrivel and die."

It took no more than that to hold me there with him, as the weeks turned into months and approached three-quarters of a year. Surely, I thought, it can't go on longer than this. And then I'd always reproach myself. I didn't want Sir Guy to die—not really. He was a good conversationalist and had a sharp, quick wit. And he had been very good to me. My cock was for sale. If not him, it would be someone else—at least until I started to grow old as well and dry out and wither and blow away as it seemed Sir Guy would do on any given afternoon.

Still, I felt isolated and trapped, and after six months of waiting for what surely would happen before the next dawn—but that never did—I started to take long walks by myself. And in search of company, I started to walk down to the harbor village at the foot of the cliff. There was a small open-air café there on the harbor wall that I began to frequent. And I was not the only one frequenting it.

One such regular was another Englishman by the name of Reginald. He was perhaps five years older than I was, close to thirty surely. A fine figure of a man, his muscle tone enhanced, I'm sure, because he was a part-time fisherman. I understood that he also was an artist and had come here a few years earlier. He'd just appeared in the village, looking for work, and an old fisherman had taken him on. One of the café's patrons had whispered between his fingers to me of a probable relationship between the young Englishman and the old fisherman and had given as proof positive the fact that Reginald had inherited the old man's boat, preferred fishing spot, and two-room flat above the small sundries shop across the cobble-stoned alley from the café.

Some afternoons I could hear the Englishman humming and singing softly to himself in his rooms above my head. One of his rooms was all windows, and I could tell that he was using it as his artist's studio. And I could tell by his humming that he was in his element when he was painting. I knew exactly how that felt. That's how I felt about my writing as well.

After I had been coming to the café for a month or more, he took notice of me, and if I was there when he came in from his brief fishing excursion of that day, he would come sit at the café. In time, there was a day when the café tables were all occupied and he asked if he could sit at mine.

We talked briefly of England and were both surprised that we had come from essentially the same area. I was from Reading and he had come down from London to a cottage outside of Caversham Park to paint. And for extra money, he'd worked a stint as an orderly in the same expensive rest home in Henley-on-Thames where I had done my physical therapy.

Then one day, abruptly, while we were drinking glasses of amber ale, he said, "I suppose the locals have told you how I came to have that fishing boat out there and the flat above."

"Ummm, yes," I said, "There was something about an old fisherman who had befriended you and who you assisted."

"They put it that way, did they?" He had a little sort of grin on his face.

"Well, no, not exactly that way," I answered, a bit nonplused.

"I'm sure they told you that I fucked my way to my small inheritance. Isn't that the exact way they put it?" The grin held on his face but was a little tighter now.

"Well, ummm, yes, that's what they said. But, you know—"

"They have that right. Exactly right. I've been watching you, you know," he interjected. "Could it be that you fancy me too?"

I paused, wondering where to take this, deciding that honesty was the best route. I hadn't had any variety in my sex life for months, and as generous as Sir Guy was, he wasn't exactly fully satisfying for a young, vigorous, highly sexed lad like me.

"Yes, I guess I could say that I fancy you," I answered.

* * * *

We fucked in the sun-drenched studio room looking down onto the canvas umbrella tops of the harborside café. I gasped when I entered the room. A single, narrow, cot-like bed occupied the center of the room, and facing that, in a great circle all around the bed, were oil paintings. All were of young, well-hung naked men. Some of single men in erotic poses. Others of couples or threesomes in various sexual positions. The paintings were very well done and very arousing, highly erotic.

We stripped and wrestled on the bed for some minutes, both tops, both fighting for control. But fishing was hard, muscle-building work, and Reginald eventually wore me down and got behind me, trapping my arms over my head in a strong arm lock, and working his knees between my thighs. When he had worked his hard cock four inches inside me, I gave up the fight and started working with him. I'd been fucked before, mostly when I was younger and was being introduced to the life by my father's best friend. But it had been a couple of years since I'd last been taken, and so it took Reginald some effort and considerable groaning and grunting on both of our parts for him to bottom inside me, and then to hold while my panting and heaving subsided. And then he ran a strong arm around under my belly and raised my buttocks to where he could rise to his knees and get firm leverage. That accomplished, he began to stroke me hard and fast. His thumb came up over my chin, and I took it inside my mouth and sucked hard on it to keep myself from crying out at the mixed pain and pleasure of his throbbing plumbing deep in my channel.

He came quickly in a flood of semen inside me, giving me the impression that it had been some time since he'd had a man. I thought that this might be so—that he walked a thin edge in this small village, considering how he had come to be one of the village residents himself. I supposed that the villagers kept a close eye on all of their young men, even without having ever said anything to each other about it. He must have been looking for someone such as me to come along for some time. All of his sexual energy must have been projected into these paintings of his. But now, for this moment, all of the sexual strength of him was concentrated on that hard cock working inside my ass canal.

40

After coming in several jerks, Reginald let me free of his tight hold and rolled me over onto my back, He sank down on the floor at the foot of the bed and pulled me down to him, his hands gripping my thighs. And I felt the warmth of his mouth come down over my cock, and he sucked me expertly to ejaculation, with his tongue fucking my piss slit as deeply as he could penetrate me there.

When I had released my seed, he came back up on his feet and pulled my body back up the bed, turning me on my side, and stretching down along my back, the two of us plastered close together on the narrow bed. He lifted my leg, and I groaned and grunted as he ran his cock back up inside me, the entry this time more of a glide, aided by the cream of his earlier coming inside me.

The urgency and lusting of our first fuck behind us now, Reginald took me again with more care and more deference, asking me what I liked and what I liked better. My cries of passion and the involuntary churning of my hips told him what I liked best. I arched my back and turned my face to him and we kissed, his tongue caressing the insides of my mouth and flicking back toward my tonsils, while he kneaded and pinched at my nipples.

Spent, at least momentarily, his dick softening but still inside me, he asked me what had brought me to Madeira. I told him of Sir Guy and my service to him and that I was only here until Sir Guy passed on.

Reginald suddenly laughed and raised up on an elbow and looked down into my face.

"Why that old fucker. He bamboozled you too?"

"Excuse me?" I answered. Studying his face, looking for clues of what he might be talking about.

"Sir Guy is why I'm here too. He brought me out here five years ago. He said he wanted to die in Madeira. He had sweet talked me to be fucking him in that old geezer's home of his in Henley. Said he wanted to die in Madeira and would I bring him here to do so? Made it sound like death was imminent. I'll bet the old fucker will survive us all."

I started to say something, but Reginald stopped tweaking my nipple and raised a finger to my mouth, silencing me. I sucked the finger and then another two into my mouth. I felt his cock stirring again, rising again inside me. I reached back and palmed one of his bulbous buttocks cheeks and held him close against me.

"Five years ago," and he laughed again. "Well, we got out here and he came to life again and wanted to be fucked hard three and four times a day. I did that for months, waiting for him to die. But all he'd talk about were these little deaths of his—*le petite mort* he called it—and how they brought him life. And then I started coming down here and found this guy who appeared to be in a lot better shape than Sir Guy was and who was satisfied with a weekly fuck. One day I just didn't climb the hill again and I heard that Sir Guy had flown back to England. So, he's still alive, is he? And still getting away with this trick of his. I guess now you'll leave him too."

Reginald was fully hard again now. He plopped his cock out of me, though, and stood up behind my butt beside the narrow bed. I didn't quite know what he was doing—at least until I looked out at his paintings and saw in one a couple in a position that Reginald was maneuvering me into. My left leg was stretched out flat on the bed, and Reginald grabbed under my hip with his left hand and lifted my pelvis, while his right hand pulled up my right leg and propped it up along his chest.

Then he swung his right leg over through my spread legs and to the other side the bed, where he dug in his heel where the mattress met the box springs. As he was swinging, I was crying out and grunting, because this maneuver brought his hard, long cock to my entrance at a side angle, and he thrust inside me and started caressing my channel walls with his cock bulb in places and ways it had never been made love to before.

He was stroking me hard and fast, and I was letting him know that I loved what he was doing to me. But at the same time my mind was processing what he had said.

No, I didn't think I'd be abandoning Sir Guy any time soon. I was fond of him, and I didn't begrudge him his little subterfuge in his clutching at whatever life and loving that was left to him. No, as long as I could occasionally break away to be mastered like this by Reginald, I believed I would be happy and content on Madeira—and in Sir Guy's bed—for some time to come.

Wait for Carnival

Ned Harrington had patiently waited for his young protégé. Ned had known for years that he wanted Devin; he'd known for more than a month he could have him. But everything had to be right, just right.

Ned and Devin's father, John Treadwell, had been long-time lovers. The Harringtons and Treadwells were among the first families of Charleston, South Carolina. Ned and Devin had gone to private school together; Ned had been John's best man. And the night before John took Helene to the matrimonial bed, Ned took John in the back seat of a Cadillac convertible. They initially had tried to stay away from each other after John Treadwell had wed, but their resolve was weak, and within a couple of years they had begun surreptitiously meeting for sex.

When Devin was six, John's wife, Helene, died in an airplane crash on her way to her usual summer retreat in Paris; John followed along behind her five years later in what would have been reported as a suspicious hunting accident covering a suicide if Charleston society hadn't closed ranks around its own. John's death left Devin Treadwell an orphan. It also revealed that the Treadwells had been living well beyond their means for decades. Ned Harrington swept in and covered the family's debt and bundled Devin off to the same private school he and Devin's father had attended.

John wasn't nearly as successful in life as Ned was, and Ned had carried the Treadwells for years financially. He didn't give John and Helene money directly, but he made sure that business came their way and that the Treadwells could hold up their head at the forefront of old-line Charleston families.

Ned mourned the passing of John, but in Devin he had the spitting image of John. Patrician Greek god looks, a ready smile, natural athletic ability, curly light-brown hair, and an innate interest in men. Ned would not have disagreed with anyone who said bisexual preferences were inherited. The Harrington and Treadwell men loved their woman, but a good many of them loved their men as well. And the Harringtons and Treadwells had been linked in this way for generations. Ned had been initiated into male-male sex by his own father in the family's hunting lodge in the Great Smokey mountains and before that evening was over he had been taken as the lover of John's father as well in a threesome. It was almost inevitable he himself one day would seduce John.

Charleston society was one that was not as unique as the local patricians liked to suppose. It was all prim and proper and almost antiseptic on the surface, but underneath it was teeming with sexuality and a wild bent toward hedonism. In truth this was the same with many an isolated, highly stratified cast system, though.

Devin, the orphan Ned had taken on to raise as his own, worshipped Ned, and Ned figured it was only a matter of time until he could relive his love affair with John Harrington through his mirror-image son. But Ned wanted to do it right, and he wanted to do it away from the searching eyes and wagging mouths of the insular old-family culture of Charleston. And he wanted the taking to be special. Once he'd made love to Devin, he wanted to have Devin with him forever, taking the "spitting image" place of his true love, John.

All of Ned Harrington's carefully and well-laid plans for Devin almost were blown to the winds, however. Shortly after Devin's eighteenth birthday, the two of them had gone up to the Harrington family's hunting lodge in the Great Smokeys. After a day of hunting deer, weary and tired but with Devin exhilarated about the stag he had bagged, the two drank a bit too much. Ned had always assumed that he would have to prepare Devin for him and methodically seduce him when it came time to take him.

Thus, he was taken by surprise when Devin put the moves on him, begging Ned to make love to him. Ned had showered and was sitting in the lounge of the lodge just in his sleeping shorts and a light robe. Devin appeared naked, told Ned he had wanted to be taken by him for years, stating that he now was of an age to make this decision for himself, and sinking between Ned's thighs and burying his face in Ned's crotch.

This put Ned into such a sense of shock that he failed to react immediately. And within minutes, he was too weak and defenseless to the unexpected onslaught to resist Devin pushing the waistband of his sleeping shorts below his balls and taking his cock in his mouth. Devin's sucking technique was wholly unpracticed, but Ned was so taken with him—and had been for so long—that this hardly mattered in his arousal and the quickening of his cock. He lay back in his chair and moaned deeply as Devin sucked him hard.

Periodically Devin pulled his mouth off Ned's cock long enough to beg his mentor to make love to him.

Ned came back to his senses Just as Devin was taking charge and was coming down into Ned's lap and holding the older man's cock in position to penetrate his ass. He rose and pushed Devin off him and backhanded the young man across the cheek, sending him onto his ass on a bear rug in front of a roaring fire in a deep stone fireplace. Standing over the young man, looking so wounded and so vulnerable and yet so desirable and still desiring of what Ned could give him, Ned had to steel himself with all of his might. This was the same bear rug and an identical roaring fire atmosphere in which his father had pushed a cushion under his belly and fucked him for the first time and then invaded his mouth with his cock while John's father turned him, Ned's butt cheeks raised on the cushion, and came in between his spread thighs and fucked him as well. Then, spent and whimpering but filled with arousal, Ned had sat on the floor, his back against the warm stones of the fireplace, and watched John's father put on a show of just how intensely and masterly he could fuck Ned's father. Ned had been taken into Mr. Treadwell's bed that night and shown just how filling and satisfying man sex could be.

"Have you done this before? With other men? Have you been fucking other men?" Ned roared at Devin in indignation. All of his plans, all of his careful work, and someone else had slipped in and taken this little bastard. The ultimate betrayal. A betrayal of all the John and he had been to each other.

Ned wasn't reasoning well; he was acting as if supposition were reality—and he was holding Devin up to standards he'd never enunciated to Devin. If Devin had been sexually active with men already, this was something he had done naturally. He had made no pledge of constancy to Ned; Ned had never asked him to do this, never demanded it of him. Now he was looking up at the man he worshipped with dismay, confusion, and deep embarrassment.

"No . . . no . . . never . . . never with anyone else. I've always wanted it to be you. I knew you went with men . . . I've always wanted that for me. Not just any man. You . . . never before. I wanted you to be the first."

Ned believed him, relief rushing in, the program salvaged. The awkward way Devin had sucked him was evidence he was telling the truth. And the young man looked so startled and contrite and openly shocked.

"I'm sorry, son. I never expected that you'd make the first move. I've always wanted you too. But it has to be special the first time. I'll think of some way to make it special. Something we'll always remember. And we'll always be together."

Ned had sunk to the bear rug and had taken a now trembling and sobbing Devin into his arms. They both immediately slipped into renewed arousal, and Ned took Devin's lips with his and they kissed passionately and deeply. Instinctively they each moved to take the cock of the other in their hands, and Ned permitted this much intimacy, a mutual masturbation to a shared climax with soft moaning and sighing. But no further than this. Beyond this, although the two came together regularly over the next couple of weeks, Ned would not permit the lovemaking to go farther for now. In fact, he wouldn't again, in those months building up to the full taking, let Devin touch his cock. Instead, he would take Devin in his arms and stretch out behind him and hold Devin tight, one hand playing his nipples and the other stroking Devin's cock relentlessly until the young man had ejaculated for him.

"I'll think of something special," he murmured as they lay entwined before the dying fire that first night.

"Please do it soon," Devin whimpered. "I don't know how long I can hold out." And then he gasped and began to groan and grind his pelvis against Ned's flank, as Ned took his cock in his fist again and masturbated him in vigorous and relentless strokes to a second ejaculation.

* * * *

Ned Harrington was perplexed about how he could make the taking of Devin special until one day, when he was walking down Charleston's Queen Street, he stopped at a corner for a light change and turned and looked in the window of a travel agency.

They were advertising special rates on travel to Carnival in Rio de Janeiro. Just the thing, Ned thought, and when Devin next lay stretched out in the arms of

Ned and being stroked to completion—and begging, in vain, for Ned to move their lovemaking to a whole new level—Ned told him where they would be this time next week—fucking in a suite at the Mar Ipanema hotel in Rio and enjoying the sounds from outside of the annual Samba parade making its way to the Sambadrome.

Ned Harrington was a world traveler and thus he completely misjudged how overwhelmed Devin, who had never been abroad, would be by the sights and sounds and sensations of Carnival in Rio. Ned's idea was to have Devin completely devoted to and in thrall to him and only him in this foreign environment. But from the very beginning—starting in the airport itself, where a group of young, hunky Brazilian men honed in on Ned and Devin and swept them up in the gaiety of Carnival—Devin started to spin away from Ned. The Brazilian men were preparing a float for the gay procession in the Samba Parade, and they declared that Devin would be perfect at the top of the float—and that, yes, of course, there would be a place for Ned as well.

From there the whole trip careened out of Ned's control. The Brazilians dashed all over town, Devin in tow, gathering materials for their float and costumes for Devin and Ned. The theme of the float was the Arabian nights, and both Devin and Ned were to be outfitted in diaphanous harem pants and turbans and nothing else but greased up torsos to accentuate their musculature. And the float needed to be prepared as well.

For two nights, Ned made careful preparations in the Mar Ipanema suite for a ritualistic deflowering of his young protégé. Devin was always working on the float with the boisterous Brazilian hunks, though. The preparations for Carnival had put Devin in high heat, so it wasn't a question of not wanting to lose his virginity to Ned—and, in fact, every time Ned appeared to check on Devin and on the progress of the preparation of the float, Devin begged Ned to take him off in a corner of the warehouse and relieve his virginity forthwith. But Ned was a stubborn man, and he had it in his head to do this in luxury and in a way that would always be memorable to them both.

At last he gave up and decided that it would have to wait for the concluding night of Carnival, when the parade was completed.

The day of the parade arrived, and all was in readiness. Ned was on the first level of the float, arm in arm with two of the Brazilian studs, while Devin was at the very center, top of the float, surrounded by several nearly naked Brazilian men. All were laughing and gay, and the Brazilians were passing around bottles of Cachaca, the local strong sugarcane rum, as the float started out in the Samba Parade, headed for the Sambadrome.

But the float never made it to that destination. The drunker the revelers on the float became and the more intense the gaiety along the parade route was, the hornier the Brazilian men got.

Ned was horny too. He looked up at the greased up, youthfully beautiful, nearly naked Devin at the top center of the float and he ached for him. He could hardly wait to get Devin alone in the hotel suite.

Sensing the heat rising off the handsome American, the two Brazilians at his side went into heat themselves. The float began to waver, the driver now being heavily under the influence of the Cachaca. The first Ned sensed something was unusual was as the float was staggering off the parade route and into a secluded park area to the west of the Sambadrome. And then he realized that his harem pants had been lowered and that one of the hunky Brazilians was beginning to suck his cock.

Ned recoiled and started to move out of the grasp of the young Brazilian making love to his cock, but this only pushed him into the encircling arms around his waist of the other strong and large-built Brazilian who was kneeling behind him and had inserted his tongue in the crease between Ned's ass cheeks.

Ned looked up wildly at the top center of the float—just in time to see Devin's ass channel being breached by the chubby cock of one of four Brazilians near him. One of the Brazilians was crouched behind Devin and holding him up in the air, while two at each side of Devin were hold his thighs wide and the four Brazilian was hunched between Devin's thighs and slowly feeding his cock inside the young American.

Devin was having a ball. Laughing and swigging from a bottle of Cachaca and egging the Brazilians on. Wanting to be fucked. Having been put off by Ned too long in the losing of his virginity.

Over the next hour, Devin's ass entertained the vigorous cocks of four virile Brazilian studs, all five lost in the hilarity and freedom of the Carnival Rio, while Ned, looking helplessly on at the ruination of all his careful planning, was being fucked from behind by his own two Brazilian companions, in succession. Ned finally broke away and waved for Devin to try to do the same, but Devin just waved a friendly smile at his benefactor and smiled broadly as several Brazilian men who had been at the lower edges of the float now start mounting the tiers for their own turn with the highly receptive and achingly handsome young American man.

Ned waited for two days for Devin to return to him. But at the end of that time, he decided he was waiting in vain—and the interest he had had in Devin had waned anyway when Devin was no longer pure and just beyond his reach. Ned left Rio never to see Devin again, although he continued sending checks regularly. He had simply waited too long.

Young Man's Gift

"Auburn and curly, you say?"

"Yes," I answered after a moment, after the directness and shock had dissipated, both embarrassed and being turned on—but trying just to convey the embarrassed part. I'd played tennis with our new, young neighbor, and, the day being hot and wanting to be friendly to the new guy on the block, I'd readily agreed to go home with him to his cliffside house on the ridge above our house and to take a swim in his pool.

"Yes, auburn. Most of us gray from the top down. As you'll probably find out." I had meant it as a joke. But it had been delivered nervously, and his youthful smile told me that he thought he was as invincible as I had felt at his age.

I'd had my flings with men back in my daytime TV acting days, but not much of anything in recent years. I'd settled in well with Marge, used my earnings to establish a comfortable, normal—safe—life. And I thought that part of my life was just something from the past, gone and put to rest. It was a shock how quickly it all could come back to me. Hank. Mostly Hank. My first. When he was about my age and I was about Jeff's age, as a matter of fact. Interesting that.

I'd been surprised when Jeff invited me to play tennis. He was half my age and was so handsome and outgoing that I thought he'd have no trouble finding partners—for anything he wanted to do, female or male. He reminded me of the way I was at his age. Young, strong, confident. I could have anyone I wanted in those days too. But I was attracted to Hank. Gray-haired, handsome Hank, who played the "all-knowing" family doctor on my first television show. Maybe I thought concentrating on the seeming unattainable would blank out my feelings, help make me ignore what turned me on.

I think I impressed Jeff when I beat him in straight sets. I'd kept in shape. Gray didn't mean decrepit.

"You know, I watched you on the television when I was a child, and I think I was in love with you," Jeff was saying. I had stretched out on my back on a lounger after swimming in his pool and he was sitting beside my hips, his arm extended over me. I wasn't going anywhere until/unless he moved.

"Or maybe it was just lust," he continued and flashed me a really, really friendly smile. He told me how attractive my gray hair was and that he had noticed

49

the mix of auburn coloring among my chest matting. That's what had led to his question of what color my pubic hair was. Forward and suggestive, certainly, but it had been successful in getting my attention and piquing my interest, surfacing old feelings. I'd convinced myself that part of my life was over. I obviously was wrong. At least my dick thought so; it was straining at the tight material of the bathing suit.

"There were rumors at the time that you and the actor playing the doctor in that program were doing it. True? He was a real hunk, as I recall. About your age now, wasn't he? Hot though. Like you still are."

"Um, ah." I was tongue tied and entirely too slow to respond—getting the sense that this was going somewhere I hadn't been in years and debating with myself if I wanted to deny that Hank Forman was fucking me at every opportunity in those days.

"Can I see it? Can I touch it?" Jeff's smile was gorgeous. He was so young and hunky. I was so turned on by this.

I didn't have to answer. He was slowly pulling the bathing suit down and off my legs even while he was asking. His voice was soft and so compelling.

"Ah, I can see you are interested," he murmured. "And so, very, very nice. Yes, like you said, auburn and silky and curly. Still young down here, I see." he laughed. A full, throaty, husky laugh.

There was no more talk. He wrapped two fingers around the base of my cock, and he was running the other fingers of that hand through my pubic hair. I felt the palm of his other hand going in under my balls, the middle finger poised at my rim.

I was immobilized. Not expecting this at all. But remembering. And sighing at the attention. It had been years, but I remembered as if it was yesterday. Hank's hands running all over me, slowly preparing me, seducing me. That first time taking so much time with me. Burying his thumb inside me near the beginning of foreplay and holding it there, pulsing, telling me all I needed to know where this would end up.

Jeff was handsome and young and well built, broad, muscled chest. And he had Hank's voice, his silky-smooth convincing tones.

Hank could have had me just with that rich, baritone, authoritative voice of his. On the examination table on the set of the television program, after hours, practicing our lines and movements for the next day's shoot. But the "examination" going much further than the script called for. That enticing, controlling, dominating voice. And those strong, sensuous fingers. That pulsing thumb. Lips, tongue. And when I had melted to him, that strong, commanding, never-ending cock—when embedded churning and churning.

I was lying on my back on the cold steel table, trembling, scared, virginal, but oh-so prepared emotionally for the older, experienced, dominating man. He was wearing that white, pretend doctor's medical coat—and nothing else—and open, so nothing was left to the imagination. I vividly remembered being surprised that his pubes were jet black, silky and curly, even though his head hair was a delicate, shiny gray. I writhed, my legs spread, my buttocks at the edge of the table, while his soft mouth went down over my hard cock and his lubricated thumb moved inside me, preparing me, loosening and opening me up for that huge member springing forth from that jet-black bush. Then that first, painful, glorious breaching and glide—

50

deeper, deeper, and deeper, as I cried out my first taking to the hard steel beams overhead—that hard steel beam of his stretching and penetrating inside me—and arched my back and he pulled my legs up and out with strong hands wrapped around my ankles and began to rotate and pump.

He was so sophisticated and serious and elegant and fatherly in reading from the script, but the unscripted Hank was crude and hoarse, muttering of ripe buns, taut nipples, young flesh, fucking, scoring, popping cherries, and, when he had entered me for the first time, not so painfully as I expected as fully as he had prepared me, of sweet tight virginal asses and of how he was going to make me beg for it and cry out at what he could do inside me. All of which was true. The unscripted Hank filled me with lust—and with his burbling cum. Again and again and again.

For months after that, whenever the filming took a break, Hank took my elbow and guided me into his dressing room and bent me over a chair and thrust inside me, possessively, strongly. And I loved it.

But I kept telling him that people would talk. And they did. But he didn't care. He just laughed and pulled me into his dressing room and fucked and fucked and fucked.

For three months. Then a younger man was added to the cast. Fresh, still-innocent flesh, and the doctor was working on a new patient. I was taken over by a lighting man, who was younger, stronger, and more cruel and demanding and longer lasting than even Hank had been—and who had a thicker, if stubbier cock. And I enjoyed that as well—until the year I moved up to a better role in a different television series—and to more variety in my sex life.

Ahh, the memories. What Jeff was doing to me, bringing back the memories. Causing me to lengthen and thicken.

Jeff's voice reminiscent. And his fingers. And then that tongue slicking down my pubes. The strong, hard finger at my rim, entering. His thumb inside my channel, pulsing and stroking. I was lost.

The tongue moving up the side of my tool, just as Hank's did. Kissing my knob, flicking my piss slit with his tongue. Me sighing and moaning and panting and lifting my hips to him—as a second finger sank inside me and Jeff's soft mouth came down, down, down over my longing, remembering cock.

My hand gripping his bobbing head, enjoying the feel of his movement there as well as on my cock, my fingers running through his hair. Auburn, just like me once. I hope when he is gray he has someone young, virile, and masterful to do this to him too. Ohhhhh.

Bad Boys

Pen Pal

Paul first saw him in the prison library. His name was Dexter, and Paul helped him find a book. An adventure book with words that weren't too difficult to comprehend. Paul felt a chill go up his spine when their hands brushed against each other—and he knew.

Dexter was an indescribable mix of races that pretty much resolved itself into "mean." Skin that came across as deeply tanned without having taken the effort to go outside, a montage of tattoos that screamed brutality, and a physique that revealed he'd been penned up for years with little better to do than work out and work at working off angry aggression.

Paul couldn't believe—couldn't hope—that Dexter would ever be in a position to leave the penitentiary, but after months of exchanging pen pal letters, it looked like that might be the case.

While he waited, Paul, who worked a couple of volunteer hours a week in the prison library, dutifully went to his accountant's job in a medium-sized cubicle in an unending bank of cubicles on the third floor of a mammoth insurance agency and quietly and innocuously put in his time. After working into the early evening hours, he'd stop at a modest grocery store on his way home and pick up his canned or quick-frozen supper. And then he'd enter his sixth-floor, one-bedroom apartment without a view in a medium-rise, thirty-year-old apartment block and sit and eat his meal with a television show going in the background that he never watched or listened to.

While Paul ate, he'd concentrate on dredging up and continually replaying the last short, seemingly innocuous conversation he had with Dexter in the prison library. When he was finished eating his meal, he'd wash his dishes and stack them back in the cupboard. Then he'd walk over and turn off the television, take a shower, and then, naked, lie on his bed and masturbate to the rereading of the letters from Dexter and the imaginings of being fucked by Dexter, being Dexter's cellmate and being taken by Dexter without his consent. Then spent and satisfied, Paul would turn off his night light and sleep until it was time to start the cycle all over again.

When he learned that Dexter was being paroled, Paul broke out into a sweat, and his hands trembled so badly that he could neither finish his evening meal nor his nightly masturbation. It was only then that he realized that perhaps the reason he had focused on Dexter was that he seemingly was unattainable. Safe. Probably never going to see the outside of the prison.

But Dexter was paroled. And on the day Dexter walked out of the prison, Paul was standing on the pavement outside the gates, as he had agreed he would be, waiting for Dexter.

"You got a room?" was the first thing a miraculously free Dexter said at the prison gate.

"Yes," Paul said meekly. And, indeed, he did. It wasn't his apartment, of course. It was a room at a good motel. And he'd prepaid for a week. He'd promised Dexter the room would be clean and his—for a week.

"Clothes first. I gotta get out of these shitty rags. And money. You said you'd give me a thou."

"Yes, here's the money," Paul murmured. He couldn't look at Dexter. He was all atremble. Scared and aroused at the same time. Being alone in his apartment with the letters and Dexter behind bars was one thing. Dexter here in the flesh out on the street and the content of those letters zinging through Paul's brain were something else altogether. "My car's over here. I'll take you to a good clothes store."

"Think they'll have something to go over these pecs and biceps," Dexter asked with pride in his voice. He flexed and made the tattoos running down his arm jiggle.

"Yes, sure, we'll find something," Paul responded. A whole other world, he was thinking. There was absolutely nothing that Dexter's world had in common with Paul's. But then Paul's life wasn't all that hot, he thought. This gave Paul a little thrill, and he felt himself going hard. Maybe this would be OK.

"A bar. After the clothes, then a bar. Then that room." Dexter gave Paul a look—that look—and he smacked his lips and sucked his teeth in.

Paul looked down and blushed.

"Hey, you really want this?" Dexter asked. "You know the money, clothes, and room will do me if you don't. I can find someone else to screw. That ain't no problem."

"No . . . no. The clothes, a bar, and then . . . the room. It's what I want."

Later, in the motel room, blinds drawn, and a underamped light bulb in a bedside lamp sending shadows into the corners of the room.

"What you said in the letters . . . what you described . . . did you really . . .?" Paul couldn't complete the sentence. He was hunched down in the chair, Dexter towering over him, naked and aglow from a shower now except for his newly purchased briefs, having wanted to wash every hint of prison from his body the first thing after they'd entered the room.

"Yeah, it's true. It's what I do. It's rough in there. And when you don't got no power in one way, it sorta shows in other ways. You either do or you get done. And if you do, you make sure everyone knows you can do."

Paul trembling a bit now. And aroused. On the edge. Those letters . . . they were quite graphic. And, as the correspondence had progressed, they had increasingly become focused on Paul. Paul knew it probably was only because of what he promised to do for Dexter—the transition from prison. But . . .

Paul looked up at Dexter, at the rippling muscles of his chest, the constantly undulating tattoo display, the barrel chest tapering down to the thin waist. The broken nose, the mean, screaming gash across his cheek. The ropy muscles with the veins popping out, the rock-solid meat inside giving them no place else to go.

The thought of what was there under the prison uniform, plus what was in those letters, had sustained Paul for months of solitary masturbation. Now, in the flesh. . . . Paul felt himself turning to jelly. He suddenly longed for this to be fantasy. It *had* all been a fantasy. Hadn't it? He attempted to transport himself back to his cubicle, among all of those other cubicles, soft, nondescript music in the background, crunching numbers as he listened to two guys down the corridor discuss the previous night's basketball game.

But there was no transporting himself to the "other side"—to safety.

"Did you mean what you put in the letters?" Dexter asked gruffly. "Do you want this?"

He dropped his briefs. He was ready. Long and thick and throbbing and ready.

"Yes," Paul murmured quietly. He hadn't meant to say that. But someone in the room other than Dexter had said it, so Paul guessed it had been him. Paul didn't want to look at Dexter's mammoth cock. But he couldn't look anywhere else.

"And you want it prison style, like you said in your letters?"

"Yes." Whispered. Surely by someone else. Paul wouldn't have said that.

"Like a virgin? First night in my cell? Guards pissy at the new pretty boy in my cell, needing to be taken down a notch. Everyone lookin' the other way?"

"Yes."

"Are you that, Paul? Are you a virgin?"

"That way. That way, yes,"

Dexter was smiling. He also was stroking his cock—which was growing in size, although Paul hadn't thought that was possible.

"You bring rubbers?"

"Yes. There. There, in my briefcase."

"Lots?"

"Yes."

"Tonight. Tonight, you understand. Then that's it. I get the money and the clothes and this room for a week. And you get lost. And no calling the cops, no matter what, Right?"

"Right. Yes, it's what we agreed."

"'Cause if you call in the cops, I got friends that'll do you good and forever, understand?"

"Yes."

"After it starts, no stoppin' it, you understand? Otherwise it ain't real. Not like in my prison cell. Not like fresh meat thrown into my cell."

"Yes." Close to tears now. The last yes whimpered. Hanging out over the edge. He wasn't safely tucked away in his cubicle now.

Paul's head snapped to the side in pain and shock as Dexter took two strides toward him and backhanded him across the cheek. An evil grin on his face. Wanting and intending to take. Brutally.

This pushed all of the air out Paul's lungs, and he was given scant chance of replacing that. Dexter grabbed Paul's head between his hands and had the head of his cock forcing its way between Paul's lips.

"Treat it right, Baby, or you'll regret it."

Paul, trapped in the chair by Dexter's hulking body hunched over his, gagged and fought for breath as Dexter filled him to the back of his throat and, grabbing Paul's hair in his hands, began moving Paul's head back and forth, back and forth on his rod.

This was only the beginning. And Dexter saved himself, wanting the virginal ass—and sooner rather than later. When he released Paul from the face fuck and turned to fish condoms out of the brief case, Paul made a struggling lurch out of the chair and for the door. This definitely wasn't fantasy. This was overload.

But Dexter turned and tackled Paul down to the floor. He held Paul down with one strong hand holding the accountant's arm twisted, painfully behind his back, Paul's face buried in the carpet, while the erstwhile inmate jerked off Paul's pants and briefs. Then, crowned, but without lubricant or any other preparation, Dexter pulled Paul up to his hands and knees, hunched over his pelvis, and brutally thrust his dick at Paul's hole again and again and again, until he was in, past the sphincter, into the tight, previously unused channel.

Paul was gasping and crying out to the ceiling and writhing. Dexter was laughing and pounding away. Having a good old time. When Paul's knees gave way, Dexter just rode him down to the carpet, and kept thrusting away.

Later, Paul laying on his back on the bed, exhausted and brutalized. Dexter, sitting, still naked, in the chair facing the foot of the bed. Swigging one of the beers they had brought back to the room.

"Stroke it," Dexter said in a guttural voice. "Stroke yourself."

"What? Why?" Paul said, his voice spent and trembling.

"Just do it. I want to see how big it gets."

After a bit.

"Ah. Good. Nice size. Keep it up. I want to see the cream. Think of the letters. You said you did it to the letters."

Heavy breathing, from both bed and chair. At last an "Ahhh," and Paul let his head drop back, spent, dribbles of cum on his flat belly.

"Spread 'em."

"N-o-o," wheedling, weakly voiced. "Please, no."

"I said spread 'em for me. I'm in a fuckin' mood again. Your jackoff put me in a fuckin' mood."

Dexter was already at the end of the bed, pulling Paul down to the edge with a fist wrapped around his ankle.

"Nooo," Paul whimpered, trying to come up in a sitting position. He started to say something else, but this was cut off by a backhand across his face that sent his head reeling back onto the bedspread.

"Here, hold this," Dexter said as he thrust his half-empty beer bottle into Paul's hand. "Don't lose none."

As Paul meekly took hold of the beer bottle, fighting to keep it upright, Dexter fisted Paul's calves and pulled them wide apart. Then he grabbed one of the bed pillows and stuffed that under Paul's hips, raising his pelvis. Dexter took the beer bottle back in one hand and pinned Paul's sternum to the bed surface with the other. Paul didn't have a chance. Dexter was twice as big and three times bulkier than Paul.

Paul cried out in surprise and pain as he felt the cold glass of the beer bottle neck being pushed into his ass. He started to struggle, but Dexter lifted his hand long enough to backhand Paul's cheek again and then returned it to his sternum.

"The more you struggle, the worse it will feel," Dexter said, giving his prey a cruel grin. "Thought we'd do it this time with some lube."

The cold beer felt strangely soothing as it spread and sloshed around inside Paul's stretched and shredded channel, and Paul just laid back and took it. Again.

Soon the thrusting bottle was replaced with a hard, thrusting, insistent cock.

Dexter was in high heat. Who knows how long it had been since he'd gotten his rocks off—years at least since he had been able to enjoy it without keeping one eye and ear cocked to the cell door in case a guard was passing by—assuming that it would be one of the few guards who cared what he was doing with and to his cellmate.

While he fucked, Dexter took Paul's cock in one hand and treated it like it was the stick shift in a drag race. He grunted and lowered his lips and teeth to Paul's nipples and neck and licked and kissed and bit and chewed, while Paul panted and moaned and groaned and moved in waves of his own intense new-found passion and lust under the attentions of a man who fucked brutally and roughly—and completely.

Hours later a bruised and whimpering Paul was dumped unceremoniously outside the motel door, on the balcony overlooking the parking lot and a Pizza Hut, and the door to what was now wholly Dexter's room was shut firmly and locked. It was several more minutes before Paul was able to rise and drag himself down to his car . . .

. . . and back to his life.

Paul saw him for the first time three weeks later, in the prison library. His name was Digger, or at least that was the name he went by in prison, and Paul helped him find a book. An adventure book with words that weren't too difficult to comprehend. Paul felt a chill go up his spine when their hands brushed against each other—and he knew.

Prisoner's Prisoner

He had chosen well. His gaze went over all of the possibilities and they fell on me. And he knew and I knew in that gaze who the real prisoner was. I thought even then that he must have had help, that someone must have researched and guided his choice. Surely he couldn't tell that about me just by looking over all the possibilities—that I was the weakest in the chain and what my weakness was and the extent of that weakness—and that he could exploit it as well as he did. I knew I was lost when I first saw him enter the room. I knew then what the outcome would be. The joke really was on him; he didn't need to do what he did to get what he wanted.

We were released for lunch, but as the others left the room, a clerk came over to me and told me I was needed briefly in a room down at the end of the corridor.

When I entered the room, there he was, sitting in a straight chair, still handcuffed. The man who let me in the room was burly brute of a man. Well over six foot and solid with muscle but also well padded with too much rich food, beer, and other forms of self-indulgence. He looked mean and unyielding, just as he should to be doing what he was doing.

But my eyes went immediately to the boy. No, not a boy. I had read the record; he was a man now, and that made his plight all the more hazardous. If he lost now, he wouldn't be free again for years. But he looked so vulnerable—or he certainly looked just as someone would who I would take as being vulnerable. Very young looking. Lithe, blond, with curls hanging down in his eyes, and almost a girlish, shy sense about him. Hooded eyes that probably could tear easily and were, to me, at least, very sensual. I certainly took the look he gave me as a sensual one, and I wondered if that was natural and if it would be his undoing if he were to lose now. Certainly the curls would go, but how much of the manner he was showing me could be changed or at least hidden from the predators? My heart went out to him, as, involuntarily did other parts of my body. He was just the sort I had always fancied.

I wonder in hindsight if perhaps he wasn't that sort at all, but only was that sort now because he needed to be.

The eerie thing, really, is that not a word was spoken by him. He conducted the whole scene with his eyes and his gestures and his body.

The other man, the dark, foreboding one, motioned for me to sit in one of the straight chairs and then, when the young man lifted his wrists, the older man brought out a key and unlocked the cuffs.

Then the young man came over and knelt before me and looked up with those wounded deer eyes of his. I looked on, mesmerized, almost in shock, as he lifted his T-shirt off his torso. I could see bruises. He had been mistreated already. (I wondered later if he might have done that to himself. If so, it worked a charm on me.)

I heard more than saw the sound of the zipper of my trousers. My eyes were lost in the young man's imploring gaze. I did break away from his control long enough to look at the other man, but he was just standing there, looking at us both, impassive of body. But he had a small smile on his mouth, and his eyes were gleaming.

I sat there as if shackled as the young man found my cock and brought it out into the open and began working it with his hands, his eyes imprisoning mine still. Even when his mouth went to my engorging tool, his eyes were lifted up to mine, imploring me, trying to convey the depth of his need.

He knew me fully even before I possessed him fully. He knew I was lost in the look of him, in the need in him, in my own need for him and for all of the other hims like him.

I just sat there, straight in the chair, my arms hanging limply at my sides, as he stood then and took off his trousers and briefs and then settled down in my lap, facing me. I moaned and threw my head back in wonder and desire as his ass passage slowly descended on my throbbing cock. This is what I lived for; this was the most intense, basic need in my life. And I had been stripped entirely by him. He was the one physically stripped and me still nearly fully clothed, but I was the more naked of the two. He had gone straight to my secret desires, had found my deepest vulnerability.

I looked to the larger man for some sense of the why of all of this, but he was just standing there, with that gleam in his eyes and the half grin on his face—and his beefy hand rubbing the front of his trousers, running his fingers along what appeared to be a monster tool.

The young man had unbuttoned my shirt, and his lips and fingers were playing with my nipples as he slowly raised and lowered his small hips on my engorged cock. I began to groan and moan my passion and the rising of my essences. And my moans were mixed with sobs. I didn't want to enjoy this, to need this, to live for this. But I did. I couldn't help myself—and the young man knew I couldn't help myself.

I was lost now. I was taking over and thrusting my pelvis up into him as he rode backward and forward on my lap. He was crying out for me now, talking dirty, biting at my nipples, bringing his mouth to mine, trying to pull every ounce of power out of me, doing everything he could to bring me to a quick finish.

And he succeeded. With a sob and the ejaculation of both my strained voice and of my seed, I capitulated to him, became his prisoner of passion.

We sat there, both panting, trying to regain our breath, me still inside him, but retreating, withering from the knowledge and shame of what I had done—what I had let him do to me; what he had lowered himself to do for his own need, which

62

really wasn't my need at all. I knew I meant nothing to him really except for the two words I could give him.

It was then that the larger man, the beefy man of the mean aspect, went into action. He was at us now, pulling us apart. The young man was roughly lifted off me and thrown down on his back on the table that was in the center of the room. The young man tried to rise, and the larger man backhanded him across the face. With one hand the man gripped the youth around the neck, holding him down on the table top with a strong strangle hold. With the other hand, he undid his belt, dropped his trousers, and pulled out a baseball bat of a hard cock.

I sat there in my chair dumbfounded. The young man's eyes were on mine, and I could see the pain and suffering in his eyes.

Those eyes woke me to his plight, and I started to struggle up, to come to his aid, although I had no illusions that the monster of a man couldn't take care of both the lithe blond and me together.

Seeing me start to move, though, the larger man turned to me, took his hand off his cock, and raised it toward me.

"Stay where you are. You'll do that if you know what's good for you."

"But you can't—" I started to say.

"He wants this," the guard declared. "This was both the deal and what he said he wanted. I get to fuck him for letting you in here and giving you both privacy. And he wants me to fuck him hard and rough so you'll know what waits him if you don't save him. So, you just sit there and watch."

The look in the young man's eyes told me that his tormentor was speaking the truth. And I just sat there, not wanting to watch, but mesmerized, sharing the young man's pain and suffering, as the large man brutally entered him with his cock in one powerful thrust and pounded him hard and long and vigorously, all the time holding him to the table with a beefy hand on his neck. And all the time the young man's eyes imprisoned mine, conveying his suffering, making me share in his suffering. And share I did. I felt every thrust of that cock and of every cock that might be in the young man's future. And I cried for him.

The next three days need not even have happened. It was a foregone conclusion. The young man sat there, impassive, the burly guard within striking distance, as I stood in the final moments and, as jury foreman of the young man's trial for manslaughter in the first degree, read out in ringing tones those two words he wanted to hear: Not guilty.

The young man hadn't promised me a thing; indeed he'd never said a single word to me. But, of course, I had had hopes. Such was the depth of my need and my obsession that I would still harbor hopes against all reason, against all evidence that he had just used my weakness against me. But after we left the courtroom that day, I never saw him again. He had what he wanted already.

BDSM

Big Boy Curious

We'd met in passing on a porn Web site and had given each other a couple of satisfying private chat cyber fucks. Without openly asking for it, he increasingly pushed our cyber play to the kinky and S&M. His site moniker was Bigboy and mine was Viper, and it didn't take me long to figure out that he turned on to bottom and domination, which was just fine with me. I could also tell that he was very curious, if a little shy and hesitant. Chances were good he'd never gone beyond the cyber but was drawn like a moth to the whole concept of what we were cybering.

His site profile was scanty—an artist in California, claiming to be bi—but the location opened up a wealth of possibilities for me.

[Viper] Located in California, bb? North, South, Central?

[Bigboy] Central.

[Viper] Ah, profile says u're an artist. frisco then?

[Bigboy] No, farther south. even more artsy. Coast.

[Viper] must be monterey then.

(Pause)

[Viper] santa cruz myself.

(Pause)

[Bigboy] Interesting.

[Viper] yes, interesting. interested, yes?

(Pause)

[Viper] u've said u wanted to see my basement room.

(Pause for three minutes, and Bigboy signed off chat)

Three days later I was cruising the chat room, and he invited me for a private chat. I was beginning to think he wouldn't contact me again, but all the time the moth was fluttering around my flame.

[Bigboy] Maybe. But here in Monterey. Out on the pier.

[Viper] no. must be something u want. u have to come to me in santa cruz.

He signed off again then, and I didn't enter the chat room at all the next evening. Toward midnight, he IMed me, eagerly agreeing to come to Santa Cruz that weekend. I put him off, telling him I couldn't make it until the following weekend, although I didn't really have anything else to do. Just stringing him out; giving him line to either slither away or hook himself. He agreed to meet, and I picked out a gay biker's bar in the rough part of town, telling him what the bar was, giving him plenty of room to cut and run.

On the designated night, I tricked myself out in my leathers and black net muscle shirt that stopped short of my belly button, showing off my abs real well, and biked my Harley over to the bar. Chances were that he wouldn't show, but I'd have me a fine evening anyway.

Surprise, surprise, though. He showed. I easily picked up on him when he entered. Nice looking; good, trim, muscled bod, but nervous as hell. He saw me when I waved at him, and I saw his eyes get all big. I didn't think he was dissatisfied, just hyperventilating at the whole concept.

He came over and sat, and after establishing we were who we thought we were, we tried some small talk. From time to time, he looked like he wanted to bolt for it, and each time I asked him if he wanted to leave alone, but he set his jaw and said no. He told me that his life had become just so boring in the sex department and he needed to give it a jolt start. I told him I could do that—and he had no idea how close to reality my plans were to do that—but that where we could go from here wasn't going to be for the fainthearted. He swallowed hard and asked me if I was going to show him my basement. I told him, no, not this time—and his body seemed to deflate as if he'd worked himself up for nothing. But I went on to say that I thought he might like to see my garage instead tonight. Asked him if doing it tied up and on my Harley appealed to him, and I felt his thigh tremble under my hand.

Out in the parking lot, he climbed onto the bike behind me. When we started off, he was sitting well behind me and having a hard time figuring out where to put his hands, but I upped my speed, and his pelvis was soon plastered tight against mine and he had to wrap his arms around my bare, steely midsection to keep from flying off the bike. I could tell he was excited by what I could feel snaking up the small of my back and getting harder as it rubbed up against me.

We sped through the town and back out into a more disserted area in the dust- and sagebrush-covered hills and pulled up short in front of the large corrugated, isolated garage building I kept to work on my cars and bikes. I zapped the high entry door open, and then zapped it closed again when we had driven into the building. The same zapping turned on the industrial-strength lights hanging from the rafters well above our heads. I ran the cycle right up to a clearing in the middle, under some gymnastic arm rings suspended from an overhead beam. I stopped the bike there and knocked down the kick stand with my boot as I hopped off. Bigboy, who I had learned was really named Roy—or at least had chosen for me to know him by this name—sat on the cycle, scoping out the surroundings in the brightly lit garage, as I went over to the side and picked up a pile of leather material and tossed it at him.

"Here. Strip and put these on," I directed, using a voice of authority both to keep him focused and because I had discerned that was what he wanted from me.

He stripped, and I was pleased to see that he had gotten the Web moniker "Bigboy" honestly. His new costume was composed of a leather harness crisscrossing his chest, leather chaps, leather boots, and thick leather wristbands lined with fleece. No pants. He seemed pleased with the outfit, and his cock was rising to attention, clearly anticipating having a good time.

"Come over here and get back on the cycle; turned facing the back, your back on the handlebars," I commanded.

When he'd done that, and after showing him what I was holding in my hands and giving him an opportunity to object, which he didn't do, I quickly attached a long chain to his right wristband, threw the chain through one of the gymnast rings overhead, and attached the other end to his left wristband. There was some give in the chain, but he couldn't bring his hands and arms to in front of him now. I then attached shorter chains through rings in the ankles of his boots to something in the wheel of the motorcycle on either side. He wasn't going anywhere for a while.

He watched me, all wide eyed, as I then stripped my own pants and muscle shirt off, and stood there only in my leather boots—and those busy tattoos and all those metal rings piercing my body, including the big, thick silver ring in the head of my penis. I already had quite a hard on, one to rival what he was showing me. His cock was something to whistle at, but I was bigger and thicker than he was. I could see that he was panting at the sight of me. Starting to sweat, and his well-muscled pecs were twitching.

I took out a camera and snapped "memory" shots of him astride my cycle and in restraints, which I promised to share only with him. I expected him to object to that, but he was licking his lips, obviously aroused at the prospect of being able to see this real-life encounter on replay. I promised to break out the video when the scene heated up.

I brought out a tube of ointment and started lathering up Roy's ass, while pumping his cock with my other hand. He was already writhing under my touch. When I had him all lathered and pumped up, I took out the camera again and took some "hard on" shots of my new Harley decoration. Then I set up video cameras on pods that zeroed in on the bike and the now-glistening-with-anticipation Roy from three different directions, turned up the lights on the "set," turned on the video cameras, and came back to the bike. I threw my leg over the bike and was sitting on the seat, facing Roy. He was trembling all over, and his skin sizzled where I touched it. The video cameras were running, as I ran my hands over Roy's torso and thighs and lathered up and stroked my own cock until it was hard and slick enough for me.

I told Roy what I was going to do to him then, and he invited me in—hesitatingly, but I could see the lust in his eyes. There was no way his libido was going to let his body back out of this now. Then I tilted his ass up with my hands on his butt cheeks and entered him, slowly but fully. He was in fine shape and was very vocal for the cameras—and so was I.

All the way in and pumping in short strokes deep. "Nice tight ass, and nice tits, Hot Shot. Gonna fuck you until your eyeballs are swimming in spunk." I was using the language of our cyber fucks now, language that turned him on for real as much as it had hard the Internet. It certainly was keeping him aroused now.

"There, you want me. Not just in the chat room. You want my cock throbbing inside you. I'm in and you're pulling me farther in. Can't get enough of me, can you? Been wanting me for weeks, haven't you? Ah, made you moan, made you flinch, made you pant. You haven't had a man until you've had me, have you?"

His "yes" answers were inserted weakly, but with determination, between moans and groans and pain cut by pleasure outcries.

69

He managed to pant out that my penis ring was driving his ass walls to distraction deep inside him, and I pulled my cock toward the surface until he could feel the ring dragging back and forth across his prostate. He threw back his head and screamed in ecstasy, the reality obviously living up to what he'd imagined and was seeking.

And I pumped and pumped and pumped, showing off for the cameras—covering his torso and thighs with my searching hands and brutalizing his nipples and armpits with my teeth. When I was about to blow, I withdrew, stood up, and sent my cream flying all over his chest and belly, good footage for the cameras.

I then got up and switched off the cameras. I went back to the cycle with a damp cloth and wiped Roy down and then I wiped myself down. I did this all in silence, listening to Roy's panting and groaning as he rattled the chains holding him on the back of the Harley and came to grips with his fantasy turning into reality. He probably wondered if it was over, but I wasn't ready to let him go yet—not by a long shot.

I glided around the garage in fluid motions, with Roy's lustful eyes following my every move, working myself up for what he'd learn was a grand finale, recharging my load.

After several minutes, I went back over to Roy and wrapped a studded leather ring around the base of his cock, ensuring that he would remain hard for the cameras when he got hard again. Then he watched me as I encased my own cock in a special sort of sheath and strapped an apparatus around my head and over my mouth, that, when it was in place, made me look like I had big, thick, black lips. I moved my new set of lips up and down, making sure that the device moved with me properly. Then I turned the video cameras back on and went back to the bike, once more throwing my leg over the saddle and facing Roy. I didn't make him wait long to learn what my new lips were for.

The lip device was electrically charged, with batteries and emitted a low-level current that registered at just above the tingle stage. It did have an electrical zap feel to it, but only just at the threshold of being painful.

My torso muscles rippled for the cameras and Roy screamed out in agony and ecstasy, as I started to kiss him with those lips from his neck to his pits and biceps, across his chest to his nipples, and down his sternum to his belly, navel, pubic region, thighs, and cock and balls, sending slight electric shocks into him wherever they touched. Pleasure mixed with shock, causing Roy to jerk slightly for the cameras with each touch of the lips. Electric pinpricks to his tender inner thighs, on his butt cheeks, across his perineum, on his balls, and firmly applied to the rim of his asshole. He jerked and jumped and cried out with each touch.

Then Roy found out about that sheath covering my cock. I tilted up his ass with hands under his butt. My cock slid into him again, and he found that the sheath was electrified too. But the voltage here was higher. I was manually operating the jolts, applying the first one as I slid my penis ring over his prostate, causing his whole torso to lift off the bike handles in shock and arousal and sending him into spasms that had barely subsided when the second jolt hit him, all along the ass canal some five inches down; another half inch and another jolt. My lips went to his nipples and held onto them, one after another, sending electrical shocks into him there. Six and half inches of my cock's journey up his canal and another, stronger, more prolonged jolt. It lifted his torso off the bike and took me with him.

He was bucking like a rodeo stallion now. I wrapped my arms around his waist and rode with him, giving the muffled shout through my electrified lips, "Whooeee! Ride 'em, Cowboy!"

Seven inches in and a jolt that made him spew his hot lead all over my belly, and seven and a half inches in, I filled him with even hotter lead of my own.

We lay there, arms and legs entwined, astride the Harley, panting and moaning and coming down off our electric high. I removed the apparatus from my head and nuzzled my own lips into the sweat-drenched hollow of his neck.

"So, how does the real thing stack up to the cyber fucking?" I whispered in his ear.

"Amazing. Can I see what you've got waiting for me in your basement now?" he croaked back at me between heavy pants.

Topsy-Turvy

I'd been working on my Chris Craft on the dock down in the keys for several hours, often looking over to admire the size and lines of a sleek, humongous yacht on the other side of the dock, before I realized that two men were sitting in the covered fantail of that craft and watching me too. I almost regretted that I'd stripped down to the Speedo to do my washdown.

Suddenly embarrassed by their close attention, I went over to the other side of my boat to work. But I took occasional peeks at the other craft, which had the name *Topsy-Turvy* painted on the stern, and couldn't help but notice that both men had binoculars pointed in my direction. From here they looked like Mutt and Jeff. The large guy was a little hard to miss—a bruising muscle-bound hulk in white shorts and a fluorescent-colored Hawaiian sports shirt. The little guy seemed no more than a boy, as spied from down here. He was in gray gym shorts and a T.

The day was hot and I'd been slaving for some time and, having raised my eyes to the boat to see if I was still under surveillance—which I was—I tuned into the fact that I had developed a deep thirst. I came around to the dock side of the boat to fish a beer out of the cooler I had sitting on the dock.

"Care to come aboard for a beer?"

I looked around and up at the main deck of the *Topsy-Turvy*. The big guy was standing at the rail, a beefy hand shading his eyes. He repeated, "I say, you look thirsty; care to come aboard for a beer?"

I was already opening the lid to the cooler, but someone else's beer was always a better idea to me than one I'd bought. "Maybe," I called over to him. "Does the offer come with a tour of the boat? That's some yacht you have there."

"Certainly can, yes," the big guy answered jovially. "We can even take it out for spin, if you like. We were going to cruise for an hour of two this afternoon anyway."

"Sounds good to me," I called back. "Just give me a minute or two to batten down the hatches over here." I'd done all I wanted to do on my Chris Craft that afternoon anyway. And I'd been arguing with myself over whether to take the boat out. It was a gorgeous day, but if I took it out, I'd have all of the scrubbing to do again when I got back to the dock. Now I could have it both ways—a short cruise in a real ship and my own scrubbed down nicely.

A couple of burly crewmen in spiffy whites appeared and started casting off on the *Topsy-Turvy* almost as soon as I got aboard and was moving to the fantail.

"Hello, there," the big guy said as I walked up to him. He was still standing by the rail. The grip of his handshake had power and authority in it. "I'm Tom, and this is Jerry. You tired us out just watching you clean your boat down over there. Come sit and select your poison."

Tom and Jerry. I almost laughed. But then that was better than Mutt and Jeff, I supposed.

I went past Tom as he turned to introduce me to the little guy. The little guy—Jerry—didn't stand up. He looked like he'd fallen down a flight of stairs, rather bruised and battered, and I thought immediately that maybe he couldn't stand. I leaned down, extended my hand, and introduced myself. His hand was trembling and was slightly moist. As I leaned down, I couldn't help but notice red welts on his inner thighs, and I wondered how the hell they'd gotten there. That would be hard to do in a fall down the stairs.

"Hello, Jerry," I said. "I'm Raymond. Call me Ray."

Jerry looked at me wanly. His eyes were glittering and much more expressive than any other part of his face. He responded his pleasure in meeting me in a rather weak voice. His eyes were boring into me, though, and I got the impression that he wanted to convey something to me, almost plead for something. But then Tom spoke again, naming beer brands they had on hand so I could take my pick, And Jerry's gaze snapped away from me and looked beyond me to where Tom was standing. I saw the little guy's eyes blaze up and then dim. Then Jerry looked down in his lap at his hands and said no more for the time we sat in the fantail, Tom and I drank beer and talked about boat maintenance and the Miami Dolphins as the yacht steamed out into the Atlantic.

I had worked hard, and there was a lull in the conversation, and both the sun I'd already taken and the beer I was drinking too much of got to me. My head went back into the cushions as the yacht steamed along and I dozed off.

My dreams were disturbed. I heard noises, disturbing noises, groans and moanings and sharp little cries. I jerked awake at the sound of a louder, muffled scream, my mouth sour from the beer, my head throbbing a bit from having had too much sun while scrubbing down the Chris Craft, and the sensation of not knowing whether the cry had been in my dream or was part of my sudden wakefulness.

Tom and Jerry were gone, but one of the white-clad crew members was standing at the door into whatever lay inside the ship's main cabin beyond the fantail porch. He was looking at me, and when I was fully awake, he pushed the door into the salon open with a hand and pronounced in a low, gravely voice, "They are in here."

I stood and walked over and through the door and then stood there, immobilized for the moment in shock. Then I turned, wanting to get out of there— and off the ship, not giving a thought to the fact that we were a good two miles off the strand of Florida keys now.

But the crewman, who was nearly as big as Tom, was blocking the door and staring at me in a way that I knew would not permit exit.

Tom turned around and gruffly told me to take a seat and watch. I collapsed into a tub chair near the door.

Then Tom turned back and flicked Jerry's naked buttocks with a leather whip, raising a little cry tapering off into a gurgled whimper. He then thrust his engorged cock inside Jerry's ass and began pumping hard in long strokes.

It was a regular S&M movie set. Jerry was naked and bent over a padded, brown-leather-covered gym pommel horse type apparatus that was closer to the ground than usual and didn't have the handles of a regular gymnastic pommel horse. He was barely in contact with the floor on his stretched toes. His wrists were cuffed to the legs of the horse on either side and his legs, straining back from the apparatus as he reached for the floor, were separated by a steel extender rod cuffed to his legs underneath the knees. This was holding his thighs wide in involuntary spread. His cries were muffled, because his head was covered by a leather harnessing that held a plug in his mouth. His buttocks and back and the backs of his thighs were red with welting from where Tom was whipping him.

I sat there aghast, unable to take my eyes away from the tableau. Tom, decked out in only black leather pants missing a crotch and black storm trooper boots, was fucking Jerry hard while flicking his legs and torso with the whip. With each upper thrust of his cock, Tom was lifting Jerry's scrabbling toes off the floor. The action stopped long enough for Tom to pull his cock out and strap a ribbed silicon extender over his already-huge member that increased its width and length appreciably, and then he reared his hips back and slammed the pole into the channel of the much smaller man. Jerry writhed under the augmented attention and turned his head back and looked at me—his eyes full of his pain and pleading.

I started to rise, to try to go to his aid, but the crewman at the door leaned over and pushed me back into the chair with a meaty fist to my sternum. The look in his eyes told me I'd better not move again.

As the fucking continued, Jerry began to writhe under the attention and to moan ever louder. I was embarrassed, but I had to admit to myself that something was stirring inside me—that I found this arousing. I turned and looked at the crewman at the door, and that didn't help a bit. He had his cock out and was beating it. My hand went involuntarily to my own cock, which was hard and throbbing inside the restricting pouch of my Speedo.

Jerry was moving his hips in a frenzy now, and he arched his back and bellowed under his mouth restraint as he jetted out cream under the powerful, relentless thrusts and whipping of Tom. I didn't know how the little guy managed it. He looked far too fragile and vulnerable against the brutish hulk of his oppressor.

After Jerry had come, Tom pulled out of him and just let the small guy collapse against the apparatus in muffled moans.

Tom turned to me and said, "You now. You fuck him now."

"Me?" I croaked in shock.

"Yes, you."

"I . . . I can't do that," I managed to blurt out. Possibly the severe tenting of the crotch of my Speedo and the spot of precum there somewhat belied that statement, however.

"We're not going back to land until you do," Tom declared ominously with glowering eyes. "Stavos," he bellowed, and the crewman at the door, who was busy stuffing himself back through his fly, came to attention. "Supplies for our guest."

75

I looked around as the guy at the door dug in his pocket. He came up with two condom packets and flipped them over to me. I let them fall at my feet and looked down dumbly at where they lay. A big hand—Tom's—reached down and picked them up and tucked them under the rim of my Speedo and then he stormed out of the door. The crewman shut the door behind Tom and then turned again, crossed his arms, and resumed his guard stance inside the door.

Jerry was whimpering and moaning. I rose and went over, and, as gently as I could, freed him from the collection of restraints, and half dragged, half carried him over to a bed at the side of the room.

"Thank you," he whispered. I turned to leave, but he clutched at me. "Please don't leave. Hold me. Please."

I sat down on the edge of the bed, and he curled up to me in a fetal position and wrapped his arms around him. I encircled him with my arms. I don't know who started it, but we began to rock back and forth, and he had a hand down the front of my Speedo and was squeezing my cock. The sensations of arousal and lust welled up inside me.

"I must go," I murmured, trying to pull away from him. But he held me fast, suddenly quite strong.

"No. You have to take me. You heard him. You won't get back to land—"

"Hush," I said, putting a finger over his bruised lips. "Don't try to talk. I . . . can't . . . I . . ."

He was pulling my face down to his with the back of his hand, the other one still encasing me cock. "Fuck me," he whimpered. "You must fuck me. It's the only way." And then he had his lips to mine and his mouth was opening to me, and we went into a passionate kiss.

I adjusted our bodies, coming up more on the bed, moving his buttocks to presentation position for my cock. When in a natural position for fucking, I opened a condom packet and, with a sigh of resignation edged with a chill of thrill, I crowned my cock.

"No . . . no . . . Bind me," Jerry whispered when I had the bulb of my cock at his rim. "Both wrists to both ankles."

"What?" I said, loud enough for the man at the door to take notice. "I can't . . . I couldn't—"

"He's watching; he'll know if you don't." Jerry was whimpering, pleading with me, reaching for the leather thongs on the bed coverlet.

So, I bound him, ankle to wrist on each side and rolled him onto his back, trussed like a sheep for shearing. And I put the palms of my hands under his buttocks and presented the bulb of my cock to his Tom-stretched anal entrance. And I fucked him. And he moaned and told me how filling and manly I was and how much he loved my cock churning inside him—loud enough for the monitoring crewman to catch it all. And, sad to say, I enjoyed it immensely.

When I was lost to any qualms about what I was doing and was fucking him vigorously in long penetrating strokes, he cried out, "Slap me. Punish me, Daddy. Slap me." He had to say it a couple of times before I complied, but when I did slap him on the buttocks and on his nipples a couple of times, he became frenzied in the fuck and his cock hardened. And he ejaculated up his belly.

Ashamed at having enjoyed myself, but unable to deny that this had been one of the hottest fucks of my life, I untied him and we went back into a rocking embrace.

"The punisher," I heard him mutter after several minutes, while our breathing was returning to normal.

"What?" I responded, in shock. I'd heard him perfectly, but I didn't quite believe what I was hearing.

"The punisher, Daddy, I want you to do me on the punisher. The apparatus. Put me on the apparatus again," he was pleading. "I want you to fuck me again on the apparatus. Please, Daddy, please." Jerry was licking his lips and giving me an intense, dreamy look full of lust and determination.

I sat up and away from him, staring down at him. Seeing him for the first time since I had boarded this boat.

"Tom," I said, accusingly.

"Tom works for me," Jerry said. "This is my boat. I told him to get you aboard." His face was set in a determined, suddenly strong expression. His voice now was equally hard. "Fuck me on the apparatus. We're not going back to land until you fuck me on the punisher."

I required Salvos's help in hooking Jerry up to the apparatus correctly, during which time Jerry became increasingly docile and started to tremble in anticipation, his cock hardening as we finished. After I had fucked Jerry on the apparatus, just as Tom had, but without the whip and the mouth restraint, substituting hand slaps in response to Jerry's angry declarations that he couldn't come if I didn't punish him, and I had unhooked him from all of the restraints, Tom reentered the room. He was still in those black leather, crotchless pants, big, thick cock at full staff and flicking his whip. And he had a mean expression on his face.

"Salvos," he bellowed. "Help our guest get hooked up to the punisher."

"Nooooo," I cried out. But Salvos already had me in his grip.

Big Cocks

Long John Silverman

"Come on, let me at least look at it. I have a bet going. I've declared it can't be true."

"No," John said. But he was smiling. He knew the British bomber jockeys were a boisterous and randy lot, and most were too good-natured to raise his dander. And there was a heart-wrenching war on. And, mostly, he was too embarrassed that he was chained to a desk and, this not being his war, at least not yet, locked into a nothing, thinly symbolic liaison job while they were up there laying their lives on the line.

"Come on, then, John. Just a peek. I'll be dead next month. Would you want me to go without knowing?"

Trevor Chelton was being morbid, of course, but they had to be that way, the British war pilots. And they had to grasp at any humor in it that they could—or else none of them could have made it this far. Six months. That was the life expectancy of a British bomber pilot in this second world war. And no one had known anyone who had retired from this. At least not yet.

When John Silverman had just arrived at RAF Mildenhall air base in September 1939 as a nominal American liaison officer to the British war effort, a twenty-one-year-old, fresh-out-of-college U.S. Army Air Corps lieutenant, the best sign of support the Americans could offer to the British at this point in their war against Adolph Hitler, he had "gotten" it the moment he had arrived. His welcome escort had taken him to a barracks building and told him to pick out the billet he wanted.

"But all of the bunks are taken," he had said, after his eyes had scanned the long room and seen the unmistakable sign of primitive, yet determined domestication around each one of the neatly spaced cots.

"No, they are all available," his British counterpart had said quietly. "You can just clear the muck away of the one you choose. None of these lads are coming home."

It wasn't until much later, at war's end that John would learn that only 10 percent of the British bomber pilots who ever flew off over the channel survived the war. But just the image of that seeming full, but empty, barracks that day was all he ever needed to see to believe the horror of that reality. And that was enough to make him vulnerable.

Which was why, in the end, John had given the young and tragically dashing Trevor Chelton the look he wanted—and why he had softened to the young man when his eyes went wide as saucers when he got that look.

And it was why that, in late November, he let Trevor come to his cot in the ghostly empty barracks and had sat on the edge of the cot and let Trevor lower his naked body into his lap, facing him. Why John had sat quietly and docilely and let Trevor rise and fall rhythmically on John's manhood, nipples rubbing nipples, hands encasing John's head so that their lips met and they kissed while Trevor sighed a satisfied sigh of fulfillment and peace—and momentary escape from the reality of the times and expectations.

For three weeks that late fall they were lovers, John progressively being won over to Trevor's desires and needs so that by that last afternoon, Trevor was laying on his back on the cot, buttocks at the edge, and John was holding Trevor's trembling legs spread wide and was actively entering and entering and entering Trevor to the tune of Trevor's cries of passion and pleasure at the depth of the never-ending, mutually engaged taking.

That had been on the 16th of December. The legendary Wilhelshaven Raids over Germany had started two days earlier. No one knew then when they would end. All suspected it would be when the last British bomber pilot was dead.

There was a frenetic, "forget the world," element to John and Trevor's lovemaking. John had never lain with a man before, but he felt so helpless and superfluous to the brave defense these young men were putting up for their homeland, their great sacrifice in the face of sure death and probably futility. He could deny Trevor nothing in these circumstances. And for these days of impending horror, he let himself go. They fucked like there was no tomorrow, for, indeed, there probably wasn't going to be a tomorrow for Trevor and his compatriots. Again and again and again, Trevor in the deepest throes of passion at what John was willingly and completely giving him now, feeding deep inside him. No need for condoms. Skin on skin. Trevor arching his back and his eyes rolling back in his head, his cries of joys lifted to the ceiling of the eerily deserted barracks room as John sank in, in, in. No thought of tomorrow. Only today, and the frenzy of the deep fuck.

And on that day, John believed that it was Trevor who held his love. No other. Trevor was his whole life. And he was no longer even thinking he was doing this because of the unusual circumstances they were in. Trevor needed him in order to get through the days, to motivate him to climb into that Wellington bomber in the twilight and take his next dark-of-the-moon run into the German, flak- and Luftwaffe night fighter-filled skies. But that was passed them now. They were fucking because they were lovers.

The Wellington Raids ended on the 18th of December 1939, the British force exhausted but having made a decisive, staving off impact on the German war-making capability.

In this last sortie across the channel in the Wilhelshaven Raids, Trevor Chelton's Wellington bomber was shot down by a German ME-109E as it had the English channel in its sights after a successful run over Wilhelshaven, with the plane ditching in the North Sea, all crew registered as lost.

Three weeks later, John Silverman was reassigned to Claire Chennault's fledgling Flying Tiger "support" aid force unit that was forming in Kunming, China, to help bolster the Chiang Kai-shek government's resistance to the Japanese invasion in the east. And it wasn't long before John was fully occupied with an entirely different sort of war and without the time or luxury of private mourning for his lost lover. Young men were dying at every turning. There was no time to think on the senseless wasting of them individually any more.

* * * *

It was late in the November of 1963 in a quiet Cleveland, Ohio, suburb, when a distraught and drained John Silverman answered the ringing at his door. If he hadn't been distracted, he might have just let the doorbell ring and ring until whoever was there gave up and went away. But he had been watching the television coverage of the assassination and burial ceremonies for the U.S. president for days, and he was confused and drained and just went to the door without really even thinking about it.

The man was young and sad looking. John immediately started forming in his mind whatever he could say to get rid of a door-to-door salesman as quickly as possible. He was in no mood for anyone else's hard-luck story or personal tragedy at this time. He had all of that he could manage himself now. He was worn out by life.

But he was wrong in thinking there was no more of this to face.

"Did he suffer?" John asked, sitting there in the dimly lit silence of his living room in the long shadows of the late afternoon, the television set turned off for the first time in a week.

"No, not really. He went quickly, once we knew for sure that he was that ill." The young man, Raymond Bock, as he had introduced himself, dragged up a swelling of old, bittersweet memories for John. It probably was his English accent.

"I had no idea that Trevor had even survived the war," John said in a halting voice. The shock that Trevor Chelton had recently died was magnified by John's assumption that he had been dead for twenty-four years already.

"He didn't want you to know," young Raymond said. Bock was a strikingly handsome young man. Lithe and blond. Fine, expressive hands. Probably an artist of some sort. Certainly artistic, sensitive. He had shown as much sensitivity as possible in letting John know that John's old lover—Raymond's most recent lover—had both lived and died in a completely separate dimension from John's postwar life.

"He didn't want me to know?" John was still stunned and a little confused. This wasn't his sharpest week. He was vulnerable.

"No," Raymond answered in a low, throaty voice. It sounded like he was a bit on edge himself, barely holding in his emotions. "By the time he found you after the war, you were married and had children. How many was it?"

"Six. Six boys. In seven years."

"But your wife?"

"Mary died in having that sixth child. I raised the boys on my own. The last of them—Phil—is off at naval training now."

"Six children in seven years. What took her? A difficult childbirth?"

"She was just worn out. I tried to get her to slow down. But she always . . . she just wanted—"

"Can I see it?" Raymond's voice was hoarse. John sensed a thickness in it. A familiar tone. He looked up sharply at the young man. As if seeing him for the first time now.

"Excuse me?"

"Trevor talked of you . . . of it . . . often. In the throes of passion, he would cry out your name. I was jealous for ever so long. Not that he cried out your name. But jealous of what he had to say about it. I wasn't sure I ever believed it. But he was so sincere. He was fixated, and I'm afraid I've become fixated too. I've come all the way from London. Please, can I see it?"

Perhaps if John had not been at such a low point, his life would not have taken this jolting turn to the past. But the last of his boys gone. No one to care for. The tragedy of Dallas. The shock of learning that Trevor had survived the war but now, just as suddenly as he had been regained, was gone. Here and gone on the breath of a handsome young, vibrant man, in a silent, lonely room in a quiet Cleveland suburb as the whole world collectively mourned the irretrievable loss of innocence. A man with an English accent just like Trevor's. A need just like Trevor's.

They fucked right there in the living room as the late afternoon progressed into dark night. Raymond straddling John's lap once they both were naked, sinking down, down, down as he arched his back and lifted his gaze to the darkening ceiling and warbled in ecstasy at the long, long, stretching journey down into John's nestling pubic thatch.

Later, as Raymond was bent over the arm of the sofa, John hunched over and behind him, and Raymond felt the renewed throbbing moving ever more impossibly deep into the quick of him, the young man thought of that suitcase he had set down out of sight of the front door on John's front porch and wondered how soon there would be an opportunity to suggest that he bring it inside.

No Pole Big Enough

He certainly looked like a big brute when he had arrived in the hotel room, and with all that muscle, he provided me the hope that he could touch me where I needed to be touched, take care of my need, and give me relief. But it hadn't happened. Once again it hadn't happened. I was beginning to think there really was such a thing as wearing your hole out, as having become so used that you no longer could be touched where you were screaming for it and spouting off all that buildup, draining yourself in satisfaction.

I had ordered and paid for a guy who, they claimed, was not only the biggest they had but could keep it working all night—wouldn't finish without me.

I had lived for three years in that remote valley in the Himalayas, where the men were elephant built and could fuck all night. Through long practice, they had reamed me a wide one and had trained me to hold out for hours. And now my sex life was ruined. I had returned to the corporation offices in New York a year ago, and I hadn't had good sex—or what I had been trained to in the way of good sex—since I landed in Manhattan. It was making me irritable. It was getting in the way of my work.

I had tried the bar scene and the classifieds, being very explicit about my need, and then I had turned to the escort services. This was my third one, and although he had a good ten incher and seemed to have a lot of stamina, I was, once again, left unsatisfied, jittery, and with an ache in my balls that just wouldn't go away.

After the fifth fuck as deep and vigorous as he could manage, he just fell off of me and over onto his side on the bed and cried uncle.

But when he left, he said, "Here, man. Nice tail, but sorry I couldn't do it for you. I've never failed before, but I felt like I was swimming around in there. Maybe you need surgery or something. But Leo told me that if this didn't work, I should give you this card. No charge. Again, sorry. It isn't that you don't turn me on. You'd be a fine lay if you weren't stretched so wide."

With much regret I took the card, and after we'd kissed at the door and he left, I looked at it. It simply said "Club Pan" and had a telephone number and an address on the other side for a side street in the Village.

Two nights later I was standing at a dimly lit walk-down door under a iron porch giving access to the main level above of a nondescript brownstone on a dark

Village street. A blinking sign saying "Club Pan" was beside the door. So I at least was in the right place. I had called the number on the card the night before, and, after I had very directly told the man on the other end of the line what the nature of my problem was, he told me he thought they could help me. He also told me not to wear any clothes I was fond of. The one-evening visit I had paid for was quite expensive. But I was willing to try anything now for relief.

After giving my name to the pair of dark flashing eyes that opened a window in the door, I was let into a small vestibule that was completely black—walls, floor, and ceiling. But what arrested my attention was the half man who ushered me through the door. He was costumed as some sort of nymph—horns on his head that were cleverly attached so there was no indication they weren't naturally his and the hairy legs and hooved feet of a goat. He was pretty cute, actually, very slender, with black curly hair, including his pubes, which were exposed. He had a long cock dangling out of pert little balls, and he had a little goatee that jerked up and down when he talked. He was giving me a very enticing look, and I wondered if he was the one who was to try to service me. If so, I didn't think this was going to work. He did have nice length to him, but I doubted his would hit my walls at all as it slid up me.

He led me past an entrance down into some sort of club room where a performance was going on. I could see as I passed that the room, which stepped down to a stage area, was dark except of the glitter of gold cylinder-type decorations hanging from the ceiling. I caught just a glimpse of the stage in passing, but there appeared to be small figures dancing on poles at the four corners of the stage, with other, more muscular nymphs then this one—satyrs really—embracing the pole dancers. And a young naked man was tied to an X-shaped contraption in the middle of the stage and seemed to be in the middle of being fucked by another satyr.

As the nymph guided me farther down the corridor, I rather regretted that I hadn't been taken into the club. I needed warm-up if there was any hope of bringing me to the orgasm I needed.

We entered a room that was all white and had a curtain at the far side with some sort of framework in front of it, sort of a large, sturdy window frame, also in white. The nymph told me to stand in the center of this, and I hardly had noticed the velvet restraints at the four corners of the frame before he had my arms spread and my wrists tied to the upper corners and then my legs spread and my ankles tied to the lower corners.

He left the room and the curtain in front of me slowly opened. A diminutive figure was perched on a low bench nearly against the far wall of the room that was revealed to me. He was dressed in what looked like a Roman toga. He couldn't have been more than four and a half feet tall, but he wasn't by any means either a dwarf or a child. He was a perfectly formed little man. Some creature of the mythical woods, I supposed, just as the nymph who had let me in and satyrs I had seen down on the stage were—or were pretending to be. It was all in keeping with the Club Pan motif, I figured. But I really had no idea what it meant as far as filling my hole to satisfaction and giving me a needed orgasm.

The little man, who had downy reddish-blond hair and a beatific expression on his handsome face, was playing a haunting tune on some sort of piped instrument. I watched him for a couple of minutes and listened to his playing and wondered what possibly could happen out of this in the way of a solution to my problem.

I blinked my eye, and in the moment of that blink, another figure had entered the other room. He looked like one of the satyrs I'd seen down on the stage. He wasn't terribly bulky or tall, but beside the young man playing the pipes, he looked like a veritable monster. He was hung like a horse. And he was ready for action in that department. His rod curved up from his belly like a crescent moon, and it was capped with a big reddish, angry-looking bulb. He strutted around the room, giving an evil leer from under his bushy eyebrows. He was swaying to the music on cloven hoofs. His legs were as hairy as a goats, and he had massive pecs with patterns of hair circling his nipples and trailing down into his bushy pubes. He snorted and moved around the room to the music coming from the pipes, giving off an air that was many things at once: cruelty, sensuality, power, grace, danger, domination, and brutality.

I found myself both fascinated by him and shrinking from his visage as far as my bonds would allow, just as the small young pipe player seemed to be doing on his bench.

But then, as I watched in horror and absorption, the haunting piping stopped and the frightened squealing began. The satyr had drawn near the bench and just grabbed the little man by the front of his toga at chest level and lifted him up with the strength of one hand. The pipes went skittering off across the floor, as the little man howled his shock and surprise.

The satyr was ripping at the little man's toga, unwrapping him in ripping fashion like a child getting into a Christmas package. As I had surmised, this was neither a dwarf nor a child, but a fully—and very nicely—formed adult who just happened to be about half adult sized. Without further ceremony, the satyr, turning sideways to the window so that I got a full view of what he was doing, held the young man in front of him with strong hands encircling his waist and crouched a bit and brought the young man's hips over his hairy thighs. He positioned that bulbous mushroom cap at the young man's hole, and I thought there would at least be some preparation, although surely the young man couldn't take him with or without preparation. But I was wrong on at least the first count.

With guttural animalistic sounds of lust and expectation, the satyr was skewering the writhing young body down on his tool. The satyr pushed the torso of the young, howling man down toward the floor and turned then, full frontal toward me, so that I could see the head of the cap poise a brief moment at the rim of the hole and then slowly get stuffed inside as the satyr pulled the young man's hips up into his groin.

The satyr was doing the impossible: Stuffing an improbably thick and long cock inside an impossibly small ass. If it all went in, I was sure it would reach the young man's stomach. And slowly and surely is was all going in, and the young man was faltering. His arms and legs were dropping and I could see the whites of his eyes. He was either passed out or near to passing out. And this was all being done for my benefit. And I'd like to claim that it was frightening me or disgusting me, but I began to feel stirring inside me that I hadn't felt since I'd left that mountain valley in the Himalayas.

I kept telling myself that this was all being done for me, that these two probably did this nightly. And sure enough, when the satyr had bottomed his dick inside the young man, I saw the little man's face begin to flush. And then, as the satyr began to play the young man's body, making it slide up and down on his cock, I saw the little man's eyes come alive once more and now he was crying out again. But he was crying for the fuck now. The fright was gone and he was crying out for the plowing.

The satyr stiffened and gave out a loud sigh, and the little man was exclaiming that his insides were being bathed in cum. I expected the satyr to withdraw then and this phase of the demonstration to be over, but he just resumed pumping the little man's ass on his hard cock, all the more vigorously now thanks to the added lubrication.

I was no longer alone in my own room. Two hulking presences were beside me. And the first sensation I got was the musky smell of their lust. Two more satyrs. But this time, big towering specimens, over seven feet tall each and with swinging cocks that put the satyr's on the other side of the window to shame. They both took hold of the clothes I was wearing and literally ripped them off my body.

Mean, determined looks on both. Cold, piercing eyes staring out from underneath bushy black eyebrows. Sharp, flashing white teeth.

One showed me the monster dildo in his hand and, while the other moved to my front and started teasing my nipples and then my cock with those sharp teeth of his—never piercing anything with them but with the continual threat of being just on the brink of doing so—the other thrust the dildo in my ass. It was thick and long, but not of filling proportions in my present stretched state. Still, the satyr worked it around inside me in circles so that I felt the first flutterings in months of an arousal that might reach a climax.

I looked in the other room and the satyr was still fucking the young man. The little man cried out in ecstasy for a second time as I watched and the satyr's body gave a lurch and I knew that there had been a second ejaculation. But still the satyr pumped on.

The tormenting satyr in front of me stood and turned and released my wrists and ankles. But I wasn't free, not by any means. The dildo had been withdrawn, and my ass canal was now descending on the huge, throbbing tool of the satyr at my rear. He had lifted me off the floor with his strong hands and just sat me down on his cock.

He was monstrously big. Bigger than the escort I'd been sent earlier in the week. Both thicker and longer. I splayed my legs out, my feet finding leverage on the window between this room and the next. The satyr worrying my nipples now dropped and swallowed my balls, vibrating them with a maddening hum and sucking hard on them. I was crying out in ecstasy myself now. I hadn't had a fuck like this for a year.

The plowing in the other room was still going strong, relentlessly. There was an obvious third spouting, and the little man's eyes appeared to be swimming in semen and he was babbling to himself, completely lost in the experience, stuffed impossibly to the gills. The obvious inference to me was that, as ordered, these satyrs were determined to stuff me on a similar scale and to continue fucking me until I had my elusive orgasm.

That was all very nice, I was thinking, but this satyr wasn't going to quite be able to satisfy me. But that's not what they had planned. Now the satyr at my front was standing and then going into a crouching position, his thighs crisscrossing those of the satyr at my rear and his gigantic, hard tool now poised under me as well.

Thick fingers were at my hole now, spreading me further apart, giving purchase to the second gigantic cock. Sliding in alongside his fellow satyr's, fingers remaining just inside the rim. Two monster cocks inside me now, as well as a couple of fat fingers. I arched my back against the hairy chest of the satyr at my back and accepted the thick-lipped kissing of the satyr at my front as the two counterpumped me.

I looked into the other room. They were still fucking away. But the satyr had turned the young man. The little man was facing me now, his feet against the window on the other side of mine, but between mine, the satyr's arms wrapped around his prey's belly. The soles of the little man's feet were scrunching in and out, no doubt in the rhythm to what was churning in his tight little ass. The satyr was behind and crouched below him and I could see that giant cock pumping up into the impossibly small hole. The little man's face was slack jawed, but his eyes were dancing and just swimming in the cum that was building up inside his body. He was staring right at me and looking totally content and fulfilled, loving the stuffing and the never-ending fuck. His eyes were telling me that I could be content in this way too with what was being done to me on this side of the window. And I believed him; I believed there was hope. I watched the scrunching of the soles of his feet to the rhythm of his fucking, and I believed I could be well stuffed and fucked forever too.

This . . . was . . . just . . . about going to do it. Plowing. Relentless plowing. I was sighing and purring and crying out for it and doubting I could take any more of it, my mind flashing back to the Himalayan mountain valley and the giant mountain men with their monster tools. I was panting and groaning and tightening. The satyr reached down and squeezed my balls hard, and I shot off all over his hairy belly. For the first time in a year.

And then so did the two of them. Deep inside me, lathering my insides with their combined jism.

I looked into the other room. Still fucking away.

I felt great. They had done me. I had had the orgasm I had paid for. The release that I wondered if I'd ever had again. I lowered my legs from the window, ready to be released and to leave. Determined to do this every week now, no matter what it cost.

But the satyr in front of me still held the cruel piercing look in his eye. And it contained that edge of lust still as well. They weren't releasing me. Their cocks were alive again. They were pumping me again. They pumped and pumped and pumped. I whimpered and cried for mercy and ejaculated, miraculously for the second time. And so did the satyrs. And then the cruel smile again, and they once more were pumping and pumping and pumping and . . .

I looked through the window and they were still fucking there as well. Endlessly

Mooaaann.

Ethiopian Cabin Boy

To my surprise, when I was training for intelligence gathering, I discovered that my line of work wasn't as pristine sexually as I had tried to convince myself it was. I should already have been aware of this, as I had already gotten hints of my spy masters looking the other direction during my assignment to Bangkok when it pleased them to do so. And in my training, I learned that they could be pleased to do so if the intelligence needed was considered very important and when the options of "getting the goods" were restricted.

I was sent into the Middle East and stationed in Cyprus, which is now considered in relationship to the Middle East somewhat like Switzerland was considered to Europe in World War II—a safe haven where spies can meet on neutral ground and where it is considered ungentlemanly (although it does happen on occasion) for "wet" (meaning doing someone to death) operations to be conducted. And it wasn't long before I learned how far I might be expected to go to "get the goods" in my job. It was also where I quickly found a new answer to one of three questions that had perpetually come up in the world of "bottoms" in my Bangkok days: This question was "What was your longest?" One of the other questions, "What was your thickest?," would also be answered when I lived on Cyprus, but during a different tour a decade later. The remaining question, "What was the most satisfying?," had already been answered years earlier in Bangkok in the form of a black Army officer (who, with his ten by two dimensions, almost answered the other two questions as well).

The "longest" question was answered in the form of an Ethiopian cabin boy on the yacht of a Saudi businessman at anchor off the Larnaca waterfront. This promenade, very European in atmosphere, enjoyed a deep, flat beach separated from a long hotel and sidewalk café front of gaily decorated umbrellas and tables by a wide boulevard. The boulevard was anchored at one end by a yacht marina and at the other by the medieval harbor castle where Richard the Lionhearted married his shipwrecked Berengaria.

After our encounter, the Ethiopian had me singing a couple of octaves higher than normal and walking around tenderly—although the later part might have been caused by the escapades later that night. I can't attest to how long the

Ethiopian's cock was, but both my eyes and my intestines are quite sure they've never seen or felt a longer one.

When he took me, we were in a lower-deck cabin of the yacht, where you couldn't stand up straight except in the middle of the room. A double berth went in under the bulkhead. The Saudi owner of the yacht and I had just agreed on some successful business of a nefarious government nature, and the Saudi had been very attentive to me and let me know he wanted to fuck me. I had met him at a couple of embassy cocktail parties earlier and apparently had made a very favorable impression on him. I could tell by the way he looked at me that he fancied me, but I didn't make the connection at the time when I was assigned to contact him. My spy masters wanted the deal to go well, and I had been told to do what it took to conclude the deal—and I subsequently came to assume that my masters knew exactly what the Saudi businessman was interested in getting in return for his vital information. So, when he so directly propositioned me and connected it with his willingness to provide what I had come for, I said I would sleep with him that night on the yacht. Clearly delighted, he responded that, in appreciation, he'd send me a gift before dinner.

An Ethiopian cabin boy—not a "boy," of course, but an adult young man—had been gliding around the yacht all day as it wallowed off the colorful Larnaca waterfront, doing this and that. He was incredibly tall and thin, really out of place on a yacht with cramped head room, even if it was large. When I opened the door of my cabin to him, he was carrying a tray with a bottle of champagne and one glass on it, but I knew right away that he was my gift, because he was nude. His pecker hung down almost to his knees, it seemed—and this thighs were unusually long in themselves. I had never really thought about whether the unusual height on some African tribesmen had a relationship to dimensions elsewhere, but just then my education in that department lengthened considerably.

There was no thought of me refusing this gift from the Saudi; he hadn't given me the promised information yet, and this was no time to rock the boat—other than the rocking the Ethiopian was about to do with his performance on my body, of course.

I was still in just my Speedo, so there wasn't much undressing required. The tray also had a bottle of KY and a couple of condom packets on it, and the Ethiopian just slid off my Speedo and knelt there and sucked me hard, while pulling his own meat to erection. I fell back onto the bed, which was low to the floor, while he lathered himself and my hole up and rolled on a condom. He wishboned my legs up and out and I dug my feet into the low bulkhead that stretched out over the berth. He then knelt between my legs and just fed and fed and fed and fed that long eleven- or twelve-incher up into me.

At first he moved my hand to my ass and had me cup my fingers there so that he was pushing his cock through my cupped fingers, giving him a hand job as well as him giving me an ass fuck, when he entered me. I gasped as he reached a depth inside me I'd rarely felt before even though he had to go three inches through my fingers before entering me. But he laughed hoarsely as I panted and moaned to accommodate him. And then he brushed my hand away and I arched my back and cried out my astonishment and passion as he just dug deeper and deeper inside me. It wasn't all that painful, because his cock was pretty thin, but he had to have gotten

92

well up into my intestines and stretched them out where they'd never been touched by a foreign object before.

I looked up as he was doing this, and the Saudi was lounging in the doorway, watching me get royally fucked. The Ethiopian pumped me that way for a while and then turned me over on my belly and got that cock even farther up into me, taking it all out and then just slamming all the way back in repeatedly until he needed to come. And he withdrew then, ripped the condom off, and shot off all over the small of my back. I was digging my fists into the bedding as best I could to hold position while he jackhammered into me. I'd already come twice by then myself, once with the help of his mouth and then with the help of his hand.

The Saudi just stood there and watched with slitted eyes, and he kept his hand busy with his own cock. His "gift" to me was even more another gift to himself. He really wanted his entertainment worth for those precious secrets he held, and the long, long Ethiopian and I gave him quite a show.

That night the Saudi and his bulky bodyguard did me in a sandwich in an all-night fuck fest in the main cabin, which was not nearly as cramped as mine was. The Saudi's equipment was nothing to write home about and he came quickly, but the bodyguard had a really thick piece and was a fast reloader and had a vigorous, long-endurance pelvis action. Lots of nice muscle. He's probably the one who was responsible for my bowed legs and shuffling walk—and big smile—the next day.

They did me in turn. Then, as a finale, the Saudi really wanted to get his cock in there with the bodyguard's, but I wasn't having any of that, needed secrets or not. The bodyguard alone was much too thick.

I never did drink the champagne, and I can only surmise that the information I collected was worth my effort—at least my masters were well pleased when I returned, and they asked me no questions about my use of trade craft in getting the goods.

Ten Slash Two

I had been jittery and conflicted for the entire two weeks since I'd seen that big black topping a guy at a pool party in Bangkok. I had been bottoming for a Swede in a nearby patio lounge when I looked over and saw this monster cock jackhammering in and out of the other guy—who clearly was in seventh heaven—and I almost melted on the spot. I was conflict, though. Obsessed with desire because the cock, even more distinctive because it was almost jet black and was attached to a bulky—but ripped bulky—milk-chocolate body, looked so desirable. But threatened because the sheer size of it filled me with fear and uncertainty. I'd only been doing this for a short time. Was it even possible to take something like that in?

I couldn't get it out of mind, and a couple of days later I had the opportunity to ask the host of the party, Ben, who the guy was.

"Ah, we call him Ten/Two," was the answer. "He's an army captain at JUSMAG. Luscious, isn't he?"

"Ten/Two?" I asked, somewhat bewildered.

"Yeah," the host said, with a little snicker. "That's like in inches, both ways."

"Oh."

"Yes, oh. Biggest combined stats we have in service here, as far as I know. Interested?" the host asked, not showing the least amount of jealously, even though he had fucked me at the party himself—and must have enjoyed that, because he had just finished fucking me again on the rattan-carpeted teak floor of his Bangkok mansion when I asked him this question.

"Just curious," I said, nibbling at one of my host's nipples to give him reassurances.

"Well, if it's more than that, forget going after him," Ben replied. "He does the picking. If he wants you, you'll get an invitation."

I don't know if Ben had passed on my interest or if the big black had seen me at that pool party and liked what he saw, but not long after that I got the invitation.

Although I wasn't military, my SR71 supersonic jet unit was under military cover, and so I usually fell in with whatever the U.S. military establishment in Thailand had going. Thus, only about a week after that, I was invited to a change of command ceremony for the chief of JUSMAG, the Joint U.S. Military Assistance Group in Thailand. The speeches were still droning on, with all of us standing, if not exactly at attention, when I felt this big hand cup one of my butt cheeks. I didn't dare look around, and it could have been one of several guys I had been meeting at Ben's Bangkok mansion. In fact, I had assumed it was Ben, because he was a JUSMAG lieutenant himself, and I knew he was attending this ceremony. But, the voice that whispered in my ear in a deep melodious tone clearly was not Ben's.

"I've heard you've been asking about me." the voice whispered.

I turned and looked up, which was humbly in itself, because I wasn't short, and found myself staring into the glittering eyes of Ten/Two. I felt overwhelmed by his muscled bulk as he stood very close behind me. I was speechless. The hand on my butt cheek applied pressure, as he continued.

"I saw you at the party at Ben's a couple of weeks ago."

A weak and breathy "Oh" was all I cold manage to squeak out. There would be no fooling him, then.

"I'd like to have you for lunch today . . . at my place . . . unless you have other plans. My car's here. I could drop you back here if you've driven or take you home after . . . lunch . . . if you don't have wheels."

What could I say—assuming that I could catch my breath to say anything at all, that is. I just nodded dumbly, wearing, I'm sure, the sloppiest of grins.

By the time we'd reached his Thai-style elevated teak house, hidden in a lush tropical garden beside a khlong, one of those waterways lacing through the city that made Bangkok the Venice of the East, I was trembling all over from fear and anticipation and could hardly make my way from the car and up the stairs into his nearly wall-less platform house under my own steam.

There was, of course, no lunch waiting for us, and, indeed, I had not had any illusions what was going to be fed into me on this excursion. The black army captain motioned with one hand, sending servants scurrying for the stairway and out to the corners of the compound, I'm sure, to afford us total privacy, while he guided me straight to his bedroom with the other hand.

Centered in this room was a gigantic, mosquito net-draped four-poster bed, set on a teak-board floor. The three exterior walls were actually wooden louvered folding doors running between circular tree-trunk columns. The doors could be shut at night for privacy, but they were all open now, and the foliage of the deep green jungle trees, laced with wild orchids, pressed in at us from all three exterior sides. A ceiling fan revolved lazily overhead. The air was heavily with humidity. I felt the jungle closing in on me, and I was immobilized by trepidation. I couldn't get that ten-inch long, two-inch thick ebony cock out of my mind.

And very soon thereafter, it no longer was in my mind, but was there before me. I stood dumbly beside the bed, as the big black stripped my clothes off me and placed them neatly on a side chair. He held me at arms' length and then drew me to him and kissed me deeply on the mouth. He let me virtual fall into a sitting position on the end of the bed, as my knees gave out and then stood and stripped before me, revealing that monster that soon would be splitting me asunder.

He came to me, pushing me down on my back on the bed, opening my legs with knees that knelt on the edge of the bed, taking my wrists in his big hands and spreading my arms wide across the bedspread, and then dipped his head, first down to mine for searching kisses on the lips, and then traveled his lips down to my nipples. After an eternity of attention there, he followed the thin trail of hair from my pecs down and around my navel and into my pubic region, his knees now down on the floor and his barrel chest between my spread legs.

I was sighing and moaning and giving little mewing sounds—and quite frankly was beginning to hyperventilate, my mind obsessed with what he was packing between his legs—both longer and thicker than anything I'd attempted thus far.

His lips, tongue, and teeth were at the rim of my asshole and then invading me, loosening me up—or at least trying to. I think that, rather, I was tightening up the longer I thought of his equipment and what it might do to me.

He obviously felt me tighten up, because he stood up then, between my legs, giving me quite a good view of his now-hardened cock, the sight of which, of course, wasn't helping dispel my gathering fear.

"What's wrong?" he asked. "You are tightening. Don't you want it?"

"Yes, of course, I want it, but I'm afraid of your size. Can't you feel me trembling?"

"Ah," he said. "I saw you with the Swede. I'm just a bit longer and thicker than he was. I'm sure you can take me. But, I'll tell you what. Unless you want to just stop—and you'll trust me—we can try something that's worked on others. Do you want to try?"

"Yes," I answered in a tiny voice. I was dying to take that cock. I'd try anything that might work.

"Have you fucked with mild bondage?" He asked.

"Once or twice," I admitted.

"And how did that make you feel? Did you tense up more or did you relax, no longer having the responsibility for what was happening?"

"I guess I relaxed at bit," I admitted.

In no time at all, I was on my chest on the bed, my wrists loosely tied with leather strips to the slats of the headboard, up on my knees, and with my butt in the air. The big black worked my ass at length with his tongue and lips, with a lubricant, and, eventually with an increasing number of fingers.

No longer having any responsibility at all, I did find myself loosening to his attention, which included hands flowing all over my body, exploring all of my curves and crevices, making intimate love to me.

The finger fucking became progressively more painful as more fingers were added and they went deeper, until a certain peak was achieved and then the pleasure flooded in. The fingers probed deeper and deeper, and I widened my stance as much as I could, trying mightily to take them all it. Deeper, deeper. Impossibly deeper.

"I had no idea your fingers were so long and thick," I managed to speak between moans and pants.

"Those aren't fingers, Sport." Ten/Two whispered with a little laugh. "I've been cocking you for several minutes now. I'm in. And now that you know I'm in, I'll run it to the end and start stroking you. You're doing fine. You've got a sweet ass. You're doing fine."

He stroked me and stroked me and stroked me, until he came deep inside me, and then he stayed in me, still filling me to the limit as he became tumescent, and reached under and stroked my cock until I came. We lay, his beefy black body covering mine, my knees now collapsed and my body stretched out under his on the top of the bed, as we both recovered, reloaded, rearoused.

Then he released my imprisoned hands, turned me over on my back, and pulled me back to the foot of the bed.

The fear was over. I had accommodated him, and I had loved being fucked by him. I now couldn't get enough of his ripped body and that vigorous ten- by two-inch muscle at his center. He was standing on the floor between my widespread legs now, hunched a bit over me, his gigantic manhood and huge balls swaying below his flat belly. My heart was racing and I was moaning, overcome with anticipation, as his milk chocolate, beefy-fingered hands glided over the creamy white skin of my thighs, belly, and chest. I groaned as rough-padded fingers rubbed, and twitched, and pinched my tender nipples.

I arched my chest up from bed, wanting to see as much of his stud-muscled body as I could as he worked my arousal zones. I cried out as his full lips found my nipples and his mouth opened around aureoles, closed tight, and gave suck. I melting to his teeth sliding across my engorged nipples. I opened my mouth wide to gasp at the hint of a bite on a nipple, only to have his heavy lips crush mine and his thick tongue push in. I Opened my eyes to his, very close now, filled with desire, determination, insistence.

I easing my back down on the bed, as he rose up below me. Breathlessly, I watch giant hands gliding across my body, slowly working their way to my center. Milk chocolate hands on soft, creamy white belly and thighs, nudging. Mesmerized, I opened my legs to him. Purring sounds involuntarily escaped my lips as hands glide around silky inner thighs.

The body of hulking black army officer sank toward the floor between my opened legs, and his grinning face dipped out of sight. I arched my back and gasped again, as his thick tongue once again rimmed, flicked in, and then invaded my ass canal. Grasping the close-cropped kinky black hair of the head bobbing at my crotch, my immediate impulse was to push the invader away, but this was quickly replaced with desire to hold the swaying orb in closer to my center. I began twitching and trembling to the dancing of the tongue, but this no longer was a sign of fear and dreaded anticipation, but of ecstasy.

Big, thick fingers snaked in, thicker than some men's cocks, exploring, searching. An agony of mixed pain, pleasure, and expectation flooded me in the brief seconds it took him to center. I writhed against his possessing hand as it found the prostate, tweaking it, rubbing it, and quickening the flow of precum from my aching cock.

I panted and moaned for him and shouted the intensity of my burning desire and pleasure to the giant rustling leaves of jungle trees pressing in on us beyond the teak columns. A bolt of electricity rushed through my body and sparks flew, as my cock's trigger snapped and my cum flew.

I heard a low, satisfied, hoarse laugh from between my trembling legs.

The muscle-bound milk chocolate army officer, with his jet-black ten/two monster cock and plump balls stood in possessing triumph between my spread legs now. His massive chest and arm muscles bulged and undulated, glistening in the heavy atmosphere and the strobing of light through the waving leaves and the languidly moving blades of the overhead fan. A big grin on his square-cut face, he captured and placed my hands so I could feel the awesome length and thickness (and the bulbous, purple-black cap and popped-out blue-on-black veins) of his hardened cock. My fearful fingers trembled at the measure of the beast, all the more imposing in its blackness against his otherwise milk chocolate, while he told me quite clearly and graphically—and breathtakingly—what he was going to do with all that manhood and how much pleasure he was getting—and expected to continue to get—out of me and expected me still to get out of his cock—to the point of making me tremble in anticipation. He told me that I never again would be fucked this completely and fulfilled to this extent—and he was right, and I suspected, even then, that he would be right, because I could not imagine any higher ecstasy that he now was giving me.

I went up on my elbows, my legs splayed up and out, my ankles held in his big hands, and watched him first, slap that monster cock against my butt cheeks, and then rub it up and down and around there, and then stroke it up and down in my crack, across my puckered asshole, teasing me, dry fucking me, driving me wild, making me beg for him to ram in back inside me. He rotated that purple-black cap around and just inside the rim, entirely with the control he had over his hips and his hardened cock—no help with his hands. And then slowly, almost magically, he made the pillar of power and strength follow its bulbous head and disappear inside me, me arching my back, trying to stretch to accommodate him and involuntarily giving him deep moans and groans of being stuffed.

"No, no; yes, yes, y-e-s. It's too big; it's the size I've always dreamed of. It's splitting me; it's stretching and filling me to perfection. I can't take this; I can't get enough of this. Yesssssss!"

Bringing his mouth down to my nipples as he plowed me, he sucked and bit me lightly there.

I felt the veins of his thick pole sliding against my ass walls as his cock journeyed in to the quick. Then he rose back on the balls of his feet again, hunched over me, and repeatedly pulled his glistening jet-black cock out slowly to where I could again see the rim of the purple-black cap, and then glided it back in to the root until he eventually lost control in his own trip to nirvana and started pumping me wildly (showing that he panted for me as much as I did for him). At the height of his passion, he dipped his mouth to mine and brutalized my lips with his. His hands grabbed my hips and moved my pelvis in and out, up and down, revolving around to meet and enhance his thrusts. He cried out. Again he was flooding the inside me with fountains of cum, so strong and full that it oozed out of me and bathed those black balls of his.

All of that was still throbbing inside me, hard for me, wanting to be inside me, and filling me repeatedly—followed by my insides being creamed again and again with his semen and him holding for a few minutes, young, virile, powerful, quick loading. and then doing it all again. And my being able to take it, each time more slippery than the last because of the accumulation and mingling of juices—and then he turned me on his cock until he was close in behind me, capable of going even deeper inside me, and then fucking me again, holding my wrists with his hands, dominating me. Him shooting off every fifteen minutes or so for what seems like forever—me climaxing repeatedly, encasing that jet-black ten/two hunk and being encased by that milk chocolate rippling network of perfect muscle.

99

The fuck of my life.

Bondage

Beautiful Bondage

I had been told that the assignment was a bit kinky, but a weekend stopover in Hawaii and three days on my own in Tokyo, paid for by the generous fee addition, were enough for me not to care. My pimp, Leon, told me to make myself blond all over, which I had grown used to in any assignment sending me to the Orient. And I was a bit intrigued because I was told up front that the client was Matsu Shinjuto, an elusive Japanese billionaire, much of whose wealth came from his Japanese ink paintings and block prints of ancient Shinto shrines during the various seasons.

The limousine sent for me at the hotel stopped at a massive set of iron gates at the base of a sharp steep slope up a hill, heavy with ferns and carefully pruned weeping trees, and I climbed slowly up to a hilltop eerie high above Kyoto, where my client had placed his many-pavilioned Japanese-style mansion floating over Japan's cultural capital. As I climbed, I looked up at the red-lacquered railings on the terraces above, sensing many sets of eyes on me, assessing me, although I wasn't able to discern any movement.

I entered the compound through a brightly painted torii gate, ushered by a black-robed figure nearly bent at the waist. We moved silently on stockinged feet through a series of white rice-papered-walled, wood-framed pavilions seemingly floating in the clouds. Between each pavilion was a austerely beautiful, uniquely landscaped stone garden atrium straight out of the master's style of painting. I was to find that his art went much beyond the scenic, however.

When I entered into the first courtyard, a deceptively small, square space that used stunted Japanese maples, mountain-like rock formations, and running water to provide the illusion of larger-than-life scenic splendor, I was escorted into a small room off to the side. I was asked by the elderly, severely demeanored gatekeeper who had taken over as my escort at the entry of the second pavilion, which seemed to mark the beginning of the core living area of the compound, to strip down and wrap an emerald-green kimono around my torso and tie it off with a royal-purple sash. There was a tube of scented lubricant on a low stool, with instructions, written on rice paper in elegant, black-inked calligraphy, to apply it generously to my channel. None of this was shocking to me, of course. I was way beyond the capability of being shocked in the world of the extremely highly paid male prostitute. I had already, by practice cleaned that channel.

When I was escorted to the third pavilion, I was motioned to sit, yoga style, with my kimono billowing about me on a cushion placed in front of a squat rosewood tea table. Another, more luxurious and plumper pillow was set beside me. As a willowy young Japanese man in a shiny silver and black kimono served me a glass of perfectly chilled Sapporo beer, I gazed, in great interest and aw, at the walls about me, where a large collection of traditional Japanese ink drawings were displayed—composed of highly graphic male-male gay erotica set in some ancient oriental era.

As a whole, the exquisitely drawn collection could stand as a tutorial in the many exotic positions men could get into in fucking each other. I was particularly drawn to the style of Shinjuto—because they unmistakably were the work of the master—used to gain maximal erotic images from the clothing. Rarely were the models completely naked; rather Shinjuto had used clothing to help enhance the senses and understanding of the paintings. By exposing only fingers on a nipple and a half-buried cock in an ass—along with the expressions on the faces of both taker and taken, Shinjuto had perfectly caught privacy and sensuousness in one work. And in yet another, by showing the clothing in dishabille as in a struggle, the bent-over position on a moss-covered rock in a garden, and the panicked look in the face of the significantly smaller, taken one and of the flailing, helpless position of his arms, Shinjuto caught nonconsensual ravishment perfectly.

"Ah, do you find my private collection to your liking, Mr. Smith? I presume we can refer to you as Mr. Smith in our arrangement?" Shinjuto had arrived, on silent rattan sandals, while I had been absorbed in his artwork and settled very close beside me in a sigh of satin and silk. He was in his early senior years, at least into his mid sixties, but he looked toned and handsome in his traditional kimono of pure white undergarments and an over dress in a blue oriental waves pattern. He was well groomed and had long, elegant, strong fingers that attracted the eye with their fluid motion and precise placement while he talked.

"Yes, that name will do, Sensei," I responded, using the term for master teacher and lowering my eyes as I had been instructed to do in a quick tutorial I had been given before I left Los Angeles. Shinjuto was paying top dollar, and I was warned to treat him as such. "And, yes. I find your art extraordinarily . . . melting. It has me . . . excited . . . with anticipation, if I might be so bold as to say."

I saw no reason to mince words. Shinjuto already had one hand behind me and at the nape of my neck, running his elegant fingers through my blond hair and his other hand buried inside the folds of my kimono below the purple sash and gently encircling my engorging cock. The preparation, the foreplay, had already begun.

"And which do you find most erotic, Mr. Smith? Perhaps that one over there, depicting much of what we are engaging in now?"

He had indicated the work where the two figures were nearly fully clothed but undoubtedly steeped in a very intimate act of taking. As he spoke, he had untied my sash and folded back the material at my breast, exposing one of my nipples. And his fist had brought my cock out from the folds of the material below where the sash had fallen away.

I sighed and trembled for him as I had been carefully taught men of refinement and an artistic temperament appreciated. In this case, I didn't have to act;

104

his tense refinement while performing the most blatant sexual advances was having an arousing effect on me. The fingers at the nape of my neck tightened as did the fist on my cock. Shinjuto pulled my head back and down, and I arched my back for him, my chest expanding and bulging out from the draped kimono.

"I wish you to come for me, Mr. Smith. In good time, while I tell you why I have engaged your services."

So, it wasn't to be just a simple fuck. What he was doing now wasn't the main thrust of why my time and body had been bought by him for top dollar. His lips and teeth went to one of my nipples as my back was arched by the tension of his closed fist in my hair and his other fist slowly and relentlessly jacked me off. He had a thumb on my piss slit, and as I flowed in precum, he thumbed the fluid around on my swollen glans.

"Yes, like that, Mr. Smith," he said when he lifted his head from one nipple in preparation for giving equal attention to the other one. "I want to see how large you can become. I was explicit about that . . . and it seems my desires were satisfied."

"I am paying well for you, Mr. Smith, as you no doubt are aware, but you are a means for me to make millions."

I moaned and trembled a bit at what Shinjuto was doing with his mouth and fist. He drew his head back and watched the effect of his artwork, as he briefly took his fist from my cock and then glided the palm of his hand up my torso, his moistened thumb, moistened by my own precum and raised outside the fold of my kimono, up to my mouth. He rimmed my lips with the moisture from his thumb and then pushed it past my lips, into my mouth, and I sucked on it.

While he was doing this, he was rearranging my body as well from where we had been sitting, yoga style, very close beside each other. He had moved one of his thighs beneath one of mine, and he was twisting my torso to the side, the arm of the hand that had been in my hair now wrapped around my shoulder blade, his arm supporting my torso in its twisted, but still upright position, and with an elegant, long-fingered hand palmed across a nipple.

"Have you ever heard of the Japanese art of *Kinbaku-bi*, Mr. Smith? Translated as 'beautiful bondage?'"

"No, no, I . . . haven't," I managed in a gurgling tone, the thumb of his other hand still in my mouth, before I involuntarily groaned. Shinjuto had moved his face inside my draped kimono, forcing my arm over my head, and he was licking his way up the side of my chest, headed for my pit. He had also pushed his thigh farther under mine, lifting my hips up over into his lap. His kimono was open below his sash, and he was naked under the elegant white silk. His thighs were hard for a man his age, and I could feel the power of a strong cock, as well. I also could tell that it was sheathed, ready for me. There would be no clumsy pauses or wasted movement in his flow toward the taking of me.

"I have a Chinese client. A very, very wealthy Chinese client, Mr. Smith. He also has an attitude toward the West. He will pay me dearly for a collection of art, using the *Kinbaku-bi* style, but depicting the East dominating the West. You are to be my model for the West, Mr. Smith. And this client has eclectic tastes. While I am painting these scenes in traditional style, one of my students will be taking still and video photography, and my son will be developing a *Hentai* version."

I grunted and strained at this point, because the elderly Sensei, showing his extraordinary strength and flexibility and sorely testing mine, had drawn my leg straight up to rest on his shoulder between our torsos, which were now bowed away from each other. His thumb had left my mouth and had returned to fisting and slowly pumping my cock.

"Does that sound interesting to you, Mr. Smith?" Shinjuto said this just before his teeth and tongue found the most tender hollow of my pit and started devouring me there.

"Yes. Oh, yes. Oh . . . OH . . . . YESSSS!" I cried out, not so much in response to his question, but because he had now opened and positioned my lubricated ass to his shaft, and he was burying his strong, virile cock deep inside me and somehow finding the leverage to piston fuck me as I found myself in a melting fuck position I'd never experience before. I knew it was a traditional position for Shinjuto, however, because, as I threw my head back in the passion of the taking by a Japanese master, my eyes caught one of his drawings depicting exactly the same position.

* * * *

The modeling project was much more involved than I had thought it would be. After Shinjuto had jacked me off and cum with a very satisfied and decorous grunt, he rose and readjusted his kimono, which more or less fell back into an innocent drape line as he stood, and glided back out of the room. While a few young male attendants cleared away the pillows and table and half-empty glass of beer, which I could have used after the muscle-stretching exercise I had just gotten, a couple more helped me groan to my feet and took me to another pavilion, where I was bathed by them in a copper tub.

All of the male attendants were handsome young men. The two who attended me were especially nice, and apparently had been instructed to please me. Their appearance, along with remembering and reliving what Shinjuto had just so expertly done to me, made me hard again, and, seeing this and while they both giggled, one of the young men leaned over from above my head and possessed my lips fervently with his and reached over and pinched my nipples while the other lifted my hips to the surface of the water and sucked me to ejaculation.

After they had dried me off with warmed, fluffy towels and left me, I had a surprise visit from what must have been Shinjuto's art students. I stood stock still and stark naked in the middle of the pavilion while four young men painted my body. What they were painting were depictions of Western arrogance and power projection—polluting mills, dollar bills, conquering armies, plundering ships, and every form of avarice and crass consumerism they could get on my body—in angry red and orange and yellow and black body paint colors. One design flowed into the next. My cock, of course, which they had to pump up to paint properly, was a guided missile. They were quick and inventive and highly skilled. I'm sure that they had worked all of the designing out in advance.

When I was "done," I was summoned to the first of several "stages." This was one of the austere stone gardens. The attendants made me lay in the center of a flattish platform rock, where I could barely touch the ground with the heels of my hands as they arched over and out at the corners of the rock toward the ground. White shiny silk runners of cloth ran out from under the rock, at the center of which, they must have crossed and been knotted, and streamed off at the four corners. I was forced to dig my heels into the sand at the lower quarters of the rock, and then the streamers were wound around my wrists and ankles, binding me on the surface of the rock to the ground in a backward crab position, my cock pointed at the sky.

Through intricate windings of the silken runners, my head was arched back with a strand running taut under my jaw, the runners crisscrossed my chest, and another of the strands wound up a leg and then under my balls and tightly encasing the root of my cock, which effectively kept my cock both pointed straight up and engorged.

Although I had sort of figured it out beforehand, I knew for sure what the body paint was about when I saw the two lithe but well-muscled and very agile Japanese young men who came out into the garden after I had, by the Sensei's definition, been "beautifully bound," or prepared for *Kinbaku-bi*. The two young Japanese were also covered in body painting—but in more subtle greens and blues and whites and certainly in more refined and artistic images than were slathered on my body. Everything their bodies depicted was the antithesis of the crass and angry and grabby images on my body.

I got it. Shinjuto was going to be used as a traditional Japanese sexual art form to give his Chinese client exactly what he wanted—an exotic and erotic collection of art showing East controlling and fucking West.

And that's exactly what they did. After the master and three of his prized art students had arrived and settled themselves in three different areas of the periphery, the two young men representing the East began to regain the dignity of the East by putting it to the bound West. Shinjuto was sitting cross-legged, in an elegant heavily brocaded vermillion kimono behind a sketching easel. Beside him sat a younger man, of maybe nineteen or twenty, and achingly beautiful—but with a melancholy aspect. He handed implements and inks to the elder Shinjuto upon command, and, when not doing this, he was sketching with rice paper pad and charcoal. Every time I looked at him, I found him slack jawed and watching me intently. I knew he wanted me. But I equally knew that he wanted me to fuck him.

Another of the students was busily moving around the garden, snapping photos and switching now and then to video—and always checking and scowling at the light sources. The third young man, the one Shinjuto had identified as his son, was sitting as his computer, doing whatever one did to adapt what was happening in real life to the Hentai world.

But I hardly noticed the actions of either of the latter two; I had my mouth and ass full with the two painted models. I was sucking one off, my head pulled back by the "beautiful bondage" so that he could just pump his cock inside my mouth by standing above my head, his fingers busy worrying my nipples. And the other one was between my legs and fucking my ass, while his hand was moving my "missile" to lift off.

In a second "beautiful bondage" setting, I was lying on my back at the last step of a rock-based water cascade formation descending down into a small pond. My wrists and ankle were bound together by the silken runners, which then rose to the graceful limb of a pine branch jutting out over the water cascade. Two runners wound around my waist, with one snaked around an ankle of one of the painted East figures and then to the other, binding him to me, as he stood at the base of the cascade between my spread and raised arms and legs and fed his cock in my mouth. The other East model was lying below me in the shallow pond at where it was cascading down between my trussed appendages. Bondage runners ran from his waist up to around mine. His cock was buried in my ass, half visible and rocking in and out for the artists to see, appreciate, and capture in their various mediums.

In the third and last scenario, although it provided a double bonding image, I was taken into a large pavilion bedchamber. In the center was a large, square bed, covered in mussed silken sheeting of the purest white. Hanging from a hook in the ceiling above the center of the bed was a silken runner, the richest red this time, gathered up so that it was well off the bed. Similarly, there were two other hooks and red hanging runners at either side of the center hook, each positioned near the edge of the bed. I was forced down on my belly in the center of the silken sheets. My wrists were bound together behind my head and encircling my jawbone and then attached to a runner around my chest at the level of my pecs. Inside this runner clips had been sown into the fabric and were clipped securely onto my aureoles, pinching my nipples closely.

Another runner ran off of this chest wrapping from between my shoulder blades and went back and was tied to my left ankle taut enough to pull my leg at a side angle. A runner encircled my waist and another, wider-banded one tied at the chest banding both at the sternum and between the shoulder blades. It wound down and through my ass crack between these two points, winding once on each side around the waist wrapping as well. My right leg was bent back upon itself with a tight wrapping holding the ankle up against my thigh at an awkward position that, by design, left my butt cheeks stretched wide.

I didn't notice that the runner going between my crack had a shallow cylinder pouch in it at ass level until the East models began fucking me. They took turns. And although their cocks weren't thick, they were long. The deeper they fucked, the deeper the pouch that now ran up inside my channel was pushed. And the deeper this was pushed, the more tension that was put on the "beautiful bindings" attaching at my chest and ultimately around my jaw and at my nipple clippings. With each thrust, my head was being jerked back, my back was arching involuntarily, and my nipples were being pulled.

From this point to the end, the photography guy was going to video only. He had his microphone down close to my head and he was capturing some sounds of taking like he'd never heard before.

Both I and the men below me on the bed were doing a lot of writhing, and the body paint was coming off onto the white silken sheets. While I was trying to focus on something other than this excruciatingly painful-pleasurable fucking, I briefly wondered how much Shinjuto could get for the framed silk sheet at an art auction in Chicago. Knowing that it could go for high money with the right background story, I was getting fully into this East fucking West scenario that had been created here.

The finale was a doozy. Before the two East models came this time, they untied my legs and undid the binding around my jaw, and I found out what the red runners on the ceiling hooks were for. The ones at the corner were let down and my legs were split wide and my ankles were bound in red well off the bed and straight out at my sides. The center streamer, which was on some sort of pulley system was lowered, and my bound wrists were bound on this and I was raised above the silken sheets in a spread-eagled form.

The two East models then laid stretched on their backs below me, their heads in opposite directions and joined at the pelvis, the thighs of one over the hips of the other. One of them held their two long, but happily not all that thick, cocks together until an attendant had wrapped a binding around the base of their cocks, making their tools one, thick cock. Then the binding between my ass cheeks was taken away, the pouch slurping out of my channel, as I was lowered onto the two cocks. Skewered deep by two throbbing, joined tools, and then raised, and lowered, raised, and lowered . . . until both of the East models had come in much jerking and thrusting up of themselves from below me.

* * * *

As I was being unbound and praised for my contribution to art by the attendants and the photographer, I looked up and saw Shinjuto standing there, half way between his easel and the bed. He stood tall and straight, but he was shaking. And I could tell how wound up he was and moved to a higher plane of desire by the expression on his face alone. His sash had come untied, and the kimono had fallen away from his body. His heavily-muscled chest was heaving, his nipples were puffed and rock hard, and there was a thin film of sweat glistening at his sternum. His erection was gigantic and angry red and slightly bobbing up and down.

The young man who had been handing implements to him and crouching beside him and sketching as well was still huddled back at the easel. I could see the want and need in his eyes as well. But I could also see fear and confusion, and it hit me at that moment that he had no experience in this. Only want and need.

"Come. I am well pleased," Shinjuto said in a wavering, barely controlled voice. "I will pay double. I will also charge double. And my client will gladly pay it upon seeing the samples."

He took my hands, my wrists still bound in "beautiful bondage," in a firm grip and led me over to the side of the room. There was a contraption in front of the rice-paper wall that looked like the side view of gymnasts' parallel bars—quite widely divergent parallel bars. The lower bar was the nearer one and was set at mid-thigh level. The one beyond it was set at shoulder height. On this higher bar, there were silken strands wrapped near each end.

In short order, my thighs were straddled on the lower bar and my ankles were bound above the higher bar at the widely spread interval. Shinjuto was crouched down behind me, his angry red, gigantic tool working its way up into my ass channel, his long, elegant fingers digging into my aureoles. My bound wrists were thrust over his head, joined behind his neck, which held my shoulder blades against his heaving chest.

I saw the young assistant in my periphery vision, at Shinjuto's elbow.

"Please, uncle, please. You said that I might . . ."

"Yes, Kanto, you may have your first taste."

The younger Japanese came around in front of me and knelt and tentatively started to taste my cock. As he worked at it, he quickly got better, no doubt having had a lot of instruction in the theory of it from his father's art.

"One last *Kinbaku-bi*, just for my own pleasure," the Sensei was muttering. "This does not go to the Chinese client. I have this part of you for myself."

I was thinking—between grunts and groans at Shinjuto's expert fucking and the young one's pleasurably learning—that it was a shame that this wasn't being captured in art if it meant so much to Shinjuto.

But even as I thought that, the pavilion wall panels before my eyes were splitting and being drawn back . . . to reveal a life-sized, obviously Shinjuto master painting of just what I would see if there had been a mirror there. The agency must have sent him a photo of me, because it clearly was me in the painting, trussed up on this apparatus—and it clearly was Shinjuto fucking me and showing a pleasure in the fuck in his face that I couldn't see in real life from where I was bound. And between my legs in the painting was the bobbing head of the handsome young Japanese nephew of the master.

Shinjuto had orchestrated it all. He was the master.

* * * *

I never saw Shinjuto again. As far as he was concerned, I'd done what I had been paid handsomely to do and now he was going to be paid even more handsomely for having created art out of his sensuous, torturous taking. He was the master, the Sensei. Before he released me from his bondage, however, he told me that before I left Japan, I would receive one more token of his appreciation. But that I should accept it—and he declared that it would be quite valuable—only if I would grant the one wish of the one who delivered it to me. I hesitated slightly in responding, but he reassured me that the present would be worth far more than I would have to give for it, so I told him I accepted.

I was intrigued about what this present might be, and it was that more than the declared value of the gift that made me say yes. Shinjuto had been very generous to me. But, despite all that I had made—and even how much I had enjoyed the exotic taking and learning of the Japanese sexual art of *Kinbaku-bi*, I was just too mischievous and imbued with the need to control in my heart to leave it all completely at Shinjuto's design and command.

I had seen that Shinjuto was holding his nephew back—that he had every intention of teaching him in the ways of men with men. But that he was going to dole it out piecemeal and almost reluctantly—and completely under his control and at his direction. That he was going to torture the handsome youth with it.

Kanto, the nephew, was in the pavilion where I was being cleaned up and given a chance to rest. I could tell that he wanted to linger when the others were finished, and I decided to help him with that and to assert a little control of my own and to leave my mark on Shinjuto's well-ordered and orchestrated life.

As Kanto was putting the towels into a bin, I went over to him and took him by the hand and walked him around the walls of the pavilion, which was the same one in which Shinjuto had first taken me. We viewed the erotic art together, going from one to the other. I felt the intake of his breath and his tightening up as we

110

stood in front of one that showed a young, willowy Japanese receiver rolled up onto his shoulders on a mat, his torso rising in the air and the older muscleman Japanese giver standing over him, one leg over the thigh of the younger one, whose heel rested on the older one's butt cheek, the older man holding the younger man's leg at the knee. The younger man's other leg was spread out wide, being held by the older man's hand under the thigh. The muscleman Japanese was fucking down into the receiver's hole, his thick cock only half buried. The expression on the giver's face was one of triumph and lusting cruelty, and the younger receiver's head was arched back in a cry of passion and overstretching.

I unknotted the sash of my kimono and let it drape open. And I searched down in the folds to ensure that the tube of scented lubricant I had retrieved from earlier and hidden there was still there. Then I came up very close behind Kanto and drew him into me.

He shuddered at the feel of my cock in the small of his back, and he moved as if to pull away from me, but I held him fast to my chest. I held his torso to mine with a palm spread on his chest and I untied his kimono with the other hand and, tugging at the kimono at his shoulders, made it drop unto the tatami mat below.

Kanto whimpered and struggled again, but I held him fast with a palm over his chest and the other hand going to his cock. He was already almost fully aroused. He was ready for me already.

He swiveled his head away from the painting, but I raised one hand to his jaw and held him there, face forward, fully looking at his uncle's masterwork of an older, muscled man dominating the younger virginal man. I got a large glob of lubricant on the fingers of the other hand, and I started working his tight asshole with my fingers. First one finger and then another.

Kanto was panting heavily and moaning, and I could feel his legs going to rubber. But I held him up with the framing hand under his jaw, forcing him to look at what was happening in the painting and with the strong finger of my other hand skewering up into his tight ass.

When I felt he was open enough to take me, I crouched down at the knees a bit and just picked him up off the floor with my hands on his waist and sat him down on the crown of my cock. He cried out at the pain of the taking, but now he had thrown his hands around my neck and locked his fists and his chest was arched out. He jutted his butt cheeks back into me, helping me to bottom.

We were united there, joined at the cock and channel for several long minutes, while we waited for his virginal channel to stretch to accommodate me and his pain and suffering to turn to wanting and lust. We were both panting, and he was groaning and moaning and telling me he never knew it could be like this and that this was his first time—which he hardly had to tell me.

Holding him to me with one arm across his panting chest as I lapped him in my semicrouched position in front of the painting, I reached down and fisted his cock in my other hand. He ejaculated almost at once with a joyous shouting that sent my own fluids spewing through me and deep into him.

Again we held the pose for several minutes as we cooled down and recovered the strength of our manhood, which he was able to do quickly because of his youth and because it was all so new and arousing to him—and I was able to do through professional conditioning.

111

Still, I had thought that would be enough. I had taken the virginity of Shinjuto's precious nephew, who he intended to slowly cultivate. I had thus accomplished my little flash of mischief and grabbing for control. And, just as important, I had thoroughly enjoyed myself.

That thought caught in my mind with a guilty twist, though, because Kanto was shaking inside my grasp. Perhaps I hadn't thought of him well enough in all of this. I'd thought he wanted to be relieved of his virginity as soon as possible, and his body had been sending out unmistakable signals to me. But he was trembling, so maybe I was wrong. Maybe he was upset at what he had lost.

"Kanto—" I started. Not really know how to say it; not even knowing what to say, what to ask. I couldn't given him back his innocence.

"I'm sorry. I can't pay you much," be blurted out, ending it with a sob. But then he continued in a flood. "I know you make a lot of money at this. I have very little, but l could send you a little at a time . . . for as long as it takes."

"Oh, Kanto," I said and then laughed with relief. "I didn't do this because I wanted you to pay me for it. I did this because I thought it was what you needed, and, frankly, because you are super hot and I wanted you. I don't have to be paid when I want to do it. You honor me by giving my your virginity. You don't know how thrilling that is to a man. To be the one to deflower a hot young man like you. So, now, shall we clean up and—"

"No. Please . . . no." His voice started off stubborn but then got shaky again.

"No, what?" I asked, surprised.

"The painting. Can you fuck me like they are doing in the painting first?"

"Yes, of course," I said, laughing again. And, taking him off my lap and turning him around and setting him gently down onto his shoulder blades, I showed that I could . . . and I did.

* * * *

Three days later as I was packing my bag and getting ready to leave Tokyo after having had a great time in the Shinjuku ni-chome bar scene—and after bar hours activities, where I picked up some extra cash from several randy Japanese men with open and overflowing wallets, I answered a knock at the door. Shinjuto's son stood there, grinning in recognition and, no doubt in remembrance, and, after bending in synch low at the waist, handed me a wrapped package.

"From Sensei Shinjuto, with regards and thanks," he said. And then he came out of his bow and gave me "the look," and I then knew much of what receiving the gift would entail.

"My father said that you would grant me my one wish," he said, and then, when I nodded in assent, he said, "My one wish is one last *Kinbaku-bi* with you. I assure you that it will not be as strenuous for you as my father was."

"Certainly," I said. "Come in."

I was already starting to strip down when he went back out in the corridor and returned with a laptop computer, which he sat at the foot of the bed, facing the headboard, and revved up. He also had red silk bindings with him.

I watched the computer screen in fascination as he put me into beautiful bondage, one wrist bound to the railing of the bed's headboard at the left corner and

112

the other wrist and my left ankle loosely bound together at the right corner of the headboard. I was then trussed up, my butt resting on the side edge of the bed near the headboard, left leg raised and torso stretched back toward the other side of the bed.

What fascinated me with the computer display was that it was of an animated Hentai of the cartoon me and Shinjuto's son in just this position. Shinjuto's son stripped down. He was slender but well muscled, a handsome young man, and his quite presentable cock was already engorged. He must have been a little self-conscious about his endowments, though, or overly ambitious, because the cock on his Hentai character was the size of a baseball bat. But then, so was the dick on my Hentai character—and my character's hole was big enough to take the baseball bat.

I watched both on the screen and in real life, as Shinjuto's son bound his forearm to my right calf with the silken bounds. Then, already encased with a condom, he just pressed between my spread thighs and fucked me as closely as he could in real life to the exaggerated good sex unfolding in the Hentai animation on the computer.

When he was finished, he just quietly unbound me, turned off and closed his computer, gave me a look and salute of full satisfaction and appreciation, and departed.

When he was gone, I opened the package to find an ink drawing, done in bold strokes, undoubtedly by the master, Shinjuto—of me fucking his nephew, Kanto, in front of the painting depicting the same act.

I had to laugh. Shinjuto had mastered me again. He had planned even what I thought I was controlling—the deflowering of his nephew—for free. And he'd managed to get a free *Kinbaku-bi* fuck for his son thrown into the bargain as well.

The Cure

I came to slowly, the flashing colored lights taking their time to form in my consciousness. Whatever Tony had spiked my drink with was slow to let loose of me. I was lying on a bed. I tried to rise, but my hands were cuffed together above me and my legs were cuffed as well to the lower corners of the bed. But the bonds were loose there. I could raise my legs as I wanted, but I couldn't rise from the bed. I was going to scream, but my mouth was gagged.

Tony was sitting on my belly, flashing a sharp knife before my eyes. As I watched, he slowly slit the buttons off my shirt and then shredded my shirt. I could feel the cold steel of the dull side of the blade moving between my body and my shirt as it was ripped away from me. Tony was smiling an evil smile. Once the shirt was torn away, his face dropped to my chest and he sucked and bit at my nipples until they ached. I arched my back and struggled as best I could, but I couldn't escape his lips and teeth.

He moved to below my buttocks and licked and bit his way down my abs and to my lower belly, paying particular attention to teething the rim of my navel. I screamed into my gag, but no one would be able to hear me—not even Tony.

He unbuckled my belt and pulled it through the loops. Then he flicked the leather end of the belt against my arms, chest, belly and thighs, enough to inflict short, sharp flashes of pain, but not enough to break the skin or to leave welts. Then he looped the belt around my neck, making it ready for who knew what.

Tony was naked. The red, blue, green, and yellow strobe lights danced across his well-muscled torso, picking out an array of tattoos going down just one side of his body. He rose up on his knees below me, and I saw that his huge cock was already half erect. His eyes were slitted in pleasure.

The knife went to work on my pants, which Tony shredded and pulled away from my body. The knife slit through the strings of my thong briefs, and then I was naked as well. Naked and open to anything Tony desired.

He moved down on the bed below me and I felt his mouth go over my shaft. Most alarming, however, was that he had laid the knife on my belly, the cool side of the blade a constant reminder of danger. His mouth pushed my foreskin to below the helmet of my dick, and Tony sucked hard. His tongue went to my piss slit and he flicked it before trying to work his tongue into the slit. I writhed in combined pain and pleasure below him. His teeth encased my shaft and slid down toward the root and then applied pressure until I wanted to scream in fear and anticipation. His mouth went to my balls, which he sucked hard and nipped and pulled away from my body with his teeth. I writhed some more for him. Then his mouth went back to my cock, and he pumped my shaft with his mouth for several minutes, always keeping me on edge as to whether he was going to take a big bite. At last, the intensity got to me, and I jacked off down his throat.

He quickly moved up my body, picking up the knife as he ascended. He jerked the gag off and gave me a deep kiss, mixing our saliva and my warm sperm. He took my tongue between his teeth, and I thought for an instant that he would try to bite through that.

But then he disengaged from the kiss and brought the blade of the knife up to the side of my neck, poised against a throbbing artery. He spoke in a low, menacing voice. "Attempt to scream—or even to talk—or to do anything funny with my dick in your mouth, and I'll cut you so deep you'll bleed out."

I took him seriously. He was kneeling above my chest, his half-hard rod hovering over my face.

"Get it hard," was all he said as he grabbed the end of my belt with his free hand and pulled my mouth up to the helmet of his dick with it. To keep from choking, I raised my head farther, taking his cock into my mouth. I gave him head, as good as I could, and he panted and moaned above me, getting hard fairly quickly.

When it seemed like he might be ready to cum, he pulled out of my mouth. He let loose of the belt, letting my head drop back on the mattress. He replaced my gag and then moved down below me again. His mouth and teeth went to my asshole, and he was pumping my cock again with one of his hands and digging the nails of his other hand in the tender back of one of my thighs.

After rimming me for a few minutes, he came back up on his knees and showed me both the knife and a small bottle of lubricant. He poured lubricant over the blade of the knife, and on his dick as well, and then he moved the knife slowly down between my legs. I was struggling for all of my might, trying to escape the thrust of the blade up my ass canal, but when something entered me, it was rounded and warm, not sharp and cold. Tony laughed and held up a long and thick dildo, with knobs and suction cup-like appendages running along the shaft, to show me that this is what was assaulting my asshole, not the knife.

I felt the head of the dildo at my asshole again. Tony rotated it around and around, moving it ever deeper, until it was past my sphincter. Then he just steadily pushed it in to the hilt. I screamed into the gag in pain, mixed with waves of desire, and twisted my body around while he was impaling me, which probably only helped send the dildo deeper. The novelties running around the shaft were driving me wild with mixed pain and pleasure. But the pleasure started to overshadow the pain—so much so that by the time Tony replaced the dildo with his own longer and thicker dick, I was meeting him thrust for thrust.

He took both of my calves in his hands and wishboned my legs up and out. He then rolled his pelvis up on mine so that I was fully open to his plunging cock. I set my eyes on the ceiling and watched the strobing colored lights play, while I listened to the sounds of the bouncing bed springs and of the skin of a shaft sliding in and out of the skin of an ass passage. I wanted the gag off. I wanted to tell Tony how much I was enjoying the fuck, that I wanted him to dig deeper and deeper. I couldn't tell Tony that, but I could tell that he didn't need to be told. He was rotating his hips and alternating short strokes and long plunges in a mad frenzy of plowing above me. His dreadlocks were flying around his head, and his chest and arm tattoos seemed alive in their undulating movements in the strobing lights. His nipples were erect and prominent and his washboard stomach muscles were tensing and puffing out with the heavy breathing of his ecstasy. He was beauty in motion in his dance of fearsome fuck, and I was proud now to be the instrument of his mayhem.

He was no more beautiful than at the supremely intense point of his strong, three-gushes of ejaculation deep inside me. I was almost at the point of coming again myself, and Tony took care of pumping me off in a fountain of sperm between our bellies before he collapsed his sweating torso on mine. He ripped my gag off, and we went into a long, tender kiss.

After several minutes, as I felt his dick softening within me, I spoke. "That was great, Tony. I feel truly fucked. The doctor was right—that bondage and the sense of danger was a way to cure our inhibitions. Now you. Release me, and now I'll do you. Quickly now. I still feel horny as hell."

Breath Control Play

Looking for It

I stood there, in front of the still-wet painting. It gripped me, pulled me in, made me tingle, feel on edge. I wanted it; I wanted to be it. I wasn't it yet. The painting was of me, but it somehow was more alive, more aroused, nearer the pinnacle. I could see it everywhere, mostly in the eyes, I thought. They were so alive, so satisfied and . . . completed.

"It's . . . it's like something you've never done before, Klaus," I murmured.

"It's in the style of Seligman," he whispered in my ear. "Well, partially the style. I like to think I bring something new, important to it. My counter to Seligman. Do you like it?"

"Yes, yes . . . of course. It makes me . . . it makes me want to be that man."

"But you *are* that man, Petro, that *is* you. You are that for me."

Yes it was of me; I was the model. I had just lain there, naked, on the divan, for hours, swirled in folds of the scarlet silk. And yet it wasn't me. It was what I wanted to be, what I wanted to feel, at the height of ejaculation. It was a level I had not attained, although I had sought it for years. The ultimate ejaculation. "No, Klaus. I wish. But there's more, much more than me, in the painting. In the style of Seligman, you say? Who is this Seligman? Where can I find him?"

"You do not want to know, Petro. You think that I am peculiar . . . have special needs. No, do not bother to deny it. But Seligman, he is a man on the edge. I shudder to think of the tightrope he would make you walk."

Moeller was standing close behind me. He too was naked. We had worked for hours, and I could tell by the way he looked at me as he painted, that he would want me again—and in his way. He was enfolding me in his arms, a hand on my cock and one strumming a nipple with his thumb. And his cock was hard and rubbing against the small of my back. He had been hard for some time, as he was finishing the painting. Looking at me in that way. Wanting fucking me to be the high point of his creation, what he would remember when he looked at this masterpiece he had created. And not just any fucking. His way.

He deserved it. It required so little of me. The painting was a masterpiece. It was alive with lust and arousal.

"I love it, Klaus," I repeated. "It makes me feel so . . . so . . ."

I couldn't complete the thought, and Moeller's hand on my cock and thumb on my nipple felt all the answer that was required.

"Please . . . the divan," he uttered in a low, hoarse voice.

"Yes."

He handed me the lubed dildo as he stood between my thighs, my shoulder blades resting on the silk draperies on the divan. I took it and placed it in position as he raised one of my feet in his hands and brought it to his lips and kissed it and stroked it lightly with his fingers.

His eyes slitted as I slowly impaled myself on the dildo, methodically drawing it deep inside me. I kept my eyes on his, knowing that was important, showing him how arousing his lips on the arch of my foot was in consort with the slow inhaling of the dildo inside my ass canal. I made my eyes burn, imploring as his mouth enclosed over my toes, one by one, and he gave suck.

I arched my back and started to slowly move the dildo in and out, in and out, inside me, as he took up my other foot and made love to it.

I moaned for him, as I knew he would want me to and that would arouse him further. I extracted the dildo—slowly—and he moved closer into me, and I took his cock in both of my hands and drew him inside me, as he continued to suck my toes and run his tongue over my feet. He was making little mewing sounds that shortly melted into the sounds of his need. He fucked me faster, deeper, and he was biting my toes and feet, and I was crying out in both pain and passion.

And then it was over and he dropped my legs and collapsed on top of me. His eyes sought out mine, and although I saw pleasure there, I saw also in the reflection in his eyes that I had not attained it—the eyes he had painted for me were so much more satisfied, completed, than the ones he was staring into.

"In the style of Seligman?" I asked in a low voice when we were both able to speak.

"Forget Seligman," he whispered. "You do not want to pursue that."

"But the painting is so alive, so much what I want. So much more," I murmured.

"It is not because of Seligman," he whispered. "I think it is because of what I brought to Seligman's style?"

"I don't understand," I said.

"The eyes; it's in the eyes."

Later, standing in front of the painting, I paid particular attention to the eyes again. They were one of the best aspects of the painting. My initial impression did not change. The eyes were so alive, so deep in passion and lust—and fulfillment. Satisfied eyes. Fully taken and satisfied. The best part of it.

And I asked Moeller again, and he would not tell me. "You do not want to know," was his repeated answer.

"Where is this Seligman?" I asked again.

"You do not want to know," he repeated.

But I would not let him take me again—in the special way he liked—until he told me. And he wanted me so much, in that way, that he did tell me.

* * * *

122

Seligman's studio was high in the German alps, carved out of the ruins of a small castle keep—what had probably been a remote watch tower and fortification for a small sentry force in centuries past. When I asked in the hostel in the small village at the foot of the mountain, they refused to tell me how to get there.

But we weren't in the dark ages. Seligman had a cell phone, and I was able to contact him. And when I had established that I had modeled for Moeller and Viscuss and even Hollimain when he was still painting—before he was incarcerated for what had been declared as both blasphemous and pornographic—Seligman seemed all too pleased to give me directions to his isolated studio.

He seemed delighted to see me and was quite straightforward. He commanded me to strip and to turn my body this way and that way, which I did expertly, being experienced in modeling and knowing what artists of the male nude wanted.

Knowing also what many of the artists of the male nude wanted to do with their models, I was not surprised when he said, without a modicum of embarrassment or hesitation, "First we fuck, and then I paint. Always I fuck first. It informs my painting."

We did not do so immediately, though. Seligman wanted to charge his paints first, to set his easel and canvas and to set the divan just so. He too used a rich, scarlet silk, seemingly carelessly thrown on the divan, but set just so, nothing careless about it. I assumed this must be some of what Moeller had meant when he said that magnificent painting of his had been done in the style of Seligman.

The walls of the studio were lined with Seligman's work, so as he prepared his paints and set the divan as he wanted it, I drifted around the walls, viewing the paintings. I could see what Moeller meant. It wasn't just the arousing pose of the model, seemingly tousled carelessly in folds of the scarlet silk. It also was the strong brush strokes. The bold strokes that, when scrutinized closely, seemed to be haphazard, wild, almost uncontrolled, but that, as the viewer moved away, all came together. And it came together in tension and unease—a feeling of coldness that was all the more alluring because it contrasted so with the lush setting and vibrant colors, not to mention the sensuality of the model.

It was here that I felt the first chill, felt myself clutch and tighten. At first blush, I hadn't seen the difference, but Moeller was right. There was a difference. Whereas Moeller's study had been alive, arousing, had made me shudder with want, these did something else. I couldn't place it. I moved in closer to the one I was standing in front of again, looking closer into it.

The skin. A slight pallor perhaps, in contrast to Moeller's, where the skin seemed lustrous. Maybe in just this one, I thought. But when I moved down to the next painting, I saw the same thing.

And the eyes. Moeller had said something about the eyes. What was that? He had especially wanted me to scrutinize the eyes. I walked in closer and studied the eyes. Moeller had made the eyes reflect his own lust as he painted me—capturing what he wanted to do with me, what he did do with me. Using me to play his own personal fetish, gaining arousal and satisfaction, for him, that went much further than just fucking.

Seligman's eyes didn't reflect anything like this. In fact, they looked dead to me, as if the model was sleeping with his eyes open—that the model wasn't even here, that he was transported to another realm and had lost his connection to the sensuality of the setting.

All of which accentuated Moeller's talent—his triumph over Seligman. Maybe that's what he was trying to tell me. That I didn't need to search out Seligman. I already was in the presence of the master.

I turned and saw that Seligman was ready, and that he was watching me, his eyes active, alive, full of lust.

I suddenly was scared—without knowing why—and my legs were taking me, slowly, but intentionally toward my clothes, where I had neatly folded and placed them on a straight chair in the shadows. I had seen what Moeller was trying to tell me—or certainly thought I had.

Seligman intercepted me, though. He took my wrist in a firm grip, and I felt all of the power draining out of me. He was a strongly built man, with a grip of steel. But it was his bearing and the power of his eyes that held me. I whimpered under his grip, but I made no physical effort to resist him. The trembling that went through my body was contradictory. I was frightened, but I was also aroused—more aroused than I had been with Moeller. I was hyperventilating, but my body was telling me that something was happening, something I'd never experienced before, something I wanted to know about, to experience.

As we moved to the divan, Seligman was unbuttoning his smock with his other hand. He was naked underneath. Powerful, barrel-chested, heavily muscled, hairy. And in full, monstrous erection.

He gave me no time. He simply pushed me down on my back on the divan, a fist buried in my sternum, holding me on the divan both physically and by overpowering mental control. I was gasping for breath. His other hand was underneath one of my thighs, high up, spreading and lifting my leg with superhuman strength. The bulb of his cock at my hole. Not giving me time. Demanding entrance—and despite my cries and the reluctance of my opening, gaining entrance and relentlessly pushing me open and moving deep inside me.

I writhed under him, entwining myself in the scarlet silk, achieving, I suddenly realized, the effect of the silk draping in the paintings that lined the walls, the paintings screaming at me to escape. Too late.

His fist was no longer on my sternum. He had raised his hand to my face, the palm of his hand over my mouth, his thumb and a finger pinching my nose, blocking my air supply.

I was screaming on the inside, gurgling on the outside, my hips churning in response to his plowing cock, one of my fists clutching at the silk, the other wrapped around my own cock and pumping away. I couldn't breathe and specks were floating in my eyes, dimming out the piercing gaze in his own eyes, holding me in thrall underneath him as strongly as he was doing with the strength of his body. But still my body wanted this. My hand on my cock, working to bring my arousal to the heights, screamed that I wanted this.

He was fucking me like I'd never been fucked before, and my hand was working my cock—involuntarily—because at the same time that I was deeply frightened, sensing that I was fighting for my life, I wanted to explode, to ejaculate.

I was close, very close to coming. I wanted to come. I wanted to breathe, but I also wanted to come. This was so much more . . . so much beyond where I'd ever been before.

But then Seligman stopped. He held me tight, not letting me move a muscle, not moving himself, held me on the edge. And he released his stifling grip on my nose and mouth.

And I gasped for air. I couldn't move, but my lungs were burning and expanding and contracting in my chest cavity—fighting to take in as much oxygen as possible, to replace what they had been denied for so long, almost too long.

But that's not what I wanted to be moving. I wanted his cock to be moving inside me. He slapped my hand away from my own cock and gripped my wrist, holding me away from finishing myself.

"No, please," I was whimpering as I felt myself moving away from satisfaction, losing the roaring sensation of the approaching ejaculation. I didn't think I'd whispered that aloud, but he reacted as if he had heard me. "Please finish me."

He smiled a sneery smile. A "look who is in control" smile. And his eyes. They possessed me. Not unlike the look in Moeller's eyes when he took me. I realized this was a fetish with me—seeing that look in my lover's eyes. There was a wildness in Seligman's eyes, triggered, I now realize, by the fear in my eyes combined with need as he took my breath away while fucking me—and took me to the edge and back and then to the edge again. This is what he liked best, I realized. This look of terror edged with lust in his lover's eyes. This was his fetish. What completed him.

Or was that true? Thinking back on the difference between his paintings and those of Moeller—the treatment of the eyes—I began to think, with increasing trepidation, that maybe it wasn't the mixed look of fear and lust that completed Seligman, that was his fetish. Maybe it was the dull look in his lover's eyes when Seligman was done—when he had choked the life out of his lover. I moaned at the thought—at the danger of it. And, at the same time, my arousal went to new heights.

I murmured, "No, please," again as I felt his hand gripping my chin again, closing again over my nose and mouth. And as I fought for breath again, he recommenced the plowing of his cock. Working me, bringing me to the edge again. I was beginning to black out again. I was . . . right there . . . on the edge. Both edges. The edge of blacking out, the edge of exploding in the most complete ejaculation I'd ever experienced. Wanting breath, wanting the ejaculation. Want fighting want.

And then the release on my mouth and nose, the gasping for breath, the pounding headache. But at the same time, the denial of ejaculation. Holding me still, making me fall off the edge of satisfaction. The jeery smile, the possessing eyes.

The approaching hand; turning my head back and forth, trying to escape the hand, writhing in the silk, but no escape. The fingers pinching my nose, the hand covering my mouth, the cock resuming its deep, possessing thrusts.

The eyes. Oh God, the eyes. Moeller had said, "Look at the eyes." Lifeless.

At the very edge of breathlessness. Not one more second. The glorious release, my release in a cascade of cum up my belly, as I feel the pump of the spurting, the flow, deep inside me. Throbbing temples, spots before my eyes, roaring in my ears. Got to . . . get . . . a brea—

* * * *

I was swimming up from a great depth and slowly becoming aware that I could breathe again—that I was still lying on the divan, entwined in the scarlet silk, but that I was breathing normally. I shuddered and started to move.

"Hold still." It was a command, not a request. And I instantly obeyed. I had known the authority behind that control.

"Stay just as that, please." The voice came from the direction of the easel. I saw from my periphery vision that he was there, behind the easel, painting furiously. Still naked; still in full erection.

I shuddered again, which prompted, "So, you thought that was it, did you? I saw you scrutinizing the eyes in the paintings. You thought of death, did you not? I would have told you—I paint death. I create it, but I do not cause it. I would have told you, but it was better this way, no? More satisfying. Bigger coming. The full range—your fighting wants. It helps with coming. You came well. It takes you to the heights. And watching you—your struggling wants—that takes me to the heights too. I came well too. Very well indeed. My member, it wants it again, now. But it must wait. I am not finished painting."

I opened my mouth to speak.

"No, do not move, please. I'm not finished. Don't speak. When I finish, we do it again, no? You give good fuck. Yes, we do it again, I think."

I shuddered again—but at the same time a chill of arousal went through my body. The height and the depth. Starting anew. The ultimate death. Who said that? That ejaculation was the ultimate death? Some philosopher. Freud? Foucault?

"Yes, yes. I fuck you again, I think. And maybe this time I go all the way. Yes? No?" This was followed by a deep-throated laugh. "No, do not speak. I just toy with you . . . maybe." And then the laugh again.

And I shuddered again. Not only at the thought of him doing it again—and maybe not joking about not stopping. But also because I wanted it again.

Cigars

Picky, Picky

The young man's hand was trembling as he handed the creamy vellum envelope embossed with the FGCC crest over to the older man. Edward Winslow held the younger man's finger between his and the underside of the envelope for an extra couple of seconds before taking the envelope and placing it carefully on the top of the cigarette table beside him. He puffed on his cigar and smiled a satisfied smile to himself. He wanted Bill Brewster to tremble at the thought of handing over that envelope. It was final nail in this particular coffin.

Bill Brewster shifted nervously in his crackled-leather-covered Chippendale lounge chair in the dim corner of the First Gentlemen's Covenant Club smoking room and moved his slender, finely manicured hands together in a tented position, his fingertips centering between his patrician-shaped nose and his full, dry lips. He was doing all he could do to control the trembling of his hands, and he didn't want Winslow to see the trepidation his face surely revealed. He wasn't looking directly at his boss at First Families Securities, but Edward Winslow was looking directly at him and was smiling, clearly enjoying not just the young man's resignation but also his discomfort.

A tall, fine-figured Hispanic young male in a smartly tailored black silk uniform materialized at the side of Winslow's chair and set down a snifter of port. In withdrawing his hand, the servant barely brushed Winslow's hand with his. The senior partner of First Families Securities, the son of a son of a son going back to the arrival of the *Mayflower* on America's shores—the very prize that qualified Winslow for membership in the Beacon Hill First Gentlemen's Covenant Club—twitched his hand back, almost as if he'd been shot, and sent the port in his glass into a brief tempest.

"Damn Mexicans," Winslow muttered, as the servant moved silently behind the two chairs and, appearing at Bill Brewster's elbow, quietly slid the second snifter of port on the cigarette table beside the younger man.

"The old club's going to the damn Mexicans," Winslow continued to mutter. "At least the darkies they had in here before knew to wear gloves."

Bill Brewster picked up the snifter and moved it toward his mouth. But his hand was trembling so hard that he had to take the crystal vessel in his other hand as well to hold it steady. He took a nervous gulp from the glass—quite out of character for a son of a son of a son, who had equal rights to FGCC membership to those Winslow had. But these were circumstances he'd never faced before.

It wasn't until this evening that Winslow had fully believed Brewster would actually go through with it. The room key in that vellum envelope lying beside Winslow's snifter settled that question.

Winslow snapped his fingers, and the liveried attendant appeared at his side.

"Casa Blanca Jeroboam. No, two. Now."

The servant vanished in search of the cigar humidor behind the massive mahogany long bar.

Winslow looked back over at Brewster, who was breathing heavily, obviously trying to contain himself. This had been a campaign of the older man's for nearly a year. When Winslow had offered the younger man the broker's position, he had made it clear the extent to which Brewster was to show his gratitude. Brewster was a natural for the firm and looked the part perfectly, but he had majored in partying and tennis at Harvard, where only his name had stood him in good stead from being tossed out on his tail, and he normally could not have expected to have been given a position in the firm, despite his lineage.

The attendant reappeared and Winslow snatched one of the cigars from him and motioned with an irritation usually reserved for the slow of mind for the other one to be placed on top of the vellum envelope. He hissed his disapproval that the Mexican had handled the cigars; they should have been delivered on a white linen napkin.

"No training whatsoever," Winslow muttered. "Can't train a Mexican. Heh, William?"

"Ye . . . yes, Edward, that . . . that's right." Brewster was obviously uncomfortable, but it wasn't about Winslow's berating of the servant, because he added the unnecessary. "Training would be a waste. He'll be slipping back across the border as soon as he's made a few bucks."

"Next time on a napkin, Jose," Winslow hissed.

"Yes, sir," the servant said, his eyes downcast, as he backed into the shadows.

"You know his name?" Brewster asked, the tone of his voice revealing how incredulous he thought the idea that Winslow would take that much notice of one of "them."

"They're all called Jose, aren't they?" Winslow said. And they both laughed, although Brewster's laugh was edged with a bit of hysteria.

"So, are you sure?" Winslow said, fingering the vellum envelope. "I've heard that Fenton and Felton are hiring."

"Yes, I'm sure," Brewster responded in a small voice. The mention of Fenton and Felton, a decidedly plebian firm, was pregnant with meaning.

"You'll have to ask for it," Winslow said. "I'll not force it."

"Yes, thank you, sir. I understand," Brewster said. "But you will . . . we can . . . you know, what we agreed on."

"Yes," Winslow whispered sotto voce, his voice laced with exasperation. "If you have a blindfold, you can use it. And I have restraints. If it's easier for you, we can do that if it makes you feel less guilty."

"Light," Winslow said in a louder voice like the flick of a whip. He snapped his fingers as he said it, and the Hispanic attendant materialized from the shadows and lit Winslow's cigar for him. And then he faded away as quietly as he had appeared.

"Well, you'd best be going up," Winslow turned to Brewster and said. "I'll be up shortly. I don't care if the lights are off and you are blindfolded. You are going to enjoy it, so don't look so glum."

"Yes, sir," Brewster muttered in misery. He gulped down his port and moved unsteadily toward the door and to the elevator.

Nice ass, Winslow thought, as he watched the young man move away. Good looker, nicely muscled and trim. Just the way I like 'em. And young men of his pedigree are hard to come by. As only America can produce through generations of residence.

Winslow closed his eyes and let his head loll back into the enfolding supple leather of the Chippendale chair and dreamed of fucking the very presentable and finely familied William Brewster. A year's campaign but all worth it. After a brief reverie of the images of taking the young man from several positions, Winslow realized his cigar had gone out. He snapped his fingers.

"Light."

Nothing happened. Winslow's eyes shot open and he looked to his left, where the Hispanic attendant should be standing. No one was there, but Winslow's empty snifter had been cleared away. No servant, though, and Winslow's cigar had gone out.

"Damn wetback," Winslow muttered. "Probably already half way back across the border. Probably an illegal too. The club standards have gone to shit."

He leaned over and smashed the ash end of the cigar in a crystal ashtray, and, while struggling up out of the mothering clutches of the deep armchair, took up the second cigar, put it in his shirt pocket, and reached for the precious vellum envelope.

While waiting for the ancient elevator to clank its way back to the public room floor, he opened the envelope and took the key out.

612, he thought. I didn't know the club even had six floors. Must be in the attic. I wonder who Brewster ticked off at reception when he checked in.

* * * *

Bill Brewster was naked and lying on his belly on the silk sheet covering the double bed in the middle of the club guest bedroom. He lay in the dark, his eyes covered with a blindfold, his eyelids held tightly shut, his breathing ragged, and his body twitching at what was about to happen.

He heard the key in the lock, and he almost whimpered in uncertainty and fear as he sensed more than saw the brief invasion of light from the hallway before the door was clicked shut and the subtle sound of the rustling of shed clothing reached his alert hearing.

This was his future. He'd made a deal with the devil. He'd been told that Winslow was cruel but that he didn't sustain interest. A couple of months, not more, and he'd move on to other quarry. And then Brewster's future would be made. He'd just have to steel himself. His ancestors had taken the risk and grabbed for the gold ring when they'd sailed for the New World on the *Mayflower*. At least Winslow had

131

the right pedigree. Brewster could still hold his head up after this. Just some pain and private humiliation, and then his future would be made.

Brewster lurched and made a little yipping sound as he felt strong callused hands taking his wrists and tying them together and then forcing them over his head and tying them off at the headboard.

Such strong hands. A little surprising, the strength, but Winslow bragged incessantly about his garden and how he worked it himself. Brewster shivered a bit. Strong hands. Would that mean other strengths as well?

Those callused hands were running all over his body as he lay stretched out on his belly. He was trembling and trying to think of anything else but what was happening—what was happening at last after nearly a year of putting it off. If he'd let Winslow bed him as soon as the employment deal was set, it would be all over now. It would be done and Winslow would probably already have moved on to fresh tail. No use crying over that now. Just bear it. Pretend to be somewhere else altogether.

But pretending to be elsewhere was becoming increasingly difficult. Those hands were tantalizing. No woman had done this to him, had taken the time to put him into a mood. Pleasurable. He had to admit that it was pleasurable. He was beginning to calm down, and he caught himself sighing.

Hands were on his hips, lifting them, signaling that he was to go up on his knees. He started to rise, and a large hand palmed him between the shoulder blades and showed that only his hips were to go up, that his chest and cheek were to stay flat on the sheet. His arms, trapped above his head were beginning to go numb and to tingle. But the skin of the small of his back and his butt cheeks was tingling too. This was a different tingle, though, brought about by the movement of lips and tongue on his body.

Brewster moaned as a hand came between his spread thighs and took possession of his dick. He hadn't realized it, but he was hard. A flash of embarrassment shot through him. Winslow's attentions had made him go hard. Letting yourself be fucked by a man was one thing, but your body showing that it was enjoying the attention was quite another. He gulped and whimpered as the stroking began. Then he didn't quite manage to swallow a yelp when the bulb of his dick felt the lips open over it. A tongue was flicking his piss slit as the lips slid farther over his throbbing dick. Fingers were probing his balls and pulling on his sacks. Brewster let a deep moan escape his lips.

He was supremely embarrassed, but he couldn't help himself. It had seemed like an eternity of sucking, but it had been mere minutes before he creamed himself from the close attention paid to his dick. His knees were trembling, and he couldn't feel his arms at all, but he certainly could feel the pounding of his heart against the bed sheet.

Brewster twitched and he gulped hard as the lips and tongues moved from his spent dick and started to rim his ass. He was moving to the rhythm of the attention he was receiving. His chest was sliding back and forth on the sheet and he was slowly rotating his hips back and forth as his hole was being loosened and softened. He groaned and moaned.

The trembling in his thighs increased as he felt the cool lubricant of the probing fingers that replaced the lips and tongue at his rim. He was being forced open by those fingers, which worked their way deeper and deeper, stretching him, preparing him.

He was panting and moaning, his attention so focused on those probing fingers, that he only barely heard the hoarse whisper.

"What?" he whimpered.

"Do you have something to ask?" The voice was deep, throaty. Very quiet, but intense.

"What?"

"Ask me for it."

"What? Oh. Please, yes, please."

"Please what?"

"Please . . . do . . . it . . . Ohh!" The nub of a forefinger had planted itself solidly on Brewster's prostate and he felt like he was going to jack off again, although he was just beginning to recover a hard on.

"Do what?" the voice hissed.

"Fuck me. Fuck me. Oh, please do it. Nowww!"

He had been prepared so slowly and methodically that he was completely caught by surprise at the swift brutality with which the fingers disappeared and big hands grabbed him by the hips and a thick, hard cock thrust inside him.

Brewster cried out, and groaned and begged and writhed under the firm grip of the furious assault. His crying for relief seemed only to excite his master, who pumped hard and dug deep. Brewster had no idea that Winslow had such strength and length and width and stamina in him.

It seemed to go on forever. When Brewster's knees could take it no longer and he collapsed fully on the sheet, his rider followed him, stretched full length on top of him and sucked on his neck as he thrust and thrust and thrust inside him.

Brewster was totally exhausted after his master's spouting and drifting off into a semiconscious state when he felt the restraints being loosened at the head of the bed and his wrists unbound, and he didn't stir again until well past dawn. And, of course, he awoke finally to an otherwise empty room.

* * * *

Room Number 612 did, indeed, seem to be in the hotel's attic, Edward Winslow observed, as he exited the elevator and moved down the dimly lit hallway. And it definitely was in need of redecoration. Winslow had no idea that the FGCC had permitted its guest floors to go so seedy. He'd have to talk to the steward, Richard Warren, about this.

After looking both ways down the hall to ensure he wasn't being observed, Winslow turned the key to room 612, slipped inside, and shut the door behind him with a quiet click. He stood there inside the door, in the darkness, waiting for his eyes to adjust. He was breathing heavily, and his cock was already stirring, in anticipation of what he had campaigned for for nearly a year. He could hear the nervous breathing of his prey as well. Brewster had wanted to be taken while bound and blindfolded to assuage the guilt, but Winslow had been more than happy with this plan. Brewster's nervousness and fear fed the rising of Winslow's cock. He loved

133

to dominate—in everything. That Bill had such a nice ass. Winslow could hardly wait.

His eyes were beginning to adjust. He could make out the outline of the bed and of a wooden arm chair off to the side. He extracted the leather restraints from his jacket pocket and took a step toward the bed.

"Ooff." He hadn't seen the fist coming at him from out of the darkness. It hit him midsection and sent him, doubled up on the threadbare carpeting on the floor. He was immobilized by the surprise and the pain in his midsection.

He didn't manage to even begin to struggle as he was stripped of his dinner jacket and lifted and thrown into the wooden arm chair, which rocked dangerously backward, kept from crashing back only by the hulking figure who had moved to behind the chair.

Winslow's arms were brutally jerked to behind the chair, and he heard the handcuffs snapping together. His own leather restraints were used to bind his chest to the chair back. And Winslow had only begun to regain his breath and presence of mind—to let out a scream of indignation—when tape was slapped over his mouth. Then he was blindfolded and totally under control.

The door clicked shut and he was alone. He was alone, bound to the chair, for hours, it seemed. Winslow seethed the whole time. What the fuck was Brewster up to? He couldn't just leave him here. The maids would be by in the morning and let him loose, and then he'd ream Brewster to within an inch of his life. So, he didn't want to be fucked. He would regret it. His future was toast. He might have cleared out before Winslow got free, but he'd pursue the bastard to the ends of the earth and make his life miserable. He'd ruin the fucker. He'd find a way to fuck him and then to ruin him.

Winslow had nearly nodded off, his inability to put his hundred-ways punishment of William Brewster into immediate effect, worn down by his spewing of bile within the restraints of the tape over his mouth, when he heard the door click open again.

He heard the movement in the room. The rustling of clothes. Then he felt the hands at his belt buckle. He struggled against the restraints as his pants were unzipped. His head snapped to the side as he was backhanded on the right cheek. And while he was immobilized, stunned by that, he felt his trousers and briefs being stripped off. His butt cheeks were cold against the wood of the chair bottom.

Winslow felt the cigar being taken out of his shirt pocket, and he barely had time to wonder about that before strong arms grabbed him under his knees, pulled his back down the chair slats, spread his legs, and hooked them over the arms of the chair.

Something cold was at his asshole, which puckered right up at the sudden attention it was getting.

The cigar. He was being probed by the Casa Blanca Jeroboam! God, what a sacrilege. The waste of an expensive cigar.

His ass was being worked well, though, and Winslow found himself moaning and groaning behind the taped mouth. That Brewster. What an actor, pretending that this frightened him. Winslow felt himself go harder than he ever had done before. This wasn't so bad.

The cigar was withdrawn and strong hands were under his knees again, lifting his hips up even farther out the chair. He heard the heavy breathing and the shared strain, as a big, thick cock started to work its way into his hole.

Winslow's pelvis was being swung back and forth and to the sides as the cock drove its way up into him. Both of them were huffing and puffing.

Winslow's assessment of Brewster skyrocketed. Boy that young man had balls. Worthy of his *Mayflower* ancestry. Worthy of being moved up faster at First Families Securities. It had been a risk, but Brewster had played it perfectly. Winslow was loving this fuck.

The fuck went on and on. It was a cruel fuck, an expert taking. Winslow shot off twice during the taking. He felt twenty years younger. This was far better an idea than the one he'd had—although he'd get his shot too.

A true American First Families performance. Pure-blooded American. Deep, thick, complete taking. Yessss!

Winslow was totally exhausted when it was over. He felt the handcuffs snap off and his bounds undone, and he just collapsed back into the chair, trying to pull himself together. When he reached up and pulled the blindfold off, he saw the light of rushing dawn filtering in through the dormer window. He was alone in the room. He painfully, stiffly raised himself from the chair and hobbled over to the cracked porcelain sink in the corner of the room. Using a threadbare washcloth, he cleaned himself as best he could and hobbled back to the chair; picked his briefs, trousers, and jacket off the floor; and put himself back together.

It took him several minutes to smooth out all of the wrinkles, but he wasn't about to walk through the halls of the FGCC without looking exactly like what he was—a pure-blood descendent of the original *Mayflower* first families of the New World. Pure American down through the centuries. Protectors of all that was patrician Bostonian against the encroaching world of the dirty, impure immigrants.

When he was what he wanted to project, he left the room and went to the elevator. It had been a stupendous gamble on Brewster's part. But it had pleased Winslow. It had been years since he'd come twice in a single fucking. He'd be fucking Brewster, of course, but he had a whole new respect for the man. He certainly had balls.

Winslow didn't even acknowledge the presence of the Hispanic attendant who proceeded him out of the front entrance and flagged down a taxi for him. But after Winslow stiffly folded himself into the back seat of the cab and had made a sour remark about the immigrants who were driving the service cars those days, the attendant rose to his full height and flipped the departing taxi the bird. Flashing a big grin, he slowly pulled a moist and pungent Casa Blanca Jeroboam cigar out of his shirt pocket, lit it, and walked slowly back into the entrance to the world of the First Gentlemen's Covenant Club.

Triple Magnum Nabilum

I had to turn my eyes away from the penetrating stare of Finn Bergstrum, so I took my first good look at his assistant, Nabil. "Satyr" was the first thought that entered my mind, and I almost was able to imagine two little horns above his ears there. Sharp, swarthy features with that almost sneer of a smile that was close to the edge of presumption and cruelty without losing an ability to claim interest and encouragement if challenged. Jet black hair and eyes, and that pointed goatee that accentuated the struggle between sensitivity and raw animalism. The struggle accentuated by the hand that reached out for his wine glass: Long, sensuous artist's finger, but curly black hair on the back of the hand down to his knuckles. He was giving me a proprietary look—which, of course, was his privilege. I'd been bought and paid for to be here.

I looked back at Bergstrum, embarrassed at the feeling that I was distinctly out of my depth and perhaps even out of my league, and further embarrassed that anything like this could ever embarrass me after what I'd seen in this business. When Leon had set this up and handed me the air tickets, he only said that this was a very special corporate arrangement, that I'd been very lucky to be selected, and that I should be very accommodating. From the amount on the accompanying check, I decided that, indeed, I could be very accommodating. I'd flown to Zurich, checked in by prior arrangement at the Softel Hotel, and had barely slept for five hours before I was called down to the hotel's intimate and heavily masculine "gentlemen's" bar.

I had known the name Finn Bergstrum even before being handed the assignment. Who hadn't heard of him? Entrepreneur on the grand scale. Instant relief to corporations in the need of being saved and even more immediate panic in the halls of corporations rumored to have been added to his takeover lists. Reclusive, eccentric, somewhere just short of God, the tabloids said. And whispers about his sexual tastes and capabilities as well—at least in the pools in which I swam. Well, I'd just met him, and already I was trembling. This didn't normally happen to me.

He was ugly as sin, a regular gargoyle. But when I looked back at him, here in the Softel Hotel's dimly lit gentlemen's bar, I was overwhelmed by his presence and the raw power he exuded. He could have tipped me over this table right here, stripped me, and plowed me in front of all of the sedate bankers and brokers sitting around us sipping their martinis and smoking their Cuban cigars, and I would have moaned and moved my hips for him.

Craggy features, chiseled in a Mount Everest rawness and a powerful body, barely contained by a tailored silk tuxedo—heavy but obviously built for stamina and speed, the muscled presence of a bison. He filled the room; he owned the room. Strong hands the size of hubcaps and thick, gnarly fingers that set my butt a twitching.

There was no doubt why I was here, what I was supposed to do for him. This is what I did. I'd been told the bare facts of the deal. He'd agreed not to take over a major U.S. corporation for certain remunerations and accommodations. I—or someone like me—was just one of the accommodations. Just for one night. All the way from New York to Zurich just for one night. What I'd found in my paycheck was more than enough to cover anything that would happen in that one night. I'd done this before—if, certainly, not on this scale.

"So, is all understood, Mr. Smith?" Bergstrum asked me, as he took a long, thin cigar out of his mouth and tapped its ash head carefully in a silver-lined wooden tray. As he did so, I noticed three silver boxes, of varying lengths and widths laying on the surface of the cocktail table between us.

His milky blue eyes, peeking out from under bushy silver-gray eyebrows, pierced me, and I looked away quickly, down to his hand, resting atop the stack of boxes. Those thick fingers. My butt twitched again. Projecting ahead. Trying to remember whether I'd heard anything specific from the rumors about his proclivities.

"Yes, certainly," I answered. "I am ticketed for an early morning flight. I assume—"

"Of course I know your flight schedule, Mr. Smith," Bergstrum said, overriding my sentence.

"Then—" I started to say, indicating that I was quite prepared to vacate the bar and get on with the evening.

"Oh, do finish your drink, Mr. Smith," Bergstrum said. "I don't think that Nabil here has finished admiring you yet. And what do you think of my assistant, Nabil, Mr. Smith? Do you find him . . . suitable?"

"Ummm. Yes, of course," I stammered. What in the hell did that mean, I wondered.

"Nabil, here, is my right-hand man, Mr. Smith. My hands and eyes and my ears and my . . . well, let's just say all of my appendages."

Well, Hokay, I thought. But I wasn't being paid to be confused or smart. So I turned my face toward Nabil and gave him a friendly smile. He gave me back a smart-assed look fully conveying that this night would be a double. Well, that was OK, too. That was no surprise. I couldn't shake the satyr image that pinged at my brain every time I looked at him. He wasn't tall or thin, but he was strongly built. I gauged him to be Turkish probably. Some Mediterranean blend certainly. Somewhat of a surprise set off against the hulking Norwegian. And much younger than Bergstrum. The image of the two of them fucking flashed through my mind. This was immediately followed by the vision of the two of them fucking me, and my hand trembled a little. Nabil would be nothing new, other than that satyrish puckishness about him. But Bergstrum. I just didn't know. I didn't usually lose control on the job, and he was such an ugly lump. But there was something about him that had me off balance. Those fingers. I looked at them again. Strong, thick. I couldn't help but thinking of—

"Three boxes, Mr. Smith." Bergstrum was holding up the top, squarish silver box over the table between us. "Perhaps you can give us some idea of your preference."

He flipped open the lid of the box away from me. Cigars. Five cigars, of varying brands laid out in a row, snuggled into red velvet as if they were the crown jewels—and, although I knew next to nothing about cigars, I had no doubt that these cigars were as preciously bought as crown jewels.

"Oh, no thank you," I said. "I don't smoke. Thanks anyway."

"Oh, these aren't for smoking, Mr. Smith." He paused and gave me a broad, friendly smile. I turned to Nabil; he gave me a leery grin.

"Let me tell you how we rate cigars," Bergstrum continued after that pregnant pause. "First, by length. All of these in this box are six inches or less in length. Sort of the standard size; but maybe a bit long . . . for a cigar." He gave me a piercing look; gauging whether I was following his meaning. I wasn't a dummy; I understood we weren't talking about cigars.

"The other rating is in girth, diameter, if you will, Mr. Smith. We call this rating ring gauge. A sixty-four ring gauge would be equal to an inch. The cigars in this box all range around fifty ring gauge. Again, a bit thick for a cigar . . . if perhaps a somewhat disappointing thickness for, well, you know."

Yes, I did know.

"But we have several cigars here," Bergstrum said, and he flashed me a broad smile.

"So," he continued, "there are some very nice cigars in this case. Indian Tabac Cameroon Legenda Gorilla—interesting name, wouldn't you say? At six inches in length and a fifty-eight ring gauge, it's quite a formidable cigar, as cigars go. Or perhaps one of my favorites; this is a La Gloria Cubana Series R., No. 6, which is slightly shorter at five and seven-eighths inches, but a bit thicker at a sixty ring gauge. Do these interest you, Mr. Smith, or would you like to see what is in the second box before noting a preference?"

"Oh, let's look in the second box," I said. Obviously I'd said the right thing, as both Bergstrum and Nabil gave me approving looks.

"You'll notice this box is longer than the first one, Mr. Smith," Bergstrum said in hushed tones. "These are the truly extraordinary gems of the cigar world." He took up the second box and flipped it open. Surprise. More cigars. Longer and thicker than those in box number one. Same silver encasing, blue velvet lining this time.

I could tell these were special to Bergstrum. He lifted them out one at a time, his hands trembling a bit. Those thick fingers lovingly handling the cigars. I could feel the heat rising in me. This was unusual for me. Bergstrum had something in him that aroused me. I had little question why he was so successful in the business world. Most probably called it charisma. I had other names for it.

"We are into the longer beauties now, Mr. Smith. Very few exist at this level. The Casa Blanca Magnum, at seven inches and a ring gauge of sixty is lovely, don't you think? Or this Padron Magnum Maduro at a full nine inches, fifty ring gauge."

He was expecting me to be impressed, and I was impressed. I was being well paid to be impressed. I would have been less impressed if we were really talking about cigars, but, of course, we weren't.

"Now we could improve upon those, but we'd have to make choices." Bergstrum was continuing on. At this point I don't think he even needed me in the room. Nabil was sitting closer to Bergstrum now, and he was looking intently, worshipfully at the older man. And he had a hand on Bergstrum's inner thigh. This was obviously something of a precoital ceremony for the two of them. I said nothing. My paycheck was already banked.

"For length, you might like the Perfecxion A Giant, at nine and a quarter inches, but only a forty-seven ring gauge. And if your preference went to thickness, here's a Special Jamaican Rey Del Rey, at nine inches, but with a ring gauge of sixty. What do you think, Mr. Smith? Are these interesting to you, or should we perhaps go back to the first box?" Bergstrum's voice was rasping now. Nabil's hand had found his basket and was gently massaging it.

"No, this box is fine," I said, trying my best to match Bergstrum's rasping voice and to show him lustful eyes. He was clearly pleased. And I'll have to admit that the lustful eyes required no acting. Nabil's other hand was on my basket now, and I was showing him that I, indeed, was following along with this game.

"Then just maybe you might be interested in the favorite of the actor Orson Welles, Mr. Smith?"

"Yes, I was wondering about that one," I said in a breathy voice, having had my eye on the last cigar in the box ever since Bergstrum had opened it. If Nabil didn't stop his attentions, I might come right here in the gentlemen's bar. I could see by the way he'd tented up Bergstrum's pants that I hadn't been mistaken about those chunky fingers of his.

"This is a Casa Blanca Jeroboam," Bergstrum said, his voice full of wonder. "Orson Welles's cigar of choice. Ten inches long and a sixty-six ring gauge."

We all sat there for a moment, drinking in the size of that humongous cigar. Nabil was still stroking Bergstrum's crotch, but he had abandoned mine for his own.

"Would you like to make choices for Nabil and me, Mr. Smith?"

I contemplated the pickings for a few brief moments, wondering what would be most acceptable. "How about the Perfecxion A Giant for Nabil?" I said.

"And for me?" Bergstrum's eyes were slitted and his chest was heaving up and down from the attention Nabil was giving him.

"The Casa Blanca Jeroboam, of course," I said.

That had been the right answer, obviously. But I pressed on. "But what about the third box?" I asked. I could see it was longer than the other two, although much narrower.

"Ah, that would be the Triple Magnum Nabilum," Bergstrum said. "Perhaps later."

Both Bergstrum and his assistant were struggling up out of their plush club chairs at that point.

* * * *

140

Bergstrum's room at the Softel, or rooms, I should say, were about twelve times larger than the accommodations I had been given. And they were about four degrees plusher even though, had I not seen Bergstrum's digs, I would have assumed that I'd been given the best accommodations in the hotel.

But I didn't really see much of the room. As far as the decor went, my eyes were mainly on the edge of the canopy over Bergstrum's massive bed. I was on my back at the edge of the bed, holding my thighs up and out, and Bergstrum was hunched between them and working my ass canal with the Perfecxion A. Giant cigar I'd selected for Nabil, while Nabil was over to the side, clearly in my vision, stripping down.

The cigar was somewhat of a surprise; the foreplay down in the gentlemen's bar hadn't been as symbolic as I had imagined it would be. I really was being fucked by an expensive nine and a half-inch cigar. But in my line of business and at the prices I commanded, this wasn't as surprising as some other moments in my life had been.

Nabil was much more of a surprise. The satyr impression held true. His dark-skinned well-muscled torso was smooth skin down to the waist, with the exception of patches of black curly hair around his ring-pierced nipples, but when he stripped his tuxedo pants off, I could hardly tell he'd done so. From the waist down, he was covered in thick, curly black hair that looked almost like a pelt. His forearms were equally hirsute. If he'd had cloven feet, I would have sworn he was a true satyr. As it was he certainly was horse hung.

Leaving the Perfecxion A Giant buried in my ass, Bergstrum moved back to the other side of me from where Nabil had stripped and sank into a chair, still well within my line of vision. Nabil cantered up to him and Bergstrum took Nabil's cock in his mouth and worked it up. After only a few moments, however, Nabil walked back over to me and retrieved the cigar. He went to a side table, put the cigar in his mouth, struck a match to the tip of the cigar, and took a few puffs. Then he returned to Bergstrum, stuck the cigar in Bergstrum's mouth, sank down to his knees between Bergstrum's thighs, unzipped the hulking Norwegian's tux fly, and fed on the huge piece of meat he found there. Bergstrum let his head loll back on the top of the chair and hummed and puffed on the cigar. After a bit, he groaned and lurched, and I could tell he had come.

He picked up box number two from a table beside the chair and handed Nabil the Casa Blanca Jeroboam cigar. Nabil approached me between my now-relaxed legs, lifted my legs up and out, and made clear I was to hold my own legs up, which I did—ever mindful of what I was being paid for this—while he fucked me with the thicker and longer Casa Blanca Jeroboam.

Bergstrum sat in his chair, legs thrown out, cigar puffing, and a beefy hand stroking his own cock back to life as he watched Nabil slowly, and inventively, work my ass canal with the Casa Blanca Jeroboam. At length, Bergstrum gave a hoarse cough, lurched up from his chair, and joined Nabil between my legs. He forced the wet end of the Perfecxion alongside the Casa Blanca Jeroboam inside me, and I now was being fucked more fully and quite deeply with two counterpistoning cylinders of expensive tobacco. Nabil was working my nipples with his free hand, and Bergstrum was stroking my cock. At the same time, they were doing a good lip lock on each other. Those strong, beefy fingers of Bergstrum's wrapped around my cock and stroking it. Oh, Gawd. And they continued this until I ejaculated.

Then it was Bergstrum back in his chair, with Nabil kneeling between his thighs and giving him another blow job.

"You asked about the third box, Mr. Smith," Bergstrum called over to me. "About the Triple Magnum Nabilum."

"Umm, umm," I replied. Still mellow after my meltdown.

He lifted and opened the third box, which had been lying under box number two on the table. He turned and showed me the contents of the box.

Surprise. Yet another cigar. But, carumba, what a cigar.

"Ten and a half inches long, 120 ring gauge. Almost not big enough to get in my mouth, Mr. Smith. I have these made specially for me. And do you know where the name came from, Mr. Smith?"

"Umm, umm," I repeated.

"Triple Magnum Nabilum, Mr. Smith. Nabilum. From Nabil, Mr. Smith. Our own Nabil here provided the specifications for them, Mr. Smith."

"Umm, umm," I managed.

"And now I smoke this, Mr. Smith . . . while you smoke Nabil."

Oh.

While I watched Bergstrum lean back in his chair, legs thrown out, mouth puffing his huge Triple Magum Nabilum, and his hand stroking his cock, he watched Nabil fuck me with his ten-and a half-inch long, two-inch-in-diameter cock through much of the rest of the night.

Despite all of my professional training, I cried out at the first entry, and moaned and groaned and bunched up clumps of satin bedspread in my fists and did what I could not to bite off my tongue as a sneering satyr of prodigious proportions and inhuman staying power fucked me to his completion. The satyr image kept floating up, as our hips swung back and forth, my legs wrapped around his waist and my hands gripping the heavy pelting of his bulbous buttocks and heavily muscled thighs. I had been trained to please a man, and I could tell that Nabil was beside himself with lust to be drawn as far as he could inside me and to explore every nook and cranny of my channel. As he was about to pull out of me for his first shooting, I contracted my canal closely around his sword and held him inside me, riding his pelvis hard as he twitched and then lurched again and again and again. A series of little cries from the direction of Bergstrum's chair gave evidence that he was joining us in release.

After ejaculating, Nabil brought his mouth down onto my nipples and ravished them while he stroked me to another flowing. Then he turned me belly down on the bed and fucked me again to ejaculation and then turned me and dug in even deeper and stretched me even wider, with Bergstrum puffing on his Triple Magnum Nabilum and coming in consort with Nabil's spoutings as if they practiced this every night.

On the plane trip home the next morning, as the soreness of my body and my inability to close my legs made me ever grateful for the first class ticket, my one regret was that Bergstrum hadn't fucked me. I left aching for that. That was the power he had.

Maybe next time.

Clothes

Baggy Shorts

I think of the year of management training in Port-a-Prince, Haiti, as my year of discovering my fetishes.

The company's other American on-location trainee, Jake, thought, I'm sure, that I was concentrating on his typically long-winded explanation of why the Miami office hadn't sent in their lists for distribution of the sack-laden pallets on the floor below to southeast coastal U.S. cities, but I wasn't. I was sitting there, rocking back and forward in my worn leather chair, with my back to the whole spread of Haiti's Port-a-Prince harbor from my desk on the hot and steamy mezzanine above the dusty warehouse's coffee bean sacking floor and looking right past Jake, over his shoulder. I was focused on what was happening down at the reception desk outside the sales superintendent's office.

That new eye candy receptionist of the milky white skin, Emilee, recently arrived from Marseilles, was having her effect on the burly black policeman who was supposed to be scrutinizing the arrival on the trucks of the sacks of coffee beans from the plantations—to keep our company from shipping sacks of drugs along with the beans. They had become quite chummy in the two weeks she'd worked here. Now he was perched on the counter across from her desk in his khaki uniform, baggy shorts and all.

He was quite a looker himself. The milk chocolate color of the octoroon, descendant of French planter and black slave of Haiti's colorful past. Strong European facial features, with carefully curled and blown hair and the physique of a serious body builder. He was sitting on the edge of the counter and pulling his legs up with his hands below his knees. It was almost obscene. When he pulled his legs up, you could follow the curve of his meaty thighs right up toward his crotch. And now he was pulling his legs apart. If I'd been closer, I know I could see right up to where it got really interesting. And he and Emilee were just chatting away. It just wasn't natural the way he was showing leg, and it certainly shouldn't be going on in an office. Why, Emilee might be getting a real eyeful.

Then it hit me. Of course she was getting an eyeful. That's exactly what the trolling policeman—and she—wanted to be happening. And I couldn't help it; I wanted to be getting an eyeful too. My balls began to ache, and I could feel myself getting hard. Jake just droned on with his half-assed criticisms of the Miami office, though, oblivious to what I was trying to cop a look at over his shoulder.

My fetishes, those brought to me by Jimbo Jacques, were intersecting again. Glistening black muscle, an even blacker cock, and baggy shorts. I probably would not have ever known this turned me on if I hadn't come to the Caribbean islands.

I'd been in a real state for weeks, ever since the day I'd gone to meet Jimbo Jacques, the heavily muscled sack stacker I had melted to from watching his dancing movements and the undulating muscles of his sweat-glistened torso on the coffee bean warehouse floor for what had become a short midday suck session in the alley behind the warehouse and found he'd returned to one of the plantations without so much as saying good-bye to me. I'd grown dependent on the boners the beefy jet-black floor worker had given me—and then had given relief to. The least thing now put me in heat, and especially that intersection of glistening black muscles, an even blacker cock, and baggy shorts.

Emilee was getting up from her desk, and she and the policeman were disappearing into the floor superintendent's now-deserted office. Jake droned on as my mind was racing, imaging the small, milky-white, thin, all curves and roundness Emilee and the black, bulky, all-hardness policeman on the top of the superintendent's desk. Her running her hands up inside the legs of his baggy shorts; finding what she was looking for—revealing a ruby-knobbed cock even blacker than him. Him hiking her skimpy skirt up, tearing at her panties. And then him lifting her and setting her small pink rosette on his thick, raised jet-black spike and fucking her, sliding the small of her back on the dull surface of the desk—jet black sliding into milking white and back out again. I felt myself panting at the image. And it wasn't Emilee I was panting for; it was the octoroon policeman, his imagined jet-black cock, and his baggy shorts—that intriguing tunnel up to his treasure chest.

I had to get out of there. I had to get laid. I had to get fucked now.

Jake was in mid sentence when I just stood up, strode out of the office, and headed for the stairs in the shadows at the back of the mezzanine. Jake wouldn't think this was unusual. He knew his sermonized complaints were lame; I often walked out on him in these circumstances.

When I hit the baking tiles of the cobble stones bordering Port-a-Prince's teeming harborside, I found myself walking away from the harbor and turning into the shadows of one of the alleyways leading to the old town's red light district. One night when I'd convinced the meaty sack handler to come home with me and fuck me into the next morning, he'd said I'd have to take him to an all-man's club to get him in the mood, and he's the one who showed me Papa Joe's. This had been no-holds-barred bar, where the local Haitian warehouse and plantation workers gathered and let off tension. It wasn't the place a visiting American looking for some male-male action would normally go. But what I needed now was to let off some tension, and I couldn't get the images of either my deserting jet-black hulk, Jimbo Jacques, or the Rosa-melting octoroon policeman out of my mind.

I walked into the dimly lit bar in my pressed khaki trousers and starched white sports shirt, which, along with my whiteness, screamed of out-of-place Norte-Americano in the realm of the Haitian local sexual underbelly. I focused on the bar and walked straight there and ordered a beer before turning around, perching on a bar stool, and surveying the room.

At the other end of the bar from me, a lithe young coffee-colored, citified Haitian, obviously not long enough in the warehouse muscle business to really beef up, had been pulled into a hulky jet-black, not long from the rice fields guy perched on a bar stool facing out to the room, the coffee-colored youth's butt pulled into the black guy's package. Baggy pants must have been the signature apparel of those frequenting this bar, because the coffee-colored youth, who I heard referred to as Philippe, had on citified duds of droopy silky basketball shorts, a muscle shirt, and high-top sneakers, and the black-black guy had on cargo shorts that hung low on his waist and a white T-shirt and heavy boots. What caused me to look in that direction was the black guy, arm muscles rippling, was pulling the muscle shirt off the younger man. I watched his huge black hands slowly glide down the youth's long, lightly muscled torso. I expected the hands to go under the rim of the droopy silk shorts, but they went down over the thin material of the shorts rested a moment on the youth's thighs, just above the knees.

Then the black guy's hands went under the hem of the basketball shorts at both leg holes, and I watched the material of the shorts bunch up and rise as the hands came up the coffee-colored Philippe's thighs and met at his still-encased package. The youth got a dreamy look in his eyes and began to purr. He was stretching his torso up inside the black guy's reaching arms and he threw his own arms around the back of the black guy's thick neck. They turned their faces toward each other and were both moaning and groaning as they kissed deeply. I watched what was going on in those thin, silky shorts, mesmerized with the rustling and tenting of the material at the crotch. The black guy was stroking Philippe off with one hand and doing something with the ball sack with the other.

The younger worker began to writhe in the black guy's lap. One of the hands of the black guy—the one that had been working the balls—came out of the leg opening to the shorts and moved to hold the younger man tight to him with a palm on his heaving belly. The youth was writhing about and he was giving little panting chirping noises, lost in a controlling jerk off that was inevitably going to bring him to orgasm as he was held tightly into the body of the black guy. I licked my lips in anticipation of what the black guy was going to do as an encore once he'd jacked the young guy off.

I sensed that someone was watching me watch the couple at the end of the bar, and I let my eyes sweep away from the coffee-colored youth being taken. I saw a man eyeing me from across the smoky room. Everyone else around seemed to be well into hooking up—some in fact were already fucking away on the cushy couches at the fringes of the room and on the carpeted stage area in the center of the room. I remember registering surprise at that point because he looked like the hunkiest of the lot, and yet he was the only one alone and not in some phase of fuck at this moment. Other than me.

He was wearing only baggy shorts and workman's boots—and a red bandana around his neck. His massive chest and bulky arm muscles also made clear that he was into heavy lifting work. Fine, heavy-muscled calves and thighs. I'm sure he could see how deeply in heat I was just from the way I looked at him—and that I liked what I saw in him. Neither jet-black nor mulatto, he looked more Jamaican. A rich brown but with European features reflecting some mix of ancestry. He gave me a little satisfied, knowing, possessive sneer, and then as he held my eyes with his, he pushed his butt forward in the lounge chair he was in and opened his legs, and, oh my, I could see a bulbous, red cap hanging low, near to the bottom edge of the bunched up shorts and I could also see all the way up to a heavy, hairy ball sack. His cock was several shades blacker than he was and his pubes were jet black, curly, and kinky.

I melted and he had me with no more than that. This was exactly what I was shopping for. I found myself rising off the barstool and gliding toward him. He had himself unzipped by the time I got to him, and he pulled me roughly to him, my legs encasing his. He made quick work of the buttons on my white sports shirt with one hand and the zipper on my khaki trousers with the other and pulled me down into his lap. He pulled the tail of my shirt out of my trousers, making no other move to strip them from me. But when he brought me down into his lap, we could not have been more intimately linked, the half naked warehouse worker and the managerial clothed Norte-Americano.

He pulled my pelvis right into his and my engorging dick entered the opening of the fly to shorts and both of our penises were there together in the tented area between where his denim and my pressed cotton met at the zippers.

He got a beefy hand in there as well and was stroking our cocks together—mine pink, long, and slender and his a regular super-sized, jet-black sausage—while his thick lips went to worrying my nipples. I arched my torso back and gazed around the room, watching others in various forms of fuck, knowing that soon, very soon, that jet-black sausage of his was going to fully possess me. I sighed and trembled as he stroked us together and worked his lips and teeth on my nipples.

I looked down at the pink cylinder being stroked together with the jet-black sausage by the lighter black fist, and I lurched and jerked, and sighed and groaned and creamed myself up into his kinky black pubes. He laughed and rhythmically squeezed our cocks, draining all he could from me.

And then he was pulling my trousers down and off my legs and he had his wide, callused palms on the backs of my thighs, squeezing them and appreciating that I was well worked too. Then he moved his hands to my butt cheeks and was raising them and settling me on his ramrod. I whimpered and protested a bit, not being ready for what he had for me—but containing my reaction, not wanting to scare him off, because this was exactly what I wanted. He wasn't the least bit afraid or reluctant; he just laughed and insisted on having me then and there. I felt the pain of that bulbous mushroom cap at my hole, straining at me, and then a sharp forcing sensation and he was inside me and sliding up and up and up. He was caressing all sides of me inside and stretching me, and my walls were starting to undulate—to work his sausage as they had worked Jimbo Jacque's prodigious jet-black cock. He was grunting his satisfaction.

I could hear myself groaning for him as he plowed up me, and I whispered dirty words in Haitian-kissed French to him, words I had learned from my short-time lover, words that aroused him in ways he transmitted down his shaft and into my center. I lifted both legs around the sides of the lounge chair and grabbed his massive pecs with my hands, my thumbs pressing on his erect nipples, struggling to maintain leverage, as he bottomed in me. And, with strong hands on my butt cheeks, he was stroking me up and down on his black-black sausage. Up and down and around and up and down. At first labored. And I was melting, and panting, and groaning, and crying for what he was so deeply and fully doing inside me, my own rehardened cock rubbing up and down on his heavily muscled, hair-matted belly, preparing to cream once again for him.

I had found exactly what I had come into this bar looking for and what a peek up those baggy shorts of his had promised me. He lifted my pelvis high off of him, pulling his cock completely out of me and then slammed me down hard while sucking hard on a tit, and I howled to the ceiling and spouted up his belly.

It was like my howl was the bell summoning the others to the main event, because some of the other muscle-bound, hulky, various-shades-of black Haitian workers gathered around.

The sausage man hadn't cum yet. And after I did for the that second time, he stood up from the chair and turned me so my knees were in the chair and my arms and neck hanging over the back of the chair and then he slammed hard into me again and began riding me quickly and deeply. He was running his callused hands along the curves of my thighs and yammering something throaty and full of mirth in Haitian French to the other delighted Haitian workers gathered around me.

I knew enough French to know that he was making boasts of putting it to all the uppity white Norte-Americans from above the Caribbean, and his compatriots were laughing in agreement to fucking the northern fuckers. But I didn't care and I laughed with them. I didn't care as long as he continued pounding my insides with that jet-black cock of his.

He pumped me for a few more minutes and then pulled out of me and came around to in front of me and I was being face fucked. Another of the Haitian workers, with a thinner, but longer cock, mounted me then and came quite quickly, filling me with his cum at the same time that the first one was creaming my throat.

And then I was taken by a succession of beefy workers, including both the black guy and the coffee-colored youth, Philippe, I had watch earlier, working inside me with increasing ease, helped by a frothy mixture of shared cum. Several of them shed their baggy shorts in my sight before moving behind me and boning me with much excited yammering in Haitian French. It wasn't long before I forgot Jake's problem and the octoroon policeman and Emilee—and even my departed warehouse worker, Jimbo Jacques, ejaculating again and again, almost as often as I was filled.

For months afterward all I had to do was see a Haitian worker in baggy shorts and I'd go straight to hard—and it wasn't long before I found that the octoroon policeman was versatile enough to do me on the warehouse superintendent's desk too when that office was deserted. I was delighted to find that his cock was as jet-black as I had imagined. I would make him lean back against the edge of the desk, and I'd reach up into the leg opening and pull his cock down to my searching lips and suck him to the top edge of arousal, the hem of those baggy shorts caressing my cheeks. And then, when he had me flat on my back on the desk top and my legs spread for him, all I had to do was lift my head and watch that beautiful black hunk of meat stroking in and out of my ass to come with loud gasps and groans just as I could hear Emilee do when she disappeared with him behind the frosted glass of the superintendent's office door.

Jake remained clueless to the end. He was flabbergasted when I put in for a permanent assignment to the company's Haiti office when my internship had been completed.

Men in Tuxedos

(From *Man's Man*)

"Man, don't you ever give up?" I asked in exasperation, removing Zane's hand from my basket and rising from the sofa and moving over to a stool by the bar. I was going to put out for Zane, but I didn't think he'd been told yet that he was going to be mentoring me for Rex Reeson's stable of male escorts, and I wanted him to work for it a bit more. Besides, there were a couple of things I wanted to ask him about while I had some hope of getting an honest answer.

"No, Brian, I never give up. Not when there's something I want like I want you."

"I should have known when you brought out the good scotch that you just wanted to get me drunk and have your way with me. True?" I'd already let Zane kiss me when I'd come back from my signup session with Reeson and his French sidekicks, so we both knew I was just playing with him now.

"Yes, that was the general idea," Zane said dryly, a smile of perseverance on his lips. "What's the problem? You don't find me attractive?"

"Yeah, you're plenty attractive all right, Zane," I said. Still, I tried to put a glint of defiance in my eyes—trying to work in some acting on him. "And well you know it too. I just don't open my legs for anyone who says he wants me."

"You sure open them for the customers down at Thunder Road," Zane retorted, the smile just as sparkly as before.

"That's different," I said. "And I don't do much of that there anyway."

"Right. They have money and position and are proper sugar daddies. You're so obviously on the make for connections to give you a start in movies. You know what that kind of arrangement is called, don't you?"

"Yeah, that's called good old American trade," I shot back. "Quality goods for quality services. And I see no reason for you or anyone else to look down your nose at it."

"Oh, I'm not," Zane answered calmly. "Believe me, I'm there myself."

"Excuse me?" I said. I gave him the surprised and intrigued act. "You of the Ivy League education and Porsche Boxster and expensive clothes?"

"Right," Zane responded, getting a glint of an opening here

"So, what do you know of what a guy's got to do to make it in this town?" I challenged. I was going to make him tell me he was a male prostitute working for Reeson and opening his legs on demand, just like he said I was doing at Thunder Road.

"I didn't come from money, Brian," Zane shot back. "I know it looks like I did from the car I drive and the clothes I wear and from my education, but I earned my education on my back—just like you are doing at Thunder Road."

"What do you mean?" I wanted him to say it. To tell me something that would open him up to me emotionally before I opened my legs to him and let him fuck me.

"I put myself through school by working for a hard-core call boy service— one that put me out on the street advertising for tricks," Zane said. "I came to this lifestyle through hard work."

There, it had been said. Now to push him just a bit farther. I returned to the sofa and started pelting Zane with some of the questions I wanted answered before I signed up for Reeson's stable. I took a couple of swigs of scotch from the generous portion Zane had poured out for me and settled back in the sofa cushions. I purposely didn't pull away when Zane put a hand on my thigh and started working it up my leg.

"And what was your strangest assignment?" I asked Zane at the end of a flurry of other questions that Zane had dutifully responded to. "I mean, can you remember any? Something involving strange fetishes. There must have been some." One of the real burning questions I had with this was just how kinky this arrangement might get—and might it be more than I thought I could handle.

Zane chewed on that one briefly—but only briefly. He had his hand on my bare belly now, under the hem of my shirt. His other arm was snaked around my shoulder. I acted like I didn't even know his hands were there, letting him play his little seduction game. I knew this would end with him fucking me just as much as he hoped that was where this was going.

"Hmmm, let's see. That might have been the night of the men in the tuxedos."

"The men in the tuxedos?" I said, showing him I was interested and also that talking to me like this would get him what he wanted. To drive that home, I put my hand on top of his and moved it below my waistband, on the warm skin of my lower belly, letting his fingers glide into my pubes. Then he started into his story.

* * * *

"Yes. As the night was starting out, I knew I was in for a workout, because the caller had specified he wanted someone experienced with men and had authorized for the full unlimited service for a four-hour period. That usually meant multiple ass work, although it's true that some out-of-town hicks just didn't realize what the various options were and had more money than brains when they set up a session. I knew there was big money involved, though, because the gig was in New York. I was flown across the country for it.

"The address I was given was for a large, but nondescript brownstone, up on 57th Street, near Central Park. A polished brass plate by the doorbell simply stated that I was at some club, Hedgewood or Hedgeneck, or something like that. I later assumed that it was one of those old-world highly exclusive men's clubs that had existed for a couple of centuries without catching the public's eye.

"I was met at the door by the epitome of a butler type who told me to follow him toward the back of the house. Outside a double oaken door set in a whole hallway of polished oaken paneling carpeted with an Oriental rug in vibrant colors, he told me to strip entirely and to leave my clothes folded on a Chippendale arm chair that was located next to the door. I did so, and then he knocked twice on the door, opened it, and ushered me into the room.

"I was in some sort of club room. Leather-upholstered arm chairs sitting on a huge Oriental carpet in the middle of a wood-paneled room with glass-fronted shelves of books on three walls and on the third wall a fireplace flanked by French doors that apparently led to garden at the rear of the building. At the opposite end of the room from the fireplace was a large mahogany desk with a leather top. The arm chairs were arranged in a circle in the center of the room, facing each other, with a clear space out in the center. There were six chairs, each with a little cigarette table beside it and a brass floor lamp behind it. All of the lamp shades were turned up so that they functioned as spotlights trained on the circle in front the chairs. Each of the chairs was occupied by a man in a tuxedo. All of the men were fairly young— none older than his mid forties—and all had the air of pampering to a high gloss and well-toned physiques and of highly successful positions. They had brandy snifters in their manicured and bejeweled hands, and each was smoking a cigar. The air was cloudy with the smell of premium Cuban cigar smoke.

"'Come to the center of the room, please, son,' a strong, willful voice commanded me from the depths of the cigar smoke cloud. I did as I was bade.

"'Turn, please. Turn completely around. Slowly please. Again please. Stand straight and tall, please. You have nothing to be ashamed of.' I slowly turned a few times, obviously letting them all see what they were paying for, for whatever purpose—which I had yet to discern.

"'Now masturbate for us, please. To completion. Do not worry about where it goes.' The same commanding voice. From the intensity of the light directed from the lamps and the thickness of the cigar smoke, I could not be sure which tuxedo had spoken.

"'Excuse me?' I asked. In shock more at the incongruity of the setting than at the request itself. I had known it would be a performance evening for me. They had paid dearly for it. This assignment would carry me nearly a month at school all by itself.

"'Masturbate, please. And do it slowly and don't hold back on your expression and response, please.'

"So, I did as they asked. I had been trained what to do with this sort of request, but I had always assumed it would be something involved in a one-on-one situation.

"I was progressing pretty well, when I sensed movement in the room behind me, and I heard the rustle of rich material close behind me and hot breath on my neck. I looked down, and an arm came around me from behind. It was clothed in luxurious black material. White starched cuffs showed at the wrist, with gold nugget

153

cuff links. An elegant, manicured hand with a signet ring wrapped itself around my engorged cock after brushing my hand away.

"Another black-clad figure was now at the other side of me. I turned enough to see the brilliant white shirt front and the satiny lapel on the tuxedo. The hand of this figure also went to my cock, and the two tuxedos worked my cock in unison and rubbed their expensive evening suits against my bare arms.

"Another figure, a commanding figure, probably the source of the voice that had given me direction, appeared through the cloud of smoke before me. He was sucking on a long cigar and giving me a very intense look. He was perhaps the oldest of the men present. Very handsome, with strong facile features and intense black eyes. The light was reflecting off the diamond studs cascading down the front of his perfectly cut tuxedo shirt. I remember thinking that one of those studs alone would be enough to get me out of the business and cover the rest of my college. He gave me a grin, almost a leer, and then he turned the cigar in his mouth, took it out, and pressed it between my lips. It was moist from his saliva. He rotated it in my mouth, adding my saliva to his, and then he grinned again and moved out of my line of vision.

"He obviously had moved to behind me, because I felt hands pulling my butt cheeks apart—in fact I found hands everywhere on my thighs and belly and nipples, in addition to the two that were stroking my cock—and I bowed my legs outward as I felt the moist end of the cigar working its way into my ass.

"The heel of a hand came up under my chin, the fingers covering my lower jaw and the thumb pushing its way into my mouth, obviously wanting me to give suck, which I did. Meanwhile, the two hands were still stroking my cock, the fingers of both of my hands were being taken into mouths and sucked, and that cigar was being rotated in my ass, being screwed in deeper and deeper and rotated around.

"I was panting heavily at the attention, the feeling of being shrouded in elegant black satin and silks and white starched shirts, flashing studs, and heavy cigar smoke. Aroused by the contrast of my being completely naked and vulnerable and being stroked and invaded everywhere by fully and elegantly clothed men.

"The cigar twisted out of my ass, and the commanding figure came back around to close in front of me. He gave me that leering, possessive smile, and then he put the cigar back in his mouth and twisted it. His eyes lit up with a mischievous gleam and I felt a strong hand cupping my balls, coming in under the stroking hands of other tuxedos, and he squeezed hard. I threw my head up in a primeval scream of pain and surprise and release to the ceiling, jerking my mouth away from the thumb I was sucking, and shot a strong fountain of semen I know not where.

"The teeming mass of black silk and satin took my ejaculation as some sort of sign, because I was lifted and carried by a bevy of tuxedos over to the leather-topped mahogany desk. At first I was bent over that on my belly. Once again hands pulled my cheeks wide. Then fingers, slippery with lubrication, of different sizes, invaded me, pulling my well-used hole wide. The cigar again now, soggy with lubricant, entering between the fingers and twirling and screwing into me. I was panting and moaning now. The cigar twirled out, but the three fingers of different sizes remained, pulling me, stretching my hole wide. I arched my back, as a thicker, throbbing object, a cock, slid in between the fingers. The fingers pulled out as the cock plowed in, deeper, deeper, deeper. And then it started a furious rhythmic slapping back and forth into me as I counterthrusted my hips back to it until I heard a deep-throated cry and felt my insides being creamed. A second cock replaced the first and I was fucked vigorously and deeply from the rear by one cock while another tuxedoed figure on the other side of the desk pushed another cock into my mouth. At no time did I see man flesh during the whole ritual. Cocks were buried in my ass and mouth, but the tuxedos remained fully in place otherwise.

"I was fully naked, being fully possessed by six elegant tuxedos, heavy, hard, virile cocks invading me from within the folds of the rich material, but never seen.

"When the first set of tuxedos had spent their seed in either end of me, I was turned on my back and fucked repeatedly in succession, each man obviously taking more than one turn at me, with two tuxedos holding my arms out and two more spread-eagling my legs.

"As something of a finale, I was lifted off the desk and a tuxedo came in under me and settled me on his black silk lap, his cock buried in my ass, and another tuxedo came in at me from the front and penetrated me with his member as well. The most athletic of the tuxedos was hunched on top of the desk, black silk pant legs against my naked chest and me deep-throating his cock, chaffing my chin and cheeks on the zipper of the only slightly parted fly.

"I found myself draped, naked and covered with repeated semen of six men over the top of the desk, moaning my elegant defilement, trying to concentrate on the fee I had earned for the evening. When I was able, I pulled myself up to a sitting position. The six chairs once more were occupied by six sedately and richly clad gentlemen sipping their brandy and puffing their cigars and looking very satiated and pleased with themselves.

"The commanding voice then thanked me for my time and told me I was to leave. I dragged myself out into the hall, dressed with my aching muscles feeling every move, and received a generous tip from the butler before I was shown to the door."

* * * *

When Zane had finished this story, the room was silent for the longest moment except for the heavy panting coming from me, and not just from the sensuous tale he had spun, but because, while telling the story, he had pulled me over close to him and leaned both of us down on the sofa and his hand was completely below my waist band and was encircling my cock. I found myself fully aroused by his story, not put off at all by the kinkiness of it—drawn to it, somewhat frustrated that it had been his experience, not mine.

"Yes, I think that might have been my strangest assignment," Zane said finally, marking closure to his tale.

"Wow." That seemed to be all I could say at the moment. I was breathing too heavily to contribute much to sophisticated conversation.

Zane sensed he had me now, and I was completely ready for him. I unzipped my fly myself, and Zane correctly took that as a sign that he could bring my cock out into the open, which he did, and began to stroke it.

"So, what do you think?" He asked.

A few more moments of silence except for my soft moaning and sighing and the rustle of the cheap cotton material of my pants in its rhythmic countermovement to Zane's slow stroking motion.

"You wouldn't . . . You wouldn't happen to own a tuxedo?" I asked in a hoarse, struggled whisper.

"Why, yes. Yes I do. I think I can find a box of fine Cuban cigars too," Zane said just before I lifted my lips to his and sank into a deep, passionate, moaning kiss.

Suits

It was a steamy, smoke-filled night at Hernando's, and I and the other two guys had been dancing to the music on the small stage for twenty minutes. I was already down to the ten-gallon hat, the pinto pony vest, the cowboy boots, and the low-slung belt and six-gun holsters with the even lower-slung eight-inch gun swinging in between and nothing else on when I felt the hand on the ankle of one of my boots.

The dude clinging to my boot looked cooler than a cucumber despite the heat and the indoor smog and even though he was wearing a suit—a finely tailored Brooks Brothers navy-blue pinstripe silk suit that was cut close to his well-cut body. He looked like money all over. His pale-blue dress shirt was as finely and closely cut to the perfect curves and bulges of his body as his suit was, and the gold studs in his shirt cuffs and his Rolex watch sparkled in beams from the strobing lights overhead. He was flashing a set of ultrawhite, perfectly capped teeth at me in a full-lipped, sensuous mouth. He also was flashing a fifty-dollar bill.

Having gotten my attention by grabbing my boot as I was undulating on the stage above him, stroking myself off, not far from giving the crowd the thrill it had come to see, he yelled up to me through the loud music and the din of cat calls and stale suggestions. "You fuck me? More of this if it's good for me."

Fifty dollars? His tie alone was worth four times that. An insult. I was having offers twice that high thrown at me by the plumbers and electricians sitting all around him. I crouched down and shot my load across the nice lapels of his $800 Brooks Brothers suit, and then I went home that night and fucked my bass-voiced boyfriend until he warbled soprano. And I did it for free.

Three nights later I was at my other evening job, the more humbling one, as a car hop at the Honeywell Hotel. They made me wear a monkey suit there; I much prefer my cowboy outfit at Hernando's. It had been air conditioned and I was watched when I wore that one. I liked being watched; I was built to be watched. Here at Honeywells I was invisible; just part of the service in getting into and out of the hotel in a jiff. But at least here I got to jockey Porsche Boxsters—at least as far as the parking lot over in the shadows beside and behind the hotel.

I was contemplating being invisible when a honey of a silver Maserati Quattoporte drove up to the entrance and out stepped . . . the suit from Hernando's.

At least he was still noticing me. He picked up on who I was right off, and I was afraid he might take a swing at me for messing up his Brooks Brothers—but he didn't. He was all flashy smiles and knowing looks. And he had been slumming the other night. Tonight he was wearing a lustrous brown Armani suit, easily worth three times what the blue pinstripe the other night had been worth, and he had on an ochre silk shirt under that, a flashy silk tie, and diamond cufflinks. All just as expensively and closely cut as the suit of the other night was. The man was dripping money. It was almost like I could walk along behind him and pick up gold coins as he shot them out of his ass like a magic bunny with diarrhea.

Two hours later he reappeared through the hotel entrance. Another one of the car hops reached for his ticket, but the suit held off from giving it to the guy and looked around until he spotted me. He walked over, flashing that big, "see what I've got and you don't" smile at me and handed me the ticket. But he also had $200 in folded fifties in the hand holding the ticket, and he wouldn't let loose of either of those or my hand as he said in a husky whisper, "Shall we up the ante?"

I was going off duty then anyway. And two hundred bucks meant a lot to me—obviously far more than it meant to him. When I drove the Maserati around to the entrance, I didn't get out of the driver's seat; I just leaned over and flipped open the passenger seat door. This was a signal to him, a gauntlet, so to speak. If we were going to do this thing, I was going to do the driving. I liked the idea of the $200, but if he thought he was going to get off as cheaply as that, he was mistaken. Tonight was going to cost him a whole hell lot more than $200.

He got in the passenger side without hesitation, and I fisted the stick shift and he fisted my stick as I drove him into the parking lot and back to the corner where I had my Chevy van parked. I clicked open the sliding side door to the van, and the suit got in without hesitation and whistled in appreciation. I had it outfitted for love. Smoked windows; floor, sides, and ceiling covered in padded sapphire blue velour; grab straps anchored strategically here and there; and an easily accessible sound system with speakers embedded all around. And that stool. He'd be introduced to the stool later.

I told him to take off his shoes in my home—just like they do in the Orient. And while he docilely did that, I climbed into the van, stripped off the hated car jockey's uniform, clicked the side door shut, and turned on the sound system. I selected Lebanese music with a good strong beat and a tortured-voice singer warbling in a manner that would disguise most any yowling coming from inside the van. I planned on there being some yowling.

First thing I did was tie up the dude's right wrist to a strap in the ceiling of the van, a little behind the front seat. I didn't want him going anywhere or getting the notion he was going to be in charge. He hunched there, in his Armani suit, his free hand searching between my thighs.

I stripped the Rolex from his left wrist and, after entertaining him with how well balanced it was when I hung it on my hard cock and spun it around for him, I tossed it into one of his shoes. I didn't want the reminder of money ticking away while I worked here. Then I got his fist off my cock, where he had found a mushroom cap silver stud that flashed in the overhead bulb just as brightly as his diamond cufflinks did, and strapped his left wrist up to the ceiling.

I unbelted and unzipped him, and I peeled the Armani trousers and Calvin Klein briefs off his legs. And I wasn't delicate about it. I heard a rip and so did he, but neither one of us showed that we cared. I was moving with determination and he was already wide-eyed and giving little panting sounds and murmured moanings. He had seen my eight inches in full erection already. He knew what I was packing for him.

He was crouched there on his knees now, panting, in fine silk socks held up with braces under his knees and above his well-muscled calves, but still fully decked out in suit coat, shirt, and tie. I crouched between his spread knees, letting my cock snake up under the tail of his shirt and bedevil his navel while our lips were heavily engaged in a sloppy kiss. I unbuttoned the two middle buttons of his shirt, just enough so that I could spread the expensive, rustling silk and expose a puffed-up nipple. Then I lowered my head and pushed his tie aside with my chin and worked his nipple through the opening of his shirt with my tongue and teeth.

He was moaning for me. Begging to be fucked.

I raised his legs, one at a time, and tied them to straps in the ceiling toward the back of the van. He was trussed up now and hanging like a deer over a campfire, face up to the ceiling. I threw a leg over his belly and put my hands on the back of the front seat on either side of his head and clicked my silver cock stud against his white teeth until he opened for me and gave me head. He gave me good head, moaning and groaning all of the time at the length and width and hardness of me. This is what he was paying for. This is what he was going to get.

When I was bored with this, I pulled my cock out of his mouth and threw my leg back over him. He watched in eye-silted lust and interest as I opened a side glove compartment and took out a handful of condom packets. I opened a packet and rolled a condom onto my cock. Then I extracted a leather-studded cock ring and wrapped that around the base of my cock. The last item I pulled out of the compartment was a small bottle of KY. All the time he was whimpering for me, begging for me to get inside him.

He did look a little concerned then, though, when I reached up and undid the cuffs on his shirt on both sides and extracted his diamond cufflinks and then tied them with string to my cock ring. I was chuckling about him getting his money's worth out of this fuck. But he didn't seem all that amused.

He probably thought I was going to take my time and open him up real well for the fuck. But he was wrong there. I soaked down my cock with the KY and squirted enough into his hole for it to be beneficial for me. But then I was rimming him with my bulbous mushroom cap and pressuring his hole and making little forced entries and pulling back a little and then worrying the tight, unready hole again. And then, when I'd gotten the cap all the way in, I just thrust in and bottomed with one lunge. And he yowled to the velour ceiling, hitting a high A even stronger and truer than the Lebanese musician was doing on the background music. And he continued to yowl, first in pain and then in consuming desire, as I picked up the beat of the music and fucked him and fucked and fucked him.

As I fucked him, I bunched up that silk ochre-colored shirt of his in my fists and literally ripped it off his body, pulling the shreds of it from underneath his tie and the brown Armani suit coat. The dude didn't seem to care; he was swinging his

159

body against my plunging cock with the beat of the music and warbling right along with the Lebanese singer. He came in great spoutings long before I did.

Sometime during the fucking, I felt the diamond cufflinks come loose and work themselves up the dude's passage with the thrustings of my cock. The dude gave little yipping sounds at this added fiber to his ass's diet, but he made no objection. He wasn't objecting to anything now except to the possibility that I might stop stroking his ass. I almost went on a laughing jag mid fuck at the image of how he'd be shitting diamonds for the next day or so. Thinking about that being close to the meaning of being filthy rich.

When I was spent, I leaned into him and encircled his torso with my arms and felt the fast beating of his heart next to mine through the shredded ochre silk until he had calmed down and I had started to reload. He was sighing and whispering endearments to me, telling me how good I was and hoping I wasn't finished taking him.

I wasn't finished. Not by a long shot. This wasn't nearly expensive enough of a fuck for this dude yet.

I released both his legs and arms, but I immediately turned him and reattached his wrists to straps at the base of the front seat on either side. He didn't object. He was licking his lips. I was giving him exactly what he was seeking from me. I pulled over a low, velour-covered stool with a hole in the seat and forced the dude down on top of it on his lower belly. His cock and balls were poked through the hole and he found that he was encased in a sleeve around his cock and sacks around his balls, which were the business end of a cock-milking machine. I strapped his hips to the stool so he couldn't extract his cock and then turned on the machine. The machine started to slowly contract the sleeve around his cock and undulate over it, teasing his cock to engorge and discharge. And the sacks around his balls also contracted and squeezed in a fascinating rhythm. He seemed to like this, and began moaning almost immediately. He'd maybe have second thoughts after he'd shot off the first time and found the machine wasn't satisfied with that.

I crouched up where he could see me and changed the spent condom for a fresh one and lathered it down with KY. And then I was behind him, making him push his knees wide, his butt waving in the air. I straddled him, my thighs on either side of his waist, above his stretched thighs, my hands on his shoulder blades. And then I reared my hips back and thrust my sheathed cock inside him and pumped hard and fast.

He was singing a loud duet again with the Lebanese singer to the heavy beat of the music.

I tore the coat off his back while I was fucking him and the stool was milking him, and I put it in front of his face and tore the lining out. He didn't care. He was going over the moon with what I and the stool were doing to him. I pulled the expensive silk necktie around his neck to his back and used it as reins as I did a bull bucking rodeo exhibit on his buttocks. I could feel the diamond cufflinks churning around inside him and he could too. I could tell that by the screams of passion he was making. The Lebanese singer was reaching a climax in his yowling and so were the dude and I. The dude shuddered and came, and then moaned as he discovered yet again that the stool wasn't finished with him. And then I gave a cowboy whoop and came as well.

After a second and then a third ride, and continuous attention from the stool, I was finished with him. I turned off the stool and untied him and he just huddled there in thank-you whimpers. As a parting gesture, I untied his necktie, rolled the spent condom off my dick, and wiped my dick and then his asshole with the silk tie and stuffed it in his mouth. His gaze told me that he was still in love. It didn't seem like anything I was going to do was going to tell this guy where he could stuff all his money, as far as I was concerned. Still, I figured when the semen had drained out of his eyes, he'd come to his senses and survey the damage I had done to all his expensive stuff and get a little mad.

I put my car jockey duds back on and made sure he could see where I was leaving the keys to his Maserati. And then I left him there, in the back of my Chevy van, and walked back over to the entrance of the hotel. Within minutes a studly black guy gave me a ticket and a look, and, when I'd driven around his shiny black Mercedes CLS55 AMG, we were driving off to his up-town penthouse apartment, where I fucked him silly and he fed me breakfast, begged for and received my bone a second time, and then brought me back to the hotel for my now-deserted Chevy van.

Two days later, I was dancing on the stage of Hernando's when I felt a fist wrap around the ankle of my boot. There, gazing up at me with love-struck eyes was the suit, now outfitted in a black sharkskin $3,000-plus Valentino, diamond cufflinks cleaned and polished and gleaming in beams from the overhead strobe lights—holding a wad of hundred-dollar bills in his other fist. Wanting me agaiin.

Condoms

All That Glitters

I was bent over on my belly on the conference table and the hunky blond attorney was riding me hard from behind. I still had on my tie; my shirt, unbuttoned; and my shoes and socks clipped to supporters wound just below my knees. But otherwise I was naked. He started a maddening rotation of his cock inside me, and I was giving little urping sounds. To let the others see the pain and ecstasy this master cocking brought to my facial expression, he pulled my head up by pulling on my tie, which he had spun around to my back to give him reins for his hot ride of my ass. All the time he was telling me what a hot performer I'd be in his nightclub act.

My own boss and the two Japanese businessmen were sitting there, mesmerized by the exhibition the blond and I were putting on, their hands in their laps, working their own meat. The blond released the tie and his hands went to holding my hips still as he stroked hard in and out of me. I could feel his gold cock ring kissing the sides of my inner canal as he pumped me.

The golden blond was telling me what a good fuck I was, that he wanted to have more of me. He was asking me how I was enjoying the ride, and I was panting and groaning my approval of his eight inches working hard inside me.

My boss rose from the table, engorged cock in hand, and came over and tweaked one of my nipples while he kissed the blond deeply. Then he told the blond that it was time for the Japanese businessmen to take over with me and that he wanted the blond's cock in his own ass now.

The blond withdrew from me, the Japanese businessmen already eagerly standing in line behind him, and a large cock was exchanged for a medium-sized one, which, however, was more active and inventive in its exploration of my ass; the other Japanese businessman knelt between me and the table and started playing my cock and balls like a flute with his sensitive mouth.

The blond had planted my boss on his back across the narrow conference table from me, and my boss and I engaged in deep kissing and exploration of each other's torsos with our hands, as the blond spread my boss's legs and plowed into his ass. I lifted my head up from my boss's as the blond brutally entered him, and I held my boss's head between my hands, both of us connecting on what was happening in our asses with a variety of expressions on our faces.

When the Japanese and their blond attorney were finished sealing our multimillion dollar deal, they left my boss and me there on the table, consoling and rejoicing in each other and at our success at and on the conference table.

In parting, the golden blond came back to me and gave me a kiss. He flipped a business card out and said that I should visit his nightclub for the experience of my life; that the card would give me a free pass and free drinks. And that he would throw in another wild, free fuck as well if I was interested.

Try as I might I couldn't get the blond out of my mind. He had ridden me hard, but he hadn't finished me off. I developed an obsession that he finish me off, that I feel the explosion and bathing of that eight-inch ring-headed cock of his deep inside me.

* * * *

Three nights later, the blond's business card in hand, I was standing at the dimly lit walk-down wooden door under the iron porch of a brownstone on a dark street. Only the blinking sign announcing "Club Pan" beside the door assured me I was in the right place. At my ringing of the bell, the door opened just a crack, but enough for me to show the business card, with the scrawl of the blond across it. Then the door opened enough for me to slip through, but then it shut again with a solid sound of finality. The vestibule was dark, black drapery on black walls, ceiling, and floor. The half man who admitted me was also dark.

I say half man, because he was togged out as a wood nymph, or a satyr, or whatever they call those horned men with the legs and feet of a goat. This one was slender as a reed, with black curly hair, a small goatee, little pointed horns above his temples, black eyebrows curled up at the ends, and an interesting array of black tattooing on his naked torso. The most prominent of these, as I could see when he turned to guide me beyond a beaded curtain into a large step-down, smoke-filled room, was a chain of interlocked heart shapes descending from the hair line at the back of his head down to where the goat's pelt started just above his crack at the bottom of the small of his back. His legs, as I already indicated, were pelted like a brown goat's, and his feet coverings were made out like cloven hooves. Most distinctly though was that his cock and balls hung free and there was a circular opening in the pelt at his rear where his asshole lurked.

The nymph swished his tail saucily as he guided me through the dim, smoky room to one of four long bars by the back walls on either side of what looked like a small diner theater, with three tiers of descending levels going down to a circular stage in the center. Everything was black. The bars were black, the carpets and walls and ceiling were black, and the couches set around on the descending tiers, more like the lounges in those Roman banquet movies, were also covered in black material. Even the stage was black; it was square but had a round, revolving platform set into it. And standing up from this platform was an eight- or nine-foot high, widely spread X-shaped apparatus, with the cross-over set so that the upper portion of the apparatus was larger than the bottom. This was made out of some sort of transparent Lucite-type material. Near the four corners of the stage, rising to the ceiling, were poles made out of the same transparent material. The poles were some sort of hollow tube filled with a liquid in which glittery gold confetti floated.

166

The theater was dark, although I could hear the sound of moaning and activity that told me that something was happening down on those lounges on the descending tiers—and as my eyes adjusted to the dimness, I could see that there were pairings and small groups of men dotted here and there, becoming very well acquainted with each other. It must have been early, however, as the theater was only about a fourth full of these fully occupied patrons.

The nymph whispered something to the bartender, yet another satyr, but a larger version than the young man who had admitted me to the club—indeed all of those serving the patrons were decked out in the same motif. The younger man pointed to the business card that I carried and then told me I could order anything I wanted—that the bartender was at my beck and call. That was very nice to hear, I thought, as I checked out the very presentable, broadly smiling bartender, not leaving out a peek over the bar at what he was packing between his legs. There was nothing there for him to be ashamed of.

As I sat back and drank my first drink and observed the atmosphere, I saw that activity had started down on the stage. The four poles now were occupied by male dancers—all young, lithe nymphs just like the doorkeeper.

Strobing yellow-white lights started to work the room, and I now was getting a sparkly feeling of glitter everywhere. That's when I noticed the decor of the room. Cylinders of glittery gold hung on wires above the stage area in thick profusion, and as the lights strobed, they bounced off the glittery gold sparkles and brought the arena to life. I noticed then that the lights were picking up glitterings on the tiers down to the stage as well—just here and there, but enough to make my eyes dart around the room, increasingly picking out very intimate embraces and activity going on at the lounges.

A few of the glittering cylinders were on the floor of the stage, and I assumed that they had fallen from the wires. But I felt a chill and a tinkling sensation going down my spine as I realized otherwise. From the third tier in front of me, my eye caught a naked figure rise from one of the lounges, and I caught the bounce of strobe light off gold glitter as he glided down to the stage and came up with one of the gold glittery cylinders and threw it down on the stage floor. Condoms. These were glittery gold condoms. Used condoms, merging the activity in the audience with the entertainment on the stage. The club's decoration was both evocative and functional. I watched in awe as the figure pulled another cylinder off a wire hanging down toward the stage and glided back up to the third tier, no doubt for another round of pleasure.

Four beefy satyrs had arrived on the stage now and were cuffing the pole dancers who had preceded them to the poles and, one muscled satyr to one lithe pole-dancing nymph, were beginning to perform a duet of love dance for the patrons. Each of the muscled satyrs was outfitted with a glittery gold condom.

The club was beginning to fill up now, and all of the patrons I saw coming in were handsome and well built. The club had developed a winning clientele. The performers on stage were turning me on. Already one of the beefy satyrs had filled his glittering condom and had thrown it to the floor and was pulling another one down from an overhead hanger and sliding it on his hard, curved up tool. He quickly was ready to resume his dance with—and inside—the younger nymph, who was contorting his body around the pole, seeking a new and interesting position to be

167

taken by his partner. All of this for the enjoyment of those in the audience, most of whom were so absorbed in filling out their own glittery tubes to give full attention to the floor show.

I felt my tool pushing against the fabric of my trousers, and I reached down to stroke myself, only to find that I'd been so absorbed in the atmosphere around me that I hadn't notice there already was a hand there. I turned to see a nice, square-jawed face with bedroom eyes. But I only caught a glimpse of the man who had taken interest in me when the bartender said something gruff to him and he was gone. I was a little annoyed, because I hadn't asked the bartender to run interference for me.

And I was about to say something to him, when the lights went brighter on the stage and the heart-stopping golden blond who had invited me here appeared. He was decked out in leather, but it was all of a glittery gold color, from the chain crisscrossing his chest, to the boots, and arm bands, and a riding crop with a billy club-like handle—but no other body attire except for the glittery gold condom trying its best to cover his eight inches of horse-hung meat.

He walked the four corners of the stage briefly, flicking bottoms here and there with his riding crop and inserting hands into this and that undulating position, and then he came in front of the revolving transparent X apparatus and spread his arms wide, muscles rippling in the strobe lights, and all action on the stage stopped in mid fuck.

"Do we have a volunteer this evening, gentlemen?" he asked the now-filled house in a booming voice.

The strobe lights revolved wildly around the theater and then all merged—on me.

Before I had time to react in any way, I was being bustled down to the stage by my babysitting bartender and a few of the other club satyrs and was finding that the transparent X apparatus had cuffs on it that, when I was trussed up, stretched my arms and legs out wide and securely in place.

I had become a focal point for the floor show. For the next half hour or more, as the satyrs returned to pole fucking the nymphs and the well-used glittery condoms from the audience and the corners of the stage continued to build up on the floor of the stage, the blond god teased and tormented me. He prodded and pinched and kissed and tongued me endlessly and to distraction, as I revolved on the turntable at the center of the arena, cuffed to that transparent X. He flicked me with his riding crop and applied love slaps to my butt and hips and thighs and chest. He twisted and pulled at my nipples and balls until I screamed my awareness of the sensual cruelty in him.

And then he fucked me with the greased butt end of his riding crop, stretching and preparing me for his even longer and thicker gold-glittered tool. All the time I was revolving, giving the club patrons a look at the glorious torment from all angles, writhing and bucking with and against the butt end of the riding crop, testing the rock-solid holding strength of the X apparatus.

The tiers running up from where I was being displayed were a teaming mass of undulating bodies and young, naked men descending to the stage and tossing their offerings of spent glittery gold condoms at my feet and then grabbing a replacement

168

off the handing wires and remerging with the slithering pile of man flesh stretched around the room.

The golden god was behind me now, his hands on my shoulders, and his glitter gold cock slapping on my butt cheeks and working its way up and down across the puckered, moist rim of my asshole as he stroked up and down inside my butt crack. The bulging head of his dick came ever lower as he stroked up and down inside my crack, with each stroke now more centered at my hole, until with one long stroke he entered me deeply, strongly, and painfully. I lifted my head and howled to the ceiling and a cheer went up around the theater.

There was more of a hush now, much of the attention on the blond god and me rather than on each other, as two of the satyrs left off tormenting their nymphs and uncuffed my legs and held them higher and stretched out more as the blond relentlessly pumped my hole with long, deep thrusts, giving all in the audience a good view of my plowing as the stage revolved slowly around and around.

I was not shy in voicing being well fucked, and another cheer went up as my ejaculate shot out across the dozens of glittery-gold used condoms littering the stage below me.

The golden god also yelled his delight and joy when he had cum deep inside me, and he swiftly parted from me and jerked off his spent condom and tossed it out into a roaring audience. Then he strutted around the stage, flicking the poled nymphs playfully with his riding crop as, one after the other, the four muscled satyrs plowed me and added their glittery gold condoms to the offerings at my feet.

When they had done with me, my wrists were uncuffed. But then I was pushed to my knees, with my heaving chest forced into the V of the X apparatus, and my wrists were cuffed again at a lower position. The blond then presented his cock to me, me knelt on one side of the X and he standing at the other side, and I sucked him to life again as the stage continued its endless revolutions to show the entire audience the full effect.

When he was once more in engorged full-eight-inch fucking form, I was uncuffed and simply sank to the floor, exhausted. But once more the golden god's tool was adorned with glittering gold and he took me one last time on the floor at the base of the X apparatus. He fucked down into me deeply and strongly as I lay whimpering and moaning on my belly on a pile of used glittery gold condoms on the revolving stage—loving every golden stroke he took.

Cops

Restrained Freedom

We sat there sipping coffee and chowing down on donuts in an all-night diner, my new partner Hank and me. I was trying to figure him out. Ever since I'd come out in the department, potential street-duty partners had avoided me like the plague. But here I understood that Hank had asked to be partnered with me. As I drank coffee and listened to him complaining about his wife, Janine, I was wondering if maybe he swung both ways. I certainly wouldn't mind if he did. He was a good ten years older than I was and outweighed me by at least twenty pounds, but he was all muscle and handsome as all get out. Dark complexioned and black curly hair matting his forearms and pushing out at the neck of his blue uniform shirt. Pale blue eyes and a smile to die for. Some kind of Latin. And you know what they say about Latins.

The open neck of his blue uniform shirt. There it was. I thought to myself, "Shit. Nailed it with that swinging both ways supposition."

"Does this mean what I think it means?" I asked, as I moved my hand to under his chin and got the round medallion on a sterling string between two fingers. It was red, white, and black enamel on silver in a design like that Oriental Yin-Yang swirling tear drop pattern, but with three swirls rather than two—the universal sign of BDSM.

"Yeah, that's exactly what it means," Hank said, staring me down real good. He moved his hand to behind his collar and pulled around another silver charm he'd been keeping at that back of his chain. It was a miniature set of handcuffs. When he brought it back around to where I could see it, his fingers lingered on mine at the other medallion.

"Do you mind?" He asked. "What I really mean is are you interested? I maneuvered like hell to get a partnership with you. I've had my eye on you since you were transferred to the squad."

"Fuck yes, I'm interested," I whispered hoarsely to him under the din of the noise of the civilians around us who either couldn't sleep or were on their way to an early shift or back from a late shift. I raised my foot and forced it between his thighs under the table, crushing the sole of my boot into his crotch to emphasize my interest. He gave me a surprised, but desired-filled look, gripped the edges of the table with white-knuckled fists, and squeezed my calf tightly between his thighs to confirm his own interest.

"But what about Janine?" I continued nonchalantly. "I'd heard you were happily married and an attentive daddy." I dropped my hand from his medallion, not wanting those around us to get the right idea about what we were discussing.

"Yeah, I am," he answered. "I can't explain it, but I've got these urges that go beyond Janine and the family thing. It is getting a little tedious with Janine. Being with a guy now and then heightens the pleasure for both me and Janine when we fuck."

"But bondage and S&M?" I asked. "That's quite a bit farther along that road. And it can get rough."

"I like it rough," Hank shot back. "And the bondage? Well, I think that helps take the guilt away. If I'm bound, it's like I really am not making the choice, if you know what I mean—restrained but suddenly free to fully enjoy it."

I sat and stared at Hank for a couple of minutes, grabbing the edge of the table hard where his fists had just been to keep my hands off him. But I could feel the juices flowing already.

"Well, when it's convenient, maybe we can hook up and—"

"Now," Hank hissed through his teeth in a voice strangled with urgency. "When I saw you in the showers this evening after the squad workout and before we hit the streets, I nearly creamed myself. I wanted you to see my jewelry. I want you take me someplace right now, tie me up, and fuck me hard."

"Well, if it's a quiet night, I know of some places we can park. The car's not the best place, but—"

I felt an insistent buzzing in one of my pockets that had nothing to do with the effect Hank was having on my cock.

"Shit," I exclaimed as I reached for my mobile phone. "It's dispatch."

I listened to the assignment call for a several seconds. Hank was already standing and flipping a couple of bills on the table.

"Trouble?"

"Yeah, I'm afraid so. But not a rush, rush. They caught up with that guy who's been kidnapping and assaulting those college guys over on the east side. We're to go pat down his pad. Guess our business will have to hold fire for a bit."

"Yeah, I guess you're right," Hank said. I kinda liked the tone of regret in his voice on that one.

Chas Sheldon, a smart-assed cop in our squad who razzed me pretty bad about my preferences was standing at the door of the small, rundown bungalow hidden in the undergrowth of a quiet east side street when we rolled into the driveway. He was giving me a snide stare as Hank and I approached.

"You'll just love this one, Lance," he said to me as we walked up to him. "It's right up your alley." He sniggered at his double entendre. Real genius; I bet he'd been working on that for a half an hour.

"Yeah, well, they couldn't have gotten this guy any too soon in my opinion," I answered brusquely. "Any sign of any of the missing men?"

"Just the one we caught him in the act with," Sheldon smirked. "He was pretty far gone, but they've sent him off to the hospital already, and the perp just left for the department in a squad car. We caught him doin' it and followed the book—

there's hardly a mark on him. So this one should be airtight. The forensics crew has started on the basement, but I think they're about ready to call it a day. We've got a crew starting to dig in the backyard too, but it will be too dark to continue with that for a while. Guess you'll want to see the scene yourself though, to, ya know, get some pointers maybe."

I could have shoved my fist down Sheldon's throat, but that would just make for good conversation and more razzing in the squad room. Hank gave a disgusted sound deep down in his throat and pushed on by Sheldon and into the house. I was senior and hadn't gotten the full assignment pass yet, so I stuck with Sheldon for the moment.

"So, what's the call here?" I asked. Sheldon saw that I wasn't going to rise to the bait, so he got through it quickly with just one more jab.

"I was just to stick around until another set of blues—which would be the two of you, I suppose—showed up. Since they won't be able to process the scene completely until tomorrow, we're to maintain a presence here overnight. I understand you've got the shift for the next four hours and then they'll send someone else. Think you can handle that without messing up the toys in there?"

"Roger, Sergeant," I said, staring right at him, reminding him that I outranked him. "By all means shove off now. Hank and I will hold the place."

I pushed by him and turned back after I'd gotten inside the door to see that he was already half way across the yard to his ride. I looked around for Hank but didn't see him in the small, drab living or dining rooms. I found him in a back bedroom, just standing there, mesmerized by the trophy photos this perp had papered the wall with of what he'd been doing to his victims. I could see at a glance that the perp had been busy and had quite an imagination. Hank was growling deep down in his throat again and was rubbing a hand up and down on his crotch. No doubt that the photos and the other paraphernalia in the room were turning him on.

I swung on my heels and made tracks to the basement in time to see that the forensics crew was struggling up the steps into the kitchen with their bulky cases banging against the stairwell walls and would be gone for the night within a couple of minutes. I quickly scanned the basement to see what I could see and then followed the technicians back up the dark stairwell. As they left the house, I looked out in the backyard and saw the last of the workers out there leaving as well. I prowled around the house quickly to ensure that Hank and I were alone now and locked the front door from the inside before I returned to the back bedroom.

Hank had his pants down around his ankles, although he still had his equipment belt around his waist, and he was all bug-eyed staring at the photos while he pulled on his good-sized dick.

With a mind to what he'd said he needed to perform, I quickly got him into a pair of cuffs hanging conveniently from the upper wall in front of him, which pulled his arms over his head and trapped him there, facing the wall. Then I stood close behind him, my crotch plastered to his exposed butt cheeks so he could feel me getting bigger down there and wrapped my arms around him. I took over stroking down on his cock and squeezing his hefty balls with one hand, while I unbuttoned his shirt with my other hand. As I went for his nipples, he arched his head back to me and we kissed deeply. There was no doubt that he was ready for this.

175

I broke and looked behind me to see what sorts of toys and aids our perp might have dropped around the room. With little effort, I came up with a leg spreader bar, a ball gag with two nipple clamps hanging from it at the end of small-linked chains, an outlandish-sized flexible dildo, and a tube of lubricant. If Hank needed bondage to get excited, then I'd see just how excited Hank could get.

Coming up behind him, I had the ball gag in his mouth and snugly tied off before he even knew what was happening to him. I then stripped his pants all of the way off his legs and clamped the spreader bar between his thighs, forcing him into a wide stance. He was squirming around now and pulling at his wrist restraints. I moved around to in front of him, between him and the wall, and lifted the long, thick dildo up to his eye level. He went all wild-eyed and backed away from me as far as the restraints would permit, but I had one of my hands wrapped around his dick, so I knew he was finding this very stimulating. I rubbed the dildo around on his cheeks for a short time to let him feel the texture and size of it.

I then slowly started tonguing, kissing, and teething my way down his chest, around his nipples and down his washboard abs. I reached up and applied the nipple clamps hanging down from the ball gag one after the other to his nipples, and I heard stifled screams from him from behind his gag. I brought the tip of the dildo to his navel and rotated it around the rim and pressed it in a bit to give him something to think about for when I moved to behind him. The gurgling sound he now was making around the rubber ball in his mouth told me he got the message. Down his belly and into his pubes my mouth and the twirling dildo moved.

I then played with his dick and balls with my mouth and slid the dildo back across the perineum through his legs and back and forth across his puckered asshole until he melted to me. I was deepthroating him, and he was making very satisfied, if muffled, noises from his mouth and had set up a rhythm with his hips. I didn't want this to get too conventional, though, so I popped his nicely engorged cock out of my mouth and moved through his legs, my tongue tracing the journey from the base of his balls all the way back to his asshole.

I rimmed Hank's ass with my tongue at first, letting my tongue flicker into his hole and pushing his butt cheeks apart with my hands. The leg spreaders helped keep him open to me. He writhed in pleasure above me, obviously enjoying the attention. From time to time, I let a hand stray between his legs to check out his cock to ensure it hadn't lost interest and to squeeze and roll his balls.

I had his asshole well lubricated with my spit now, and it was nicely open to me. I stood up and stripped down and reached for the tube of lubricant and lathered up the dildo real well. I moved to behind Hank and slapped my half-hard cock around on his butt cheeks. I'd seen him eyeing me in the showers, so he knew I was horse hung. I wasn't as horse hung as the dildo I'd lubed up, though. After that, he wouldn't have trouble handling me at all.

Hank seemed to like the feel of my cock beating against his butt cheeks. I soon had substituted the dildo though, and I worked it ever closer to his asshole. He arch his back, brought his legs back, and dipped his chest when he felt the head of the dildo gently rimming his asshole. He'd seen it and knew how long and thick it was, and he was doing all he could to ensure it didn't split him in two when I'd worked it in—which I proceeded to do slowly but relentlessly. I had nearly a foot of thick dildo to work inside him, and I took a long time doing so. It had an extra bulbous mushroom head on it, so there was no buildup of strain as it moved up his canal—the biggest was always right up front.

Hank was straining and grunting and groaning through the experience, but I could tell that he was with me on this, that this was exactly what he wanted and that was keeping him on edge. I was getting excited now too. The way he was straining back, there was a shelf at his waist above his big, round butt cheeks, and when I'd gotten the dildo all the way in, I hiked my right leg up onto this shelf and nestled closely into Hank. My now-engorged cock was rubbing up against his left hip, and I knew he was aware of it there. My right hand held the dildo inside his ass and corkscrewed it inside him and slowly churned it in and out, while I wrapped my other arm around him and my left hand pinched on his nipple clamps and stroked down to his cock and balls and gave them some more attention. I kissed and nuzzled his shoulder blades while he trembled underneath me, a background of pain swept over with intense pleasure.

He came in my hand then in a prodigious fountain of pent-up man juice.

I untied and pulled the gag from his mouth and ripped the clamps off his nipples. Free to speak, he told me through gasps and groans that the dildo was awesome but that he wanted me to fuck him with my own cock, that he had wanted my cock inside him for some time.

But I hadn't ungagged him to hear this. I had wanted him free to scream through the next procedure—to be able to tell me if and when he really couldn't endure any more.

I lifted my leg off the small of his back and slowly pulled the dildo out—but when I could see the rim of the mushroom head, I plunged it back in up to the hilt. Hank threw his head back and screamed at the ceiling, but I covered his mouth in a brutal kiss, as I pumped the dildo deep inside him for another thirty seconds. I could feel his knees going to rubber, and I pulled the dildo all the way out and threw it to the side.

"Now you," Hank gasped. "Now your cock inside me. That ring through the head. I want to feel that ring deep inside me."

"Eventually," I whispered in his ear. "First some police work, though."

He felt me pulling his billy club out of the equipment belt that still encircled his waist, and he started to moan and hiccup in fear.

"No, man. Not that. Please."

I lathered the belly club up and leaned my mouth back to just inches from his ear.

"I've heard you've used this in perps before," I whispered. "Haven't you ever wondered how it felt?"

"No, no, Lance. Not that. NO! A-u-g-g-h!"

The billy club wasn't nearly as thick or as long as the dildo had been, but, although it also was rubberized, it also wasn't as flexible as the dildo, so it could only go straight up his canal.

"Oh Gawd, oh Gawd, Ah, FUCK!"

"Precisely," I said in a deep-throated voice, now on the edge myself. "I wonder if the perp who owns this place ever let his victims scream like you are. I wonder if the neighbors heard nothing—or if they heard and did nothing. If they can hear you, maybe they'll just think it's business as usual in here."

Hank had obviously had enough of this, so I stopped, wiped his billy club off on the edge of the bedspread and sheathed it back on his equipment belt.

"But I want you to fuck me now, Lance. No more of this dildo shit. Get that big prick inside me."

"OK, sure," I said. "But I was kind off wondering what our perp might have down in the basement that the forensics team was so interested in checking out." I, of course, knew precisely what was in the basement awaiting us.

I looked around and found some leg shackles and exchanged these for the leg spreader, clamping them at his ankles. I released his wrists from the wall restraints but quickly had him locked up again with my own handcuffs. I shuffled him through the house and down the basement stairs, and, I quite enjoyed Hank's excitement when we found a black-painted, padded-walled room with a sling on chains hanging from the ceiling in the middle.

I pulled Hank's shirt off his back as I pushed his butt down into the center of the sling. He didn't fight me as I uncuffed his wrists and recuffed them high on the suspending chains running up on either side of his torso and then unshackled his ankles and cuffed those up high on the two suspending chains running up on either side of his butt.

I unpopped the gag then and let him talk—and grunt and pant and moan— me through what he liked and what he really liked—and what sent him over the moon. It turns out he liked ten minutes of tonguing his asshole and fifteen minutes of fingering and nearly fisting his asshole. And he really liked throwing his head back and sucking me off while I pinched his nipples. He also really liked thirty minutes of my cock churning inside him with a string of beads I'd found nearby attached to the silver ring piercing the head of my cock combined with what my hands were doing on his torso and with his dick and balls. But what sent him howling over the moon was the twenty minutes of deep fucking with the electrified cock sheath and extender I'd found that made my cock thicker and longer—and more highly charged—then the dildo had been.

During the two hours we spent in that basement room, we each came two more times and Hank admitted that this session had far surpassed what he had been expecting.

In the time we had left, I smoked a cigarette and tossed off some of the perp's scotch while Hank moved around in the nude, cleaning up after our use of the facilities. When he'd finish, I slammed him down on his back on the kitchen table and scrambled up and crouched on top of his chest, my knees pinning his arms against his sides. I forced him to suck me off one last time, with me bobbing his head back and forth on my cock with my fingers buried in his hair and brutally fucking his mouth and throat. He seemed to enjoy that as much as anything that had gone before and gushed over with the regret that we couldn't have access to the toys in this devil's den any more.

As we were leaving, I assured him that we'd have plenty of opportunity to explore our fetishes and that what I had in my basement made this place look like a nursery school.

Rough Riding to BARUF

I had found him through a friend of a friend of a friend. He didn't look like much when we met in Starbucks to discuss particulars. In fact, he didn't look at all like what I wanted.

"So, how did you settle on this?" he asked me.

"It was a costume party," I answered. "I hadn't, you know, been much interested in or turned on by anything until then, and—"

"Well, you look mighty fine to me," he said. "Surely you've gotten offers by real studs."

"Yeah, but this was different," I said.

I was, of course, flattered by what he was saying, but he didn't turn me on at all. He was a bit on the rangy side and more hippy like than authoritarian, so it really was kind of a waste of breath. In fact, this whole idea, this obsession—this fetish I had—seemed a waste of breath and effort now that I'd actually moved to do something about it. Perhaps it was just as well. Maybe the obsession would die as quickly as it had been born. But it hadn't died yet. I still melted at the mere thought of it.

"As I was saying," I continued, "I was at this party and several of the guys were beefy and were in uniforms and that really got to me. And then they got a little rough, and that got to me even more." I stopped there.

"And?" he said, egging me on to say it.

"Well, I went wild and jacked off like I'd never done before." Another pause.

"And?" he repeated.

He was going to make me say it. "And I want it like that again. I checked around, and it led to you. But now that we've met, I don't think—"

"It would cost you a hundred bucks," he cut in. "That's if we're including bondage, which is what I was told you wanted included."

"Excuse me?"

"Here. You'll paste this in the back window of your car when you want it and go cruising a little above the speed limit down on 301 on that stretch between the cutoff from Route 50 to the beaches and the Maryland-Delaware line. Afterward, if it goes through, you'll mail a check to this address made out to this name." He was taking a cardboard sign and a slip of paper out of his knapsack. On the sign, in big, black capital letters was printed the term BARUF. What sort of word was baruf, I wondered.

But while I was thinking about that, he was getting ready to leave.

"You mean you're not—?" I said, confused and not as sure about this as I was when I started calling around.

"With me? Hell, no, kid," he said with a snort. "Just do what I told you."

"But the payment. How can you be sure I'll pay up."

"Oh, I'm sure. If you get the service, I'm sure you'll pay up. You'll see what I mean. You'll get the idea of what it means if you don't pay up."

Bewildered, I watched him walk out of the coffee shop. I picked up the sign. It was on a board about eight inches by eleven. It could probably be seen at a good distance. Baruf. What in the hell does baruf mean, I thought again.

But, hey, I hadn't been turned on and creamed like at the costume party in, like, forever. And it was worth a try. I had come this far with it. It was worth a try.

Two days later, the day was sunny, the Naval Academy had been on recess for more than a week, and I wouldn't have to be back there for several more days. And I had nothing better to do, and I felt horny. So, it was into the old Jag sedan and out onto the road across the Bay Bridge and the narrows and toward Wilmington. I had remembered to paste the sign up in the back window. Baruf. What the hell was that supposed to mean?

When 301 forked off to the north from 50, I let the engine rip and built up some speed. The road was straight and flat and there were few cars going my way. Everyone on the road was going to the beaches, and those were behind me now.

I passed a Maryland rest area. Beyond those there was nothing else out here except flat, sandy land that was once ocean bed and that now supported large fields of corn. I slowed down a tad when I saw a state police building coming up on my right, but I was still going a bit over the speed limit. But, then, who didn't? And the road was flat and straight and nearly deserted.

No more than three miles beyond the state police building, though, I heard a siren and was pulled over to the side of the road. I sat in the car, wondering what I had done wrong, as a solid-looking policeman decked out in a tight uniform and shiny black boots strutted around and took a look at both license plates, all the time swishing a mean-looking night stick with a short leather whip on one end. I wasn't going any faster than anyone else would go on this road. There wasn't anything out here to hit that was worth anything. I rolled down the window as the cop approached. He leaned an arm on the sill and looked intently at me through very dark sunglasses.

"Let me see your license and registration, son."

"Umm, just a minute," I said, as I struggled to get the glove compartment open. "What seems to be the problem, though?"

"License and registration please."

I handed them over to him, and he took them back to his cruiser and did some communicating into a mike on his dash. He got out of the car and sauntered back to mine. He was a tall, muscular Hispanic dude with an obvious attitude toward non-Hispanics.

"Is that your sign in the back window of this here car?" he asked.

"Yes, sir," I answered. "But it isn't obstructing my vision. Both of my side mirrors are working fine and I really can see out the back. The sign isn't blocking much."

He didn't answer and he didn't hand my license back to me. "Now, I have to do some more checking, so I want you to pull your car up in the overgrown driveway up there. Pull in a good fifty feet, beyond those trees. I'll be right behind you." I did as he asked. The place he indicated obviously had been abandoned. There was a burnt-out wooden house at the end of a broken-asphalt driveway that was choked with tall weeds. And I don't think either my car or the cruiser could be seen from the road where we pulled to a stop. He came back to my window.

"Officer, what seems to be—?"

"Step out of the car, please."

"But—"

"Get out of the car now, hands showing, and assume the position on my police ride over here, hands out wide on top and legs apart."

I got out of the car, although I couldn't open the door all the way. The copy was in tight, not giving me much room to maneuver.

"Farther away from the car, now! Over to my ride. Assume the position. Feet wider apart."

He tapped me. No, more than tapped me, bonked me pretty hard on the thigh. It hurt. But I did what he said. I was a little off balance now, concentrating hard to keep my weight balanced on my hands. I figured this was probably the point.

"Got any drugs in the car?"

"Drugs? Me? No, I don't do drugs."

"That's not necessarily what your rap sheet says."

"My rap sheet? What rap sheet?"

"Got any drugs on your person?"

"Certainly not. Listen, officer—"

"Save it."

He started patting me down, doing a real thorough job, not excepting my privates. When he was finished, he stood there beside me. He seemed to be breathing a little heavy, which probably should have clued me in.

"Afraid I'm going to have to do a cavity search."

"Excuse me? A what?"

"Now don't go resisting an officer, he said," as he tapped me meaningfully on the cheek with the big end of his nightstick.

"Open wide," and he had his fingers in my mouth and was roughly feeling around on all sides in there.

"Now, these pants are going to have to come off."

"My pants!?"

"I said a cavity search." He tapped me on the cheek with his nightstick again, and then he put the stick under his arm and held my butt in his left hand as he unbuckled my belt and zipped down my pants with his right.

"Pull your legs together." Down and off came the pants and underpants in one movement. "Now, take the stance again." I was about ready to cry in frustration and bewilderment, but I did as he told me. His left hand was on my bare butt now, and his right was searching around my balls and cock, which was beginning to come to life.

"Can't be too careful; you guys are hiding it just about anywhere these days." His voice was thick, and he was breathing heavier. He got behind me, and I felt his searching fingers going for my asshole. He entered right in. I winced and turned my butt to get away from him, but he whipped me one good one with the whip on the end of his nightstick and stuck the larger end of it between my legs and into the back of my ball sac.

"Seems to me you're resisting, son. You're going to have to pay for that."

I'd had about enough of this, cop or no cop, and I began to push off the car, but quick as a flash he had two pairs of handcuffs out and handcuffed me to the ends of the racks on the top of the police car. Then his fingers went back to digging in my ass.

"Oh, God, no," I cried out. "Stop that! You can't—"

"I can't what, Pretty Boy?" he said close to my ear as he grabbed a handful of my hair and arched my head back. "I can do whatever I please. And you're going to let me do whatever I please." Swish, swish went the whip across my butt cheeks. And now the nightstick was being pulled back across my perineum and to my asshole and being rubbed and pushed against my puckered rim. All of my attention went to my asshole now and to doing all I could to open up to business end of the billy club. I was sure that he was going to fuck me with that big club and was wildly wondering if that would tear me apart so badly that I'd die. Another part of me felt a shiver of excitement and arousal shoot through me, however. This is what I'd come out here to find. He did get the stick pushed in an inch or two, and then he suddenly pulled it away.

Swish, swish. He stroked the whip end against my butt cheeks and then he slapped me on the butt a couple of times. And then I felt another rod back there, between my thighs. Not as big as the billy club, but more insistent. He pulled my T-shirt up over my head and onto my arms as far as it would go.

Then he entered me from behind with his fair-sized hard prick. Pushing pretty quickly and steadily, not really giving me enough time to open to him. I arched my back into his chest and cried out in surprise and pain as he went in to the root, and he swished his whip across my chest and belly and thighs. Not sharp enough to cut but enough to raise welts and to cause flickers of pain. He must have had a strap with studs on it wrapped around the base of his cock, because the rim and entry of my ass were being chafed by something nobbly.

He pumped me for a good fifteen minutes before he came inside me, filling the head of condom enough for me to tell he was done, all the time slapping my butt cheeks and swishing that leather whip across my body and giving a little nasty laugh at the moaning and groaning I was doing.

I cried out for what he was doing to me but not in fear or loathing really. It was really turning me on. My cock was ballooning out as it never had done before. The uniform, the surprise, the rough treatment. I was panting and moaning for what his cock was doing inside me.

He was pulling out of me when I heard the roar of a motorcycle coming down the road from the same direction I had been traveling in. The sound got loader and I realized it had turned into the overgrown driveway. My senses were heightened. Was someone coming to rescue me?

The cop was patting me on the butt cheeks with his billy club and telling me what a nice fuck I was as a second cop pulled up on a motorcycle, cut the engine, and stood the cycle up on its stand.

He strode over to us, and I could tell in an instant that he wasn't here to help me escape the first cop. He also looked a lot younger and more fit than the first cop. I was shivering in anticipation.

"He had the sign in his window?" the second cop asked the first one. "You're sure the sign was in the window?"

"Sure thing. Look for yourself."

The second cop proceeded to walk behind my car and take a look at the rear window. He grunted a sign of satisfaction, and came back around to where I was cuffed to the police car. "Nice ride," he said to the first cop.

"The Jag or the guy?" the first cop said, and then he gave a hoarse little laugh in appreciation of his own joke.

"Both," the second cop said, and he too laughed. My ears burned from the comment. It was a silly thing to do, of course. The first cop had fucked me, and the second cop could see me with my naked butt hanging out, and I was embarrassed that they were talking about how nice a fuck I was. This wasn't a time for logic, however.

I watched in anticipation mixed with consternation as the second cop stripped off his shirt. He was obviously a bodybuilder and very impressed with himself, as he had every right to be.

"You wanna do him here or on the bike?" the first cop asked.

"On the bike, I think. He looks like a real fun one."

Cop number one uncuffed me from the rack on top of the cruiser and manhandled me over to the motorcycle, swung my leg over the seat, and pushed me down, chest up and bare butt on the smooth leather of the seat. I was handcuffed on either side to the handlebars of the bike. Cop number two unzipped his tight blue pants and pulled out a thick piece that was already loaded. He rolled a condom on, swung a leg over the bike below me, took my calves in his gloved hands, and spread them wide. My butt dug into the cold leather of the saddle. Then he took aim, his barrel was rifling into me, and he was vigorously stroking. His hands moved up to take a strong hold on my thighs, and as he stroked in with his piece, he was pulling my hips back to meet him and then pushing me away as he pulled out of me. He was coming all of the way out of me and then stroking quickly and strongly all the way back in to the root. Cop number one was hunched over my chest, and he was working my nipples with his teeth and tongue.

I gasped and yelped in pain, but more because of what the first cop was doing to my nipples and because my tender butt was chafing on leather of the saddle. Otherwise, this was a glorious fuck. I plastered my eyes on those of the second cop, and I thrilled at the look of lust in his eyes as he stroked me. I could tell the instant that he was ready to fire off his rifle, and I gave a little lurch to my hips that made him explode, which also made firecrackers of satisfaction shoot through my own body.

And then the cops were all business. They both pulled away from me and adjusted their uniforms. I was released from the bike, and the first cop pulled my T back down onto my body. It stung where the material came into contact with the welts from the whipping. He then had me step back into my pants and he fastened me up. He forced me back into the driver seat of my car and handcuffed both of my hands to the steering wheel.

"Gotta take you in, Pretty Boy. Can't resist arrest and not be taken in for a spell."

"But, but, I didn't . . ."

"Drive behind me. Dan here will be driving behind you. No use trying to slip away, 'cause you can't get out of those cuffs. Just drive along behind me, like a good little piece of ass."

We drove in tandem back to the state police building, where it appeared that the two of them were the only ones on duty.

"Okay, back in the tank," cop number one said, as he manhandled me out of the car, through the door of the station, and toward the back room. I didn't see cop number two again, which I sort of regretted, because he was the better looking of the two and had given me the better fuck.

There were four cells in the back room of the station, but only one occupant, a big Neanderthal trucker type wearing a gas station work uniform consisting of dark pants and a greasy striped shirt that was so dirty I couldn't read the name on the pocket. He was so barrel chested that he was almost busting out of the shirt at the chest. His feet were stuffed into muddy construction-worker boots. He had been dozing on one of two cots in the cell when we entered the room. Even though the other three cells were empty, the cop forced me over to the occupied cell, unlocked the door, and pushed me in.

"Here, I brought you a present, Jack. A pretty boy; I've already tried him out myself. Good meat, if I do say so myself."

"No, please, don't," I whimpered, as the cop took first my right arm and cuffed it over the bars above my head and behind me and then my left arm to the other side, stretching me out, my back to the bars and me facing the inside of the cell and the grinning cop and the slobbering trucker type. There was a wooden bench below me, behind my thighs.

"Gotta go make some calls, Jack. Enjoy." And the cop left the cell, shot the lock home, and started whistling as he sauntered back to the front of the facility.

"I do'n know, Juan," the other prisoner was calling out to the cop's disappearing back. "We could get into a lot of trouble over this."

"Naw, it's cool, Jack," the cop called back over his shoulder before he disappeared up the hall. "He had a BARUF sign in the back window of his car."

Once again he caught me wondering what the fuck baruf meant.

"Well, all right then," Jack said to no one in particular. He stood there in front of me for about a minute, a sloppy grin on his face, drinking me in.

"No, please don't . . ." I whimpered, but that was as much as I could get out, before he reached over with a big mitt, grabbed hold of the collar of my T, and just ripped it off my torso. Then he came into me with his beer breath and tried to kiss my lips while his was fiddling with my belt buckle and the zipper to my jeans. I turned my head, and his mouth landed in the hollow of my neck, where he bit me and then moved down to my chest and nipples, slurping and nipping. He took a couple of steps back as he pulled the jeans off my legs.

"Hot damn, Merry Christmas," he exclaimed. He pulled his shirt over his head, his biceps and chest muscles rippling and bulging. Even his muscles seemed to have muscles. And when he'd pulled his pants off, I saw the most impressive muscle he had. He was almost as big and thick as cop number two had been. I gulped with arousal and anticipation. I had thought that my hundred dollars had been well spent on the two cops. This was quite a bonus. He gave an unearthly scream and plowed right into me. He pushed me up the bars with his hands under my thighs, and after a couple of swallowing pumps of my cock, got his mouth applied to my asshole and slobbered that up pretty well. I had my feet on the bench now, but he lifted my right leg off the bench and up almost to the bars with his left hand, while he was positioning his rod at my asshole. And then he was in, plunging to the root. Up went my other leg, and I was "hammocked" there, my wrists cuffed to the bars behind and above me, my legs being held up and out by strong hands, my welted back rubbing up against the bars, and my butt suspended in air, as my ass, firmly skewered by his big pole swayed in and out with his pumping motion.

He took even longer than the cops had to shoot off up my ass. But when he did, he just let me collapse against the bars, pulled his shirt and pants back on, went back to his cot, turned his back to me, and soon drifted off into satisfied snores.

Exhausted and trying to escape the pain and this filthy cell, I forced myself into sleep. I was wedged in a sitting position on the bench, handcuffed to the jail cage bars and propped on one butt cheek to relieve the pressure on my ass. It had been a truly rough ride, but it had really hit the spot. I was aroused and satisfied as I never had been before, and it had been well worth the effort and risk. I slowly came to as voices became louder from the hall of the station. One of the voices sounded familiar. As two figures came in sight, I wasn't surprised to see the guy I had settled this deal with in the Starbucks. He was wearing army fatigues now, though and he looked a good deal more "squared away" than he had when I last saw him. Another uniform. My cock took a lurch. A uniform really made a man.

"Ah, look at him," the familiar voice was saying, "I haven't seen one of our clients strung up like that before."

"He was resisting," cop number one said with a big grin.

"Yeah, I'll bet. I knew you'd do him, but you didn't rough him up like that all by yourself, did you?"

"Naw, it wasn't all me, Stretch. Dan and Jack here took a dip too. This guy got his money's worth."

"Not quite yet," Stretch said with a dry laugh. "These welts look pretty nasty. Your work?"

A little giggle from the cop. "Yeah, you know me real well, Stretch, I guess. And what I like. But he ain't none the worse for wear. I didn't do any of my black leather stuff on him. Well, not much, anyway."

Stretch was standing over me inside the cell now, the cop right behind him, and the trucker-type dude still snoring over on the cot.

"Hey, kid, it's me, the guy from Starbucks." He was talking down at me now, but he turned to the cop.

"Let's get those cuffs off him now and get him into another room. You got any salve or something we can use on him?"

"Sure thing, Stretch." My hands were freed and I just collapsed onto the bench.

Cop number one came back with the salve and they got me into another room, some place that looked like a small interrogation room, with a small beat-up wooden table and two rickety chairs. I was still naked, but the cop brought my underwear and pants along. My T-shirt was in shreds now.

"Here, stand up and lean over this table," Stretch ordered. I did so, and he gently applied the salve to the welts all over my body. The cop just stood there, watching, a little grin on his face and breathing pretty heavily. Out of the corner of my eye, I could see him rubbing his basket from time to time. Before Stretch was finished, the cop turned and left the room; off getting his rocks off at my expense again, no doubt.

"Okay, I think that will help," Stretch eventually said. "Put your pants back on and let's go."

"Go where?" I asked suspiciously. "I was on my way down the road and plan to be back on my way down the road."

"Well, you'll have to drive me back to Annapolis first," Stretch said. "I got a ride right out here from a meeting as soon as I heard you were here. I know you were having fun, but any more of that and I'd have to charge you another hundred. I'm without wheels, so you're going to have to drive me back first."

What could I say? He had sprung me from the jail and, more important, seemed to have full power to put me back there if he so decided. So, we went out the door and to the Jag. As we were leaving, I could see cop number one off in a side room, slumped in a chair, his pants off, beating himself with one hand and flicking his whip across his legs with the other.

We weren't more than a couple of miles down the road, when Stretch started gently tracing the welt marks on my chest and belly with his right hand.

"Please, don't do that," I said.

"Do they still hurt?" He asked.

"They do sting a bit," I answered.

His hand went down and covered my basket.

"Hey, don't do that," I said. "Just stop, all right?"

But it wasn't all right. He was unbuckling my belt, unzipping my jeans, and running his hand into the opening. He bypassed my cock and my balls, and his big index finger slid on across my perineum and stopped at the rim of my ass.

"Stop; just stop that," I said. He got his left hand under my butt and pushed me forward on the seat, which gave him better entry to my ass with the fingers of his other hand, and enter he did with that index finger. He was moving it around, driving me crazy.

"We're going to have an accident if you don't stop that," I said, trying to put irritation in my voice. But he was really turning me on.

"Then pull over," he said huskily. "There, up ahead. There's a closed shopping strip mall. Pull in behind that."

"No. Certainly not!"

His finger pushed farther in and my body jerked and the car veered out of the lane.

"God, you're going to kill us!"

"Not if you do what I say. Not if you pull over where I told you to."

"Okay, okay. Pull that finger out and I'll pull over." He did, and I drove around and behind the closed line of stores. As soon as I'd gotten stopped, he had his hand back in my lap, this time stroking my cock, pumping me up. His mouth was on mine in a long, drawn-out kiss.

He broke away and opened his door. He was holding my right wrist in his left hand with a strong wrestler's grip.

"Here, out of the car. This side. I don't want to have to chase you down, but I could if I had to."

I first tried to fasten my pants, but he just said, "No, you're not going to need to do that."

"But—"

"Just take the damn seatbelt off and slide in this direction."

I did as he demanded. When he had me out of the car, he slammed the front passenger door, opened the back door, and pushed me down on the back seat. He produced a set of the cop's handcuffs from somewhere, snapped one end around my right wrist, and then pushed me down along the back seat, passing the linking chain through the seat belt two-thirds down the seat, and then snapped the other cuff on my left wrist. I was stretched out on the seat, my torso and arms inside the car, my butt on the edge of the door side of the seat, and my legs hanging out of the car.

He stripped my pants off and stepped back and pulled his own clothes off. He produced his ointment and a condom from somewhere and sheathed and lathered up his cock, pumping it up to its gigantic proportions.

I should have been horrified. But my body was aching to be taken by another man in uniform.

He took a gob of ointment and started working it into my asshole. I was lying on my left side, and he lifted my right leg up to give him an good view of my channel. When he had me moistened up to his satisfaction and his own pole standing at magnificent attention, he slapped my butt and said, "Get out here. Get your butt out here, feet on the ground, chest on the seat." I wasn't moving fast enough for him, so he dragged me out of the car and brought my rear end up into the air.

"Stand wide," he said. "Stand as wide as you can for your own good." I believed him and did so. He pulled my butt cheeks apart and brought his mouth to my asshole and tongued it briefly. Then he was only holding my left butt cheek, and I felt his cock at my hole. It reminded me of that cop's billy club. He took his time entering me, and when he was in all the way, he rocked me back and forth, pumping deep. I moaned and groaned and he grunted and sighed. After a few minutes, he turned me, rotating me around his embedded cock, and had me laying on my left side again, raising my right leg and side splitting me with continued deep pumps.

"So, dude. Do you like this? Do you love this?"

"Yes," huff, puff.

"Too rough? Should I stop?"

"Oh, God, no. Don't stop."

He rotated me yet again. This time my back was on the seat, and he was supporting my butt up in the air with both of his hands, suspending me and moving both his cock and my pelvis in a rapid, deep fuck. I got my legs and feet back in the car. My right foot was in the corner of the back window, and my left foot was on the ceiling above the passenger door.

He pumped and pumped and pumped, and then he pulled out of me. I felt his withdrawal as a loss. I was on the point of coming. I wanted to come while he was inside me.

"What do you want me to do now?" he said, knowing full well what I wanted.

Silence. "I don't know, what do I want you to do?" I couldn't bring myself to say it.

"You want me to fuck you, fuck you hard; fuck your brains out. Say it."

"Fuck me. Fuck me hard; fuck my brains out."

And he did that as best he could. He got a pillow off the floor and stuffed in under my hips, and just fucked me and fucked me and fucked me. His hands came over my hips. His right hand went to my cock and he pumped me until I shot off all over his belly. His hands then traveled slowly up my torso and buried themselves in my chest. With a heave he pulled his rod out of my ass and shoot up my belly. Then he lowered his belly to mine, and moved it around, mingling my cum with his.

He stood up, put his clothes back on, made a clumsy attempt to push my pants back on as well, pushed me all the way into the car, slammed the door, and came around to the driver's side and got in.

"I'll drive the rest of the way. You can drop me off down by the harbor and then drive on back to the Academy yourself. Any problem with a check being in the mail tomorrow?"

"No," I said with a sigh.

"Satisfied?"

"Yes, very?"

"Anything else we need to do here?"

A long pause.

"Well, there is something else," I said. "What in the hell does baruf mean?"

He laughed and then he told me. "BARUF is an acronym used to tell the cops along this route what you've paid to have done. It stands for bondage and rough uniformed fuck. You were just picking from the menu."

When I dropped him off, I was happy to note that he hadn't taken the sign back. There was no telling when I might want to take a fast ride down that straight and level section of Route 301 again.

Cybersex

Konan to the Rescue

"Hey, look at that," Ronda nudged Jerry. "I told you we could set the clock by him."

The bank's loan officer and new accounts clerk, whose desks were set side by side in the bank branch's lobby, were leaning into each other and marking the rapid progress of the senior teller to the exit door. Kevin Radcliff had stepped out from behind the bank counter precisely on the stroke of five o'clock. As he breezed past the customer service desks, Jerry made an exaggerated gesture of resetting the time on his wristwatch.

"Hot date, I suppose," Ronda murmured, just beyond—she hoped—Kevin's hearing.

"I wouldn't count on it," Jerry responded sotto voce.

But Kevin Radcliff wasn't listening to either of them. Kevin Radcliff was intent on getting home. It was Thursday. And on Thursdays there often was a new Konan story posted. Thursday was the day that Kevin lived for.

He raced to his car and drove straight to the Taco Bell that was located on the straightaway between the bank branch and his apartment. He was hungry—he did have to eat. If there was a new story there, he'd be lost until late in the night and wouldn't even think about eating. So, he did need to eat. A stop at Taco Bell, though, would be the shortest sacrifice of time between the office and Kevin's computer.

Having ordered, received, and wolfed down a couple of tacos and a Coke within ten minutes of pulling into the Taco Bell lot, Kevin was quickly on the move again. He raced up the stairs at his apartment house, having no patience to wait for the elevator to arrive. And he was stripped and sitting in front of his computer and firing it up within a half hour of having stepped out from behind that bank branch counter.

"Come on, come on," he muttered as he waited for the Literotica erotica story Web site to load.

And there it was. A new Konan the Barbarian story. Kevin sighed and clicked on it and immediately was lost in ancient time.

Within two paragraphs, the timing and atmospherics of the story had been set. The hulking brute of a barbarian—but one of honesty and fairness, not to mention bulging muscles, a monster dick of cartoon proportions, and an unquenchable sex drive—who went by the name Konan had met up with a caravan traveling the Silk Road and had helped the treasure-laden caravan, led by the young and comely son of a merchant prince, stave off an attack by brigands.

In paragraph three, which—making Kevin gasp and lick his lips—was illustrated, the young merchant was showing his gratitude for the hunky barbarian's help by spreading his legs and giving Konan an unmistakable "take me" look. Without hesitation, the barbarian had unhooked and dropped his loin cloth and torn away the young merchant's tunic. He was already magnificently and hugely hard, as shown in no uncertain terms in the story illustration.

Kevin whimpered and reached for his own cock, which was filling out and beginning to throb. He wrapped his hand around it and began to slowly work it. It had been two weeks since he'd been transported like this. There hadn't been a new Konan story last week; he'd had to do with rereading an old one. He had other sites on the Internet to follow to help give him release, but nothing did for him like a new Konan story. Nothing transported him out of this dull life of his and into a hugely arousing world like a new Konan story.

The young merchant had been sitting on the driver's board of a covered wagon containing a fortune in trade goods. Once they both were naked, Konan had pushed the young man down on his side across the board and lifted his thigh. Konan then stood up on the spokes of the wheel at the side of the driver's board and started working the young man's hole with the head of his cock. The young merchant screamed out to the night as Konan impaled his tight hole with an impossibly thick cock. Miraculously, and after taking his time, Konan had managed to bury his cock, though, and the young man's screams had been reduced to weak groans and moans.

Kevin shuddered and released his seed into a washcloth he kept conveniently nearby. Since there had been no story the previous Thursday, he had been ready to ejaculate at the mere assurance that a new story had posted earlier in the day. He lay back in his chair for a few minutes, gathering himself and luxuriating in having gotten himself off with story to spare for another—and perhaps even a third—release this evening.

He waited for his breath to regularize again, but that didn't come easily. He was sitting and looking at the illustration. It told him what came next, and Kevin melted down into a puddle at the mere thought of Konan doing that to him as well. Calm now, Kevin's eyes went back to the computer screen.

Having managed to bottom in the young merchant's channel and having reduced the writhing and jerking of the young man's body as a result of the seemingly impossible journey of a monster club in a virginal channel into a semicomatose state and a sloppy grin of master possession, Konan just lifted his prey off the wagon bench with strong hands that nearly met as they circled the young man's thin waist. Gracefully for a rough and massive hunter such as the barbarian was, Konan swung the young man off the wagon—still bottomed in his channel— while he stepped down from the spokes of the wooden wheel. Standing on the ground, Konan crouched down, knees bent and the young merchant's legs straddling his hips, and held the young man's hips to his pelvis. Using the hands encircling the young man's waist, Konan began moving the merchant's channel up and down on his cock, fucking him deep with long strokes. The young man's torso just arched back, and his head lolled to the side. The expression of total satisfaction and surrender on his face showed that he was getting the fuck of his life.

Kevin didn't have to imagine this. The illustrator had captured it all.

Kevin moaned, totally lost in what was happening in the story and illustration. And it wasn't just a silent or half-hearted moan. It was a moan that started deep down inside him and rumbled forever up to the surface.

Startled, Konan the Barbarian suspended his pumping action of the young merchant's hips, He lifted his head and sniffed the air and started looking around in the dimness of the dying fire set in the middle of the circled wagons and kneeling, snoozing camels.

Suddenly fearful, Kevin shrank into the camel saddle that he had been crouched behind.

But Konan, with the eyes of a desert cat, saw Kevin in the dimness of the light. His mouth turned up in a smile, and he slowly let the body of the young, totally fucked merchant slide off his cock and down his massively muscled legs to lay in a panting and groaning heap at his feet.

Konan was moving across the shadowed clearing—toward the source of the moan—Kevin's moan. Kevin at first shrank down behind the camel saddle, trying to meld into the smooth leather and heavy wool blanketing. But quite unsuccessfully. Realizing this, Kevin gave a little cry of fear and managed to get to his feet and turned to flee into the desert. He cried out as his foot came down on a rough stone, and he momentarily wondered why his feet were bare—in fact, why he was completely naked. Then he remembered that he had stripped down as usual as he had sat down to the computer, all set to pleasure himself as he read the latest Konan story.

Something was still wrong with this scenario, Kevin thought, somewhat idiotically, but he couldn't put his finger on it. In the meantime, there was a hulk of a barbarian, naked and with a huge erection, bearing down on him. Kevin stumbled back up on his feet and turned to run.

But the barbarian was faster than Kevin, and Kevin was hampered by the surrealism of what was happening.

Grabbing Kevin with two strong hands encircling his waist, Konan the Barbarian simply lifted the retreating Kevin off the ground and turned him and pushed him down on his belly on top of the camel saddle.

Kevin cried out in pain, as Konan straddled his hips and began working his huge cock inside Kevin's hole. He cried to the heavens and flung his body about, trying—quite unsuccessfully—to escape the slow but relentless skewering of his virginal channel by the impossibly thick cock. He was begging for mercy and crying of being split asunder. But Konan just continued to impale him, not paying a bit of attention to Kevin's pleadings.

And of course he wasn't answering, Kevin reasoned between the flood of pain, which was arousing other sensations as well—welcome sensations, sexy sensations. Konan was a barbarian, after all. What language did an ancient barbarian speak anyway, Kevin wondered. He briefly wondered if he should plead for mercy in the broken French he knew—but then he decided he was being stupid and probably was just suffering from shock.

The barbarian was beginning to fuck him in long, strong strokes that bottomed deep in Kevin's interior, and Kevin was moaning and groaning to the barbarian's unabashed grunts of pleasure. The barbarian was breathing heavily and Kevin was panting, taking long breaths in each time the barbarian bottomed, usually just a fraction of an inch deeper inside Kevin than the last assault. Kevin had never been ass fucked before, but he found he had fallen into the rhythm of the fuck now, and was moving his hips to meet the barbarian's thrusts.

The barbarian was covering him close from behind. Kevin felt teeth lightly close on the hollow of his neck and the barbarian was sucking him there while fucking him. Waves and waves of pleasure flowed over Kevin, and he was feeling as one with the barbarian—a combined fucking machine. Konan was enjoying the taking, and Kevin was flooded with a sense of accomplishment and satisfaction not only that he was pleasing the literary character who he had fallen in love with several months earlier but also that he was able to accomplish a cock of cartoon proportions.

And then Kevin's insides were being flooded by a sea of cum. It was seeping deep inside him and was simultaneously burbling up between softening cock and beleaguered channel walls and dribbling down Kevin's legs.

They lay together, their breathing in unison—slowly calming together, the sweat of Konan's massive chest slicking down Kevin's trembling back, Kevin feeling a slight chill as the breeze cooled their bodies. Kevin looked over across the embers of the fire and saw that the young merchant was still lying in a heap. But he was on his back now, watching Konan fuck Kevin and working his own cock. He had a satisfied grin on his face. Kevin found himself wondering if his own eyes were swimming in Konan's come as the young merchant's eyes seemed to be doing.

But then all of Kevin's attention was concentrated on the cock still buried deep inside him. Konan was saying something to him—but in a language he couldn't understand. From his reading of previous stories—and of the fairness and honesty of the bulky barbarian—Kevin somehow understood that Konan was asked for permission to fuck him again.

"Yes, oh yes," Kevin murmured. "Again and again."

Pleased, Konan rose, pulling Kevin up with him, not giving up the purchase his cock had established in Kevin's channel. Kevin was turned, his back on the warm sand of the Silk Road verge and the small of his back running up the saddle. Konan spread-eagled his legs and crouched over the saddle and fucked down into Kevin. Kevin put his hips into motion, meeting Konan's downward thrusts with upward thrusts of his own, and soon ancient barbarian and senior bank teller were lost in the rhythm of the ultimate fuck once more. The fucking was even more pleasurable now, Kevin's channel having already taken the measure of Konan's cock and now being lubricated with Konan's earlier ejaculation.

Konan had the palm of one of his hands pumping Kevin's cock and the other one was cradled under Kevin's chin, forcing his head back, where he was now watching—in upside-down view—the young merchant being fucked roughly by one of the caravan's camel drivers—and by all appearances enjoying it immensely.

In a third taking—and to the total delight of Kevin—Konan duplicated the fuck of the story illustration, standing on his feet, heels dug in the sand, holding Kevin's hips to his pelvis, and slowly marching around the clearing while fucking

Kevin up and down on his hard tool. Kevin just arched his back and let his head loll to one side and let exhaustion and total surrender slowly overtake him.

Kevin was stretched out on the rug beside the computer chair when he awoke. The computer screen was in save mode, but ready to flicker back on at his command. He was still fisting his cock, but it was tumescent now. Sticky cum was spread through his pubic hair and on his thighs and fingers—not to mention the stickiness from the can of Coke that had spilled over into his lap. He had the most wonderful feeling of total satisfaction and fulfillment that he connected with both sexual release and a good workout at the gym. The combined feeling was incredible. This was why he hurried home on Thursday nights—what got him through all of the intervening dull days at the bank, putting up with the twittering of Ronda and Jerry behind their fingers over there at the customer service desk.

He couldn't wait for next Thursday evening.

Dreamworld

It's not that Sean didn't see and understand the effect he had on other men; it's just that since he entered his dreamworld with jacko242, he didn't really give a shit. And it wasn't as if he hadn't been a player before he had succumbed to his new world.

His boss in the architectural firm had known Sean would put out—and he certainly had no inkling why Sean still wasn't putting out. There was that corner office on the second floor he'd been grooming Sean for—and that he'd been holding over Sean's head to get every ounce of tail out of his young and winsome employee that he could get. Phil Ocksen thought of Sean as his last fling, a delicious confection he could poke at will, his little joke on his up-tight society wife. Phil wasn't exactly decrepit yet, but he was moving along in age. He was doing all of the right things in diet and exercise and grooming, and, yes, although he wouldn't admit it, a bit of a nip and tuck here and there.

He was just as presentable, however, as the day he trapped Sean in the filing room and almost blatantly asked Sean what he would do to get that raise he wanted. This had led, just as he'd hoped it would, to fucking Sean on the Xerox machine— with the machine scanning and flipping out images of Sean's flattened buttocks and spread thighs and the underside Phil's very nice cock as it buried itself in Sean's ass and reappeared only to bury itself again. Far from being ashamed of his cock and balls—which have never seen the edge of a plastic surgeon's knife, he wants to make quite clear—Phil had saved the Xeroxes and to this day takes them out now and again to reminisce about the day he conquered that particular conquest. It amused him to think that he'd make them his wife's in the inevitable divorce settlement.

But Phil didn't know about jacko242. So that afternoon when he was leaning over Sean to look at some blueprints on Sean's drafting table and was murmuring about how the light was so much better to view these blueprints in that now-empty corner office on the second floor *and* was undoing a button on Sean's sports shirt and running his fingers in to find a nipple hiding in the soft blond down on Sean's chest, Phil had no idea why Sean wasn't reacting as he wished. Sean was being polite and attentive, but he was making no effort whatsoever to warm up to Phil's signaling. Only four weeks earlier this nipple play would have had Sean on his back on the floor, reaching up to Phil's belt buckle as Phil knelt between Sean's spread legs, and pulling Phil's cock inside him while sighing sweet nothings about "big daddy."

Sean had clearly shown that he wanted that corner office—and he sure as hell wanted the subsidy Phil gave him for the house on Queensbury Row—so Phil assumed that there was some pale of desirability and acceptability that he himself had passed beyond that made him less attractive to Sean. He checked himself in the mirror on the way back to the office. Yep, same forgivingly matured face and full head of hair with distinguished graying at the temples. Same straight back and flat stomach. He reached his hand down. Yep, the same nice cock dressed left in his tailored slacks. But were those crows' feet at the corners of his eyes? Surely that couldn't have been enough for Sean to spurn him. Still, he'd have his secretary, Mavis, call his plastic surgeon.

And, as an afterthought, he called that retired cop he had watching his wife for signs of grounds for divorce as well. Maybe it wasn't that he was losing his desirability but that Sean had found some cock on the side he wasn't talking about. The live-in guy was OK—it was just the one. But Sean had agreed there wouldn't be in whoring around. Phil had made clear to Sean that the corner office came with conditions.

Sean left the office that afternoon, not even fully aware that he had cut off an advance by Phil. He wasn't thinking of Phil at all. His mind was in that small room at the end of the corridor on the second floor of his house. The one he padded to naked, on bare feet, at night when the house was dark and silent other than the soft snoring of Rod.

He almost absentmindedly entered the backseat of the Lincoln Town Car. Phil had thoughtfully provided this service to take the senior staff members into the exclusive old section of the city where parking was at such a premium and life was so self-contained that many did not have cars and those who did preferred not to take them out of whatever premium parking space they had finally scored.

Phil had instituted the car service two years previously, and Julio had served as the executives' chauffeur from day one. Julio liked the job. The transport hours for the firm's executives worked quite well around his sessions at the gym, where he was training hard to be a champion heavyweight boxer. Other than driving and working out in the gym, Julio had only one vice: cute-looking and saucy blond male tail. Of course the boss, Phil Ocksen, didn't know anything about Julio's fetish, or he wouldn't have let him chauffeur Send. Sean had been a hot little number when Julio had come on board, and it hadn't taken long to figure out that the boss was fucking this nice piece of tail. Julio wanted some of that for himself, and within two weeks of coming on board, Sean had been game for the long ride home and a somewhat shorter but very explosive ride from Julio in the back of the Town Car, with Sean's heels leveraging off the back of the front seat and Julio knelt between Sean's legs and pile driving his puckered ass.

Since that first fucking, Sean had been willing to drop trou and spread legs on just one meaningful look from Julio in the rear view mirror. The cute young blond was a veritable male nympho. And Julio enjoyed manhandling him and listening to him groan and moan as a dark tan Hispanic monster cock slowly buried itself inside him and Julio started a fast and furious ride that benefited greatly from many hours of thrusting and parrying in the practice boxing ring.

All of this was right up until a couple of weeks ago. And then the arrangement had died cold, very dead, turkey. Julio didn't know what was wrong—he half expected that Ocksen had found out what they were doing on those long drives home, but time went by and the boss didn't show any signs of knowing about it. Even so, Julio might have gotten the message not to fuck so close to home, but his cock missed the tight warmth of Sean's channel.

Maybe Sean was getting that promotion he was always talking about and it just hadn't been announced, Julio thought. Maybe Sean was going up in the world—he certainly had a tight fist on Phil Ocksen's balls, so there was nothing he couldn't ask for in the architectural firm—and maybe Sean was getting uppity. He was a really, really nice piece of ass, and up to recent weeks he'd been so randy for the fucking Julio could give him that he almost begged for it whenever he entered the Town Car. But not now. When Julio gave him "that look" in the rearview mirror, Sean wasn't even looking. His eyes were glazed over, and he was off in some dreamworld somewhere.

Uppity or not, Julio felt like driving into the woods and parking and coming up over the seat back into the backseat and giving Sean the rough fuck of his life. A couple of weeks ago Sean even would have loved that. But not now. Now he was off in a world of his own where Julio was transparent. Julio's cock and balls ached to be fucking the blond little piece of ass. But most of all his pride was aching. An Hispanic fucking the lights out of a little blond Gringo. Now that had been worth talking about down at the gym.

It wasn't anything Sean was holding against Julio specifically or Hispanics in general, though. Julio just didn't know about jacko242.

Sean barely waved an acknowledgment of Julio's good-bye when they arrived in Queensbury Row, and, anger rising inside him, Julio flipped Sean off—but well below the window sill of the Town Car, as Julio wanted to keep his cushy job—and there was always a chance he could get back into Sean's ass. Julio then pulled the Lincoln away from the curb and into traffic a bit faster than was really warranted.

Hearing the squeal of the tires, the occupant of the townhouse next door to Sean's, one Professor Steven Connolly, paused at the door while rummaging around in his mailbox and cast a forlorn eye on Sean ascending absentmindedly to his own front door. Steven almost called out something to Sean. But then he stopped, sad, in resignation, and stepped back into the shadows of his foyer.

That phase of Professor Connolly's life was closed now. And although the professor didn't know why it had been cut off so abruptly and so definitively, not more than a month earlier, he could recognize "the end" to an affair as well, if not better than most. Sean had been such an open and fun-loving young man. When Connolly's long-term companion had died, Sean had been so sympathetic and understanding and had provided just the medicine the grieving professor had needed. He had pulled Connolly out of his blue funk one gloomy afternoon in the study in his home, when Sean had taken him by the hand and pushed him gently down into his desk chair. He then had knelt in front of Connolly, slowly unzipped his pants, and sucked Connolly's cock to paradise. After that Sean had stripped off his own clothes and sat on Connolly's now-very-hard cock, facing him, and had slowly fucked himself to their mutual completion and satisfaction.

Subsequently, on most workday evenings, Sean had mounted the stairs to Connolly's Queensbury Row townhouse before entering his own when arriving home from work. Connolly had waited for him, trembling, in the foyer, and then the two had ascended the stairs, hand in hand, and in silence moved to the bedroom where, for decades, Connolly and his companion had made love. And just then, for that brief afternoon period, Connolly was transported back to happier times as Sean laid down on his back on the bed and spread his thighs and Connolly sank his cock deep into the younger man's world.

And then, just when Connolly was building up to the suggestion of a more permanent arrangement, Sean had just stopped coming for their late-afternoon assignations. No explanations, no harsh words, no formal ending—just an abrupt, total ending. Now Sean mounted his own stairs when he returned from work, no longer visiting the house next door to be mounted by Professor Connolly. And always that blank expression on Sean's face as if he was totally off in another world.

Steven Connolly had no idea what had changed—but then he knew nothing about jacko242. All Connolly knew was that he had not left his house since Sean's last visit—everything he needed he had had delivered—and that he spent his late afternoons tangled in the sheets of his lost companion's bed, naked, and writhing against the sheets, fucking the sheets, until he had exhausted himself and relieved his grief and loneliness in spent cum and tears.

When Sean entered his Queensbury Row house, his senses were immediately assaulted. There was humming in a deep baritone coming from the kitchen and from there as well the smells of an oregano-laced spaghetti sauce. The combination of the two meant that it was Italian night. It also signaled that Rod was in high heat and wanted to fuck on the bearskin rug in front of the fireplace.

Sean sighed and checked through the mail. All of the time he was doing this, though, and listening to his live-in lover's humming from the kitchen, Sean's mind had already mounted the stairs and walked deliberately down the hall to the small room at the end—and to jacko242. It just wasn't time yet, though. Sean ached for the hours to slip by until the appointed time.

Sighing again, Sean turned and moved toward the kitchen. He knew what he would find, and he was right. Enhanced aromas of the cooking sauce, two glasses of Burgundy on the island top, and a smiling, naked, black-skinned god in full erection. Rodney Singleton had come into Sean's life just a bit more than a year earlier. A star receiver of the metropolitan area's professional football team, he had come to Sean's architectural firm, annual bonus in hand, wanting to build his dream house on the cliffs overlooking the sea in a nearby suburb. At this point Phil Ocksen had made possibly the biggest mistake of his life. He had turned the big black hunk over to Sean for drawing up the concept layouts for the project, and within an hour of their meeting, Sean was bent over the toilet in the small bathroom off his office and Rod was crouched over him from behind, palming Sean's pert little nipples in his big football-receiver's mitts, and giving Sean as deep a doggy fuck as he'd ever had.

Rod moved in with Sean rather than building that house, and Phil lost not only the client but also a good chunk of Sean's sexual favors, not that Phil had noticed any wavering in accessibility to Sean after Rod had moved in—a least until a couple of weeks ago. In fact, though, Sean had been stretched to the limit to continue to service Phil, because Rodney's sexual demands were enough to exhaust a horse. But he'd managed them all until a couple of weeks ago.

Rodney was highly sexed and not all that observant, which was probably just fine for his mental well-being. He had barely even noticed that Sean had been somewhere else—in his own dreamworld—for weeks.

When Sean had entered the kitchen and taken a sip of Burgundy with hardly any greeting at all—or any appreciative look at that magnificent cock rising below Rod's washboard belly and bulging, barrel chest—Rodney completely failed to notice Sean's vacant expression when, as he so often did, he murmured. "So glad you're home, baby. I'm so full of cum, I'm about to explode. Strip for me, honey. We have a good hour before the sauce is finished."

Sean absentmindedly stripped down as requested, took another sip of Burgundy, and then docilely followed Rod into the living room, to the bearskin rug, in front of a fire set in the fireplace. He laid down on his back and raised his trim ankles to the shoulders of his magnificent black lover who was kneeling between his thighs. Sean turned his head toward the mesmerizing fire and let his mind wander to that little room on the second floor and to jacko242, as, with a grunt, Rod entered him strongly with his throbbing cock and drug that thick silver cock ring along Sean's channel, deep inside him. Sean raised his hips and let them slowly drift into the familiar undulation of the rhythm of the deep fuck, his body responding, if minimally, but his mind off in its own dreamworld.

Rod didn't notice that some part of Sean was missing. He hadn't had a fuck in nearly twelve hours and he needed to get his rocks off. And Sean had the sweetest passage in town. Rodney just grunted and thrust away, coming in great gobs of milky-white jism, deep inside Sean's sweet hole, just as the timer was going off for the bubbling tomato sauce.

Rodney was equally unobservant that night, when, balls once more aching for sex, he trapped Sean's compliant, docile body, belly down on the sheets, under his, gripped Sean's hips close between his knees, and rode his little blond pony hard through two mighty ejaculations. Then spent and satisfied himself, Rod rolled Sean over on his side, cock still buried, still deeply sheath even in flaccidity, and spooned Sean into his chest. Rod went into a deep, satisfied, fulfilled sleep, not needing another fuck for a good eight hours—in the morning he'd take Sean up against the tiles of the shower before Sean left for work and then he'd putter around the townhouse all day—this being his off season—except for a three-hour session in the training room down at the stadium and then be cum filled again and hard for Sean's return from work.

All a good, fulfilling day for Rodney—and especially so since he was blessedly unaware that Sean hadn't really been there, other than providing a compliant hole to poke, for several weeks. Sean had been off in his own dreamworld and in the thrall of jacko242.

Hours later, in the darkest of night, with Rodney snoring contentedly in his ear, Sean slowly and quietly disentangled himself from Rodney's possessive embrace and sat up on the side of the bed. His cock was hard and dripping with precum, and his breath was ragged—in anticipation. He was in heat for the first time today. Neither the advances of the elegant, experienced Phil in the office; nor what most young men would see as the enticement of the delectable Hispanic chauffer, Julio;

nor the hopeful—eternally grateful—proffering gaze of Professor Connolly at his door—nor the exuberant attentions of the masterfucker black stud Rodney had set Sean's juices going.

But the thought of that little room down the hall and of jacko242 had done so.

Sean stood up beside the bed, still naked. He ran his hand up from his hard cock along his belly to his nipples and flicked them with his thumb. Already puffed out, hard. He padded out of the room quietly and down the hall and into the small computer room. He shut the door behind him. He knew that he might cry out upon release, and he didn't want to wake Rodney—although a temporarily well-fucked Rodney could sleep through an earthquake.

Sean sat down on the terrycloth covered desk chair and fired up the computer. When he had a browser screen, he tapped in www.mandate.net and then clicked on the profile of jacko242.

There he was, the love of Sean's life, in all of his naked glory. Beautiful, sun-kissed body. Turkish features, a well-muscled hunk with black, curly body hair. Square-cut facial features and that knowing smile. Knowing that Sean had returned to him.

Sean clicked on "live-chat," and he was there, waiting for Sean.

"You're late."

"Sorry. I'm here now. Hard to get away tonight."

"Are you hard?"

"Yes, for you always, Jacko," Sean tapped out. And that was true. He was as hard as he could be.

"Stroke it."

Sean complied.

"Is there precum yet?"

Yes, there certainly was.

"Taste it."

Sean did so. A little moan escaped his lips.

"Look at my cock in the photo. It is for you. Is it big enough for you? And thick enough?"

"Yes, oh yes."

"Close your eyes. Run your hands up my belly and into my chest hair. Feel my nipples? Hard for you."

"Yes, oh yes," Sean replied. He was leaning back in his chair, running hands up to his own nipples. As hard as he imagined Jacko's to be.

"Do you have the cock? Is it lubed?"

"Yes and yes," Sean tapped out. He reached for the dildo he had lubed up while the computer was warming up.

"Close your eyes. Work it in. It's my cock. Inside you. Making love to your walls."

For the next couple of minutes, while the computer screen murmured words of instruction and lovemaking, Sean moaned and groaned in ecstasy. His thighs were spread and hooked over the arms of his desk chair, his hips rolled forward on the front edge of the chair and one hand stroking his cock and the other working the dildo deep in his passage . . . as the honeyed phrasing of the words on the screen fucked him masterfully.

As long last, at the height of a passion that Sean had felt at no earlier point of his day, Sean gave a little cry and jerked several times as he ejaculated into the hand cloth he held over his cock head.

He looked up. The screen was blank. Jacko242 had left him. But jacko242 had left him feeling deeply touched to the very quick of him—once again. Sean would somehow have to endure through another day. Jacko242 was only there for him for this one hour of the night. Sean had no idea whether he could wait for his next deeply satisfying encounter with his jacko242.

* * * *

At a dingy workbench in the back of a double garage in suburban Jefferson City, smack dab in the middle of the flattest, most monotonous Midwestern U.S. state, Elmer Dent had quickly switched from one profile on Mandate.net to the next. It had been a touch-and-go thing. Piningblond had been late this evening—again, for the second time this week. Jacko242 thought perhaps he'd have to cut him off; he wasn't fitting into the schedule well. He flipped open to Legsopen4u, who was already there, on time, as usual.

"Are you hard?" Elmer tapped out under his jacko242 name. He ran his hand inside his robe and scratched his belly, not even bothering to look at the response from legsopen4u before tapping in the next sequence. "Stroke it." The response was always the same—as were his instructions. These computer sex junkies never seemed to notice the sameness of it all. Elmer took a swig of his beer and burped.

A faint sound, coming through several of the thin walls in the squat tract rancher. "Elmer. You out in the garage again? Come to bed and do me, hon. Turn off that computer."

Elmer sighed. That Hazel was so demanding. If she weren't the one with the job—down at the Laundromat . . .

"Just a minute, Sweetcheeks," Elmer called back, pulling his robe closer together over his paunch and reaching down and scratching his hairy balls. "Just about done out here."

And he was, in fact, just about done. Legsopen4u was his last computer sex junkie of the evening. While he'd waited for piningblond to click on, he'd browsed the new members. There was a nice-sounding profile obviously just aching for it who he might like to ride for a while. Maybe he'd give him piningblond's slot. That one was about to play out anyway. It had been four weeks.

He took another swig of beer and turned to the computer and tapped in, "Is there precum yet?"

Daddies

Big Birthday Wish

I was an impressionable teenager and prone to fantasies I couldn't shake. And, like any teenager, I was raging with hormones. One such fantasy was Mr. Walker, who lived down the block from us. He was a former Marine in his thirties, who worked hard to keep himself in tip-top shape. He was a runner, and I'd frequently see him running around our neighborhood, wearing no more than skimpy shorts and running shoes without socks. He wasn't muscle bound by any stretch of the imagination, but he was finely built, and there wasn't an ounce of fat on him anywhere. His buzz cut and exercise regime screamed that once a Marine, always a Marine.

The first thing that started me to fantasizing about Mr. Walker was his wife. She was a cute little blonde thing who always looked so satisfied with herself and who popped out a baby every twelve or thirteen months or so. In my adolescent mind, this suggested to me that every minute Mr. Walker wasn't out running, he and Mrs. Walker were in their bed "doing it." The mere image of that turned me on. As I said, I was suffering from raging hormones then, and I found myself fantasizing about being in bed with the Walkers—for several weeks about being in bed with Mrs. Walker, and then for a while with both of them, and finally, distressingly, I fixated on being in bed with just Mr. Walker.

The Walkers belonged to the same community club my family did, and in the summer of my sixteenth year, I found myself at the pool the same afternoon the Walker clan was there. Mr. Walker looked mighty fine poolside in that Speedo of his. He was in the shower of the men's locker room soaping himself up when I entered the shower after my swim. A lump went to my throat. His body was magnificent—all sinew and muscle in motion and rolling veins lacing his body, having been pushed to the surface by his muscle and lack of any fat in which to hide. My eyes went directly to his dick, which was the biggest and thickest I'd ever seen as it plunged out of a clump of red hair at his groin. I hadn't thought of Mr. Walker as a red head; his buzz cut was just too short to tell from that, and the rest of his body appeared smooth and hairless from a distance. I could see now, when he was soaping himself all over, that he had tufts of red hair at his pits as well. My own cock came to quick attention at what I was seeing.

Mr. Walker obviously saw me staring at his package as well as what my own was doing in response.

"Hey, you're the kid living up the block from us, aren't you?" he asked in a pleasant tone, not bothering to stop soaping around his dangling dick.

"Yeah," I managed to burble out. "I see you running in the neighborhood sometimes."

"Well, how old are you, kid?" he asked straight out.

I told him.

"When's your birthday?" he then asked, which seemed a strange question at the time.

I told him that too.

"Well, on your eighteenth birthday, we'll meet again," he said. "Until then, keep yourself clean, ya hear? And you could stand to do some running of your own." With that, he rinsed off and left me and my boner alone in the locker room shower.

I started running after that, but I never stopped fantasizing about Mr. Walker.

On my seventeenth birthday, I was out running a woodland trail. I'd gotten myself in great shape with my running, and I was grateful for that little nudge Mr. Walker had given me a year earlier. I was doing real well on the cross-country team now.

As I was steaming down the trail, I heard another runner coming up behind, someone, incredibly, who was opening it up a lot faster than I was. When he came up level to me, I saw that it was Mr. Walker in his skimpy shorts and sockless running shoes. He hadn't aged a day in that year, and my mind went immediately to the image of him in the swimming pool locker room shower.

"How's it going, Sport?" he called out to me in a voice that showed no signs of breathlessness. "Happy birthday. Today is your birthday, isn't it? I remembered right, didn't I?"

Besides being breathless from the exertion of running myself, what he was saying—having kept track of my birthday like this just from a chance encounter at the swimming pool—bowled me over so that the most I could do was mumble an affirmation that today, indeed, was my seventeenth birthday.

"I see you took my advice on running," he said with a grin. "Lookin' good, Sport. See you on your eighteenth. Keep clean." And then he was off in front of me, leaving me in his dust as if I weren't even flat out running myself.

This encounter didn't cut down on my fantasy time about Mr. Walker for the next year.

It was my eighteenth birthday, and I was moving up the walk to my house after school, when a big SUV with smoked windows stopped beside me, and the passenger window rolled down. I came over and looked inside. It was Mr. Walker. He was wearing a loose, long-sleeved shirt, worn blue jeans, and shiny black boots.

"Happy birthday, Sport," he said with a big grin. "Climb in."

I opened the door and climbed in. As the door shut, he rolled up my window. We were alone now, in his big SUV with the smoked window.

Without fanfare, he took my right hand by the wrist and brought it around and laid it on his basket. I could feel him hard and massive through the worn material of the blue jeans.

"This can be your eighteenth birthday present, Sport, if you still want it," he said in a husky voice. "You wanted it two years ago. Do you still want it, Sport? I won't go any further unless you want it."

"Yes, oh yes," I managed once the frog had been cleared from my throat. He'd remembered. I knew I should say no and just get out of the car and bury myself in a safe, normal life. But this had been my fantasy for years.

"Well, then, let's take a little ride. Buckle yourself up, but you don't have to take your hand back, if you don't want to. Here, let's give it some air." He pushed my hand to the top of his thigh and worked his zipper down. Then he went back to putting the SUV into gear and driving away from the curb. I worked my hand into the gap in his pants, not believing I was even doing this, imaging it was happening to someone I was watching from across the room, and his big plump dick just popped out of his pants. I gently ran my hand up and down and around it as we drop into the countryside. It had this large, popping vein running up the underside. His dick got impossibly large and hard as we drove along, and I was smearing some precum around the knob of the head when we pulled up to a small cabin in the woods, well off the main road.

Mr. Walker was breathing pretty hard when he came around to my side of the SUV, pulled me out with a strong hand on my wrist, and guided me to the door of the cabin. I was wondering if he had been fantasizing about me that past two years as much as I had been fantasizing about him. He certainly had made a point of knowing exactly when we could do anything about it.

He unlocked and pushed open the door to the cabin, but then he turned and looked hard into my eyes.

"Last chance, son. We can go back now if you're scared. I like to do this kind of special like. This probably won't be like anything you'd imagined it to be. Birthdays should be memorable, I think."

I just set my jaw and moved closer to the door. He got the message, and spoke again, in a softer voice.

"I can see you've kept up with the running as I suggested, Sport. But did you keep clean too? You do understand what I mean by that, don't you? No one before me? And don't you go lying to me about that. You'll still get what you came for, but it makes a difference whether someone's been there before. So, you've kept clean, right?"

"Yes," I answered faultingly, trying to keep my eyes connected with him. "I mean yes to both. I understand, and I've kept clean."

"Good," he said with a satisfied tone. "It's better, it feels better, if cleanliness can be assumed—if nothing has to get between skin and skin. And it means something to me to be the first." While I contemplated if I'd really understood what he meant, because there had been a hand job now and again, although I didn't really think they were what he meant, he put the palm of a hand in the small of my back and guided me to a door. He opened this, and we were descending stairs to a basement. The door at the bottom of the stairs was locked, but he unlocked this and pushed me into a small, square room. The walls, floor, and ceiling were a stark white, and in the very center of the room, prominently located, was a black leather sling suspended from overhead beams by strong chains. Half way up each chain was a black leather cuff, now open, padded on the inside.

I just stood and stared at this. Something inside me was stirring. This was beyond my fantasy, but I found that it was turning me on. I heard the door close behind me and the key turn in the lock, but I just couldn't take my eyes off that black leather sling. When, at last, I was able to do so, I turned and my eyes popped open.

Mr. Walker had taken off his shirt and jeans and stood before me, nearly naked. He was still wearing the black boots that came up above his bulging calf muscles, but, beyond that, all he was wearing was a black leather harness crisscrossing his chest, studded with silver studs, and studded black leather wrist bands and bands around his biceps. His horse-hung cock was at full staff, and he was wrapping a black leather, studded cock ring tightly around its base as I watched.

"Strip, Sport," he said in a throaty voice. I just stood there, mesmerized by the sight of him.

"I said strip, Sport," he said more insistently. "And climb into that sling. I told you this would be special. But it won't be any more of a cherry pluck than any other way we might have done it."

I then did as he directed, somewhat self-consciously pulling off my clothes and hunching over before him, trying to cover my manhood without any real means to do so.

"Stand up straight, Sport. Push it out. Ah, very nice. Very nice, indeed. It was well worth the wait. Now, into the sling."

Not knowing quite how to get into the sling, I walked over to it and turned around, and tried ineffectually to hoist my butt up into the contraption. Mr. Walker walked over and lifted me with strong hands at my waist, as if I were a rag doll, and plopped my ass into the sling. He then walked around to above me, and took, first one wrist, and then the other, and locked them in the black leather cuffs up the chain. He repeated this below, with my ankles, and there I was, spread-eagled helplessly in the sling. The bottom edge of the sling cut into my buttocks just where the small of my back flared out to my butt cheeks, and the upper edge hit between my shoulder blades.

Mr. Walker walked away from me and the lights went out in the room, to be replaced by colored lights, beamed from several positions, swirling about the walls, ceiling, and floor, in undulating waves of blue, green, red, and purple.

Mr. Walker was above me now, pushing my shoulders down and then taking my head in his hands and pushing that down as well. He had his enormous cock at my mouth, pushing at my lips from above, and then he was inside my mouth, and fucking my mouth in ever more insistent thrusts. I didn't have to do more than gag for him; I couldn't do more than gag for him, either, because I was completely trussed up and at his mercy. I wouldn't have known what to do anyway. But he told me what to do.

"Just relax, Sport," he said. "Open wide, unlock your jaw, and get your tongue below it and let it slide in easy. Ahh, yes, like that. Ahh, yes, a sweet mouth. Teeth out of the way, lips closed tight on it. Yes, that's better. Take it all, now. You can do it. Just loosen up and relax. There, just a bit more. Ahhhh, yesss. Feel the studs of the cock ring at your lips? That means you've taken it all. Now, letting it slide in and out. Yes, like that, in and out. Ahhhhh. Ah, AH, AHHH! Hot Damn!"

I started gagging again, as his cum burbled up in my mouth and overflowed on my chin. He pulled right out of me than, and his lips and tongue were at mine, cleaning me of his jism, and kissing me now.

He leaned his face into my ear and whispered to me. "That was nice, Sport. I think you're going to learn to give head real good. But I bet what you really want is your birthday present. I'm going to give that to you in about fifteen or twenty minutes. Gotta reload from that nice blow job. Won't take long to reload. Got some good advice for you on that. Eat healthy, live clean, stay fit, get plenty of sleep, and fuck often with a lot of variety and guys who are a real turn on, and you can keep your reload time down. Now, I'm gonna do you."

He walked away from me, and the next I saw he was below me between my spread-eagled legs. He held my balls in the palm of one hand like they were eggs he was about to crack, and he lowered his lips to my throbbing cock, licking it all over and then going down on it with his mouth. I almost lifted out of the sling in response to teething and sucking he was doing on my cock. The meeting of fantasy and reality were just too much for me, and I shot my load down his throat in short order. I was embarrassed that I'd come this quickly, but Mr. Walker seemed to be pleased. At least he gave me a big grin and then moved his lips and tongue to my asshole and wetted me up real well there. All the time he was sucking and rimming me, he was encouraging me to tell him what I liked and what I liked better, and, although words pretty much failed me, I think he got the answers he needed from the differing timbres of my moaning and groaning.

After a short while, he seemed ready to go again, because I saw him rise up below me and I felt the head of his cock at my asshole. It was just pressing at my asshole, with its head rocking back and forth, straining the rim, and I already felt I wouldn't be able to take him. My torso and limbs went rigid, and I arched my back against the sling.

"Relax there, Sport," he was saying. And then he left me for a minute, and when he came back, he had a black rubber plug with straps attached to it, which he plopped into my mouth, pushing my tongue down and filling my mouth, and he then pulled the straps around my head and tied them at the back.

"That isn't to keep you from screaming, Sport. You're going to want to do a lot of screaming, especially at the beginning. But we're way out here in the woods. There's nobody to hear your screaming. This is to keep you from biting your tongue off."

He went around to below me again, and with a sudden thrust of his hips, the head of his cock was inside my ass. I screamed in pain and went all rigid again. There was no sound, however, beyond a muffled grunt of pain, and I was biting down so hard on the rubber plug that I thought my teeth surely would bite through and meet.

"Not much else to do at the start, Sport," Mr. Walker was saying. "Your ass is new to this, and my cock is extra big. Trust me, it's going to be bad for a few minutes, but then it's going to get very, very good. And keep remembering that you wanted this. Ugh!" And with that his cock head and breached my virginal ring, and he held there.

"The worst is passed, now," he was saying. "The rest will be easier, especially if you'll relax and let all of the tension flow out of your body."

He placed his hands on my belly and worked them up to my pecs, massaging me, helping me to relax. They came back down and then glided up my outstretched legs.

"Breath deeply and regularly," he was saying. "And as I snake up you, take short, panting breaths. It will help. But however you breathe, remember to continue to do it. Don't hold your breath. This is your eighteenth birthday. I want to give you the fuck of your life."

I watched his strong, thickly veined hands, with those sensuous fingers, gliding across my body. One came back to my belly, palm down, and his finger spread out on my abs. I watched that hand, rising and falling as I breathed, and I relaxed as I could see my breath becoming more regular. And as I relaxed, his cock started its long, slow journey up my ass canal. My ass walls were welcoming it, the muscles moving in waves and closely caressing his pulsating rod.

"Nice, very nice," he was murmuring. "Your ass wants me, I can tell. It's making love to my cock. You're tight and sweet. Everything I'd imagined. There, can you feel them? The studs of my cock ring are at your asshole now. You've managed me; I'm all in."

And I could feel those studs, and it didn't hurt so much anymore. And I was exhilarated that he was all in me, fulfilling my fantasies. He'd told me it would be a lot easier and less painful the next time, and I believed him.

He lifted his hands and wrapped them around the chain and my bound ankles now and started the sling in motion. My ass was being stroked, but it was happening by the motion of the sling Mr. Walker was setting with his hands. The swinging of the sling increased, both in arc and in speed, and soon Mr. Walker's pelvis also was in motion, and he was fucking me in deep and long strokes. He was losing control of himself and giving me a wild ride, as I watched the motion of the studded leather harness across his chest. At length, he gave out a primeval scream, and I felt his cum jetting off deep inside me, and backing up along his buried cock and dribbling out of my asshole.

"Happy birthday, Sport," he exclaimed to me with a big grin, and then he helped me out of my bonds and the sling and supported me in his strong arms as we went back up the basement stairs to a small table in the kitchen. There he pulled food out of the refrigerator, and we both sat there, naked, at the kitchen table and ate like we hadn't seen food for a week.

After he'd had his fill, Mr. Walker winked at me, and said. "Think it's been twenty minutes again, Sport. I can feel the power coming back. And my birthday is coming up soon. Let's see if I can find a present too."

He pulled me up from the table by the wrists and marched me into a small bedroom that took up the other back corner of the house from the kitchen. He had leather thongs out and, after pushing me down on the bed on my belly, he tied my wrists together and strapped my arms to the rods at the center of the brass headboard and then tied my legs, from the ankles, to the opposite bed posts at the bottom of the bed. He then came up behind me and between my legs on his knees, and a felt that big, hard cock at my backdoor again. He lifted my pelvis with his hands on my hips and skewered me with his cock in one long gliding motion, having already stretched my ass to his specifications not more than an hour earlier. I gave him plenty of noise, while he rode me like a show bull. And rode me and rode me and rode me.

When he'd shot his load, he reached around and released my arms and legs and then went over on his side, pulling my butt into his pelvis. We cuddled and kissed and joyfully explored each other with our hands until he'd reloaded again and then he lifted my leg, nuzzled his pelvis under my butt, and took me in a side split one more time, this time more gently and languidly, as if we had all of the time in the world to meld to each other.

It was near dusk before we had finished fucking and had gotten cleaned up. Mr. Walker drove me back into town, leaving me off a couple of blocks up the street from my house and then just driving on by my house and into his driveway before I reached our section of the sidewalk. He was greeted at the door by his pert little wife, who kissed him, and I saw him give her a little pat on the butt as they turned and went into the house. I wondered if he would take her straight to their bedroom and feed that enormous cock into her just like he'd done with me, and a little jolt of jealously shot through me. I knew then that Mr. Walker wasn't a habit I'd be giving up anytime soon.

My family held a grand eighteenth-birthday party for me that evening, oblivious to the fact that I couldn't bear to sit on the hard dining room chairs for any length of time. My gifts from that significant birthday were memorable—my parents gave me the keys to a red Mustang convertible—but none was as memorable as the gift Mr. Walker had given me in that cabin in the woods.

Please, Daddy, Please

I knew he was the one I wanted as soon as he walked into the bar. Clean cut; maybe mid-to-late thirties; business suit; hiding behind sun glasses in the dimly lit bar; hesitant at the door; picking out a table back in the corner, one with a full sweep of the room. I moved a little to my right at the bar, under a light, well within his vision.

I called Chuck, the bartender, over, and we went into the routine he'd always been agreeable to. Chuck and me got along real good. He'd do me maybe once a week back in the bar's storage room and then he'd help me the rest of the week.

"No beer for you, kid. Whatcha' doin' in here, anyway?" Chuck asked me, raising his voice high enough for the mark to hear and knowing full well that I was of legal age. I looked over toward the corner with my peripheral vision to make sure he'd heard. If he hadn't, Chuck and me would have to do it again. But he'd heard. I saw him sit up in his chair, tensed.

"Geez. Am I gonna have to show ID till I'm thirty," I groused back. I pulled out my wallet and laid it on the counter. Flipped out my driver's license and put it under Chuck's nose.

"Those things is a dime a dozen, kid." Chuck puffed out his chin for effect. I brought my other hand up a bit, so's Chuck could move his attention there. I had a greenback clutched in my fist, enough showing for both Chuck and the mark to see.

"Well, OK," Chuck said, noticeably palming the money. "But don't plan on getting' drunk in here or causin' trouble. A beer and then move on, OK?"

The guy at the back table was trying to act like he wasn't looking, but I knew he was. And I knew I was well on my way to hooking him. Size and looks had always been my disadvantage in high school. But I was turning them to my benefit these days. My friends were out workin' the street corners, rain and all, havin' no more than a couple of minutes to size their marks up before gettin' into their cars. Thanks to my size and appearance, I could stay inside, in bars like this, pretending I might just not be legal, which really turned some guys on, and decide who was worth pursuing—and I made about twice the money on half the men that my friends out on the street did.

I hadn't grown much, if at all, since I was fifteen. The doctors had told my folks just to give it time. Now it could take all the time it wanted. My size and young

215

looks were keepin' me alive and ahead of debt. And it told me just exactly the kind of man to go after. Saved a lot of time and energy, and thus far I've picked well enough to avoid a lot of fuss as well. That's because I've picked guys like that one over in the corner. I knew what he wanted—what he really wanted. I could give him the next best thing. And whatever happened afterward, he couldn't squeal about it to the cops—not without getting himself into a lot more trouble than he got me.

"Hey, guy, you want a drink? The tables are for customers." Chuck was calling past me, over at the guy I'd marked. Chuck and me had this down pat. This type was a runner just as likely as a buyer.

"Umm, yes . . . please. A beer I guess. Whatever you have on tap." Kind of a wavering voice. I knew he was close to bolting. But he hadn't. Sometimes they left at this point. But if we got them this far and we were positioned this way, Chuck and I had worked out the closin' of the trap door.

"Comin' up," Chuck sang out. "And stay put. I'll deliver."

While we were workin' this out, Chuck had sometimes screwed it up by saying either I would bring the drink to the mark or just that it would be brought to him. As long as he didn't have to think about me, Tim, comin' to his table, comin' closer to him—temptation actually approaching—he'd stay put for the drink.

He panicked, as I knew he would, as I started walkin' toward him, both of our drinks in hand. But I did a little maneuvering around the tables, looking natural but putting me between him and the exit. So he stayed put at the table.

"Here ya' go," I said. "Don't mind if I sit, do you?"

Of course he didn't mind/of course he minded.

"Cause' it's just, just that you look sorta' like my dad—just not mean like him. Is it OK if I just sit a while?"

"Yes, yes, of course, sit," he replied. His breath was ragged. I could feel him torn between runnin' and movin' deeper into what he'd come here for—maybe, just maybe, taking a step across the fantasy/reality divide. And it was just talk. Nothing needed to actually happen.

"Hi, I'm Timmy," I said, giving him a smile and extending my hand out after I'd set the two beers down and sank into the chair next to him, where he'd turn away from the bar area to be talkin' to me. "But you could call me Tim, if you wanted to."

"Hi, Timmy," he said and then "My name is Joe . . . Joe Clifton." I knew that was a fake name, of course. But I hadn't missed the preference for "Timmy." That was a good sign.

"I don't usually come into places like this," I said.

"Neither do I," Joe quickly agreed.

"But I wasn't feelin' well, and when I get like this, I start thinkin' about my family—my dad and all—and I need a drink or somethin' to keep me solid."

"Not feeling well?" He was following along just like I wanted him to.

"No. I get these weak sessions. Can't move too well. The doctors tell me just to stay in my room then. But it's almost spot on the time last year that dad left me, and I couldn't just stay cooped up thinkin' about that and all."

"That's really too—" he said in a low, sympathetic voice.

"And then I saw you," I interrupted, workin' to keep him with me and not doin' too much thinking on his own. "And you reminded me of Dad. Sort of. The dad as I liked to think of him, and . . . oh . . . excuse me. I feel a little faint."

"You OK?" Joe asked, his voice full of concern. He'd laid his hand on my arm as I swayed just a bit, and I could feel the heat and tremble in his touch.

"Uhh, yes. Just a passing spell. Do you have family, Joe?"

"Yes, yes, I do," Joe said. And then I drew it out of him. His wife and two daughters and his son, Johnny. I heard the extra clutch in his voice when he talked about Johnny. I knew as much as he did what that really meant to him. I knew exactly what he was struggling with. Why he'd come here today. What he'd put himself up against the edge to try to satisfy. I was banking on bein' the scratch for that itch. Which I figured would be a service to him—and his son.

Then I told him about my family and how I worshiped my dad but that he'd turned away from me when he found I had this strange sickness. Didn't stick with me. I spun quite a story but left out the part about the nice suburban home and my mother's Escalade. A lot to swallow, of course, but these guys always believed just what they wanted to believe.

I'd gotten the beer down by the end of the story, and then I went back into the faint routine.

"Here, here, steady, Timmy," Joe said, now holding me up with both hands. "Maybe we should get something more to drink and eat into you."

"No, no," I answered. "Not here. The bartender said I was only welcome for one drink. Maybe you could just help me home. All I need do is lay down for a bit. It's not far."

"Of course," Joe said. Hooked.

"Home" wasn't really home, of course. It was just a room in a gay fleabag nearby that I rented by the half day on working days.

"Hot, so hot," I muttered when Joe had helped me to the bed and I laid down. Taking the hint, he stripped my T-shirt over my head. I knew my hairless, Twink torso turned him on. He was sitting on the bed beside me, and I could see his basket tent right up inside his tailored trousers.

I gave him that dreamy, "I'm ever so grateful" expression as I whispered, "Please, Daddy, Please. Don't leave me."

I drew his face down to mine, and despite the shocked expression on his face, he didn't resist me.

His kiss was warm and increasingly passionate. I opened two of the buttons on his shirt and ran my hand in and pinched at his nipples. He was sobbin' and groanin'. Making sounds like we should stop, but not being able to stop. I made sure of that.

Holding the kiss, I twisted down around him and off the bed and down on my knees between his thighs. His kiss became more possessive, more insistent as I unzipped his pants and pulled his half-engorged cock out.

Then we were no longer kissing, I was kissing and licking his cock. Sucking at the head of it. He was panting hard, his breath rasping. I didn't want him to catch his breath. I didn't want him backing away from this. As I sucked, I pulled his trousers and his briefs over his hips, him raisin' his butt off the bed at the right moment for that, and cleared them away. He was stripping off his suit jacket and tearing at his dress shirt. Within moments all he was wearin' was a tie and socks—and a big hard on.

He was in good shape, nicely muscled, a nice-sized cock. I was going to enjoy this.

When he was stripped down and trembling under my touch, I looked up into his face, and whispered, "Please, Daddy, please. I want your love."

Joe shuddered. "We can't . . . I didn't . . . we mustn't . . ."

I smiled, searched on the floor under the edge of the bedspread, and pulled out the condom packet I had hidden there, among others, earlier, and showed it to him. "Please, Daddy, please."

There was a deep rumbling in Joe's throat, and he sat immobilized, slipping irrevocably over into reality from fantasy as I stood and stripped off my pants, straddled him, and held his cock up and steady while I rolled the condom on it and then descended my ass on it. A growl started up from far down inside him as I slowly pumped up and down on his engorged cock, pulling him farther inside me with each descent.

Then he was freed, a wild man, a daddy in full control, taking his pleasure. He came up off the bed, carrying me with him, and stood in the center of the room, crouched slightly, bent at the knees, lapping me, his palms on my buttocks as I locked my fists behind his neck and he pounded me up and down on his cock, endlessly, until his lust was released deep inside me.

I wasn't at all surprised that he was crying out, "Johnny, Johnny, Johnny," as he fucked me in his primeval frenzy. I have no idea, though, if he realized what name he was calling out. If he did, he didn't let on.

Spent and starting to regain control of himself, he turned and gently laid me down on the bed. He was red-faced, nearly overtaken by embarrassment and remorse. I tugged on his arm, bringing him down onto the bed, and, following my guidance, he stretched out beside me. His face was buried in the hollow of my neck and he was sobbing. His body was trembling all over. I took his hand and guided it down to my pert cock and made him fist me. I put my hand over his and guided him in stroking my cock till he was doin' that with his own rhythm. Then I left him to it and moaned and sighed for him. I took his head in my hands and moved his lips to mine, and we kissed. When he melted to me there, I moved his lips down to my nipples and arched my back and moaned deeply for him—and ejaculated for him too. He shuddered then, as if the struggle inside him was over, as if all his secrets were stripped away.

"Please, Timmy. Please . . . I want you again," he murmured in a halting voice.

That's when I told him how worried I was—that I couldn't become involved. That I didn't want to be hurt. That I could barely make ends meet. That I planned to move on to another town where there might be work for me. A hint of him having taken advantage of me—in my weakness. Of how big and powerful his cock was. Of how I melted to havin' him inside me. But, no, that I didn't think I could risk it again. All of the time I was stroking his cock and moving my body against his.

"I have money," Joe croaked. "Lots of it. I'll take care of you. I won't abandon you like your father did."

"Shush, Daddy," I whispered. Then I pretended to realize for the first time that he had a finger at my hole again and was slow-fucking me with it.

"Oh, oh, OH!" I cried out and ground my ass against the palm of his hand. "Please, Daddy, Please. Fuck me again. Now!"

Joe lost control again and rolled me onto my stomach on the bed, pulled my belly up with the palm of his hand as he straddled my hips and crouched over my ass cheeks and thrust inside me. Fucking me hard now. Just as I wanted. And I moaned and groaned for my daddy.

Hours later, when he had left me, I looked over at the nightstand and saw several more twenties than I had imagined I would end up with. Quite satisfying. And a service, I told myself. Joe would be back. And as long as he—and the others like him—came back to me, I would be financially solvent and his Johnny would be safe.

Or so I told myself.

Ready4Daddy

I was just messing around on the computer, checking out the male-male dating Web sites, looking for something to turn me on.

On one of the sites I had gotten a view hit of my profile from someone named Ready4Daddy. Well, at sixty, I was definitely a daddy. I also was pretty randy.

I clicked on his profile. An immediate sense of nice looking, tall, slim, in his forties, good, angular features, elongated face. Looking casual and laid back in an Adidas sweat shirt. Good smile. That smile, though. Oh my god, I thought, I knew him. He was the singer in that band at the club I sometimes went to. Nice tenor voice. I had latched into his singing, because I was a tenor too—and I'd sung in a band in my younger days. And when I sat in his club and listened to him singing, I hoped that my voice had been as good then as his was now.

I had liked the look of him in the club. And here he was, saying he was looking for a daddy. But his profile was unlike most. He wasn't coy; he was straightforward. He liked to suck cock. And he declared he was an expert in it. But he posted that he didn't like being fucked. Not my concept at all about daddies. When I was being a daddy, I was fucking someone who liked being fucked by older men—usually holding him in a close embrace from behind and fucking him slow and deep, while he murmured how good daddy was being to him, which helped keep my cock hard. I didn't think of sucking cock in that way.

I felt my juices rise. I didn't get much sex anymore, but when I did—finding a young man on the street who I fancied and who claimed he fancied me—it was usually a furtive fuck behind a park building in the bushes, me holding him close from behind and fucking him slow and deep. I had this really nice, long, thick cock—it was really the best feature I had now. And, if I had a guy to fuck, I no longer went through all the preliminaries. I just turned him and bent him over and stroked him until he whimpered that he'd had enough.

But here was a guy who was proud of his blow jobs—who declared that he would and could suck off a daddy—deep throat and tongue and teeth him—so that he would be fully satisfied. He was proud of being a singer, but he boasted that his best instruments were his lips and teeth on a daddy's cock.

He had me dribbling precum here just in reading what he said he could and would be willing to do to me. It was all such a new and different way of looking at sex for me. And he was right here, in town, where I knew where to find him.

I didn't believe he could do what he claimed he could. But I was willing to let him try.

My hands trembled as I tapped out a message to him on the Web site. "You've seen a photo of what I have. I know where to find you. I don't believe you can make me warble as you claim. But if you want to try, tell me where and when."

Without hesitation, the response came back: "I know who you are too. I can make you hit a high A. Here at the club, now, if convenient."

He was still singing a set when I entered the club. The crowd was sparse, but the club wasn't deserted. All guys. It was that sort of club. And, although the music was great, not all of the guys were paying attention. There were booths lining the two side walls, with translucent screens between them and the central room where the band was set up on a low stage at the far end of the room. Some of the sounds coming from these shadowed booths were not in keeping with an attentive band music crowd. Some of them were moans speaking of other activities going on in the shadows.

Now that I was here, I wasn't as sure of myself as when I had impulsively sent Ready4Dad that message, and I hesitated, ready to turn and leave the club.

But he had seen me enter and he stopped singing and moved quickly to me and took my forearm in his hand. He was as tall and slim and willowy as his picture on the Web site had indicated. He certainly didn't look strong—certainly not as strong as I was, having been a serious body-builder all of my life—but that firm grip on my forearm held me there, in place.

"You want the blow job of your life?" he murmured to me. "I know you were a singer once—a tenor—when was the last time you hit a high A?"

"Almost never," I responded nervously. "Are you always this straightforward?"

"Yes, it saves time," He answered. And then he laughed. "Guys either want a blow job or they don't. Why should I beat around the bush? I love sucking cock. That's what gets me off."

"I am a second tenor. A high A was a real strain, even when I was well practiced."

"Well, when I go down on you, we will practice and practice and practice until you do hit that high A. I'm more interested in whether I can deep throat you. I saw that photo of your cock. Impressive. I'll cream myself if I can swallow it all."

I couldn't believe we were having this conversation. It was surreal. Standing here at the door of the club, in the main hall, with him just having a hand on my forearm, and he was telling me in straightforward terms what he claimed he could do to me with his mouth. I could feel something else straightening out, and, looking down, he could see it too. He smiled.

"Come with me," he said and he started to gently guide me with that hand on my forearm.

"Where?" I asked dumbly.

"I have my own booth," he said. "My own sucking booth."

As I meekly followed, trembling from head to toe at what was happening, he led me down the line of booths on the left side of the room, toward the back booth, which was around the corner of the band platform that extended out into the main room. Very private, very shadowy, the seat pulled back from the table farther than was the case with most of the booths.

We stopped and stood, him very close into me, beside the booth. He unbuttoned the middle button on my shirt and slid a hand in and found a nipple. Already erect. Already anticipating—but not knowing what it anticipated exactly.

I turned my face to his and he leaned down, being several inches taller than I was, and gently kissed me on the lips.

"Have you ever been sucked dry before," he whispered. "Ever gotten a really, really masterful blow job?"

"No," I squeaked. "It's almost always been straight to the butt fuck," I answered. There, I was being straightforward too—and using language I didn't normally use. It was all overwhelming to me.

He smiled and leaned in for another kiss, and I put my lips to his, expecting a repeat of the sweet-tasting kiss. But this time, he forced my lips open with his, and he was sucking my tongue into his mouth, far, far into his mouth. He had his teeth holding it close back near the root of my tongue and he was sucking hard on my tongue with his cheek muscles.

Flames of sensations were shooting through me—sensations I couldn't identified, but I was breathless and wobbly at the knees and moaning. He wouldn't release my tongue and was sucking hard on it. Applying pressure and releasing and then pressure again. I struggled with him, but he proved to be stronger than me, and held me there, in the tongue-sucking kiss, until I almost fainted from the lack of oxygen. And then he released my tongue and released the embrace he had me in with his arms and let me sink, gasping for breath onto the booth seat.

"Anyone do that for you before?" he asked with a little sly smile.

I shook my head, unable to speak.

"That's what I'm going to do to your cock. I'm going to suck everything out of it. I'm gonna leave you breathless."

I shuddered and whimpered from the thought of it. But my cock didn't seem to mind. It was at full staff now.

"Strip off your pants and briefs," he said as he scooted into the booth across the table from where I had collapsed.

"What? I don't . . ." I was trying to form the words, but my tongue had not recovered from the sucking and I was in somewhat of a daze.

"I said remain seated and get those pants and briefs off."

I unbuckled my pants and pulled down the zipper. He grabbed the material at about the knees and helped pull the pants off my legs as I raised my butt off the vinyl of the booth seat. Then I stripped off the briefs myself.

He gave me a grin and then his head went under the table.

He pushed my legs into a wider stance, using both of his hands and then I felt a hand fisting my cock at the root.

"Nice, very nice," I heard in muffled voice from below the rim of the table. "The photo doesn't do this justice. I'm going to enjoy this."

I lurched and gave a little cry and gripped the edge of the table as I felt the other hand pulling the foreskin off my uncut cock and moist lips come down over its bulb. I gasped as teeth gently closed down over the rim below the bulb and then again as I felt the tip of his tongue flicking at my piss slit.

I alternated from going rigid and collapsing into a puddle of Jell-O as he sucked just the head of my cock, holding it steady with his teeth, and fucked my piss slit with his tongue.

I begged him to stop, to take it slow, that this was sending me over the top—but he relentlessly carried on until it did, indeed, send me over the top and I ejaculated.

Ten minutes. It was all over in ten minutes. And although I certainly had had nothing like this done to me before, I had not hit a high A.

"Thank you. That was nice. That was . . ." I was mumbling to him, not wanting to disappoint him. And I was reaching under the table for my briefs.

"Hold still. This is not it," he said, giving instruction in a way that showed he was still in total control and that this wasn't a less than stellar performance at all. And, indeed, he still had his fist around the root of my cock, which was still half hard.

"I want you to move your legs onto the top of the table," he directed from underneath the table.

"You want me to what?"

But he was already lifting my legs up and folding them into my belly himself, and I got the idea and moved them up to the top of the table myself and spread them out. I certainly hoped there would be no waiter coming by this table for an order anytime soon.

He was holding my cock in his fist again and licking up and down on it, and then his tongue went down to my balls and he was licking them, cleaning them real well. His tongue went down to my perineum and licked down that to my hole as I rolled my hips up to him. And then he was back at the balls and, just like that, popped them into his mouth, one in each cheek.

And he began to hum. The vibrations on my balls from his humming drove me crazy. And my cock began to harden out once again and his fist started to pump up and down on my cock, bringing it back to full erection.

I gave a little cry and jerked as a thumb went to my dick head and started to rotate across the piss slit, which immediately began to produce precum again.

"Oh god . . . oh god . . . Oh GOD!" I warbled. And the pitches in the tone of my voice were rising. You could tell I was a tenor now. I was yipping on an F above middle C.

My legs were uncontrollably shuddering and I was scrabbling at the vinyl booth covering with my claws, finding rents in the plastic and digging down to grab onto springs between the padding.

My balls popped out of his mouth, and his lips were coming down over the head of my cock. And slowly descending on me. He would come down a few inches and then retreat and suck the bulb hard and then down a little further and retreat and suck the bulb hard and then down . . .

My hips were going in motion, and I was singing for him—a concerto in high G. Getting there. I'm sure the guys in the band and everyone else on the floor were enjoying my tenor aria.

A thumb was entering my hole and finding my prostate and rubbing and rubbing and rubbing.

"OH God! Oh Shit! Oh F-u-c-K!"

Faster and faster now his mouth worked on my cock, taking more in with each swallow. Still sucking the bulb hard on the exit.

A thumb rubbing my prostate, the fingers of the other hand stretching my balls away from my groin and squeezing, and the lips reaching my curly hair at the root of the cock and teeth closing on the very root of me. And me rocking up and down, eyes rolling in my head, ejaculating strongly for a second time, and . . . hitting and holding that high A.

I was collapsed in the booth, completely drained dry, and gasping when he came up from under the table. He stood up and folded his cock back into his pants—he'd obviously been jacking himself off as he sucked me dry—flashed me a "told you so" smile of victory, and turned and walked away.

He left me to recover and redress. He was singing in falsetto to the tune from the band as I struggled up out from the booth. Having no trouble with those high As himself. And with a broad, satisfied grin on his face.

I paused at the edge of the platform and slipped a fifty into the jar they had sitting out on a high wooden stool.

He winked at me and said, "Another music lesson next Thursday at five?"

I just gave him a sloppy grin—not sure I could wait until Thursday.

Docking

Doner Kebabed

I'd barely made it through a rough day in paradise. I had paperwork up to my eyeballs, and the ambassador was being a real bear toward the Country Team. He was being crushed in a vice between Washington, the Greeks, and the Turks over the latest failure of the Cypriot settlement talks to move just when the Greeks and Turks were both teasing us with the possibility—the false possibility, as usual—of inching ahead in the decades-long struggle. And the ambassador didn't like being put through the crusher—so he was deflecting his pain onto the members of his Country Team. Despite the real work we each had, he had peppered us all day with petty little memos designed to irritate us all as much as his superiors and the Greeks and Turks were irritating him. This was hardly the moment I wanted to think about what brand of sedan my office could next buy.

I hadn't planned out the evening I ultimately had, but I couldn't face going to what was waiting for me at home. Lena was off in the States on one of her periodic shopping trips—which I didn't begrudge her, because it was her dad who was paying for those and so much else we both enjoyed in life. I never slept alone, though, when I could avoid it, and so Marios, the actor I'd been working with in my cultural attaché capacity at the Theatro Ena, the Greek Cypriot national experimental theater housed inside one of the old gates to the ancient city fortress of Nicosia, had moved in temporarily the day Lena left.

But Marios was high strung—and quite opinionated himself on what the Americans should be doing in the current peace talks. After having had the ambassador chew on my butt all day, I was in no mood to go home and have Marios chew on my dick.

So, I avoided going home. I took up the paperwork I should have done today, putting the classified material in the vault adjacent to my office and the unclassified work in my briefcase in the hopes that it would solve its own problems overnight, and walked out to my BMW convertible, part of the reverse dowry Lena's father had given me to marry his flighty daughter and give her instant cachet in the diplomatic community. Neither Lena nor her father cared that I was bisexual; they both were more interested in how I looked in a tuxedo beside her in the newspaper society section snapshots—and, of course, my access to diplomat status and world travel at government expense. And the arrangement was quite agreeable for both

Lena and her father. She was happy with my cocksman skills with her—and her father had enjoyed taking me himself more than once since before we'd married.

I decided I'd eat dinner out and only go home later, when I was less on edge from the day and when Marios had drunk enough Cypriot brandy to be maudlin and I could use his cock for relief of my tension without being lashed by his sharp tongue as well.

But I didn't really want to go to a Greek tavern, either. They wouldn't be in full swing until 10 PM, and I'd been on TV today, in the background, as the ambassador was being subjected to a trying press conference. I found that on those days, when I then appeared in public, I was swamped by Greeks who bent my ear mercilessly about what the Americans should be doing for them and not doing for the Turks—thinking that I had something to do with the formulation of the policy since they saw me on TV. If I went to a taverna and dined virtually alone, I'd be a helpless target.

And so, I nosed the BMW toward the Ledra Palace checkpoint, the only border crossing in the city, which was divided by a UN-monitored green line no-man's zone. I'd catch a quick meal on the Turkish side and then slip back across the border and go home to face Marios. Marios was between plays at Theatro Ena, and I was ambivalent about that. When he wasn't working, he drank hard and could be a mean drunk; but when he was working, he worked hard and came away from the theater wrung out and not always capable of fucking the way I liked it. I tried to slip into the in-between when he was mean enough to fuck rough, which is what I liked from him, but sober enough to actually deliver it.

I had intended to drive on to Kyrenia, on the northern Mediterranean coast, as dinner by the harbor was always soothing, but the BMW was more practical—or thought it was—and parked, as if having a mind of its own, not more than a hundred yards beyond the Turkish checkpoint at the Ledra Palace crossing.

Mehmet's was one of Lena's favorite restaurants—and I enjoyed it too. That's where we went for our doner kebab, that national Turkish dish of shaved roasted lamb covered with yogurt and a marinara sauce and served atop freshly baked pita bread. I'd found out about Mehmet's from the son of the owner, who naturally enough was named Mehmet. The son, Jelal, was on the Turkish national tennis team, and I had played him in singles a couple of times in the diplomatic club league—and we were pretty even on wins and losses, which thrilled me because he was a good five years my junior and looked like he got a hell of a lot more exercise than I did.

The restaurant was directly on the Ininci Selem Caddesi, the road leading from the Turkish checkpoint around the western side of the fortress walls of Nicosia—called Lefkosa in the Turkish zone. As close to the road as the restaurant was, it still opened to the outside with large plate-glass windows, a rarity in an area where most restaurants were either inside ancient rock-walled caverns or in the open air. The glass expanse gave the restaurant's waiters notice that I was approaching.

Jelal waved me to a table as I entered and arrived there the same moment I did with a heaping plate of doner kebab. I didn't have to look at a menu; I never had to look at the menu at Mehmet's. If I was eating there, I was eating the doner kebab.

"And is madam meeting you here?" Jelal asked me as he set the plate down even before I had settled in my seat.

"No, just me this evening, Jelal," I answered. "Is that convenient for you?" The smile he gave me sent chills up my back and let me know that it, indeed, was convenient. We both knew what it meant when I dined here alone.

The proprietor, Mehmet, came from behind the cooking counter and took up a position beside the cash register and stared at me intently.

I brushed Jelal's crotch with the back of my hand as he walked by my chair, on the side where Mehmet couldn't see what I'd done, and I had my second chill. I could feel that he was hard.

Mehmet and his son weren't fully Turkish, which was not all that uncommon for Turkish Cypriots. Mehmet's family had roots in London, where they ran another Turkish restaurant, and each was the son of a Turkish Cypriot father and a British mother. In both, it made for an exotic mix, the British origin softening somewhat the rougher look and manners that were purely Turkish. Turkish men are often gorgeous in youth and ogres as they age—in both aspect and disposition. Mehmet wasn't an ogre, though, which held promise that Jelal wouldn't be either. Both were muscular men of tall stature, straight of spine and well-proportioned. Both had dark curly hair, but whereas Mehmet was hairy all over, Jelal was not. Both were olive skinned and handsome of face, though, and of dark, brooding, sultry looks that, in Jelal's case, were offset arrestingly by milky blue eyes. With Jelal, it was always the eyes that attention went to—at least at first. The rest of him was very nice to look at too.

His eyes reminded me of his British connection, which then reminded me of the single other characteristic that set him apart from all of the other Turkish men I knew. But even though that image was making me tingle all over, I did what I could to control myself in the restaurant this evening—there were a good number of customers at the other tables—mostly Turkish Cypriot, as this was one of the culinary treasures residents of Lefkosa tried to keep to themselves—and there also was Mehmet, standing by the cash register, taking it all in.

I ate my meal slowly, enjoying every morsel, pairing it off with half a bottle of Chankaya wine, while Jelal buzzed around my table like a bee, attentive to my every need—and Mehmet stood at his station and observed every pass by me that Jelal made. I could not have asked for better service, and I left a tip that was, in itself, four times the cost of the doner kebab and wine.

Jelal looked at the tip and gave me a smile that made me melt. I knew, of course, as soon as the BMW stopped and parked in front of the restaurant that I wouldn't be driving back into the Greek zone—indeed, I probably knew even before I crossed over into the Turkish zone.

Feeling full and satisfied and already beginning to sense the tension in me lessening, I climbed into the BMW, and rather than turn around and approach the Turkish checkpoint, I drove in the opposite direction, around the walls of the old city and then north, toward the Kyrenia mountains. Driving over the mountain pass and into the outskirts of the northern-coast castle harbor town of Kyrenia, I turned east and was almost immediately climbing back up the northern slope of the mountains to the old abbey village, now a den of artists and writers, of Bellapais. Here, with pretensions of being a writer myself, I had rented the villa once occupied by the British novelist, Lawrence Durrell, as my Turkish side residence. As American cultural attaché to both of the zones, I maintained a residence on each side.

In all, the drive up from the restaurant took just under an hour. I parked my car in the village square, near the Tree of Idleness restaurant that sat across the square from the ruins of medieval Bellapais Abbey, and walked up the steep cobble-stoned road—not more than a path, really, which is why I didn't drive the car up it. Some people did drive to their villas higher on the hill than mine was, but none of those people were driving new BMW convertibles—and they held a death wish against the high likelihood of meeting another car coming down the narrow, winding path.

The house was dark when I reached it, but I didn't turn on the lights. I lit an oil lamp in the great room and then candles in the bedroom and a few candles as well out on the stone terrace perched over a cliff and with a stunning view of the northern Cypriot Mediterranean Sea coast and of the harbor town of Kyrenia. I set the candles near the edge of the small pool, where the reflected light could dance on the water.

I then went to the bathroom and cleaned myself out well and took a shower. I padded out into the bedroom naked and took up a silken robe, wrapped it around myself, cinched up the sash, went to the refrigerator for a bottle of wine, and poured a glass. I went out onto the terrace and sat on the rock wall for a while, watching the lights of Kyrenia below. I knew I should go back into the great room and tuck into the paperwork I had there, but I just wasn't in the mood. Tomorrow was Saturday. I just wouldn't report to the office, so that the ambassador couldn't make new, silly demands on my time. I'd work on the paperwork here in the morning before returning in the afternoon.

Marios would be furious, but fuck him. I laughed, because when Marios was furious he also was horny—and when he was horny he was a forceful lover. My staying the night here would most probably work very nicely to my benefit tomorrow afternoon—assuming he hadn't started drinking early.

I knew it would be a long wait tonight, and when I had finished the wine and grown bored with watching the northern coastline at night, I went over to the chaise lounge beside the pool and stretched out on it on my back and dozed.

I didn't hear the opening of the front door or the footsteps across the great room and out onto the terrace. The first that I knew he was there was when he was crouched beside the chaise lounge and unknotting the sash around my waist and brushing the robe open.

His hands were gliding over my torso and I sighed, still only half awake, as he lowered his lips to my nipples.

"You seemed tense in the restaurant," he said. "Would you like to have a massage?"

"Yes, please. That would be very nice," I murmured. I sat up on the chaise and shrugged the robe off my shoulders, as he pulled it out from underneath me and told me to turn over. Then, using the oil from the bottle I kept beside the chaise he began to rub me down, giving me a professional quality massage. I felt tension flowing out of my muscles, and I knew that my instincts had been right—that this was the best place for me to be tonight.

I gave a little lurch and gasp as his tongue went to my asshole. He had been kneading my butt cheeks and rolling them and pulling them apart and blowing air at my opening, so it wasn't a great surprise that he went on to tonguing me there. Oil was dribbling down into the crease between my cheeks, and he stopped tonguing me and spent some time and effort in working oil inside the entrance to my channel. I mewed softly, knowing where this was leading.

At his command, I rolled over, and he began to massage my chest and arms and then my calves. His searching hands massaged up my thighs and he started to oil my cock and balls, and my cock hardened for him. I moaned softly.

Opening my eyes, I saw Jelal standing at the foot of the chaise. He was naked and fully aroused. His powerful body was beautiful, and I already was aching for him.

I turned my head and said, "Please, Mehmet. Will you disrobe for me as well. I want to see you both."

Mehmet moved away from me and stood by his son as he slowly stripped off his clothes. The two, father and son, couldn't be both more the same and more different. The same beautiful, heavily muscled and well-worked bodies. The difference was in the slimness and smoothness of skin of Jelal contrasted with the Zeus-like build and silky hairiness of Mehmet.

In one other, strategic, manner they were the same—and for my purposes, this was the most arousing feature of all.

They were both uncut. That was almost unheard of in any Turkish area. Turkish men are almost always circumcised; there's even a traditional coming-of-age ceremony for that in the Turkish world involving a pubescent boy, a white horse, a parade through the street, and a cleric's sharp blade. But Mehmet and Jelal had been born in England to a British mother, and circumcision isn't a custom there. And those mothers apparently had had stronger influence in the raising of their sons than had their fathers.

Circumcision was a Hellenic custom, but I preferred my men not to be cut because of two fetishes I had, and, as much pleasure as I got out of normal Greek and Turkish men, only Jelal and Mehmet had been able to fully satisfy me since I had been posted to Cyprus.

"Would you like Jelal first?" Mehmet asked.

"Yes, please," I answered "You know what I want first."

Mehmet walked over and held out his hand and helped me up from the chaise lounge, and we walked, arm in arm and arm, making little darting grabs at erect cocks and slaps on bare butts as we went into my candlelit bedroom.

I stretched out in the middle of the bed, and Jelal lay beside me on one side and Mehmet sat beside my waist on the other. I put my left arm behind Jelal's neck and shoulders and he put his right arm under the armpit of that arm and stretched it behind my neck and fisted the wrist of my right arm, drawing my arm over my head. He was strong enough that he now had an arm hold on me that would keep my arms immobile. He moved his hip over my thigh, which spread my legs and, with his torso tilted toward me, brought our erect cocks together.

Jelal held our cocks together in one bundle and slowly stroked them. I moaned quietly and trembled, knowing what was coming, knowing that it was one of my favorite fetishes.

Mehmet was tonguing my nipples and moved his lips and tongue up into my exposed armpit. He had a hand on my balls and was rolling and pulling on them. He moved his mouth up to mine and was kissing me deeply when I shuddered at what Jelal was then doing—what unnerved and aroused me so, the main reason I paid these two four times what their doner kebabs sold for when I visited their restaurant alone—which was the signal that they were to visit me here that night in Bellapais.

Jelal was raised higher over my pelvis now and was docking our cocks—placing the bulbs of our dicks together, piss slit to piss slit and pulling his generous, uncut foreskin over my bulb until it was fully covered and our cocks were one unit. Holding the docked cocks together in his fist, Jelal started stroking them together, while friction rubbed our two glans together inside Jelal's stretched foreskin, my hips undulated at their own volition, and I gasped and sighed and moaned. Jelal brought his face close to mine, and he and his father took turns possessing my mouth with their lips and searching tongues, and Mehmet stroked my oil-slicked torso and thighs with his free hand.

I murmured my love of what they were doing, as Jelal continued the stroking. I knew that he would not stop until I, at least, had come, and I luxuriated in the feel of being connected—docked—so intimately with him.

I did come—and so did Jelal—with our semen mixing and bloating his loose cock skin until it burbled out onto my pubic hair.

Then Mehmet laughed and drew away from me and rose off the bed. As Jelal was still holding me tight, Mehmet moved around to the foot the bed and grabbed my ankles and pulled me down to him, with Jelal releasing me and straddling my chest and rubbing my cheeks and neck with his cum-slathered cock.

Mehmet asked formally, "Me now? Do you want me now? May I fuck you, sir?"

"Yes, oh yes," I answered, no longer a bit worried about the world of diplomacy and whether the ambassador would still be in a snit tomorrow or not. All tension and cares drained from me. "And after you, Jelal again, please. Fucking me, in one of his special positions."

I loved Jelal's flexible and athletic positions—but what was coming next was the other fetish that had me coming back again and again for the special doner kebabs at Mehmet's restaurant.

Mehmet, much thicker than Jelal—much thicker than almost any man I knew, was working his cock inside my channel. I gasped and grunted at the effort, a sound that Jelal cut off by offering his cock for sucking.

And then it was happening, and I was going straight to heaven by the feel of the loose foreskin of a hard-as-steel working inside my channel, the movement of uncut skin working the walls of my channel, a sensation like no other in the world.

Dom/Sub

Marine's Choice

Mitch was a lot older than the rest of us in the college program. He was an ex-Marine. Back from a second tour in Iraq, catching up with his life. He would be a natural leader among the students even if his playing skills didn't shine brightly above the rest of ours in all of the intramural sports we played to let off steam. Even in choosing sides and getting anything going, we'd all hem and haw and throw out suggestions, until, at some point, in a few, not-to-be-questioned, barked-out words, Mitch would tell us what we'd do. And we'd do it.

Even though he was graying at the temples now, which was barely discernible with that buzz cut he maintained, and had some tested-by-life lines in his handsome, square-cut face, he was still every inch the in-control Marine. When I'd go down to the basement of the intramural gym to swim my laps early in the morning before classes started, he'd be there in the weight room, stripped down to gym shorts, lifting weights and doing push-ups and pull-ups a couple of hundred reps at a time. Not an ounce of flab on him, all steel and muscle, with his veins popping out on his arms and legs and along his torso because there wasn't any fat for them to run through under the skin.

Other than the gym and the class and the pickup sports games out on the basketball and tennis courts and intramural football field in the afternoons, he didn't really fraternize with the college students much at all. He was a man of few words and of hard, serious stares that made you feel compelled to pay attention to him, to make him approve of what you were saying and doing. He never talked about what he'd done in life, what he'd done in combat or what combat had done to him, but his bearing and the intensity he approached everything with, whether it was classroom work, the pickup games, or those solitary morning gym workouts, made you want to accept whatever he said as basic truth the rare times he said anything.

He had the exact same effect on our professors that he had on the students. If there was a discussion or argument going on in class, all Mitch had to do was to start a sentence, and by the end of just one sentence, the discussion had been decided and the room was quiet.

He really was reclusive and totally apart from the other students, something that went way beyond the difference in our ages, life experiences, and his manner of being above any argument or discussion rather in it, of being the last, authoritative word. He didn't live in the dorms with the other students; he had a small house out on the edge of the college town. At one time it probably had been the gatehouse of some estate, although the bigger house was no longer there.

That's where he held his study sessions with a select set of students.

The study sessions became somewhat of a mystery that students whispered about but never reached any conclusion on about exactly they were and how much of a help they were in passing tests and completing winning papers. No one even could—or would—say for sure who was in the study group, or had been at one time. The only common denominator in the names tossed out were that you had to be a serious student, not into the party scene, good looking—and male.

Mitch did spend a fair amount of time studying at the library in the late evening. That's where I'd see him the most. We shared a few classes; we'd been in a couple of afternoon pickup basketball games, where he'd chosen me for the skins side and we'd shared wins; and I'd occasionally see him standing at the weight room door, panting in shallow, controlled breaths between his marathon one-armed push-up sessions, watching me come out of the gym pool some mornings. But it was really seeing him at a nearby table at the library that caught my attention the most—probably because in the most recent weeks it seemed like he wasn't really studying much there at the library; he seemed more sitting there and watching me study.

It should have made me uncomfortable, I suppose. But it didn't. I found it flattering. Mitch was taking an interest in me. Mitch, the natural leader, the one with all of the answers, all of the experience. Mitch, who already had met life head on and who had his own house and camouflage-painted Hummer H2 that made all the heads snap whenever it floated across campus. Mitch, the man of the world, who even the professors listened to and obeyed.

Chuck Albert stopped me on the quad one day. He pulled away from a group of guys he was joking with as I passed by and said he wanted to tell me something in private. Chuck, the college team's quarterback, a guy I wouldn't have thought even knew I existed. Quiet Chuck, the guy who aced all of his tests, had a solid-gold passing arm, and who I assumed could pop the cherry of any coed on campus just with one of his sultry gazes.

"Big test coming up in calculus," he said to me when we had withdrawn to the verge of the quad's tree line.

"Yeah," I said. "I've already started studying."

"But you'd like help and would be willing to contribute, wouldn't you?" Chuck asked. He was looking at me with a hard stare. He seemed a little more serious than the test was worth.

"Yeah, I guess so. I usually study alone, but . . . it's a big test, and—"

"Mitch wants me to invite you to his study group. Seven next Tuesday, at his place. You know where it is?"

"Mitch's group?" I was practically speechless. The mystery group. Something like a golden ticket. Of course I couldn't say no. Especially to Chuck. "Um, yes. Yeah, sure. I'm sure I can make it. Out at the end of Pine, right?"

"Right. Seven on Tuesday. I can tell him you'll be there, then?"

"Yeah. Yes, I'll be there."

Chuck gave me a hard look and then he turned and was gone.

Tuesday night, almost exactly at seven, I pulled into the asphalted area at the side of Mitch's cottage. The house was right off the road, but there was such a thick fringe of trees and bushes between it and the road that you'd never know a house even was there if you didn't know it was there and if you didn't see the mailbox at the edge of the drive.

Mitch's Hummer was there and just one other car, a BMW convertible I thought belonged to Bud Howard. That figured. Bud was one of our math brains in addition to being a star basketball player. No other cars, though. I looked at my watch. No, I wasn't early. I would have thought that anyone invited to be in Mitch's study group would be prompt. I'd think they would know that much about Marines. Well, maybe I'd rack up points with him for being on time.

The front door was ajar when I got to it and there was a note taped to the knocker to come on back to the back of the house, so I didn't knock or ring the bell. I entered directly into the living room, which was sparsely furnished, but all of the furniture looked like it was good quality. And the place was neat as a pin. Another Marine trait, I assumed. The living room was only dimly lit, but a hallway running off it toward the back of the cottage was brightly lit, so I just moved on back. I could hear the murmuring of voices from somewhere in the back of the house.

A door was open as far back down the hallway I could go, and a light was on in that room, so that's where I headed.

And I stopped dead in my tracks, in shock, as soon as I walked through the door.

I was in a sparsely furnished bedroom. A double bed against the wall to my left. A straight chair immediately to my left beside the door, with a wooden bureau beyond that.

And directly in front of me, in front of a draped window, under a pole light, the only light in the room, in a straight chair set at a three-quarters angle to me—Bud and Mitch.

Bud was the first one I identified, because Mitch was behind and below him in the chair. Both were nude. Tall, lithe, almost gangling, sandy-haired, ruddy skinned Bud, sitting on Mitch's lap, facing me, his long, thin legs hooked over Mitch's muscular, widespread legs. The balls of Bud's feet planted on the carpet, giving him leverage for his rising and falling hips. Bud's chest was arched out, and Mitch's arms were wrapped around him, his hands palmed on Bud's pecs, Mitch's thumbs and forefingers playing Bud's nipples.

Bud's face had a mixed expression of pain and ecstasy and wonder and panic all at once. Bud was the one who I heard murmuring. He was panting and moaning and making little gurgling sounds. He was the one doing most of the moving as he rose and fell on Mitch's thick cock. On the rise I could see a good three inches of condom-sheathed cock appear above the short, curly pubic hairs at Mitch's crotch. And then the three inches would slowly disappear as Bud descended on it. Bud was also doing most of the huffing and puffing. Mitch was more or less just sitting under him, solid as a rock. Muscles taut, bulging. A slight smile on his face—slight, but more expression than I usually saw from him. The only movement from him those thumbs and forefingers rolling Bud's nipples and a slight undulation of his pelvis as he rolled, almost imperceptibly, in countermovement to Bud's rising and falling, moving back as Bud rose, and forward to meet Bud's downward thrusts.

When he noticed me standing, dumbstruck, unable to move from the doorway, to retreat from the shocking sight, Bud looked surprised and more than a little embarrassed. But he just kept on pumping, his eyes searching mine, seeking understanding and acceptance.

"Sit in the chair." It was Mitch's voice, clearly Mitch's voice, although it had a guttural edge to it. The voice of the Mitch who was to be obeyed.

I stumbled to my left and fell more than sat in the chair.

"Faster." The voice again. I was confused. Faster what? But then I saw that the command wasn't for me. Bud dutifully picked up the rhythm of his rising and falling. Bud was moaning louder now, his eyes still on me, but I couldn't hold the gaze. I was watching that three inches of hard, thick, condom-crowned cock disappearing and reappearing. I'd never seen anything like this before. Shock, dismay, interest, arousal.

"Unzip." I sat there, hearing him but not comprehending him.

"Unzip your pants. Pull it out." The voice was for me. I realized that now. No, I certainly wouldn't do anything like that. I would stand up right now and leave the house. Never speak to either one of them again. Transfer. Put this all behind me.

All the time I was thinking that, I was unzipping my pants and fishing my cock out. It was half hard already. Gawd, why was that? I couldn't find this arousing. Could I? I'd never . . .

"Thought so. Stroke it." The voice that was to be obeyed.

"Rotate." The commanding voice again. But this time for Bud. Bud moved his hands back to cup the back of Mitch's head and, leveraging off the balls of his feet, began to rotate his hips back and forth and in a circular motion. Mitch moved his hands to Bud's small waist and helped control the movement. Moans in harmony now, Bud's tenor and Mitch's bass. Bud's louder than Mitch's, but Mitch was softly grunting and groaning now too. And I could see his muscles straining and the veins popping out on his ropy forearms.

My cock was hard already, rising to my involuntary stroking. I moved my other hand up under the hem of my T-shirt and up to a nipple. Three-part harmony in the moaning now. Bud's tenor, Mitch's bass, my baritone.

"Up on your feet." Who was that for? Must be Bud, although he didn't seem to fully comprehend.

"Up on your feet. Now!" Mitch brought Bud up out of his lap with the grip he had on the basketball player's waist. Bud stood, but still crouched over Mitch's lap. I saw a good five inches of the condomed cock now, but the head was still embedded in Bud's ass.

Mitch's pelvis came up off the chair and he thrust up into Bud's ass, again and again and again. Six, seven inches sliding out and then disappearing in a quick upward jab. Bud lurching and twisting and gasping and yelping. Muscles rolling, bulging, straining. Both straining and breathing heavily.

Bud's legs were trembling uncontrollably and his knees gave way and he fell back into Mitch's lap, fully impaled. Mitch snaked a hand around and fisted Bud's engorged cock in a steel grip and started pumping, slowly but relentlessly. Bud was trembling and writhing under his grip. Mitch had his lips buried in Bud's neck. Loud oohs and ahhs and gruntings and groanings now. All tenor, all Bud.

Bud cried out in a shooting of cum and collapsed like a rag doll in Mitch's lap. Mitch's pelvis was still slowly churning. He wasn't finished, although Bud certainly was.

Bud raised his head and searched out my eyes with his. He had a languid, well-taken expression on his face. I don't know why, but I somehow knew this had been his first taking and that he was lost to the Marine now. Whatever Mitch, still churning inside him, wanted, he would do. And there was another look in his eyes. A message for me. A "you're next" warning.

I gathered strength and fled the room and the house.

Another week and nothing. I spoke to neither Mitch nor Bud, nor Chuck, for that matter, during that time. I went to a college basketball game on the Friday following that Tuesday and Bud was there and was the star of the game. He was all smiles and fluid movement and jazzed-up energy. So, no crushing experience for him there then.

After a week, I stopped trying to avoid seeing any of the three and started looking for them. In the meantime, I found I was jacking myself off at every opportunity. I was embarrassed and ashamed, but that didn't stop me from doing it and from thinking about what I'd seen in Mitch's house.

A week and two days later, there he was. I was studying in the library and looked up, almost in expectation, and there Mitch was, at the next table, a book open in front of him, but his eyes glued to me. Trembling, I pulled my books together and stumbled out of the library.

The next night I returned to the same table in the library. He already was there, sitting sideways to the table, his muscular legs spread. He knew I'd come back. It was the last thing I planned to do, but here I was. I opened my books, but my eyes were on him. His eyes were on me. He moved one of those strong, sensuous hands to his crotch and let it just sit there, cupping his power through the material of his jeans. I couldn't take my eyes from him.

A slight imperceptible smile, and then he uncoiled from the chair in one fluid, graceful moment. As he passed my table, he leaned down and whispered in my ear, "Tomorrow, six thirty, my place."

"Nooo," I moaned softly back to him. But he already was gone.

* * * *

"Strip and lay on your back on the bed." The voice to be obeyed.

When I was laying back on the sheeted mattress, Mitch stood at the foot of the bed and slowly stripped himself. He was just as strong and powerful all over as I knew he'd be. Thick and long, ball sacs full and hanging low. Every muscle fully developed and taunt and bulgy. Every muscle.

"Stroke yourself." I wrapped my hand around my half-hard cock and started doing what I'd done at least daily ever since I last was in this bedroom.

He was standing over me, stroking his own cock. Within moments we were both hard. he leaned over me and wrapped his hands around the underside of my thighs and pulled my butt to the foot of the bed.

"Sit up. Suck me." I sat up, my face right at the level of his hard on. But I was at a loss of what to do now. I'd never done this before. I had no intention of doing anything here. I shouldn't be here at all. I wasn't staying here. I, in fact, wasn't here. This was all fantasy. I was in the library studying.

"Kiss it." He touched his bulging dick head to my lips. Moist, salty taste. And then I was gagging slightly and having trouble breathing, as his moist bulb pushed my lips open and he was inside me, moving it from cheek to cheek, sliding back over tongue. My eyes were tearing and I tried to move my head back, off the invading tool. But strong hands fisted my hair at the back of my head and held me to him. Held there for several moments and then I felt my lips sliding along veiny, smooth skin of thick, warm cylinder, and my jaw was aching to open wide enough and my throat was clogging. I wrapped my hands around his hard, bulging thighs and started to go with the rhythm he was setting.

I heard sighing, in that bass voice. I was pleasing the Marine. Mitch was pleased.

"Lay back." It seemed to have been an eternity that I had that thick cock inside my mouth, but it surely was only moments. As he drew it out, I closed my lips tightly over the rim of the glans and gave a little extra suck, flicking the piss slit with the tip of my tongue. I felt Mitch shudder. Good. At least I had retained that much control.

Mitch moved away from the bed. When he returned, he had a big black dildo in his hand and a tube of lube. He extracted a big glob of lube and then tossed the tube to me.

"Lube your ass."

"Nooo." I don't know if my whimper was audible to him, but he got the hint of rebellion.

"Do it, Now! You'll be glad later you did."

Back in full control. Any sign of resistance evaporated. While I worked the cool lubricant into my tight, virginal ass, Mitch lubed up the dildo. He was going to fuck me with the dildo!

But, no he wasn't. He handed it to me.

"Fuck yourself with this. Slowly, shallow at first. But you'll want to open to a good eight inches of it. You'll want to be stretched."

This was the most painful part of all. I slowly worked myself with the dildo, as Mitch stood between my spread legs, stroking his cock and pulling on his ball sacs.

"Stroke yourself. It will help." My fist went back to my hard cock.

Mitch disappeared from my vision.

"Come over here and sit on it."

He was in the chair I'd seen him in the previous time I'd been here. The only light on in the room was the pole lamp, its beam of light trained on the chair. Mitch was rolling a condom on his huge cock.

I cried out in first taking, in pain, and wonder, and awe, and arousal, and ecstasy, as my ass channel descended on his possessing cock, my channel stretching as best it could, caressing his cock, feeling every veiny contour of it as it moved up inside me. I was faced away from him, my legs spread wide on either side of his thighs, the balls of my feet dug into the carpet, ready to leverage my rise and fall on his impaling cock. I arched my back and Mitch reached around me with his sinewy arms and covered my pecs with his palms; his thumbs and forefingers went to my

242

nipples, and I grunted and sighed as he started to pinch and roll them. I could feel his hot breath between my shoulder blades.

"Fuck yourself. Up and down on my shaft." The voice that must be obeyed, thick now with lust.

Leveraging off the balls of my feet, I began to rise and fall on his cock. All of my senses going to that thick rod running up inside me, electrifying my walls, stuffing me, fully possessing me to the quick. Up, down. Groan, moan, sigh. Up, down.

I sensed more than heard the other presence in the room. Then the heavy release of breath that wasn't mine or the Marine's. A slight gurgling noise.

"Sit in the chair." Mitch's voice. But not speaking to me.

I looked up in time to see a dark, chocolate brown, trim figure collapse into the chair by the door. The shocked look on his face. I'd seen him before. Tennis team, I think, and in a couple of my classes. Smart. Achingly handsome. Confused now, torn.

I sought his eyes out with mine. Not a warning. Warnings already useless. A sense of sharing, of inevitability. "You're next," my eyes said.

"Faster." I picked up speed in the rising and falling. Overwhelming ecstasy. Taking it deeper. Moaning.

"Unzip yourself. Pull it out." Familiar, but not meant for me.

Gasping at the depth and stretching of it. Pinching of nipples overwhelming. Up, up, and away. A feel of a sudden twitching and further engorging of the hot poker inside me, constriction of Mitch's thigh muscles under me.

"Ah, I thought so. Stroke it . . ."

Beyond the Beaded Curtain

Fuck Julia, I was screaming in my head, as I pulled on my jeans and a dress shirt and my leather vest, slammed through the apartment door, and stabbed at the buttons on the elevator door.

She didn't feel satisfied. SHE didn't feel satisfied. Well, what about me? She didn't satisfy me either. Maybe I could satisfy her better if I ever was made to feel satisfied.

Well, fuck Julia, I muttered as I slammed my fists against the metal elevator walls while it descended twenty stories to the street level below. I'd told her I needed smokes and dressed and headed for the door before she could go into that litany of how Jim had fucked her so much better than I did. Well, fuck Jim too for that matter.

I hit the streets. It was drizzling rain and I knew I couldn't just walk it off. I didn't really need smokes, but I sure could use a drink. There was an open bar up ahead, Big John's. I'd never been in there, but it was beginning to rain harder now, and I couldn't go back to the apartment—not just yet. Anything but facing Julie's mocking eyes right now.

I pushed the door open and entered the smoke-filled room. A rock band with a sound much too big for the size of the room was doing its thing over in the corner. The first thing I realized, though, was that there was nothing but men in the room. Not a woman in sight. Well, that wasn't all that bad. If I looked into the eyes of any woman just now, I'd probably only see Julia's mocking eyes staring back at me.

A skinheaded guy who appeared to have far more muscles than brains motioned me to a seat next to him at a table. He was wearing a big smile, but I just smiled weakly back at him and moved slowly toward the bar at the far side of the room. I passed men dancing with men. I surprised myself by not being the least bit turned off by this; in fact, I felt a little thrill, like I was going on an adventure—like I was detached from my body and somehow sparring with Julia across the divide between this danger-filled smoky room and the sterile environment of Julia's apartment up in the clouds not more than two blocks away. This was a whole new world to me. Maybe I'd check out this world a little more closely.

I leaned up against the bar and ordered a beer and then turned and watched the rock band and what was going on around me for a while. This was obviously a pick-up joint at the height of its evening activity. Connections, some of a blatantly intimate sort, were taking place all over the room. For some reason I found this exciting, even sexually arousing, in a way that I didn't find Julia arousing. It didn't take long for me to realize that some of the men were starting to buzz around me as well, sensing a new player in the room. I started to become a little embarrassed. I wasn't really planning on being a player; I was just playing on the edge of this world, observing it, considering the "what ifs." And I hadn't the foggiest notion of how to play here even if I had intended to do that.

I ordered another beer. I momentarily wondered how long I could stay away from Julia's apartment on the pretense of buying a pack of cigarettes, when it hit me that I didn't really care. Fuck Julia. I downed my beer and ordered another.

I had waved off several guys in obvious search of a pickup when the mystery man appeared at my elbow. As time went on, the Rock band was getting louder, the beat getting heavier. I knew I was drinking too much; the beat of the music was beginning to transfer into my head as a headache.

Tall and dark, with curly hair cascading around his head, he moved into the empty stool beside me I had been protecting to keep some distance between me and the circling crowd. His eyes seemed to be violet. He had a mustache that met his sideburns and a sensuous mouth with an engaging, ready smile. There was a small scar running down his chin that made him seem a little dangerous and kept that question in my mind of what the story was there.

He trapped me with his eyes, and I couldn't lie when he asked if I was alone and if I'd let him buy me a drink. We didn't really say anything to each other, but, although there were loud conversations and music and the smoke of cigarettes all around us, I felt that we were the only ones there. I could hear my heart beating, and I thought I could hear his as well, moving to match the rhythm of mine, matched the rhythm of the band music. It wasn't long before he had his arm around my shoulders in a possessive manner, and on my fourth drink and his second, his arm had drifted down and he was cupping my buttocks with his broad hand. I let it stay there. I was feeling dangerous and exhilarated and aroused all at once, something I hadn't felt with Julia an hour earlier. Above all, I was feeling wanted and desired. I'd play the game for a while longer and then leave and get those smokes and see if I could transfer these feelings into another go at Julia.

All the time he was holding my eyes with his. He set his drink down, fished the cherry out and put it up to his lips. I watched him slowly draw the cherry in, move it around his mouth, and produce the pit in between his lips with that smile of his. He obviously wanted me to do something, so I reached over and went to take the pit out of his mouth, whereupon he captured my thumb with his lips and drew it into his mouth.

At the same time, I felt his hand on my thigh. He held my thumb while his hand moved to my crotch, and he felt the full engorging length of me with his hand. I could feel his intake of breath, clearly pleased at what he had discovered. I was pleased that he was pleased. I sensed the growing danger here, though. Just how close to the edge was I here? And on which side of the edge. It was about time to put an end to this pleasant little fantasy I'd entered and return to my world.

He released my thumb and gave me a broad smile. I rotated my hips, in a half-hearted attempt to get free of his grasp. He was moving too fast, but I wasn't sure I minded. All I could think of was punishing Julia for those mocking eyes of hers. She didn't want me? Well, here was someone who was showing he wanted me—even if he was from another world altogether.

His hand traveled with me as I rotated my hips, intending to shake his grip off. Misjudging my intentions, he grasped my cock through the fabric of my pants and his other hand squeezed my butt cheek, holding my hips in place. It was obvious where he was going with this. I relaxed, giving up, bordering on the intoxicated, whether by the drink or the promise of some form of satisfactory sex as a punishment for Julia's mocking eyes.

He pulled away from the bar and led me around the bar by an elbow. I was drawn through a beaded curtain into a alcove with dark velvet walls. We were just a beaded curtain away from the raucous, revolving crowd and the steady beat of the music, but were fully private in our own world in that dark alcove.

He pushed my back to the wall just beyond the beaded curtain and leaned his hips into mine. I could feel the strength and urgency of him. He held me with his eyes again, as his face came to mine. He pressed his lips onto mine, opening me to his urgency and his surprisingly sweet kiss. His mustache tickled my nose. It was time for me to put a stop to this brief fantasy—to stay on my side of this divide. But, although my mind was screaming "break and escape," my legs felt like lead, glued to the spot.

I sensed that it was too late, that I no longer could pull back, and decided to go with the flow, to see and sense what this world looked like, if only for a brief time. I could always go back to my world. I'd probably be better with Julia when I'd seen and been able to reject this world.

His hands were working on the buttons of my vest and shirt, which he pulled off my body and dropped beside us. He quickly pulled off his T-shirt, and we were bare chest to bare chest. I ran my hands up his sides and onto his pecs. He was in magnificent shape, obviously a bodybuilder, and was covered with dark curly hair. I pushed through his curly chest hair and found his nipples, both pierced with rings. I let a hand follow hair down his washboard abs, finding another ring in his navel-- curly hair everywhere. I wondered if it continued on down. But I wasn't in a hurry. This would be my one fantasy encounter. I might as well make the most of it.

He was in a hurry, however. This was all moving just too fast for me, but I couldn't have stopped it now if I'd tried. He had me trapped with those violet eyes. He had one hand on my crotch again, and with the other one, he was unbuckling my belt, pulling down my zipper, pushing my pants and briefs over my hips and encasing my stiffening cock. He quickly had his own cock out, and he held them against each other; mine was being measured with his. Mine was a good size, but neither as long nor as thick as his was. He encased both of our cocks in his hand, mine lying atop his. I sighed, letting my hand travel on down below his navel, through curly hair and sliding across the underside of his cock and finding his heavy, hairy balls. He reacted with pleasure, intensifying the sucking motion of his kiss, his exploration of my mouth with his searching tongue. I could have continued at this stage for some minutes, maybe even have left the whole encounter here, but he obviously couldn't.

I gasped as he disengaged from our kiss and quickly worked his lips and his tickling mustache down my neck, over my pecs, down my abs and belly, through my pubic hair, and to my cock, which he took into his mouth and started to work back and forth in a frenzied manner.

I grabbed his head, burying my fingers in his hair, in an involuntary maneuver to stem this full assault on my body. He roughly grabbed my hips with his hands to hold me steady, and when I relaxed and gave into his victorious breach of my crotch, he moved his hands around to cup and dig into my buttocks, still holding me firmly in place while he pumped my rod with his mouth. He pulled his mouth up to where he just held my glans in his mouth, sucking hard, flicking his tongue around my piss slit and then forcing the tip of his tongue into my slit, tongue fucking me there, in that smallest of all entrances to the body. I groaned and tried to escape, but his hands, digging into my buttocks, held me in place. His strength was incredible, and I was weak from the buzz of the drinks. He slowly swallowed me whole again, his teeth scraping down the sides of my penis as he drew me in, applying pressure all the way in. I couldn't help letting loose with soft moans and writhing under his attack. It all was surreal, a party blithely going on in the bar, and a mad man beating down my defenses and eating me alive just beyond the beaded curtain. I grabbed his massive shoulders, beating on them, scratching at them, trying to push him away from me. But all of my efforts were fruitless. His brutal mouth began his pumping of my cock again. The beat of the band beyond the beaded curtain was steadily increasing, and his pumping of my cock matched the rhythm of the band.

Without lessening his pumping of my cock with his mouth and tongue, he took my balls in the fingers of one of his hands and rolled and pulled on them, causing me to give out little yip, yip sounds and to moan more deeply. The fingers of his other hand had found my asshole, and I lurched and writhed and increased my moaning as they worked their way into my ass, not giving me time to adjust, plunging past my sphincter muscle and finding, and roughly rubbing my prostate. Not long after this, I came under his unrelenting onslaught. He just took my cum at the back of his throat as I spasmed three times and went limp against the wall. His hands went to my hips and worked their way up my sides and onto my pecs, He was digging into my chest, nipping and kneading my nipples. I begged him to stop, to let me rest.

He just laughed and told me to turn around and to spread my legs, which I did, meekly, at his sharp command. I felt his hands roughly spread my butt cheeks and he had his mouth and tongue at my asshole, licking, rimming me, and pushing in. One hand went back to kneading the muscles in my belly, the other one was working my cock and balls.

He had me all wet and moaning again in a short time, when, without ceremony, he spun me around, lifting me up the wall with his strong hands, got his arms under my legs, and folded my knees up so my feet were completely off the floor. I was yelling for him to stop or at least slow down, but the noise in the bar was so overwhelming that there was no one to hear me or to come to my rescue.

I felt the knob of his huge, erect cock at my asshole, and I tried to lurch and escape him, without success, as the head entered me up to the rim of the glans. He stopped then, but only briefly, as we gasped and panted in unison. He captured me with those violet eyes again and commanded me in a hoarse whisper to kiss him again. As our lips met, he brutally pushed mine open with his and buried his tongue down my throat, stifling any screams of pain and pleasure I might have given, as his long, thick cock slowly but steadily pushed its way up my ass canal, keeping just ahead of my ability to stretch to accommodate him. When he was in up to the hilt, he started to pump me, keeping time with the beat of the band beyond the beaded curtain, slapping and ramming my back against the velvet wall with his thrusts, and didn't stop until he had come.

When he was finished, he let me slide to the floor and then stood over me, smiling that smile and holding me with his violet eyes, while he adjusted his clothes. He told me that he'd enjoyed me immensely and would like to see me again. He flipped a business card down into my lap, and then he was gone. And I was again alone in the alcove, with the sounds of a raucous party drifting through the beaded curtains. The band had stopped; was probably on break. My whole world had also stopped.

As I lay there on a heap of sore but strangely satiated flesh on the floor, trying to come to grips with the brutal but glorious sexual encounter I'd just had, I also was coming to a realization that maybe the problem with Julia and me wasn't Julia and her mocking eyes at all. Maybe I was meant for something different than Julia. But did it always have to be this brutal and, what concept was I striving for— both intimately personal but also impersonal at the same time? I had no idea where I fit now, but after what I'd just experienced, I couldn't honestly tell myself that I could go back to the other side of that beaded curtain, to Julia, ever again now.

I scrabbled around with my fingers until they closed over the business card.

Double Penetration

Doubling Bets

I should have known that the sneaky Dutchman had all the angles figured when he suckered us into betting against a myth in the Men Only back room at Cowboy's Bar in Bangkok's Patpong district. He waited until the third revolution of the happy hour clock—when we were all soused and sluggish—and then entered with a boy-built Thai. I recognized the Thai immediately as a champion bantamweight kick boxer from the arena over by Lumpini Park. Knowing the Thai, I figured he probably was a lot closer to thirty than he was to twenty, but he wasn't much over five feet tall and was skinny as a rail. All corded sinew, though, and I'd seen him put opponents in the hospital over in the ring. He still had all of his facial features where they belonged and was quite well turned out in looks, so it's obvious he'd been able to defend himself successfully.

Those of us holding up the bar couldn't isolate—even when we revisited the issue several days later—who exactly brought up the question of whether the supposition that two guys could fuck another one in the ass simultaneously was fact or fiction. But it must have been the Dutchman. He must have had it all planned before he brought the Thai kick boxer into Cowboy's.

It came down to the boys at the bar against the Dutchman. We all said it was a myth, something they dummied up in the videos they made of it, and he asked us if we wanted to take up bets on that. Suckers that we were, we did. We even thought we'd put one over on him, when one of us had the presence of mind to stipulate that we could pick the cocks that would be buried and, that stipulated, took the time and effort to do some comparing and measuring. The Dutchman even let us check out the Thai's hole on a surface inspection, and led us into doubling the stakes when we saw there was nothing especially slack about the Thai's backdoor.

I came up second longest and thickest, so I was picked as one of the house champions. Dennis, a news agency journalist, who was a good fuck buddy of mine, got highest honors, which pleased me; we'd taken turns with each other as top and bottom, and I enjoyed either position with him.

After Dennis and I had stripped down, I was pleased to see that the Thai was showing that he thought this was all a good idea. He was all smiles and winks and lustful looks. It should have been another signal for us when he didn't seem to mind what was going on—but for all we knew, he hadn't been clued in on the plan at that point yet—or, indeed, just didn't understand English very well. We cleared a space in the center of the room and someone found a cot mattress from somewhere in the depths of Cowboy's back establishment, and we had our arena.

Dennis, the Thai, and I engaged in a good half hour of three-way feeling and kissing, and stroking, cocksucking, and greasing ourselves up lavishly with lube to get us all in the mood and to get Dennis and me lengthened and thickened to the point where we assumed our bet was well covered. In time, though, I found myself on my back on the mattress and the Thai straddling my hips with his thighs. And then he was settling on my cock. Dennis had a hand under there, fingers wrapped around my cock and rotating my dick head in what felt like a tight ass opening. But then the Thai arched his back above me, settled his pelvis, and he was coming down on my cock, swallowing it with his ass, the muscles of his canal walls undulating along the sides of my cock as he settled down into my lap. He was driving me crazy down there, and I managed to tell Dennis between gasps what was happening. The boxer had magic ass muscles and was going to make me come and start going flaccid before Dennis got his cock into position.

The Thai was grinning above me, going for my nipples with his strong fingers, trying to bring me past the brink.

Forewarned, however, Dennis pushed the Thai's chest down toward mine, tipping his hips up, and I felt the giant mushroom head of Dennis's cock at the base of my dick where it was encased by the Thai's asshole. Dennis was grunting mightily from the effort to enter the Thai, and the Thai, his face very close to mine, was registering pain in his eyes and panting with exertion himself.

But slowly, ever so slowly, Dennis's cock was sliding in and I felt its warm, hard, yet pliable skin pushing in on the underside of my own cock. All three of us were straining now from the effort. But somehow the Thai took us both. He reached a point where we were both beyond the entry-level of muscles in his ass, and I could see the transition in his eyes from overriding pain and some sense of uncertainty to triumph and "ride me hard" lust.

We'd lost the bet to the Dutchman, who was showing no pain or exertion at all as he walked around the circle of oglers, pulling in cash. But, without the exchange of audible signals, Dennis and I managed to agree to get a good ride for the money. We started pumping the Thai in counterpistoning that produced arousing friction I've never felt in a corn-hole encounter since. And good sport and magnificently conditioned athlete that he was, the Thai went with us and we all bucked to near-simultaneous ejaculations.

So, now, whenever I hear anyone pooh, pooh the idea that double penetration can even be done, I just smile a little smile and remember how I got more value in losing a bet in the backroom of Cowboy's bar than I'd have gotten if I'd won.

White Beards

If what happened to Bernard could be traced back to anyone, it probably would be his grandfather, Heinrich. He was just too good to Bernie. When Bernie's parents died in an automobile accident, Bernard's grandfather took him in and raised him without hesitation and without denying the boy anything he needed. Thus, from an early life, Bernie trusted elderly men with white beards and gravitated to them for comfort. Klaus Keller, who owned a clock shop near the square in Bamberg down near where the Regnitz flowed by, had been a good friend of Grandfather Heinrich's—and was of much the same age. When Heinrich died, Klaus took the nineteen-year-old Bernie in as an apprentice in clock repair. And Bernie trusted Klaus and was comforted by his white beard.

Bernie was a fair and finely formed young man. And Klaus comforted him. In time Klaus took Bernie into his bed on cold nights in the cold drafty flat above the ancient clock shop near the square in Bamberg, where, eventually, Klaus came to comfort Bernie closely and deeply. And Bernie, who had no one else but Klaus to care for him, was grateful and comforted and felt needed when Klaus embraced him close and filled him with his love.

When Klaus died, Bernie was barely twenty-four. He had learned enough about clock repair in his apprenticeship that he managed, if only barely, to keep body and soul together in the shop that he inherited from Klaus. It was a very lonely profession, though—and not one where a young men would meet many more young people.

There was a hole in Bernie's life. Since he had been a child, there had always been a gray-bearded man to comfort and protect him. Bernie missed that—and, in particular, he missed the way in which Klaus had shown how much he valued the young orphan, Bernie.

Not long before he died, Klaus had bought Bernie a computer and had helped him learn how to use it. Bernie found the Internet. And in those dark months after Klaus died, Bernie spent his lonely evenings exploring the Internet.

He found a Web site named Whitebeard.com, where, when Bernie had paid a fee to discover what lay behind the intriguing name that made him feel so comforted and mellow, he found, to his delight, that there were stories of young men seeking connection with something called "daddies" and nice-looking white-bearded men saying they wanted to be daddies to young men.

Bernie was a young man who felt the loss of several men who had been good daddies to him. He looked at the stories of all of these white-bearded men who were looking to provide just what his grandfather—and later, in a more intimate fashion, his mentor, Klaus—had given to him—back when he felt protected and comforted and needed.

Bernie decided he would put his story on this Web site too, and maybe he would find someone as comforting as his grandfather and Klaus once again. He looked at the stories—which they called profiles—of the young men who seemed to have the most notes from white-bearded men, and he used many of the same words in his profile so that he might find someone to talk to as well. He had no trouble describing his body—which was some of what was required in the profile—because he did indeed have a very nice body. He didn't want to mislead anyone, though, so he did admit that, although very well proportioned, he was quite small for his age—almost boyish—and he felt it only right to acknowledge that his penis was really quite small. Klaus had said he shouldn't be ashamed of that, though, that it was one of the reasons that Klaus loved him all the more—that he looked almost exactly like a statue by a Renaissance sculptor.

When it came to what Bernie would write that would tell anyone else the void he was seeking to fill from the loss of his kind and attentive grandfather and mentor, Bernie was at a loss for words. In the end he just said he was interested in someone who would love him and hold him close—and, having seen how well it worked for other young men in encouraging older men to contact them on the Web site, at the last minute, Bernie added "group and 1-on-1," whatever those meant. Bernie figured out how to add to his profile a picture that Klaus had taken of him in the park one day when he was very happy and then he pressed the submit button and went off to open his clock repair shop for the day.

Johan and Hans were gray beards, and very nice looking ones, as well. They were not all that old—Johan was fifty-five and Hans was sixty—but they certainly would seem like the grandfather type to Bernie. And they were just the type Bernie would find comforting. They were both tall and well filled out, but not fat really. And they were prosperous looking—and both had benign smiles—in the photos they put on a shared profile on the Whitebeard.com Web site. They posted a shared profile because they were very good friends indeed and they wanted any young man interested in exchanging messages with them to know they liked to share. They put it right their in their combined profile—they liked to share. Bernie thought that was very nice and unselfish of them. It was good to share, he thought.

Johan and Hans lived in Nürnberg, where Johan was a banker and Hans was a lawyer. They saw Bernie's profile on Whitebeard.com, and they were excited, because he was just the sort of young man they were interested in and Bamberg was not all that far away from Nürnberg.

They messaged Bernie to his Whitebeard.com account.

And Bernie, when he came upstairs into the flat after a day of repairing clocks and talking to almost no one, was delighted to see that he had a message in his Whitebeard.com account on the very first day—and from not one, but two, men who were much like his grandfather and Klaus. For the first time since Klaus had died, Bernie felt that someone else might exist who could comfort him and make him feel special.

In no time, Johan and Hans had convinced Bernie that he deserved a day off from repairing clocks and could think of nothing better to do with that day off than to come to Nürnberg and have lunch with his new friends at a little café they told him they were sure he would enjoy.

"It's a very nice café," Bernie said after he met his new friends Johan and Hans in a downstairs room on Jacobsstrasse in Nürnberg. "But I'm not sure I see anything special about it. Except maybe that there are no women here. Just a few young men—mostly sitting with older men. But it's a very nice café. It has a comfortable feel to it."

"Come, let us find a nice booth and have a nice drink and become better acquainted," Johan said.

"Yes, let's," chimed in Hans.

And Johan slid into a booth and beckoned Bernie to slide in beside him, which Bernie did. But then Bernie was surprised that Hans slid in beside him—leaving the other bench free. The three of them were wedged together like sardines in a tin. And although Bernie found this strange, he also found it very comforting. And Johan and Hans seemed to find it very pleasant too. They had their arms around Bernie and were hugging him and saying very comforting things to him.

Bernie had not had anyone pay attention to him—focus on him—since Klaus had died. And he found himself opening up to these two very nice white-bearded gentlemen and talking of things he'd never talked to anyone before. This included the nature of his relationship with Klaus.

Johan and Hans were very interested to hear of this—and they were smiling and Bernie could almost feel them trembling in pleasure of how good Klaus had been to him.

"We can be very nice, too," Johan said in a low, hoarse voice. "I think we could be as nice and comforting to you as your good friend Klaus was."

"Yes, I quite agree," Hans agreed. "Would you like that, Bernard?" Hans squeezed Bernie close to him in assurance and affection.

Bernie didn't quite fully comprehend what his two new friends were proposing, as he was noticing for the first time that some of the young men were going through a door at the back of the café with some of the white-bearded men who had been sitting at the café tables with them.

"Yes, that would be nice," Bernie said absentmindedly. And then, "I wonder where those men are going? I wonder if there is another room back through that door."

"Yes, I think there are several rooms back behind that door, Bernard," Hans said almost in a whisper.

"Would you like to see the rooms back there, Bernard?" Johan added in that low, hoarse voice he had acquired while Bernie was talking of the comfort Klaus had given him.

"Yes, that would be nice," Bernie said—again absentmindedly—wanting to return all of the good feelings these two nice white-bearded men were bestowing on him with their hugs and friendly smiles.

Within minutes of finding a room of their own beyond the door at the rear of the café, Johan and Hans proved they were not that old at all. First, they managed to undress Bernie quickly even though his enthusiasm for their friendship was waning a bit in the process and, although he didn't fight them, he didn't exactly help them either.

And then they showed that they each had a very nice long, although not all that thick, cock that could still get quite hard.

And then, Johan embracing Bernie from the front and Hans embracing him from the rear, his legs lifted off the ground and straddling Johan's hips, the two white beards showed just how well they shared, as they both managed to get their cocks into Bernie's channel together and fucked him until he was exhausted in perfectly choreographed counterthrusts, all the while making love to each other over his shoulder with their lips.

To show him how comforting they could be, they each fucked him separately as well on the cot in the small room behind the Nürnberg café on Jacobsstrasse.

Although Bernie did enjoy the first close attention—and sexual arousal and release—he had gotten since Klaus died, he wasn't sure he wanted the comforting that was going on to be more between two others rather than toward him—when he left the Nürnberg café, Johan and Hans were fucking each other and didn't seem to notice him leaving at all. Thus, when he got back to Bamberg, he opened his profile on Whitebeard.com and made a few adjustments. In his description of what he was seeking, he changed the "make love to him" part he said he was looking for to merely "seeking a daddy"—he'd seen how this had seemed to have gotten a good response for other young men on the Web site, and he certainly would like to correspond with someone like his grandfather, Heinrich. And he struck out the "group" reference—as he seriously suspected that Johan and Hans had rather misinterpreted his interest on that one—but left the "1-on-1" because, if he had marked that out, there would not have been much of anything else in that space.

Almost immediately, he received a message from a very nice looking white-bearded man named Bigdaddy10inch who said he lived in Heidelberg and had some toys he thought Bernie might like to see. Perhaps, he said, Bernie could come to Heidelberg on his next vacation day—Bamberg wasn't that far away from Heidelberg. Bernie thought he just might do that. Grandfather had played with him with toys—and he'd found that very comforting.

Edging

Malta Intervention

It was Giorgio's own fault. Really. Sandy and I were quite happy to do our part. But if Giorgio hadn't been such a snotty little bitch, we would have never done him that way.

For three glorious years Sandy and I had thought we'd found paradise on the Mediterranean island of Malta. We'd managed to live well on his stipend from the British Royal Navy and were quite pleased with our pleasant little art gallery on the St. Julian's waterfront. And we were more than pleased with our association with Rocco and Sebastien, both professionally and as partners in bridge, travels, and just sitting in the cafés on the promenades of whatever quaint Maltese seaside town or village we were exploring on any given day and making catty remarks about the passing tourists. Sandy and Rocco were of an "age" that neither wanted to discuss any more and Sebastien and I were much younger but fully satisfied by our respective "daddies." We were still somewhat different, however, because Sebastien enjoyed serving under his master whereas Sandy preferred me riding his waves. The differences all made for conviviality and some very torrid and amusing conversation.

From the beginning Sandy told me that we were destined to last longer than Rocco and Sebastien and to lose them as friends and coconspirators—and he was right. But he wasn't right for the reasons he supposed. He continually told me that when the top was older, the fire would burn out quicker; that as long as I was young and vigorous, however, we could fuck until Sandy was senile and incontinent. But Rocco and Sebastien had their break a long time before reaching that stage. Both Sandy and I felt the loss greatly when our little foursome broke up. And the split came on artistic differences, of all things, rather than any diminishing of their sex drive or ability to perform.

Rocco was the fine artist. We met him when we started to fill our gallery with his charcoal pastels. And we had started carrying his art before we realized that he lived in the old stone villa high on the hill on the road from St. Julian's to the capital city, Valletta. Sandy and I had often remarked on how intriguing was the villa's blood-red double-entry door and garage door set in a solid wall of ancient gray stone broken only by a curly-rodded black iron balcony over the door guarding a single French window in the second story. The front of the house was right up against a curve in the road, and once you cleared that wall on your way back to the sea, the east coast of Malta opened up in a breathtaking view. Until we met Rocco we never could discern how good the view was from the side of the old house that faced the sea. And after we met him we fully understood what inspired his art as he worked in the room behind that French door to the street, but with broad windows open to the view of St. Julian's harbor.

When we were first invited to enjoy that view and he introduced us to his "other," we realized that we had known his resident lover, Sebastien, even before we ever heard of Rocco or his art. Young Sebastien, at once sensual and high strung, was the art critic for two Valletta newspapers, the *It Torca* in Maltese and the *Malta Today* in English. He had the best of art credentials from the Sorbonne and had even worked at the Louvre for a couple of years despite his young age. He had come to the Mediterranean for his health and had hooked up with the best artist he could find who was inclined in his direction—as, in truth, most of them were.

It seemed an arrangement made in heaven, but it proved to be their downfall. Just when Sandy and I thought that our foursome could not get any better, there was a bitter battle royal in the old villa above St. Julian's that we could hear down at the art gallery in the harbor. Sandy and I made a mad dash up the hill in his Alpha Romeo, but we were too late. When we got there, Sebastien had already packed up and was gone.

Rocco met us in the doorway waving a copy of *It Torca* in his hand.

"Did you see what that little turd did?" he yelled at Sandy. "Could I have been knifed in the heart by any greater treachery?" he turned and yelled at me?

Sandy and I were both mystified. Neither of us spoke Maltese, so there wasn't a prayer we could read the paper he was waving at us—and we were quick to remind Rocco of that.

"No problem," Rocco yelled again, and he disappeared into what functioned as his main-floor parlor, a particularly nice, warm-colored room overlooking a hillside terrace and a small, but inviting swimming pool. We could barely see the rim of the St. Julian's coast beyond the boxwood hedge marking the lip of the hill.

"No problem," Rocco screamed again, as he rushed from a back room with yet another newspaper, this time the English-language *Malta Today*.

"It wasn't enough for him to have stabbed me in Maltese; he did it in English as well."

Sandy and I gathered around and read the article in the newspaper, as a steaming Rocco fiddled around behind his bar, looking for some scotch to douse on the flames.

I could see Rocco's point and said so, in a way. Knowing something of art by now, I could also see Sebastien's point. I didn't want to see this break, though, so I tempered my comment. "I'm sure he didn't—"

"No, I'm sure the little prick didn't given two thoughts to my feelings, either," Rocco said as he moved back from behind the bar, scotch sloshing out of a glass far too large for anyone's safety.

That wasn't quite what I meant to say, but I let it ride. Sebastien's article praised Rocco's work but suggested that his talents were wasted on charcoal pastels—that he would develop his skills much farther by moving to colorful acrylics, and that a locale like Malta was just begging for him to do so.

"I don't think—" I started. Sebastien had been unthinking and not a little disloyal, I had to agree, to put that in print, but—

I didn't get any farther. Rocco gave me a murderous look and sank down into an overstuffed chair and began to blubber. The glass of scotch, still largely untouched, teetered on the edge of a glass-topped coffee table.

Sandy leaned down and moved the scotch to safer ground and put his hand on Rocco's shoulder. Rocco huddled even more into himself, however.

"We can stay if you like," Sandy said. "Whatever you like. If you'd like to be alone, however, we'll return to the gallery and wait for you to call us. Whatever you like. You know we will be here for you when you need us."

Rocco continued to sob, but he did mutter his thanks and say that, yes, he didn't like for us to see him this way and it would be best for him to be alone for a while.

As we shut the blood-red double doors behind us and climbed into the Alpha Romeo, I whispered, "Is it really safe to leave him like this? Do you really think it's good of us to?"

"We had to leave just now," Sandy answered grimly. "You were tipping over the edge of saying the wrong things, and if I had remarked, I most surely would have said the wrong things too. It was disastrous for Sebastien to write that, but he's been trying to tell that to Rocco to his face for months now, and he's absolutely right. Rocco is limiting himself with the pastels. And they aren't selling well—or at least as well as his work should sell. His talent goes beyond that. Sebastien was right; he was just a stupid prig about it. And I didn't want to join him in that. And neither did I want to lie to Rocco."

That night, after the gallery closed, Sandy and I went up to the roof of the gallery with a futon and a triangular bolster, and we made wild, exhausting love under the stars and clear skies. Sandy wanted me rough and hard and deep inside him, repeatedly, and I obliged, pushing him first belly over the bolster and fucking hard down into him from the rear and then turning him with his back on the broad side of the bolster and rocking him on my cock back and forth on the edge of the triangle until we collapsed in a satiated heap. We fucked as if it was our last time, both of us thinking of the unfortunate split between Rocco and Sebastien—and feeling very vulnerable and sorry for ourselves as well. We kept looking up the hill to the old stone villa that was usually fully lit up at this time of night and alive with the sound of conviviality. But tonight it was dark and brooding. And then with nothing else I could do, I centered my frustration on twisting and turning and churning my cock inside Sandy until his cries for more subsided into whimperings of being well and completely undone.

The situation remained dark and brooding for weeks, as Rocco sank deeper in his depression. And often he was not there when we went up the hill to check on him. When he was there, we saw that he wasn't working on anything in his studio. He didn't even have his charcoals out and set up. But there was a mounting collection of empty scotch bottles lined up on and behind his bar. He was polite and welcoming to our presence, but in an absent, quiet way he had never displayed before. For a brief time then we thought that he was coming out of his depression. There were signs that he was painting again. And when his first post-Sebastien work was delivered down the hill to be hung in our gallery, Sandy's eyes flashed with pleasure. It was an acrylic painting; it caught the gaiety of St. Julian's harbor and the separate blue-greens of the Mediterranean and the bright sky perfectly, and it was far better than the charcoals Rocco had been doing before. And, justifying much, it was snapped up at the asking price by an oohing and ahhing buyer within days.

But then no more paintings came down the hill and we saw little of Rocco for two weeks. It wasn't long after that before we heard where he was going most evenings and what was absorbing his time. There was a new bartender from Venice at Tom's Bar in Floriana. Sandy dragged me over there one night just to check the rumor out, and it was confirmed and we were totally distressed. Rocco was sitting there at the bar mooning over a swishy little transvestite who was serving him scotches. Giorgio was a cute little trick, but not something that we'd ever seen attract Rocco before—and he certainly wasn't any Sebastien. Sebastien was elegant and glib and had a great sense of humor. This Giorgio was pretty all right, but he was also coarse and a little piggish and reminded me of a ferret searching for food to steal.

Rocco saw Sandy and me lurking in the shadows of the club. He called us over, and we tried to be polite and inviting, but it was obvious that Giorgio saw us instantly as an intrusion and a threat.

Rocco suggested that we all meet at a seaside café over in St. George's the next day for one of our "catty gatherings," as we called them. He said he had missed our outings, and we readily—and genuinely with pleasure—agreed. We had sorely missed the outings as well. It was, of course, a disaster. Whereas the delicate balance of Rocco, Sebastien, Sandy, and Hank had been a perfect, made-in-heaven, meringue, the replacement of Sebastien with Giorgio was a flopped soufflé. Giorgio resented every word spoken by Rocco to either Sandy or me; he was crudely vocal while saying he failed to see any of the well-crafted digs we made about passers by; and his own contributions were consistently dumb and off key. Rocco didn't seem to notice, but the rest of us certainly did. As stupid as he was, the odd-transvestite-out message certainly wasn't lost on Giorgio.

This being the case, and Giorgio being Giorgio, and Giorgio already having learned what a good deal living under Rocco's roof was, it was obvious to Sandy and me where this was heading.

The declaration of war came within a week. We had included Rocco's pastels we still had on hand in a gallery opening cocktail party when a cruise ship ripe with rich Americans was scheduled to dock at St. Julian's. We sent Rocco an invitation to be present and to use his abundant charm to help flog his work to the tourists. He didn't answer the invitation; but, then, he never had before and still he'd always shown up. This time he didn't materialize. At the height of the opening, when it was evident that Rocco could sell some of his pieces if he only was there, Sandy suggested I take the Alpha Romeo and zip up the hill and bring him down.

No one answered the door, so I pushed it open, as we had been given permission to do, and went in. I was about to mount the stairs to the studio when I heard low moaning coming from the terrace. I went over to the French window to discover that it was Rocco who was doing the moaning. He was sitting, naked in a chair by the pool, his back to me. Giorgio, in full dress, was straddling his lap, facing him. Giorgio's face was fully made up with a vivid slash of red lipstick across his face. He was wearing a wig of long, black hair, which he was swishing around on Rocco's knees with his head thrown back. The bodice of his dress was pulled down to his waist, and his black, lacy brassiere was hanging open. His skirt was also hiked up to his waist and he was waving two, thin, shapely legs on either side of the back of the chair. His legs were encased in long black stockings, and he was pointing the toes of stiletto heels at me. Giorgio was in motion, his answer for a pussy being moved back and forth on Rocco's cock. The transvestite was mewing softly, and Rocco was moaning and grunting at the effort of the fuck. Giorgio lifted his head and saw me standing inside the French window. He gave me a languid, self-satisfied stare with mascaraed slitted eyelids. With one hand, he pulled Rocco's face into his chest, and I heard the suckling sounds of lips on a nipple. And with the other hand Giorgio, slowly lifted his palm and gave me a distinct, universally understood one-finger salute.

There was no doubt in my mind that the invitation to the gallery opening had never been brought to Rocco's attention.

When we had last met at the café in St. George's, we had set the next gathering date in the harbor at St. Julian's. At the appointed date and time, Sandy and I were at the café, willing to try our best to make this work, both for Rocco's sake and for our own. A half hour after we were supposed to meet, we saw Rocco and Giorgio strolling on the other side of the harbor. Giorgio, a shapely and saucy blonde this time in a smart morning dress, was compelling Rocco to look at the displays in the shop windows, turned away from the harbor. Giorgio was giving Sandy and me looks, however. They were looks of hostility and triumph. And once again there was that raised one-finger salute out of Rocco's view before the two turned into a street running up the hill from the harbor and disappeared.

If Rocco were happy and if he was making the most of his art, Sandy and I would just have left him alone. But even though Rocco thought he was happy, we could see that he was growing older by the moment and losing his health. He had bags under his eyes whenever we saw him and seemed a little dazed. We decided that Giorgio must be giving him drugs. And there were no works of art coming down the hill, either pastels or acrylics. We could only surmise that Giorgio was getting at Rocco's money as well and was fucking him in many more ways than one.

We achingly missed the company of Rocco and Sebastien together. We even briefly considered selling the gallery and moving on to someplace else. But then we got angry. We didn't think we were wrong that Rocco was coming out of his depression before he was taken over by Giorgio and even was coming around to a reconciliation with Sebastien. Premier in our thinking in this direction was that he had painted an acrylic masterpiece, as Sebastien had been after him to do, and that he couldn't have been unaware that the acrylic was far superior to the pastels—that Sebastien had been right and had been trying to help make him the best artist and happiest lover that he could be.

Sandy and I decided to save Rocco from himself—and for us. That meant Giorgio had to go. No guilt there; he had declared war first and had conducted dirty maneuvers. We would have made room for him even if the quality of the foursome obviously was going to make a nosedive. He was the one who had struck first and hardest. We had to intervene.

It turned out quite simple really. We arranged for a cousin Rocco cared for who lived on the sister island of Gozo, in Victoria, to be conveniently indisposed and needing to see Rocco just in case this was "it," the end of life for him. Then we arranged for another friend to pick Giorgio up at Tom's Bar in Floriana, near Valletta after closing for a well-paid fuck. We were sure that Giorgio was still taking tricks on the side when he could, and we weren't wrong. We even had the friend specify that Giorgio would probably be servicing several men that evening—and Giorgio hadn't blinked an eye at the prospect.

The friend brought Giorgio in through the back of a leather bar in Valetta, to a private pool room, where we had gathered a smattering of leather-swathed toughies.

While Giorgio screamed out his indignation—presumably wholly because he spied Sandy and me—we laid him flat on his back on the pool table. Sandy held his arms and our friend and one of the leathermen each held a leg wide with strong fists around his dainty ankles. I then slowly unbuttoned his blouse and his bra and pulled them open and hiked up his skirt, all the time telling him that Sandy and I just wanted to become better acquainted with him. He had black silk stockings attached to a garter belt, but he wasn't wearing any panties, no doubt ready for the after-hours extra money he planned to make.

To bring home our regard for him, I took my wallet out and fished out a few lira and flipped them on the table beside where he was laying. I told him that Sandy and I would certainly pay him for his time, just as he had expected would happen—just as we would make sure that Rocco heard was happening—but that I thought a few lira was all a whore like him was worth.

Then I stripped; rolled on a condom that had been proffered to me; got up on the table, my knees under his butt cheeks; and in front of a cheering audience, I began to work my tool inside the writhing body underneath me. I had learned to be very good at what I did, and it wasn't long before Giorgio's curses of indignation turned into more passioned pleas to ride him hard and deeper. Sandy, still standing above him, let others hold Giorgio's arms and unzipped himself and presented his cock for sucking, and Giorgio readily serviced him with his mouth and his ruby-red lips. Giorgio didn't seem to mind now at all that Sandy and I were involved in his taking.

Giorgio's cock was getting bigger and bigger and he begged to have a hand released so he could pleasure himself. When we refused him, he begged for one of the spectators to oblige, but we refused that too. I just kept pumping and pumping him at one end, as Sandy was doing at the other.

When it looked like Giorgio's cock was about to explode, Sandy gave a command and I stopped pumping, Sandy withdrew his cock from Giorgio's mouth, and the other handlers held Giorgio very still, not letting him move a muscle until the surge toward ejaculation had subsided. We then started working him again, and, each time he was about to come, we stopped and held him off from release. He was whimpering and moaning now, begging us to finish him, crying that his balls were aching from the built up, unspilled seed. But we didn't allow him to release.

After the fourth standoff, I pulled out of Giorgio and Sandy joined me on top of the adjacent pool table, and we made Giorgio watch as I turned Sandy, stretched out, onto his belly, pulled his hips up with my hands, positioned myself between his thighs on my knees, and fucked him deeply and vigorously to our shared, passion-filled release.

Then, giving Giorgio a contemptuous look, we had him released, and we all just filed out of the room.

Needless to say, we never saw Giorgio again. He left Malta the next day, having cleared out of Rocco's villa that night before Rocco returned from Gozo.

We went to see Rocco the next afternoon, and although he seemed sad and distracted, as well as we knew Rocco we could also see the underlying, unspoken relief. We found him sitting on the terrace, clothed and in front of an easel.

After we'd said our good mornings, Sandy, the cleverer and more sensitive conversationalist of the two of us, said, "What are those paints in your paint kit, Rocco?"

"Acrylics," Rocco said simply, offering no further explanation.

Not needing any, Sandy merely said, "Good. You know the one you did more than a month ago sold quickly at the gallery."

"Indeed?" Rocco said. He returned to dabbing his fast-drying paint on the canvas. But he was smiling.

"We found a telephone number for Sebastien in Nice," Sandy then said. "Hank and I miss him and are thinking of inviting him over for a weekend for a café crawl. Would you mind terribly if we did that? Of course, we won't if you mind."

Silence for a few seconds, and then Rocco said, "No, no, I wouldn't mind that at all." He was still stroking his painting on the canvas and looking squarely at what he was creating there. But he also was still smiling.

Exhibitionism

Cairo Captive

He had his dick inside me a half hour after we'd met. Jorgen was that good, he was. It also was like I was fucking myself. Almost a mirror image, which was no less surprising because he was Scandinavian and I'm an American—never knowing before then that my ancestry might have been Scandinavian too.

Granted I'd entered the beach bar in Brindisi, Italy, to get pretty much what I got. But I had no idea it would happen so fast—or that it would lead to what it did.

I had come to Rome as international financier Theo Gamboni's boy toy, having picked him up in New York City when he was slumming in a gay bar. Gave him such a good ride in his hotel room, making all of those noises and responses that made him feel like he was first and had the world's most potent tool, that he asked me to stick around. That surprised me. I'd gone with him because I'd seen the wad of bills he was flashing and I figured I'd lift it off of him sometime during the night. That was what I usually did. I primarily was a pickpocket; and I was really good at it. And I'd found a good angle on it. Most marks were too embarrassed to contact the police after I'd fucked them and fleeced them; most didn't want to explain the circumstances to the police or their families.

Theo couldn't get enough of me. He'd attend all of those nerve-wracking meetings on Wall Street and come back to his hotel room all keyed up—and there I'd be. On the edge of the bed, or in a chair, or leaning against the frame of the sliding glass door out to the balcony, naked and posed for him. He'd drop what he was carrying and start stripping as he moved to me. And I'd get all "Daddy, yes, yes" and spread my legs for him and cry out like it was the first time—each time—as he thrust inside me.

It worked a charm. If I'd known being taken care of was this easy, maybe I wouldn't have become a pickpocket in the first place. Maybe not—but, again, maybe I still would have. It was like a compulsion with me.

Theo Gamboni so much couldn't get enough of me that he invited—no, begged—me to go back to Rome with him. Which, I did, not having anything to speak of holding me to New York.

For a couple of weeks that worked out all right. Until two things happened. Theo started sharing me with his friends, and I started picking their pockets.

The first time was rather a surprise—to me, at least. Theo and I were having dinner in a swank Rome restaurant and one of his business associates, older, bulkier, and uglier than Theo, joined us. I gathered from what they were talking about that Theo was trying to get the other guy, name of Aldo, I think, to come in on a business deal. Ugly Aldo kept eying me and saying maybe, and Theo got the message long before I did. Aldo said he wanted to see Theo's new apartment. And when we got there, I didn't have a chance. Aldo knew how to control and to undress and to fuck. He might have been ugly, but his cock was long and thick, and he knew what to do with it. Theo watched. And after Aldo had left, Theo fucked me too—and the ardor with which he did it told me he had found a whole new game he liked to play.

There were other "chance" encounters after that with other men who also wanted to see Theo's apartment. And Theo always watched while they fucked me and then took me with added lust himself afterward. After the second one, I decided I needed to be recompensed over and above what I was getting from Theo. So, I put my pickpocketing talents to work and relieved these men who just had to see Theo's new apartment of some of their wallet cash—not all of it, but enough to make me feel this was worth my while.

This, of course, could not go on forever, so I left Rome before Theo and the Italian police could catch on to what I was doing. And not really knowing all that much about Europe, I headed south, down the boot of Italy, rather than north up into Europe proper, and wound up on the Adriatic Sea at the port city of Brindisi.

I nosed around when I got there and found out where the best place was to pick up middle-aged men, the ones likely to have enough money to make it worth my while, and that's how I ended up at the beach bar overlooking the Adriatic at the edge of the city.

There was a fairly good crowd in the bar when I got there. A lot of good possibilities for getting my fingers into their wallets. I was a fool, I guess, for letting Jorgen take me.

He stood out in the crowd. A tall, well-muscled blond with blue eyes and a smile that drew me right in. I guess I first latched on to him because of the striking resemblance between us, but the more I looked, the more I decided that he had more than I did. The facial expressions he used were manipulative in the most arousing of ways. He drew me in just with that smile of his—a knowing smile, knowing that within a half hour he'd be fucking me. And somehow this message was conveyed to me and I didn't fight it. I didn't care. The middle-aged men would wait, I was sure. If he motioned to me, I knew I'd follow him.

He did motion, and as I passed him, he turned and placed the palm of his hand on my butt and guided me out onto the deck of the bar, facing the sea. We weren't alone. A couple of men were in a deck chair in the shadows, one lapped by the other, slowly and silently fucking. They might not have actually been silent, but whatever they were voicing was lost in the screaming of the surf reaching out for high tide not far from the railed edge of the deck. It was windy too, which also would snatch words out of one's mouth and scatter them to the elements.

Jorgen guided me over to the railing, facing me out to the sea, and covered me closely from behind, his hands gripping the railing hard on either side of me, imprisoning me there at the rail.

He kissed me in the hollow of my neck and then on the cheek, and then he took an ear lobe into his mouth and put pressure on it with his teeth. I sighed and turned my face to his, and we kissed. He unbuttoned my shirt and let his hands glide all over my chest and belly. He whispered in my ear how nice I was. And I believed him.

He murmured what he wanted to do with me as he was unbuckling my belt, lowering my zipper, and pushing my jeans and briefs down off my hips. I believed him and turned my face to his again, giving him a kiss of acquiescence.

I felt an engorged cock rubbing up and down inside my crease, across my hole. He whispered then that he was going to do it, that he was going to fuck me there and then. And I moaned and said nothing to disagree with him.

He flashed a condom packet in front of my face, still covering me close from behind, against the railing, and said I would have to tear it open if I wanted him. No problem—other than the trembling of my hands.

And he fucked me there, from close behind me, taking me in long, deep strokes, nibbling on my ear, whispering what a good fuck I was, me gripping the railing for dear life, him stroking my cock with a fist until I spouted off in long arcs toward the pounding surf—all within the first half hour of walking into the bar. I didn't even know his name until afterward.

After, when I asked if I'd see him again, him still holding me prisoner against the railing, his cock still buried deep inside me, he said I could see him every day if I wished.

"See that sailboat out there?" he asked. "The one anchored off the pier over there?"

"Yes."

"That's mine. I sail for Alexandria tonight. I live in Egypt. You can come with me if you want."

* * * *

The journey across the Mediterranean to north Africa, across the Adriatic Sea to the Dalmatian coast and down the coast of Greece, along the southern stretch of Crete, and then the dash across the Mediterranean to the Nile delta, was a progression of five things: trim the sails, fuck, eat, fuck, and sleep, with little time available for eat and sleep.

I learned little about Jorgen other than his first name and that he owned a dive of a gay bar in Giza, outside of Cairo and near the pyramids, which he had to keep on a very low profile because of the supposed Egyptian taboos about homosexuality, a taboo many of them paid no heed to in their private lives. The bar was named Amr's, and Jorgen said he thought I'd like it there. I didn't tell him much about myself, either—certainly not about my pickpocketing proclivities. I wondered if the middle-aged men of Cairo had wallets as thick as those of Rome.

Off of Alexandria, within sight of land, Jorgen hove to and anchored. It was twilight. He said that I should go ahead and sleep, that he'd take the dingy into the harbor and smooth our entry into Egypt—that after his trip into harbor, we wouldn't have to worry about Customs, that he'd be back by sunrise. He floated off into the night toward the lights of Alexandria, and I went to our berth below, nagged suddenly by the question of whether we were transporting—or had just finished transporting—something Jorgen didn't want to declare to Customs the normal way. I hadn't asked what Jorgen was doing in Italy; perhaps that was a mistake. Not that he would have told me the truth if he was smuggling something one way or the other—or both.

I woke with a jolt—the slamming of the side of one boat against another. And my first thought was that it was the authorities, having caught onto whatever Jorgen was up to—and me being left here holding the bag. And it occurred to me as well that I looked enough like Jorgen that they might think I was him if they were looking for him in particular.

I only made it to the hatch leading onto the deck before hands grabbed me and a cloth bag was pulled down over my head. I was bound and gagged, and I realized that I was being transferred from one boat to another and that we were casting off and moving under the power of a muffled motor.

Was I Jorgen now? Unfortunately I probably looked like him to an Egyptian. What had Jorgen done for this to be happening?

I started to squirm and then I felt a tight grip on my arm and the prick of a needle, and I was dead to the world.

* * * *

When I came to, I thought I'd been dropped into an Arabian nights film set, if a rather seedy one. The room was stone-walled with a vaulted ceiling and high-off-the-floor, heavily barred arched windows. Although the furnishings, such as they were, were composed entirely of oriental carpets and a scattering of large, damask-covered pillows, the Arabian nights theme hit me because I had been bathed and powdered and perfumed and was only wearing diaphanous, billowy harem pants and lace-up sandals. I also had gold serpent bracelets banded around above each of my biceps and around my ankles.

I wasn't alone. There were three other guys, all of Middle Eastern extraction lying around on the pillows too, each with the same wary, scared expression I knew I had, and each dressed, or, should I say, undressed, in the same manner as I was. And at the four corners of the room stood four guys looking like thugs and wearing Egyptian caftans. All were muscle men. Three were obviously Mideasterners; the fourth looked European. The European stepped forward and addressed me.

"Good. You're back with us. Good timing. They will send for you soon."

"They?" I asked. "Where am I and what am I doing here?"

"You're here for the auction," he said, and then he gave me a sardonic little smile.

"What? What the hell," I asked. "I'm not interested in any auction . . . what's being auctioned?"

"You're not a buyer," he answered, and I thought he'd break out into a laugh. "You're what's being auctioned."

"Good joke," I responded. "Now, really, what's going on? People can't be auctioned in this day and age. Slavery's dead, haven't you heard?"

"It isn't dead here in Egypt. You're in Cairo. And, Caucasian to Caucasian, let me strongly suggest that you convince the auctioneer he wants to keep you. I can

274

guarantee you won't want to go with any of the other men who are at today's auction."

The European briefly explained while we were being herded down the narrow, stone-walled passageway what was going to happen now. We would be sent in, one by one, into an entertainment room where we would see five men spread in a semicircle around a small platform stage, reclining on pillows. There would be music and we were to dance for them. If we danced well, one of the men might bid on us. If we didn't, we possibly were living our last day. Of course, the men could take their purchases away and do whatever they wished with them, so there were no guarantees past today anyway.

A small, lithe, but well-built Lebanese young man was sent in first. We all stood out in the corridor, waiting our turn, as we heard the music begin. Shortly, we heard the raised voices of men, bidding enthusiastically. Then a period of silence.

I was the second one to be sent in. Four men were sitting in a semicircle around the spotlighted platform I was led to and made to stand on. I had been told that there would be five, but as my eyes adjusted to the contrast of the spotlight in which I stood and shadowy, smoke-filled edges around the platform, I saw that buyer number five was already trying out his purchase over on a pillow-strewn divan at the side of the room. The young Lebanese man who had preceded me was on his belly on the divan, half on and half off it. A large-bellied, middle-aged Egyptian, caftan lifted up around his armpits was crouched between the young man's legs, already ready to mount him.

I tore my eyes away from that scene and looked back at the four remaining men. Three of them were pretty gross, fat and middle-aged and ugly. The fourth one was younger and more comely and well-muscled. He showed that he was in charge by gesturing for the music to start.

This was where I was supposed to dance and, the European captor's warning ringing in my ears, convince the auctioneer, obviously the younger, more presentable of the men, that he wanted to keep me. I started to undulate with the music, never having been a dancer before, but being a dancer now for dear life.

I was egged on by the cries from the side of the room, where the older man was slapping the young Lebanese man hard now, on face, arms, legs, and buttocks, while he drove his cock inside a barely ready hole. The older man had the younger man by the hair with one fist now, and he reached for a riding crop with the other. The cries from the younger man rose and the expressions of the three older men watching me dance—whose eyes were flicking at the fucking at the side and then back at me—left no doubt of how this combination aroused them. They all had hands inside their caftans.

I could see interest in the eyes of the younger man, but not yet a "sold" sign.

In panic, I pulled out all of the stops. I danced, but I danced only for this younger man, the man holding all of the power. While I danced, I traced my cock through the diaphanous fabric, leaving little to the imagination of what I had in there and that it was getting hard, hard for the younger man among the bidders. I had had much practice in getting hard for men I didn't desire, and I brought all of that art to play here. By the time I had pushed the front of the harem pants below my ball sack and shown what I had and was stroking it, I could tell I had sold the younger man. He had his caftan open and his hand was in his lap and he was stroking himself too.

I heard him cry out one word in Arabic. He had raised a hand—the one not teasing his cock—in the air, and the music stopped immediately.

The other three had been no less impressed and aroused with my dance as he was. The fifth bidder was much too busy ravishing his purchase off to the side to care what was happening in the center of the room. And the young Lebanese man's cries and screams had decreased to whimpers and groans as his new master continued to beat and to fuck him roughly.

There was a cacophony of sound as the three older bidders went into overdrive, trying to assert their bid for me over all others. But the younger man cut them all off, and I discerned, to my temporary, partial relief, that he had withdrawn me from the bidding. I was led over to the side of the chamber and chained with metal cuffs to a ring in the stone wall.

I watched then as the two remaining captives were auctioned off. The one loser of all bids stood in a semi huff, a sour expression on his face, and left through a doorway behind a tapestry hanging. One of the other bidders led off his new slave through that door as well. But the last one started enjoying his purchase on the pillows on which he had been sitting. And I could see that he was going to be as cruel as the first master, who was still enjoying himself at that other side of the room.

The younger man, the auctioneer, walked over to me, undid the chains that had attached me to the wall, and, with me still handcuffed, led me through yet a different doorway behind a tapestry that led directly into an opulently furnished Oriental-style chamber with stone walls, high clerestory windows that let in filtered sunlight, and a gurgling pool in the center, complete with central fountain of a young boy pissing water into the pool.

The man released me from handcuffs, then disrobed, showing a magnificent body and good-sized cock, and sank down into the pool. He waved to me, and I stripped down my harem pants and unlaced my sandals, which apparently was what he wanted me to do, and also slipped into the pool. The man had lifted himself to a sitting position on the side of the pool and I swam to him, took his cock in my mouth, and started working all of the wiles I could think of on him. I was fully in his control now. I knew it and he knew it, and I wanted him to want me—for him to always want for there to be a next time. No matter how long it took. No matter how much time it took me to escape from here.

I could tell that my willingness and the mastery of my attentions were very arousing to him. He came almost immediately after becoming rock hard.

He lifted me out of the pool with the strength of his arms then and guided me over to a nearby pillow-strewn divan and laid me down on my back. Then he showed me that he was a master of lovemaking too. He handcuffed me again to rings at the side of the head of the divan on each side. Putting his knees between my spread thighs, he lowered his face onto my torso and tongued and kissed all over my body. And I sighed and moaned for him, not all of it being an act, but all of it focused on pleasing him.

I was laying there, on my back, my legs spread and him sitting on the edge of the divan between my legs. The touching had stopped, and I looked up to see that he had a huge ivory phallus in his hand. He was rubbing oil all over it. And then there were oiled fingers at my hole too, opening me up. I whimpered as I saw that phallus descend, and the bulbous cap of it was at my hole. I cried out and arched my back as

276

the bulb invaded my canal, stretching me wide. He put a palm on my belly and pressed down as he pushed the oiled phallus in another couple of inches. I widened my stance as much as I could and lifted one of my legs to hook on his shoulder at the ankle. He turned his face to the muscle of my calf and kissed and licked me there . . . as the phallus sank in a couple of more inches.

I was panting and moaning and the phallus kept creeping up into me. When it had bottomed, perhaps nearly a foot inside me, the man lowered his mouth onto my cock and started to suck me, pushing his tongue as far as he could into my piss slit. He also slowly pumped me with the ivory phallus, keeping up the same rhythm he was using with his lips on my cock. It didn't take me long to come.

Then he removed the phallus, uncuffed me, turned me, forced a couple of pillows under my belly to raise my buttocks to me, and fucked me long and slowly until he had ejaculated.

Leaving me and rising off the divan, he clapped his hands and two of the thug guards entered and bundled me back to the room I had started in, which was now deserted. There was a dinner tray waiting for me, and then the guards left and I was alone, counting myself lucky. I decided I must thank the European for the advice he had given me if he ever showed up again—and perhaps if I could weave my thanks around him, I could find some means of escape through him.

* * * *

The European captor did reappear. He apparently was the one who was assigned to watch over me for my new master. On each succeeding day, I was brought to the master's chamber. And each time I was fucked in a different way. And each time the master seemed to want to go a little farther, seemed to be working his way in the direction of the point at which the other bidders at his auction had started off. I pretty much figured we were headed to the same goals the others had reached—just taking the slower road.

During my second visit to him, he used an even bigger phallus on me than the first time before he fucked him, this time with me bound to the divan even when he was fucking me. And on the third visit, I was chained to the wall of his chamber, closely attached at spread wrists and ankles, while he swished, with increasing force, a many-thonged hand whip against the tender flesh of my back, buttocks, and thighs. That he then had me taken down and licked my wounds and lap fucked me in the cooling pool, did not go far in mitigating my fear of what was to come. The fourth visit I was cuffed, straddling the divan on my belly, on all four corners, and the whip cut deeper as he rode me hard.

I had tried, but I'd been wrong. I thought I could teach this man to love me—and thus save myself. But there was no indication that he even was beginning to see me as anything but a toy—to be used for his personal enjoyment—and then, probably, to be discarded without feeling for a new, unused toy.

That evening I stopped the European captor after he had placed my dinner tray in my chamber and before he left by means of the locked door on the opposite wall of the door to the passageway that led me to my daily taking.

"Tell me, lesser master," this being what I had been told to call the European, "If this is an auction house, where are the new slaves?"

"New slaves are not needed until the old ones have been used up," he answered. And then I saw the expression on his face, an expression of dismay, as if he had revealed some secret to me. And perhaps he had. This seemed to agree with my observation that perhaps it wasn't that my master was less cruel than the others who had been at the auction. Perhaps he just took longer in using up his slaves. It was obvious to me now that time was of the essence.

"I have never thanked you properly for your advice that first day, lesser master." I told him, and I turned my body—naked other than the gold serpent bracelets at biceps and ankles—in as provocative a pose as I could. "If only there was some way I could show my appreciation. But I have so little. There is only my body—and it withers with each passing day."

This more than gave the European pause. I knew he wanted me. He hadn't been able to hide that from me, not since that first moment when I had come out of my drugged state and had seen him looking at my body.

But he hesitated. At least he was calculating.

"I'm not sure how long I can go and still properly show my appreciation, either," I then said. Shooting home the reality that we both knew, but that neither one of us had been able to give voice to.

"What lies beyond the door you come through?" I asked. It wasn't all that innocent of a question. I had seen him go out that door and come in from the other passageway. Whatever was through that door also had access to other parts of whatever building we were in—and, conceivably to the outside world.

"My chamber," he whispered.

"Your bed chamber?" I asked.

"Yes," he answered in a husky voice.

* * * *

I had gauged the European rightly. He didn't want to take me. He wanted to be ridden. And that worked perfectly with my plan. I prepared him, on the bed of his in the chamber beyond my prison, sucking his cock to his creaming and letting him suck mine big. And then he was wholly mine. I turned him on his belly on the bed and crouched between his spread thighs, and, leveraging the balls of my feet off his stone floor, plowed him until he begged alternately for mercy and for deeper penetration.

After I had come, I turned him on his back on the bed and stretched out on top of him, assuring him that I would not leave, that he would be fucked royally that night.

He was dozing off in a satiated reverie as I started to make love again to his cheeks, ears, the hollow of his neck, his nipples, the pits of his underarms with my tongue and lips. He was fully relaxed. I started teasing him, saying he needed a reward for his sweet channel and expert receiving. He laughed and reminded me that I had no rewards to give other than my body, although he was quick to say that my body was enough reward.

As if just thinking about it, I unwound the gold serpent bracelets at my biceps and, lifting his arms above his head, one at a time, began winding them back around his wrists. He was so besotted with me and off guard, that I was nearly finished when he realized that his wrists were now bound to the corners of the railings at the head of his bed, imprisoning him there as neatly and tightly as any metal handcuffs.

He started to bellow when he saw me searching around for clothes to put on my naked body and was cursing me when I was standing at the other door of the chamber, the one leading to a deserted courtyard where I could see an open gate out into a busy Cairo street. My last cheery gift to him was to remind him that he still had a royal fucking to come—and I assured him that, as far as I could see, he now was truly and royally fucked.

* * * *

It took me a couple of days to make my way across the Nile and to Giza. I took furtive tricks off the street to get enough for food; jeans, a T-shirt, and some sandals; and somewhere I could take a shower from a tap that did no more than drizzle. I had remembered what Jorgen had said about owning a gay dive there named Amr's, and I slowly worked my way in the direction. If Jorgen was OK, if he hadn't somehow been captured as well or taken by the Egyptian police for whatever he was doing, he most likely could be found at Amr's. At least this would be my best bet for getting out of Cairo and somewhere where they didn't trade in human bodies.

I was in luck, I found Amr's and Jorgen was there. He was delighted to see me and pulled me over into a relatively quiet section of the room. He was doing good business. Mostly Egyptians, I thought, but an American or European here and there. Mostly middle-aged businessmen types, but enough of the younger crowd there to keep the middle-aged ones circling and hoping.

Jorgen settled me down in a banquette and wanted to hear all of what had happened to me. He said when he'd returned to the sailboat, near dawn, as he had promised, our entry into Alexandria all worked out, he'd found evidence that the boat had been boarded and I was missing.

He said he'd been looking frantically for me ever sense. This was the first discordant note I heard. He looked anything but frantic when I entered. He did look relieved when he saw me enter Amr's, but there was a hint of something else. It was almost as if he wasn't surprised to see me.

I stumbled through my story, while Jorgen, sitting close beside me, encircled me with his arms and clucked at me like an old mother hen, occasionally taking my lips in his and calming me down with his attentions. Men swirled around us, and several showed interest in us—but none intruded. We could be fucking, naked, in the banquette and none would have taken that as unusual. All the time Jorgen was cuddling me, he also was twisting one of the red cloth napkins on the banquette table around his fingers.

My story stumbled out. Jorgen then said he had to go to the gent's and that he'd return in a moment and would order drinks for us at the bar on his way back. He stood, still fingering the napkin in his hand, and headed for the back of the room and into a corridor. I'd already been to the gent's, however, and I thought the door to it was off to the right of the corridor. But Jorgen went straight back and entered a door at the end of the short hall.

Order the drinks on the way back? I thought. Why didn't he order the drinks on the way to the gent's and bring them back with him?

When he returned, having stopped, as he said he would do, and ordered drinks at the bar, Jorgen was all sympathy and gliding hands again. He hadn't brought drinks back with him. He wanted me to start going over my story again, slowly, with him asking questions as I went. At one point I looked down at the space between us, and I saw that the red napkin he had been fingering was now in my side pocket, half in and half out.

I had wondered how this was going to work.

I took a deep breath and pulled away from Jorgen, saying I thought I saw that our drinks were ready and I'd go get them. He thought that was a fine idea. They were, in fact, sitting on the bar. When I got there, I saw the three thugs—the European noticeably absent—from the "master's" auction house come through the front door of Amr's. I called over to Jorgen and motioned for him to come to me. Instinctively, obviously not having given it enough thought, he did stand and move toward me.

The red napkin was now hanging out of Jorgen's side pocket—the Jorgen who was a spitting image of me. I took the drinks and scooted into the shadows of the corridor back to the toilets and, obviously, Jorgen's office with its telephone, and watched, sipping on one of the drinks, as the eyes of the thugs honed into the red napkin in Jorgen's pocket, and he was dragged kicking and screaming out of Amr's.

I reached down and took Jorgen's wallet out of my pocket. I had lifted it while I was moving the red napkin from my pocket to his. Enough documentation— even his passport. This should be enough to get me out of the country. Not quite enough money though.

I downed one of the drinks, and took a swig out of the other. Then I took a deep breath, walked back into the bar room, all smiles, scanning the room for the wealthiest looking middle-aged businessman here.

Firemen

Fireplugged

I awakened with my butt spooned into Jesse's groin, both of us on our sides, his placid cock inside me, me encased in his arms, his strong hands fanned out over my pecs. I felt for the ring. It was still there. I didn't care what the courts had said, Jesse and I were married. One unit. As solidly linked as we now were in one body, linked irrevocably by that cock now at gentle rest inside me.

Jesse felt me stir and kissed my ear and nibbled at my neck, while his fingers started to make little swirling movements in the curly, downy hair around my nipples. I felt his cock stirring, that long, slender rod with the upturn that caused his dick head to drag along my inner walls maddenly as he stroked me. I pushed back into him with my butt. His mouth started to suck on my neck, more insistently, more awake. One of his hands dug into a nipple; the other fanned out over my belly, holding me there, while his hips began a rhythm. The rhythm of the early-morning deep, slow, languid, sensual fuck. I lifted a thigh over his, giving him deeper access. I sighed and moaned for him.

But he wanted more. He was fully awake, fully reinvigorated. He wanted to fuck me wildly. He always wanted to fuck me like a wild man. We didn't really have time for this; I wasn't really in the mood for this. But he was my partner. He wanted me, and I loved him for that.

I allowed him to pull me up onto my knees, and I widened the stance of my legs, opening wide to him. My chest was flat against the sheets, and my arms were flung out wide, my fists gathering and releasing bunches of bedspread and sheeting in rhythm with the furious stroking that he, on his knees between my legs, was applying with that long, draggy cock of his inside me. As I knew it would, that cock of his was putting me in the mood for him. I cried out for him, loving those long deep strokes. I writhed underneath him, as he plowed me hard and long. I loved the feel of the sliding uncut cock inside me.

With a cry of exultation, he came inside me, flooding me, no need for any protection between us now beyond the rings of pledge on our fingers.

We collapsed on the bed, and he stroked me off to ejaculation with his hand. The loving, caring partner. I could feel him stirring again, and he wanted more, but one of us had to be sensible. He had a class to go teach and I needed to get to work on the new chapter of my novel.

283

Stolid against all of his protestations, teasings, and attempts to arouse me, I forced him out of the bed and lay there, half asleep, contentment filled, as I heard him patter about the apartment and then leave for the university. I would not make the mistake of stirring before he was gone. The last time I had done that, he had taken me, roughly and wildly on the kitchen counter and almost not made his class.

I waited until I was well sure that Jesse was on his way, and then I groaned my way out of the bed, showered, threw my favorite white, diaphanous caftan over my head, and padded out to the kitchen. Immediately, my mind became lost in thoughts of where to pick up the threads of my writing for the morning. I put the coffee on and wolfed down some cereal in milk while my mind was a thousand miles away. The coffee brewed, I poured a cup and moved out to the balcony overlooking the back garden. I just stood in the doorway there, breathing in the clean air through the aroma of the rich coffee. Not seeing the garden, but my mind calming down, preparing itself for what I had to write this morning, the mere presence of the garden helping me to focus inwardly.

I loved a morning fuck from Jesse, of course, but I still wasn't fully satisfied. I had begged him to enter this monogamous relationship, I know, but I had no idea how hard it would be for me. He tended to be the one who went from one long-term relationship to another in a consecutive stream, never overlapping his lovers. I had been the one who sought variety—who fed off that variety to enrich, I had thought, each of them. My insistence on a more permanent arrangement with Jesse was really my struggle with myself to settle down, now that I had found the right man.

But this wasn't getting me anywhere on my novel, I thought. I shook my head, sipped at the coffee, and tried to pull myself back into what I had to write today.

"You know that when you stand with the light to your back in that white thing you're wearing, I can see every contour of your body, don't you?"

My head snapped around. I had no idea I wasn't alone on the balcony. I'd been so lost in my thoughts when I'd come out here that I hadn't even bothered to check. The apartment that shared the balcony had been vacant for months. I vaguely knew that someone was rumored to have moved in—a young fireman, I'd been told—but I'd forgotten. I instinctively wrapped my arms around my chest, trying to withdraw into myself.

"No, don't bother with that," the bronze god, who evidently had been doing his morning stretches, said with a laugh. "I've seen it all now, and it's much too nice to cover."

"Uh, umm," I stammered as much lost for words because he was a hulking beauty, all hardpacked muscle, with massive chest and arms tapering down to a divine six-pack and, from what I could see below the gym shorts he was wearing—the only thing he was wearing—massive thigh and calf muscles as well. And his face—a regular poster model. He no doubt posed for those sexy calendars fire stations put out to help pay for their wild parties.

"You're Jesse's partner, aren't you?"

"Ummm, yes," I managed to dumbly mutter. He was beautiful. He was all I looked for in a man before I had decided to settle down. Gorgeous, smiling, and gregarious.

"I've met Jesse already. He told me about you."

"Uh, he did?" I said, not yet together enough for intelligent conversation. Jesse, I thought, was possibly gossiping a bit too much with strangers.

"Yeah, he told me you were a sweet fuck."

Lost for words altogether now. Jesse had, indeed, been saying entirely too much around the neighborhood. But had he used that bald language? I rather thought this guy was putting me on. Maybe he hadn't even met Jesse; maybe he'd just our names off the mailbox down in the lobby.

"Here, come here," he said with a big smile, as he moved around to an iron patio chair with arms on it that sat on his side of the balcony and settled himself in it. "I'd like to get to know you better."

"I'm sorry, Mr. Mr. . . .," I said, trying to keep this on a civilized basis, although my knees were knocking and my hands were trembling to the point of slooshing coffee out of my cup and onto the front of my caftan.

"Ah, you've spilled that on yourself, come on over here and I'll lick it off for you. Chet, you can call me Chet. And I'd like to fuck you. Come on over here."

"Well, excuse ME . . . Chet," I almost bellowed. "But that's just a bit forward. I have a partner and we are loyal to each other."

"Ah, it's just a little fuck," Chet was saying, still dazzling me with that smile. "I don't want to marry you, I just want to fuck you. And there, I can see you want it too. Your cock is at attention under that tent of yours, and you are trembling so badly you're spilling that coffee all over yourself and I think you're about ready to buckle at the knees. At least put the coffee down. It's very hot . . . just like you."

His first good idea. I managed to get the coffee cup over to the table on our side of the balcony and set it down. But I went much farther than that. I also slipped my ring—my partnership ring pledging me to Jesse and only to Jesse—off my finger and laid it beside the coffee cup. I knew, of course, what that meant. He was just so beautiful and hulky and hunky and forceful. If I couldn't resist a muscled hunk, I simply melted at a cocky dominator.

I turned toward him, he put out his hand to me and simply said, one more time, "Come," and my feet betrayed me and my pledge of fidelity to Jesse. Even with the rationalization that it was all Jesse's fault anyway—he and his big mouth about my being a bottom—the guilt at what I was doing flooded me. It had made me decide to believe that Jesse had talked about me like that to a stranger. I was rationalizing.

The guilt kept me silent, as he pulled me into the chair, my knees between his thighs and the chair arms, and began sucking on the coffee stains on my caftan. The guilt kept me silent as his lips found my nipples through the diaphanous material and sucked on them too. The guilt kept me silent as his lips found mine and searched and possessed. The silence turned to moans, however, when his hand went under the hem of the caftan and found my alert cock—aching for the touch and stroking that he was giving it.

Strong hands pulled the caftan over my head and discarded it to the side. And warm, moist lips went to my nipples, buried themselves alternately in my bushy pits, taking in the clean, post-shower man smell of me, and worked their way down my sternum. He lifted my body up under my armpits, and my knees found the arms of the chair.

All the time, I was whimpering and whispering pleadings for him to stop, that I couldn't, that we mustn't, that it wasn't right. But all the time sighing and moaning for him, not wanting him to stop. Hardening for him; melting for him. My plaintive, verbal "nos" became compliant, body talk "yeses," as I let him know in murmurings and body responses what he was doing was driving me crazy.

His hands were dancing on my cock and balls, and I was hugging his searching lips to my chest, burying my fingers in his fine, blond hair. He put his hands under my butt cheeks and brought my body up to him. I instinctively reached up and found a couple of chains hanging from the balcony ceilings, chains that could hold flower pots for the more fussy tenants, and I hung on tight with them with my hands. The tenant before the fireman had had a veritable jungle of hanging pots out here.

I arched my back and cried out an "Oh, Gawd!" as he swallowed my cock and started working it with his mouth. He was relentless and didn't stop working me until I had come and collapsed into the chair, my hands losing hold on the chains, and my knees slipping down off the chair arms and back down between the arms and his thighs.

He took one of my hands then and placed it on his basket, letting me feel the strength of him there. He felt massive, even there. He freed the monster with one of his hands, and brought my hand back to it. He wasn't particularly long, but he was thickest I'd ever seen and felt—he had a regular fireplug between his legs.

"Do you like my club?" he asked in a hoarse whisper. "All of this goes inside you. I'm going to fuck you good."

"No, noooo," I whimpered. "I don't think I can."

"Sure you can," he said. "You just have to be loosened up a bit."

With that he turned me and brought my knees back up onto the arms of the chair. I grabbed for the chains again, as he buried his face between my butt cheeks and wettened and tongued, and widened, and ate my ass out until I was a burbling mass of jelly under his talented attentions. I don't know how good he was at putting fires out, but he was the tops at starting them and making them rage.

He must have had a tube of lube nearby, because he was now lathering my ass up and sliding his fat fingers in and out of me, checking me, preparing me.

I panicked when he turned me and I could see that he was about to set me down on that greased up monster cock of his.

"No, oh no. A condom. Gotta be sheathed." This was one pledge to Jesse I couldn't give up. We had foregone condoms ourselves, both loving the feel of skin on skin, as the reward for only having sex with each other. This would have been the final betrayal. I could not have returned to Jesse if I had gone back to multiple bareback partners.

The hunky fireman gave me a pained look, but he dutifully reached around and fished out a condom packet from somewhere, a bit too conveniently at hand, I later thought. Just to make clear that I was cowed and under his power, he made me roll the condom on his cock, which was no easy chore, even though he had the largest size made. His cock was just gigantic in circumference.

I had been well prepared and had a long history of taking cock, but, even so, I howled to the breezes crossing the balcony as he rolled that massive mushroom cap around the rim of my hole and forced himself into me. A few excruciatingly painful moments, and my ass decided it would take him—in fact, that it had to have this fireplug inside it, and my muscles gripped his club and pulled it inside me, with me groaning and grunting deeply to stretch for him and him laughing his delight at splitting me asunder. He soon had my butt cheeks nestled into the tops of his thighs, and that giant cock grinding around inside me and stretching my walls almost beyond the limit.

I moaned and writhed for him. I arched my back way back so that I was draped down his legs and hanging onto the legs of the iron chair with my hands. One of my legs was running up his torso and the other one hung out over the chair arm. And all the while, with those big, strong hands on my hips, he was stroking me back and forth on his fireplug. When he got tired of that, he lifted me and set my butt down on his monster cock in an ever-faster rhythm.

He was a virile stud, fast to reload, and he took me twice more as our encounter stretched over the hour point, once with my knees on the chair arms and the back of the chair biting into my chest, and him standing, straddling the chair and fucking me from behind and, at last, down on all fours on the steel grated floor of the balcony, me huffing and puffing and staring down three flights of balconies to the ground and him covering me from behind and making magic between my legs.

In all that time, neither one of us said anything outside of what we wanted in the fuck and how it was affecting us. We were both concentrated on giving and taking—mostly taking—and getting every ounce of satisfaction we could out of the chance encounter—he because he showed that he expected this anytime he wanted it from whomever he wanted it. Me in the guilty pleasure of knowing he could take me to fuck heaven better than Jesse ever had.

At last we collapsed in a heap on the balcony floor. I was breathing hard and moaning from the exertion and the stretching of my ass. He had hardly broken a sweat.

"Jesse was right," he muttered at last. "You are one sweet fuck."

I was feeling totally guilty all over again. Mostly because I had betrayed Jesse and gone with another man. Partly, though, because if I was going to go with another man, and a hunk like this didn't want to use a condom, I was not taking full advantage of the sin. "I'm sorry about the condom," I murmured back to him. "It's just that—"

"Oh, that's OK," the fireman hunk responded with a little laugh. "Your Jesse made me use a condom when I fucked him too."

Mascot

Chief had first noticed him when they did the Smithson 4th of July parade. The young man was Hispanic with a dark complexion and jet black hair and dashing eyes, also, with an easy smile and a "gosh-died-and-gone-to-heaven" look as the fire trucks rolled by with the firemen all decked out in their firefighting equipment and hanging off the sides of the hook and ladder truck.

The next day Chief saw him again, standing outside the firehouse, waiting patiently for a call that would bring the trucks out. An hour later, Chief looked again, and the young man was still there, sitting on the curb. Chief was the only one around for the next couple of hours, as the rest of the day crew was off at a practice tower performing an exercise.

The young man looked familiar. It was only after searching his brain that Chief realized he'd seen him out at the Loredo Ranch—a place where men went to meet other men and maybe to get a little action. Most of the guys at the firehouse liked to go out there. They were comfortable with each other—having the same interest bonded the men into a good firefighting team. They were considered the best in the region. They all kept in good shape, which encouraged appreciating the bodies of other men, and they backed each other well—and you could say they backed each other up real close. But there was no particular need for the other firehouses to know why they jelled as well as they did.

For the life of him, however, Chief couldn't remember in what capacity he'd seen the young Hispanic man at the ranch. Chief certainly hadn't paid for time with the guy there. Although he would have been happy to. He was a real sweet piece of tail. And those doe eyes of his. Chief ducked back into the firehouse and continued the inventory he was taking of the equipment—a job he performed every three days to make sure that everything was right there where it might be needed in an emergency.

Chief fantasized about latching his eyes onto those of the young Hispanic's while he was fucking him—watching the change of expression on the guy's face when he realized that he was being mined deeper than usual and that the man riding him had the stamina to fuck him into the ground. Firefighting made a MAN of a man. Chief liked to watch for the point at which the guy he was fucking realized that—and realized that he was in for one royal fucking.

An hour later and the guy was still there. Chief thought that showed a remarkable stamina itself, as the day was scorching hot and the Hispanic guy had been out in the sun for hours just from the time Chief had first seen him.

So Chief went out into the drive and approached him.

"I'm just watching," the young man said as Chief came closer. "I make no trouble. I just like to watch."

"No problem," Chief said.

"Really, I stay to sidewalk. I make no trouble."

Again Chief said, "No problem. Really. I'm just afraid you'll fry out here. You want to come in and get a drink of water?"

"Me? Come into the firehouse?" The young man was incredulous.

"Yes, come in and get out of the hot sun for a bit. Do you like firehouses, firefighting equipment? What's your name?"

"They call me Ricky. Ricardo, but Ricky for short is OK to call me."

"I'm Chief," Chief said. "That means I'm in charge here, and if I ask you in for a drink of water, there's no one to tell me I can't."

"You are kind. Yes, please. Thank you."

They started to walk toward the door next to the bay truck windows that were now closed. Chief guided the young man with a hand on his upper arm, and he could feel Ricky trembling at the touch.

"I think I've seen you . . . out at the Loredo Ranch." Chief said it to try to make the young man less skittish, more comfortable. He could feel he was intimidating the young man. Chief was a man and a half himself. All of the firemen were. Most of the time they weren't out on call, they were working out in the gym at the back of the truck bays. They had to be strong and agile to do what they had to do.

But the young man was still trembling. "Maybe. You go to the Loredo Ranch?"

"Yes, we all do here. It's part of keeping our edge—keeping in shape and calming our nerves. It's a tense job, you know."

The youth said nothing. But Chief could see he was processing it. And Chief didn't want to withdraw his hand even when they entered the cool interior. Ricky was turning him on. He liked the little guys, and although Ricky was a good third the size of Chief, he was a very nice little piece. And those eyes alone were making Chief go hard.

"You like firehouses, Ricky?" he asked as the Hispanic youth drank first one glass of water and then another and then another.

He hadn't looked like he was sweltering out there, but Chief could see that he was having a lot of trouble quenching his thirst.

"I don't know. Maybe. We don't have them where I come from."

"I saw you at the parade yesterday. You looked like you liked the equipment—the hook and ladder truck and the red water truck."

"Yes, maybe. They were nice."

Chief was perplexed. Ricky had looked like what he was seeing was way beyond just "nice."

"It *was* the firefighting equipment you came to see, wasn't it, Ricky?"

Ricky hesitated. And then he hung his head low and said, "It was more the men—in their fire suits. If you go to Loredo Ranch, I think you must understand."

"You like seeing the men in their uniform?" Chief asked.

"Si." Given a bit reluctantly. "Out at the ranch, on the stage, some of the men dance in fire suits. I like watching that best." And then. "Thank you for the water. I guess today not a good fire day. I hoped to see men racing to fire. My friend Miguel, he tells me men come running out of firehouse still dressing in their uniforms."

Ricky looked up into Chief's eyes, and Chief could see the arousal deep inside the young man.

"You like to see the firemen half dressed?" Chief asked.

"Si." Again somewhat reluctantly given.

"And you like to see firemen dressing—and, maybe more, firemen undressing."

"Si."

"And you work at the Loredo Ranch, yes?"

"Si."

"And maybe you like seeing these half-dressed firemen doing each other?"

No "si." Just a shrug and a failure to meet Chief's eyes with his.

"You see the building above the truck bays, Ricky? That line of windows up there?"

"Si."

"Do you know what's up there?"

"No."

"That's where the firemen sleep much of the time. And that's where they begin to dress. And it's where they undress. And sometimes it's where they fuck. As chief I have my own room up there. And I do all those things."

"Oh." Chief chose to interpret that as a glimmer or more of interest—and maybe understanding. And if Ricky understood, it was a good sign he wasn't backing out of the firehouse right about now.

"If I let you see me dress in my firefighter's gear will you let me see you undressed—and more maybe? If I pay you. You lay with me if I pay you?"

"Me? You want me to lay under you. With you in your fireman's suit?" Ricky asked.

Chief could see the interest in Ricky's eyes.

"Come with me, Ricky. The stairs are over here."

The young man was still trembling and Chief was still holding his arm, guiding him, willing him not to back out now. Because now Chief had an aching hard-on.

Chief asked Ricky to undress first—and Chief was delighted with Ricky's nicely formed body—and heartened by the young man's own half hard-on. That was the real gauge of his interest.

Then Chief stripped, giving Ricky a full view of what was waiting for him, and Chief was pleased to hear the intake of the young man's breath when he saw the length and girth of what Chief had and the bulging muscles that went with the demanding job.

And then Chief began to suit up in his firefighting gear. Ricky stammered a request as he was dressing, though, that Chief not put anything on his upper torso other than the suspenders.

"I like chest. And the hair," Ricky simply said. But there was a catch in his voice and his cock was at three-quarter staff now when he said it.

There was a full-length mirror in the room, and Chief looked at himself with just the suspenders and the heavy pants and boots, and he couldn't help thinking, "Damn I look good. This kid knows his fetishes."

"Fireman's hat too?" Ricky asked, almost as if it would be a great favor.

Chief motioned the young Hispanic to him when he'd put the hat on and adjusted the chin strap, and Ricky slowly moved to him. Chief took Ricky's cock in his hand, while Ricky tentatively touched Chief's bulging arm and chest muscles and paused at the fireman's nipples, which were now hard and the size of quarters. The young man gently played his fingers through Chief's chest hair, and Chief took one of Ricky's hands in the one Chief wasn't stroking Ricky's cock with and moved Ricky's hand down the hair trail to Chief's abs and to his belly and then into the opening Chief had left unbuttoned at his crotch.

Ricky gasped at the size Chief had grown to. Now it was Chief's turn to shudder at the feel of Ricky's hand on his freed cock, and he pushed gently down on Ricky's shoulders, signaling he wanted the young man on his knees.

Ricky gasped and choked on the cock working inside his mouth. He was giving a valiant effort, but Chief knew it wasn't going well.

Pulling the young man back up on his feet, he whispered. "You haven't done this before, have you? What is it you do at the ranch?"

"No, no. I'm sorry. I'm a cook there. A new cook. I must go now?"

"You can go, if you want. But I still want you. I'll still pay you to let me have you. If you still are willing. I won't be rough."

"I stay. I want it."

"Then let's do it right. Come with me." Chief led the naked young man back down the stairs. He hopped up on the running board of the hook and ladder truck and opened the passenger door, which yawned wide outward. He'd gathered a tube of lube and a handful of condoms as they left his room. He handed Ricky up and laid his back on the passenger seat and told him to lift one leg and brace it in the corner of the windshield. Then he moved the other one to reach for the ceiling at the post between the front seat and the back.

Chief spent the next glorious half an hour standing on the running board and rimming Ricky's nice, tight hole and then slowly opening it up with his tongue and lubed fingers so it could take his cock. As Ricky arched his back and moaned, Chief also gave him a good example of a blow job—which ended with Ricky's first ejaculation of the fuck session—and nipped at Ricky's nipples, while Ricky groaned and sighed and clutched at Chief's chest through his matting of hair.

All the time Chief was opening Ricky's channel up for the first time and Ricky was crying out and moaning and grunting and groaning and hanging onto Chief's suspenders for dear life, Chief kept his eyes locked on Ricky's, watching in an experience he so much wanted to see and that he'd never forget, the change from pain to ecstasy to exhaustion but full satisfaction at the taking. And then the confusion and fear—and the resignation—when Chief didn't stop plowing him.

Ricky had been moving with him, but he couldn't sustain it—all of the rhythm and muscle work slowly went out of him until he lay there, completing open and defenseless to Chief's mastering, pistoning staff, not able to do more than whimper and moan and quietly groan. God, it was great taking a virgin.

"Thank you, Ricky," Chief murmured at the end, when he'd taken Ricky for the second time doggy style from the rear, as both stood on the running board and Ricky's chest was buried in the passenger seat of the hook and ladder truck and Chief's hairy chest was rubbing up and down on Ricky's back in the rhythm of the fuck—and Chief was holding the young man up with a grip on his hips because Ricky no longer could do that for himself.

"No, thank *you*," Ricky whispered as he turned his head and Chief took his lips in his. "Sorry I know not what to do. Sorry I could not stay with you."

"You did just fine. You could be our mascot."

"What does mascot job pay?"

"All the dick you can eat at both ends for starters. No, no, that was a joke. We'd treat you right."

"You mean other firemen fuck me? Like you did? Dressed like you?"

"Yes, if you liked. And I'm just an old man. Some of the younger guys can ride you into tomorrow."

It was just banter, but they were still in a pretty compromising position when the day crew—six burly and boisterous young, virile, in-shape men—returned from the fire tower exercise.

Chief immediately had work to do that took him off to the side. Ricky dragged himself up the stairs to retrieve his clothing, but not fast enough that two of the guys didn't see him go up the stairs naked. They followed him and cornered him in the room.

"Hey, lookee, Frank. We got a real nice piece of Cuban ass up here with us," said firefighter number one.

"Has Chief been doing you, cutie?" asked firefighter number two.

"He say I could be mascot here," Ricky answered, almost indignantly, not wanting to lose the ground he thought he'd already gained.

"He say what a mascot would do for us?"

"What you want, mascot would do."

Frank and friend immediately started to strip as both reached out for Ricky.

"Only the shirts, please. I like rest of it on, please."

"Whatever you want, cutie."

Chief was busy talking with the men in a group, but it wasn't long until he realized his "group" was down to one and a firefighter in full gear except for a bare muscled upper torso was standing on the stairs and motioning to the only guy still with Chief.

"Oh, my God. Ricky," Chief exclaimed and he headed for the stairs—in time to find the third guy in the second round standing between Ricky's spread legs and feeding his channel deep and vigorously.

"Off him, Clint. He's fresh—or was."

He looked down into Ricky's eyes, glittering now more than ever before, a sloppy grin on his face, and limp as a rag doll.

"God, I'm sorry Ricky. I didn't mean for this—"

"You mad at Ricky?" the young Hispanic asked in a weak voice. "I no good as mascot?"

"You're OK with this?" Chief asked, incredulously. "You want to stay?"

"I want to be mascot," Ricky said in a faraway, but determined voice.

"OK, then. I guess you're up, John," Chief said. As he stepped aside, firefighter number six was already stepping up to the plate and unbuttoning his fly.

"The shirt. Wear everything but shirt. Yes, keep fireman's hat, please," Ricky requested in a small voice.

Fisting

Heartbreak

I feel like a fool. Many would say I should have seen it coming. But I didn't, and it wasn't something that crept up on me and that I might have adjusted to—although I have no idea what comes after being a stud top. Do you? Still, when it came, it fell on me like a load of bricks, because I didn't see it coming. It's a heartbreak.

The hiatus may have had a lot to do with it. I'd held down the end-of-bar available stud fucker position at a popular gay beachside bar near a major university in Miami throughout my thirties. A former Marine, however, I jumped at the opportunity to go to Iraq with a private security firm to work as a protection unit scheduler. I worked at that for six years before returning to Miami. It wasn't only because the money was phenomenal but also because I wanted to do something for the effort and I was years past being able to go in on the ground as a grunt. That probably should have clued me in on what was happening. But it didn't.

And maybe it didn't because there was no change in position on the sexual chain throughout my Iraq duty. There's a whole lot of tension and need there to be served in a warfront situation. And although the need hasn't lessened in the Iraq action world, it's gotten increasingly difficult for the soldiers to relieve each other in their own environment. My situation was ideal. I had a storefront office in the Green Zone and my living quarters were right behind the office, complete with vibrating queen-sized bed. The young soldiers would stop in when they could to shoot the bull and drop the hints about how keyed up they were and what they wanted to do to relieve that, and I'd usher them through the door into my bedroom. They would strip and open their legs to me, and I'd fuck all of the tension out of them. And they kept coming back. No one complained that I was getting too old to make them moan and groan and to fuck the stuffing out of them.

I knew my body was changing. I still had the bulging biceps and pecs, but I knew the midsection was thickening. Not to any significant degree, though. My stomach was still flat in spite of the military grub and beer—thanks to spending a good fifth of my life in the weight room—where my dicking was quite popular in the shower room. I may not be an Apollo—in fact, I never was—but I was a perfect Zeus now. And there is no end of young men, I don't think, who melt at being manhandled by a beefcake Zeus. And my sideburns may have gone gray in my years in Iraq—but, then, whose haven't? Iraq does that to a man—or at least to a man who manages to keep his hair.

And significantly, a man's dick—as long as nothing happens to keep him from getting it up—doesn't change in size and his balls are as heavy as ever. And most important, a man gains in knowing just what to do with that dick as he gets older. I won't mention that a man looses endurance and recharge powers over time. And I won't mention it because I still haven't fucked a man who I couldn't power drill to exhaustion.

So, it was without a single twinge of fear or self-doubt that, within days of returning to Miami from Iraq, I stood in front of my full-length mirror and studied my body in a Speedo—not one of the Speedos I'd worn when I worked this bar before, because I'd lost my narrow waist—but one that showed off my beefcake muscling up from the Baghdad Green Zone weight training to good effect. I'd been very careful to tan up all over on the flat roof of an American State Department official's residence, while enjoying myself in working his asshole while his wife sat and watched us—and then doing her. I am happy to say I'm an equal opportunity fucker.

Satisfied—falsely it seems—with what I saw, I tucked my car keys, a credit card, and a couple of condoms under my waistband and drove my Sebring convertible down to the beach.

As in days before, I went straight into the surf to slick myself down and swam over to the beach right off the bar. Looking into the bar from out beyond the surf line, I saw that it was as crowded as it had been six years earlier and that most were young, snotty chicken types from the nearby university. I enjoyed fucking twinks. I liked to hear them squeak when they realized they were getting a bigger and more vigorous dick then they dreamed of and when I was only beginning when they thought they were already at their limit. And I had learned a trick or two with the toughened soldiers in Iraq that probably would make these little tight asses faint. And even more, I liked fucking the snot out of the snotty ones. I liked leaving them sobbing and unable to close their legs. And they liked it too, because they had always come back for more—just as soon as they recovered from the first dicking. I was giving them more of an education than their university did, I think.

And then there were the bodybuilders who came in because they heard of my specialty. Guys who wanted to be the biggest, baddest fuckers on the planet—who wanted everyone to know they would and could take anything. For them I had a fist, and I could work that fist, slathered with cream in them to the wrist. And I could make the guys they hung out with marvel at what they could and did take and treat them all with more respect then ever before. And they'd always come back for more too.

As in days before, when I'd parked my ride within sight of the open bar, I slowly walked out of the surf, posing all of the time, and padded into the open-walled bar, drawing the attention of all, as I knew I would. I got the same little thrill I always had as I heard the raucous conversation die out under the thatched roof as I approached. I entered under the roof and walked down to the end of the bar—to find my spot occupied by a late twenty-something, dangerous-looking Hispanic hunk.

I stared at him, but he didn't move—at least not until I'd given up and taken another stool, where I perched, facing the table area and spreading my legs and letting the edge of the stool seat push up my package.

I could have moved into my old place within a couple of minutes, but by then I was in shock. While I watched, one of the university twinks, a dirty blond, thin guy, with an almost too-pretty face, had come up to the hunk and backed his butt into the hunk's package, and the two had done a dry-fuck lap dance to the rhythm of the rock music coming out of the speakers up in the rafters.

I went into a slow burn when they moved over to a thick palm and fern fringe at one of the side the wings off the bar, which, however, wasn't so thick that I couldn't, in short order, discern the soles of pale-white feet set wide apart and waving in the air and the hint of a moving brown bare ass between them, the toes of the feet scrunching up in rhythm with the movement of the butt cheeks. This was a location I'd used hundreds of times myself to draw attention and advertise my wares. How dare he, I thought. He'd not only ruined my entrance but stolen my turf and my moves at the same time. All eyes would now be on the greenery until they saw the final curling of the toes on the feet and the jerk on the brown buns and heard the cries of release.

But that wasn't really true. The twinks huddled around several of the tables were actually watching me. But they were whispering among themselves and smirking and laughing and pointing while trying not to make too obvious that they were pointing at me.

At me!

My world collapsed in that instant. And I could feel my heart breaking into a hundred pieces.

I looked around the bar area. Realization set in that everyone there was at least twenty years younger than I was. Even the bartenders. All except one, though. There was a guy, probably in his late thirties, trim and ivy league-looking even in his baggy orange swimming trunks, sitting at a table by himself at the outer edge of the bar area. One of the twinks had approached him as he caught my eye. He waved the student away, though. He had his eyes trained on me.

If my tan wasn't so good, everyone there could have seen that I had turned red as a beet. I'd always been a little older than the clientele. That had been part of my package. The twinks liked getting laid by someone obviously a little more experienced than they were. Most of these kids wanted a dominating daddy fucker. Many the time it had been my buns undulating between those spread twink legs in the palm and fern fringe until toes curled and some young university snot felt the filling out of the bulb of my condom deep inside his ass.

But a twenty year difference between me and all but one other? And I had about ten years on him even. Why hadn't I seen it coming.

My hope now was that the rustling of the palms and the moans increasing in volume from that direction would galvanize all of the attention under the thatched roof there and I could pick the pieces of my heart off the floor and quietly melt away.

But the thirty-something guy was rising from the table and walking in my direction. When he reached me, he smiled and leaned over and whispered to me, "You got a car and a location and want to ride me?"

299

Grateful for any sense of an honorable exit, I croaked, "Out on the curb; the silver Sebring convertible."

I drove to a secluded spot just short of rocks and surf at the back of a burned out mansion down the coast toward the keys, while the hole—that's how I thought of all the guys committed to getting fucked, because by this point I was only focused on getting my dick sheathed someplace warm and tight and shuddering and backed up by moaning and begs for mercy—rolled the waistband of my Speedo down under my nuts and expertly sucked me off, time after time bringing me to the brink and then backing me off and, when the ejaculation finally came, swallowing me and holding me inside him until I'd softened.

I'd checked the location out beforehand and it was still available and private. So many of my favorite places had changed and lost their usefulness in the six years I'd been gone.

Once in place, I turned to the hole and took his mouth with mine and swabbed his inner cheeks, tasting the essence of what I'd deposited there while we were moving down the ocean highway. I didn't usually do much kissy face; my technique was based on taking the hole's breath away and making him immediately lose control and either go frenetically wild in surrender or beg for his life in the face of fast-developing power drilling. But I'll have to admit that I needed some time to recharge from the hole's surprisingly expert blow job.

I made the hole strip his trunks off. Then I spread an extra-large terrycloth beach towel on the rear decking of the convertible and pushed the hole down on his back on the towel, with his legs hanging down into the backseat compartment.

Than I overpowered him with my body, still stinging from the revelation at the twink bar, angry and, for the first time, thinking I had something to prove to the world. Panicked, because, as I've already asked, where does an aged-out fuck stud go from there that isn't humiliating?

I knew I could dick him into melting submission, but I wanted to prove there was more to me than that—especially since he had sucked me better than I knew I could do. And he was a little smirky at how well he'd held me in check during the blow job and had made me want it.

Having him on his back on the trunk of the Sebring, I covered his body with mine, one arm laced around his back and holding his chest tight to mine. I outweighed him by quite a bit and out muscled him by even more. Pushing my thighs between his, I reached down with the other hand and grabbed his balls and squeezed.

His eyes bugged out and he yelped. This had been completely unexpected, as I meant for it to be.

"You came out here to be fucked, good buddy. But you are going to be fucked with a big F. You understand that? You want to back out?"

His eyes were watering, and I knew he was having difficulty forming the words because all of his attention was centered on his aching balls.

"Uhhh."

"No need to answer, because you aren't getting out of this. You are going to feel fucked before I even dick you—and then you are going to feel fucked with a capital F."

300

Holding him close just like that and staring down into his face to savor every tortured and impassioned expression there as he writhed under me and shuddered and trembled and shot off twice before I even got my dick in him. I'd brought a month's supply of lube and used it liberally with my free hand to slowly open and spread his ass. His hole was slack, which fit my plan perfectly. I worked it with my fingers until I could get my fist in, him screaming and groaning and moaning as I stretched his ass channel as he'd never been stretched before. And then the surprise on his face when he realized that my fist was in him and he'd taken it.

I fist-fucked him—something the real macho types in Iraq had loved as much as the bodybuilders in this town had and that I had sorta looked forward to surprising some snotty college twink with—while he went from yowling and writhing and panting and struggling against me to softly moaning and whimpering and just laying there, his eyes glazing over, all of the fight out of him. Then I withdrew my fist but left my fingers in and spread them and inserted my hard dick between them and slowly withdrew them as my dick plowed deeper inside him.

The cocking, when it came, came in a flood of relief to him, even as big and thick as I was, and he was pushed over the edge of lust and passion—paradise so much closer now after having gone through hell. He wrapped his legs around my hips and started going with the plowing. We were moving as one, ultimate fucking unit. We came simultaneously and then I turned him on his belly and we fucked on and on and came almost simultaneously once again.

My spirits soared. I hadn't lost it. He was putty around my pistoning dick.

He begged me for more, and I turned him on his side and side-split him back into paradise.

Spent, we both lay there, arms entwined, staring up into the sun, our chests heaving from the effort.

And then he calmly told me the fuck would cost me $100 and he could take credit cards.

My heart broke into a million and one pieces.

Fur

Hair's the Thing

I let him buy me a drink at the beach bar—and then another and another—because he had those big tuffs of hair in his pits. I found that intriguing—and arousing. He was a good-looking guy, probably a stevedore or something on vacation, because he was built solid like a tank. But he was also virtually hairless everywhere else I could see, including billiard cue baldness on his head. But there were those bushes of hair in his pits, with dark hair peeking out even when he held his heavily muscled arms down.

I couldn't take my eyes off them. And he was watching me watching him and quickly got the impression I found him attractive. Which was at least partially right. I found the bushes in his pits attractive.

He was wearing a Speedo with an athletic T—with the arm holes cut real low down his sides, which had drawn my attention to his pits.

It was an open beach bar, but it was known to cater to a specialty, so all the guys there were comfortable about hanging out and dancing freely and being loud and boisterous and getting plastered—and sometimes getting nailed without anyone around raising an eyebrow.

A party boat was in at the pier adjacent to the beach bar, and the guys from the boat, a fancy catamaran with a large, squarish cabin area straddling the shells and good decks for partying at the front, back, and up top, were augmenting the Saturday night party.

I'd come alone with the hopes of not leaving alone. It had been a rough week at the office, and I'd come down to the beach to let loose.

I was wearing just baggy cargo shorts, no briefs, and sneakers—knowingly ready for action. Even if I hadn't been, though, the drinks I had would have dissolved my resolve tonight. There were a lot of hunks out tonight—including those who had come in on the catamaran—and did I mention I'd had a rough week at the office and wanted to let loose?

The third drink and the fascination of those hairy pits set off against the otherwise hairlessness of the stevedore—Steve Adore; I'll call him that, because we never did get to the name stage, or he did give me his name and I reciprocated, but that was on the first drink, long ago forgotten and lost in the noise of the music and the crowd—had me ready to give him anything he wanted, and I had let him lap me while he sat on a stool at the bar.

He lifted his arms and let me nose up into his pits and tongue him down there, a fascination of mine, while, in turn, I let him pull his Speedo half way down his thighs to below his balls and snake his dick up a wide leg of my cargo shorts and skewer me. I'd known he liked the arm-pit tonguing because I could feel him hardening up for me.

I rose and fell on his cock there on the stool, right there at the bar. We weren't fooling anyone. They all knew what was going on. I had the heels of my feet leverage on the rungs of the barstool and was slowly rising and falling on his cock. And we were both making sounds of appreciation. So, anyone really interested in what we were doing, knew what we were doing. But some of them were fucking in even more obvious ways.

It was a busy night at a free-loving beach bar.

Someone yelled out that they were taking the catamaran out into the bay for an even freer party and anyone who wanted to come aboard was welcome to.

Steve Adore seemed to want to, and I went with him, lost in the fascination of his hairy pits.

The catamaran was making good time to wherever out in the bay, maybe toward the three-mile limit, considering the sort of stuff being passed around now beyond the booze. Didn't know and didn't care, not the least because someone had broken open a capsule under my nose as we boarded and I was feeling really, really great and so welcomed by all of the faces wafting through my vision.

Guys were swirling around us on the foredeck, having a good time. The music was blaring from loudspeakers at the corners of the cabin area. There was a bucket full of condom packets set outside the door into the cabin from the foredeck, and guys were already liberally dipping into that in passing. I was sitting on some sort of bench seat with a vinyl cushion on top of it and Steve Adore was hunched between my knees and fucking me, his arms held at the side of my head, gripping the top of the back frame of the bench seat for leverage on his pumping action. I had my face up in first one of his pits and then the other, enjoying the bush of hair there. He'd lost his Speedo, but I'd lost my cargo shorts too. Having too good a time to wonder where they were, though.

I came up for air, to spy a man standing on the deck on the cabin's roof and staring down at Steve Adore fucking me. He seemed to be focused on me and smiling slightly. He was beautiful. Hairy all over. Black curly hair on his head, dipping down his forehead almost to his eyebrows. A matting of black hair, also in short curls, swirling around his chest and falling in a thick trail down his sternum, across his belly, and into the rim of the low-slung bathing trunks he was wearing. His arms and legs were hairy. Even the knuckles of his hands and their backs were hairy. And my cock lurched when he raised his sandaled foot to the rung of the railing around the top deck to where I could see that the tops of his foot and toes were hairy too. The same fine, curly black hair.

He must have seen me melt to him. Because as Steve Adore finished inside me and rolled off of me to the side, still possessively holding me in his arms—the hair of his pits rubbing against my shoulder in a way that made me feel tingly—the guy with the terrific black curly body hair was down on the foredeck and standing in front of me and talking to me. He and Steve Adore had some words too, none of which I caught because my ears were buzzing from the effect of the capsule shot I'd been given. All of the voices sounded far away and under water. But if I concentrated, I could get the gist of what a single person talking straight at me was saying. Picking out words in the crowd noise, given my buzz on and the volume of the music was impossible.

Steve Adore was gone, and the black curly guy was getting across to me that he was the host of the party—and the owner of the catamaran—and would I like to see his cabin.

I didn't know if I wanted to or not, but, given his beautiful hairy body, I would have followed him anywhere. He was sort of ugly in the face, but he had a good body. And that hair.

His cabin was really nice and plush. It had a window out to the side and out to the rear deck, and the curtains were open in both windows. I could see the party going on in the rear just as anyone there could see into the cabin. I didn't care. I wanted to see how hairy Black Curly, who I guess really should be named "host," looked under that bathing suit and on his back.

It didn't take me long to be satisfied—in several dimensions. Other than those two windows, the walls of the cabin were almost completely mirrored. And a double, platform bed was bolted to the floor in the very middle of the cabin, with floor access all around it.

When we embraced to kiss and for him to feel me up, I ran my hands up his back and then back down to cup his buttocks and thrilled at the feel of curly black hair there as well.

When he laid me on his bed and I opened my legs to him, he assented to my request to take me on my back so I could run my hands through his chest hair and down into his black curly pubes and watch him fuck me—all titillating hairiness—in the mirrors on the wall from all angles.

He kept telling me how nice I was, and how he wanted to keep me. He had a mammoth, extra-thick cock, which was nice—but not as nice as his hairiness—and was considerably more filling than Steve Adore had been. He had trouble cocking me at first, and I whimpered and struggled a bit, but he reached into a drawer next to the bed and came out with another one of those capsules, which he broke under my nose, and then a didn't feel much of anything and opened right up to him.

While he pumped me hard, he asked me how many days I could be out to sea before needing to get back to land, and I told him I needed to be back by Monday morning.

It was all a dreamy swirl, but I noticed a guy standing at the window out on deck and watching us. He was an older guy, maybe in his forties. Built like a bodybuilder, though. And what caught my attention was that the nicely groomed hair on his head was white gray, but that he had chest hair that was salt and pepper.

As Host pumped away and leaned down into me to play with my nipples with his tongue, my attention focused on that guy at the window, and I found myself wondering what color his pubic hair was if his head hair was white gray and his chest more salt and pepper.

Host was pumping me with short, vigorous strokes, when he tensed and gave a little cry and I felt the stretch of the condom head deep inside me.

"Stay right here," he whispered. "I want you again. I'll get hard again soon, you're such a good lay. Got to go to the head first, though. Stay right here until I can get the party closed down and the guys back on the beach and then we'll cruise and fuck through Sunday."

"OK," I answered in a thick-tongued voice. I was still clutching his chest hair in my fist when he pulled away from me, rolled the spent condom off his already-reengorging dick and padded over to the adjoining head.

When he shut the door to the bathroom, I turned my eyes to the window to the front deck, and the older guy was still there. He gestured for me to come out of the cabin.

I really wanted to know if his pubes were gray or salt and pepper.

They were even darker than the hair above—a soft brown, which continued onto his legs.

Whatever was in the capsule was setting in pretty good now. I almost slipped on used condoms already littering the floor of the deck when I emerged from the cabin. I still had the strength to grasp the edge of the overhang of the deck above, though, with the help of two guys on either side of me, pulling my legs back and out with one hand and supporting me with their other hands grasping my pits, while the mature, multicolor guy fucked up into my channel from behind. A group of guys were gathered around us and counting the strokes. The older guy had good stamina. I had to be let down and bent over and held up by him with his arms wrapped around my belly before he had come.

As he was finishing me, I noticed that one of the guys watching us was a redhead and had a magnificent carrot-red bush of pubic hair.

I ran my fingers through the fine, almost golden pubic hair as I gave him a blow job.

Host was back on deck by then. He only gave me a cursory, half angry, half disappointed look as he corralled another young guy to give a tour of his cabin.

I woke up the next morning on the beach on my back between the now-deserted beach bar and the pier. There was no catamaran in sight. A guy with a heavy bush of chest hair was walking along the beach at the water's edge, carrying a pail for a toddler who was collecting sea shells. My eyes remained riveted to him until they had passed me. Disappointingly his back was hairless.

One of the guys I often go with, Jamal, a thin black guy with wonderful dreadlocks that sway back and forth in the rhythm of the fuck when he does me, laughs and says I have a fetish. I don't think so. I just like hairy men.

Gynemimetophilia
(Dressing Up)

The GED

He came to me in the night. It was always in the night. In the daylight we both pretended that there was no nightly visitation. But he was highly sexed, and since my mom died, he came to me often at night.

"Dad . . ." I murmured, still only half awake.

"Shush. Take this."

I was on my back and he was straddling my chest with his knees and leaning over me, holding my arms out and above my head with strong fists encasing my wrists. I felt the tip of his erect cock at my lips and I opened to him, and we both moaned quietly in the dark as he stroked his cock in and out of my mouth, hardening it and arousing him further—and slicking up his tool for what he'd do later.

When he was sufficiently aroused, he moved his knees and lips down my chest and belly and swallowed my balls as his hand went to my cock. His hand went to join the other to cup and raise and separate my butt cheeks as his mouth went to my entrance. His hand on my cock was replaced by one of my own, and I lay there, looking dumbly toward the window, watching the wind sway the branches of the willow tree, and stroking myself. For a moment I had the sensation of someone being there, watching us, but I had shut my systems down. I didn't care and my senses weren't on alert. I was trying to transport myself to someplace else altogether.

He pulled my sleeping shorts—all that I was wearing—off my legs.

"Turn on your belly." The voice was low, raspy, needy.

"Dad . . ." I murmured again. It was all I could manage, and I knew it had no effect.

"Turn on your belly, son."

With a sigh of resignation, I did as he commanded. I always did as he commanded, whether day or night.

A heavily muscled arm went under my lower belly and lifted me to my knees, while a palm between my shoulder blades pushed my chest down on the cool sheet. He was crouched over me from behind, his thighs encasing mine. I felt the stretch and filling of the entry. But no pain. There hadn't been pain, really, for months. My channel was fit to his cock now. He just slid up into me as I gasped slightly and groaned the almost nightly possession by him.

One of his fists went to the wrist of my left arm and pinned it to the bed above my head. He let me have the use of my right hand—he'd done so for nearly two months now—and I moved it to my cock and began stroking it again to the rhythm of his fucking cock.

He moved his other hand between gripping my waist and pinching my nipple and turning my head toward his face when he brought it down to my head. When he did that, we kissed, deeply, his tongue invading and searching my mouth cavity. This was something else that had only entered the ritual in the last month or so.

My lips freed, I once more turned my head and gazed at the window—and once more had the sensation of someone or something pulling away from it out there as I turned my head. Then I closed my eyes and concentrated again on not being there.

The nature of pretending I wasn't really involved in what was happening to me in the night had changed in the last month or too also—and it scared me. In the initial months, I had zoned out to deny it was happening. Now I was zoning out because I was beginning to need it—to look forward to it each night.

Of course he really wasn't my dad—not my biological dad—and nothing that he was doing was something I could report him for, something I could stop, short of fighting him, which, considering our differing sizes and physical power, was a comical notion. And leaving was something I couldn't do, at least not yet.

My real dad had died when I was eleven, and Tyler had been with us for six years now, arriving a little more than a year after Mom was widowed. I say us, but he really was only with "us" for a bit more than five years. My mom died six months ago. She had been sick for some time before she died, and I think she understood Tyler's interest in me before she went. But by then she was too far gone to do anything about it. She seemed to be hanging on mostly to be there until I got old enough to leave the house and go on my own.

My real dad's death and her own quick decline there at the end had bollixed up that idea, though. I'd worshipped my real dad, and his death had been a real blow to me. I just shut my life down for nearly a full year though—and that included school work. So, I was set back a grade. And, so, when mom died, I was no more than a week past eighteen, but I had a year and a half more to go in high school. And what were almost Mom's last words to me stuck.

"Stick it out until you graduate high school, Chris," she'd said. "Promise me you'll get your high school. Then go in the service for a while or something. Get away from this. But promise me you'll get your high school in first. A man can't do much of anything without that diploma."

And so, I promised.

And the way it worked out with Tyler wasn't wham bang, either. It was gradual. He worked me. He seduced me. And he was smart. He waited until I was eighteen. And when he finally had me, there I was, an adult, and not able even to claim rape. And the longer I stayed, the less anyone would care what I let happen to me. They would have asked, "Why didn't you just walk?"

Well, I didn't walk, because I promised my mom I'd get in that last year and half of school, and I didn't have any other good options. I had no living family left, and I had no means really to live out on my own. I didn't mind the idea of signing up for the military—I was leaning toward the Navy—but it stuck in my mind that one

312

thing my mom had asked me to promise to do was to get that high school diploma before leaving.

And, as I've said. Tyler was clever. And he took it slow so that by the time I really was over the edge, it was done.

It had started the day after I turned eighteen. Mom was in the other room, dying. She'd been to the hospital and was back, under Hospice care, to die at home. I was keyed up and confused and into self-denial and wanting to make it all go away—transport myself to some fantasy land—and because I was a teenager with raging hormones, that meant a flashlight and dirty magazine and beating myself off in the middle of the night.

Which was all fine, but Tyler found me that night, right after my eighteenth birthday. I was terrified and paralyzed in place when he found me. But he came into the room and was calm and sat down on the side of the bed and told me all sorts of mumbo-jumbo over how it was normal and understandable under the circumstances. And while he was talking and holding my attention, he had his hand on my cock. When I noticed and flinched and began to object, he shushed me, reminding me that Mom was just in the other bedroom and that, although what I was doing was normal and understandable, it wasn't something we wanted to worry her about.

"So, just lay back, and I'll take care of it."

And so I did. And he did. And I was surprised at how much different and better it felt when someone else did it.

Three days later, the night before Mom died, Tyler was back and sweet talked me into letting him take care of my fears and tensions again. And this time he ran his other hand over my body as he was slowly jacking my cock off.

When we came home from Mom's funeral, I was a basket case, and Tyler sent me to my room and told me to try to get some sleep. But I couldn't and I couldn't stop crying. And Tyler came into my room and sat on the bed and hugged me close and soothed me with his calm, soft voice—which was really something coming from such a big, muscular man—and with his hands patting and stroking me here and there. He had my cock out of the fly of my sleeping shorts before I knew it. And I was in such a state that I didn't care—in fact it was comforting. And this time he didn't relieve me with his hand. He did it with his mouth.

Mom was dead now and there was only Tyler. And he'd already given me a blow job. And I was already eighteen and had promised my mom I'd stick it out through high school. And not only wasn't I thinking too straight, but I was a teen with raging hormones and Tyler was giving me release and pleasure that, though I knew it was evil and not right, was overwhelmingly hard to resist.

Everything was fine during the day. Tyler was a coping single-parent dad by day. Fitting in getting me to school and being there during my ball games and other activities while still holding down his job. I took up more of the cleaning and cooking duties, but Tyler was hanging in there on those as well. And we said nothing during the day of what was happening at night. The dark covered all of our sins.

But he was coming to me more often at night now. And he cajoled me into taking head, and one night he introduced a dildo into the ritual as he was sucking my cock. The first time I just thought it was his thumb, which he had started strumming rim of my hole with while sucking me, but it wasn't—it was a dildo. And the second time I knew it wasn't a thumb—and that it hadn't stayed at the entrance. By the time he fucked me with his cock, he had me asking for it. And I was over eighteen, and with nowhere else to go.

And now it was four months later.

Tyler had just been to visit me the night before. But he was here, at the door, tonight, as well. I'd heard it. He'd had a video on out in the living room. A male porn film. He was standing at the door, breathing heavily and giving me a scary stare. He was stark naked and had a raging hard on. I was sitting on the floor, on the thick cushion I'd taken off the overstuffed chair in my room; my back to the bed; earphones in, with the music set to something I liked to listen to before I went to bed; and doing my last-minute homework. I already was in my sleeping shorts.

Tyler was on me like a flash, grabbing my wrists with his hands and pushing my arms back on the bed. His cock was assaulting my mouth, pushing my head back on the bed as well. And I was gagging and gasping as he face-fucked me.

Then he pulled me up on my feet and kicked the cushion out into the middle of room as he was stripping off my sleeping shorts. He pushed me down on my shoulder blades on the cushion and grabbed my hips in his hands, and pulled my pelvis up into his crotch and my hole onto his cock, and started fucking down into me with long, deep strokes, thrusting down with his cock, while he pulled my pelvis up into him. Pushing me down as he moved his hips back and then pulling me in again as he thrust forward.

He was fucking me with a fury as he'd never done before, and I hooked my legs on top of the flare of his butt and hung on for dear life, my soothing "go-to-bed" music still playing in my ear from the earphones.

Above the sound of the music, I could hear the sound of the sex. Grunting and groaning and moaning in harmony, but above that, a plaintive cry of "Oh, shit, oh yes, oh gawd yessss, Fuck ME!"

I was shocked—and scared—at the realization that it was my voice.

* * * *

By this time, Tyler wasn't the only one fucking me. By now, I knew what was done was done—and that I didn't mind it when I wasn't thinking real hard—and was thinking why should I give it away just to Tyler for free. I was scraping together whatever money I could to help my escape from here, which was coming within a year. I kept the money in an old can out in the rafters of the storage shed in the back yard.

I figured I knew where I would make some money off this. And I was right.

For years, Mr. Collins, a bachelor living in a house twice as large and tidy as ours just down the street from us, had been giving me the eye and trying to make friends with me when I walked past his house. I wasn't so dumb that I didn't know what his interest was—and there were whisperings going around the neighborhood and at school that bore this out.

All it took to get him to come out of the house was for me to stand out on the front walk by his white picket fence one day and look around like I had nothing better to do than stand there. Sure enough, it wasn't long before he sauntered out, acting like he had a reason to be on the move and "accidentally" noticing I was there and coming to the fence to greet me.

"Hi there, Chris," he called out in a chipper voice. "Great day, isn't it?"

"Yeah, yeah, it is," I answered. "Might rain tonight, though. The rains will be heavy this summer, they say."

Mr. Collins was trembling like a Chihuahua on speed at this string of words from me. It was more in total that I'd ever said to him in all the years he'd been living in the neighborhood. He literally wagged his tail as he came out to the fence, obviously thrilled that I was still standing there.

"Yes, it's good for the flowers, though."

"Nice flowers," I said. "And you got a gardener to take real good care of them, I see." I was searching for words. The gardener was kneeling at the rose bed that lined the front porch of the house. He was facing away from us, an Hispanic, I guessed, maybe in his thirties. An outdoor worker. I wondered if he could hear us— and if he could understand English if he could.

"I try to keep the grounds up," Mr. Collins said, his voice full of pride. "Say, I was real sorry to hear about your mother. I—"

"Thanks. Thanks, Mr. Collins. You're a nice man for saying that." I turned my eyes on him and smiled.

He practically melted on the spot with pleasure. He had his hands on top of the fence and they were trembling. I put a hand up there too, trying to make it seem like a natural move, and I could see him shudder as our hands touched each other.

"Nice house too. Real nice house. Big. Bet you have lots of rooms in there. Bet you have some nice things in there."

"Would you like to see inside sometime?" Mr. Collins asked. His voice sounded so hopeful that I felt kind of sorry for him.

"I'm not doing much of anything now," I said. I tried to keep my voice low, because I could see that the gardener had turned his head toward us—that maybe he was listening to us.

I thought that Mr. Collins was going to melt down to a puddle on the spot at the prospect of getting me in the house.

The gardener looked up from the rose garden as we passed and gave me a tentative little smile. I wondered if he figured any of this out. But then I didn't care. He was just a gardener.

"How's school and the baseball going, Chris?" Mr. Collins asked me as we entered the foyer. I walked right on into the living room, which showed that Mr. Collins made a whole heap more money that my stepdad did. "I've always been interested in how the kids of the neighborhood were doing."

"Yeah, I know you have, Mr. Collins. I've seen how you watched me over the years. Well, I'm here now. And I'm over eighteen."

He turned his head toward where I was standing in the living room, surprised by what I said and by the hard tone I'd taken when I said it. And there I was, standing in the middle of his living room, with my fly open and my dong hanging out and cupped in the palm of my hand. I was kind of proud of my cock, and Mr. Collins seemed pretty impressed too. He went to his knees with a loud moan and began sucking my cock in a way that assured me that, as suspected, I probably wasn't the first neighborhood boy who had visited this house.

We were naked on his bed with him stretched out behind me and stroking his cock inside me from the rear as I propped my knee up on the bed to give him better access when I told him what the deal was: "$15 for you to suck me; $25 if I suck you. $50 for a fuck; $60 for the whole package."

He didn't object and signed up for the next visit to be on my way home from school three days hence. My stepdad didn't get home from work for nearly three hours after my school finished for the day.

The gardener was in the front garden the next day I visited Mr. Collins, and he turned his head and gave me a little smile again when I reached the stairs to the porch and started climbing. I instinctive smiled back, a little nervous because he was there, and because I couldn't think of a plausible reason to be approaching Mr. Collins's house by myself if the gardener asked. But he didn't ask.

The door was slightly ajar when I got to it, and I heard a faraway voice call out from upstairs. "Come on in. It's open. I'm upstairs."

I went in and began to climb the stairs. Half way up I stopped dead in my tracks and let out a "Holy shit." I began to turn to flee the house, when Mr. Collins said probably the only thing that kept me there.

"$75. I'll give you $75. And you won't be doing anything special or different. This is for me. This is to make it more interesting for me."

I turned back and looked up at him again. He was wearing women's lingerie. A black lace bra, with matching panties and black mesh stockings and black stiletto heels. He also had on a red-haired wig, and his face was made up like a baby doll, a mean slash of shiny, deep-red lipstick across his mouth. He was talking in a funny, high voice like he was playing some sort of game. And I guessed it was pretty obvious that he was.

"It's no different for you, honey," he repeated. "It's just me. It's just what I like. $75, OK?"

He didn't look all that bad as a woman. Younger even. And he wasn't fat; he had good muscle tone and firm arms and legs. A flat belly and a nipped-in waist.

If I closed my eyes. . . . And it wasn't like I had to get it up. He said it would be no different. And he had topped me earlier, although for the money, I was willing to try going either way.

I started walking up the stairs again, and as we crossed the hall to the master bedroom, I was impressed on how well he walked in the heels. I guessed he'd done this a lot.

"Please take your clothes off and sit on the side of the bed," he said.

I watched myself—and him/her in the mirrors as I stripped. That was the thing I'd remembered the most about his bedroom from the other day. The mirrors. He had them everywhere. It had been arousing to me to see myself being fucked no matter how I turned my head. I assumed that the mirrors were there because he found it amusing as well. He wasn't bad looking for an old guy and was a good cocksman—or so I thought, only having Tyler to compare him with. But I thought Tyler must be good at it as much as he was fucking me—and I knew he and my mom really went at it before she got too sick to enjoy it. And, surprising, Collins was as good at it as Tyler was, although he must be at least ten years older than Tyler.

We didn't do it just like we had the first time. This time Mr. Collins spent more time in setting it up—and he had an extra fetish thing going with the lipstick. The color was something that rubbed off easily. Collins made a point of paying attention to nearly every inch of my body with his lips, and I could see that the

316

lipstick was rubbing off on my skin. And he got up every once in a while and renewed it, so that it was always leaving fresh lip marks.

I found quickly that the panties had a slit in them in front, so that his cock came out without having to remove the panties. I sucked him and then he sucked me, being careful to leave distinctive lip-shaped red markings on my cock. He followed this up with lip attention to the rest of my body, and then he had me lay on my back on the edge of the bed, and he came between my thighs and fucked me to mutual ejaculations while we watched ourselves and each other in the mirrors. Although I had been worried about being able to get it up, the setting was so exotic and he was such an expert cocksman that I didn't have any trouble at all. The mirrors helped too.

Afterward, Mr. Collins made me stand in front of a full-length mirror and he took photos of the artwork he'd done on my body with his ruby-red lips before he let me shower and gave me four twenties and told me to keep the change.

I had a pretty busy extracurricular activity schedule at school and on the baseball mound, but I did have Tuesday afternoons free, and Mr. Collins signed up for that time slot. He must have had quite a closet, because he was wearing a different set of lingerie each time—and a different shade of lipstick.

Tuesday's must have been one of his set days with the gardener too, as he was always there, kneeling by the roses and giving me a little nod and smile when I mounted the porch stairs to Mr. Collins's front door.

* * * *

I rather enjoyed the fucking with Mr. Collins, and it worried me that I did, but the money was too good to deny myself and put the brakes on this stuff. At $80 a week, my tin can in the storage shed was going to need company soon. I'd made it to late summer. One more year, my senior year, and I could just walk away from here—and with some serious cash in my pocket. I'd put it all behind me, or so I thought.

I was getting old enough now to accept that I was just fooling myself. I began to become obsessed with the women's lingerie—and wondering about it in connection with my nights with Tyler. I have no idea what caused me to do it, but one afternoon, when rain had wiped out a baseball practice and Tyler wouldn't be home for hours, I stole into the master bedroom and started browsing through the drawers in my mother's bureau. Tyler had done nothing about getting rid of her clothes.

I found her intimate lingerie in one of the lower drawers and I took a pair of black lace panties back to my bedroom and stripped and put them on and walked around the house for a half hour. It didn't give me quite the thrill I thought it might, but just the idea of how I wanted it to make me feel made me hard.

And then Tyler went four nights without visiting my bedroom. I didn't think he was doing this on purpose at the time, but now I think he did. Now I think he wanted me to take that last step. The first two nights I luxuriated in a full night's sleep. The third night I couldn't sleep and kept looking at my door, waiting for it to open and for Tyler to slip into the room and into my bed. On the four night I was in a stew, wondering what was wrong, why he wasn't coming.

On the fifth night I could take it no longer. I padded out of bed, stripped off my sleeping shorts, and slipped on the black lace panties I'd purloined from my mother's drawer.

Tyler was awake, on his back, no doubt waiting for me—although I didn't know it at the time. I climbed onto the bed and straddled his pelvis. He laughed and pulled my face down to his and kissed me deeply on the mouth. I could feel his cock come alive. He moved his hands over my bare torso as we kissed and then down to my hips, and I felt the jerk in his cock and heard the low gasp when he learned I was wearing lace panties. He let me know he enjoyed that a lot—but he didn't enjoy it so much that it prevented him from gripping the flimsy material covering my buttocks on both sides and rending it apart with a low ripping sound and then settling my channel on his cock through the slit he'd made.

He laid there, providing the ramrod, and smiling up into my face as I did all of the work, riding his cock in undulating waves. When he had shot his load up into me, he laughed his ultimate victory over me, the fulfillment of my conditioning.

Later, in my own room again, I couldn't sleep. I had come in the panties in Tyler's room and he'd kept them as a trophy, so I was in my sleeping shorts once more.

It had already rained once and then stopped, and I could hear the splatter of precursory rain drops once again on the window. They were promising quite a storm tonight.

I liked watching storms, and Tyler's laugh at the conclusion of our sex had awakened me to what he had conditioned me to do—that final step of me coming to him, wanting it, and willing to do all of the work to get it. This depressed me, and for the first time I wondered if staying around to complete high school was going to be the end of it—whether I could break away from Tyler even after that. And, even more depressing, I was beginning to doubt if the high school diploma was the real reason I was staying around—whether I wasn't completely under Tyler's spell now.

I couldn't sleep, so I got out of bed and took a Coke from the refrigerator and walked out onto the front porch, just in my sleeping shorts, to welcome the coming storm and to try to force my racing brain to be lost in watching the thunder and lightning show.

I had finished the Coke and gotten tired of waiting for the storm to arrive. I turned to go back into the house, but I was grabbed from behind and tossed out into the yard. I landed on the wet grass and someone was on my back, his knee in the small of my back, and my hands were pulled behind me and being tied off. A burlap sack was pulled over my head and I was roughly pulled up and frog marched across the yard, tossed into the back seat of a car, and, after doors slammed, the car was on the move.

I have no idea how long we drove; I was too stunned by the sudden assault to keep any sort of track, but the car eventually stopped after a particularly bumpy ride at the last. I could hear the pattering of rain on the metal roof. The storm was starting. I heard a door open at the front of the car—and slam shut—and then one of the doors to the rear seat opened, and I almost tumbled out of the car. Strong hands grabbed me, though, and lift and tossed me toward the other side of the car. Someone was in the back seat with me. His chest was pressing in on mine—he was bare-chested, so I knew it was a man, and heavy muscled and slick with sweat. I

318

heard and felt the ripping of my sleeping shorts—and heavy breathing. Whoever it was was too agitated to just pull my pants off. I was wedged, facing up, in the back corner of the seat. The seat was wide and plush, I figured some older model car—something American and from the 60s, maybe.

Rough hands were forcing my thighs apart and raising my legs, and the man was between my legs, and I screamed as a cock far thicker than either Tyler's or Mr. Collins's split me and forced itself deep inside my channel and I was being furiously fucked. He bit into my nipple and I cried out in pain again. I began to sneeze from the dustiness of the sack over my head. I tried to suppress it, thinking, "No, please don't take the sack off, please don't take the sack off"—knowing that if he did I would see what he looked like. And if he didn't care if I knew what he looked like, then . . .

I couldn't suppress the sneezing, though, and also began to cough. And the sack was drawn off my head.

It was Mr. Collins's gardener.

"Why?" I cried out.

He backhanded me across the face and growled, "Shut the fuck up."

And I turned my head toward the window in the passenger door I was wedged up against and watched the storm roll over us. There was thunder and lightning aplenty, and it seemed like each clap of thunder and flash of lightning was accompanied by a ramrod splitting me asunder. Each time the thunder clapped, I lurched at the thrust of his cock inside me, each time thinking he couldn't go further down inside me, widen my channel with his monster tool any wider, but, with each thunder clap, he did.

He fucked me with intense purpose and abandon, and I moaned and groaned at how much fuller and more intense his taking of me was than Tyler's and Collins's fuckings were. He wanted me and drilled me in ways they hadn't done, moving deep inside me, relentlessly fucking, making me writhe and whimper and cry out, afraid of what came after this, and then, because he was at it so long and so deep, afraid that this was the last of me—fucked to death. I had ejaculated a long time before he exploded and fell on top of me, sweaty and panting. Holding me tight, his breathing becoming less ragged but his cock coming back to life inside me the longer he held me there.

The second fucking, in consort with the abating of the thunderstorm into a gentle rain, was slower, more methodic and longer, with his hands now searching my body more, as if assuring himself that I actually was here, that the snatch and furious fuck that went before were real, not just one of the longing wet dreams that had driven him to do this.

When he was finished, he covered my head with the sack again and went over the front seat back into the driver's position while I whimpered, exhausted and taken as neither Tyler nor Mr. Collins had ever done with me.

We drove on for a half hour or more, and I sensed when we turned off asphalt and onto gravel and then, eventually onto dirt—probably mud now. The last quarter of a mile or more was on jarringly rough road.

I was bundled out of the car, across uneven dirt, and up onto a wooden porch—which I discern because I was barefooted, and then through a door which

319

was closed behind us. I heard two bolts being thrown on the door and the scrape of a key in a lock. The sack was jerked off my head again.

He had prepared for me. This wasn't a casual snatch. We were standing in a log cabin that was about twenty feet square. The windows were all shuttered from at least the inside. There was a double bed in one corner and chains were welded to the wall above the headboard. At the loose end of the chains were wrist clamps, and this was where the gardener herded me—over to the bed, where he pushed me down on my belly. He untied my binding and turned me over on my back on the bed and forcing my wrists into the wrist clamps. The chains attached to the walls were short, and I couldn't move my hands below my shoulders as I lay on the bed.

The gardener stripped off his wet jeans and his briefs and came down on the bed, forcing his knees between my thighs and sliding them under my buttocks. Then he thrust his cock inside my channel again, and fucked me for a third time—long and hard, with animalistic noises like he'd been building up to do this for months and hadn't had sex in the meantime.

He said nothing to me, didn't answer my whimpered questions or respond to my pleadings. If he hadn't told me to shut up in the car in half-decent English, I would have thought there was a language barrier between us. There certainly wasn't any other barrier between us.

He got out of the bed and padded around turning off lights. I had only a brief opportunity to see what was there, while he was doing so. Just one room. A small kitchenette area over on the front wall by the door we'd come through. This bed was in one back corner and a raised tin square about three foot square was in the other back corner. A shower head was on the wall above this. A toilet was set in the wall at one side of the open shower square and a white porcelain sink on the other. Thus, the room was completely exposed. There was an old couch with the stuffing coming out. A small desk against the front wall, on the other side of the door from the kitchenette—with a laptop computer on it—a round wood table with three mismatched straight chairs in the center of the room, and an overstuffed chair that didn't match the couch.

Just this one bed. When he'd turned out the lights, he came back to the bed and stretched beside me and almost instantly started to snore. It took me longer to go to sleep, and shortly after that, he was waking me again, turning me on my belly—with my chained arms crossed above me—and straddling my hips and fucking me again.

When I woke in the morning, he'd changed the chains. They were longer now, enough so that I could get out of the bed and stand and walk maybe three feet from the bed. There was a hunk of bread and a cup of cold coffee on the nightstand next to the bed and two tin bowls on the floor below that. One was about a third filled with water and there was a sponge floating in it. The other was empty and had a half of roll of toilet paper in it. I could pretty much tell what both of those bowls were for.

The gardener was pissing in the toilet on the other side of the room. He was still naked, as, of course, was I. I listened as he emptied his bladder in a long, steady stream going on for almost a minute.

I wolfed down the bread and drank the coffee as the gardener moved to the sink and brushed his teeth and shaved. He still looked like an Hispanic to me. But he had a well-worked body, muscles bulging on muscles, and his cock and balls were hanging heavy. He was taking side glances at me as I sat on the edge of the bed and chewed on the bread, and I could see that he was getting hard again.

So, I wasn't surprised when he put his razor down when he'd only half shaved and came over and grabbed for my legs while I sat on the bed. I slapped at his hands as best I could and told him no as emphatically as I was able, but he just stunned me again with a backhanded slap across my face that snapped my head to one side, and roughly grabbed my legs, tipping me back on the bed, and crouched been my thighs and fucked me to his ejaculation.

When he was finished with me, he just left me there, my heels dug into the corners of the bed and my legs spread and trembling, and me moaning softly, and went back to his shaving. He took a shower, dressed in his gardening work clothes, and was gone for the rest of the day.

The first thing he did when he returned to the cabin that night was fuck me again. He obviously had been building up to this and looking forward to it for some time. After that, he usually didn't do it more than once a day, but he never got tired of doing it.

When the first weekend came up, he brought out some red lace panties he had been keeping hidden somewhere, put a slit up the middle of them in back with a knife, and forced them over my legs. He then sat on the edge of the bed, forced me onto his lap and cock—through the slit in the panties—with me facing away from him and stroked my cock through the material of the panties until we both had come. He hung the torn panties with my cum in them on the bedpost, where they remained for a week. I now knew that he'd been peeping on me at Mr. Collins—and probably at my own house too while Tyler was fucking me.

And I now also knew what had prompted this elaborate scheme.

I stayed with Julio—for after the first few weeks I ascertained at least that much about him, that his name was Julio—for thirteen months. I knew it was thirteen months, because he had a calendar hanging above the desk and he delighted in marking off the days. He delighted even more in the first few weeks he held me captive in marking off each time he fucked me. And there were more of the latter marks than the former.

Slowly, over the initial months, he lengthened my chains in stages of trust. The longest addition, permitting me full access to the cabin so that I then could shower in the corner stall too and go to the toilet properly and have access to food and drink was the night I woke him up and straddled his cock and fucked myself on him. That was a watershed of him believing I wanted him now and that he'd won me over.

He took the shutters off the windows soon after that, and I discovered we were in the deep woods, with a clearing for a power line not far in front of the cabin and railroad tracks in back. I'd already ascertained that a train ran by somewhere near at three set times a day, as it was about the only sound of life outside the cabin I'd heard for two months at that point. It didn't escape my notice either that the train ran slow in this section of the forest.

By that time I'd figured I was here for good—or at least until something drastic happened. No one had come for me; there was no hint that anyone was looking for me. And I thought that figured. I was over eighteen. The school system couldn't touch me if I'd decided just to drop out. And Tyler wouldn't come looking for me; he would just have figured that I'd had enough and had cleared out that night I disappeared. I had screamed obscenities at him the night I'd left—mad, frustrated, and angry that he'd tricked me into coming to his room on my own for the fuck and begging for the fuck—and taking all responsibility for it. Tyler would neither wonder at me leaving that night nor want anyone to look into my disappearance too closely.

So, I was on my own. And seeing the effect of initiating the fuck on Julio—which I had tried as an experiment—had given me hope of being able to work on his vanity. I was making use now of what Tyler had taught me in his conditioning—he had taught me to move from one frame of mind to another just by gradual reconditioning. In Julio's case the method could still be sex, which Julio was obsessed with, but the goal would be developing a level of trust that would, I hoped, eventually set me free.

I made him believe I couldn't get enough of his cock now—and I admitted even to myself that it was, indeed, a very nice cock. I went after him and gave him master head, something he'd never had done before, and more often than not I was initiating the sex—and complimenting him on what a great lover he was. I asked him to bring more lacy and silky panties, and we repeated the fetish that he seemed to enjoy so much.

Increasingly, he was giving me little freedoms and favors here and there. And I was showing appreciation for them and doing my best to convince him that I was here by choice now.

Then, purposely, I went into a blue funk. He, of course, asked me why, noticing that my end of the lovemaking had become lethargic. I told him I was bored—and wanted to use the Internet. He said that wasn't possible. I cried and pouted and told him that I wanted to study—that I could complete my high school via the Internet by taking GED—general education diploma—classes on line. He told me he couldn't really trust me alone on the Internet, and I said, he could use the keyboard and I'd just sit there and do the class work.

He wanted good sex again, so he gave in to me. I started working on a GED on line to complete my last year of high school—thinking that if nothing else in life I could try to fulfill the promise I'd made to my mother. And, in turn, I gave Julio great sex again.

After a month of acting as intermediary for my studies, Julio got bored and let me do the classes myself. I was careful to stick to only that on the Internet, though, as he tested me several times to make sure that was all I was doing. And I gave Julio really great sex, thinking of inventive positions that he'd never even dreamed of before.

I had him convinced in the first eight months that I couldn't live without him, that all of the police in the state couldn't close in on the cabin and pry me from his bed.

The chains came off completely. But I was still naked. Julio had never permitted me to wear a stitch of clothes. That was one hedge on me not going anywhere. He had locks on the doors of the drawers and closet he used for his clothes and he kept them all secure.

For a couple of more months he still locked me in the cabin and shuttered the windows, using the outside shutters, when he went to work. I gave him no reason to think I'd even thought about trying to escape, and I always had my legs open for him, begging for it, when he came home.

He was the world's greatest stud. I couldn't go five hours without a cocking by him and by him only. I made him believe that.

I had complete freedom of the cabin and its environs for a full month during which he laid many a scheme to catch any sign that I'd tried to leave him.

At the end of that month, I completely finished my online GED work. I went to a virtual graduation ceremony, without inviting Julio to it or telling him that I had finished the work—and had a graduation certificate waiting for me on line for whenever I wanted to download it.

The next day, a Tuesday, while Julio presumably was pruning Mr. Collins's roses, I put on trousers and a T-shirt of Julio's that I had kept out of the wash and Julio hadn't noticed were missing when he'd locked his clothes away, dug the pair of old boots out from under the bed that Julio had thought he'd taken to the dump with other trash, and held my breath until I heard the whistle of the train somewhere down the track, where it blew its whistle three times a day at almost exactly the same time.

I caught the train, which was moving slow by the house and hung on to the side of one of the cars while the train chugged into a town—happily, my own town. I walked for two hours in Julio's glumpy boots to my neighborhood and, staying well clear of Mr. Collins's house, slipped into my own back yard. It was a work day, so Tyler was at his office. I busted a pane in the kitchen door and entered the house and found my room just as I had left it—suspecting I would from the example Tyler had set by not getting rid of my mother's things after she died. My wallet with my driver's license and all were right where I'd left them the night I'd been kidnapped. My clothes were there too, and I changed into some of my own clothes, being surprised at how they hung on me after my more than a year a Julio's sex slave. And I put enough clothes for several days in my duffle bag.

I went to the computer and turned it on and went to where my GED diploma was waiting for me. I printed off two copies and folded one of them and put it under the picture of my mom on the mantelpiece. I then took up the duffle, took one circuit around the house to say good-bye to the spirit of my mom, and went out to the storage shed in the back and retrieved the money I'd saved and hidden there.

Within an hour and a half I was back downtown and pushing my way into the door of the naval recruiting station.

And starting a new life, not thinking much where it would take me—but knowing it was a whole hell of a lot better than some of the places I'd already been.

Painted Laddie for Mr. R

(From *Second Coming: Emile LaCour Unleashed*)

Gabe had had many strange photography assignments for the eccentric, but very rich Mr. R, an avid collector or erotica, but this was perhaps the most challenging. The money was better than good, however, and when he'd put a little thought into it, Gabe saw little problem in the execution of the assignment. It was something different. He might even enjoy it.

When Ms. Tulip came off the stage at the Bourbon Street female impersonators' club and swished into her dressing room that Saturday night, Gab was waiting for her. The meta hunk had worn a muscle shirt barely covering the firm bulges of his torso and a silky pair of shorts that barely held the bulge of his eight thick inches. So, when he asked her if she'd come pose for him for photos, her quick answer was, "Honey, you can take me anywhere you want and do anything you want to me." She would have cause to reconsider that comment.

They went straight out to the alley and Ms. Tulip hiked up behind Gabe on his motorcycle, stiletto heels and all. "She" wrapped her arms around Gabe and hugged him tight. By the time they reached the plantation house on the Mississippi, Ms. Tulip had fully examined every curve and hard muscle of Gabe's torso under his muscle shirt and had determined for herself that everything in that bulging basket at his crotch was the real deal. She was purring when they stopped in front of the old mansion.

Gabe had a room set up with still cameras pointing from different angles at a floodlit ivory chaise lounge backed by a white curtain. These cameras were set to automatically fire off photos at seven-second intervals. He had another handheld camera for close-up shots.

Ms. Tulip hadn't liked the idea that Gabe wanted to photograph her as she was rather than the image she wanted to display, but she made only one demand in compensation as she stripped down to black silk net stockings, garter belt, and stiletto heels and wrapped herself in a red silk lounging robe.

"If I show it all, Dear Boy, you must as well. I want you to be nude for the photo session as well."

And then, when Gabe had stripped down, her response was. "Holy, Mother, Jesus, Joseph, Herod, and Pilate, you stud you. Is it legal to be as beautiful and big . . . everywhere . . . as you are? Love the rings in the ear, nipples, and navel, and, Oh my God, there too. Come to Momma, you horse-hung beauty, you. I gotta have me some of that, Baby."

"Photo shoot," Gabe answered. "Concentrate, woman. You can keep the pout if you want, but drape yourself on the chaise, please. Back to me. Yes, like that. Robe off your shoulders and look back at me. Yes, just like that. A beautiful woman; soft shoulders, beautiful face, brunette hair flowing down your back. Work it for me, and I'll work it for you."

Click, click went the cameras.

"Okay, same position, but let the robe all the way down to your waist. Beautiful rounded shoulders tapering down to that tiny waist, and glowing, golden tan skin. Right."

Click, click, click.

"Half turn around, now. Show that nice perky tit. Yes, that's nice. Now full around and lean back into the chaise. Arch your back to me; give me a full frontal on those nice tits. Now, fingers to tits and work them. Luscious red nails against the glowing skin and big, pink taut nipples. Wonderful. Make love to the camera."

Click, click, click.

"I'd rather make love to you, Sweet Cakes," Ms. Tulip said, as she blew Gabe a kiss. "You're making me all hot and bothered, Honey. Come over here and cool Ms. Tulip off, won't you?"

Gabe just laughed. "Now, move your hands slowly down your torso and slit the robe so that we can see the nice long line of your legs in those silk stockings."

Click, click, click.

"Yes, that's nice. That's hot!"

"I sure can see that, Honeybun," Ms. Tulip purred. "Don't look now, but you're getting hard. I can take care of that. Although I may need help from the rest of the girls in the show, because I've never seen such a big and thick one."

"OK, now, slowly open the robe the other way. Show the cock."

"Sweetie, Ms. Tulip doesn't like to show Mr. Albert. He destroys the illusion."

"Depends on what illusion you want to make. It was a deal. I stripped down, and you show it all."

"Oh, very well," and Ms. Tulip slowly uncovered "her" cock, although then "she" arched "her" back even more, trying to draw the attention of the camera back to the melon-sized breasts that had cost her so much effort and a small fortune to acquire.

Gabe started clicking away with his handheld camera, coming closer and closer to Ms. Tulip until he was straddling the chaise at the level of her hips and taking close-ups of her beautiful woman's face and those nice breasts.

Ms. Tulip writhed sensually below him. She reached up and took his huge cock in both of her hands. "Ooooh, uncut. And that divine gold ring in the foreskin. Wonderful." She slid the loose foreskin off and on the bulbous head of his cock, and his eight-inch half hard stiffened right up and went to a full ten inches as he clicked away with his camera. Some of his shots were straight down his flat belly to the hand job Ms. Tulip was giving him. But then she pulled his hips up and had those big ruby-red lips opening wide. She slid the foreskin off the helmet of his cock and took the head in up to the rim and sucked and tongued him there.

Click, click, click.

Gabe pulled the robe off her back and turned her over on her belly.

"Up on all fours, he said. Rest the side of your head on the top of the chaise and look into the camera over there. Show it how much you are enjoying this."

He widened the stance of her legs and gave her breasts a little pat, sending them shimmering as they hung down from Ms. Tulip's chest. Her dangling cock could also be seen by the camera. Gabe pushed her butt cheeks apart and kissed and tongued her asshole for a few minutes. She wiggled her butt and sighed and moaned for him.

Click, click, click.

He got out a tube of KY and lubricated her ass real well and then slicked down his own cock with the lubricant. Then he took up a six-inch length of small beads and attached them to the ring in his cock.

Click, click, click.

"What's that, Sweetie?" she asked.

"Pearls. Every woman loves her pearls."

"Well, I don't . . . Oh, my Gawd!"

He had come up close behind her and entered her to the rim of his glans.

"Oh, you big, big, naughty boy," she moaned. "God, I've never had it this big. And that ring. I can feel that ring. Oh, I love this."

Gabe worked his way in a couple of inches. The cameras caught the shine of the ruby-red lipstick encircling his cock head and the beads as they disappeared into Ms. Tulip's ass. Ms. Tulip was writhing around, her tits and cock quavering.

"Ahhh. That ring and those beads," she moaned. "Nobody's given it to me this good." She rotated her butt in appreciation.

Click, click, click.

Six thick inches in, and Ms. Tulip was moaning and grunting. She had her knees off the chaise now and she was standing on the floor straddling the chaise, her stilettos digging into the carpet, and trying to get her ass canal as open as possible.

Eight inches and Gabe had stopped drilling to do some slow pumping at this depth. Ms. Tulip's tits were jiggling as her chest and belly heaved. He was still holding a good two inches in reserve, and he undulated his hips, rotating his cock in her hole and dragging the golden ring and the string of beads around her ass canal walls. She was giving little yipping sounds. Her cock was standing at attention, and she was stroking herself off.

"Yes, yes. Fuck me deep. And, Honey, those beads are driving me crazy. I'm going to have an orgasm!" And she did.

Click, click, click.

Nine inches and Ms. Tulip had adjusted. Her eyes were dreamy, swimming in Gabe's precum, which had given her an energy boost. It had helped widen her ass canal and strengthened her to take him deep. She arched her back up and managed to swing an arm around his neck and bring his lips to hers. She was stroking her cock, which was hardening again. Gabe cupped her breasts in his hands, his thumbs stroking her big nipples, as he kissed her deeply. Her knees and arms buckled.

Without losing purchase in her hole, Gabe brought her down on the chaise on her side, stretched in front of his body. His pelvis was cuddled under her buttocks. He had his left arm under her chest, with his hand still cupping and squeezing a breast and his right hand was lifting a long, lean mesh-stocking leg in the air and pointing the toes of her stiletto heels toward a corner of the ceiling.

Stroke, stroke, stroke. Side-split pumping her at the depth of nine and a half, and then over ten inches. She was sighing and purring for him. Deep strokes, almost pulling out all the way and then plunging back in to the hilt and undulating his hips in rhythm with hers.

Click, click, click.

Gabe pulled out and flipped her over on her back before he came all over her breasts. He slowly licked his cum off of her melons as she moaned her satiated pleasure.

After that, Gabe rose from the chaise, gathered the wilting body of Ms. Tulip up, walked out into the hall, and mounted the stairs to the second floor.

"Where we going, Hon?" Ms. Tulip murmured in his ear, not sounding as if she really cared where they were going, her free hand tracing the star-burst tattoo encircling his nipple.

"Your evening's not over, Sport," Gabe answered. "Mr. R wants to meet and greet you. He's got a few tricks to show you."

"Loved the pearl beads," was Ms. Tulip's only response, as they mounted the wide staircase toward the candlelight flickering through the open door at the top of the stairs.

Coming to Savannah

I'd come out here to the park to try to calm down. The slight wedge of a townhouse I'd rented on Savannah's Lafayette Square was hardly big enough to turn around in, let alone pace in. It was essentially one continuous shot-gun room downstairs, a twelve by eight-foot foyer with a spiral staircase—entered from the street, followed by the "big" room, a twelve by fifteen-foot parlor, dominated by a period fireplace, followed by a twelve by twelve-foot dining room, and then the afterthought kitchen, added, probably a good hundred years after the house was first constructed. Overhead was just the one bedroom, a bath that had taken over another small room, and the glorious sun porch perched on top of the kitchen afterthought. This porch looked down into a small, but exuberantly lush garden encroaching on a brick patio with a wrought-iron table at which I could sit and compose what my overzealous agent told my publisher were literary masterpieces even while she was telling me to "fix this garbage."

The house's one modern convenience, a Wi-Fi connection, had been the selling point when I'd been dickering from New York over a down-south rental. But once down here, I fell in love with the house; with Lafayette Square, one of the original squares in the first truly intentional urban design in the New World; and with Savannah itself. And it's a good thing I loved the house, because I hid out in it for weeks at the beginning.

I didn't want to love it; I wanted to take one look and go back to New York and tell Todd that he was wrong, that I hated it. That he was wrong about everything. But once here in Savannah, I had to admit he'd been right about this. And then I had to start reconsidering everything else he had said.

"How about Savannah, Georgia, Mike?" he'd said. "I've always thought of you as the slow, easygoing Southern gentleman."

It sounded nice, but I knew that, coming from the Jewish "I can git it for ya wholesale" Todd, it wasn't really a compliment. And now that Todd was leaving me, I was dissecting everything he had to say since we'd driven out to the Hamptons—to see what the underlying dig was.

"You can live anywhere you want to," he said. "You can take your work anywhere, and you've already socked away enough for a cushy retirement."

Was that a dig, I wondered. I hadn't been generous enough to him? That was why he could take all of this so calmly after thirteen years of living together? He hadn't told me there was a problem with his allowance. I'd just found out there was a problem the hard way.

"And I don't think you'll want to live here in New York—at least for a while," he said.

And I supposed he was right about that. I did have to get away from New York—at least for a while—after what had happened. All of the mutual friends we had, standing around, not knowing quite what to say to me—whispering among themselves their "poor Mike" comments. Most of them had never known either of us other than as a couple. No, Todd was right about that. I'd have to be out of New York until the memory of the two of us together had faded.

"Forget me," Todd said. "You'll find someone new in Savannah. I'm sure that will be a good place to get back into circulation."

Yeah, right. As if I could ever forget Todd. And how could I get back into circulation. Thirty-five years old, over a decade of not even speculating about being with another man—which, when I'd tried that on Todd, he'd gone all amazed and speculated whether that even was possible. This only added to my frustration and sense of abandonment, because as closely as I could remember, it was utterly true. How could I just start up again—in Savannah or anywhere else?

In the end, I didn't say good-bye. I couldn't bear to say good-bye. I just got up off that uncomfortable chair beside Todd's bed and walked out of the hospital. We both were moving away from the old and toward something else, something unknown to either of us after all of the years we had shared a bed and a life. Somehow I was sure that it would be tougher on me than on Todd. Even Todd had acknowledged that. But he'd smiled when he said it. The bastard.

So, here I was, sitting on a bench in the Lafayette Square Park five months later, my front door at my back, and facing the scene of the coming assignation, the Café Marquis, across the square from me, the cornflower blue of its outdoor café umbrellas shimmering in the light beyond the shaded square with its flower beds stuffed with dark purple seasonal flowers whose name I never could remember.

The first place I'd ventured to after moving here and hiding on my garden patio for a month with the excuse—very real, actually—of a tight deadline for my new novel manuscript was under those blue umbrellas in front of the Café Marquis. One late morning I had been stuck for just the right word and lost my concentration long enough to realize that I had rushed to the computer with an idea I'd awakened to without eating any breakfast. Since I was at a temporary impasse anyway, I walked across the square.

I was in a bit of a funk because I was in a corner with my writing as well as stuck for a word—and also because I'd been in Savannah, where I was supposed to "get on with it," for a month, and I hadn't "gotten on with it."

The first face I saw upon approaching the blue umbrellas was a smiling one, though, and that started to change my mood. The waiter was young and small of stature and delicate of facial features, a coffee and cream mulatto, as seemed so prevalent in this inexplicably French-flavored genteel southern coastal city that had somehow been tucked away out of sight during the industrial revolution. He introduced himself as Vallois, to be called Val, names that stuck with me even though I was pretty much a dunce at remembering names. And he introduced me to rich, dark-roast coffee and reintroduced me to flakey beignets that I hadn't tasted since my last visit to New Orleans.

By the time I emerged from under the umbrella, I was content for the first time since I'd come to Savannah—and, perhaps more to the point, I'd surfaced the elusive word I'd been looking for and had devised how I was going to get out of the plot corner I'd painted myself into.

After that, the question of where I was going to breakfast every morning was settled—under the blue umbrellas of the Café Marquis and the attentive smile and service of the small mulatto, Vallois, "call me Val."

After three months in Savannah, I couldn't avoid the assignment Todd had set forth for me any longer. I was running out of excuses. I had finished and delivered the manuscript, and my agent had, unexpectedly, been delighted with it and suggested no changes. She sent it directly on to the publisher, and where I thought I'd be able to hide behind the need to rewrite for the agent, I suddenly had time on my hands.

I turned to the Wi-Fi capability and tried the Internet connection route. It was a stupid, naïve thing to do. I got several responses to my listing at the Internet gay male dating service, with at least four from the Savannah region.

I picked out the one most like Todd. I didn't do this on purpose—although maybe at least subconsciously I did.

I was extremely nervous with this whole "scene," so I insisted that we'd meet on my turf. I picked the Café Marquis—for breakfast. It couldn't get any more in my comfort zone than this. If we hit it off, my house was just across the square. I hadn't done any "on the first date" connecting for thirteen years. But then, I hadn't had a date, hadn't gone with anyone but Todd, for the same thirteen years. I had no idea what was expected these days. A whole generation of the gay "scene" had come and gone in the space of Todd's and my exclusive relationship. I didn't want to call it a marriage, but that was what it had been in every sense other than the legal one.

Of course the man who showed up, insisting that he indeed was Phil from the on-line gay male dating service, was nothing at all like either his picture or his profile. Couldn't have been any farther away from Todd if he'd flown in from outer space. He was heavyset and loud and opinionated, and he talked a mile a minute. Poor Vallois. He fluttered around us, giving me the evil eye, signaling that it was ludicrous for me to be having breakfast with someone like this, let alone at the sedate and understated Café Marquis. I wasn't sure whether he was protecting me or the café.

I appreciated Vallois's concern, but it was wasted. I knew the minute Phil convinced me he was "the Phil," but a different Phil than advertised, that we wouldn't be walking across the square to my house together.

In the end, I excused myself from the table to go to the men's room inside the restaurant, and with Vallois's help, I escaped through the service door on Albercorn Street and doubled around to where I could slip back into my house on the square without being seen from under the blue umbrellas. Vallois later told me that Phil had rattled on for another twenty minutes, talking to himself, before realizing I wasn't coming back to the table.

That put me in a panic, and, although I shouldn't have, I made a date with another man from the dating service almost immediately. He'd been pretty far down the list as my second choice. He'd been less than forthcoming on his profile, and although he looked squared away enough in his photo, there was something just a little off, a little dangerous looking about him even in the photo. Maybe it was the tattooing around his neck, peeking out above his shirt collar in the photo, something I didn't really notice until I checked back in the files after the debacle that was that date.

Once again we met at the Café Marquis. Once again Vallois was signaling me that this wasn't right from the moment Sligh was riding up on his motorcycle, filling the quiet, genteel square with smoke and the rumble of an illegal muffler.

Gone were the ivy league shirt and khakis of his photograph, replaced with something in shinier black leather. Now it was quite clear that he was tattooed from his neck down and his wrists up.

He told me in no uncertain terms that he liked what he saw in me—unfortunately. And I made the mistake of letting him know my house was just across the square.

In my anxiety to "get on with it," I ignored my instincts—and Vallois's frantic signaling, and I let Sligh hustle me across the square—where we made it no farther than the foyer, where he efficiently stripped me down and fucked me on the spiral staircase.

He apparently hadn't read the part in my profile that stated that I preferred the top.

Needy slut that I was, though, I went with the fuck. I actually found his full-body, full-color tattooing arousing. And I hadn't had sex in months. After being fucked was a foregone conclusion, with him bending me over the stair banister and fucking me from behind with a stubby, but thick cock, I sank down to the stair treads, and he turned his belly to me and worked up his cock with my mouth and hands until he had recharged, and then I spread my thighs and raised my pelvis to him and ran my hands and tongue along the curves of the tattooing on his chest as he fucked me hard to a mutual release.

He left me exhausted and panting—and strangely relieved and satisfied—in a heap on the stairs. I would have had no regrets, really, about that encounter, if he hadn't taken my laptop as a souvenir.

That had cured me of the on-line dating service approach—even if I didn't have to take some time and hassle in replacing my laptop—including a declaration for the dating service that they'd never had such a man in their files. But it had given me impetus to be a little bolder in my seeking of a new life. Sligh's fuck may have been run-of-the-mill for him, but it had been exotic for me and had aroused me in ways I never would have suspected I could be aroused. I was amazed to find that I even loved having a man's cock up my channel. That had never happened with Todd.

Looking back on my "marriage" to Todd, I could see that we had fallen into a very vanilla relationship. I began to feel a little less betrayed by the circumstances that had split us apart. Todd was probably right. It was our time to part anyway.

It was Val—I started calling him Val now, as I finally owned up about my preferences to him, so we were "no secrets" friends now, or so I thought—who came to my rescue at that point. It took me a couple of more weeks after the Sligh incident to build up the courage to go back to the Café Marquis for breakfast. I could see now that my behavior had been far too obvious. And I was embarrassed.

But the Café Marquis made the best dark, strong coffee and beignets I'd had, and there came a morning when I was starting my new novel that I got stuck for just the right word and realized I was painting myself into a plot corner—and woke up to the fact that it was late morning and I hadn't had breakfast yet. And, without thinking, I strolled across Lafayette square, drawn by the blue umbrellas in front of the Café Marquis.

Vallois was there, as always. Smiling his welcome smile, as always. Greeting me in hushed tones, not a hint of smirk on his face.

But this morning, unlike any other, after he had served me my coffee and beignets, he sat down in the chair beside mine at the table under the blue umbrella.

"I'm sorry," he said.

"What?" I asked in surprise. "Sorry? Sorry for what?"

"That you can't find what you're looking for. You are looking for a man, aren't you? A man to love. A man to be a lover to."

I was flustered and I couldn't answer, but it was in not answering, not standing up indignantly and walking away right there and then, that Val knew everything he needed to know about me.

"That Phil guy told me how you connected. I looked you up on that Web site. It's OK. You aren't the only man doing this. I'm looking for a man too," Val whispered. "A man to love me. We're all looking for something."

"But I'm so . . . so ashamed," I said. Not knowing until now that this was why I had shied away from the Café Marquis.

"Ashamed?"

I might as well say it, I thought, now that I realized it. "You saw that guy, that last guy I met here. The biker. I'm ashamed because I let him take me home—and I enjoyed it. I knew for the start it would be a one-time thing. That's not what I'm looking for, but I let it happen anyway."

Val laughed. Then he looked stricken and apologized profusely.

"I'm . . . I'm not really like that," I said. "I'm not." I was trying a bit too hard—to convince myself, not just the waiter.

"You know what I think," Val then said. "I think maybe you've been a bit too much 'not like that.' This is Savannah, Honey. Live a little."

I felt sheepish, and I knew I looked the part too.

"Say, I think I know what you need," Val said. And then he stood up and fished around in his shirt pocket and took out a business card and laid it down on the table in front of me.

"Club One?" I said, looking at the card dumbly.

"Yes, Hon, I think you need to let your hair down a little. You go to that club one night and see if you don't get a whole new perspective on your life and on having fun. It's at the corner of Jefferson and West Bay Streets. Just start walking toward the waterfront and listen for the beat of the drums."

I took the card, but I didn't do anything about it. I was scared to. That bout with Sligh the biker had frightened the spit out of me. Especially because I'd enjoyed it. Who knows what I'd unleash if I didn't keep myself reigned in?

Each morning when I went to the Café Marquis, Val met me at the edge of the blue umbrellas with a smile on his face and an urn of steaming coffee in one hand and a basket of beignets in the other. And each time I sat down, he placed one of those Club One cards on my breakfast plate.

And I took each one, and as soon as I returned home, I dropped it in a brass plate on the bureau beside the front door like it was a hot poker. I was building up quite a collection of those cards on the bureau inside the front door.

That was until the day I got the letter from Paris. Nothing in writing, just a photograph in the envelope. Todd and Edward standing in front of the Eiffel Tower, all smiles, arm in arm. Todd had a walking cast on his calf. The break from his spill off the horse when we'd both been invited out to the Hamptons by Edward and Todd had tried to bluff himself into being an expert horseman had been really bad, I thought, for him to still have to wear a walking cast. Of course the date on the postcard was almost two months old. It had been redirected from New York.

Edward had been mortified about Todd's accident, and Todd had simpered as only Todd can. Edward had found Todd's simpering precious—and, I would suppose, arousing. I had found Edward fucking Todd in the bed in that private hospital Edward had insisted he go to for convalescence. And everything had gone downhill from there. Edward was richer than I was, which, I guess was the bottom line for Todd.

I turned the picture over to what the exuberant underlining and exclamation point told me was the breathy written comment, "He proposed at the top of the Eiffel Tower."

And one of them—it must have been Todd, as it would have been Edward's place to propose—had seen fit to send me the photograph. Me. Good old stuffy, dull Mike.

That night I dressed carefully and closed the door to my house on Lafayette Square behind me with a solid click and turned to the right on East Harris and walked slowly west, crossing Madison Square and half way across Pulaski Square. And then I turned north, walking through Orleans Square and Telfair Square and what would have been Ellis Square if they hadn't leveled that, back when historical preservation was an unknown term, and made a parking garage there. It was being made back into something like a square now, but I bypassed the construction there, and moved on toward where Bay met Jefferson. I didn't have a Club One card with me. I didn't need it. The location had been burned into my brain—and, besides, by the time I reached where Ellis Square once was, I could hear the rhythmic beat of the drums.

Club One was a real eye-opener. I had my choice of sins. Val had specifically mentioned the Cabaret one morning, though, so that's where I set my sights.

It was a transvestite extravaganza. I'd seen nothing like it before. I'd had to give my name to the host at the door, and there were several couples—mostly men—waiting ahead of me, but the host took me ahead of all of them and led me to a table right down near the dance floor. The other tables climbed in rows of occupied banquettes behind me—all in a red leather—or, more likely vinyl.

I didn't have to ask for a drink. The host had snapped his fingers, and a topless male waiter—all muscle and hunk—met us at the table with a bottle of good, chilled champagne and two flouts at precisely the moment we got there.

As soon as the lights went down and the music started up and the beautiful women started sliding out onto the stage, I was lost in the show. They were fantastic. Some were celebrities and some were in a class all of their own. All of them were dressed to the nines and prancing on stiletto heels and mouthing the words of the songs in perfect synchronization to the original songstresses—and all, I knew—but only because I'd read the billboards outside—were men.

Several of the performers were particularly good and alluring. One in particular, a small, cream-in-coffee colored Ertha Kitt look-alike, showed particular interest in me whenever she wafted by in her routine and with the periodic parade of beauties—and I, in turn, thereby paid particular interest in her.

As the lights came up in the room at the end of what was a mesmerizing show, the performers fanned out into the audience, to the appreciation of the clientele.

The Ertha Kitt look-alike folded "herself" into the booth where I was sitting and scooted over to me close. The topless waiter hunk materialized instantaneously and filled her flout with champagne.

She cooed at me and asked me how I had enjoyed the show. I told her I had enjoyed it very much, thank you. And it was the truth. I hadn't felt as loose and alive in years. It was like I could feel every muscle and bone in my body, down to my fingertips in a tingling sensation that was highly sensual.

The performance had given me a raging hard-on.

She asked me how I had enjoyed her performance, in particular. I told her I had enjoyed her performance in particular. And as I said it, I knew it was true. And I equally knew that my hard-on was for her.

She told me that she was Miss Savannah, and that she liked me and that she thought I might be more comfortable in her dressing room. And then she tossed off her champagne and reached her gloved hand around my neck and pulled my face slowly into hers and we kissed.

I didn't feel squeamish at all in kissing her. She tasted of champagne, which was sort of a "duh" realization, even though it had taken me by surprise. And her kiss made my nipples go hard and ache.

She rose and took my hand and led me back through a door beside the stage, one of the doors that she and her sisters had come through before my life had started—back before I felt alive and sensual again.

We fucked on the red satin-covered chaise lounge in her small, sweet-smelling dressing room. She insisted that I be naked. And she slowly undressed me and made love to me with her tongue and her gliding gloved fingers while she did so. She remained dressed in her shimmering silver gown, with its plunging neckline, and her long white gloves. Merely standing after rising from kneeling in front of me and giving me the most divine blow job I'd ever had and pushing me down on my back on the chaise lounge and reaching up under her billowy gown and pulling off her red G-string. Then she straddled my hips with her knees, her silky dress caressing my body in folds, and positioned her entrance on my erect phallus. And fucked me to paradise.

She sighed and moaned as I unzipped her bodice and let it fall down to her waist and played the best set of pert globular breasts a surgeon can give with my hands and my lips and my teeth. All the time she was rising and falling and rocking back and forth on my deeply buried cock. I moved one hand under the folds of her silver gown and found her own erect cock and slowly hand pumped that to the rhythm of her moving pelvis on my tool.

We came nearly simultaneously, and then she lowered her breasts on mine without dislodging my quivering cock, and we kissed and nuzzled and whispered sweet nothings to each other.

I whispered—in halting hesitancy—a burning question: would she come home to live with me on Lafayette Square?

I surprised and shocked myself. It wasn't a preplanned question. It came directly from the heart and the dick. I was suddenly mortified at my boldness and at my behavior. I never in a million years would do this when I was being my rational self. And yet, here I was, flat on a chaise lounge in Savannah, being fucked by a transvestite named Savannah. And I felt like a million dollars.

But then I shouldn't have been surprised. I knew. I think I knew as soon as the host started ushering me to my table.

She brought her lips to my ears and said the word I was yearning to hear. "Yes." Just that. "Yes." But with that "yes," that new world that Todd said I would find if I came to Savannah had begun. And I decided that Todd—and Edward—could go to hell.

Exhilarated, walking on the clouds, I took control. I rolled on the chaise lounge until she was under me, moaning and sighing, the heels of her stiletto-clad feet rubbing on my calves, and I fucked her into the dawn. I came in Savannah. Again and again.

The next morning, I rose early, not hungry—or at least not hungry for dark-roast coffee and beignets—and could barely dress myself, my hands were trembling so hard. I couldn't believe that it would happen. I kept telling myself it hadn't all been a dream, but the practical side of Mike kept whispering, "Yeah, it was," in my brain. I was a novelist. I was used to living in a fantasy world. Most people could tell the difference between fantasy and their real life. I couldn't. My career depended on not being able to do so.

So, it was a not-fully-convinced me who walked out of my door and down my front steps and across East Harris Street and into Lafayette Square, where I sat on a bench momentarily, my eyes glued to the blue umbrellas in front of the Café Marquis across the square rising above the purple flowers I couldn't name in the square's flowerbeds.

When I could breathe somewhat steadily and decided it was now or never, I stood up and continued my walk toward the blue umbrellas. As I drew closer, there he was. The waiter, Vallois. My waiter; my Val. Standing there, a suitcase on the curb of the road at the edge of the line of blue umbrellas. The sun was shining on this side of the square, and Val's eyes were glittering—there at the corners, where Savannah hadn't managed to cream off all of the silver Ertha Kitt glitter from the previous night.

Crystal Ball

Clarence was one of the most timid men on earth. And yet Clarence craved adventure. In his mind he engaged in the most dazzling exploits. Exploits with other men. Whole scenes and novels ran through his mind of "Clarence of the monster cock," fucking other men silly. Clarence, in fact, had a very nice cock. Clarence just had never used it in anything remotely like his fantasies in his entire thirty-six years. Oh, he used it all right—but always alone, in his own bed, as his mind wove tales of super cocking. Clarence the Superfuck.

Clarence was getting a little worried about his failure to get laid. I mean he was thirty-six, for god's sake, and although he knew he could be considered to be a handsome man and he kept his body in tip-top shape and had this very nice cock that he knew men would just love to have churning inside them, he was beginning to lose his hair. And he noticed an extra laugh line appearing here and there—despite this not being a laughing matter at all—and was there a hint of a little extra padding around that formerly washboard stomach of his?

He was just too damn timid—unable to cross a certain barrier. It's not that other guys weren't attracted to him, didn't sense that he had something they'd like to share. It's just that whenever Clarence came to the point of "getting it on" with another guy, he shrank away in indecision and shyness.

His problem had become accentuated of late. He had this little heart matter that he couldn't help chewing on—and letting chew on him. The doctor had said it was just a bit of heartburn, but, well, you know, one could never tell. And, perhaps worst of all, Clarence hadn't been able to get it up the other night. He was tired that night, for sure, and had watched a couple of DVDs that afternoon that had done a good job on him. But he'd never been unable to get it up on command before.

Maybe that's why he perked up when he was in Chuck's Bar the other night. It was a gay bar Clarence went to so he could get a good buzz on to work off alone in his bed later that night—having nervously pretended not to understand a couple of perfectly fine come ons in the bar earlier. While there, he'd heard two guys talking about a small carnival that had settled on an absentee farmer's field a couple of miles out of town—of how it was a traveling gay troupe on the sly—the usual offerings out front and gay shows at the back of the tents—and how they were planning to go out there and get their rocks off.

Clarence decided that was a good idea. He was growing tired of the DVDs—and he was afraid maybe they were part of why he had failed to arouse himself the other night. Or at least he hoped that might be a reason. When he contemplated becoming too old to get it up—especially when he'd never really used it with anyone else—his mind just shut down in a blue funk. Maybe if he saw a live show . . .

* * * *

Eric was sitting, fidgeting, in the folding chair in the front section of the tent. As he was driving by, he'd seen the "Maximus Circus" sign over the somewhat bedraggled collection of tents and small trailers pulled up in a small double ring in the field at the Chapman farm. He'd heard about this carnival—that it was a front for a traveling gay show. He had immediately wondered if there would be good action there, and, against his better judgment, Eric had pulled over into the parking lot. This was Eric's problem. He was promiscuous beyond all reason, willing to bend over and spread his cheeks for any man who put a hand on his belly.

Eric knew he couldn't keep on doing this. At twenty-two Eric already had the urge to settle down with just one man. That's what he craved. But, still, he had these urges he couldn't control. Even as he was parking the car in the muddy lot next to where the Maximus Circus tents were pitched, he knew he needed help; he didn't need to be stopping off at a dive like this in hopes that some man would give him that look and lay a hand on his belly. With a sigh, Eric had put the hand brake on the car and gotten out and walked toward the double ring of tents and vans.

As he entered the first circle, Eric saw the sign beside the open flap into one of the tents. "Madame Toni, Clairvoyant," it said. And in smaller letters under that "I can change your life."

Eric certainly did need his life changed. He hesitated momentarily. There was a big bruiser of a guy looking at him from across the circle. He was giving him the eye in that old familiar way. Eric wavered, and then, disgusted with himself, he abruptly turned to the right and entered the tent. The tent was divided into sections by plywood screening. There was a small area with four rusty metal folding chairs in the section Eric first entered, and there was a sign hanging next to the beaded curtain-covered door into the next section that said "Please wait. In Session." So Eric plopped down in one of the folding chairs.

He had no idea, really why he was here. There was just something about that "I can change your life" statement that had gotten to him. He knew it was all hooey, but he needed to do something to stop this insatiable appetite for having another guy's cock inside him. He needed someone steady, someone permanent. A daddy who would take care of him. Just one lover. Oh, and he should be well hung too.

As he was ruminating, the flap at the entrance to the tent fluttered and another guy entered the tent—or rather came inside the opening to the tent. Once there, and having seen Eric, however, the other man wavered.

Eric looked up to see an almost panicked expression in the other man's face. Otherwise a good face, though. Quite handsome. Sandy haired, hazel eyes, a nice smile—a few laugh lines to indicate a humorous, gentle nature. Good build. Very presentable. Maybe ten or fifteen years older than Eric. Eric couldn't tell, but he could see that the guy wasn't too young or too old. Eric liked being fucked by guys not too young nor too old.

Nice clothes, too. They looked expensive. He looked like he could afford someone with Eric's tastes.

Eric could tell, however, that his presence was disturbing to this guy, so he did what he could to be invisible. He shrank into his chair and looked the other way. It's OK, guy, he was thinking. I'm not here. I'm no threat to you.

The other guy hesitated for a few more moments, but then he straightened up, somehow resolved not to break and flee, and sat down in one of the folding chairs on the other side of the tent enclosure from Eric—as far away from Eric as was possible.

The more Eric was alone with this guy, the more he lost his own resolve that had brought him into the tent to consult with Madame Toni on how he could get off this wheel of casual promiscuity. And the more his resolved flowed from him, the more Eric, the problem child, took over. He began to fantasize about this other guy in the small tent enclosure with him—about what they could be doing. Wondering about what the other guy was packing.

He looked at the other guy's midsection, at his basket, and the other guy nervously crossed his legs—as if he could divine what Eric was thinking. Eric slouched down in his chair, instinctively spreading his legs, gazing steadily at the other guy now. The other guy was trying to look everywhere but at Eric, but that wasn't working so well. From time to time, he took peeks across the enclosure. Eric let his hand go to his basket.

Silence for the longest time, with Eric doing his "available" signaling and the other guy taking occasional—actually, more frequent—peeks and getting pretty fidgety.

"Wanna fuck me?" The question was posed in a low voice so that the other guy could pretend he didn't hear Eric if he wanted to.

But the other guy had clearly heard what Eric said, and they both could tell that he had said it. The other guy's hands were trembling; his whole body was shaking, and he popped up out of his seat, ready to flee the tent.

"Oh, two sweeties. Two honeys waiting to see Madame Toni." The husky voice cut through the exploding tension in the enclosure. A blowsy "woman" in full-drag gypsy dress was standing at the beaded curtain into the back section of the tent, a monstrous, high-color figure that suddenly filled the space, both with "her" presence and with "her" strong perfume—to capacity. A middle aged man, working on his zipper, tucking in his shirt tail, and sporting a sloppy grin was passing from the back to the tent opening, and was quickly gone—barely an illusion of whatever had been going on in the back of the tent while tension was building in the waiting enclosure.

The other man was already standing, and Madame Toni jumped to the conclusion that he was next.

"Come on back with me, Honey," she was saying in that melodic husky voice of hers. She turned to Eric. "Be with you in a few minutes, Sweets."

The other man opened his mouth to say something—either that he had changed his mind or that Eric was the next one in line, but Eric was already demurring, conceding his rightful place to the other man, and Madame Toni had a pudgy, bejeweled hand on the other man's forearm and was guiding him beyond the beaded curtain.

* * * *

Clarence felt trapped and was close to hyperventilating as Madame Toni manhandled him through a second, darkened compartment of the tent, which appeared to be her sleeping and cooking quarters, and into the section at the back of the tent, which was set up in some tacky perception of the Arabian nights, as envisioned by someone who had never been outside of Kansas. There were candles and large carpet pillows strewn everywhere, and in the center of the area, a small, round table was strategically positioned, covered down to the ground with a green felt cloth. On one side of that was another one of the rusty metal folding chairs and across the table from that was a white wicker fan chair that was listing a bit to the left. In the center of the table was a crystal ball, all aglow, with a murky milkish cloud swirling inside it.

Madame Toni pushed Clarence down onto the metal chair, and she moved around the table and lowered a gigantic butt into the fan chair.

Clarence was still in high panic over the near-thing encounter he'd had out in the waiting area with that dark-haired, dreamy-eyed young hunk. The guy had been coming on to him. Clarence had known that long before the guy had asked him if he wanted to fuck. And Clarence had found the young guy irresistible—or would have, that was, if he didn't have the block against contact with another man that was driving him crazy—and, he suspected, sending him to his grave.

When he'd popped up out there, even as he was doing it, he didn't know what he would do next. He wanted to grab the saucy little hunk and take him into the woods and fuck his lights out—and, in fact, that night when he got back to his apartment, all alone in his bed, he would weave a fantasy of doing just that as he masturbated himself to sleep. But the rational side of Clarence's brain was telling him that he had jumped up to escape once again—that he just couldn't slip over that divide from fantasy to reality. He needed something to explode him across that divide.

"What is troubling you, my dear? Tell Madame Toni. Madame Toni can help."

Clarence looked up, realizing for the first time that the larger-than-life figure across the table from him was addressing him. He looked around the enclosure, with its cheap movie set props of the mysterious Orient—seeing them for the first time—and he wanted to laugh. And to get up and march out of there. This wasn't going to give him any answers. But then, that young hunk was out there. And Clarence would have to see him again and be struck with the reality that he just . . . couldn't . . . take that step.

Madame Toni had one palm on her glowing crystal ball, milky cloud aswirling, and she was holding one of Clarence's hands in her other hand. She had her thumb folded under so that it was stroking Clarence's palm, and it brought chills up his spine—and, he was almost embarrassed to admit, stirrings in his loins.

And then he blurted it all out. How he'd dreamed of having sex with another man—of mastering another man. And of the block he was having doing that. And of

340

how he was getting older—and, he was afraid—infirm. He even told Madame Toni that he was beginning to have trouble getting it up.

All the time Madame Toni sat there, looking comforting and confident and sympathetic, stroking Clarence's palm with her thumb, and clucking that she was certain she could help him.

Inside, though, she was calculating. She'd heard this story a hundred times before. This was probably the number two reason the men came to see her. The number one reason was that men just liked to get their rocks off and hers wasn't any more expensive that any other quickie blow job.

This seemed to be an extreme case, though. The guy seemed to be on the edge and tipping over it. For no particular reason at all, really. He was quite good looking and in great shape. Madame T wondered for a moment if he was just tiny down there. Well, that wasn't a problem, either. She could pretend delight with the best of them and if there was anything down there at all, she could get it hard between her lips.

He was so skittish, though. The approach would have to be delicate and she'd have to gauge what he would be willing to pay—what amount she should charge him that wouldn't scare the rabbit off.

Clarence was trembling and shuffling his feet nervously under the edge of the green felt table covering. Madame T knew she'd need to move this session along quickly to close the deal. And there was another one waiting out in the waiting area. A real cute one. She could tell what his problem was. He'd want to be fucked. Well, she could manage that, as well, although the blow jobs were a lot more convenient, took less time, and were less messy.

"Let's just see what the crystal ball has to say about this," Madame Toni murmured, letting go of Clarence's mitt now and covering the ball with both of her palms. She raised her face to the ceiling and closed her eyes. "Let's just see what the crystal ball has to tell us about your future."

She was humming, in a low, husky baritone, her tone becoming darker, more possessed, the light in the room seemed to be dimming.

In fact, it had become a whole hell of lot darker in the room. The crystal ball had blacked out. No glow. No milky-white swirl. Nada. Black.

Clarence gave a strangled little cry and stumbled up from the folding chair, which fell away behind him with a metallic clang. Panicked, knowing instantaneously what the crystal ball was telling him about his future, and gurgling his horror, he turned and hobbled out of the room.

He stumbled through the intervening, dark section of the tent, and his eyes were blinded by the light as he pushed through the beaded curtain into the reception enclosure.

"There is no future. I have no future. I knew it. I'm doomed. I'm going to die," Clarence was muttering to himself as he entered the reception area.

His eyes, when they focused, lit on Eric, still sitting there, jaw dropped, eyes bugging out, as he viewed the ghostly apparition bursting through the beaded curtain.

Clarence leaned down and grabbed Eric's wrist and pulled him out of the folding chair with superhuman strength.

"Now. You. Me. The woods," Clarence roared as he pulled an astonished Eric toward the tent opening.

Clarence fucked Eric three ways from Sunday on the moss in a little glen of the woods between the field and the house of the Chapman farm. Clarence was a superfucker. Masterfully taking Eric in several positions—all that he could remember from his built up fantasies—with a master cock that made Eric melt and writhe and cry out in ecstasy.

At length, both spent and exhausted and still panting, Eric lay in Clarence's arms on the soft moss as they watched the leaves in the trees above them sway in the evening breeze.

"God, I have never . . . never . . . never been fucked like that," Eric muttered in awe and admiration. "Can I come home with you, Daddy? I mean like in forever?"

"Yes, why not?" Clarence answered in a small, dreamy, well-satisfied voice. Why not indeed? Clarence had had no idea it could be this good. He was at least half in love with Eric already. And what was forever, anyway? He had seen reality in that crystal ball. Forever was fleeting.

* * * *

Back in the rear enclosure to Madame Toni's tent, Madame T broke her trance and humming and looked, in surprise and confusion, at the retreating figure of Clarence.

Then she looked down and saw her blackened, dull crystal ball.

"Damn. Damn, damn, damn," she muttered as she bent and ran her hands under the table until she found the two loose ends of the electric cable that Clarence had knocked apart with his shuffling feet. "I keep telling myself I need to get a battery-operated ball. Shit."

In****

Prodigal Father

At last Steve felt he'd gotten the dimensions just right on the sailing sloop they were building for the Connecticut banker. He'd been concentrating for hours on the task. This was the project that should put them into the black for the year, and it was barely October yet.

It had been a good year. Sonny had left him in March, but Raul had hired up in the wake of Sonny's departure, and Raul was every bit the man Sonny had been and more. The tall, beefy Cuban émigré had the talented hands for all of the tasks Steve had for him—around the Shrimp Cove Boat Builders yard and, just as important, in Steve's bed. This was the fourth man Steve had had in the nine years since he left Baltimore and came down to Key West, where the hot men to be had were plenty. And although Steve was pushing his fifties, he still kept a forceful and willing twenty-something hunk around to make him feel young. It had been his good fortune that the last two—Sonny and Raul—had both been expert boat builders. It helped Steve to focus his activities.

Steve stood and looked down at the drawings spread across his work table. He was pleased with the morning's work. The Connecticut banker was getting himself one honey of a yacht. And he was buying at just the right time too. The downturn in the market made materials cheaper, and so many of the big boat builders up and down the East Coast had bitten the dust that the smaller, more specialized operations like Steve's had more breathing room. All they needed was just a couple of yachts like this a year and they were sitting pretty. And the banker was good for the money. What he had already written a cleared check for was more than enough in itself to keep Steve in business until he had to scrounge up another sugar daddy in the new year.

Steve laughed. The Connecticut banker had been quite a sugar daddy too. Raul had taken care of him when he'd come down to the keys. By the time he went back up to New England, he would have done anything for Raul.

Yes, indeed, Raul was a real asset.

With the thought of Raul, Steve lifted his face toward the double-wide garage door that opened the design and construction floor of the ship-building works. He looked out onto the marina on Stork Island, the last key save Key West down the chain of islands strung out between the Florida tip and Cuba. The sunshine

345

streaming through the bay doors was strong and hot, and Steve gauged the breeze—of which there was practically none—by the slight swaying of the two palm trees between the office building and the business' dock and slipway.

As he looked, his eyes narrowed and his heart began to race as Raul sauntered up and stood, leaning, at the corner of the open bay. He'd been working in the hot sun, finishing a sailboat for a local customer. And he looked hot in more ways than one. The rays of the sun made him little more than a silhouette from where Steve stood, leaning over his drawing table, but Raul was body beautiful in a tableau like this. He was wearing only shorts, and his dark skin was even more golden from the tanning of the fleeting summer in the keys. All muscle and beef and a full head of black curls. The sultry look of the Caribbean. His casual stance and his torso taut from the pull of his arm resting over his head on the frame of the doorway sent flames of arousal through Steve's body, and he began to breath heavily.

"God, it's hot out here, mon. Time for a beer break?"

"Sure," Steve answered tightly. "Take one from the fridge and bring me one too, please. I just finished the Walker specs. I think we have a winner."

It would be good to have a beer, but what Steve really wanted was Raul over here, behind the table with him. Giving attention to the raging arousal he'd given Steve merely by standing in the doorway in the sunlight.

"Oh, I think Walker can't help but be pleased," Raul said as he sauntered over to the drawing table with two open bottles of Corona dangling from one of his hands.

"Yes, thanks to you."

"Thanks to Mighty Moe," Raul said and then he laughed.

Steve laughed too. That's what Raul called it. Might Moe. And mighty it certainly was.

Raul stood close behind Steve and set a beer for Steve down on a square of space on the surface of the drawing board that wasn't covered with drawing and spec charts. His other hand snaked around Steve's waist and palmed Steve's flat belly after snaking up under the hem of his Polo shirt. Raul took a full pull on his beer bottle while Steve's breathing turned raspy and he began to tremble.

"Let me see what you've drawn," Raul said, as he came in even closer behind Steve and looked over his shoulders at the charts and drawings on the surface of the table. "Yes, very nice. I think we will enjoy building this one."

"Raul," Steve whispered, with what emitted from his mouth being more of a groan than a spoken word. He was leaning over the table, arms wide, supporting his weight on the heels of his hands, legs splayed, because he felt Mighty Moe, all ready for action, at the small of his back, stroking up and down along his spine. Raul knew full well what he was doing—and how it would be received.

Young, hot, muscled, virile. Steve had given up a normal life in Baltimore for this. A family, a reputation, more than half a fortune. And at this moment, it had all been worthwhile. God, he loved Key West. No end of young, hung talent. No worries if one took a walk. There would always be another one—or at least there would be as long as he had money and kept his own body in shape.

"Raul," he rasped.

"Time for more than a beer break, mon?" And then that happy, deep-throated laugh. Raul knew his worth—his talents. And he enjoyed life to the fullest.

346

Both of Raul's hands were free now. They were working Steve's belt buckle and his zipper, and then they were pulling his trousers down off his legs. Mighty Moe was already free, and Steve began to moan at the feel of the power and heft of it at the small of his back.

"Raul," he whimpered.

"What is it you want, Mon? Tell Raul." And then he laughed again. A husky laugh.

"Fuck me, Raul. Please."

"Here, now? It's cost you some cotton. You know that. You know what I like."

"Yes. Yes. Yes." Steve reached down and fumbled with the drawer under the rim of the drafting table and pulled out the lube and one of the condoms he kept there and dropped them on the table within Raul's reach. This wasn't a unique scene in the construction hall. Steve enjoyed being taken in various parts of the hall. Raul wasn't taking liberties.

Raul didn't answer. He just laughed and reached over and picked up an Exacto knife from the drafting table.

Steve trembled, as he felt Raul pull away from him and heard the ripping sound the knife made behind him in the briefs he was still wearing.

Raul flipped the knife back onto the table and squeezed lube out onto his hand and then, as Steve leaned over the table, arms wide, supporting his body, Raul palmed his belly with his free hand and Steve began to grunt and groan as thick, slick fingers snaked through the slit in his briefs and entered him and began to open him up to the power of Mighty Moe.

With trembling hands Steve took up the condom package and slit it open and freed the condom for Raul to take up when he was ready.

Steve felt like Raul had his whole fist up there now, and he was hyperventilating and moaning and moving his butt on the invading fingers. He didn't notice when Raul had taken up the condom and rolled it on Mighty Moe, but the strength of Raul entering him almost lifted Steve up off the floor and would have slammed his chest down on top of his yacht drawings, if Raul wasn't palming his belly with a strong support hand.

"Oh Shit, Raul. Yesssss!" Steve cried out. Raul hunched his chest over Steve's shoulder blades and gripped Steve's wrists with his fists and fucked hard and fast up into Steve's ass. And then slow and deep. Steve moaned and moaned and moaned as Raul fucked on, breathing heavily now and still laughing, thoroughly enjoying himself.

Steve almost collapsed on the table as he came, but Raul moved his hands in time to Steve's side, a finger on either side reaching for and finding and rubbing Steve's nipples under his Polo shirt as Raul rode on and on.

Steve looked out toward the marina as he held there, in exhaustion, while the young and vigorous Raul continued to plow him through the hole he'd rent in Steve's briefs.

The figure of another man was silhouetted in the door. A young, lithe man. Blond and tanned. He was peering into the interior of the construction hall, but it was debatable what he could see—and what he could discern was happening over the drafting table—because of the dimness of the interior and the brightness of the sun beaming into the door.

"Be . . . with you . . . in . . . a minute," Steve managed to vocalize, hoping that his voice sounded somewhat normal. "Wait by the dock . . . Please. Be . . . with . . . in . . ."

Steve hoped the moan he gave as Mighty Moe pulled out of him and the condom was jerked off and Steve felt the wetness spread up the small of his back wasn't audible as far as the doorway.

The young man turned and disappeared from the doorway. Raul laughed and went back to finger fucking Steve through the hole in his briefs—just long enough to establish that he was finished when he wanted to be finished. Steve loved this aspect of the younger man.

* * * *

"Yes, may I help you?" The young man didn't look like a buyer. He's was too young, for starters, and he was leaning against a venerable Camaro, which looked like a speed ticketer's delight. "Are you interested in a boat? . . . or maybe employment."

The young man leaned against his car and gave Steve a searching look back. He was a very presentable young man, just the type Steve liked. Young, and hunky. Blond, with curly hair and a chiseled face and torso. He wore his T-shirt and jeans and moccasins without socks well.

"Umm, maybe employment," the young man said. But he said it almost like a question, and in faltering tones, like maybe there was something else heavy on his mind. Steve didn't think it was because he saw that Steve was being fucked by Raul just now—at least Steve hoped not. The interior of the drafting and construction hall was dark and the young man hadn't come inside. From the doorway, it would have just looked like Steve was hunched over the drafting table. And if the outline of Raul behind him could have been seen, it would have only looked like Raul was looking at the material on the table top over his shoulder. Surely, Steve thought. Surely, that's the most that it would have looked like.

And, anyway, the young man hadn't left. So he must not have been embarrassed by anything.

"You old enough to work?" Steve asked. He didn't need any more workers, but this guy was gorgeous. It wouldn't hurt not to just say no and send him off.

"Yeah, I'm nineteen. Nineteen in June. June 19th." Again that searching look, but then he shrugged and said, "Old enough."

"Know anything about boat building."

"A bit. My old man is a boat builder." The young guy was looking at Steve as if Steve was supposed to know something he didn't.

"From around here?" Steve asked.

"No. I'm down from Maryland." That pregnant pause again.

Steve was beginning to feel like this was pulling teeth.

"Got a name?"

"Ty. Ty Taylor." He pronounced it like it was some sort of answer to a million-dollar TV quiz question.

"Well, hello, Ty. I'm Steve." Somehow the name sounded familiar, and Steve went over the names of customers and local families. There were a lot of Taylors around. He was always being stopped and asked if he was related to so and so. He didn't want to just turn the guy around if he was here through a connection that meant something to the well-being of Steve's company.

"Yes, I know your name . . . You don't recognize me at all, do you?"

His voice sounded a bit piqued and Steve looked at him sharply, his mind racing. But the young man's mouth was faster than Steve's post-fucked brain could compete with.

"Ty Taylor. Your son." The young man said it with a hardness and bitterness that slapped Steve right in the face.

"Oh," he muttered. "I'm sorry. It's just such a surprise. So much time . . . how's . . . how's your mother?"

"She's dead. Cancer. Went fast. I need a place to stay until I can regroup, and boat building is what I do in Baltimore."

Steve felt the presence of Raul at the door to the drafting and construction hall, and when he looked around, he saw that Raul was looking at the young man—his son—rather than at him.

* * * *

"You can't stay here, son."

"You were about to hire me before you found out I was your son. Is it because of who you are? What you do? Why you left us?"

"I couldn't stay in Baltimore," Steve answered, a note of defensiveness in his voice. "It would have hurt you and your mother more if I had stayed. And I took care of you—both of you."

"You didn't even know who I was," Ty answered softly. "You didn't recognize the name you gave your own son. And you didn't know mother was dead."

"It was best," Steve said stubbornly. "My activities were blown all across the newspapers. He was a deputy mayor, for Christ's sake. It was best that I just leave."

"You didn't answer my question," Ty now said. "You were about to hire me before you found out I was your son. What makes my presence as your son rather than just another workman so impossible?"

Steve said nothing, so Ty picked up the conversation again.

"Is it because of that guy standing in the doorway? The guy who was fucking you when I started to enter your office? Is that why you don't want a son around? Because I know men fuck you? You can't get it up if your son is here?"

Each accusation was like a hard slap across Steve's face, and he lowered his head and couldn't look at his son.

"If that's it, I know you fuck men. I came here for a job, for someplace where I can shack up for a while and take stock and see what I want to do in life. I didn't come here to pass judgment or try to keep you from doing what you want to do. You proved where your priorities were when you left us in Baltimore and came down here. I just need a job and a roof over my head for a few months, god damn it."

"You got money for a meal or do you need some?" Steve said.

"I got money. Money's not the problem. You sent us money."

"Well, go get something to eat and come back in an hour or two and I'll be ready to show you where the house is. There's a room. But I share a room with Raul over there. If you have a problem with that, don't come back."

"I don't have a problem with that," Ty answered.

Steve turned and walked back to the office, his heart thumping in his chest, his feet feeling like lead, every ounce of him screaming out that this wouldn't work.

As he walked past Raul, the Cuban put a hand on his arm. He was grinning. "New tail in town? He's a cutie." Then he lifted a pair of ripped cotton briefs to his face and took a good whiff of his trophy.

"Don't even start with me," Steve hissed through clinched teeth.

* * * *

Miracle of miracles, it turned out that Ty knew his way around a boatyard and also was the model of discretion in Steve's house.

He didn't lay a guilt trip on the father who had deserted him and jilted his mother for another man—well, for a series of men, most of them young enough to be Ty's brother.

Ty came with boat-making skills, but under the tutelage of Raul on the construction line, his talents and abilities blossomed even further.

The months rolled by. By Christmas, Steve had decided that he wanted to have Ty around and that he loved making boats as much as his dad did. In early spring, Steve stood out in front of the drafting and construction hall as sign makers hoisted a new sign over the bay doors and hammered it in place. The company name had been changed to Steve Taylor and Son. Ty was given greater supervisory responsibility out on the dock and was spending time with his father at the drafting table. Steve didn't think his son would ever actually design the boats, but he wanted him to know enough about the process to be able to see whether they were designed well after Steve was no longer doing it.

Ty was given keys to the company offices, his name was put on the company bank accounts, and he was given title to a brand-new Camaro.

There was no discomfort between father and son at all. If anything, it was Raul who seemed put off kilter by the presence of Ty in their lives. Steve decided that Raul might have had ambitions vis-à-vis the company, but if so, that was really just too bad for him. Steve had never intended to make Raul a partner in that sense. Steve *had* thought of making Raul his life partner, though, and this is where the presence of Ty was having a bit of negative effect.

Not that Ty was a problem. The problem was Raul. Raul just wasn't as impetuous and forceful as he had been before—and he didn't surprise Steve with the sex urge as often.

They still fucked often enough for Steve, though—so if there was a problem, Steve saw it as Raul's problem.

At least he did until the evening he came home from work and decided to do a wash and went into Ty's room to gather up anything he'd thrown on the floor that might need laundered—and found the ripped briefs.

They were laying right there at the side of the bed. A rip in the rear. Right where Raul liked to split them apart when he fucked Steve. Steve had learned early that Raul had this fetish with briefs.

These weren't Steve's briefs, though. These were Ty's briefs. And Raul and Ty had gone off early that afternoon to look at a boat that might need reconstructed up on Long Key. Or at least that's where they had told Steve they had gone.

* * * *

Steve thought that he could live with sharing his son with Raul. And if that had been what it was about, maybe it all would have worked out.

The next time Ty told him that he and Raul had to drive off somewhere for the afternoon, Steve waited a half hour and then drove back to the house. He parked down the street and approached the house from the back and quietly entered through the kitchen.

They were there. The company's pickup was in the drive. And Steve could hear them, down the hall, in Ty's room. He quietly approached the door and peeked through the half-closed door, around the hinges. What he saw caught him by surprise and was something he couldn't forget.

Both men were naked, their bodies beautiful, Ty's lighter skin on Raul's. But what was unsuspected was that it was Raul who was lying back on the bed and Ty rubbing his briefs on Raul's face for him to sniff them and then pulling the briefs up Raul's legs. And then turning the Cuban hunk over onto his belly. Ty's mouth went to the bulge of Raul's buttocks and he was ripping a hole in the cotton material with his teeth, while Raul was moaning and writhing under him, which only increased as Ty's tongue went to Raul's hole through the rip in the briefs.

Steve watched in utter surprise and arousal as Ty then straddled Raul's hips with his thighs and began to fuck the Cuban through the rip.

The father backed away from the door and quietly retreated down the hall. He jacked himself off when he reached his car, unable to get the image of the two men fucking out of his head—not Raul fucking Ty, but Ty fucking Raul.

Steve did his best over the next few days to forget and not reveal what he had seen, what he knew. But it was becoming an obsession, and one that Raul could not miss. Sex with Raul wasn't the same now. And Steve's obsession was not that Ty was fucking Raul, but that Ty wasn't fucking Steve. Steve knew it was wrong, but it wasn't like he had raised Ty as his son. He hadn't seen Ty since he was ten. Ty had grown up to be another man, not his son. Just a stranger. A gorgeous stranger with a master cock that he was using to cock the man who was cocking Steve.

Inevitably there was a small disagreement over something minor that blossomed into a shouting match between Raul and Steve that ended up with Steve spilling out a sarcastic remark on what he knew was going on between Raul and his son.

The atmosphere in the house for the rest of the evening was decidedly frosty. Raul didn't come to Steve's bed. In the middle of the night, when Steve awoke and Raul still hadn't come to his bed, Steve rose and padded down the hall to Ty's room. Raul wasn't there either. But Ty was there, naked, lying on his bed, and looking absolutely delicious.

Steve stood in the dark outside Ty's room, watching Ty's body bathed in moonlight. And his hand went to his cock and he masturbated, half dreaming of Ty working his body like Steve had seen him fucking Raul.

The next day, Steve discovered that Raul had cleared out. He didn't appear for work and he wasn't at the house that night. Or the next night.

But Ty was there. Ty took up the slack of Raul's disappearance at the docks, and he was skilled enough now to manage it. Ty became indispensable at the boatyard. And he was there, in the house, in the evening.

Ty began to walk around the house in next to nothing. And he brought home porn videos, and he'd sit on the couch in front of the TV and watch them and play with his cock.

He was driving Steve crazy. At first Steve would hang back in the dining room, working on company papers on the dining room table, within sight of the gay porn showing on the television, but where he couldn't see Ty. But all the time he was sitting at the table, his mind was seeing Ty even if his eyes couldn't.

After a few days, Steve would knock off working at the table before the porn video finished, and he'd come into the living room and sit in an overstuffed chair where he could watch Ty climax at the high point in the film. Then he'd get up and go down the hallway to his own room and shut the door—and jack himself off to the vision of Ty.

The first time Ty fucked his father was a couple of weeks after this pattern had set in. The night was dark. It was raining and there were flashes of lightning. The air was hot, and close, and sticky. Steve was in cotton sleeping shorts and laying on his belly on his bed, trying to go to sleep, but held awake by details of the mornings work running through his mind—and being pushed aside by thoughts of Ty's body. Of Ty's smooth, youthful muscles, the beauty of his blondness, the strength of his fucking of the Cuban, Raul.

Steve heard a noise and he looked up at the open door to his bedroom. He thought he saw the naked body of Ty leaning against the door frame there, illuminated by a flash of lightning. But he assumed he was hallucinating and he shut his eyes tightly and opened them again. Another flash of lightning revealed the doorway to be clear.

But then he felt the heaviness of Ty's body coming down, full length, on top of him, the slickness of Ty's hot body on his, the muskiness of his scent, the hardness of the muscles.

Steve felt fingers digging at the cotton material covering his butt, and he heard the ripping sound of the material, and he felt the cool, lube-slathered fingers at his entrance. And he groaned and gave a small yelp as the fingers entered him, roughly and deeply.

Ty's body was covering his, trapping him completely, holding him within constraining bounds as Steve writhed at the rough opening of his channel. Then Ty's cock was invading him, stretching and punishing him. Skin on skin. No condom here. The skin of the son rubbing against, chaffing, the sensitive channel of the father.

Steve tried to spread his legs, tried to widen the access to his channel, but Ty tightened the vice of his thighs encasing Steve's, wanting him tight, wanting his channel to feel the full fury of a young, vigorous, monster cock.

The father moaned and whimpered and cried for mercy, but Ty fucked on, the moaning of the bedsprings matching those of the father. Steve reached over his head and grabbed at the slats of the headboard as Ty rode him hard.

After an eternity, Ty put a hand under Steve's belly and brought him up on his knees and then continued fucking him doggy style, his hand now reaching around and grabbing Steve's dick and pumping it until Steve came with an exhausted cry and collapsed on the mattress. But Ty just followed him down and fucked on.

Ty came twice inside Steve before Steve drifted off into sleep in exhaustion. When he woke, it was morning—more than an hour after he should be at the boatyard—and the only evidence he had that the night had been real was mussed sheets, a sore channel, and ripped sleeping shorts.

Ty wasn't in the house. But when Steve reached the boatyard, Ty was there, working away on a boat hull as if nothing had happened the night before.

Neither father nor son said anything about the fucking in the night—not that day, or the day after it happened again, or the day after the next time.

Steve was horrified, confused, and frustrated by it all. Ty was his son. But Steve also was totally aroused by what was happening. The Ty who fucked him was a vigorous hunk in the night. There was little connection to be made to the snot-nosed ten year old Steve had deserted in Baltimore.

Steve told himself it would have to stop. But the more he told himself that, the more of an obsession it became for him. And now being taken in the night, in secret almost, wasn't enough. Steve wanted to fuck in the daylight—joyously and like any committed couple would. It didn't matter that Ty technically was his son. He wanted Ty to be his life partner. They already were partners in the business. There wasn't anything Steve had that he wouldn't give Ty—just as long as Ty fucked him.

He spilled out to Ty what he wanted one sunny afternoon in midsummer after Steve had stood in the bay door of the drafting and construction hall and watched Ty, shirtless, work on fitting and polishing a teak deck on a small sailboat. Steve couldn't take it anymore. He told Ty that he wanted to go back to the house with him then and there and wash and fuck with him in the shower, and then to fuck the rest of the day away on Steve's bed—in the daylight. Acknowledging to the light of day that they fucked.

Ty merely put his hammer down, smiled, and led Steve to the pickup. They fucked under the running water in the shower, Steve's legs hooked on Ty's hips and his face buried in Ty's chest as the younger man pushed Steve's back up and down on the soapy stall wall tiles with the strength of his cock.

And then, in the full daylight, Steve laid on his back on his bed, his legs spread, while Ty stood between them and fucked Steve interminably while kneading his nipples with strong, calloused fingers, the two men's eye's locked on each other's.

Three changes of positions and two comings deep inside Steve's channel, and Ty left Steve to drift off into fully satiated sleep, while the younger man went back to the shower.

When Steve came out of sleep, it was twilight and the house was silent. Too silent.

He rose off the bed—painfully, as Ty had worked his channel like never before—and went to the door to Ty's room. Ty wasn't there. In fact, there was little of Ty there. His closet was bare, and the room looked like it had been stripped of everything that had made it into Ty's room.

Steve drunkenly moved down the hall, swaying and hitting both walls as he stumbled.

The note was on the dining room table. Next to it was the company checkbook. The balance had been zeroed out.

Through blurry-eyed tears Steve struggled to read the note: "You fucked the family. Now I hope you know how it feels to be completely fucked."

Steve sank into a chair by the table. He didn't have to look around to know that Ty had taken everything that wasn't nailed down—all that Steve had worked for for nine years. And even then, wherever Ty was, he still owned half of the company. And everything was in the company name, including the house.

He was trembling—trembling from frustration and anger. But the anger wasn't directed at Ty. Steve was angry with himself—because all that Ty had taken didn't matter a bit to him. What mattered was that Ty was gone. That Ty wouldn't be there tonight to fuck him.

Hook or Crook

I wanted to fuck Nathan from the moment I saw my son, Seth, fucking him. And I didn't just want to make love to him like Seth was doing, but to really give him a good fucking. I happened upon them in Seth's bedroom. I heard the moaning from the hallway and couldn't resist checking it out. Seth had won the neighbors' new pool boy—a golden blond surfer type with heavenly cut features, brown-tanned as a berry, and unruly curly hair flipping up at his shoulders. This was fast work even for Seth. Nathan had only been working for the Carnadays for two days. I'd seen him too and masturbated to the thought of fucking him twice already. But I'd barely thought of a scheme to get him for myself, and here he was already, on his belly on my son's bed, moaning, and undulating to the fuck my son was giving him.

Seth had the blond's thighs closely encased between his knees and his chest pressing on the pool boy's shoulder blades. He was running the fingers of one hand in the blond's golden mane and kissing him in the hollow of his neck. They could have been resting in postcoital repose, except the hips of both of them were moving like a ship on a rolling sea. Seth was slow fucking Nathan in a rolling undulation and Nathan obviously was enjoying it. His hips were moving in consort with Seth's and he was sighing and moaning.

They were making love, and the coupling made for a beautiful tableau. It got my juices going. Not because I wanted to make love to him like Seth was doing, but because I wanted to enter Nathan like that and make his eyes bug out because I was longer and thicker than Seth, and I wanted to slam my cock up into him again and again and make him groan and grunt rather than sigh, and cry out alternately for me to stop and for me never to stop.

This was not Seth's way, though. He fucked for the intimacy of love. And all these young hunks who gravitated to him left him eventually. He always seemed to be bewildered by not being able to find something permanent—a young man worthy of him who was willing to stick with him. I knew, however, that it was because the young men who gravitated to him really wanted to be fucked to exhaustion. They wanted to be dominated and squeezed to the limit and plumbed to the depths.

That was where I was entering dangerous waters with my son. My son was a romantic; he fell in love with those he was screwing. I just wanted to get my rocks off with a delicious hunk—to fuck the living daylights out of him, to dominate and leave him exhausted and moaning. It was probably my son's bad fortune that he attracted just the sort of young man I wanted to bang the living daylights out of.

The last time I'd taken after someone my son was wooing was that young Israeli Ely on the Elat resort beach. He had been a waiter in our hotel and had his tongue out and panting for my son that first morning on the balcony café overlooking the Red Sea. As he was pouring coffee—almost putting mine in my lap because he couldn't take his eyes off Seth—I asked him if he ever was able to get off work to enjoy the beach himself, and when he said he did and wasn't working that afternoon, in fact, I asked him if he wanted to come out on the beach with Seth and me—that I had a cabana reserved. He didn't hesitate in saying yes.

I could tell that Seth was taken with the dark, hirsute Israeli immediately. But I didn't suggest the assignation for Seth. I knew I wanted to fuck the stuffing out of the Israeli hunk myself. I regret to admit that I often used Seth like this, as bait for my own needs and desires—almost regret, I should say.

And I never took more than the young men wanted. They enjoyed the fuck my son gave them, but I'd leave them with their tongues hanging out, their asses steaming, and a look of total satisfaction on their faces.

I watched from a stretch of sand in front of the cabana as the two played in the water, becoming increasingly frisky and intimate. I could tell the instance that Seth's dick first entered the Israeli, because the Israeli, who was one of those kind of men who always had to be in motion, suddenly went rigid and his eyes took on that "Oh fuck, yes!" expression I so often saw on the young men my Seth was fucking. They were out in the water almost up to their nipples. Seth was close behind Ely, and I could see below the surface of the water well enough to know that Seth's hands were palmed across Ely's lower belly. They were moving with the gently rolling surf, but I could tell that they also were in the rhythm of the fuck, Seth crouched a bit and controlling the rise and fall of Ely on his cock by pushing off from the sandy sea bottom with his heels. I retreated to just inside the cabana, pushed the waistband of my bikini trunks below my balls, and masturbated as I watched Seth and Ely fuck in the gentle surf.

There were few other bathers around, and those that were there seemed focused on enjoying their own time in the sea and on the beach. No one appeared to be paying any attention to the coupling except me. I sat there in the shadows just inside the entrance to the cabana and slowing jacked off to the sight of my son making love to a dark, curly haired Israeli beauty who seemed totally lost to the experience. All the time I was scheming my own taking of him.

The three of us lunched together on the hotel terrace, with Seth and Ely already comfortable with each other, happy and satisfied, and likely to become even closer the longer we stayed in Elat. This was my son's way. Other men were comfortable and immediately smitten with him and prone to dropping their current lives without giving it a second thought and turning themselves over into Seth's hands—willing to rise and fall on his cock forever in some sort of love-filled mystical world. That wasn't my way. My way was fuck 'em hard and leave 'em gasping for air. And few had objected to that.

After lunch, Seth and Ely left me sipping a brandy sour on the terrace and went back to the cabana, closing the entry flap behind them. A half hour later, Seth emerged and came up to the terrace and said he was going up to the room to shower and dress and would be meeting Ely in the hotel lobby—that Ely wanted to show him around the area on his motorbike. I could tell by Seth's contented look that not only had he fucked Ely again in the cabana but also that he was completely smitten with the Israeli. I was happy for Seth, but a part of me was jealous. A part of me wanted to see that contented look on Seth's face after I'd fucked him—and not in his gentle way with others, but fast and hard.

I waited only long enough for my son to turn toward the door into the hotel and then rose and strode down the beach to the cabana. Ely was still stretched out on the day bed on his belly, his eyes closed and a huge smile on his face. He was naked, having just been loved well, I'm sure. His hole was still puckered and slack from where it had taken Seth's cock, and the small of his back was still splattered with gobs of my son's semen.

Already hard from the anticipation of what I was going to do, I stripped off my bikini, rolled one of the condoms that had been tucked below my waistband onto my cock, swung a leg over his pelvis, and thrust hard between his dark curly-hair covered bubble-butt cheeks, finding the slack and well-lubed hole opening to me immediately.

I had picked up the belt of my terry cloth hotel bathrobe before pinning Ely's belly to the day bed with a deep thrust of my cock, and when Ely's body flopped around from the surprise and pain of the assault, I grabbed for his wrists and got them bound to the railing at the head of the daybed. And then, crouched over his hips with my pelvis and leveraging my feet off the sand of the cabana interior, with my hands pressing down on his shoulder blades, I fucked Ely hard, deep, and brutally. He cried out and cursed and begged for relief at first, but he quickly subsided into groans and whimperings.

When he had quieted down to accepting the fuck, his hips rolling with the rhythm of my plowing and Ely sighing his enjoyment of my technique of rotating my pelvis as I dug in, I moved a hand below his belly and onto his cock. His hips were moving in perfect harmony with mine, and I squeezed his balls and cock and jacked him off, making sure that he had come before I did.

We held there, panting. He was still whimpering, though, when I pulled out of him, felt myself ready to rise again, and changed condoms. Then I turned him over, and ignoring his weak entreaties to leave him be, I straddled the narrow daybed with my thighs again, between his spread legs, and gave him another, even deeper, rapid-pistoning fuck. He flopped around under me until he had cum again and then he just lay there, collapsed, his tongue hanging out and a silly grin on his face while I piledrived to my own release.

He was exhausted and semicomatose when I was done this time. I just pulled my bikini trunks back on and turned and went up to the room and showered. Seth returned to the room while I was drying off, a sad expression on his face. He told me that Ely had not shown up in the hotel lobby as arranged, and, like a dutiful father, I clucked my condolences that perhaps Ely had flitted off to somewhere else, having gotten what he wanted from Seth. We never saw Ely again—and although Seth had not said anything to me about it at the time, I couldn't be sure that he didn't suspect some of his boyfriends just disappeared after I gave them a proper fucking. Seth would have to be a dope not to suspect some sort of pattern in play—and my son wasn't a dope.

I had tried to lay off after that and had usually managed to do so—with one or two lapses. I was a highly sexed guy and needed to get my rocks off regularly—in something beyond personal release. I needed the affirmation that I could completely dominate my partner and fuck him to his exhaustion—that I wasn't too old to do that to a younger man. And Seth and I had identical taste in men—we just had different things we wanted to do with those men.

I watched Seth and Nathan making love on Seth's bed. As usual, Seth was the one controlling the fuck, and Nathan was the one loving whatever Seth wanted to do to him—knowing instinctively that Seth would be gentle, would give Nathan time to adjust to him, and would take care of Nathan's needs and desires so that they plateaued and released almost simultaneously. Seth's sex was loving, giving as well as receiving. Nathan was in ninth heaven, the two moving in perfect harmony and rhythm. After a long, lingering kiss, Seth raised his chest off Nathan's shoulder blades and held Nathan by the hips as Seth moved his own hips in circles—a technique he had inherited from me—making deep cock love to every aspect of Nathan's channel walls. At length Seth raised up and pulled his dick out so that his bulb was just inside Nathan's entrance, rubbing up and down on Nathan's prostate.

Nathan was panting hard and making mewing sounds. His hips lifted up off the bed and one of his hands went and encircled his dick. He was dragging his cock head along the sheets under him, fucking the bed.

Seth pulled all of the way out of Nathan, jerked off his condom, and languidly went into a 69 position with Nathan, with both of them deep throating each other and swallowing each other off in a nearly simultaneous ejaculation. It was like they had been lovers forever, knowing exactly what to do and when, even though they hadn't laid eyes on each other before three days earlier.

I knew four things then—that Seth was really enthralled with this one, that I couldn't keep my hands off this one for however long he would be in our life as Seth's lover, that I as going to fuck this one hard myself by either hook or crook—and, most surprisingly, that I longed to fuck Seth too.

The avenue to my scheme was given to me that evening at dinner. Seth was bubbling over about his new friend, Nathan. It seemed that Nathan wasn't just the neighbor's pool boy. He also was one of those computer technicians who went to people's homes and helped them get their computers set up and troubleshooted.

After dinner I went up to my study and sat down at the computer. I knew the Web sites I wanted to use, and for the next hour I went through them, going to the pages that evoked what I wanted to the most and earmarking them in my favorites list. The next day, when I was sunbathing by my pool in the nude, I watched the Carnadays' yard until I saw that Nathan was out there, dipping leaves out of their pool. I went up on my diving board and did a few expert dives, giving Nathan every opportunity to check out the goods, which, if I must say myself, were plenty good. Then I sauntered over to the fence and called out to Nathan.

"Hi, I'm Seth's dad," I said.

"Yes, I know, Mr. Arrington," Nathan answered. A very nice, tenor voice. Steady. He didn't seem at all nervous talking with the naked, forty-five-year-old father of his new lover. Well, I intended to fuck some fear into him before I was done.

"Seth tells me you work with people's computers . . . sort of work out the kinks. True?"

"That's right. You got kinks in your computer to straighten out, Mr. Arrington?" He was giving me a smile that I couldn't figure out. These open, hunky surf dude types can be hard to read. I didn't know if he was being half snotty or just friendly. But I knew I did have something for him to straighten out. In fact, it was already straight, and if I backed off from this fence between my patio and the neighbors', he could see how straight—and fat and long—my cock could get for him.

"Yes, I can't figure it out. My favorites list is all fucked up," I answered. "When I click on one URL, a different site comes up."

"That's strange," Nathan said. "I've never encountered that." And I could tell by his smile—he was almost salivating—that I'd given him a challenge that no computer geek could resist.

"Do you have anything to do at about eight this evening?" I asked, knowing that Seth planned to be off to the gym then.

"Nope, I can come around then." Nathan answered. I was thinking that both Nathan and I would be "coming" a little later than that, but I just smiled and nodded and turned and walked away from him, giving him a great shot of my still-tight buns.

Nathan arrived promptly at eight and I took him up to my study. He was wearing loose shorts and an athletic T, all of which would be convenient for me and set his blond hunkiness off quite nicely.

I sat him down in my chair and turned the computer on for him, and he was soon working his way through the favorites I had set up the previous evening—all of fuck sites of daddies taking on blond hunks just like him, all earmarked to hot fuck scenes.

He spun through the dials for a while and eventually said, "Umm, I don't find anything wrong, Mr. A. All of the URLs seem to go where they are supposed to go." His voice was husky, though, so I knew he'd been looking at what he'd clicked on.

Time to make a move. Either it worked or it didn't.

I pulled the chair away, forcing him to get up on his feet, crouched over the computer. Then I covered him close from behind, with one hand snaking up under the hem of his T and up to a nipple and the other hand moving around to his basket. He was hard. And so was I.

I pushed the front of my shorts down—that's all I was wearing—and the back of his shorts down, and I had the underside of my cock running up and down along his crack.

"Umm, Mr. A. Ohhh, Mr. A." His voice was cracking.

"Don't speak. I want you. I want you now. You can feel my cock; I plan to slam that as far up your ass as I can. If it's not what you want too, you can just break away and leave. I won't stop you." He stayed put, and that and his ragged breathing told me that he was mine.

I crouched down behind him and went for his hole with my tongue. I kept a hand wrapped around his cock, and he has hardening nicely and panting hard for me as well.

359

And then, hands grabbing his hips hard, I was standing behind him and fucking him deep—brutally—in a pistoning action that had him yelping and writhing under me.

And then the surprise. He was turning and grabbing me in a wrestler hold—showing that he was a lot stronger than I was and well trained as a wrestler.

Here it came, I thought, he was going to punch me unconscious and leave me unfucked—and I didn't know what disturbed me more: that I would be black and blue or left sexually unsatisfied.

But he wasn't punching me. He was pushing me to the floor on my back and straddling my pelvis with his hips—and bringing his channel down on my erection. And he was fucking himself hard on me. He wasn't rejecting me; he was showing that he liked a rough fuck like I liked—in fact, that he loved it.

We were really going to town when Seth entered the room.

I was momentarily shocked that he'd found me in a compromising position with the young man he was currently wooing. But this didn't seem to be the case. I watched him strip off his shorts, and then he was sitting in the chair from the computer desk and watching Nathan fucking himself wildly on my cock and slowly jacking up his own cock.

When I had come, surprised that Nathan could bring me to the boil so expertly and quickly, the blond hunk pulled off me and then went and sat on Seth's cock and the two of them fucked in slow, sensual undulations that had me hard and masturbating myself again.

Later, on my bed, with Nathan wedged between us and Seth and I sharing him, Seth told me that he had no trouble sharing like this—that it turned him on.

"In fact, Dad," he said, moving his hand from Nathan's cock to mine, "having seen what you do to Nathan, I think I'd like to have a little of that myself."

"Thought you'd never say that, Son," I said, with delight, as I reached for him with both hands and brought him up to his knees straddling Nathan's prone figure, and the two of them were kissing and Nathan was stroking their cocks together, and I hunched over Seth's hips and piledrived him until his knees buckled and he fell onto Nathan. By then, however, Nathan had rolled up his hips to Seth, and Seth was fucking him almost as furiously as I was fucking Nathan.

Later, all satisfied and weary and once more with father and son sandwiching Nathan, I leaned over and whispered to the computer geek, "So, you like it both ways, Nathan?" I asked. "Both the loving Seth can give you and the rough fucking I prefer?"

"No problem. No problem at all, Mr. A." And Nathan was giving me that sunny surfer-boy smile of his. And I was content for the first time in my life and not feeling guilty about my son anymore at all.

"I think we may have found a new high-paid houseboy," I murmured around Nathan's nipples to my son who was sucking on one. "That is, if Nathan feels he can do better here than at the Carnadays,'" I said.

"No problem," Nathan squeaked, whether at the tonguing Seth was given his nipple, or the slow hand job Seth was giving him, or at my dick pumping him deep, or at my hand on his belly, I didn't know—or care.

Interracial

Snowball Effect

I couldn't resist Michael Dabney's proposition in the Checkers Lounge at the LA Hilton Checkers hotel during the Entertainment Industry Advertisers' Association convention—well either of his propositions, really. I'd never done it with a black man before, and that had become somewhat of a special fantasy of mine. I was attending the EIAA convention because I'd been working with a small firm that had exclusive contracts with a few actors' agencies for commercial TV work. Dabney worked for a much larger and more influential black-owned firm representing the recording and advertising portfolios for black singers—mostly bad-boy rap artists.

"But why me?" I asked.

"You mean other than trying to get your luscious body in bed?" Michael asked. But he was smiling that enigmatic smile at me that I found so engaging, and he was so glib and given to turning of phrases and playful double entendres that I didn't take him seriously. Besides, he was far more luscious than I was. Not American black, but a transplant from the Caribbean and all hot sexy looks and lean and trim body, emphasized by his graceful, fluid movement. And he had a smooth, rich voice and an expert grasp of the disarming sales pitch technique. He could talk the chastity belt off a nun. Which probably was why he was head of the marketing department for Johnson Brothers, the rising black advertising firm in the music industry.

"No, I mean that I'm a white guy and Johnson Brothers is an all-black firm representing black musicians only. Why are you offering me a job under you?"

"You mean besides the desire to have you under me?" he asked. That enigmatic smile again. "Well, being all black has put us at a barrier to advancement," he continued after that pregnant pause that put me off balance again. "Our clients are all black, but the industry is pretty much white—and some of it is pretty racist white too. Clarence and Maurice Johnson want their business to grow. They think having a white guy in place to work with sticky situations will enhance our business. We've been over the likely candidates in the field, and we think you are our white guy."

"I guess I should feel flattered," I said with a laugh. "And how much would a token white guy be worth in your firm?"

I whistled at the number Michael tossed out. It was nearly three times what I was making in my current position.

"And you wouldn't be token," Michael said. "We think you'd be worth your weight in gold with companies that aren't giving us the time of day now."

"Because of my résumé?" I asked, trying to keep the sarcasm out of my voice.

"Yes, that—and, of course, because of your terrific bod," he flashed back. I still couldn't read whether he was toying with me, making fun of me.

"My bod," I said in a flat tone.

"Just being honest here. Advertising is all about appearances. Sexiness sells. We wouldn't have anyone on our marketing staff who didn't come across as sexy. And you're sexy plus—in a white way, of course." That disarming teasing smile of his again. I think he could tell me I'd had spinach in my teeth throughout an important briefing and I would just nod and give him a silly "happy smile."

I knew that sex sold and was important in the advertising business already, of course—I'd let many a woman and man lay me on the way to closing a contract—but it wouldn't have taken more than a glance at the suave, achingly sexy Michael Dabney, Johnson Brothers' marketing director, to see the truth of that.

I said I'd think about it. And when Dabney pressed, I said I'd most likely accept the offer.

And that's when I realized that he wasn't joking with me with his suggestive double entendres. Because that's when he hit me with his other proposition.

Michael was an astonishingly attentive lover. He held me in his arms just inside the door into his hotel room and kissed me deeply—and expertly, I might add—while his hands were stripping me of my clothes—also quite expertly. He then guided me to the bed and lay me down on my belly and gave me a deep massage from neck and shoulders to the soles of my feet, taking his time and making sure he'd covered every inch of my backside with his sensuous massage. Then, me already fully aroused, he turned me onto my back, and lay, shirtless but still with his trousers on, stretched beside me on the bed, his arm encasing me, and glided his free hand all over my body, becoming increasingly intimate. All the time he was kissing my lips and the hollow of my neck and my eyelids and running his tongue into my ear cavities. His hand went to my engorged cock, and he began stroking me off slowly while still holding me closely in place with his other encircling arm.

"Now doesn't that look nice?" he murmured to me. "My milk chocolate on your milky white body. Don't they meld nicely?"

"Umm, umm," was the best I could respond under his attention.

"And how about some milky white cum on my chocolate thigh?" he whispered.

I couldn't answer, as I was arching my back and panting shallowly to try to prolong the pleasure before that happened.

He made love to my body in this manner for more than a half hour, until I was writhing under him and begging him to fuck me—and ejaculating in great gobs of milky white cum under the attentions of his stroking hand and his thumb rubbing back and forth on my piss slit.

Then, as I lay there all mellow and moaning for him, he stood up and slowly dropped his trousers and briefs. He was a true black. His skin was the chocolate color of the Caribbean quadroon and his features delicately European, but his cock was black as coal and hung low—except that now it was at full staff.

"Want to watch a black cock moving in and out of that nice white hole? I know I do," He murmured.

I moaned at the mere thought of that image. I'd fantasized about being taken by a black man, and here it was, happening in reality.

Smiling down at me, he took my hips in his hands and pulled me down to the foot of the bed and then knelt between my spread thighs. His mouth went down on my ejaculate-slicked cock head, and he was sucking me into his mouth. The image of my whiteness being pulled between those full, brown lips had me hyperventilating. At the same time a moistened thumb went to my asshole and he was beginning to open me to him.

I undulated my pelvis at his attention and fisted the bedspread and cried out for him to fuck me—the foreplay had gone on for an eternity, and I was burning for him to finish me—to bury that luscious black cock in me and pump me hard.

He moved his lips and tongue to my asshole and by the time he was finished there, I was so open that he merely stood between my legs and slid that long, black tool into me. He pumped me deep for a few minutes as I moaned and groaned and arched my back and pulled his torso down to where we could kiss. After we parted, he put a hand behind my neck and raised my head so I could see that black cock appearing and disappearing inside my hole—and I began to pant and melt.

Then he turned my body on his cock so that I was belly down on the bed, cock hanging off the end to be found by his stroking hand, and then he was fucking me from the rear in deep, long strokes. I turned my head and sought his mouth while he thumbed my nipples with his free hands and I felt him jerk and could feel the strong flow of his come even though he was sheathed.

* * * *

Strangely enough, Michael was mostly business with me once I had joined Johnson Brothers and, although we did fuck again on occasion, it certainly wasn't as often as I was willing to be taken by this master lover—nor was it as intense or as fulfilling as that first encounter was. Over time, I developed the suspicion that the lovemaking was mostly just part of the job offer pitch—and testing me out, perhaps on just what I too would be willing to do to close a deal. Still and all, it was the best attention I've ever gotten—and it fulfilled every fantasy I'd had of sex with a black man.

Michael must have talked around the office about me, though, because there wasn't much in the way of checking out preferences or willingness on the part of one of their premier clients, the black rapper Sledge, when the firm assigned the marketing department to help find a home for his newest album recording. Michael asked me to take a crack at getting him into Top Ten Records, which had just started including rap artists in their offerings, but wasn't yet into the heavy leather type of music that Sledge put out.

I make an appointment with Top Ten Records, whose name pretty much said it all as far as market position was concerned. I didn't really think there was much hope, because they were an old-white boy, tight-assed sort of organization that only went for surefire projects. But, miraculously, they showed interest, even though a flagrantly bad-boy tricked-out Sledge, complete with minimal clothing coverage of his heavily muscled and obscenely tattooed body and his fake fur coat and platform shoes, insisted that he attend the session. One of his homeboys drove us from our offices over to Top Ten Record, and I was shocked to see how much floor space there was in one of those Hummer stretch limousines.

After the meeting, with Sledge euphoric over how well the talks with Top Ten had gone, I got a personal lesson in why Sledge had all of that floor space in his limo. As I was starting to climb into the back outside Top Ten's entrance, Sledge pushed me in and onto the floor of the vehicle with a meaty fist to my back. And then he showed me his appreciation for the extraordinary sales job I'd been doing for him by pulling me up to my knees with a fist in my hair and gagging my throat with a big, black cock with a heavy-duty silver ring in its head. He stripped my trousers and briefs off as I was trying my best to suck him, and when he was satisfied that he was prepared, he simply picked me up and slammed my butt into the seat at the back of the Hummer and spread my legs wide with his hands.

"Lay down nice for me, white bitch," he said. "Gonna ream you a whole new hole with black cock. Your ass is mine. You put on a good show in there; so's now put on a good show for me. Nice tight hole." He was digging the fingers of one hand deep into my ass while pulling my lips up to his bulging nipples on a hard chest with a fist in my hair.

I whimpered and gasped as he then fucked me hard and deep until I was crying out. He was so good at rough cocking, though, that I was soon crying out for more. He laughed a deep-throated laugh as he felt me give in to him and then to clutch his bulbous buttocks to hold him deep inside while I sighed and murmured my involuntary ecstasy.

Sledge kept declaring that he owned my white ass while he was jackhammering me—and perhaps he did in the cutthroat world of entertainment advertising. I certainly wasn't in a position to naysay him without backing in my own office, which I wasn't likely to get if this cushy Top Ten Records deal went through. So, in effect I was fucking myself by having won him a chance at the deal.

After he was done with me and the Hummer was pulling back up to the building in the low-rise parklike office campus that housed the Johnson Brothers offices, he grunted at me to dress and then we went back up to marketing division's second-floor offices. He just sat there all smiles and all innocence as I reported on our success to an appreciative Michael Dabney, while I tried to cover my embarrassment of having a twitching butt that was asking for more attention from Sledge's cock ring.

I had to walk Sledge back to his limo and found it hard to walk a straight line as out of joint as my legs were from Sledge's power cocking. When we reached the foyer, though, Sledge saw a couple of muscle-bound homeboys lounging at the door to the shipping department and went over and chattered with them for a while in low tones that I couldn't have deciphered even if they were loud enough for me to hear. I didn't need an interpreter, though, to figure out that Sledge was talking about me. He kept sniggering and pointing to me, and the two bulky black homeboys were muttering back to him with big, knowing smiles on their faces.

When he returned to me he palmed my butt as we walked to the car and he smiled back at the two shipping clerks with a "I own this white boy's ass" look that they fully appreciated. I thought I was seeing him to the door, but he wasn't finished with me. He took me back to his place and pounded my ass so hard all night that I called in "ravished" the next day and had to soak in the tub for hours.

The day I returned to work, I made the mistake of stopping by the shipping department when leaving on my lunch break to drop off some outgoing packages that I just as well could have let an office boy take care of. And before I knew it, I was lunch for Ham and Sly, the muscle-bound shipping clerks. Without so much as a "May we fuck you, kind sir," they lifted me and hustled me out of the shipping dock and over to the picnic table they'd set up for themselves in a copse of trees next to the building.

They stripped me, and Ham fucked me hard and rough doggy style, while Sly pushed his thick cock between my lips. And when Ham was done, he turned me and changed places with Sly. Once again, though, I melted at the image of being fucked by big black cocks and watching hard, chocolate muscles rippling against my white skin as they worked me.

Each of my fuckings at the hands of the black dudes of Johnson Brothers was getting rougher and involving more. I likened it to a snowballing effect. We were building to something it seemed—something that made me tremble with fear. So far, although I objected to the lack of choice after my taking by Michael Dabney, I must admit that I thoroughly enjoyed the plowing by these hunky black studs.

I just wasn't sure I liked being taken for granted like this—or how much rougher it could get and I'd still be able to endure it.

While Sly was standing being my legs and pistoning my ass and Ham had already finished getting his blow job, I had a chance to look up at the building. Several of the windows had black guys standing in them. More than one of them had his dong out and was pulling on it while watching me being porked and squealing for mercy on the picnic table. The two Johnson Brothers themselves were standing at the window of the corner office on the third floor. I saw more black men in my future at Johnson Brothers.

* * * *

As I looked up at that window, I realized that I'd never seen the Johnson brothers, Clarence and Maurice, alone—I only saw them in tandem. They attended meetings together; whenever they were in the lunchroom, they were together; whenever they left for lunch, they left together. When one went golfing from the office, so did the other one. It was almost like they were Siamese twins. They did look like identical twins. The same meaty, but nicely proportioned build. The same bull necks and bald, bullet-like heads. The same smirky smile, following a tandem track, as they watched me walk in the corridors in the days immediately after my public fucking on the picnic table by the shipping department.

Days later their secretary called me and told me to meet them in the lobby—that they wanted to take me out to lunch and give me my three-month initial performance evaluation. I wasn't surprised to see them both there in the lobby, wearing identical business suits and smiles as I exited the elevator.

Their limo drove us way out into the Watts area, deep into a section I've never dared travel in before. I probably should have felt safe in the limousine, but I was sitting in the center of the backseat with a big black man about twice my bulk hemming me in tight on each side, each looking at me with an identical "could eat you up" grin. I was relieved when the limousine pulled up in front of the restaurant—although there was really no reason I should have felt relief. The block looked derelict and the street was littered with—well, litter. The sign over the one-story, windowless building hunkered between a sleazy-looking liquor store and a parking lot read "Club Doblar" in green neon lights, with the light out on the "B."

The light inside was dim, the furnishes something out of a 1950s burlesque house—and all of the clientele other than me looked very, very black—and very, very male. I felt all eyes on me as we were guided to a table near a small stage with a curtain in back of it.

The Johnson brothers ordered drinks—identical brands of beer, and, being keyed up and on edge, I made that three of the same.

The lights went down even lower—except for the spots on the curtain—and then the curtain drew back and I gasped in shock.

I wasn't the only white man in the establishment. There was now a young white guy on the stage as well—completely naked. And there was a naked black guy under him, working his ass with a black cock, and another naked black guy saddled up over his spread legs, and the audience was getting a clear shot—to the accompaniment of bump and grind music, of a dance of double penetration by the black guys in the white guy's ass.

I started to pant and continued to gasp, as the Johnson brothers, one on each side of me, came in closer to me and were wrapping their arms around my shoulders and running their hands all over my body—and eventually meeting their fingers at my crotch.

The eyes of the white guy on the stage were as big as saucers, and his mouth was formed in a big "O" of consternation and emitting a yip, yip sound of being stretched to within an inch of endurance, as the black cocks buried themselves deeper into his hole and started a rhythmic pumping in concert with the bump and grind music.

I wasn't around for the finish, because the entertainment had gotten the Johnson brothers all hot and bothered and I was being hustled through a door covered with a beaded curtain at the back of the room and through a dim, narrow corridor. I was pulled into a small room with a red-velvet-covered dais in the center and full-length mirrors on the walls and ceiling and beeping video cameras at various levels on the walls.

Clarence was working my lips with his and undressing and squeezing and prodding me with what seemed to be a dozen hands, while brother Maurice was stripping himself and laying down on the dais on his back and working up his cock.

Before I knew it, Clarence was sitting me down on Maurice's cock, facing away from his chest, and Maurice wrapped his arms around me and pulled my shoulder blades back to his chest and was stroking his cock up inside me and making me moan and groan. Clarence stood below us and stripped down and worked up his cock. And then he was moving in, straddling Maurice's thighs and pushing mine up and spreading them with his hands. And his cock head was at my already-filled hole as well. And I was crying out and being invaded by a second cock—and pumped and pumped and pumped. I watched myself get double fucked by my hulky black employers, the Johnson Brothers, from all angles in the mirrored walls and ceiling as the video cameras beeped away. My mouth formed a big "O" just as the white guy's on the stage had, and I was yip yipping my stretching and the feel of two cocks in counter fucking motion inside me.

I was indignant and in shock, yes. But if I said I didn't enjoy it—not least just because I survived it—I'd be lying. So I won't say any more about that experience.

I will say, however, that two days later, when I was invited up to the Johnson Brothers' office near closing time and was met by a naked Clarence and Maurice—and introduced to their third brother, an equally naked larger version of them named Roosevelt—and I could see the videos of my double fucking in the Club Doblar running on a couple of TV screens in the background, I decided that this had snowballed far enough. I beat a hasty retreat and mailed in my resignation letter from New York City.

Licorice-Centered Milk Chocolate

Heart racing, moaning, shimmering with anticipation, as milk chocolate, beefy-fingered hands glide over creamy white skin. Trembling as they search for and explore curves and crevices, zeroing in on heaving pecs. Groaning as rough-padded fingers rub, and twitch, and pinch tender nipples. Arching chest up from bed before the hovering milk-chocolate monolith, rising to the inevitable. Crying out as full lips find nipples and mouth opens around aureoles, closes tight, and gives suck. Melting at teeth sliding across engorged nipples. Opening mouth to gasp at the hint of a bite on a nipple, only to have heavy lips crush mine and thick tongue push in. Opening eyes to his, very close now, filled with desire, determination, insistence.

Easing back on bed, as he rises up below me. Breathless as I watch giant hands gliding across my body, slowly working their way to my center. Milk-chocolate hands on soft, creamy white belly and thighs, nudging. Mesmerized, I open my legs to him. Purring as hands glide around silky inner thighs.

Hulking Marine sinks between opened legs, grinning face dipping out of sight. Arching back and gasping again, as thick tongue rims, flicks in, and then invades. Grasping close-cropped kinky black hair, immediate impulse to push away, quickly replaced with desire to hold in closer. Twitching to the dancing of the tongue. Big, thick finger snaking in, thicker than some men's cocks, exploring, searching. Agony in the brief seconds found to center. Writhing as it finds the spot, tweaks, rubs, and quickens the flow. Panting, moaning. Can't . . . get . . . breath. Electricity, sparks, release and flow. Low, hoarse laughter from between trembling legs.

Muscle-bound milk chocolate Marine, with his jet-black monster cock and plump balls, standing between spread legs, ham fists squeezing calves as he wishbones my thighs, telling me what he's going to do as I moan in anticipation. His massive chest and arm muscles bulging and undulating, glistening in the strobing of light through the languidly moving blades of the overhead fan. A big grin on his square-cut face, telling me to hold my legs stead, out, as he captures and places my hands so I feel the awesome length and thickness (and the bulbous, purple-black cap and popped-out blue-on-black veins) of his hardened cock. Fearful fingers getting the measure of the beast, all the more imposing in its blackness against his otherwise milk chocolate, while he tells me quite clearly and graphically—and breathtakingly—

what he is going to do with all that manhood and how much pleasure he is going to get out of me and expects me to get out of his cock—to the point of making me tremble in anticipation (and having the added pleasure that, out of all those he could pick to fuck this day, he is here with me).

Going up on my elbows, my legs splayed up and out, my ankles held in his big hands now, and watching him first rotate that purple-black cap around and just inside the rim, entirely with the control he has over his hips and his hardened cock— no help with his hands. And then slowly, almost magically, making the pillar of power and strengthen follow its bulbous head and disappear inside me, me arching my back, trying to stretch to accommodate him and involuntarily giving him deep moans and groans of being stuffed. No, no; yes, yes, y-e-s. It's too big; it's the size I've always dreamed of. It's splitting me; it's stretching and filling me to perfection. I can't take this; I can't get enough of this. Yesssssss!

Bringing his mouth down to my nipples as he plows me, sucking and biting me there. My imagining I can feel the veins sliding against my ass walls as the cock journeys in to the quick, and then him standing up from me and repeatedly pulling his glistening jet-black cock out slowly to where I can again see the rim of the purple-black cap, and glide it back in to the root until he loses control and starts pumping me wildly (showing that he is panting for me—at the height of his passion, dipping his mouth to mine and brutalizing my lips with his). His hands grabbing my hips, moving my pelvis with his thrusts. He cries out. Again the flood inside me, oozing out of me, bathing those black balls.

All of that throbbing inside me, hard for me, wanting to be inside me, and filling me repeatedly—followed by my insides being creamed yet again with his semen and him holding for a few minutes, young, virile, powerful, quick loading. and then doing it all again. And my being able to take it, each time more slippery than the last because of the accumulation and mingling of juices—and then turning me on his cock until he is close in behind me, capable of going even deeper inside me, and then fucking me again, holding my wrists with his hands, dominating me. Him shooting off every fifteen minutes or so for what seems like forever—me climaxing repeatedly, encasing that jet-black hunk of licorice and being encased by that milk-chocolate rippling network of perfect muscle.

Massage

The Caregiver

Perhaps I gave in so easily because Lenny embodied the best of two worlds. First, he was a wonderful, gentle caregiver. He had been coming to my house twice a day for several weeks to take care of my bed-bound grandmother, who was recovering from a broken hip. Second, he was drop-dead gorgeous. All blond Swedish muscle with a shy smile to accompany his sensuous mouth.

I'd had a rough week trying to take care of my grandmother's needs when he came to change her bedding and to give her a massage that Thursday evening. He found me in the kitchen at the table when he was finished getting her ready.

"There," he said, "I think she will go right to sleep. My massages usually take all of the tension out and she goes out like a light."

"Here, sit and have a cup of coffee before you go, Lenny," I told him. "I envy her." Lenny sat across the table from me, filling out the chair and bulging chest and leg muscles stretching his T-shirt and shorts.

"You envy her sleep, her release of tension, or her massage, you mean? Surely you don't envy her age and her pain." He gave me a smile that made me ache.

"Well, the release of tension and the massage, at least," I admitted. "It's been a rough week so far."

"Yes, I could tell. You do look like you could use a good massage yourself. I'm off duty now; I could release that tension for you."

"I don't know, Lenny," I said. "I've never had a massage before."

"I do a great full-body massage, Tim," he said, not taking his eyes from mine. "I sense that's exactly what you need."

"A full-body massage? I don't think I know what that entails."

"Well, the best way to explain it is to do it. Come on, I'll give you a very good free massage. I can get rid of any sort of tension you might have."

I began to suspect what he was proposing, but I was too afraid and hesitant to ask. I could fanaticize, though. I had been dying to be touched by him for weeks. "Well, OK, what do I need to do?"

"That sounds great, Tim. I've been thinking about your building tension and wanting to give you a massage for some time now. All you need to do is strip down and hop up on my table; I'll do the rest. This can be such a difficult time for everyone involved, not just the patient. I care about the whole family. And I like you. I think you've got a hot body, and I enjoy massaging hot bodies."

Lenny cared about me. Great, he thinks I have a hot body. Even greater.

"So, I've noticed you have plenty of room in your bedroom for me to set up my massage table. Why don't you take a shower and wrap yourself in a towel and I'll go out to the car and get my table."

When I came out of the bathroom, Lenny had already gotten the massage table set up and had stripped off his T-shirt. What a beautiful bod.

"Up on the table, on your back," he commanded. "Strip the towel and I'll put it over your privates."

I did as he asked and thought he took a bit longer than necessary before draping the towel over me. I wasn't sure how this was going to work out, as I already felt I was losing control over my cock.

He came around to above my head and started working on rubbing my temples and my head. I looked up and the view from under his bulging and moving pecs was very interesting. He raised my head and massaged my neck muscles. I could clearly see the tenting of the towel over my loins; I could feel it, of course, but the important thing was that if I also could see it, so could he. He worked my shoulder and upper arms muscles and then moved both hands down to my pecs, where he massaged my nipples just as much as he worked on my muscles there. I could feel my rod rising even more. his massaging worked its way down my abs and to my belly. I sighed and moaned in appreciation. Then he came around beside me and whipped the towel off. I knew it. I had a Grade A hard-on. I was embarrassed, but Lenny didn't seem to mind at all. He moved down to below my feet. I looked down and was surprised to see that now his shorts were off and he was barely encased in a thong that didn't hide a thing. My cock hardened even more at the sight. Lenny saw my response to what I'd seen and just gave me a shy smile with those sensuous thick lips.

He worked on my toes and feet and then lifted my legs one at a time and did my calves and lower thighs.

"Flip over," he said, and I did. He came back to above me and did my back and shoulder muscles and then the muscles of each arm in turn. Then, starting with my calf muscles, he worked his way up. He did a good job on my lower thighs and pulled my legs a bit apart as he worked higher and higher. He was at my inner thighs now, way up next to my groin. His sensuous fingers touched my balls as he massage. I couldn't help letting out a little moan of pleasure.

He moved his hands, moistened with oil, onto my butt cheeks, which he kneaded and rolled in a sensuous motion. My cock came alive, and before I knew it I was grinding away with my pelvis, fucking the towel under me on the surface of the massage table. Lenny was helping me with the movement, lifting my hips a bit and revolving my pelvis around and helping me pump. The underside of my engorged cock was sliding along the surface of the table, stroking up and back, and before I knew it I spouted off up my belly and into the cleavage of my chest. All the time, Lenny was murmuring how well I was doing, what I nice big cock I had, and how nice my butt cheeks were.

After I had shot off, Lenny gently pulled my legs down off the end of table to where I could stand on the floor with my still-heaving chest on the surface of the board. I felt my butt cheeks being spread, and a cool mouth and tongue found my asshole. Lenny licked and sucked and tongued me there, as I groaned and moaned and sighed. He was rimming me. I'd had no idea what this even meant before now, but now it was making me into a blob of jelly—and, for the first time, he was making me want something else inside me, past the rim.

After several minutes of this, his tongue slurped out of my hole and he stood and placed his left hand firmly in the small of my back, holding my torso down on the table. The fingers of a well-oiled right hand went to my hole, and Lenny ever-more-intensely finger fucked me, getting the oil well up into my ass passage and opening me up and helping me to relax my ass muscles.

The fingers were pulled out, and I felt the big helmet of his cock at the hole. He pushed the helmet in to its rim and stopped there briefly.

"Are you ready for the internal part of the massage, Tim?" he asked in a breathy voice. "I won't go further unless you want the whole massage."

"Yes, yes," I whispered. "Do me. Just be gentle. You're not too big are you?"

"Just seven and half inches hard," he replied and then gave a little throaty laugh. "But we'll go slowly and I won't go deeper than you can take."

I groaned, "Seven and a half inches! You gotta know, I've never done this before."

"I didn't know that," he said. And then I was afraid he'd stop, but, although he hesitated, he didn't pull back. "But you've thought about it, haven't you?"

"Yes."

"And you want me to continue?"

"Yes."

"All the better for both of us then," he said with a laugh. "Good to know, though; I'll take my time and care."

I jerked as he pushed in past the sphincter muscle. And then his helmet was at my prostate, rubbing it and causing little sparks of pleasure to fly through my body.

"So, is that OK, Tim?"

"I groaned a yes."

"Do you want me to fuck you deeper?" He was dragging his helmet back and forth across my prostate and had taken his hand and was rotating his well-oiled cock around in the canal, giving my ass channel walls special attention.

I gasped and moaned and was rotating my pelvis, wanting to feel all of the big cock everywhere at once. "Yes, yes," I managed between gasps, "Fuck me, deep and thick. Fill me up, you beautiful Swedish stud."

And when, taking his time, he slid up into me, deep. I arched my back, breaking the pressure of his hand on the small of my back and rose up, throwing an arm around his neck and bringing his lips to mine in a deep kiss. He grabbed my hips with his hands and pumped me slowly with his cock, in long oil-slicked slides in to where his helmet dragged back across my prostate and then deep glides, loving and churning and stretching my channel walls.

He broke the kiss and laughed, and pushed my chest back down on the table. Then he started pumping me in earnest, in long, gliding motions.

"Ahh, Ahhhh, Ahhhh," I cried. "Give it to me, Lenny, shoot off in me. Deep, like this."

"Deep like this?" Lenny asked, the amusement in his voice dancing. "I haven't gone deep yet, Lover. *This* is me going deep."

And he pushed my legs out wider with a slap of his feet, grabbed my butt cheeks and pulled them wide apart, and plunged his oiled rod a good two and half inches deeper than he'd gone up me before.

"No . . . No!" I screamed. "It hurts. I don't think I can . . . Ugh . . . Ahhh . . . Yes. Oh, yes, Lenny. Lenny! Lenny!!! Give it to me. I want it all. Just like that! Pump me, Man. Fill my stomach with your sweet cum."

He was deep fucking me wildly now. Staying deep, but pumping in and out. Then he stopped and rotated me around and pushing me up on the massage table, until I was facing him, still able to stay deep. He buried his hands in my chest and massaged my nipples. I wrapped my legs around the small of his back, wanting to keep him in me forever, and I stroked my cock vigorously. And he stroked and he stroked and he stroked; hard and deep.

I came before he did, shooting my load off on his chest and up mine. He gave a little yelp of delight then as he ejaculated in heavy bursts deep inside me. Then he collapsed on top of me, nuzzling his face into the hollow of my neck, savoring the moment. I kept my legs firmly wrapped around his waist, holding him in me, feeling that long, thick cock soften and retreat, but not all that far.

"God, to think I've had seven and a half inches in me," I whispered, pride and awe spilling over in my voice.

"Sorry, I lied," Lenny responded, with a little laugh. "I'm a good eight and half inches hard; didn't want to scare you. Wasn't sure how much I could stuff in you. But you took it all. You're a fucking amazing screw."

Silence for a few minutes, while I thought that over.

"So, do you want a massage now?" I then asked. "I'm wondering how much of that dick I can get in my mouth."

"Not tonight, Tim, as tempting as that thought is. I'm wasted. I come back to give your grandmother some more care tomorrow. How about tomorrow then? But rest up. There are some other tricks to a good Swedish massage."

"Can't wait."

Medical

Prepped

Not for the first time I didn't like the gleam in Leon's eye or the lilt in his voice when he told me I had an assignment. He was much too pleased with himself when he handed me the envelope containing the address and the gate key. We'd been getting along better than usual lately—or had been up to the time he seemed to think that meant I was warming to him and he propositioned me again and I turned him down flat again. But if there was a little twist to this assignation, at least it would be short-lived. The address was right here in the city. The Gordan Institute up in the Hollywood Hills.

I knew this to be a tony private plastic surgery hospital for those who wanted to be recarved without losing sight of their swimming pools and movie star mansions. Not because I'd done anything like that myself, of course. I was still at my peak, thank you, very much, and wouldn't need any of that sort of help for a good ten years more. Depending, though, I guessed, on what I did between now and then to earn my pay. And when I did need plastic surgery, there was no way I was going to be able to afford the Gordan Institute.

I just hoped that Leon hadn't agreed to let me get sliced up.

"So, what costume?" I asked.

"Oh, just go as you are," Leon answered. And then he laughed. "Chances are you won't be wearing it long anyway."

I took the envelope from Leon's claws and gave him a wan "you don't intimidate me—much" smile and headed my Beamer convertible up slope. It was late afternoon on a Sunday and it was "another damn beautiful" day enhanced by the relative lack of bumper-to-bumper traffic.

I halfway knew where the Gordan Institute was, and I found it without too much trouble, hulking behind a high stuccoed privacy wall next door to what had once been Bela Lugosi's haunted manse. Leon had given me a plastic key card like they use for hotel room entry, and it opened up the iron gates at the institute a charm. No one was about as I drove in and parked next to a silver Mercedes convertible in an otherwise empty, bricked-over parking pad. By the time I got to the front entrance, hidden in the shadows behind a porte cochere, no doubt designed for privacy in arrival and departure of the well-heeled patients, the entry door was opening and I could see there was at least one other person than me here on a

Sunday. The absence of other cars disturbed me a bit. This was a residential facility; was there some sort of law against rich people getting tummy tucks on weekends in May? I wondered.

"You were sent by the agency?" a well-modulated baritone voice asked from the depths beyond the opening door.

"Umm, yes. Alphonse?"

"Come in. Yes, yes, you'll do nicely."

I knew that. He didn't have to tell me that. They charged three thou an hour for my attentions. And for that I did quite a bit more than "nicely."

The door swung open, and I was facing "Alphonse." He wasn't really Alphonse. I knew that, and I'm sure he knew I knew that. His mug, no matter how many times it had been redone, was well known in town. He was Grant Gordan, the celebrated magic surgeon of beauty. This was his institute.

He was playing doctor. Starched, stark-white three-quarter-length doctor's smock over soft-cotton, institutional green scrubs that somehow still gave the impression they had been tailored and cost a bundle. Crinkling transparent plastic booties on what looked like gray bedroom slippers. He was tricked out to be playing the senior physician in a long-running television medical drama. Gray-haired, in his fifties, but handsome, and chiseled to an epitome of perfection that only a millionaire's billfold or an "in the business" discount could provide. A very nice bedside smile that, alone, would have cost me a fortune.

"Oh, excuse me," I stammered. "Did I get the day or time wrong? Have I interrupted a procedure?"

"No, no, of course not. You're right on time. No procedures today. We're undergoing renovations this week, so no procedures at all. No patients in residence."

"Oh, but—"

"Oh, these. I was just trying on a new shipment of surgical wear. Dr. Gordan just had these sent in."

Hokay, I thought. It's your ten thou, "Alphonse," I thought. I had peeked at Leon's chart—as I always tried to do so I knew when I should be going off the clock. This guy had bought four hours and gotten a discount of two thousand for booking that block of time. This almost always meant at least a double, but I was just as happy if they thought of that in advance and padded the time. Often trying to hammer a recharge and second fucking into an hour—or even two hours—became quite frustrating for the client and often played out in their attitude as something unpleasant.

"Follow me, please." And with that, "Alphonse" turned and walked briskly down a corridor leading off to the right of the plush reception room that, with its yawning stone fireplace, vaulted ceiling, and big expanse of glass overlooking a sea of green grass, majestic pines, and parts of the city looked more like the living room in a mountain lodge than a hospital waiting room.

I followed in the wake of the crinkling noise his surgical booties were making with the thought that, if I had known we were going to play doctor, I would have seen if Leon had a nurse's uniform in his wardrobe room.

I was ushered into a large, wood-paneled room with book-lined walls except for one well-lit panel that sported what I'm sure was meant to be an intimidating number of framed university diplomas, medical licenses, honorary plaques, and photos of "Alphonse" shaking hands with various extremely well-preserved movie stars and industry titans of old—or at least of older than they had been made to appear.

The mahogany desk was massive, the throne behind it that "Alphonse" perched in momentarily was massive, and the sort of wheel chair contraption he waved my butt into was nothing short of strange. It was a comfortable chair and all that, but did he put his prospective clients into wheel chairs this early in the sales pitch? I didn't have time to let this thought percolate, however.

"I trust you've been told the scenario and the service."

"Ummm. No, actually," I said.

"Oh, well, then," Alphonse said. "I do have a contract, you know. And the money's been paid."

"Good, fine," I said. I couldn't think of anything else to say. I was busy racking Leon over in my brain. I knew there was a reason for that evil little smile. Holding the particulars back from me again. Such a poor loser.

By then Alphonse had bounded back out of his—or, rather, Dr. Gordan's—throne and was moving around the room.

"Strip down, please. I want to see if my directions were followed."

I stood up from the wheel chair and started to take off my clothes, in the slow, provocative way I'd been taught to do, wondering all the time whether I was supposed to wear something I hadn't been told about. As I did so, Alphonse came around to the edge of the desk facing me and perched there, closely scrutinizing my every movement. I imaged that I was a client asking for a little more here and a little less there, and I wondered if he also was thinking about how I could be recarved to best advantage.

But his eyes were slitted, and he was humming softly to himself. From long experience, I recognized this as a sign of satisfaction with the goods.

"Ah, yes," he said when I was stripped down, giving out a sigh and letting his hand run across his crotch. "Nice body hair. And a natural blond, I see."

Well, no, but he didn't need to know all that was entailed in that.

"Sit, please."

I did so, and Alphonse was back on the move. He was behind me, and I heard the noise of something being dragged toward me. I looked around in time to see some sort of steel contraption on wheels, supporting a large cylinder rolling up to my chair. But that's all the time I had to see anything, as the doctor was right behind me then, throwing his arms around my chest, holding me down into the wheel chair with one arm and clamping a mask over my mouth and nose with the other. I struggled briefly, but not for long. The gas was fast and effective.

When I came to, I was strapped down on my back on a white-paper-covered vinyl operating table. My wrists were bound close behind my head, which pulled my arms up and close beside my head on either side. My ankles were bound too, but to flexible appendages that extended beyond the end of the table, which only reached to the small of my back. It was apparent that these appendages could be manipulated apart and up and even folded to bend my legs.

I awoke to a whimper. It was mine.

"Ah, good, awake. Be aware that I contracted for the specific service."

I focused on the voice. Alphonse—Grant Gordan—all smiles and standing over me with an aerosol can in one hand and in the other—a straight razor.

"Oh, God, no," I muttered. "Please—"

"You must hold very still, or this will undoubtedly hurt you more than it does me," Gordan murmured. And then he smiled. I knew the look in those eyes. He was aroused.

He started squirting foam onto my torso and into my pits. It was cold, and I squirmed a bit. I said nothing; I was still assessing the situation and how and whether to get out of it. Just how crazy was he? Was this just the first stage of something? He lifted the razor and I stopped squirming. I wasn't that stupid.

He had music going on in the background. Just what I was used to hearing when I went into a dentist's office. And he was humming as he worked.

The razor moved from my right pit to my left pit. This was followed by Gordan's tongue, as he lapped up the residual lather there, which must have been something other than soap, because he was having a good slurping time of it.

"You know," he said as he finished there and was carefully shaving around my nipples and along my hairline down to my navel, "For years I watched my patients being prepped by the nurses before surgery, and I never realized why I got a hard-on before surgery. For the longest time, I thought it was the surgery itself that was a turn on for me. And I was ever so grateful that I had gone into a profession that could give me so much pleasure in addition to paying me so well. But then I slowly caught on. I was aroused by the prep. The shaving and the cleaning off of the lather."

"I can show you a really good time without this, you know," I stuttered out. "I can give you a fuck like you've never had before." It was grabbing at straws. But I was worried about where this might lead. Whether he had even darker fetishes. I usually liked to be very sure of a client before I was tied up.

"Yes, yes, I'm sure—and perhaps you shall," Gordan said in a faraway voice, which told me that he was locked into his fetish. "You know, though, that after I knew what it was that I wanted, I had a dilemma. I couldn't really take the risk of pursuing this on a real patient. Besides the fact that the operating room is full of people in this stage, there where phenomenal risks with the patient's lawyers. So, you know—"

He had broken off because his mouth was full of foam and nipple now. He had shaved my chest, down to my navel and was cleaning up the lather with his tongue. He was really good at it, and I wondered how much practice he had had with this. How many before me? If other guys in my profession had gone missing, I think I would have known. The agency would have known. But, what if I were the first?

I was so deep in worry and thought that I didn't know how long it had been since he'd stopped tonguing me down. When I looked around, I saw that he already had his scrubs off and was putting his white lab coat back on over his naked body. For his mid fifties, he really looked good. But, at the same time, too good. Plastic. I bet he'd had every inch of his body done and redone. And I wondered if they really could enhance a penis like that with plastic surgery. His body was hairless, so at least he carried this fetish of his through to himself.

He opened a condom package and crowned his pride and joy. Time for something I was more familiar with.

Gordan moved to below me, and I felt the lower appendages of the operating table, the arms to which my legs were strapped, being widened and bent so that I was in what I imaged to be the "birthing" position. Gordan was standing between my legs, and I saw the gleam of the metal aerosol can caught in the glare of the overhead operating lights.

Cold, wet. My pubes were being lathered up. And then my asshole too. I tensed up as I felt one of his fingers breaching my rim and pushing into at least the knuckle, taking lather with it. I did my best to relax as I looked down and saw the razor hovering over my pubes.

I panted shallowly and tried to be professional and not whimper or beg as I felt the razor scraping across my groin. Gordan was fisting my cock with his other hand, holding it out of the way and stroking it up and down. I was involuntarily engorging. Which was fine. He'd paid for the service, and I would give the service. If I was going to beef, it would be to whoever I could find in the agency above Leon. It would be no good to let Leon know I thought I had a beef about this assignment; he'd delight in listening to me whine. If I ever got home from this assignment, of course.

I watched Gordan's head come down to my groin and lick at the lather and then up the side of my cock, and he swallowed me and constricted his cheeks around my tool. I groaned and strung a series of appreciative-sounding yeses for him and started a shallow rhythm in my hips to let him know that he was a superior suck.

After a bit of this, he lifted off my cock but still held it in a fist as he lathered up my inner thighs and began to scrape and tongue again.

Then the razor wasn't scraping. The finger wasn't in my hole. I almost lifted up off the table as Gordan thrust his cock inside me, running thickly and deeply at the first thrust, his entry smoothened by the lather he'd shot up into me.

The shave was finished. He was fucking me in deep thrusts, fully aroused by his fetish, ready to finish off the surgical fantasy.

I knew this part. I cried out for him, telling him how good he was and how I wanted it never to stop, and Gordan rode with it. Thrusting and thrusting and thrusting. Making animal noises, while I moaned and groaned and told him he was killing me but not to stop.

He was as good with his cock as he had been with his razor. And I was enjoying this part—but doing all I could to make him enjoy it too. Enjoy it far more than the shaving part and certainly far more than any part he might be planning to proceed to after this. I wanted him to want me to be giving him the best of times and wanting me back some other time. Not carrying on with any possible terminal plans in this session.

With an exclamation, Gordan pulled out of me, jerked off the condom and shot up over my balls onto my now-smooth groin.

I sighed deeply and collapsed back onto the paper sheeting, only then realizing that I had arched my back and had brought my buttocks off the surface of the table to meet him thrust for thrust in his wild, exuberant fucking.

I did everything I could do act like what we had done was totally exhausting, if totally wonderful—for both of us—and that we had done what we were going to do. But then I looked up at the clock on the wall and realized that he had nearly two hours left on his contract. I groaned, and this time it didn't have anything to do with sex.

I refocused on Gordan. He was opening another condom packet. This time he rolled the condom onto my cock, which, conveniently, was standing at full attention and was hard as a rock. He let loose another cloud of lather on my capped tool.

Then, moving real well for his age, Gordan came up onto the operating table and knelt, straddling my hips, facing me. He held my cock rigid while he slowly encased my cock with his channel and began to slowly ride me. This was another maneuver I was adept at, so I lifted my hips off the surface of the operating table and gave him a good time and appropriate sounds of pleasure and, in the end, a good feel of the bulb of a condom billowing forth to capacity well up his canal.

I wondered if the clock had stopped. He still had more than an hour when we were done with that. He went back to the razor and the lather, and my legs and arms were completely denuded and exposed to the breezes.

We had come to what I thought of as the danger point, but Gordan's fetish turned out to have its limit. He released me from the table and started talking about how good I was and how he was pleased with the service.

This was when the customer service I was known for and that brought me return requests kicked in. Comfortable now that nothing threatening was going to happen, I turned to him and took his cheeks in my hands and gave him a big sloppy kiss on the lips. Our eyes were inches away from each other, and I watched him turn from surprise to pleased to renewed arousal.

"God, you're a superb cocksman," I whispered when we disengaged. "You have time left on the clock. Could you fuck me again, please?"

Flattered and delighted and immediately up to the challenge, he told me how much he'd like to do that in a flustered voice, and I turned and bent over onto the operating table on my now-hairless belly.

I felt the cool, wet lather at my asshole again, and then he was fucking me, slowly at first, and then in a frenzy, as I writhed under him and screamed out at the thick, deep taking. He covered my back with his torso and I turned my head and we kissed. He was trembling almost uncontrollably as he came again deep inside me.

I was whistling as I folded the extra thou into my billfold and settled into the BMW for the drive back down out of the Hollywood Hills. Leon wouldn't hear a whisper of complaint or description from me about this assignment. I knew that would drive him crazy.

Trail "Doctor"

I had never tried to seduce another guy before, but Dale was just there at the right time and place. We were both runners—he because he was on the college football team and running up and down the Pine Mountain trail helped keep him in shape and I because I wasn't that long out of college myself and I was doing the best I could to keep my fine form in shape.

We had passed each other a couple of times going up and down the trail that morning. It was a hot one, and as I was coming down the mountain, I saw that Dale had his sweaty shirt off as well, as his shoes and socks, and he was just standing under the shower by the maintenance hut, letting the water cascade down his beautiful body. He was a square-cut blond, with great pecs going down into washboard abs and a small waist. He had his heavily muscled arms over his head, and all of the muscles of his torso were stretched out to perfection. His calf and thigh muscles showed that he was both a football player and a serious runner. I just stood there and watched him in awe for a few minutes. The shower was sticking his running shorts to his legs and I could see that he had a pretty fine basket confined by his jock. He turned the water off as I was approaching and gave me a shy smile.

"Hi, Jack. It's just too damn hot out here. I couldn't wait to get cooled down."

"I'm right with you, Dale. There's a picnic table over behind those bushes. Let me shower too, and I'll come over, and we can jaw a bit while we both dry off."

"Sounds good," Dale said, and he headed for the picnic table. After making a short instinctive visit to the car for a tube of lubricant, which I plopped in my pocket, I returned and stood under the shower for a couple of minutes. This was crazy, I thought. There would be no way I was going to pull this off. But, just maybe so. I had seen Dale look me over on the trail before, and if he was at all inclined, there just might be some fun to be had here.

Besides, one of my favorite games was playing doctor. It was a real turn-on when I was able to get away with it. I liked it with the white coat and all, and I didn't have that here. But I'd think of myself as a doctor and try to get Dale to think of me that way too—and maybe it would be a lot of fun and I'd get my rocks off like I'd like to do. You could say that playing doctor was fetish of mine.

When I sauntered around the bushes, I saw that Dale was sitting about two thirds down the bench, his back to the table, and his legs v-ed out at a good angle. He seemed to be wincing.

"What's the matter, Dale?" I asked, as I sat down beside him.

"You don't wanna know," he said morosely.

"Sure I do. You look like you're in pain."

"Yes, I guess I am a bit."

"What's the problem?"

"There are two problems—and you probably don't want to hear them."

"Now you have me interested. Shoot."

"That's the main problem. I can't shoot. And my girl, Cheryl Ann, and this here tight jock are the main problems."

"Now, I'm intrigued, spill." This was almost too good to be true, I thought. I could feel myself hardening right up at the chance to play doctor.

"I can't," he answered with a little grin. "As I said, that's the problem. I have the hots for my girl, Cheryl Ann, and she won't put out. I've got all this stuff built up, and this tight jock is driving me crazy this morning."

"Well," I laughed, "I can't do anything about Cheryl Ann, but you're out here alone this morning and you've finished your run. There's no reason you can't just take your jock off and hang free."

"Hey, I guess you're right," Dale said with a chuckle. He stood and turned his back to me, pulled his shorts down, pulled his jock down and off, pulled his shorts back up and sat back down in the same stance he'd been in. I hadn't seen his package, but his bulbous butt cheeks had been mighty interesting. I took a peek and saw that his shorts were tented up real nice now. I could actually make out a huge knob against the wet material.

"There, is that better?" I asked.

"A little, but not much," Dale said sadly.

We sat there for a few minutes.

"You know that guys have a way to take care of that themselves," I ventured.

"Yeah, I know, but that doesn't really do it for me. I apparently build up a lot and fast, and it just never seems complete when I do it myself."

Another short pause.

"And you know that sometimes guys let other guys help them with that when it's really bad. I mean it isn't a queer thing or anything. Just playing around and releasing some tension when their girls won't put out. It's really unhealthy to just let it build, you know. It might hurt performance later."

"Really? I hadn't heard that." Dale sounded a little scared.

"Yes, really. I'm a doctor, and I'd do something about this if I were you. You wouldn't want to ruin yourself for later, when you and your girlfriend have finally hooked up."

Dale looked both dubious and scared now. And he was still wincing.

"Go ahead and do yourself, Dale. You obviously need some release right now. No one else is here. I'm a doctor, and I've seen it all. Just pull your pants on down and give yourself some relief while we talk."

Dale hesitated, but the tension must really have been getting to him, because he lowered his shorts to his thighs and took a very nice, erect cock in his left hand and began to slowly jack off.

I could hardly keep my hands and eyes off him, but, beyond a few glances when he was looking away, I kept off him. I could feel my own cock hardening even more and giving me some of the same jock problem he'd had.

"You said I should do something about it. What could I do?"

"Well, guys come to me all the time for this sort of relief. There's something we can do called prostate massage. It's all medical, of course, not a gay thing. It's just that some guys have to be what we call 'milked' manually regularly because they can't get enough sexual release otherwise. It isn't a sign that you like guys; it just means that you are extra virile. It's usually young guys like you who have this problem."

"It's all medical? Is there much pain in the procedure?"

"Sure it's medical, and, on the contrary, there's the same or more pleasure you'd get from penetration sex. It's just a medical procedure to alleviate a normal medical problem. The pleasure is just a bonus. And you'd lose that tension and pain you've got for a couple of days at least," I said, making it up as I went along and hoping this sounded reasonable. And before he could raise more doubts about this, I steamed on. "You've heard about the prostate, haven't you?"

"Yes, guys get testicle cancer from that, don't they?"

"Well, yes, they can, and that can be an added risk for someone like you who doesn't take care of the problem at this stage. The prostate is a gland behind the testicles. It's where all that sperm is being manufactured that you can't get rid of fast enough. Surely you've had a prostate exam during a medical checkup before."

"Oh, yeah, that's where the doctor put his finger up my ass."

"Did it hurt?"

"Naw. It felt a little tight and strange down there, but it didn't hurt."

"Well, in that exam, the doctor was just checking to see if your prostate was enlarging, which would be sign of trouble. In prostate massage, the doctor massages the prostate from inside your anal canal for several minutes, which milks the built-up sperm out of you more effectively than jerking off does and also gives you more pleasure than jerking off can. I hope you can follow what I'm saying; I'm trying to use words that you would understand rather than the fancy medical terms for all this. In extreme cases like yours, the doctor milks the penis at the same time."

"It sounds . . . interesting, Doc. And you say I can get this done by going to a doctor?"

"Yes, certainly."

"And could you recommend such a doctor for me?"

"I can do better than that, Dale. It doesn't require sterile surroundings. I can save you the money and give you immediate relief by showing you how it's done right here and now."

"Right here and now?"

"Absolutely, you're already in a good initial position, and I just happen to have a tube of lubricant with me—I'm on my way to see my girlfriend after this run is why I have it. Got condoms here too." I gave him my best "we're all heteros here" smile before I proceeded. "Lube is all we need. Just strip those shorts off. I'll need you fully erect, so I'll have to do some preliminary work on you, and, with your serious condition, I'd better take charge of the penis for a while." Dale pulled his shorts off and put both beefy arms back on the table.

"There, that's right; arch your back for me." I put my left leg over the bench so that I was facing his side. I tentatively wrapped my left hand loosely around his cock, which made him twitch. "Okay?" I asked. "Any problems?"

"No," he answered, although not really sure. I continued quickly, not wanting to give him too much time to think about this.

"Okay now, I'll do some preliminary rubbing of your pecs and nipples until I feel your penis fully engorge, and then we can begin. Okay with that?"

A muffled affirmative; my right hand went up to his chest and I lightly ran it around his pecs and nipples, slowly increasing the pressure and taking a few nips and squeezes of his nipples. I could tell he was stifling some grunts.

"Our goal is to release the tension here, Dale, not compound it. Just let those grunts and moans out. There's no reason not to enjoy this medical procedure."

"But it's so . . . weird. I mean it doesn't seem right."

"Would it seem right to have sex with Cheryl Ann, if she'd let you, Dale? Of course it would. Why would it be wrong to take care of a medical condition and still have sexual pleasure out of it? Everything's just fine, Dale. Ah, there, your penis seems to be ready. I'm going to be manipulating your penis now with one hand and doing some checking and preparing for the prostate massage with the other one now. We'll move slowly, and I'll tell you what is happening as we go along. I was slowly pumping his cock and he was beginning to pant and moan.

"There, yes, that's good. Just go with the flow of your feelings, Dale. We're alone out here, and this is just a medical procedure. Be natural." I took his balls in my right hand and weighed and teased them, rolling them around gently. Dale flinched.

"This is the testicular part of the procedure. I have to examine your testicles to make sure everything is okay there. And it does seem to be. And you were right; you seem to have a lot of semen backed up in here. We'll see what we can do about getting all of that cleared out. I'm now going on down toward your anus, Dale. Don't be alarmed, I won't enter the short way I have to go for this procedure without having you well lubricated. So, there will be only pleasure, no pain."

Dale tensed up a bit as I put the heel of my hand under his balls and ran my finger to the rim of his ass. I would have liked to have gotten my mouth on that asshole too, but I couldn't think of any medical excuse to do that. So, I just left my finger there on his hole, applying a little pressure, while I took the fingers of my left hand up to the glans on his cock.

"Any problem with the glans, Dale?"

"The glans? What's a glans?"

"The head, the knob, on your penis. It seems a little distended. But that might be because of how long you've gone without fixing this problem."

Dale answered with a moaning, "No, I don't think I've had a problem there."

"Well, I'll have to put some lubricant on it to examine it well. Here this will feel cool." I rubbed a small glob of lubricant on his dick head and swirled it down and around the rim. Dale flinched and moaned. I squeezed the spongy bulb and watched his slit open up. I moved my index finger there and pushed it open farther.

"Oh, oh," Dale moaned, and he brought a hand down to mine.

"No, hands up Dale, this has to stay medical. There, I guess all is in order with you there; just lubricating up for the medical massage now." I lubricated the fingers of my right hand well and took an added glop to start lathering up around his asshole. My left hand went back to stroking his cock, but I didn't do this too vigorously, because I didn't really want him to release yet.

I did a lot of work on his entry, making it large enough for what I was planning. I made a few forays farther in, just to let him know I was continuing the procedure. When he had relaxed and his hole opening had loosened up, I slid my middle finger in to the sphincter. He gave a little lurch and yelp when the sphincter picked up the finger and sucked it into place at his prostate.

"There, can you feel that?" I asked.

"Yes," he moaned through pants.

"It will take time to build the sensation up, but this should give you release." I started a gentle massaging of the prostate, and Dale slowly started to writhe and moan and grind his pelvis.

"Here, this isn't the best position now, because you are naturally going to be moving around in response to the procedure. Here. Get up and move around to the end of the table here. Perch up on the end. There, that's right. Now lay back on the table and wrap your arms around the other end to give you support. There, that's right. This is now more like the table in the examination room. Now, we don't have stirrups. So, can you get your left foot on the edge of the bench there and keep a wide stance with that leg. Good. And now, your right leg, I guess will have to go over my left shoulder so that I have you open enough down there to proceed with the massage. There, that's good. Now I'm entering again." I gently slid my index finger in to the prostate again and restarted the massage. Dale went back to panting and moaning and gyrating his pelvis slightly. His pants came louder and more quickly together, and my left finger on his glans felt some precum dribbling out.

"There, is that feeling better, Dale? The milk is beginning to show."

"Aw, shit yes, Man. That feels great—waves and waves of great. But I think I'm gonna come."

"Well, ejaculation is the whole point of this procedure, Dale. We need to clear out that sperm backup, don't we? Here, I can increase that and quicken the flow. I'll use my thumb rather than my finger. Just stick with me here, Dale, I've got a large thumb." I quickly slipped my shorts and jock off with my right hand and lathered up my cock with lubricant. I put my dick head up against his now-open asshole and slowly pushed in.

"Oh, God, that's big," Dale yelped. I had gotten it in to the prostate, and was manipulating my cock head against his prostate. "Oh, but it feels so good," Dale continued.

"Yes, big thumb. Just the right thing to get you off when you need it."

"Oh, oh, oh, Gawd Damn!" And Dale was spurting several weeks of backup into the air and back down on his chest. He arched his torso up and then thumped it back down on the table. The last time he thumped it down, I slid my cock past the prostate and right on in.

"What the fuck?" Dale screamed, and thrashed about on the table. He grabbed for me with his arms, but I got his legs in both of mine and lifted them up and out, bringing his butt up to a more open position. I pulled out nearly to the end and then stroked all the way back in to the root.

"Still workin the prostate here, Dale. Want me to stop."

"YES!" I gyrated my hips in a rotating motion while fully encased. "Oh, Gawd. No, no."

"No what, Dale?" I asked, pumping and pumping and pumping.

"No, don't stop. Don't stop," Dale whimpered. And he began to move his hips in syncopation with my thrusts, and dug his fingers into my chest hair and nipples. We came—he for the second time within a few short minutes—at nearly the same time. I released his legs, which just flopped down beyond the table, and I ran my hands up his abs to his pecs and collapsed on him. We looked each other in the eye and both leaned into a long, lingering kiss. I started to withdraw from him, but he moved his hands to my butt cheeks and kept me in place.

When our lips parted, he looked into my eyes with a satisfied smile and said, "You aren't really a doctor, are you?"

"Yes, of course I am," I answered. "I wouldn't lie to you. I have a doctorate in geology, which means I'm eminently qualified to get your rocks off. I'm not a medical doctor, but I can do a prostate massage for free, and a medical doctor will charge you $100, and it won't be half the fun I can give you. You'll need another good milking in a couple of days, if Cheryl Ann keeps holding out."

Another kiss, after which he responded. "Good. I'll stick with the doctor I've got. . . . and who's Cheryl Ann?"

"That's my boy."

Phone Sex

Phoned

I should never have been flip when Vincent asked me about that photo of Phil and me I kept on the shelf in my cubicle at work. I didn't really want to talk about Phil. We'd been roommates at the university. He'd been the star athlete and I'd been the quiet, studious geek. Still, we'd gotten along real well. Night and day we were called at school. But I'd had no trouble with his color and he'd never expressed having trouble with mine. He'd been destined for the NFL, and I'd been teased I'd have made my first million off of some dot-com enterprise before I was twenty-five.

It hadn't happened that way—for either of us. The dot-com revolution collapsed before I could grab my brass ring, and the best I could do was doing "pretty good" as a stockbroker. Phil decided that a tour in Iraq would toughen him for professional football. But all it did was kill him. That's why I had a picture sitting on the shelf in my work cubicle of the two of us, half looped at a frat party, arms draped around each other, and silly grins on our faces. Sort of a shrine to not taking life for granted, for going with the moment, in case there are no more moments.

But when Vincent, the broker in the cubicle next to me, asked, I was flip. I said the other guy in the photo was my boyfriend.

I have no satisfactory idea why I said that. I think mainly it was because Vincent was so crude at the office, always cracking dirty jokes and making with the sexual innuendo—and I didn't want an intrusion like that in the tragedy I saw in my link to Phil. I just wanted to shock Vincent and make him stop asking about the photo. And especially, maybe I told him that because I had a hard time looking at Vincent and not seeing Phil.

Vincent was a real good looker, just like Phil had been. He said he was Jamaican. And maybe he was. He had a build just like Phil's, and he was always flashing a winsome smile and was so self-assured, just like Phil had been. All the women in the office ate him up despite what any one of them could claim was sexual harassment, if they'd wanted to—if someone not as hunky as him was doing it, maybe.

But I also might have blurted it out with half-way wishful thinking. There had never been anything real between Phil and me, but I'll have to admit that he aroused me and I'd had a crush on him that I never got up the courage to fully acknowledge to myself, let alone to Phil. And now that would never happen. Any possible moment of it happening was gone for good.

From the moment I'd blurted that flippant response out, though, Vincent had turned his innuendo onto me—asking me if I liked him, pointing out that Phil was black too. Asking me if I was especially attracted to black men. And, in time, asking me if Phil and I were still doing it, and, if so, which one of us topped.

Always whispered and in passing, at first covered so that I couldn't tell if he was just joking, trying to get a rise out of me. Maybe baiting me for an office joke. But it continued, and when he moved on to touching me when and as and where he could do it when no one was looking, I knew he wasn't joking. He suggested we go for a drink after work, he complimented me on my clothes, and then on my physique. He even started dropping notes on my desk, asking me to meet him in the men's room, the notes becoming increasingly more explicit. Saying we should compare cocks. Saying he was built especially long and thick. Asking me what Phil was swinging.

I don't know if I could have stopped it. I just know I didn't try. I tried to hold back, but it was arousing. I'd never had attention like this before. I could have just told him exactly who Phil was and why that photo was on my cubicle shelf. But I didn't.

He got my home phone number somehow and he began calling me—almost always at about the same time in the evening, so I'd know it was him. One phone call after another, progressively more suggestive, more demanding.

"Hey, Jeff, I'm bored. Let's go play some pool."

"Hey, guy, it's me. What'yer doing. Want to do it together?"

"Thinkin' about you, Jeff. What are you wearing right now? Know what I'm wearing? Nothing."

"Hey, guy. I'm all alone and lonely. I've got something for you. It's long and thick and hard, and it wants you."

A phone call entirely of heavy breathing and the whispering of my name.

"You have it out, don't you? You are stroking it, aren't you?" And, of course, I was, although I didn't admit that to him.

". . . A big black, hard cock churning around in your tight white ass . . ."

It had been weeks. Almost every night. A phone call almost every night at just about the same time. I could have changed numbers, gotten an unlisted one. I could have arranged to be out three evenings in a row and see it if stopped. I didn't. I started clearing everything away so that I could sit by the phone. Waiting for the call. Being disgusted when it came. But disgusted with myself, not with the call. Being frustrated when there was no call that night. Wearing less and less as the calls progressed. Something loose; something that didn't hinder access.

A Saturday night. Just about that time. Me, sitting by the phone. Naked.

It rang.

"Something special tonight, Jeff. I have Manuel here. Say something, Manuel."

A groan in the background behind Vincent's smooth, velvety, baritone voice.

"Manuel's nice, Jeff. I met Manuel at the gym. He's cut and oh so nice."

Moaning in the background and a distant voice, "Gawd, Vinny. Oh Gawd. Ahhh."

"You and Mani have something in common, Jeff. You know what that is, Jeff?"

"No," I whispered down the line. I had rarely responded previously, not after my initial attempts to tell him to stop got nowhere. But I was mesmerized. I already had my hand wrapped around my cock and was stroking. This was way beyond any of the previous calls.

"Mani loves black cock, Jeff. Just like you do. I'm fucking Mani now, Jeff. And he loves it. Listen to Mani, Jeff."

The other voice no longer distant. Heavy panting and groaning, "Oh, fuck, Vinny. Oh gawd. Yes, like that. Harder, deeper. Oh Fuccckkkkk."

The phone back to Vincent. "Mani can't stay, Jeff, and I'm still horny. In fact I'm even more horny now. It's time, Jeff; it's time for you to come for your big, black cock. You know where I live."

The phone clicked off. I was stroking, but not anywhere near completion. This was too much. I let out a long sob.

I knew where this was going. I certainly wasn't fooled. I put on just a loose T and baggy gym shorts. Something had to give here, though. Either it was all a big joke and I'd be the laughing stock of the guys at the office Monday morning, or something would explode. But one way or the other, something was going to happen.

I stood at Vincent's door and knocked.

The door opened to a room that was dark except for strobing lights in blue and red and a blast of sound. Some sort of primeval recording resounding around the room; heavy breathing and panting and moans and groans, evoking high heat and lust. Directly across from the door, hung on the far wall, a giant flat-screen TV, screaming out the image of muscle guys fucking. Between the door and the TV some sort of black vinyl cube, not really a chair, not really anything but a waist-high black vinyl cube.

An overwhelming cacophony of sound and sensations of high heat and lust. No time to think, the images and sounds pushing all reason out of my mind, making my heart pound.

And out of the darkness, a big, black, naked Vincent pulled me into the room, and the door closed behind me as if on a spring. Bulging, shiny muscles. Gorgeous musculature. Everything that was boasted of, promised, swinging between his muscular thighs below and full chest V-ing down to a tiny waist overlaid with a hard slab of belly muscle. The spitting image of Phil in all his athletic glory.

Vincent pulled my T-shirt up and off my torso and, while my arms were lifted for that, another set of arms, behind me, caught me in a full Nelson, trapping my arms above my head.

I flinched and squirmed, trying to pull free.

"Just relax, Jeff," Vincent said in a low, hoarse voice. "It's just Manuel. He decided to stay. Don't fight it. You came to be fucked. You decided. Let's all just enjoy it."

Before I could respond, Vincent had leaned in close and had taken my mouth with his big, thick lips, pushing my lips apart and inserting his tongue. Taking my breath away. The moaning sounds of lust reverberating around me. The flashing lights, the swirling images on the far wall of men fucking.

Vincent's hands were on my hips, insinuating themselves under the waistband of my shorts, hot palms on my hips. Manuel was holding me close from behind. And I knew he was naked too, I could feel the heat of a cock pushing up my lower back, the heavy pectorals against my shoulder blades. His lips and teeth buried in one of my arm pits, licking and nipping and licking.

Vincent slowly kissed and nipped his way down my chest and belly, and he nibbled in my thatch as he slowly pulled the shorts down until my cock popped out—and into his mouth. In one movement, he stripped off my shorts.

I was overwhelmed with sensations as never before. I had no idea that cock sucking could arouse me this way. Manuel pushed his hardening cock down to between my butt cheeks and I writhed and whimpered. Both wanting it all and being scared shitless at what was happening to me. The sounds and lights and the sudden sexual stimulation was overpowering.

There were three men fucking on the TV. A black and a white and a Hispanic, the black and Hispanic sandwiching the white. This couldn't be some coincidence. I nearly fainted when I realized that this was no professional movie. The black on the screen was Vincent, there was no doubt. And if the Hispanic was Manuel, he was every inch the hunk that Vincent said he was.

It was all just too much too fast for me. I came in a fountain of semen across Vincent's face. He merely laughed and went down deep on me, sucking me dry.

Manuel had forced my head to turn with pressure from his enslaving bicep and his mouth was now attacking mine, possessing me fully. Big brown eyes, what I could see of the face was chiseled and handsome. Straight, silky dark hair of at least shoulder length. The pressure of his cock between my legs had forced me into a wide stance, and he was dry fucking me rapidly across my perineum, pushing my ball sac and the root of my cock up. Vincent was sucking my balls into his mouth and rolling them around against his inner cheeks.

The sounds of the moaning and groaning from the stereo system were becoming more stereo like. Or so I thought, until I realized that it was me who was adding to the moaning and groaning.

Vincent moved from in front of me and Manuel frog marched me forward— onto the vinyl cube. I was pushed over onto the cube on my belly, and Manuel released my arms from the full Nelson. But as quick as he did that, Vincent was grabbing my wrists and tying them off on plush-lined leather restraints at each side of the cube.

On the screen, the white guy was bent over the arm of a sofa. The black guy was on the sofa cushions on his knees and was stuffing his cock into the white guy's mouth. The Hispanic was hunched over the white guy from behind and plowing his ass vigorously.

But that had barely registered with me when my view was blocked by a close up-and-personal of a mammoth black cock, which was forcing itself between my lips. Vincent took my head between his hands and was guiding me on giving his cock a tour of my mouth cavity and the back of my throat.

Manuel was restraining my legs in a wide stance at the base of the back side of the cube, and then I felt the wet roughness of his tongue on the rim of my ass. He was squeezing and lightly slapping my ass cheeks and pulling them apart with his fists and seeing how far, first, his tongue, and eventually, his lubed fingers could get inside my ass.

I was gurgling and sobbing and whimpering at what both of them were doing to me. I was overwhelmed with the surprise and the threat of it. But I also was steeped in the arousal and lust of it all.

I tensed and lifted up as much as the restraints on the cube would allow as Manuel started working his cock inside me. He was murmuring to me, though, advising me to relax and go with the fuck, that I'd enjoy it. When I was able to relax, after Vincent had pulled his cock out of my mouth, I found that it was at least somewhat closer to enjoyment than to intense pain.

Manuel was stroking faster and faster and getting noisier and noisier about his enjoyment of my ass canal. Vincent left, leaving me to watch the white guy on the TV get just about the same thing I was receiving—which, I have to admit, I found to be quite hot.

As Manuel was in the last throes of his fucking, however, Vincent came back into my vision. He stood there, purposely in front of me, giving me that "I got you" smile of his, letting me watch as he split open a condom packet and rolled the transparent film onto his tool. It didn't roll back much more than half onto his cock and it was straining at the thickness of him.

"Manuel's real nice, Jeff," he murmured to me. "But, you know, he's no horse like I am. He fucks, but he doesn't FUCK, If you know what I mean. Is your Phil a stud like me, Jeff? Have you had eight thick inches before? Do you know that I fucked a guy for forty-five minutes once?"

I heard Manuel cry out and felt his condom bubble out inside me, and he bent over and kissed me on the shoulder blade and mumbled something about a nice, tight ride.

And then Vincent disappeared from view, and I felt Manuel sliding out of me. And I watched the Vincent of the TV video slowly working his cock into the white guy bent over the sofa arm. And I saw the white guy on the TV open his mouth wide and yowl to the ceiling, all of his muscles and veins straining hard at the invasion. And I felt the heaviness and thickness of Vincent's cock head at my entrance, and I opened my mouth wide and yowled to the ceiling, all of my muscles and veins straining hard at the invasion, as a far superior club to Manuel's started its digging into me.

The moaning and groaning of the sound system changed to cries of overstretched taking and groans and heavy panting, begging for release, begging for deeper, faster taking. All of which was matched from the TV screen and the vinyl cube.

At length, at great length, I both sensed and heard Vincent tense and give up the rhythmic plowing and a burst of release. I felt him relax down on my back, covering me close, his chest expanding and contracting close against my back, and his hands running down the length of my restrained arms. He kissed me at the nape of my neck and whispered, "You done good, Jeff. That was worth the investment."

My whimpers subsided into sighs, just as what seemed to be happening on the screen flickering in front of me. I'd done it. I'd thought about doing it. I'd worried about doing it. I had fantasized about it—nothing like this, of course—but about doing it. And I let it possess me and control me. But now it was done. I felt slight embarrassment and triumph. Which was disconcerting. I should feel anger. But I didn't. I sighed, in almost contentment under Vincent's trembling, sheltering body.

I sensed a change in the air; a new sound. The ring of a telephone cut through the other sounds still circling around the room.

I heard Manuel answer it. "Yeah. That's right. OK."

Then he came into view in front of me—and I saw for the first time what a hunk he really was.

"That's the other guys. They're on their way up from the lobby."

The OTHER guys?!

Piercings

Pierced

I moaned softly as the dark-haired man ran his tongue over my nipple and then over it again, chills running down my spine at the feel of the hard, round metal stud rubbing on my nipple. I was thinking hard, although having a hard time organizing my thoughts—Steve was his name, I thought. I had met up with him in the bar downstairs. I don't know what had drawn me here. I'd carried the card for the tattoo parlor with the handwritten address of the bar downstairs around with me for nearly a week before I'd come here. It was just general curiosity nagging at me. Once in the bar, when I saw him again, it was the stud in his tongue that won me over—that had me simply getting up from the bar stool and following him up the stairs at the back of the dark, smoke- and men-filled room. This was something I'd never done before. Still curious, I also felt the danger and arousal of it.

* * * *

It had been a busy Saturday afternoon at the airport when I first saw him—busy enough that he was mostly a blur in my memory other than that nagging curiosity he surfaced at the back of my mind. I was working security, and Fred Stringfellow, Wanda Miller, and I were on the metal-detection wands. If someone set the tunnel machine off, they were handed off to us and we'd run the wand over the passenger and make sure they weren't packing anything we didn't want on a plane.

This young, dark-complexioned guy wearing a sports jacket over a clean, white polo shirt and well-pressed khakis, his head covered with a reversed baseball cap, set the tunnel machine off like the 4th of July fireworks on the Hudson, and Fred and I took him aside.

"Sorry," I said as I waved the wand down his chest to his thighs and heard the counter go off like a swarm of angry locusts. "I'm afraid you'll have to go over to that booth over there, we'll have to check this out more closely."

"No problem," he said to me, with a big smile. "I'd be happy to go into the booth with you and show you what I got," he said.

I let that slide, although I reddened up a bit. I was sure he couldn't tell just like that that I liked men—although he looked like a great specimen of one. The passengers were usually too nervous to wisecrack like that. This was one cool customer.

Fred cut in at that point. I don't think he heard what the guy had said—but another man had set off the tunnel machine and one of us had to see to that. "I'll take this guy," Fred said. "You can get that one."

When Fred and the passenger came out of the booth, the passenger was still smiling a secret smile, but Fred looked a little flustered.

The guy went on to the bin at the end of the bag security belt, and I saw him take out his wallet and a pen and scribble something on a card. And then he was at my elbow, smiling, and he handed me the card.

"If you want to know what the other guy found out, go to this bar," he said. "I've written the address on the back of this card. I would have rather shown you than him. You're hot. I'll be back in town on Tuesday." And then he laughed and walked off.

And we were so busy afterward that I forgot to say anything to Fred about it. But the card burned a hole in my pocket for the rest of the week, and the more I felt it when I put my hand in my pocket, the more curious I became. Fred had gone off on vacation after that work shift, so I couldn't ask him. The address was in a part of town I'd never been to. And I meant to go down there one of these nights anyway. I'd heard it was a good area to cruise in, although I hadn't done a whole lot of that. And it came Friday night and I was bored and didn't have anything better to do.

* * * *

It was the first thing I noticed about him when he moved into the stool next to me at the bar. His self-assurance. He stubbed a cigarette out in an ashtray in front of me before ordering a beer over his shoulder from the barkeep and then turned sideways toward me. One hand went to the back of my barstool, the heel of his hand warm against my tailbone. The forearm of his other arm laid across the rim of the bar between me and my drink, and he was leaning in toward me.

"I see you kept the card. Haven't seen you in here before," he said to me. It was the guy from the airport who had given me the card with the address of this bar on the back. He opened his mouth in a friendly smile. It was a nice smile. He was a leather kind of guy, but he didn't look too rough. He had a full head of dark hair with a tendril of curl hanging down over what appeared, in this light, to be a violet eye. The lustrously dark hair was mostly on one side; the other side was cut short in a buzz cut and when he turned his head I could see that he had two initials, a capital *B* and *D*, shaved into the side of his head. I hadn't seen this at the airport, but he'd had it covered with a baseball cap there.

"Haven't been in here before," I said.

"Lookin' for some action?" he asked. I let my gaze float down from his well-tanned face to take in how he filled out the cut-off athletic T he was wearing—which was quite well. He swelled and bulged where he should if he was spending quality time working his body, and he V'd down to a trim waist with armor-plate-like abs. There was a metal ring in the navel I saw peeking out below the hem of the cut-off T.

"Yeah, maybe," I answered. "But maybe just curious. I'd wanted to check out this part of town. This looked like a good bar."

"It's a good place. A good place to get your itch scratched."

As he talked, I could see that something was going on with his mouth. A flash of a reflection off something. And then when he brought his beer around to take a swig, I saw that it was a gold bead he had pierced in his tongue. I noticed then that he had small rings pierced elsewhere on his face too—an eyebrow ring and then two in one earlobe—in all three cases, it was on the side where he had the buzz cut. It almost seemed like he was two people. A punker on one side and the captain of the college football team on the other.

"You've got a pierced tongue," I said, almost involuntarily, an observation I half thought I'd made in silence to myself, but he laughed and followed up on that, so I must have said it out loud.

"Yep. That defines me. It's what I do. It's sexy. I believe it's what every man secretly wants—what every man should have."

"I didn't notice those . . . the tongue and the ears . . . at the airport."

"Ah, so you do remember me," he said with a little laugh. His smile conveyed that he'd scored a point. It really was his invitation that had brought me here. "I take them out when I fly. Having hardware like that is a sure invitation to security scrutiny. As it was I didn't strip down enough."

I was going to say something to that, but wasn't quick enough in deciding what to say, and he went on. "Your mug is dry. Can I buy you a beer?"

"Yes, I guess so," I said.

That must have been some sort of code, some sort of signal in this bar, because he smiled, and when the barkeep delivered the beer, the guy moved his hand up under the hem of my T-shirt and palmed my lower back. His hand was warm to the touch, and I felt myself getting into the mood.

"Those must hurt, though. I can't imagine eating with a stud like that."

"What, can't imagine being eaten with a stud like that?" he asked in mock horror. And when I reddened up, he said, "That can be easily fixed. And no one has ever said it hurt. Everyone's liked it . . . a lot."

I covered the embarrassment of the moment by taking a deep drink of beer.

"My name is Steve," he said.

"Oh, I thought it was something like Billy or Butch," I said, coming up for air from my beer.

He turned the punk side of his head toward me and said, "Oh this? These ain't my initials. These define me too. Know what they stand for?"

"No," I said, with a smile. "Tell me."

"Well I'll give you a hint. The *B* is for big. I could show you what the *D* stood for."

I laughed but changed the subject. "You said the piercings defined you. What does that mean? And how many do you have."

I took another big swig of my beer as he sat there and smiled at me with some sort of secret smile like maybe I'd bitten on exactly what he wanted me to ask. He ran the tip of his tongue out of his mouth and moved it around on his lips. I couldn't help but watch it move, and he knew that was what I was watching.

"Thirteen. Lucky thirteen. That's how many piercings I got now. And it's what I do. Mainly I do tattoos at the parlor just down the street. You probably passed it on your way in. But I do piercings there too. In the back room."

"Thirteen. I can't imagine where you'd put thirteen—and no tattoos."

"A tat or two, yes, but not where most would notice. Just some close friends. You could be a close friend, though."

He stood up from his stool then and came in close beside me. The hand that had been on the small of my back moved slowly but quite noticeably around my side, under my shirt until he was completely embracing me with his arm and his palm was on my lower belly. The tips of his three longest fingers were pushing into the upper reaches of my bush.

"Here's another one," he said as he ran his free hand down to his navel. The thumb of his other hand was thrumming my own navel gently—and my dick was definitely starting to take more notice.

"That other security guy at the airport didn't tell you about the other ones?" he asked in a low voice. "Didn't tell you whatall hardware was setting your machines off?"

"No. I didn't talk to Fred about it after that," I said. "We're trained not to talk about the passengers that way."

"And yet you came anyway? I feel honored. Hey, it looks like you could use another beer. OK?"

"OK," I answered. I was breathing a little heavy, though, because of the hand on my belly, which was pushing a little lower. I moved my own hand down to cover it—I thought to let him know that this was far enough. But he took it as recognition that he had his hand there. And that it was OK with me. He moved a finger on each side of the root of my cock, and he'd somehow moved a thick ring he had on one of the fingers down near the tip and jammed it on top of my cock where it rooted, rubbing it on the vein there, which was hardening me right up. I started to tremble, which wasn't lost on Steve.

I looked around the room in panic, thinking we were on exhibition. But all the other guys there were pretty well paired off—and some of them were in more intimate poses than we were.

"Another beer here, Tony," Steve was calling out in a horse voice. "A special, please."

The barkeep came over and set another mug of beer down. And as he winked at me, he also flipped out two condom packets on the bar top. So much for wondering what a special was.

Steve leaned into me and moved his mouth to the side of my neck, and I felt the golden tongue bead move along the jugular vein there.

I moaned quietly and shuddered.

His lips went to my ear. "I have a room upstairs. I want you to count all thirteen piercings. And then I want to fuck you."

"Uh, no, I don't . . ."

"It's what you came for."

* * * *

406

He had me arched over the double bed, his arms encasing my waist, the stud in his tongue rubbing over my nipples, first one and then the other as I moaned softly, my fingers laced in the hair at the back of his head. He ran his tongue up onto my neck and took my mouth in his, rubbing his tongue stud across my tongue. One piercing.

He released my lips and I moved mine up his face and kissed his eyebrow. Piercing Two.

He held me in place with one hand while he unzipped first my jeans and then his with the other and pushed our jeans and briefs to the floor. Meanwhile my lips went to his ear and played with the two small rings there. Piercings Three and four.

I moved my hands between our chests. One hand went to one of his nipples. Piercing five. And the other to the other nipple—piercing six—before descending to his navel. Piercing seven.

Steve leaned down more into me, arching me back onto the surface of the bed, until my shoulder blades rested on the surface and then he raised his chest from me. He was smiling down at me, his hands going to encase my cock and gently working it, making it engorge as I moaned and sighed under him.

I watched the muscles of his chest move with the motion of his arms as his hands worked me. I saw then that he did have tattoos. There was a small green lizard poking its head and the front of its body out from underneath his arm pit, the lizard curved up under the bulge of his breast. Another, smaller lizard was curved up toward that one from the other side of his body, coming up from the hollow above his groin and beside his lower belly.

I played with those with my fingers and watched his violet eyes with my needy, imploring ones while he smiled down at me and slowly masturbated my cock with his hands. Increasingly I wanted him. I wanted to know about the other six piercings, but I was heating up fast. He no longer was moving his hands as they encased my cock. He was just holding them, and I was moving my hips, sliding my cock in and out of his hands.

He moved his mouth and that golden tongue stud down to my nipples again and then slowly slid it down my sternum, stopping briefly at my navel, on its way into my bush, as I started to writhe under him more insistently, fucking his hands. He still wore the ring, and it was rubbing up and down, up and down, on the vein at the root on the top of my cock.

The tongue stud went onto my cock and began to play with it as his hands, the fingers slick with lube, went to cupping my buttocks, pulling them apart, and his lubed fingers working closer to the rim of my ass, until they were there—and then beyond there, invading me, teasing my hole open. And then more open, the fingers sinking deeper and beginning a slow, counter rhythm inside my hole.

The tongue stud was driving my cock crazy. It moved from root to glans and the stud was working my piss slit, working its way inside me there, slowly, gently fucking my piss slit.

I writhed and cried out and groaned and grunted and warned him I was coming—at which he just raised his head and smiled up at me and said "I know you are," and then went back to work—until I did.

Panting and moaning, in exhaustion, I lay on the bed, trying to regain my breath—never having come like that before. I looked down, and he was standing over me, grinning and holding a huge, hard cock in his hand. I gasped, not so much as the length and girth of it as at the thick metal ring piercing its cut head. Piercing eight.

I was going to be fucked with a thick metal ring. I shuddered and began to tremble.

"This is what the BD was about," Steve said in a proud voice. I just moaned in acquiescence. He didn't require confirmation.

"Have you have been fucked with a cock ring before?" he asked.

"No," I replied in a low, gaspy voice.

"And that's not all. Here, feel this." He took my hand and brought it down to the underside of the cock that was standing straight out from his belly. Piercings nine, ten, eleven, and twelve. A line of thick metal beads ran down the length of his cock with the largest one right at his root.

"This one," he said, holding my finger to the one at the root, "is going to make love to the rim of your asshole."

I moaned, as he ran my fingers up and down the beads. "I'm told that each one can be felt separately as it slides inside you," he murmured. "Doesn't that sound tasty?"

I moaned, already imagining the sensation. Afraid of it. Wanting it. Wanting it so badly.

But he wasn't finished. He moved my hand lower, to his perineum, under the scrotum sack, where there was yet another ring piercing. Lucky piercing thirteen.

I trembled and entreated him to hurry as he stood over me and opened a condom packet and crowned his cock. And then I was pulling him to me and inside and thrusting with each of his thrusts, as he hunched over me and drove into me, thrusting deeper and deeper, and I cried out and writhed and felt each and every metal bead that followed along behind the gloriously rubbing thick cock ring. "Oh god, OH GOD, O-H GAWWWD!"

Before he came, but not until after I had done so again, he turned me on my belly and let the other side of my channel feel the full benefit of the beads, as my fists bunched the bedspread and my teeth bit into the sheets attempting—but not successfully—to stifle my screams of ecstasy. Never, ever, had I ever . . .

Later, his cock still deep inside me, he leaned over and opened a drawer in the nightstand and took out a pad of paper and a pen. "Here. Write down your cell phone number and address."

"I don't think . . . it was a great fuck," I said, ". . . but I don't think . . . again. I don't . . ."

"Write them down."

I was scared, frightened of the effect of this taking of me. Never had I been so fully fucked before. The studs and beads were a nice novelty. But this wasn't me. This wasn't my world. I didn't want to . . .

But I wrote my phone number and address down and then he was gone, leaving me, in emotional and physical tatters. Dominated and scared. And more fully fucked than I'd ever been before. Ashamed. Remembering how I had begged for it—how I had taken his cock and guided—no, literally stuffed—it inside myself. How under the feel of the cock stud and the beads, my hips had gone into a frenzy. This was just too much—too exotic, too far into fetish. I couldn't . . .

* * * *

In a meeting, sitting at the back of the room, bored at the droning on about that week's changes in security check procedures, I heard the quiet buzz. I'd forgotten to turn the cell phone off. I'd do so, but I might as well check the text message first.

The stud revolving around your nipple, rubbing the tender flesh, sending signals to the very quick of you.

I stifled a moan, reddened up and switched the phone off.

In the cafeteria, instinctively clicking on the phone when it buzzed. Another text message.

Sliding the tongue stud down to your navel. Exploring. My hand going lower, possessing.

I clicked it off and acted like nothing was happening. But I had to hold my glass with both hands, I was trembling so hard.

At home, in the evening, trying to read, the cell phone sitting next to me on the table. Trying not to look at the phone. Not wanting it to buzz. Knowing it would. Wondering why it hadn't. Then it did. His voice this time.

"Are you home?"

"Yes." A faltering reply.

"Alone?"

"Yes."

"Are you wearing a ring?"

"Yes."

"Unzip your pants. Take your cock out. Run the underside of the ring on your finger up and down the top of it, along the vein."

At each instruction, there was a pause. And without thinking or resisting, I responded to the command in his voice.

"I hear you breathing harder. You have done it, yes?"

"Yes." Almost a whimper.

"Go to the door. You'll find a package outside. Bring it in. Go to your bedroom, strip, and lay on the bed and open the package."

"Steve . . ."

"Are you going to the door?"

A pause. And then, in a low, tortured voice. "Yes."

"Are you there, on the bed, now, naked?"

"Yes."

"Open the package and do it. Do not hang up. I want to hear you come."

The package contained a thick dildo with knobs on it and a small bottle of lube.

"There, that was nice," he said when I was finished. "Now, come to me. We begin."

"Steve . . . I can't . . . I . . ."

Using all of the strength inside me I switched the phone off.

It was raining, and dark, and I hadn't ever driven in that section of town at night. I didn't even know if I'd be able to find the tattoo shop that was advertised on the card he'd given me that first Saturday at the airport. My hands were trembling and were slick on the wheel of the car. I wanted to turn around and go home—to get rid of the cell phone. To get a new one. To move, even, because he knew where I lived.

I couldn't do this. This wasn't me. I didn't want to be dominated this way.

I found the street. I could see the bar up ahead. It's lights were on. That made sense; it was the height of the night there. But a business. It surely wouldn't be . . . but there it was. The tattoo parlor had its lights on and an Open sign was blinking in the window.

He was standing behind the counter when I entered—smiling. A new piercing, one at a nostril. Piercing fourteen.

"Come into the back room," he said, holding his hand out to me. With his other hand he lifted a stainless steel tray holding needles and forceps.

I whimpered, hardly managing to croak out, "Steve . . . I don't want—"

"Yes you do, you want. It's what I do. Come with me. We begin."

P.A. Club Night

"God, Leon. An M-8 special? Eight? I have to take eight of them in one gig? And what the hell is an Edwardian?" I knew what this was really about. I damn well knew that Leon was ticked because I had told him I was taking three months off.

"Hey, you're the one who told me in almost exactly the same breath that you were taking a whole chunk of time off but that you also needed a big-money assignment. Eight fucks in one night will be big bucks for you. And Edwardian would be Victorian era, like Lord Byron and Oscar Wilde. We've got stuff for that in the stockroom here—or near enough. You wouldn't likely be wearing it for very long anyway."

"But eight men in one night, Leon. Can't you . . .?"

The voice on the phone went flat. Leon obviously wasn't the least bit interested in helping me out here. "Do you want the assignment or not?" he said in that "discussion closed" voice he used when the big gang bang assignments came in and had to be allotted to someone—usually to whoever he was irritated with that week. And the chief irritant obviously was me this week. I didn't have much leverage if I was planning to set the contract aside for a large chunk of time anyway. And I had no intention of telling him why I had to do that. I'm sure he wouldn't have approved of what I was going to do with the time.

"As I said, it's big bucks. We've got other studs here who would take it in heartbeat. But these guys asked for you specifically."

"Asked for me specifically?" I asked. Suddenly I was a little interested in this. "And so, if you give them what they want, it will be costing a bit more if it's really, really inconvenient for me to do the night?" I asked. "You'll pay me more than scale for this?"

Heavy breathing on the other end; Leon trying his best not to explode, maybe even popping a couple of those ulcer pills of his.

"Yes, of course, he said at last. A 25 percent bonus. I was going to tell you about that anyway, but you haven't given me a chance."

Sure, like hell you were going to do that for me, I thought to myself. But it was big bucks, and after you've had the first four cocks inside you in an evening, I guess cocks seven and eight wouldn't mean much.

411

"So, who are these guys? And do they have a track record with us?" I asked. "And who gets off on a stripper dressed in stuffy old Victorian costume?"

"I don't know who they are," Leon answered. "This is the first time they've used us. As far as I can determine, it's some sort of small rich men's club that meets every couple of months. I guess they're bored with fucking each other and wanted a little spice in their lives."

I took the job, and beyond that initial whining—which we all did so management would know who was taking the brunt of this operation—I didn't let Leon know how angry I was that he had come to me with this assignment. I knew what this was all about. This was all about me taking three months off from their call boy stable. I knew I was one of their biggest money earners. And I knew they'd feel my absence in their pocketbooks too.

The costume looked good on me, even though it was too warm. The Edwardians were stuffy and so were their clothes. They seemed intent on covering everything in hot fabric, which wasn't anything like the amount of coverage male strippers usually had, even at the beginning of the gig. But the Edwardians seemed pretty much a contradiction, too. The costume was actually pretty sexy in its own way. I'd heard that the Victorians were stuffy on the surface but that they could be quite sensual people under all of that—and I knew that they had done some pretty wild partying in their era. This was borne out by what I had to wear.

The billowy white shirt, with a flamboyant red cravat thing at the neck, looked good on me, especially topped by the tight form-fitting vest. The coat over that was pretty bulky, but that would go as soon as I entered the door, I knew. But what really showed the interesting little contradictions of the Victorian era were the trousers. They were tight-legged and so tight in the crotch that you could see exactly which side my cock was dressed on and you could follow it's entire length down the inside of my thigh. I told the dresser I thought I must have gotten trousers a couple of sizes too small, but he just snorted his prissy little snort and said this was exactly the way the Edwardians wore them, and that, in fact, Prince Albert, Queen Victoria's husband and the most Edwardian of the Edwardians, was well known for dressing down the left side contrary to the style of the time to dress down the right side. He apparently had the whole high society changing sides overnight, so whatever he was offering had to be readily apparent. Whatever, I thought this was a sexy idea that probably wasn't lost on the Victorians—apparently very modest dress, but putting the goods very much on display. I saw this as well in the bodice cleavage of those Victorian women who otherwise were buried in yards and yards of billowy material.

"A fashion revolution about where you put your cock and how you put it on display when you weren't fucking," I said. And then I laughed at my own joke, and the dresser laughed with me as he patted down my dressing to the left. He'd been trying to get my attention since I'd started working here. I wasn't interested, but at least it kept him laughing at my jokes. And he got a good feel off it, so we both left happy.

Later that evening, as I walked along Rodeo Drive in my Edwardian costume and with a shiny black beaver-skin top hat at a jaunty angle on my head, I decided this Victorian shit wasn't half bad. I was attracting a good bit of favorable attention, and if I'd left for the evening's work an hour or two earlier, I think I probably could have made a couple of hundred extra bucks in incidental blow jobs along the way.

I was surprised when I finally found the address I was looking for. There aren't that many of these old brick pile buildings left in downtown L.A., if indeed there ever had been many of them. I didn't know much about architecture, but if someone had given me a picture book and told me to pick out an Edwardian building, this one probably would have been my pick.

It wasn't a house, though, or even a gentleman's club, which is what I was sort of expecting. It was professional offices. And the address I was looking for proved to be a plush doctor's office that took up most of the building's second floor.

The place had good security. I had to stand out on the big porch on the front and ring the office. After a husky voice verified who I was, I was buzzed in. And then I had to repeat myself through a solid-looking door at the top of the main staircase and stand back for inspection through an eyehole.

When the door was opened, I immediately caught onto why they were so cautious about opening it up for just anyone. The man at the door—and all of the men I saw beyond that standing around in little groups with wine glasses and cigars—were stark naked. There were more than eight of them, which irritated me a little. I'd have to keep count while they were doing me so I'd know they weren't throwing a freebee in—and there was always the possibility that they would just force the extra dicking count. If so, I'd take it in my stride and keep count and take it up with Leon later. I'd learned that if you got too huffy about it, the situation might get a little dicey. Still, it was quite bothersome that there were more than eight of them.

The good news was that most of them were in fine shape, even though most of them appeared to be in their forties and fifties.

They welcomed me nicely and plied me with a glass of wine—well, several glasses of wine—and they didn't seem to be in any sort of rush for either a striptease or the gang fuck they had paid for.

We were in some sort of plush waiting room that was decorated more like a period parlor—like the building in a style I'd pick out as Victorian if I knew any more about furniture styles than I knew about architecture. One of the older men, very possibly the doctor whose name was on the door of this office suite, walked me around the room to show me off to his fellow club members. In each group, I was engaged in some small talk—some really small talk; no one was revealing in any way who they were or what would make them stand out from any of the other nude men in the room. But in addition to the small talk, they were getting to know me a whole lot better. They were feeling me up, checking out the goods. And they were doing so as if this was the natural thing they all did at parties—get naked and all feel up the only dressed dude there. They were almost clinical about it, and the thought crossed my mind that maybe all of them were doctors.

But not all of them, I could see. My eye caught sight of a vaguely familiar blond hunk across the room who rang a bell at the base of my cock. This undoubtedly was why Leon had been asked for me specifically. The blond hunk had been the best man and an especially good swordsman at a B-6 Cowboy Special bachelors' party I had done a month or so earlier. He smiled and waved at me from across the room, confirming with the sloppy lustful grin he gave me that we, indeed, had met before. But he was a Mercedes salesman, I thought, not a doctor. And he also had a new toy between his legs he didn't have the last time we met. His newly acquired Prince Albert was a shiny gold bar bell with big balls that matched the scale of his own.

While the other men crowded around me were talking to me about nothing and running their hands down the inside thigh of my trousers to make sure I was "dressed" in the Prince Albert style, my mind was doing calculations on the name I had been given for their club and trying to figure out if that had a medical connection. But for the life of me, I couldn't put a definition to what a P.A. Club might be.

So I asked.

"Ah, the P.A. stands for Prince Albert," my doctor escort said in a matter-of-fact tone that indicated it wasn't a secret.

"Ah then, you're named for the Victorian period," I said. "You're all nineteenth-century England buffs." I almost choked on my own tongue, though, when I realized I had used the word "buff" in a roomful of naked men.

"Not precisely," the doctor said. "We're actually named for this." And as he said that, he took his very presentable cock in his hand and waved it at me.

And then I saw it. The men weren't completely naked at all. They all had something in common. All of them had jewelry things poking out of their dick heads. Some were open loops with rounded beads where the loops stopped, some closed loops, some looked like miniature barbells, and some were studs made out of various things: gold or silver cubes or knobs or gem stones. One of the younger, studlier guys had a loop with what looked like a ruby heart charm hanging off it.

"These are Prince Alberts," the doctor was saying. "The members of our club all have them. This is our annual initiation meeting. We'll initiate a new member tonight. Prince Albert was said to have originated this idea for Victorian gentleman and to have had one himself. His name stuck on penis piercing."

Fascinating, I thought, about the Prince Albert jewelry. Absolutely fascinating. Who would have thought it of the husband of the stuffy old Queen Victoria? Those Victorians. Gotta love 'em. They had us fooled about them being so uptight. And, of course, a doctor's office would be a natural place for a party like this.

As the evening wore on, the club members became friendlier to me and friskier with their hands—and some with their lips—and increasingly helpful in equalizing our circumstances by slowly helping me off with my hot clothes. And I became more and more taken with the good wine they were sharing around.

I began to earn my fee in earnest. The party spread out from the waiting room into the examination rooms, and the club members were becoming as friendly and frisky with each other as they were with me. They were pairing off in couples and threesomes and a few of them were disappearing into the area of the examination rooms. But a few of them were also fucking right there in the waiting room, on the floor, in the chairs, and on the reception desk.

The doctor and a few of the other members, the younger ones, I was happy to note, guided me through a door and toward the back of the building. As we passed doors, I could see that the smaller groups that had come this way earlier were having no trouble amusing themselves with the medical equipment and with each other in the examination rooms branching off from the hallway.

I was quite woozy from the wine at this point, but it was time for me to start keeping count. I was down to just the billowy shirt, which was fully open, and that silk red cravat around my neck. Several of the men had me backed up to an examination table and were running their hands and lips all over my body. My doctor escort left briefly but came back with a box full of condoms and a bottle of what must be lubricant. As my first customer, a short blond guy with a short, but fat cock, was kneeling on the examination table, with me facing him and him using my mouth to get his cock as pumped up as it was going to get, the doctor escort was rubbing the lubricant into my hole and on my cock as well.

He told me the lubricant would help me take several men easier and that I would feel a bit numb after only a few minutes, but that this would keep me from tightening up.

The table was really too high for the little blond to do anything to me, so when he came off the table, he pulled me over to a chair, sat in it, and pulled me down on his lap, facing the other men, and made me fuck myself on his cock while the other men gathered around, licking their lips, stroking themselves, and waiting their turn. I felt his Prince Albert, a gold cube, rubbing along the side of my passage as he stroked me. Very intriguing. In fact I could feel all of the different Prince Alberts—and in different ways—that I took that evening. They were truly awesome toys, and I wondered briefly if Queen Victoria cried out with passion as I did for the little blond and all his successors when Prince Albert played her with one of those.

The next man, a tall, thin redhead with a long, slender cock to match, had me kneel in the chair, facing the back, and he fucked me from the rear, taking long strokes into me that were quite pleasant, really. He was good about putting his hands under my shirt and onto my chest and tweaking my nipples in rhythm with his fuck. He had one of those upturned cocks and had a Prince Albert that was an open ring with two big silver knobs. They dragged in unison across my upper canal walls as he fucked me, and I rewarded his efforts and those talented silver balls with my first ejaculation of the evening to the delight and encouragement of a very attentive audience.

Then I was taken from behind by number three while I was standing on the floor and my chest was pressed to the top of the examination table and my mouth was working black and curly-haired number four's plump cock. Number four's Prince Albert was like a bar bell, so my passage walls got extra loving on both sides as he slid in and out of me. He wanted to cuddle close in behind me and kiss me on the neck as he was stroking, and I found that curly-haired chest of his rubbing up and down on my back as he fucked quite arousing and satisfying.

Number five wanted me on the floor beside the table, me on my back, and him holding my pelvis up and my legs out and pumping me fast and furiously while his teeth worked my nipples. His cocksmanship was especially inventive and I arched my back and thrust my pelvis up into his as his Prince Albert found and kissed every square inch of my insides. Number six liked that position as well, but he had me on the top of the examination table. He was the hunk with the heart-shaped pendant on his Prince Albert loop, and he was quite pleased that I wanted to closely watch that disappear into and emerge from my hole while he plowed me. I erupted and flowed for him. Number seven just flipped me over onto my stomach and covered me close with his arms and torso, told me to come up a bit on my knees, and slowly pumped me with the longest and fattest cock I'd had yet that evening. He took his time and had me moaning and groaning for it. I had felt the distinct Prince Albert feature of all them as they dicked me—and I loved the feel of what they all had, but this seventh miner had the biggest, thickest ring of all on his longest and thickest cock. And he had attached a string of beads to the ring. These were swirling around inside me while he fucked me, and they sent me straight to bottom heaven.

I'm not sure that there was a number eight—and for all I was able to be aware of at the time, there might have been a number twelve and thirteen as well. Number seven had me royally fucked and the wine had me woozy as hell, and that lubricant had me numb on the surface, if not inside my canal.

I was aware of a muscle-bound bald guy sitting on my chest with me stretched out on the examination table on my back. I had some impression that my wrists and ankles were bound to the table, but I was too far gone to be sure of that. The bald guy was feeding me with his cock, fucking my face and making me suck him, while he held my head very still between two beefy palms. Many men—it seemed like the full contingent of men who had been at the party to begin with—were gathered around the table and ooing and ahing and making small talk to each other in whispers. I saw the escort doctor, a blur of white now, no longer naked, come around below me, and I felt him thrust inside me with his crowned cock. He had a fist wrapped around my cock as he fucked me, but my cock was so numb that I couldn't be sure of that. After some deep stroking, the doctor just held himself deep inside me, very still. The bald guy on top of me kept holding my head still with his hands and feeding my mouth with his hard cock. He was cooing to me, whispering words of encouragement for I know not what—nor did I really care at the moment; I was well-gone drunk and very well fucked.

For a short time, the room was swathed in an eerie silence. And then there was a buzzing of voices and some healthy applause sweeping around the room, and the party seemed to be taking off for a second round of frivolity.

The room nearly emptied out, and I found I was pulling myself up to a seated position on the table and rubbing my wrists as if they had, indeed, been bound. The bald guy was gone as well. Only my doctor escort remained, and he was decked out in a white surgical costume now and had a white gauss cup over his mouth.

He removed the face mask and gave me the broadest of smiles and said, "Welcome to the club."

I looked down, and there it was. I had a thickish loop pierced through my mushroom cap. It was gold and it had a gold bead on it.

I had been initiated, crowned, pierced, made a colleague of Prince Albert. I celebrated by rolling my eyes up into my head and falling back onto the surface of the examination table and passing out.

For days thereafter, Leon wouldn't take my telephone calls. I did, however, receive a hefty check in the mail for the evening's work and I'd received a nice fat tip from the guys in the P.A. Club on the spot as well—although there was no reason for Leon ever to know that.

I'm sure he figured that I was, by right, totally pissed with him and might do him bodily harm if I caught up with him before the post-surgical pain wore off. I'm sure, though, that he also was crowing to himself that he had punished me for wanting to take three months off, especially since someone had to take this eight-male-fucks assignment—the payoff was much too good to turn it down—and anyone who did would be out of commission, recovering from the surgery, for three months.

For three months, the exact time I had said I needed to take off. Which meant I wasn't trying to contact Leon to ream him a new one; I was trying to call him to gloat. I was taking the three months because I had decided I wanted my dick head pierced and a nice gold loop put in it, although I had no idea at the time that it was called a Prince Albert. Before this assignment came along, I would have had to swallow the cost of both the surgery and the recovery myself. Thanks to the P.A. Club, however, I'd now gotten that all for free—along with a club membership, membership in a club that included a master fucker number seven with a mean string of ass canal beads.

Pool Tables

Family Day on the Pool Table

I had always thought that about the only thing you could do on a pool table was play pool, but the Taylor brothers went to great length and depth to teach me otherwise.

I'd met the three brothers on the beach at Pataya, Thailand. Their family owned a hotel construction company and was making money hand over fist in throwing up fancy hotels in downtown Bangkok and at the Pataya and Hua Hin beach resorts. All three brothers, in their late twenties and early thirties worked in the family firm, mostly on the construction sites themselves, which had helped them to stay trim and to bulk up nicely.

I met them on the sand below their fancy beach house in Pataya one Saturday afternoon. I was just passing by, walking the water line, when they called out to me and invited me to play doubles volleyball with them for a while. They lacked a fourth, and I was the first one who came along, I guess, who they figured was athletic enough to give them a workout. And, as it turned out, I really did give all three of them a good workout before the afternoon was through—and then some.

I was happy to play volleyball with them, because all three of them were real easy to look at, all bulked up in small Speedos that showed off very promising baskets. I'd already seen one of them, the younger brother, Randy, at a cast party after a play in Bangkok, which had ended as a major male fuck fest, and where I'd been bottomed twice, so I knew they—or Randy, at least—knew that I had been fucked before. Volleyball is a contact sport, and there was a lot of touching and rubbing, which is nice when the bodies are hard and well-cut, which pretty much defined the Taylor brothers.

After an hour of volleyball and beer, Randy invited me up to the house to shower off and to play some pool in the area under their house, which was raised on stilts, during the heat of the day. I accepted, and we all showered at an outdoor shower on the path leading up to the house.

I didn't know how to play pool all that well, and when it was my turn to stroke the ball, Randy got behind me to show me how to hold the cue, and everything just sort of developed quickly from there. He was close in back of me. I could feel his basket against my butt, and knew from that that he was getting really interested in me. He had his arms around me, holding my arms on the cue to show me how to hold it, his chest touching my back, and his chin on my shoulder, and I just turned my face to him, and he came in for a deep kiss. The time of my tour in Bangkok was the anything goes period of my life, so I just went with the kiss.

Then he had his hands all over my chest and nipples and belly and down onto the basket of my Speedo. He flipped me around and lifted me on the table, pushing the pool balls aside, and laid me on my back with my butt at the edge of the table. Then he went for my tits with this tongue. I have large aureoles around my nipples, and they are an especially sensitive point of sexual stimulation for me, so I got all hot and bothered quickly as he thumbed, stroked, pinched, and sucked on my nipples.

I let him know that I liked what he was doing to me, and he said he'd figured that out already, as he'd seen a big Swede doing this to me at the party in Bangkok, and he'd wanted to do it to me ever since. The Swede had stuffed my ass real good with a juicy Swedish sausage too, so I knew where Randy was headed with all of this.

After giving my nipples a good workout, he tongued his way down my chest, gave me some head, and then dove for opening up my asshole with tonguing, kissing, and licking. When he was satisfied that he had me moistened up and opened, he pushed me on up the table and climbed on top with me. He knelt, with his knees under the small of my back, holding my left leg wrapped around his waist, and my right leg being lifted up with my calf on his chest. I was arching my back, with my head and shoulders resting on the surface of the pool table, and I had a good view of him entering me with a supercock. I did some groaning, heavy breathing, and slapping of the table top with my hands as his cock slowly disappeared into my hole.

Randy's brothers, Andy and Frank, had just been standing around and watching us with big grins on their faces, but when Randy had run his cock all the way in and had begun to pump me, the older brother, Frank, stripped off his Speedo and hopped up on the table and straddled my head with his knees and started eating out my cock. He had a nice eight-incher and heavy balls, so I gave those head.

Randy came pretty quickly, and pulled out of me and hopped off the pool table. Frank had saved his load, and, when Randy was gone, Frank flipped me over on my belly, straddled me on his knees with his calves on either side of my thighs, lifted my pelvis up with his hands on my hips, and drilled my ass with a cock that must have been about the same size as Randy's. And I'd been able to handle Randy without much trouble. With Randy, though, I'd managed to stretch my legs and butt cheeks to accommodate his size. But Frank held my thighs in tight together and he really filled and stretched my ass canal as he entered my tightened asshole and slid and drilled up to his root. I'd been working his cock while Randy was fucking me, so he came almost as quickly as Randy had.

And then it obviously was going to be Andy, the middle brother's, turn. He was the hunkiest of all and had an even longer cock than either of his brothers did. And when he came up on the table, I saw that he'd enhanced that. He had some sort of sheath covering his cock that had little rubber knobby and spiking things all up and down it and it was ribbed.

Frank laid me on my right side, with my right leg bent. He came in behind me and took my left leg and pulled it out and over his body. He was holding my torso up with his right arm around my back. His right hand was cupping my right breast, and he was thumbing my nipple. I turned my head to him, and he came in for a deep kiss as his cock entered my ass, which was now open, loose, and well-lubricated with the cum from both of his brothers. I felt every knob and spike and rib on his cock sheath rub at my prostate and canal walls, as he slowly pushed in nine inches or more. He filled me a good bit deeper than either of his brothers had managed. As he started his pumping action, his lips went to my left nipple, and he gathered it, big aureole and everything, into his mouth and started to suck. I writhed and bucked under him, joining in the rhythm of his fuck. I got my hand on my dick and was stroking myself, when Randy came back up on the table and swallowed my cock and took my cum when I shot my load.

I never did learn how to play pool. I might have, but old man Taylor had arrived during my last skewering and had stripped, sat in a rattan chair, and stroked himself while I was servicing his oldest son and being serviced by his youngest. When the brothers weren't at me, they were over being diddled—and, eventually, fucked by old man Taylor, so I didn't have any trouble figgering out where they boys had gotten their playfulness from.

Frank unloaded up my ass canal, and then, before I knew it was going to happen, Randy and Frank had delivered me to their dad's lap. He lifted me off his lap and had me place my knees on the wide rattan arms of the chair, facing him, and he cupped my butt cheeks in his big, rough hands, and tongued and kissed my belly and balls for a while and then sucked me off. And he was really good at giving head.

After I'd cum, he sat me back down in his lap, held me by my hips, and skewered my ass with a cock that wasn't nearly as long as any of his son's dicks but that was considerably thicker and had a lot more experience behind it in how to drive a man wild with rotations and various rhythms of pumping. My left leg was hooked on his shoulder, and my right leg was out to the side of the chair. I arched my back, and he brought his mouth back down to my belly and chest, while he pumped me in short strokes from below and got his hand down there and rotated his cock around in my canal. I made little appreciative purring noises for him. I knew the father was far richer than any of the sons. And he was probably harder muscled than any of them too; I certainly felt his most important muscle harder than I had with any of his sons.

He must not have liked the leverage he was getting, though, because he rose from the chair on powerful legs and marched back over to the pool table. I had my arms and legs wrapped around him, his hands were under my butt, and he managed to keep his dong buried in my ass. At the table, I wound up right where I had started with Randy—me bent over the table on my chest, and the old man pumping me from behind. At one point, he had me take my legs up with my heels on the edge of the table and my ass waving way out for him, and he swung me against the pressure of his cock, but that got a little much both of us, and he had me stand back down on one leg, with the other one stretched up on the table, and he sort of side split me from in back. And, boy, did he have stamina. He pumped longer than all of his sons put together. A real family man, he seemed to be immensely enjoying his cum mixing with the sperm of all three of his offspring in my ass canal, and nearly a half hour after he'd begun his expedition trip up my ass, he shoot off his load inside me.

I had a really good time, but I'm just as glad that there weren't any other Taylor brothers or a funny uncle or two visiting Pataya to service. The joke was sort of on them, though. I had fucked Mrs. Taylor—and we'd had orgasmed together once for each of her sons—in a suite in the Montien Hotel in Bangkok just two days before this little party.

Public Sex

TRTrade.com

We were in the study of Professor Hendrick's house, in the late evening, nearing the end of the tutorial he was conducting. At least I assumed it was nearing the end, because I was very close to coming. We were in a straight chair facing his desk. Professor Hendricks, his hands wrapped around my waist was sitting in the chair; I was sitting on his hard cock—or, rather, fucking myself on his cock in slow risings and fallings and me moaning in tenor to his groaning in baritone.

Professor Hendricks was murmuring how nice I was between his groans of churning inside me—as well he should, because I had had no intention of letting him fuck me and had fended him off for weeks.

Yet here I was, not only letting him have me, but doing the fucking myself—skewered in his lap and pushing off the oriental rug under the desk on the balls of my feet. Up and down, up and down. I'd never done it this way before. But I was in full heat, total rut. Today I wanted a cock inside me; I wanted to fuck myself on a nice juicy cock—and here was a more than willing Professor Hendricks, handily providing a hard pole.

Laying in front of me on the desk top, open, was what had finally won the day for Professor Hendricks. It was a coffee table book of glossy pictures—although not exactly the sort of book most people would lay out on their coffee table. The photos were of men fucking—and not just fucking. They were fucking in public places, sometimes with people strolling by and not taking notice at all. I had no idea how some of these photographs had been taken. Naked male couples fucking on the grass or on the benches in a public park on a sunny day. People sunning on the beach, with a couple of men right there fucking on a towel in their midst. Commuters packed into a subway car, hanging on straps—and there, one man with his pants down around his knees and another man crouched behind him fucking up into him.

I had been sitting at the desk in the straight chair with Professor Hendricks off to the side in his arm chair, running over the mathematics tables with me. Trying from time to time to touch me, but, as usual, me not having anything to do with it. Not saying anything, not accusing him of anything. We both knew that was out of bounds. He was the professor and I was the student. Anything in the open would mean I wouldn't pass his class. And no good reporting it; all the students knew he fucked his male students like a rabbit—whoever's pants he could get into. Surely the university administrators knew that. But he was a big name in applied mathematics; he gave the university stature. In a dispute between him and a student, it wouldn't be the professor who would be packing his bags.

"Perhaps this is something that you might be interested in," he had said. And then he had put this glossy photography book in front of me.

And I'd made the mistake of opening it. I went into instantaneous, intense heat. I had no idea that seeing guys fucking in public would be such a turn-on. My interest was obvious to the professor, as I'm sure he had hoped it would be, and he was leaning into me from behind. Touching me. And I wasn't pulling away as usual.

I turned a page, and the professor was pulling my T-shirt over my head. And I was letting him do it. My eyes were pouring over the photographs. Drinking in every pixel of them. Searching the eyes of the passers by for any sign of recognition that there was fucking going on within their sight. And here and there, seeing a reaction and stirring at the thought—actually at the thoughts: both of stumbling upon such a scene in public and of being the guy being fucked. Doing it in public. Seeing who was attracted. Who might be bold enough to join in.

All of the guys having sex in the pages of this book were real hunks. The professor had his arms laced under my pits and his hands on my nipples, pinching them. He had brought down another book—this time a photo album. Even more real and more erotic to me. Not just glossy, quite possibly staged or photo-shopped photos in a book of guys fucking in public, but actual, real life photos of the same. And in these photos—the professor—doing the fucking. A younger, more muscular, achingly handsome professor. My reaction was intense—I wanted to be fucked by the man in these photos. And somehow it didn't matter that he was older now.

He was naked and his hard cock was rubbing between my shoulder blades. And he turned my face to him and kissed me. I let him do this, but only briefly. It was the photographs I wanted to see—it was the "him" in the photos I wanted fucking me. But the photo wasn't real life. Real life was the professor, here, in his study, dominating me.

I stood at his guidance and leaned over the desk, face close in to the photographs. Turning pages, examining the photographs closely. My pants and briefs gone now. The professor sitting in the straight chair, his hands spreading my buttocks cheeks, his mouth and tongue at my asshole.

And then me, in a frenzy of lust and want. Rising and falling on the professor's dick as he sat under me in the chair, moaning, his hands encasing my waist. And me scrutinizing the photographs of the guys fucking in public places. My eyes went to the captions in the glossy book. Repeated references to an Internet URL. TRtrade.com.

Fucking myself on the professor's hard cock in the quiet evening of the wood-paneled study and repeating the URL over and over again in my mind.

* * * *

I could hardly wait that night when I got back to the dorm for my roommate to drift off to snoring before I huddled down behind my desk, out of view from his bed, and tapped out the TRtrade.com URL on my laptop. The full name was

428

Tearoom Trade. I hadn't the foggiest what that meant, but, with trembling fingers, I clicked on the "join" button. I had to pay a fee, which was a bit stiff—but within moments of the images of public male fucking popping up on the screen, I too was stiff and happily masturbating away.

The images almost immediately took over my life, and I found myself checking the latest additions to the Web site whenever and wherever I could settle in a place that had an Internet connection.

I was crouched over the laptop in the university library one day, checking out the Web site and trying to be discrete about holding my throbbing dick through the cloth of my trousers under the rim of the library table top. I don't know how long I had been at that before I realized that someone was standing behind me and looking over my shoulder. I turned. It was a guy a couple of years older than I was— Mediterranean darkness of complexion and with a profusion of black curly hair. The hair was not only on his head but heavy on his forearms as well and welling up at the v in the neck of his sports shirt. He had what I would call bedroom eyes and full, sensuous lips. His features where angular, almost craggy, but everything fell together in a highly attractive, attracting package.

I didn't know how much he had seen, but I only became aware of him when he had laid his hand on my shoulder. In shock, I looked around. Long, thick fingers, with curls of black hair on them above the knuckles and on the back of his hand.

I mumbled something—I don't know what—and snapped my laptop shut and stumbled out of the library building. When I reached my car, I turned as I was throwing my stuff into the backseat, and saw him there at the top of the stairs up to the library entrance. He was scanning the area around the library.

Before his eyes turned in my direction, I instinctively shut the car door again and slipped across the street and into the large city park that ran across the road from the older, main buildings of the university. I was well down the path and turning onto one that rimmed a large grassy area when I looked back and saw him again at the entrance I'd used to get into the park.

I went off the path and into a grove of trees. I found one where the trunk split into two about four feet off the ground so that I could hide behind it and peek out between the tree trunks and view the path rimming the grassy area. I couldn't be sure he was following me. If so, I should be able to see him from here when he passed on the path and then double back and be gone. I was so embarrassed that he might have seen what I was viewing on my laptop screen in the library. Still, I was all a tremble and aroused. The new sensations were delicious. And here I was in a public place.

I waited a few minutes, but no sign of him, although a couple, very much taken with each other did pass by not more than twenty feet from where I was half concealed between the two trunks of the tree. Two young guys had come out onto the grassy area, throwing a Frisbee and being pretty noisy about it. They looked pretty hunky, and my imagination went to what the three of us could be doing out on that grassy lawn.

I was about to leave, when I felt hands on my hips from behind and a deep voice was whispering in my ear. "Hold still. Just hold right there."

I turned my head in shock, just in time to see a mop of black curly hair dipping down at my side. Hands were fumbling at my belt buckle and then my zipper, and my pants and briefs were being slipped down off my hips.

I flinched and moaned as a cool tongue lapped between my butt cheeks, seeking out my asshole, and a hand encased my dick. I should have pulled away then and stumbled out of the park, but the lust filled me immediately and I was going very hard. The reality was even more arousing than the photos on the public fucking Web site were.

I gave in to it—just as I had for the professor. I stood, leaning into the crotch of the tree, my legs spread out behind me, locked and in a wider stance so the dark guy could kneel between them. I was depicting as fully clothed for anyone spying me from the park path or out on the grassy area, but I was revealed from the rear as naked from the waist down, with, first a tongue, and then fingers, digging into my ass canal and a big, calloused hand pulling at my engorged cock.

I came almost immediately, as an older couple was passing by on the pathway. The woman glanced around at me in slight surprise of seeing someone there. But it didn't seem to register with her that I was spilling seed against the tree trunk with the callused pad of a finger rubbing my prostate. I found that thrilling.

"Come with me to the tearoom," A deep voice was whispering in my ear as my pants were being pulled back over my hips.

"The tearoom?" I responded in a confused voice.

"Yeah. The public toilet. Tearoom, as in the letter 'T'—standing for toilet room. You know, like in the name of the Web site you were looking at in the library. Tearoom trade fucking—TRtrade.com. You like being fucked in public, don't you? I want to fuck you in the tearoom."

"I . . .uh." I wanted to scream out that, no I didn't know anything about this lifestyle, and I wasn't at all ready for the risk of being fucked in a public park bathroom. But I was in high heat too. It was all just so arousing—the intensity and reality of it just so much more than even looking at the photos of it. And it dawned on me that he thought I already was into this public fucking and that I had purposely led him from the library to the park for this tryst.

I just let him lead me deeper into the park.

We reached a narrow, boxwood-lined path leading back to a one-story building that was nearly covered with vines and that had a discrete "public restrooms" sign posted on a metal board stuck into the ground.

I hesitated, but my new Greek god companion of the sultry Mediterranean looks had a strong grip on my arm and was pulling me back toward the men's side of the building. When we entered, there was another guy, dirty blond hair hanging down in his face, rangy body, a good bit older than either the Greek god or me, standing at one of the urinals, one hand up on the wall in front of him and the other at his open fly.

I stopped at the door. "I guess . . . there's someone already here," I whispered to my companion. "I guess we can't . . ." I still wasn't sure. It was almost a relief that there was something that would prevent this.

"It's just Danny," my companion said. "Hey, Danny, want to take the watch position for a few minutes?"

"Yeah, sure," the other guy said with a big grin on his face. He turned from the urinals and I saw an especially long, but thin dong hanging down from his open fly, a bush of dirty-blond hair at the root. "That is if I get seconds."

"Done," my companion said. We passed each other, Danny toward the door and my companion bustling me up to the urinals and jerking my pants down again.

I stood, leaning into a urinal, my cheek against a damp tile wall and my arms out in front of me, palming the wall—at least until one hand went to my dick to masturbate myself—while the dark Greek guy rolled on a condom and covered me from the rear and fucked me in slow, even strokes.

I was terrified that someone would come in and catch us—and that heightened my arousal so that I came again in short order.

The Greek went into a fast flurry of plowing me hard and then grunted and shuddered. And then he was moving to the door, and Danny was saddling up behind me, holding his piece in his hand, and sliding his cock in a long, swift movement up into my channel. He wasn't as thick as the Greek had been, but he reached a whole heck of a lot deeper up into me. And he had an off-rhythm way of fucking that made me catch my breath at each change in the upward thrust.

I moaned and masturbated into the urinal again, as he took me in swift motions.

I turned in shock as he was finishing at the sound of voices at the restroom door. My worst fears. A blue uniform. A cop was standing there talking to the Greek. I'd been caught. On my first real public fucking experience, I'd been caught and would be taken into the police station, stared at knowingly and mockingly, and booked and branded. On just one time.

But the policeman was walking into the restroom and unzipping his pants. His cock was already hard—and thick and long.

Danny drifted away, and two strong hands were gripping my hips, with thumbs pulling my butt cheeks apart. And I was being fucked again by a man in blue. I sighed with satisfaction and thrill, with my cheek against the cool, damp tile above the urinal, and the sounds of clanking police gear jangling at the policeman's belt as he fucked up into me, deep and hard.

As he was walking me out to my car, the Greek told me that his name was Ted and that he wanted to see me again. I had already let my name slip and that I was a student at the university, but I didn't commit to seeing him again and didn't tell him how he could contact me.

The first day I spent in regretting the experience and feeling so lucky that I had gotten away with it without being dragged down to the station house. The danger of it all sent electric chills through me. The problem, which I acknowledged on the second day, was that I found the danger of it intensely erotic and arousing. And now that I had experienced it in reality, I was hooked. By the third day, I was regretting I hadn't given Ted my phone number. On the fourth day he called. The power of the university telephone directory.

I told him no, that I had too much to do that day, but when I came out of the front door of my dorm, he was parked there and leaning on his car, sport shirt over swimming trunks and holding a skimpy Speedo with those long, hair-backed fingers of his.

He took me to a swim club and paraded me around the pool a couple of times wearing that skimpy Speedo. A couple of beefy guys took interest and he gave them a look that I guess was a known signal in the tearoom trade world. Fifteen minutes later, he was standing in the doorway between the shower room and the men's locker room. I was being held parallel to the wet floor in the steam coming down from the shower heads and off our bodies by one beefy guy who was supporting my torso from behind with his arms laced under my pits, while the other one crouched between my legs. He was holding my thighs spread with his hands and standing between my legs and fucking me in long, vigorous strokes. They exchanged places after the first guy was finished. A third guy had entered the showers during my second fucking and then took me from the rear, up against the wall tiles, while Ted and the other two guys watched.

I loved every risky minute of it.

Back at my dorm, the car idled in front of the dorm entrance, with people walking back and forth on the sidewalk, while Ted lowered his face to my lap and gave me a blow job while I tried to keep my face from exposing to all who passed by what was happening in the car.

* * * *

Two days later Ted called and asked me if I'd go to the gay film with him, and I said I would. I'd never been to the 0 Theater before, but I'd heard about the gay movie and bathhouse, and I was lost to Ted. Each time he'd fucked me and watched others fuck me since we'd first met in the park, he'd been more inventive, more bold publicly. And each time it made me harder and more keyed up and the lovemaking had been more intense.

He asked me to wear just gym shorts and a T, and I had no doubts he planned to fuck me in the theater while we were watching the movie. I had no idea how intense it would be, though.

He stripped the T off me as soon as we entered the theater, and he made a point of finding a seat in the middle of the theater and exhibiting how well muscled I was. The atmosphere in the theater became electric, and all of the guys who were scattered around, some isolated and hunched down in the seats, beating their meat while watching what was going on on the screen, others in little clumps, being sucked or sucking or lurking nearby and watching, turned their attention to us.

A sucking scene had started on the screen in a tableau of one young guy as the center of attention of four burly truckers. Ted went down on the floor between the seats, slipped off my shorts and slid his lips over my cock. I spread and lifted my legs over the back of the chair seat in front of me and began to moan as I watched the young actor on the screen sucking at four proffered cocks, he on his knees and the four truckers surrounding him and playing with and kissing each other as their cocks each got a full share of attention.

Guys in the theater started moving toward us at the sounds of my moans and the sight of my bare legs stretched over the seat back. The ones drawing the nearest were intently watching my face to catch the expression of my ecstasy. Three bold men came right up to us. One was behind me and had his cock out and was rubbing in on my neck and shoulder while watching Ted go down on me. Another one sat in a chair in the row in front of us right next to one of my legs and started sucking the toes on one of my feet. Another sat down right beside me. When he did that, Ted stopped sucking me and lifted my hips up out of the chair with palms under my butt cheeks and started working my anus with his tongue. The man who sat down next to me had his cock out and was stroking himself. And when Ted let go of my cock, that man snaked his other hand over and started slowly pumping my cock. His eyes were intently watching my face. I was letting him know I was enjoying this attention.

I looked up at the screen. The truckers were beginning to fuck the young man doggy style. It was clear they were going to take turns.

My eyes swept the theater. Everyone was looking our way now, and most were on the move toward us. Every man standing had his cock out and was stroking it.

Ted stood up in a crouch in front of me so that I no longer could see the screen. I could hear the moaning and groaning coming from the screen, though—and from around me—and from me as well.

Ted was lifting my hips higher with his hands and the guy behind me who had been slapping my shoulder with his cock, put his arms under my shoulder blades and his hands at the small of my back, and, between them, they held me up, parallel with the floor, my torso in full view of those gathering around me. I cried out and arched my back as Ted entered me with his hard cock. The toes of both feet were being sucked now and the guy in the seat beside me was now bent over me and sucking my cock.

Ted was pumping me slowly, his cock digging deeper with each motion. While still supporting me from behind, the guy behind me drew his belly back. My head dropped back, and his cock was at my lips. I opened to him, and he began to slowly fuck my mouth.

Hands. There were hands all over me. Gliding. Trembling. Pinching, prodding. Tongues on the soles of my feet and in my arm pits. The groans and yelps of hard fucking on the screen and the hum and buzzing in full life around me of an aroused crowd of men. Me giving them satisfaction.

I came in the mouth of the guy hunched over me, and he faded back, satiated. Ted came deep inside me, but then I heard him give a little cry and he was drawing out of me and my hips had fallen back into the theater seat. The view to the screen was open now. The young man on the screen was being held up, sandwiched, between two of the truckers, one fore and one aft. They were doubling him with their cocks, pistoning away in countermotion to each other. The young man was writhing in both agony and ecstasy. Being stretched to the limit but loving it—or at least acting like he was.

I saw what had drawn Ted away. A trucker-type who could have been one of the actors on the screen. He had Ted bent over the back of one of the theater seats in the row in front of me and was doggy fucking him.

The man behind me, who was equally as large and heavily muscled, lifted me over the back of the seat and gathered my back to his front. I was bowing out from the pelvis and instinctively reached back with both hands and locked my fists behind his neck as he grabbed both of my thighs and pulled them around his hips. Willing hands from either side grabbed my ankles and wishboned my legs as he thrust his cock up inside me from behind. His hands locked at my belly as he held me steady,

433

bowed out from his pelvis, and fucked me with deep, hard thrusts. A face appeared before me and then lowered, as a man went into the seat I had been occupying in reverse with his knees and took my cock in his mouth.

The other two truckers on the screen were now worrying the young actor's hole hard. He seemed to be semiconscious, although he was smiling wanly.

I felt as much as saw a renewed swirl of motion inside the theater. Down toward the screen and to the left two guys were double fucking another guy, mimicking what had been happening on the screen, holding him sandwiched between them, and double skewering him.

I no longer felt the press of a crowd around me. The tide was moving toward the screen and to the left. The hands on my ankles disappeared, as did the mouth on my cock. And then, having finished, the guy behind let me slowly drop, bent over the back of my theater chair, and he too was gone.

Ted came over the back of the row in front of me, grinning, and plopped down in a seat. He helped me come across the seat back from the row behind and settled me down in his lap, both of us facing the screen and my ass channel sinking on his cock.

He wrapped his arms around my chest and nuzzled my neck.

The actors on the screen were shooting their loads in impossibly prodigious milky-white cum. Our attention went to the double fuck scenario still going on inside the theater closer to the screen, although there was little of the action we could see now because of the chanting crowd gathered around it.

"I just love going to the theater," Ted murmured with a chuckle, as he reached for and started stroking my cock.

* * * *

The phone is ringing and I'm answering it, hands trembling, because Caller ID is revealing that it's Ted.

He wants to take a public bus ride out into the suburbs and wants me to wear shorts with extra large leg holes.

I am already beginning to get hard.

At the Reservoir

I take three- to five-mile hikes about twice weekly. I have five nearby nature trails I rotate through (in addition to a few more urban walks). The park I went to recently—at the town's reservoir—has been on the Internet for years as a male pickup spot, although the police seemed to have stopped that a few years ago, I thought—and the pickup spots (the restrooms and an old barn) aren't near where I walk.

I was coming down a wooded trail slanting down to a bridge over a stream in a fairly isolated part of the park, when I noticed a young man down near the bridge, just sort of milling around. I don't often meet other people on this trail, and those I do meet seem to be on the move, just as I am. He was looking up the side of the ridge at me while I was descending to the stream and bridge. He looked college age—some sort of pleasant, just OK looking guy with dark features, curly black hair, about 5 foot 10—my height, eyeglasses. My mind said local university, helped, I'm sure because he was wearing a university-logo T-shirt (but, then, so was I).

When I was about down to the bridge, he smiled and said it was a nice day for a hike, and was that what I was out here for? I agreed that was why I was here (it seemed fairly obvious; this was a hiking trail and I wasn't tuned into other possibilities). As I got up to him, he pointed to my T-shirt and asked if I'd gone to the football game Saturday night. I said no, but I'd listened to it on the radio. We exchanged a few pleasantries about the game—our university had won in the last second by one point when the opponents failed to convert a touchdown extra point. He seemed to want to chat, but I was hiking, so I moved on.

About ten minutes later, I encountered him again where trails intersected. I'd taken the long route; he'd taken the short. He had stripped off his T and was sitting on a fallen tree. Big smile, pretty good musculature. He asked again whether I was only there to hike. I was starting to get the message and answered that, yes, that was all I'd come to do and what else would there to be to do on a hiking trail in the woods? Well, there's sex, he answered, and gave me "that look" up and down. Then he said he'd be moving off "there" in the woods, and if I was interested, I could follow him.

Now, I don't get all that much now and have been thinking a lot about sex recently. So, I thought, what the hell. And I followed him into the woods. He went straight for a secluded spot, well away from the trails and near the shore of the town's reservoir. He obviously had picked the spot out already. There was a big fallen tree there where you had to perch up just a little to sit. He laid his shirt on top of this and then turned to me as I approached, and I just went into his arms. He stripped my shirt off and laid it on the fallen tree with his and then we did some kissing and chest rubbing and hand exploring. He pushed my shorts and briefs down and off and I did the same for him, and then we did some more kissing and rubbing together of tits and navels and cocks. We both murmured that we liked what we found. Kept our voices down, because, although we probably wouldn't be seen, we likely could have been heard at some distance, especially with the lake so near by.

This was going on for a while, and I was wondering who was supposed to fuck who here. It had been so long since there hadn't been clear signals on that before we got to this stage from someone I was with. Funny what people think and worry about in these situations. But he then knelt and started sucking me off, which made me decide he was expecting to do me, saving his hardening for right before the fuck. He was good at cocksucking and wouldn't stop until I had creamed his tonsils. Then he stood and pushed me down on my knees and I worked him until he was hard. He had a nice piece; not as long and thick as mine, I don't think, but nice enough anyway.

When it was obvious that we were getting to the fuck part—he had lifted me and turned me toward the fallen tree, I let him know he'd have to use a condom and that I didn't have one. I just went out that day for an exercise hike. He'd come prepared with condoms and KY, though, so that part was taken care of. I went belly down on the tree on top of our Ts, with my legs out wide and my hands holding my butt cheeks open, and he put his face into my crack. He was good at this too. Then the KY and a some fingerfucking and then the real thing. Just slid on in without any trouble. Nothing exotic—other than being outdoors and a surprise—but nice all the same. held me with hands on my shoulders and pushed hard with his hips in the thrusts. Half way through the fuck, I did get him to turn me, saying I wanted to watch what he was doing, and he got my butt up on the tree, and his cock buried again. His arms went under my thighs, holding them out, and then around to my back and he held his hands together in a locked fist at the small of my back. After getting jolted there back and forth by his short thrusts and my counterthrusts with our eyes locked closely together for a while, I was able to arch back and grab a few saplings at each side to hold myself and he took longer and faster strokes.

After he'd jacked off inside me, he pulled my chest up to his, one arm around me, and stroked me off again between our bellies with the other hand. Nice enough not just to fuck and leave me. Did lip work for a couple of minutes after I'd shot off. Said it was very nice and asked if we could exchange e-mails and meet again—but I told him I didn't do this regularly and already had a steady. But that maybe we'd run across each other in the woods again some day. It would be another couple of weeks before that park came up again in my hike rotation; I did tell him when it would be likely I'd be hiking there again.

It's been a couple of weeks now. And that park is coming up in my rotation and I can make it there on the day I told him I might be there. I am wondering . . .

Rimming

Loosening Therapy

I was standing in the small room, in front of a curtained window. Paul's hot breath on the back of my neck was doing little to dispel the tension that was tying me in knots, even though that's exactly what we were here for. The room was pretty dreary really; just this curtained window and a padded massage table behind us against the wall. Tired paint on the walls, scuffed tiled floor and ceiling, as if men before us had been walking the ceiling and dragged across the floor, which, for all I knew, was exactly what had caused the scuffing. A set of loudspeakers above and at the corner of the curtained window. Paul's arms came around me, and he started to unbutton my shirt and pull the tail out of my jeans even before he pulled on the curtain cord.

I didn't want to lose Paul, and this might be my last chance to keep him. We'd met at a book event. He was the author, and I was the fascinated reader. We'd talked while he autographed my copy—and I'm afraid I'd gushed about his book. He had taken that in stride and had invited me for coffee after the signing. I was a young, impressionable college student, and he was a good twenty years older than I was—but very distinguished and handsome. Gray at his temples and dancing green eyes that held mine. Thick, sensuous lips, a cleft chin that made him look very urbane, and a well-toned bod. We weren't finished discussing the exotic substory line in his book when the café was closing, so he invited me to his place for a nightcap. His apartment matched my suppositions in sophistication; we kissed on his deeply upholstered couch, and he had my fly open and had sucked me off, with me shooting off quickly, before I managed to escape in embarrassment and confusion.

Two days later, he saw me loitering on the sidewalk in front of his apartment building, and, without words, he came down, took me by the hand, and led me back inside his door. We 69ed on his bed for hours, with him trying to take it farther, and me breaking it off in fear. I'd given and gotten both hand and blow jobs over the past year, but it had never gone beyond that.

Paul wanted to fuck me. He had no interest in me topping him. I wasn't adverse in theory, but I'd tighten right up whenever we got to the brink. He was big and thick and long—and I was terrified of the pain. After our fourth meeting, he was positioned and entered me, but as soon he had, the pain was just too much for me. I tightened right up and screamed for him to stop. His frustration was palpable, and I declared I wanted it but just couldn't do it—that perhaps we needed just to give up on the effort and on any idea of a relationship in the fullest sense. I could tell that he was conflicted, though. He said he was smitten with me, but I knew he couldn't be satisfied with just hand and blow jobs. I cried, and he gently massaged my body and then tried again, but I just couldn't take him; it was just too painful. He then said he had an idea that might help, and so here we were, two days later, in a back room of a men's club, standing in front of a curtained window.

Paul had my shirt open and he was stroking one of my nipples with his hand. He reached over with the other hand and pulled the curtains open, and I let out a shocked gasp.

We were looking through a wide, full-length two-way mirror into another small room, almost identical to the one we were in. Hung by his wrists from straps only about two and half feet away and facing us on the other side of the window was a young man of only nineteen or twenty, with a thin, twinkish, boyish build. He had a mop of curly red hair that almost came down into his eyes as his head hung down, and, as he was stark naked, I could see a patch of red pubic hair surrounding a smallish, pert cock hanging down between his legs. Despite his thinness, he had good muscle tone and was a handsome lad. He looked like a lad, but I vaguely remembered him from one of my college classes, so I'd say he couldn't be much younger than I was. The pads of his feet barely touched the tiled floor.

I started to say something to Paul, but he told me to hush and just to closely observe what was happening in the other room. One of his hands was still massaging my chest, and the other had moved to undoing my belt buckle.

I heard a hollow sound and looked toward its origin, which was the speakers at the top edge of the window on our side. These were conveying the sound from the other side of the glass. A door had opened in the other room—behind where the young man was hanging—and I let out another gasp when I saw the man who had entered the room. He was massive, but not in any way fat. He was heavily muscled, and sharply defined in every respect. He seemed about the same age as Paul, but he obviously was a fanatical bodybuilder. He was dark to the point of swarthy, with salt and pepper-colored hair that covered his body in short ringlets that kept him from being defined as more than borderline bear. He had a short-cropped beard and mustache and a buzz cut hairstyle. Gold rings gleamed at his left ear and in both of his nipples, and there were barbed-wire tattoos encircling both of his arms across the biceps. The only thing he was wearing was a black leather, studded harness across his chest and leather over-the-ankle boots. What had made me gasp, however, was the horse-hung cock and tennis-ball-sized balls swaying back and forth between his legs as he approached the bound young redhead from the rear.

I felt my pants and briefs hit the floor. Paul had freed them as the dark monster had entered the other room.

The monster stopped and stood very close behind the young redhead. He nuzzled the young man's neck with thick lips in a lingering caress, as his big, thick-fingered hands ran up the sides of the youth from the hips to his elbows. The redhead lifted his head, showing me a frightened expression, and murmured in low tones I could barely hear, but I thought they sounded something like, "No, no, please don't," repeated over and over.

I flinched as I realized that Paul was naked now, his cock running up my back. He pulled my shirt off and nuzzled his lips into my neck and mirrored the hand movements of the monster on the other side of the window.

"Paul?" I asked, a shiver of fear in my voice.

"Hush, hush," we whispered to me. "Just concentrate on the young man on the other side of the window. Watch him carefully, and keep constantly in your mind that he is slighter than you are and that the man behind him is much longer and thicker than I am."

I watched in mixed horror and fascination as the older man on the other side of the window ran his hands all over the body of the redheaded youth, paying particular attention to his nipples and his cock and balls. Paul was doing the same with me, and I found myself moaning in just a slightly lower tone than the youth facing me was. His pert little cock was standing straight out from his red bush, as my longer and thicker one was doing out of my blond bush. Paul turned my face to his, and we lingered in a long, juicy kiss. I was willing myself to loosen up for Paul—but this concerted effort, of course, only kept me tight and fidgety.

When I was able to look back around, the bigger man appeared to have disappeared, but as I focused more closely on what was going on, I could see that the redhead's chest was arched forward and his hips pulled back, and he was standing on his very tiptoes. His tormentor was crouched behind him, his face firmly wedged between the youth's butt cheeks, and his hands wrapped around to the front of the youth's thighs. The redhead was grunting and giving out little yip yip sounds and writhing his hips back and forth as much as his precarious position would allow.

Paul's lips and tongue were at my asshole as well now. He was forcing my butt cheeks open with the palms of his hands, and I almost lost my balance as my chest arched forward. My hands involuntarily pushed out in front of me to keep myself from falling, and my arms were now widely spread, palms against the window. I pressed my forehead against the glass, my eyes glued on the eyes of the redhead, and groaned and grunted at having my ass wetted and eaten out by the man I idolized.

The redhead couldn't see me—or so I assumed—but by watching his eyes, I could see his fear and resistance melting and his eyes hooding with desire. And I was going with him on this, moaning and groaning and sighing at Paul's tongue work inside my hole, on my tender inner thighs, and up through my legs on the underside of my cock.

While our asses were being worked, the redhead's cock and balls were getting attention from big, swarthy hands, and so were mine from Paul's long, elegant fingers. I began to move my pelvis in rhythm with Paul's ministrations—and the redhead was moving his as well.

The monster and Paul rose up on their feet behind their objects of desire almost simultaneously, and both produced gobs of lubricant and started to lather up holes and cocks.

The redhead was back to begging for mercy in a low, hoarse voice, and I felt myself getting more tense as well.

One palm on bellies and the other hand loosening and widening up holes with lubricated fingers, both dominators were working their targets.

Paul hissed at me to keep my eyes and senses locked onto the redhead, and I concentrated there as best I could.

I watched in horror and fascination, as the giant in the other room lifted the legs of the redhead and pressed the soles of the younger man's feet wide apart on the window separating us. His feet were precisely on the other side of window from where my hands were pressed. I was closely staring into his face. Paul was pushing my legs wide, but I was lost in the gaze of the redhead, the intense concentration he was showing. The palpable fear mixed with anticipation. The giant crouched his thighs under the raised thighs of the younger man. When the redhead screamed at the pain of first entry, I screamed too, feeling the cap of Paul's cock rotating around, corkscrewing just inside the rim of my hole. We'd been here before, but I hadn't been able to go any farther.

The redhead was sweating, his muscles knotted tightly, his head thrown back. He was crying and babbling incoherently at the ceiling. having lost eye contact, I looked down between the redhead's legs and I could see the bulky sausage of that horse-hung cock slowly working its way into the young man's hole. An inch in, a half inch withdrawal, and then another inch in. I felt Paul tugging back on my hips, widening my legs farther and opening my butt cheeks more as he pushed inside me. We had never been this far before. It hurt like hell, but, for the first time in our attempts, his mushroom cap had reached my prostate and he was rotating his cock around inside me with one hand—his other hand still holding me to him with palm on belly—stroking my prostate with it and sending little electric currents of pleasure and engorgement through me that were fighting with the pain.

I heard a scream of "Yes, yes," through the loudspeaker, and looked back up through the mirror, catching sight of the redhead's eyes again. His countenance had completely changed. His eyes were wild and shining with desire now. The monster's cock was completely sheathed inside him and was pumping inside him with little strokes.

The redhead was thrashing his head back and forth, yelling, "Gawd, yes. Gawd, yes. Fuck me. Deep, deep, split me in two." He obviously was enjoying the fuck now, having a huge cock buried inside him. The pleasure and lust in his eyes were revelations to me. This is where Paul had been trying to go. All I needed to do was get past that first pain, and I could have this. I could be crying for it just like the young redhead was. There was no doubt now what he wanted the big monster to do to him.

I laid my head back on Paul's shoulder and whispered to him. "If it could only be like that, Paul. If I could only loosen up enough—get through the pain enough—to get to where that guy is, the pain would be worth it."

"Guess what, Sport," Paul whispered back. "I'm in to the root now, and I'm pumping you deep too. You did open to me. You relaxed to me."

I cried out in surprise as I realized that Paul was right. I could feel him churning and throbbing deep inside me now. We had done it. I felt the remaining tension draining out of me. My butt cheeks and ass canal were relaxing. I was opening more. Paul felt it to, and I heard the intake of his breath as his cock lengthened and thickened in response and he reached new depths inside me. We were a unit now, moving as one. I had a masterful lover.

I looked at my hands. The fingers were scrunching against the window in rhythm with the stroking of Paul's cock inside me. The redhead's toes were scrunching just on the other side of the window in the same rhythm. He was using his own hip and butt muscles now, rising away from the giant's pelvis as the giant's cock slid out of him and then pistoning back down as the older man plowed back up into him. It was fascinating to watch; nine or ten inches of juicy veined monster cock sliding out of that impossibly tight hole and then alternately gliding and plunging back into the root. They were both pounding away furiously now, and I heard the scream of release from both of them as the monster flooded the redhead's insides with his spunk.

I was imagining Paul's cock doing the same thing in my hole, and I trembled and moaned at the feeling of finally being totally fucked. Paul was going wild at my back door, yelling at how sweet my ass was and how he'd never had such a glorious fuck.

After coming, the giant was holding there, jerking the redhead to ejaculation with his big mitts, as Paul pulled me away from the window, backed up to the massage table at the rear of our room, and turned me on his cock until my back was on the surface of the table and he was between my legs. He held my legs up and out then and pumped me in long, slow strokes, until he brought his mouth down to my nipples and tongued them and nipped them. I sighed and moaned deeply for him, begging him never to stop, to ride me and ride me. I never thought I could want it this bad, to open this wide and unconditionally to a man standing between my legs, churning his cock inside me.

I felt him tighten up, ready to shoot, but he buried his cock deep inside me then, and held himself very still, while he draped my legs on his shoulders and both of his hands went to my cock and balls. With him still rigid against me, I writhed all over the table in never-before-imagined pleasure while he beat my cock and squeezed and pulled my balls until I shot up his belly in three fountains. Then, with a grin, he wishboned my legs again with his hands and fucked me in short, rapid, deep strokes until he unloaded inside me.

He then came up on the table, laying beside me and cuddling me in his arms, as he roamed my body with his hand. I looked through the window into the other room, but the other men were gone now.

"Don't worry about them," he cooed to me in a whisper. "They were there just to help you get beyond your fear; to show you what was beyond the brief pain—why getting beyond the pain was worth the slight inconvenience."

"But he was so big and the redhead was so small," I murmured, still concerned about the physics of it all.

"Oh, don't worry," Paul snorted. "They're a team; they do that a couple of times a night. Very good at it too."

We were silent for several minutes, while we kissed and cooled down.

"What now?" Paul asked. "Shall I drive you back to the dorm?"

"Hell, no," was my spirited reply. "Take me back to your apartment and fuck my brains out again. I want to work some more on this therapy thing."

Servicemen

Elevator Man

I had sniffed the plumber guy out myself and he had seemed interested, but I was a pretty good judge of men and I didn't think that two resolved tops would work out. I was still mulling whether I had misjudged him when my instincts were confirmed.

I'd been warned that this movie guy was crazy before I started out from Eureka to Trinidad, but just the motoring itself along Scenic Drive up the northern California coast was worth a little weird at the other end. To work in Los Angeles and live on the rugged coast above San Francisco didn't sound all that stupid to me if you had the means and opportunity to do it, but when I reached where my directions stopped just south of Trinidad Head and looked up, I was beginning to understand what they said.

A mailbox and parking pad for maybe six cars right on the inland side of Scenic Drive where it hugged the coastline close and a little path leading to steel piers and a winding staircase that led my eyes up and up and up gave me a real shock when my gaze was brought to what looked like a disk-shape alien spacecraft right out of one of those science fiction horror flicks reflecting the sun's rays off curved metallic walls.

Not all that inappropriate for a perpetual child movie star who had wound up as a director of B movies, and, if the tabloids were even half right, a lush, coke head, and pants chaser of insatiable appetites. But still? A space ship hovering in the clouds high above the northern California coast? For starters, it must have cost him a mint, and people were flocking away from the expensive northern California coast, not to it. And, I mean, the view would be great, of course, but, gawd, look at all of those steps you'd have to climb to it. It must have five stories up the sheer side of a cliff to the underside of the thing.

But that's where I came in. One of those steel piers, the thickest one, contained an elevator. And I was the elevator man.

I parked beside a panel van with the name of a Trinidad plumbing company on the side and walked up the path to the thickest pier. I sighed in resignation when I saw that the elevator cage wasn't at ground level. It would be no use trying to summon it down from the house, because if it was in working order, I wouldn't be here. I was here to activate it for the first time, make sure it was running smoothly, and show the new owner how to operate it.

I hoped the new owner was electronically inclined. Otherwise, I sure wouldn't want to be stuck out in the boonies like this and trapped inside an elevator I couldn't get open. I wouldn't say anything to him about this, of course; you don't sell many home elevators that way. But I'd certainly try to make sure he understood how to operate it and what to do if it malfunctioned.

I took a look at that winding staircase, huffed and puffed a couple of times to fill my lungs, and started the five-story climb. I wouldn't have to go to the gym this evening. I took pride in my body; it was part of what sold me at pool hall and movie house. So, I worked out three times a week—pretty hard. I might make the gym tonight, but I probably wouldn't need much leg work after this climb.

Ricky Drake himself, the child star-turned bad movie director, met me at the double front door. The ID was unmistakable, even though the heavy makeup he had slathered on his face gave me a turn. It didn't convince me a bit, however. He couldn't have been more than five foot four and had the perpetual boyish look that kept him fed with teen roles until he was pushing thirty. He was pushing somewhere a lot further down the road now, though, and the wrinkles were showing. A little weird to see the age on what still wanted to be a boy. He'd kept the fat off his body, which was a good thing.

After lifting his eyebrows when he greeted me at the door and giving me that hooded-eyed smile I knew so well and was willing to satisfy for a price, he floated down the hall toward the center of the circular house in a little more of a swish than I preferred. Still, if the price was right . . .

"I've come to test out the elevator and make sure you know how to use it and what to do if it breaks down," I called out to his retreating back.

Other than saying "Yum," at the door he hadn't spoken; he'd just turned and walked back toward the center of the house. He was wearing powder blue cotton sleeping shorts with a matching robe, open and flapping about him as he sauntered away. And barefoot. It was 11:00 AM. I wondered if I had awakened him. I could imagine that these crazy movie folks weren't morning people.

"That's good, Honey," he said in a high, boyish voice, "but there are a couple of e-mails I have to answer right away. I'm showing you to the kitchen, where you can get a beer out of the fridge and cool down that fine bod of yours from the climb up the stairs."

He led me into a light-filled, circular kitchen at the very heart of the disk. It had sort of an atrium feel to it from a full circle of clerestory windows around the ceiling, which extended above the surround structure.

But that's not what arrested my attention really. My eyes latched onto the guy who was kneeling down in front of open cabinet doors at the sink, on the balls of his feet, comfortably balanced on his haunches. Tight jeans, muscle T, showing tufts of dark hair at his pits, which I liked. He looked around as I entered the kitchen and flashed me a welcoming smile. God was he luscious. Hispanic, all dark beauty and fine form. Instant interest from both of us. And almost as instantly I sensed another exclusive top. Oh, well.

I got that beer out of the refrigerator and leaned back against the counter and watched the plumber work his magic on applying the finishing touches on pipes and faucets inside that cabinet. Off and on, he'd turn his face to me and show that smile. He obviously wasn't as aware as I was that we were both pegs—or maybe he was just more hopeful that I was interested in some slot work. No chance of that, though.

It wasn't long before Drake sashayed back into the kitchen and beckoned me back toward the front foyer and the top of the elevator shaft. The cage was there.

"Wanna ride while I go over the controls and show you a few things?" I asked as the door to the cage opened?

"Yes, I'd love for you to give me a ride and . . . show me a few things," Drake answered, and then that inviting smile. "There's something I wouldn't mind being shown right now, as a matter of fact." He'd drawn close to me and was touching my thigh with his fingers. But I brushed past him and entered the cage. He followed and stood against the side wall, a little smirk on his face. Used to getting what he wanted, as soon as he wanted it. The bane of child stars.

I'd been here a thousand times. I don't know why, but guys like Drake just got direct with me fast. Like they couldn't wait or didn't have the patience to go through the foreplay.

"Let's get your elevator working," I answered. "Maybe more later. But anything beyond the company clock . . . well, I've got expenses and lots of things I could be doing with my own time." I had learned that I could be direct too, that there was no use wasting time spinning wheels. I didn't find him all that attractive for a free ride—on the margin of too old and a little freaky, trapped in that boy-man's body and trying to stay on the boy side with that heavy makeup.

"And I've got plenty of money and time," he answered, with that smirk.

For a good half hour, we rode up and down on the elevator and I showed him everything there was to using the controls. He used the excuse of following my instructions closely to come into my body closely. He had his hands everywhere, not just on the buttons and switches as I showed them to him. He copped a good feel of my basket, but I just ignored it while he was doing this. Let him assess the goods, I thought. They were good enough if his money was good enough.

But, God, it wasn't just the makeup. He was wearing perfume, even if it did have some male designer's name on it, It was still perfume. If this is what they did down in Los Angeles, I was just as glad that I was up here in Eureka. Good honest male sweat and the musk of man sex, they were fine with me. But perfume? Geez, give me a break.

"You see this switch here?" I said near the end of our session. "This is important, now. If you'll look behind the panel, you'll see it's attached to a cable going up there and attaching up there. This model of elevator is known for that cable becoming dislodged and stopping the elevator wherever it is right then. Doesn't mean the cage will fall; it just will freeze. So, if you get stuck dead, check out that cable first. Often all you need do is reattach it. And, if I were you, I wouldn't get on the elevator at all without a cell phone handy. You never know what might get fucked up." The company would skin me alive if I went any farther in scaring customers with remote homes about being trapped in an elevator. But I thought I needed to at least make them as cautious as possible.

"OK, I think I've got that," he said.

I brought the cage back up to the space craft level and reached over to push the button to open the doors, but he covered my hand with his. And I noticed he was trembling. I looked over at him. His nipples were popping out and the front of his sleeping shorts was tented. He was ripe.

"About getting fucked up," he murmured. His other hand came up, A fifty was palmed in that hand.

A fifty. Mr. big spender.

"I don't know, guy," I answered vaguely, looking pointedly at the fifty. "I've gotta test out this elevator some more and its getting late. I don' know. Makeup and perfume . . . I just don't know."

I obviously pushed his buttons, because he gave me a venomous look, punched the "open door" button hard and flounced out of the elevator, headed toward the center of the house in flapping powder-blue cotton robe.

I mulled and mellowed as I put the elevator through its purring paces for a good twenty minutes without finding anything remotely troublesome with how it was working. I'd let old guys suck me off at the pool hall for twenty. Fifty would get me a good meal on my way back to Eureka. And the boast of doing a Hollywood director, no matter how weird or queeny he was, would have some boast value down at the movie house.

I made my decision—not having any better offers on the table and obviously not being a matched set with that hunky Hispanic plumber I'd rather be poking—and walked back into the house after finishing the elevator jiggling and test ride. I'd left the clipboard in the kitchen and I'd have to get Drake to sign off on the call sheet on that anyway.

And maybe there'd be another look at the plumber. Just maybe my assessment hadn't been right.

But, when I got to the kitchen, I could see that my assessment had been spot on. Both the plumber and Drake were starkers and Drake was up on his butt on the kitchen counter, his legs spread wide and folded and his heels dug into the edge of the counter, giving him leverage to move his hips back and forth against the plumber's groin. The plumber was standing between Drake's legs. He had the heels of both of his hands plastered to the doors of the overhead shelves. Drake was holding the plumber's waist at both sides with his small, boy's hands.

Drake was giving little yipping sounds, and the plumber was doing real good with his plumbing. He had a nice circular movement to his pelvis that indicated that Drake was getting wall-to-wall servicing inside his channel. The plumber turned his eyes to me, and he flashed me that brilliant, welcoming smile. I got the impression he would have enjoyed me joining in the fun, and I did stay and watch for a while, fascinated with the plumber's technique and wondering if he had length to go along with the width of what I could see at the root of his buried and rapid-stroking cock.

But then I looked down at his feet, where his jeans lay. On top of those, next to a split and empty Trojan packet, was a bill—a fifty—my fifty. Then Drake decided for me.

"Your clipboard is there on the table, if that's what you've come for," which he hardly got out before his cried out, "Oh, God, yes. There, like that . . . just like that. Again. Oh, God!"

450

I leaned over to the table and picked the clipboard up. He'd already signed for the elevator inspection. So, I obviously was finished here.

I took the elevator back down to the car park. Let him wait to summon for it to come back up.

I didn't think much more about what had happened. After two more stops for lift inspections closer to Eureka, I ate at a carryout on the outskirts of the town that night and was cruised by a nervous middle-aged accountant type, who propositioned me tentatively, but who was willing to part with $60 to get fucked doggy style in the back of my van. He had wanted to pay less, but it was a matter of pride for me to get something better than Drake had offered—or that the Hispanic was willing to go for on the rebound.

And then I thought that was that and let it clear out of my mind. But that wasn't that. Three weeks later, I got an emergency dispatch call while I was doing regular inspection of the elevators at a hospital north of Eureka. And I found myself parked on the apron off Scenic Drive and in the shadow of the alien space ship house again.

Drake had called in that he was trapped in the elevator inside the shaft, below the residence level, and he couldn't get out. Nothing in the elevator was working, he'd reported. At least he had been listening when I told him to have a cell phone with him when he used it. Pretty strange, I thought. The elevator had been working a charm just three weeks ago, and this model was quite reliable other than that loose cable quirk. And I'd shown him what to do about that.

I went to the shaft at ground level and used my special tool to get the doors open. Peering inside and training my flashlight up the shaft, I saw that the cage was way up there, near the top. A tromp up that staircase again. I sighed, but there was no alternative, so I mounted the stairs.

Luckily I found the front door unlocked. Drake probably felt there was no reason to lock it. What burglar was fool enough to climb five flights of stairs at the edge of busy Scenic Drive just to toss an alien space ship?

Once inside the foyer, I turned to the elevator shaft and opened the doors there with my tools. The cage was just below the living level. A little hop and I was on the roof of it, and just a turn of a latch and lifting of a hatch and I was looking down at Drake, inside the cage, sitting on his butt on a thin mattress he'd dragged into the elevator, his back against the back wall of the cage.

Drake was looking back up at me with a silly grin on his face. A face without makeup. He was naked, and as soon as he saw me, he lifted both of his hands up, showing me what he was holding. In one hand he held two hundred-dollar bills. In the other, he held three Trojan packets.

He was lubing his gaping hole as I came down into the cage and stripped down, and he sucked me big while I stood over him and leaned into him, my weight balanced on hands against the bronze back wall of the cage in which I could see my reflection and enjoy the pleasure he was giving me in stereo by watching the reflection of my face in the bronze. Then I pulled his small, seemingly weightless body up off the mat with hands on his waist and thrust inside him to the tune of his boyish cries, pushing his back up and down on the bronzed wall with the strength of my cock stroking up into him, while he hooked his thighs over my hips and arched his back in abandoned pleasure.

I fucked him for an hour and then he laid me on my back and fucked himself on my tool for another hour. He'd learned positions I'd never even imagined were physically possible, and he showed me that lack of size and age had no relationship to the quality of stamina. He showed me such a good time that I almost felt I shouldn't take the $200—almost.

When I was near exhaustion, responsibility started to lean on me heavily, and I moved out from underneath him with a grunt and started to raise up on my knees.

"I want you to stay the night," he said in a dreamy voice. "I want to fuck in my bed—in the shower, on the floor. Another $200?"

"Well, first we'll need to get this elevator going," I said to the little bunny, as I struggled toward an upright position, every muscle of my body overworked and sore.

"Oh, no problem," Drake said in that perky little voice of his, and he bounced up onto his feet. He moved to the control panel and opened it.

"You see this loose cable here?" he asked. "A real hunk of a an elevator man told me that all you have to do is stick it back in place and the elevator's fixed."

Scratching the Service Worker Itch

"Bummer," I exclaimed with a pout, as I threw the telephone book half way across the room and collapsed onto the sofa.

"What's up?" Nick asked, looking up from his computer where he was checking out the latest Literotica stories.

"I've got the service worker itch, and they don't list who the hunky, well-hung plumbers and electricians are in the phone book ads."

"Fancy that," Nick said as he turned back to his computer. But then he swiveled back around and gave me a level stare. "And what the fuck is the service worker itch?"

"I've got this itch deep inside me that can only be reached and satisfied by a hardworking muscled hunk with honest-work, callused hands, a big, thick dick, and rough technique."

"Well, between the two of us, I've got the biggest and thickest dick. Let's go back to the bedroom and I'll see what I can do for that itch," Nick said, with a smile.

"I said rough sex and burly handyman hunks, Nick. You don't even come close."

"Thanks loads, Mr. White-collar Picky," Nick retorted.

"You know what I mean, Nick. You're too refined and sensitive to scratch this itch. Sometimes I need someone who will skip the preliminaries and just pork me hard, deep, and quick—wham, bang, thank you, ma'am. It's a fantasy I have occasionally. Just go with me on this."

"Well, OK, if that's what you want," Nick said with a sigh, as he logged off the computer and unfolded himself from his chair. "You're in luck. I happen to have met a couple of construction workers last evening at Club 216 who were quite explicit about what they could do with me if I came over to their construction site. I think they were hunky enough for you. Let's take a ride."

Three guys were standing around a pickup truck at the construction site and taking a smoke break when Nick and I drove up. I could tell at a glance that they'd fit my bill: all big, square-chinned sonovabitches, with big hands, muscles on their muscles, and big broad grins on their faces when they recognized Nick. Nick told them what I wanted, and their grins got even bigger as they circled around me, eyeing me lasciviously and whistling at and talking dirty to me. Just what I'd ordered. My cock began to throb; my ass began to twitch.

They led us into what would be the basement of a half-finished McMansion at the back corner of the construction area, and, at my request, two of them stripped down to just their hard hats, their tool belts, and their boots, as the third one slowly stripped me down, feeling me up as clothing items were shed, and sucking me off. When they'd striped down, the other two construction workers and Nick watched me get a blow job. I was just standing there leaning against what was going to be a load-bearing pole. The one working on me was actually the youngest and best looking by far. He was stripped down to just cutoff jeans, and I didn't at all mind him giving me a slow and easy blow job; I knew there was rough action coming later. The other two construction workers were licking their lips and fondling and pulling on their horse-hung meat as they watched the younger one going down on me.

I enjoyed watching them watching me. They looked real hot in just those construction belts, hard hats, and chunky boots.

When I had shot my load, one of the other construction workers came over and took me roughly by the hand and led me over to a makeshift apparatus that the other one was pulling together. He had taken two low sawhorses and slapped a pine board between them. The first construction worker pushed me over on my belly on top of the board, and the second construction worker spread my legs and lashed them at the ankles to the legs of the sawhorses with rope, while the other one was tying my wrists together in front of me with my own leather belt. Construction worker number one then got between my legs in back and started shoving his big, engorged dick at my asshole, finally managing to push in and, with loud grunts from him and groans from me, plowing me to his root. The tools on his belt made clanging noises and chaffed my inner thighs as they swung back in forth in rhythm to his stroking. I could feel him reach my itch, deep inside, and rub it real hard. He was rough with me, just like I wanted, slapping my butt cheeks, pinching my nipples, and thrusting me hard up the ass.

The other construction worker came around in front of me, grabbed my hair with his hand, shoved his dick in my mouth, and fucked my face. Meanwhile, the worker who had blown me came back under the sawhorse and began licking my balls and cock again. After a good twenty minutes of this, construction worker one unloaded inside me, and the two workers who were stuffing me changed positions. The second dick was even thicker and longer than the first, and it found whole new itches to scratch.

When the one behind me had shot his wad, he withdrew from me, released the ropes at my ankles, and pushed me over to a picnic table that was being used as a work bench. Reinvigorated construction worker number one now came at me from the front, pushing me down on the table on my back, wish-boned my legs, and fucked me hard and furiously from the front, while construction worker number two found a hook to hang my wrist bonds on over my head that stretched my torso tight across the picnic table. My itches were being satisfied nicely. The worker who boned me in the number two spot got up on his knees on the bench seat at my head, held my shoulders down on the table, and took another turn face fucking me. Just before my mouth got turned and stuffed, I looked over and saw that Nick was allowing the younger, better-looking construction worker to plow his ass at the sawhorse position.

Lots of itches got scratched well that afternoon, and everyone left the McMansion basement happy. I never again had to explain to Nick what my periodic service worker itch was all about.

Shaving

Bearded No More

We're in a barber shop at night. I'm lying in a barber's chair, chair back reclined. You are straddling my loins, facing me. We are both buck naked, and you have just languidly fucked yourself on my tool and have now settled down into my lap, feeling my rod go tumescent inside you.

You run your hand over your cheek, telling me that it burns and that my beard has scratched you while we were passionately kissing. I tell you that we can't have that—that I must passionately kiss you again—so you have my permission to shave the beard. But I say I'm afraid you won't recognize me if you do, that I no longer will be the man who lights your inner fires. You rotate your hips on my cock and tell me that it's not my face that sets the blaze within you—and that only that same fireplug you are sheathing now can also quench that fire, as it has just done.

You lean over and take a razor and a can of shaving cream from the barber's table. The shaving cream is a special blend—minty to the taste, tingly to the feel, a soothing lubricant no matter where applied. You spray it liberally into a hand and run that hand lovingly around my jaw and cheeks and, with delicate touch, under my nose, spreading the cream in great mounds. You bring your mouth to mine and kiss it then, bearded for the last time, the hair softened now, not scratching you now, permitting you to linger with your tongue swabbing the insides of my cheeks and my teeth. You lift your head and smile down at me, white cream on your cheek and dribbling down your jaw line, reminding me of just a short time earlier when you were making love to my cock with your luscious, soft mouth and brought me to orgasm and then raised your head and smiled at me, that innocent smile celebrating your victory and my release—my cream dabbling your cheeks and jaw.

You take the razor and gently shave off the cream-soaked beard and mustache, stopping briefly from time to time to kiss and lap up the cream residue from where the razor has separated hair from skin. When you are done, you smile down at me radiantly, telling me that I am far more handsome and desirable without the beard than with, assuring me that I arouse you even more now than before, wondering out loud if I can bring you to even greater heights of arousal by being further liberated of the soft, downy auburn hair elsewhere on my body. I can tell you are increasingly aroused; I have a hand wrapped around your cock, and your cock tells me that the unmasking of me has given it great pleasure.

The can spits a mound of cream, which is spread across my chest, and you shave the thin line of hair running down my sternum and under my nipples, two spritzes on the nipples, and you suck off the cream, lingering with your teeth and lips there. I raise, first my left arm, and then my right. You bury your face in my pits, one after the other, to enjoy the last lingering man scent and to tongue my curly hair there to moist softness, followed by cream and shave, and ending with drinking in the new, clean, fresh mintiness, with just a hint of male, with your nose buried in the smooth, shaven hollows.

My forearms are spritzed and shaved and kissed from wrist to elbow, and then you are off my lap, standing hunched over my body as it reclines in the barber's chair, and the cream, the shaver and your lips are following the erstwhile trail of auburn hair down my six pack, around my navel, and to the edge of my curly auburn bush.

You desist from that approach for now to spread my legs and cream, shave, and kiss my thighs and calves. Gobs of cream are applied to my toes, and you lick and suck each one, individually, clean. Slowly and sensuously. My belly is heaving at this, and I am stroking my cock. I tell you I want you now. No, I cry out my need for you. I want you to take me now, to fuck me.

But you are not finished revealing me, unmasking me everywhere. You brush the hand aside that I have been stroking myself with. You find some twine in the barber's drawer and bind my wrists together and hook the coil on a hook on the back of the barber's chair, just over the top rim. My arms pulled up and back, the muscles of my now-smooth arms and chest are fully flexed for you, on exhibit for your approval. And your eyes slit and burn with desire, showing that you do approve of your handiwork.

The hand I had wrapped around my cock is now replaced with your left hand, as you release mountains of cream across my loins with your right hand and slowly shave my pubic region to total nakedness, total openness to you. You kiss and lick the clean canvas you have created, well pleased with what you have done. My standing cock is buried in a mound of cream, and your mouth takes this luscious éclair in one long enveloping. You play with the hard center of this pastry with your tongue and teeth and soft inner cheek walls and stroke up and down, up and down, up and down on me until my cream mixes with the minty shaving cream, while I am writhing and moaning and sighing at your attention.

You hold there, savoring your midnight snack, while my muscles relax and my breathing turns from ragged to a soft purr.

When all is calm once more, you rise, unhook the coiled twine imprisoning my wrists, and tell me to turn as you raise the back of the barber's chair. You then tell me to straddle the back of the chair, my chest to the chair back, my knees on the chair arms, and, as I comply, you have me embrace the back of the barber's chair and you rehook my wrists to a latching in the midback of the chair.

You stand where I can see you spray cream from the can liberally on your erect, throbbing cock, and then you are behind me, first kissing and tonguing my hole, and then pushing the tab of the can into my hole and filling me with the last of the minty shaving cream. I feel you come up into the chair seat behind me on your knees, and then I am granted what I have been begging for for the last several minutes, as your cream-covered dick slides into my cream-filled hole, and strokes me and strokes me and strokes me, until the shaving cream has evaporated from the vigorous friction, to be replaced with a warmer, far-more manly flood of cream—your cum, filling me, flooding me, and making love to my inner crevices.

Size Difference

At Sea with Maurice

"So, you fancy him, do you?"

"No, I fancy you, Maurice," I answered, trying to make a joke out of it. But I was beginning to get a little irritated with Maurice. We both knew why he'd offered me this trip home, and I was getting tired of him just not getting to it.

"But you do fancy him, don't you?" Maurice persisted. "I mean you have nothing against mixed Orientals, have you? What would you say? A fourth White Russian, half northern Chinese, a fourth Thai, I would say. And I've been around in the region taking on deck hands long enough to be a pretty good judge of that."

"Yes, I suppose that could be right. Hell, I don't know anything about that. I'd only been in Singapore two weeks when you and I met."

"I was very selective, Paul. I always am," Maurice continued. If he could tell I was on the edge of irritation, he wasn't admitting it. We were in the dining room of his container ship bound from Singapore to Miami by way of India, South Africa, and up the coast of South America. "Nine days and eight nights to Mumbai, India," Maurice was saying. "Eight deckhands taken on in Singapore and exchanged in Mumbai for the run to Cape Town with a new set. In each port, a new set. Just like always. Carefully picked."

I wasn't half listening to what Maurice was saying. He owned this container ship—and apparently several others—all plying the equator route, picking up here and letting off there, enabling the exchange of goods by countries across the tropics. I guess that made him quite wealthy. He was egalitarian, though. The passenger accommodations on the ship had proven to be surprisingly comfortable and plush. He must have had at least ten well-appointed cabins for passengers beyond the ship's crew, but only he and I occupied any of these cabins on this run. And all—owner, passenger, and crew alike—took their regular meals in the common dining room.

I looked over at the sailor Maurice was prompting me to show interest in. It didn't take much effort to show interest in him. He was a well over six feet and muscle hardened, as a veteran commercial sailor had to be. Maybe thirty-five, maybe older. As Maurice noted, he seemed to have enough of the Oriental in him to be somewhat inscrutable, but to my eyes, he was mainly Slavic. Maurice had mentioned he came from Harbin and claimed to be a descent of tsarist refugees. Certainly enough White Russian in him to have a sturdy, if extremely well-toned, physique and a well-chiseled face. And his hearty laugh and the way the others at his table responded and accepted him—obviously a well-liked man of good humor.

David hadn't been like that. As he'd gotten older—and especially as he came to choose to think that I never aged along with him—and his maladies had set in, he'd gotten more ill-humored and snappish. "When will you grow into looking like a man," he'd mutter at me whenever we had a fight. But what was I supposed to do about that? There were certain attributes that made for a horse jockey type. The grand tour of Asia was supposed to make him happier. Well, that didn't happen.

"So, you fancy him, don't you? Our quarter White Russian."

"Yes, yes, I fancy him," I answered in barely controlled exasperation.

* * * *

"So, you fancy him, do you?"

"Excuse me?" I responded. Surprised to hear myself addressed. It was midday in the Raffles Hotel Long Bar, and I hadn't realized that anyone was sitting at my elbow. I was slinging gin and tonics down in some sort of wake, although I had no idea how an official wake should go. I didn't even like gin and tonics. But this is what David drank, so this is what I was drinking. It was, after all, David's wake.

"The bartender. You two have been chatting it up and you both look quite good. I thought you were working up to getting it on."

"No, no, of course not," I said. I might have been a little short with him, but the barkeep and I had been saying enough for him to know what our preferences were.

I turned and focused on the man sitting beside me at the bar who had asked me this strange question. He was maybe pushing fifty, but he didn't drive a desk, I could tell. He had that hands-on worker aspect about him. Salt and pepper hair, and a lot of it. Thick curlings at the V of his open sports shirt and matting on the backs of his thick-fingered hands where they extended from his sports coat. But he also exuded money and power. Germanic would be what I'd guess if I had to make a guess. I wasn't surprised he was chatting me up. I seem to have something that attracts these older men. David had been about his age when he had transitioned from me riding his horses to him riding me and eventually asking me to move my toothbrush into the main house.

"No," I started again. "I just needed someone to talk to, I guess—to share a last salute with. And I thought the bartender was the only one here. I didn't see you at the bar."

"I wasn't at the bar. I was over there in the corner. Waiting for you to come in."

I didn't have time to process this, because he continued. "Someone to share a last salute with. I don't—"

"My companion . . . Oh, hell, my lover, the man who fed and clothed me . . . died the other day here in the Raffles Hotel. In bed . . . with me. I've just now gotten the paperwork finished and seen his body off for the States. But there wasn't room for me in the box to Boston. So, I'm here, high and dry. I don't know if I'm here to mourn him or to feel sorry for myself."

What was I saying? I blushed in embarrassment. "I'm sorry. I shouldn't have said all of that. I guess I'm still in shock. I hope I didn't say that to the bartender. I just don't remember. Too many gin and tonics, I guess. I'm such a bore."

"No, no, you aren't a bore at all. You're endearing. And, yes, you did mention to the bartender that you had been a race jockey some years past. That caught me by surprise. You don't look hardly old enough to have had a past—or to be in this bar, for that matter. And you've said enough to the bartender that I thought you might fancy each other."

I could tell a pass when I heard one. I started wondering whether I might string my Singapore stay out for another meal and a night. That was pretty hard as nails of me, I knew. But after tonight my suitcase would be in the hall, and Singapore's welcome mat would be jerked out from underneath me, and I had no more prospect of leaving Singapore than I had of staying here. It was unfair, really, I thought. I'd given up a promising Jockeying career to go with David; you didn't just dip in and out of that, you had to have a progression of recent successful rides to get anywhere. And I'd been nursemaid and lover to him for nearly ten years—all to the horror of his family. There would be no succor in that direction. I'd not get a dime from any of them to get home on, even though I'd been more family to him for nearly a decade than any of them had been.

The man beside me backed right off of what he was getting into saying, though. His whole expression changed. He became jocular, as if he was afraid he'd been too forward. But in my straits, I'm not sure what too forward would look like. I'd given out for my keep for some time now; I hadn't honed any other skills.

"Say, I'm starving," he said—as if he'd been thinking for some time how to move this proposition along and this was the best he could come up with. "You wouldn't like to join me for a bit to eat in the Palm Court, would you? I hate to eat alone."

"Umm, the Palm Court isn't exactly in my budget . . ." I mumbled.

"Oh bother that," he said. "My treat, of course. My name's Maurice, by the way. And yours is . . ."

"Paul . . . just Paul."

"Well, Just Paul, tell me, *do* you fancy the bartender?"

I must have given him a very peculiar look, because he immediately steamed back into the conversation.

"Ummm, well. Pity that. But come, the Palm Court awaits us."

Over dinner Maurice established that he owned container ships plying around the world in the tropic zones and that he had one he was taking to Miami via the India, Africa, and South America route that was about to set sail.

"I get the impression your David's sudden death has left you here high and dry," he said over coffee. "Would it help to get you to Miami?"

Would it ever. I'd do just about anything for him to get passage to Miami.

"It wouldn't be the fastest route, of course. It would take more than a month actually . . . but if you're interested, I could take you on board tomorrow. No, no problem, no cost to you. It would just be good to have someone to talk with during the journey. I'm not taking on any other passengers this time; you'd be no added cost to me; more than enough provisions are already on board, and what's not consumed will just have to be thrown out."

Manna dropped from heaven. I didn't even try to pretend that I wouldn't jump at the offer.

"Would you like me to come up to your room with you tonight?" I asked as we were rising from the dinner table. I didn't want there to be any misunderstanding how grateful I was and what he had a right to ask of me in return.

"No, no. Not tonight. That's not necessary. Have your bags down by 9:30 tomorrow and we'll leave straight for the docks."

* * * *

We hadn't set down to our evening meal in the container ship's dining room until we had cleared the Singapore Straits and were steaming into the Indian sea. All alone now on the sea; no land and no other ships in sight in any direction. The sun was still bright outside; it wouldn't set for another couple of hours. The ship's mate came into the dining room as deserts were being handed out to report that we also seemed to be steaming into a squall. All hands were called on deck to methodically walk through the stacks of metal containers as big as box cars and ensure that all of the cabling holding them in place was as tight as could be. One container dislodged could roll the whole ship over in a high sea. It was going to be hard work and the sun was still hot, so all of the hands pushed their desert plates aside, stripped down to their waists, and headed for the hatchway.

I sucked in my breath at the look of the White Russian's physique when he was stripped down. Heavily muscled, bulking, a regular Zeus. In fact, all of the deckhands were large-boned, particularly well muscled; and strong looking; it obviously was a career necessity.

Maurice left with them, but he returned in a few minutes, and we finished our deserts and coffee in an otherwise deserted dining room. He was being extremely polite and solicitous—almost fatherly—toward me. Not for the first time did I feel embarrassment at my slight size and young looks. I wondered how I was going to get past him treating me like I might break in two if he touched me. David had never shown me this regard.

Over the day on board, Maurice had grown on me. I was used to going with older men, and, although "of an age," he seemed in better shape than most. And his curly salt and pepper hair intrigued me. I wondered if he was as hairy under that shirt as the back of his hands and the V at his neck implied. And whether he had such a luxuriant bush at his pubes—and how low he was hung. The hair leading me down that path. I was resisting the urge to run my hands under the hem of his shirt and up to his nipples and trying to start the inevitable process of the taking—right here on the dining table. I leaned in a bit toward him and moved my hand to the edge of the table near him.

But then Maurice abruptly rose again from the table and took a step back. "We should turn in early," he said. "If we run into the squall, it will be a rough sailing night."

"Shall I come to your room tonight?" I asked. Maurice had still not openly expressed the price of my passage, and I wanted to make clear that I knew what I owed. I also knew from how he looked at me that he wanted me, even though he was withdrawing from every signal I was sending him.

"No, no. It's not necessary," he answered.

I found this very frustrating. David—at least after my jockey career was shot when I stopped competing and putting horses through their paces so that I could respond to his every whim—had never let me forget that sex was my price for any favor or spending money. I hadn't needed to beg for the responsibility or right to pay my own way with the only coin available to me with David. I couldn't figure Maurice out.

My confusion and funk continued after I had gone back to my cabin, stripped down to my sleeping shorts, and tried, unsuccessfully, to read from one of the paperbacks I'd brought. The ship wasn't churning in the disquieted seas too violently yet, but it was pitching and yawing enough so that my eyes couldn't remain focused on the small print of the paperback. I had left the night lights on as Maurice had cautioned me to do with the comment that you never could tell where the furniture would wind up at night at sea and it would be best to be able to get your bearings if you had to get up in the night. But the lights cast an eerie red glow around the cabin and fought hard with every attempt I made to sleep.

I rose and padded barefooted out to the covered deck at the back of the passenger cabins, overlooking the wide span of the open hold in which the containers were stacked. Those of the deck crew who so recently had been heartily eating and laughing in the communal dining room were still hard at work, checking cables and tightening up anything loose on deck. It had grown dark now, as much from the black clouds scudding in from overhead as from the end of day. The White Russian, still naked to the waist, torso gleaming from sweat and salt water spray in the lights beaming down from the bridge, was there, not more than ten yards from where I was standing at the railing of the covered passenger deck. What came next came to me as if in a dream.

* * * *

He has come to me in the darkness of night in a stormy sea, riding me on the crest of the waves. I have had to raise the side the rails to stay in the berth as the ship struggles through the squall, rolling and churning through the stormy sea. He comes down heavily on my back as I'm stretched out in the berth on my belly. He is heavy with undulating, insistent muscle, invading, consuming.

Unable to sleep in the tossing sea, I had come to the rail and watched the deckhands moving like dancers, tightening the ropes, securing the cargo. I watched him, the burly White Russian, for hours as the ship raced toward the twilight horizon, just ahead of the storm, losing the race by the minute, inevitably being enfolded from behind in consuming embrace.

Stripped to the waist, he worked hard with ropes at the bow of the ship, letting his muscles and hands work as they knew so masterfully to do. Beauty in motion. Sensual. Arousing. No longer watching what he was doing, because he was watching me.

"What was that you said?" I called out over tumult.

"Your cabin number?" he called back. "I can come soon. I want to fuck you."

"Fuck me?" I cried out in shock. Maurice had told him, had told the White Russian I fancied him.

"Your cabin number," He called back. No longer a question.

I wonder if he would have come anyway, even if I had not told him the number.

Heavy, stretched out, covering me. Wet and salty, just come from the sea. Too strong for me, even if I had wanted to struggle. He gives me no choice, however. His strong arms lace under my armpits and back over my shoulders and make a fist with his hands at the nape of my neck.

His knees are forcing my thighs apart. His club of a dick is at my channel, pushing, pushing, pushing. Entering and rising up inside me. And he just holds me there, letting the rolling and lurching of the tossing, storm-cast sea move him deeper, deeper inside me, Rolling this way and that, the hot bulb of his cock kissing and assaulting my sensitive inner walls at all angles in the rhythm of the tossing sea. Ahhhhhhh.

* * * *

He was grunting hard and I was groaning even harder. I felt the bulk of him slip away from me and both heard and felt the slurping of his impaled dick pull out of me, and I thought he'd finished with me, short of my release. Short, I was sure, of his own. I had not invited him in, but I felt a sudden loss of him.

But he wasn't leaving me; his weight momentarily removed, he turned me over on my back, and in one swift movement pushed his knees between my thighs and grabbed me above the hips, his hands so big and my waist so thin that his fingers almost met, and pulled my torso down hard into him as he thrust his dick strongly up in me once again. I cried out and arched my back, writhing and trembling under his new, stronger assault. I reached over my head and grabbed the rungs of the headboard to hold myself in place against the tossing ship and the White Russian's digging cock.

My head lolled to one side, and that's when I saw him. Maurice, sitting in a chair across the cabin. Naked under a robe, which was hanging open at his sides. Sitting there, one leg hooked over the arm of the chair to give him a wide stance, intensely watching the White Russian fuck me, a little smile on his face, his hand pulling slowly, rhythmically on his meat. The reddish glow of the night lights made the curled wisps of his heavily matted silver-colored chest hair stand out prominently. He was breathing heavily, his barrel chest expanding and contracting, bringing movement to the thatch of chest hair that reminded me of a breeze passing over a field of wheat. His engorged cock was big and thick, extending from a luxurious bush, its bulbous head angry red in the glow of the night lights—and glistening with precum. His eyes glued to the spectacle of the slight me being manhandled and fucked by the burly White Russian deckhand.

The rolling of the ship and the thrusting of the White Russian's cock was too much for me. I gave a gasp and my muscles tightened, and then I gave a little scream, collapsed under the relentless pounding, and released my seed up into the muscular, flat belly muscle of the thrusting deckhand. He, in turn, roared in triumph and jerked and ejaculated deep inside me.

Then he was gone but was almost immediately replaced by Maurice, who took up the just-vacated position, his knees pushing under my ass cheeks and thighs, his strong hands digging into my hips, a thicker cock than the deckhand's thrusting inside me. And thrusting and thrusting. Fucking me hard, the rolling of the disquieted sea tossing and turning and churning me on his relentless cock. I ran my hands up through the enticing thick hair on his chest and took his nipples between my fingers and gently squeezed. I smiled into his face, a smile of welcome, of gratitude for the free passage. Wanting him to enjoy the fuck. Enjoying the fuck myself.

But Maurice had worked himself up into a frenzy in his voyeuristic foreplay. My welcoming him wasn't really the image and the fulfilled fantasy he was seeking.

"Fight me," he demanded. "Struggle for your freedom or I'll fuck you unconscious." Then he backhanded me across the face, and I began to writhe under him, trying to escape. But this was probably why he had selected me. I was small and light, and although I was strong, I wasn't strong enough for the White Russian or for Maurice.

I did manage to dislodge his cock and scramble over to the side, but the safety slats on the side of the bed were insurmountable, especially as the ship had taken that moment to lurch to port and roll me back into Maurice.

He laughed and grabbed me around the waist with one hand and scooped up two pillows with the other. He turned me on my face and forced the pillows under my belly, raising my hips to him. The lurching of the ship was tossing us about, but Maurice was used to this. He crouched up over my hips, his thighs encasing mine. I felt his hand positioning his angry red knob at my hole, and then he reared his pelvis back and brutally thrust inside me and started pumping me hard. Going with the lurching of the ship, using the ship's motion to delve deeper into my channel and assault and caress every inch of my channel walls as he drove up inside me. Driving me to distraction. Sensations I'd never felt before. Completely taken, wholly controlled and invaded.

He was riding me like a jockey in a closely contested race, the image not lost to either one of us. He ran the fingers of one hand into my hair, and grabbed, and lifted my head up toward his face, arching my back painfully. Bringing my ear to his lips, he whispered in a throaty, lust-driven tone, "Did your David ride you like this, my little filly? Was he this big and thick, and did he thrust like this . . . and . . . umph . . . like this . . . and like THIS?" Each brutal thrust made me jerk and spasm. Then he bit me on the earlobe.

I gasped and yelped a reply, but it didn't matter what I said. He wasn't listening to me. He wasn't interested in what I had to say. He had been so reserved and mannerly in the light of day. In the light of the reddish night light and on the tossing sea, he was something else altogether. He was a vengeful god; King Neptune. And he was splitting me asunder with his spear. I was completely in thrall to him. Alone out here on the sea. Completely at his mercy.

And his mercy was very thin at the moment. He was riding me like a rodeo bull performer, tossed by the wallowing ship, duplicating the fury of the gale thrusting against the creaking ship. He was slapping my butt cheeks with stinging blows from his hands, and pistoning inside me, and riding . . . riding . . . riding.

* * * *

The next morning, the sea was calm as glass. I remarked on this to the third mate as I was entering the dining room, and he said, "Yes, that's not unusual. But the weather charts say to expect another rough night at sea tonight."

The deckhands—and the ship owner and passenger as well—were quiet and a bit groggy after a hard night at sea—harder for some than others; harder in a different way for one than for the others.

We were all withdrawn into ourselves, needing that first cup of coffee before we could even think of being decent to each other or to struggle for something to say.

Maurice was already there, nursing a steaming mug, when I fairly hobbled in, not all from lack of sea legs.

The eight deckhands were huddled over their own coffee, hoarding their cups from each other like they were treasure chests. They all looked at me as I came in. They had had their heads together, listening to the White Russian whispering, when I entered the room. He stopped whispering as soon as he saw me come in.

I went over and sat next to Maurice, not saying a word. I was trying to think of something to say, when I felt the nudge of a hand against the one I had laid on the table top. I looked up into the eyes of a smiling, blond giant of an Australian. Open smile, a gleam in his eye. A steaming coffee mug in his hand.

"A cup of Joe, mate?" he asked. All smiles, super friendly.

I smiled wanly back at him and took the cup. "Thanks . . . mate," I managed.

He smiled again and backed his way to the table of the deckhands and slowly sank into his seat, his eyes still on me. The eyes of all eight on me. One set satiated; seven sets in lip-licking anticipation.

I turned my eyes to Maurice, who was also giving me "that look."

"So, you fancy *him*, do you?" Maurice said, gesturing toward the Australian, his eyes telling me all I needed to know about the rough nights at sea with Maurice.

Sounding

Dark Angel

(Chapter One of *Dark Angel Sounding,* which is out in e-book, and included in the paperback *Sounding: Ultimate Control*)

My angel was taking me to the darker side, introducing me to new sensations and passions, higher levels of arousal than I had ever known before in my heretofore vanilla sex life. He was an addiction, a dangerous habit to feed, I fully realized, and I had come back to his den willingly, wanting to know what more there was, what new heights my passion could reach. My head kept saying no or at least go slow, but my body yearned for his touch, for his domination, for reaching new heights of body awareness and pleasure under his guidance.

I had returned voluntarily to his basement room, as he knew I would. My hands were handcuffed to the brass headboard welded to the wall, and I was kneeling, facing the wall, on a stained mattress. We were beyond the spankings and light lashings that had made my tender ass, inner thighs, and cock and balls red swollen and ultrasensitive to the touch. We were even beyond the soothing and arousing attention his lips and tongue had paid to my swollen thighs, tender kissings that had crescendoed to bitings that had me screaming for mercy and then to the rimming and invasion of my asshole with his searching tongue with its tantalizing knobbed stud.

We were now on to a new phase. He was knelt between my thighs, very close into me now, the studs of the leather harness crisscrossing his bulging chest rubbing against my shoulder blades, his rock-hard cock, with its Prince Albert pierced head ring rubbing between my swollen thighs. He had one hand firmly palmed on my lower belly, holding my ass into his pelvis, and he held a purple silicone ribbed and nubbed dildo in his other hand, pressing it between my lips. I took it in as I would have willingly taken in his cock—as I, indeed, already had taken in his cock before I'd been handcuffed to the wall—and I made love to it as I knew he wanted me to, taking in its measure, knowing that it soon would be working its thick eight inches or more into my puckered hole.

The dark angel was humming. He had done this before when he was engrossed in what he was doing and when, it seemed, that he was being especially aroused by the activity. I had learned in our earlier session that this marked his being in a zone of his own while he worked my body and that as long as he was humming, it made no difference what I might feel or want—he was going to pursue what he felt and he wanted.

He pulled the moistened dildo from between my lips and sat back on his haunches briefly, lathering the tool up with lube, all the time telling me how nice my body was and how he was going to play me like a violin. No, he said, not like a violin. That was too refined. He was going to work me like a factory machine, roughly and strongly, one that worked with a punching rod, pistoning the rod inside it endlessly and forcefully. I moaned at the image he was providing and longed for him to cover me once again, to hold me close and dominate me.

And then he was covering me again, and I felt the bulbous-capped end of the silicone dildo against my throbbing asshole. He told me not to hold back in voicing my responses, which he hardly needed to have done, because I lurched and arched my back and cried out my mixed pain and ecstasy from the moment the slick dildo entered me, until it had screwed in all the way to the hilt. I screamed out the stretching and rubbing and rough digging it was doing as I felt each ripple and nub working the walls of my canal.

All the time he was telling me how the dildo was nothing as a take-no-prisoners invader as his own cock would be, and he soon was proving that. He made me stand up on the mattress, my legs spread wide, and my torso slanted down to where my hands were cuffed to the wall, and exchanged the swirling rotation of the dildo for his own thicker and longer cock. I groaned and grunted and screamed out again in both fear and welcome as his heavily veined cock, with that ring in the tip—thinly sheathed with a condom that didn't interfere with the sensations provided by stroking of the ring and rippling of the veins as he plowed up into me.

When I felt the studs of the cock ring at his root attack the rim of my hole, he covered my nipples with both his hands and started to worry them with his pinching fingers and nails. Then he leaned his lips up to my ear and asked me if I was ready for the piston machine to be turned on.

I moaned back my desire for him to take me long and hard and furiously, and then I cried out once more as he bit my ear lobe and continued chewing lightly on that as he began to pump me hard, in long strokes, punishing my ass walls with that twirling cock ring of his.

My knees gave up to the onslaught of his vigorous fucking, and I collapsed down onto the mattress, the dark angel coming down with me, without losing purchase on my hole. He covered me close from on top and kept pistoning his rod into me. I was pushing my ass back at him with each stroke, which caused my engorged dick to slide across the mattress, and, at length I added my own cum stain to the mattress to join that of so many who had preceded me there.

With a lurch and a cry of victory, the dark angel also spent himself within me, and we lay there panting and sighing until we had regained a regular pattern of breathing.

While he was uncuffing me and leading me off to the shower, he said, "Dress after we've showered and then I want to take you somewhere."

I was mildly disappointed, because in our previous session, it had been after we had showered that he had really shown me what I had been missing for so long in arousal and a fantastic fuck. But he was the boss, and I was the slave in our relationship.

After we showered, he fed me, telling me that I'd want to build up all the strength I could for his surprise and then we were on his motorcycle and moving into an even more "iffy" part of the city than where his digs were located.

He pulled up in a warehouse district and we entered a nondescript door in a blank wall and followed the stairs to the basement. We were in a low-ceilinged, smoke-filled room that was teeming with men in various stages of undress, arousal, and release activity. There were bars set up on three sides and small tables, with chairs, most occupied, not all by a single person, all circling around a center platform, with a spotlight shining down.

Two men were performing on the platform. There was a wedge-like cushion in the center of the platform, with arm and leg restraints at each corner. A youngish, lithe red-headed guy, with a flowing mane of hair, was reclining on the wedge, ass tilted up on the higher end of the slant, and torso draped back toward the lower end, with head propped up on a slightly elevated end. His arms were bent up and his wrists were cuffed in the restraints on the sides of the wedge beside his head. His torso was stretched out fully to show off his fine musculature. His ankles were cuffed at the sides of the other end of the wedge, although there were lines attached to the wedge that permitted the wide spreading of the young man's legs. A burlier, muscle-bound, completely hairless man, wearing a headsman-style mask that covered his head and came down to below his eyes was hovering between the young man's legs. I could tell the young man was both beleaguered and enjoying himself by the screaming he was doing.

I no more than gathered the impression that the burly man was covered with jewelry piercings and that the trussed youth had one of the longest dongs I'd ever seen, however, before the dark angel pulled me over to one of the bars, perched on a barstool, and pulled my ass into his pelvis between his spread and possessing legs. He encased his arms around me and rested his chin on my shoulder.

He had ordered beers while we was folding my body into his, and while we waited for them to arrive, my eyes adjusted to the dimly lit room, undulating with men in heat and full rut, many of their eyes riveted on the stage. As the dark angel worked his hand under the waistband of my trousers and cupped my balls and played with my cock, my attention went back to the stage, where I saw the young man straining his muscles, his head thrown back, emitting loud moans from a slack, stretched mouth.

And then I saw why, and I involuntarily tensed inside the dark angel's embrace. The burly dominator was kneeling at the end of the high side of the wedge, between the receiver's wide-spread, cuffed legs. He was holding the end of a silver, curved, rather thin wand between two of his fingers. And he was slowly pushing it into the piss slit of the young man. As it slid in farther, the young man was panting hard and crying out a series of "yeses," which was the only indication I had that he was enjoying this invasion of the most intimate area of his body. The burly man twirled the wand slighting inside the slit, and the young man groaned and grunted his ecstasy.

And then the wand was being extracted—slowly and dramatically. A sigh went through the audience. When extracted, it looked like a good six inches had been inside the slit.

I felt like I couldn't breath and discovered that this was largely because the dark angel was holding me tight, almost smothering me in his embrace. And he was humming softly to himself.

I wiggled and his embrace slackened, but it tightened up again as we both watched the burly man take a thicker and slightly longer wand from a case and slowly insert that inside the slit in the younger man's cock, now harder and even longer than before. The younger man strained at his cuffs and screamed to the ceiling. Once more a slide in and a swirl and the wave of a heavy sigh across the audience. And then the long slide out. The third wand was even thicker. The youth's piss slit was being stretched open to where I could see, even from the distance that I was standing, that the hole was gaping.

I closed my eyes tight as this third wand disappeared inside the young man's penis. I couldn't watch this; I didn't even want to think of this. My own penis was feeling the pain in sympathy—or so I thought until I realized that the dark angel had a finger at my piss slit and was trying to force the finger into me.

I tensed once more and the dark angel whispered in my ear, "So what do you think?"

"What do I think?" and whispered back dumfoundedly. "What do I think of what's happening up there?"

"It's called sounding," the dark angel murmured. "I take it you aren't impressed."

"Impressed is not the word for it," I said with a moan, which told him all he needed to know about what I thought about it.

He changed tactics, "I meant, though, what do you think of the restraint wedge. Does that look like fun?"

"Yes, yes, it does," I admitted, opening my eyes again to take another look at the wedge, and seeing the fourth, thicker wand being inserted.

While this wand was going in, the young man, who had remained calm for the third wand, cried out again, declaring that he was about to cum—to get the wand out. And the burly man followed the direction and slid the wand out just ahead of a prodigious spurting of semen onto the burly man's belly. Amid scattered applause in the audience, the burly man laughed, licked off the young man's penis and started forcing a pinkie finger into the now greatly enlarged piss slit. The young man was moaning and writhing again.

"Well, that's why we're really here," the dark angel returned to our conversation. "I've rented a cell here for this afternoon. It features one of those wedges."

He stopped in mid thought, however, the attention of both of us going to the stage now. The young man was being uncuffed, the wedge was pushed off the stage, and it was replaced with a thicker rectangle. Some sort of pillowy-padded platform with cuffs at the four corners again. The young red head went down on this on his belly and his wrists were cuffed at the upper corners. His legs were bent up on the sides of the platform, with his upper thighs strapped at the sides and the ankles cuffed in close to the bottom corners. This arrangement presented his ass to the bottom edge of the platform, and his long dong hanging down the bottom edge. The burly man was kneeling at the young man's ass and was tonguing his hole and stroking down on his cock.

"As I was saying," the dark angel went on. "Are you interested in trying a wedge?"

"Yes."

"Now?"

"Yes."

As we worked our way through the crowd to a door at the other side of the room, the burly man was working his cock into the ass of the young red head. He had one palm pushing down on the small of the young man's back and had the other fist buried in the young man's flowing mane, pulling his head back, so everyone could see the contortions on his face and clearly hear his cries as the burly man's cock plowed into him.

I was all atremble when we reached the small cell. Only a centered platform supporting another one of those wedges occupied the room. The dark angel slowly undressed me and cuffed me, facing up, on the wedge. The wedge was extremely comfortable and sensual. Then as I watched, he undressed himself. He looked good and evil, and I started to precum at the mere sight of that thick dong with the Prince Albert cock ring.

Then he did the unexpected. He blindfolded me.

I objected, but he said he wanted me to experience everything this time from just the sensation of touch. He crouched over me and kissed me on the lips. Then he kissed me on each nipple in turn—right before he attached clamps to my nipples. This was an entirely new, not fully pleasant experience, for me, and I whimpered a bit, but he was humming now. I could tell that I was going to be entirely at his mercy. And this is what I had wanted. I was addicted. I wanted to experience the edges of arousal and sexual stimulation. As I relaxed and he thumbed the nipple clamps, I began to enjoy what they were doing to my sense of touch.

He was tonguing and biting my inner thighs now and working his way to my asshole. When he thought me prepared, he started fucking me. He was riding me bareback now, and the sensation of his veined and ringed cock sliding across my ass canal walls had me moaning and groaning in appreciation. He was digging his fingernails into my thighs, and every once in a while lifting a hand to tweak the nipple clamps, hit my hard pecs with a closed fist and slap my flat belly with an open palm. Giving me a full range of sensations.

The wedge was wonderful. It opened and imprisoned me fully to the dark angel's onslaught. The domination was total. But not really total yet. He had more planned.

Before he jacked off, he pulled out of me and I felt his thick, hard cock being slapped against my thighs and then my belly and then on my chest. He took my lips in his and punished my tongue with his tongue stud. Then he was kneeling on my chest, between my upraised, imprisoned arms and was slapping that dong of his on my face. He forced his cock between my lips and I deep throated him to ejaculation, gagging a bit as I swallowed his repeated spurts of semen.

Then he was off of me, and there was a foreboding silence. Then the humming started again. I hadn't been aware of when he'd stopped the humming while he was fucking me, but he must have—because the humming unmistakably was back and in full force.

I felt a hand on my cock, cupping my cock at the root, on the underside—holding my cock up at a raised angle, my hips already being raised by the wedge. Then I turned stone cold and a chill went through my body as I felt the cold steel tip of the wand at my piss slit. I screamed out as the first of the wands slowly entered me there. Violation, stuffing, remarkably little pain, an electric zing through my body, my cock engorging, an indescribable feeling of sensual pleasure—enhanced by the mere thought of now having had every orifice of my body dominated and fucked by my dark angel.

"Relax, relax," I was hearing in a soft, soothing, hummed tone. "Relax and go with the feeling. It will be so much better,"

A sucking, emptying feeling as the wand slid out. A strange sense of loss and emptiness when it is gone.

Then a thicker wand, entering me, making me scream again despite myself. Tightening up, but then remembering, and relaxing. But as this wand glided up through my urethra, I knew I was about to come. I yelled out to the dark angel. Asking for mercy. Letting him know I was going to blow. And the wand glided back out and I did blow my wad.

A husky laugh from the dark angel and a cleaning of my penis with his tongue.

That's it then, I think. Yet another, deeper, darker experience. That was OK then.

But then an even thicker wand at my piss slit. pushing in, stretching me. Loud humming. I cry out. "Oh, God, oh God. Noooo. Yessss. M-o-o-a-n-n . . ."

Career Guidance

"What is this shit?" Bernie Wasserman grabbed up tabloids in both fists and threw them across his desk at his client, who sat slouched and defiant in a club chair on the other side of the big mahogany desk.

"Those stories are exaggerated. I didn't know she was a man."

"Good god, Danny," Wasserman continued to bluster. "You are playing parts of a sixteen-year-old still. Caught being fucked by a transvestite in the back of your Hummer. What were you thinking? And a Hummer, god almighty. Who told you you could buy a Hummer? Your fans think you're riding bicycles. I didn't sign off on any of those bills."

"I'm almost nineteen," Danny blustered defiantly. "I don't have to tell you about every job I go out on anymore."

"You sure as hell do, Danny Delmonte," Wasserman yelled. "I've got your contract. I've represented you since you were ten. I own your ass."

"That's it, isn't it?" Danny shot back. "This is all because I moved out when I was eighteen. You'd convinced my folks to let me live with you and you were just licking your lips, playing it safe and waiting to fuck me when I turned eighteen—and I moved out instead."

"No, Danny," Wasserman said in a carefully controlled tone after taking a minute to pull himself together. "This is about your life. I've been lenient with you—and you've lived high on the hog. You've been spending it as fast as you make it. You've got maybe two more good years in your category and then it's iffy if you can transition to anything from the child roles. Very few are able to. And whoring around and getting high and making a fool of yourself in public isn't going to get you there. You need to come back under control. You need to move back in with me."

"No. You just want to get me in bed," Danny spat back. "And I'm going to beat that drug rap. The lawyer you got for me says it's a slam dunk."

"And what are you going to say about being caught in the backseat of a vehicle with a male prostitute in a car you weren't supposed to be driving as a condition of your release on the drug charges? Tell me about that. Tell me how happy the Children's Express Theater is going to be with this now if you sign this contract." Wasserman was waving a thick sheaf of paper that constituted a contract for three high school musicals.

"Fuck that. Fuck you. Fuck it all," Danny muttered as he sank down into his chair.

"This is your future," Wasserman said, his voice ominous and full of venom. "This is the only contract we have on the table. You already were aging out of these roles and now you've really fucked yourself with this stuff you are feeding to the tabloids. You are out of control. Do I tear up this contract and show you the door, or do we start this conversation all over again with you saying 'yes, sir' to me?"

Silence for a long minute with Danny looking at the floor. But his eyes came up fast enough at the sound of the tearing paper. Wasserman had torn apart one of the tabloid newspapers, though, instead of the contract.

"That got your attention, didn't it?"

Danny mumbled something into his chest.

"What? I didn't hear you."

"Yes." Just getting that word out seemed to be torture for Danny.

"Yes, what?"

Another moment of silence and then a muttered "Yes, sir."

"Stand up."

Danny looked up, he eyes showing confusion.

"I said stand up. And strip."

"What?" Now Danny was shocked.

"You said you were off the drugs. I don't know if I believe you. I want to check for evidence."

"I never was on drugs—well not that kind," Danny said, his voice still showing his shock. And maybe a bit of fear now too.

"If not, then I won't find any marks on your body, will I?" Wasserman declared. "I can maybe clear this up—but only this last time—if you haven't fucked up your life more than just what's in these tabloids. If you're shooting up, you won't pass the studio tests and it doesn't matter if you sign these contracts or not. If not— and if I'm convinced you're not shooting up—I can get a doctor to say you were on prescription medicine because you were overworked and headed for a breakdown and that this is what has caused your behavior—but that you are back on the road to full recovery now. That always goes down OK in this town for at least the first time. So, if you want this contract, strip now and I'll check you out."

Danny looked all of the vulnerable sixteen-year-old role that he played so well as he meekly stripped down and stood there, naked, shivering slightly. He was a beautifully well-formed man—but still boyish looking, still about to pass as a teenager.

Wasserman sat behind his desk and looked Danny up and down as Danny's head hung in embarrassment and his hands crossed over his privates.

Wasserman opened a drawer in his desk and took out a couple of items and then, on his way around the desk, he dragged over a Chippendale straight-back dining room chair and plopped it down between where Danny was standing and trembling a bit, as if it was cold in Wasserman's office—which it wasn't—and his desk.

"Here. Sit," Wasserman commanded.

Danny looked up in confusion and just stood there.

"I said sit. And what do you say?"

Danny mumbled something, and Wasserman pushed the young actor down on his bare butt on the chair cushion. "What? I didn't hear you."

"Yes, yes, sir," Danny muttered. There were tears in his eyes now.

"This is all for your own good, Danny. You've gotten very cocky and beyond yourself. And you've lost control and you are this close to losing everything. And not just for you but for me too. I have given representation and career guidance priority to you for nearly ten years now. You need to learn control and discipline. You're fucking this up for both of us."

While he was saying this, Wasserman placed a wooden box and a couple of more items on a small cigarette table between the club chair and where he'd plopped the straight chair down.

To Danny's consternation and confusion, he was then strapping Danny's ankles to the front legs of the straight chair and pulling Danny's arms behind his back and tying off his wrists together.

"What the . . . ?"

"Just shut up, Danny. You've been building up to this. It's time you understood who's the boss around here."

"God, Bernie, what . . . ?" The exclamation was set off because Wasserman was stripping off his own clothes now.

And then Wasserman, naked, was pushing himself in under Danny's buttocks and thighs and onto the seat of the straight chair. Danny was blustering and objecting in words that no child star even should know how to pronounce and then whimpering and pleading as Wasserman got his body below Danny's and Danny was lapped.

After he had lapped Danny and his engorging cock was running up the small of Danny's back, Wasserman reached over to the adjacent table and retrieved a condom packet, which he torn open, and a tube of lubricant. He rolled the condom on his cock and he began to diddle lube into Danny's asshole with one hand palmed under the young actor's butt and, after lubing up his own crowned cock, slicking up Danny's cock as well.

Danny was moaning and pleading and cussing up a storm.

"Your trannie do this for you in the back of the Hummer, smart ass?" Wasserman asked darkly. "How many other cocks have you had up there? Ones I didn't know about. Ones before me. Oh, yes I waited. But who didn't wait? Tell me, Danny?"

"Oh, God, Bernie, no. No, not many. None before I left your house. Oh, don't do this, Bernie. I'll behave."

"Who's the boss, Danny?" Bernie said.

"You are; you are the boss, Bernie . . . just don't . . ."

Bernie was lifting Danny's buttocks and hovering it over his erect phallus, the bulb of which was touching the rim of Danny's hole. Danny was panting and whimpering. "Who's your daddy, Danny?"

"What?"

"Who's your daddy, I said."

"You. You. You, sir."

"No 'sir' now, Danny. Say it. Call me Daddy."

"Daddy. Daddy. Oh, no . . . oh my god, noooooo."

Wasserman was pulling the younger man down onto his cock, slowly bringing him down, as Danny groaned and moaned and writhed within the close embrace Wasserman had him in. At length, he was bottomed—fully skewered—and defeated. He just sat there in Wasserman's lap, fully impaled, moaning softly, tears streaming down his cheeks, collapsed.

But he had taken all of Wasserman with a minimum of effort. Danny wasn't anything close to a virgin—and this ticked Wasserman off. He had wanted to be the first and had waited and schemed for it for years.

"Who was the first, Danny? Who? Tell me."

Danny was moaning but Wasserman lifted the young actor's buttocks half way off his cock and slammed him back down, and Danny yelped and struggled out an answer. "Sid, Sid Soltan."

"Soltan? The director of your last movie. When? When, Danny? And where?"

"My eighteenth birthday. In his studio trailer."

Now Wasserman was upset—really upset. "Why that old fart," he thought. "All of my plans and he sweeps in with a trump card."

Wasserman sat up very straight in the chair, forcing Danny to arch back into his chest and Wasserman's cock to be driven deeper into him. Danny groaned. "It's all for our own good," Wasserman was growling in Danny's ear. "You were running away. Weren't paying attention. Completely out of control. You need discipline. You need control. You need to be dominated. Is that right, Danny?"

Danny was sobbing quietly.

"I said, is that right Danny? Aren't I right?"

"Yes . . . yes, Daddy," Danny murmured through his tears.

"You've been ass fucked before," Wasserman said, "enough to make the papers. There has to be something else, something more, to impress on you who is the boss here, who dominates."

"Please . . . please, Daddy," Danny muttered.

Then his eyes got really big and his body tensed and went rigid as he watched Wasserman open the wooden box on the table to reveal a series of size-graduated silver medical instruments—wands with slight bulbing at the tips—long, thin phalluses—arranged neatly in indentations in a blue-velvet foundation.

"What? What?" Danny's voice was filled with question and fear.

"The instruments of discipline . . . of ultimate domination, Danny," Wasserman said in a low, hoarse voice. "I want you to understand. I don't want to ever have to do this again—not as long as you have a career. Consider this career guidance. The best lesson you will ever learn from me; your salvation in being able to prolong your career. Your utter understanding of who is in charge here."

"No, please . . . don't, Daddy. I'll be good. I'll . . . Oh, noooo."

"Hold still. Hold perfectly still. But not rigid. It will be much easier if you are relaxed. But very still. Very, very still."

Danny was whimpering again and Wasserman couldn't feel him breathing he was holding so still. Wasserman had taken one of the smaller wands out of the box and was holding it in front of Danny's terrified eyes.

"Breath," Wasserman commanded. "Don't hold your breath. You won't be able to do so. We will be at this for a while."

Danny was panting hard and Wasserman felt him relaxing and collapsing on his body.

Wasserman reached over and exchanged the wand for a larger-sized one.

Danny cried out in fear and frustration, knowing now that the ordeal was not over, but he was reduced to soft whimpering and shallow pants as Wasserman moved through two more sizes of wands and a second coming by Danny and until he felt there was no resistance in Danny at all anymore.

"I think we've made our point now," Wasserman said at length.

"Yes, Daddy," Danny murmured.

"OK, I'm going to unbind you now and I want you to reverse on my cock and face me and I want you to fuck yourself on my cock. Of your free will. You do that and we'll sign those contracts and get on with our life—together. If not, your career is over. Do you understand?"

"Yes, Daddy," Danny whispered in a voice of resignation.

And then, after he was unbound and turned himself in Wasserman's lap, Danny proved what a good actor he was by fucking himself to Wasserman's ejaculation—and giving an Academy Award performance on selling that he couldn't get enough of his master's cocking.

Tattoos

9:30 Bus from Abilene

Sometimes I think I was born with a "fuck me" sign painted on my butt. But then, I seem to have been born with that young and vulnerable look that turns some men on, and I'll have to admit that I love being touched—especially in one particular sensitive spot below and to the left of my navel, where I have a blue rosebud tattooed. Ever since I started having sex, if a man touched me there, I hardened right up and softened to anything he might suggest. It didn't help that, no matter how much I fought it, I loved being cocked. And so I had the spot marked with a tattoo for reference.

I was trying to fight it that morning I caught the 9:30 bus from Abilene headed up to Denver. Dave didn't want me to go. He agreed to drive me down to the bus station, but up to the very last minute I'm sure he didn't think I really was going. But I'd pole danced in Dave's men's clubs for a couple of months now, which was as long as I'd stuck around anywhere since I'd gotten old enough to hit the road. And as nice as Dave's cocking was and as good as the tips for the extra service to the men in the club were, I had gotten myself in an old familiar rut, and I had started to tell myself that there must be something else out there for me to do other what whoring in sleazy little bars.

And something got into my head that if only I could get to Denver, I could start a whole new life and that this weakness in me—these urges, this vulnerability to the wants of other men—would just go away.

Just before I got on the bus in Abilene, Dave tried his last ploy. He pulled me around to the side of the station and pulled me in close to his chest. A hand sneaked up under the hem of my athletic T, and he pressed a thumb into that blue rosebud tattoo. His lips clamped down on mine, and I involuntarily danced on his pole for a few moments. First one leg went up around his hip and then another, and then he was dry humping me up against the wall—and I was loving it.

I was saved by the loudspeaker calling the "all aboard" for the 9:30 bus from Abilene, though, and I managed to break away and head for the bus without a look back. Instead, I looked up along the windows in the bus and saw that two cowboys were eyeing me real close. I wondered what they could have seen in the shadows at the side of the station house.

489

I climbed up into the bus and found a seat near the back on the side away from the platform. I didn't want to see Dave out there. I was fighting with myself, telling myself that life with Dave and in his little clubs wasn't what I wanted. That I wanted something more from life. But I was afraid if I saw Dave out there, looking oh so forlorn, as Dave was so good at when he wanted something from me, I'd lose my resolve to leave Abilene.

The bus started out, and I felt a sudden sense of freedom. It was going to work. I knew it was.

As the bus moved out into the dusty countryside outside of Abilene and headed north, I looked around to see what there was in the way of travel companions. An Hispanic family, a man and his wife and three children, the oldest a sullen-looking teenaged boy of fifteen or sixteen, was sitting near the front. From the way they were dressed, I thought maybe they were field workers moving north to start the harvest up there and to work their way back to Abilene again over the season. A couple of elderly ladies, all dressed out in their Sunday best—off on an adventure. A young woman who always seemed to be huddled close to the window and asleep. And the two cowboys I'd seen in the bus window from the station platform. They must have been together, because they were sitting side by side on a row about two thirds of the way back until the bus got started and then one moved to the window seat in the same row on the opposite side of the bus. One was older than the other, wiry with ropy muscles. Clean shaven, graying at the temples, with startling pale blue eyes in a deeply tanned and weather-lined face. Piercing eyes when he stared at you—eyes that told you you'd better do what he asked if he told you to do something. The other, younger one, was dark-complexioned, probably half Hispanic, equally tanned, but chunkier than the older one. Not fat by any means, but heavily muscled. Both were in checked shirts and jeans, with fancy leather cowboy boots and big fancy silver belt buckles. Both had tattoos running up their arms and the hint at the neckline of more on their chests. And both were occasionally looking back at where I was sitting and then whispering to each other.

Buses weren't popular anymore as a means to move long distances, but what with the cost of gas and the overall economic conditions in the States at the moment, I thought they'd probably come into their own again. I had chosen the bus because I'd never owned a car, couldn't afford the plane fare, and there were no rail connections between Abilene and Denver that didn't go hundreds of miles out of the way and that didn't, in the long run, take longer—and cost more—than the bus.

I don't know why I picked Denver. I just had seen posters of it sitting right there next to the snow-capped Rocky Mountains and it looked so prosperous and clean and open that it had become somewhat of a Holy Grail to me, the symbol of a new, cleaner, less-complicated life.

We stopped at a gas station-convenience store just off the highway in the middle of nowhere for a lunch break. There was a small dining room off the lunch counter with only three tables. The young woman didn't leave the bus, but the elderly ladies took one table and the Hispanic family another, and I sat down at the third after I'd gotten my burger and fries.

The two cowboys sat down at my table.

"Hi, I'm Tex," the older one said as he sat down. "This here's Dusty." They were both wearing the traditional ten-gallon cowboy's hat and Dusty just tipped his hat at me without saying anything. But he had a big grin on his face.

"Hi, I'm Glade," I answered.

"Glade. That's an unusual name," Tex said.

"Yeah. I sorta picked it out myself," I said. "Didn't much care for what I'd been called before that." I didn't tell them that it was my stage name. All of us pole dancers picked out names that the customers would find intriguing and easy to remember. Most picked out suggestive or downright explicit names. I had wanted to be a bit more subtle with mine.

"Goin' far?" Tex asked.

"All the way to Denver," I answered.

"Dusty and me are gettin' off in Durango. We work a cattle ranch west of there. Been down in Abilene to see the sights. Were you in Abilene long or just passing through from somewheres else?"

"I was there a couple of months," I answered. I was feeling a little disconcerted. Dusty wasn't saying anything, but his leg was touching mine and I felt those old yearnings building up inside me. Dusty was a real hunk. The strong silent type. And he was touching me. Any man who touched me set me going.

"Found something to do in Abilene, did you?" Tex asked. He was eyeing me with those piercing blues of his. It made it scared to lie.

"Oh, this and that," I answered.

"You look kinda familiar, like we've seen you before. Dusty was remarking on that when we saw you climb into the bus. Spent any time around the tenderloin district? That's mostly where Dusty and me sat drinkin' our beers. Place called Rapier mostly. Any chance we'd have seen you there?"

"I've heard of it," I answered in a rather tight voice. More than heard of it, it was one of three clubs Dave owned. I'd pole danced there. I wondered if Tex was establishing something with me—not just about me, but about him and Dusty too. You didn't go into the Rapier looking for women.

Tex started to say something else, but the bus driver was tooting his horn, and it was time for all of us to make that last rest stop and to return to the bus.

When we climbed back into the bus, Dusty returned to his seat, but Tex followed me back to where I'd been sitting and sat down in the aisle seat right next to me.

The driver started up the bus and got back onto the road. I tried to settle my nerves. Tex's leg was right up against mine, as was his upper arm. I could feel the hardness of his lean body through his checkered shirt. I was wearing an athletic T, so my biceps were bare. Just a thin layer of shirting between me and Tex's hard, warm skin.

"Born and raised in Texas?" Tex asked.

"No," I responded. "Lived here and there before that—mostly in the Midwest."

"Family in Texas or in Denver? Going to Denver to visit family?" Tex asked.

"No. No family," I answered. "No family anywhere."

"None at all?" Tex asked. His face was turned to me and his pale blue eyes were full of sympathy.

"No. I was an orphan. Floated around a lot. A couple of foster families, but not anything I'd want to talk much about." I certainly didn't want to talk about those foster families. If I'd gone down a bent path, it could all be traced back to that part of my life. I'd had a pretty rough life up to now; it looked like the only way I could go from here was up. I turned my head toward the window. My eyes had suddenly gotten a little watery, and I didn't want Tex to see that.

"No one at all waitin' for you in Denver, either?" Tex asked. His voice was soft, full of concern.

"No. No one at all," I answered. "Just startin' out again. I do that a lot. I start out again a lot."

I was still looking out the window, but I could see the reflection of Tex's face in the window, as I thought he could see mine.

He had a hand on my thigh, just above the knee now, and I'm sure he could feel me trembling.

"Just relax, Glade," he was whispering to me. "You're so tense. I can help you with that."

His voice had gotten low and guttural and his hand had moved up my thigh and was gripping me hard.

"Nice name, Glade," he was murmuring. "An unusual name. I think I saw that on a poster at the Rapier. Not a name you'd forget too fast. Not a body, either. Some even had distinctive markings. Dusty and me like tattoos. We've got 'em all over our bodies. Would like to show them to you. Would you like that?"

My trembling increased. He had fingers at my waistband now, very near my belly, with the grip of that other hand still on my upper thigh.

"Tex . . ." I said in a choked voice.

"Shush, it'll be fine. No one can see us back here." Tex stripped off his shirt to reveal full-body tattooing in a riot of colors and patterns against a rock-hard muscled chest. "Do you like my tattoos, Glade? If I remember rightly, you have a very nice one yourself. Somewhere near here, wasn't it? That's what I remember of you on that pole, dancin' away. That nice little tattoo. A rosebud, isn't it?"

He was pulling the T out of my shorts and a finger was moving across my belly and his thumb was on the rosebud tattoo. He was rubbing it and his other hand was on my basket, and I was falling apart.

"Happy day. You're just aching for it, ain't you?" Tex muttered through his heavy breathing. "Hot damn, you harden up fast." His hand snaked under the waistband of my gym shorts and he was pulling them down below my balls. My dick was standing straight up, betraying my arousal from his thumbing on my rosebud tattoo.

"Tex . . ."

"So tense. We must do somethin' about that," Tex was whispering. His ten-gallon hat came off and he dropped it onto my lap and fisted my cock under it and started to slow pump me. I turned my face to him and he could tell from the look in my eyes that I was lost to him. He leaned over and gave me a kiss and then he just pulled away and we sat there, staring into each other's eyes from six inches away, our cheeks resting on the nubby material of the seat backs, and he slowly beat me off, enjoying the look in my eyes as I was transported by his hand job.

"You can touch my tattoos, Glade. Go ahead."

I tentatively, involuntarily reached out with my fingers and ran than over the markings on his hard chest. His nipples were taut—ready for me. He could feel the trembling of my fingers as I got lost in the sensuousness of his tattooing.

When I had jacked off up into his hat, he gave a little laugh and leaned over and kissed me again. Then he stood up in the aisle and rummaged around in the overhead compartment. He opened a duffle bag he had up there and took something out and then reached up and pulled down a blanket.

"Time for a little nap, don't ya think?" he said, and then he winked at me.

What he'd gotten out of his bag was a condom packet and a small tube of lubricant. When he sat back down, he leaned over and pulled down on the waistband of my gym shorts and, out of instinct, I raised my hips for him so that he could strip them off.

I knew what was happening, but still I made some effort to resist. I was trying my best to get beyond Abilene. "Tex . . . No, I don't think . . ."

"Shush," he whispered. "I wanted to do this back in the Rapier. But you'd gone off with some other customer before I could get to you. Come on. You know you want it. Look at what I got for you." He unbuttoned his jeans and fished out a nice plump cock, already hard. Tattooing wound down around that too, and I moaned.

But still I fought the cravings. "Here? Now?" I asked incredulously. "There isn't much room . . . and there're other people here."

"Hush. We'll manage. Just don't do much yelling. They always yelp for me. Just try to keep it quiet like. Too bad it's dark in here and we have to use the blanket. They always like to see the designs on my pecker disappearing into their holes. You know you can see them through the rubbers. I buy ones that you can do that with."

"Tex . . ."

But he just kept going. I watched as he opened the condom packet and rolled the transparent condom on his cock. Then he slathered himself with lube. He covered us with the blanket and turned me toward the window onto my hip and I felt the cold lubricant at my hole and searching and stretching fingers. The palm of his other hand was on my belly and his thumb was on my tattoo and he was rubbing it. All of the resistance drained out of me. It was almost as though he knew that that was the key to my ass channel.

I shuddered as he worked his hips under mine, both of us turned toward the window. And then we was entering me, slowly, but relentlessly—showing me that indeed we could do it in bus seats. He slowly pumped up into me. His thumb was stroking my rosebud tattoo, and I was moaning and sighing softly for him. My head was against the cool window, and I watched the desert landscape drift by, as in another dimension I could also see the reflection of Tex's face and see how deeply he was enjoying the fuck.

I pretty much cleared my mind, enjoying the fuck myself, but being frustrated that I was doing so. Why was it so hard to leave Abilene and all that was Abilene so far behind, I wondered.

Tex left me under the blanket with no more than a kiss on the neck and a pat on my naked butt cheek. He pulled his shirt back on and buttoned up and went back up and sat down with Dusty, and the two of them whispered in low tones and laughed.

Near dusk we stopped for dinner and a change in drivers at a stop almost identical to the lunch stop, and I got my burger and fries from the fast food counter and took it out and ate it standing up by the gas pumps. As I ate, the young woman stumbled out of the bus, looking dazed and her eyes all puffed up. She came back moments later with a sack of food and climbed back up in the bus. I wondered what her story was and whether it was any rougher than mine. It made me feel a little better, if a little guilty, that there may be folks in the world worse off than I was.

In my case, I enjoyed the cocking. Couldn't get enough of it really. What I was having trouble with was the guilt of enjoying it and wanting more of it. That and the somewhat downtrodden feeling that I was being taken advantage of all of the time. What I really needed and wanted was just one guy. An older man, maybe. One with a good income who would stick by me and give me a somewhat normal life. I'd want him to be virile and have a nice cock, though. I knew myself enough to know I didn't want to stop the cocking. Maybe in Denver. Surely in Denver that's what I'd find.

When we got back on the bus, I waited until Tex and Dusty had gotten on and settled themselves before I climbed into the bus. I wasn't in the mood for Tex to visit me again—at least not this soon. He cocked real well, though, and those tattoos of his were a real turn on, so I wouldn't mind having him again at some point.

Dusk turned into night, and I managed to go to sleep, huddled under the blanket that Tex had covered us with earlier in the day.

It was quite dark when I felt a nudge on my shoulder and swam up from a groggy, unsatisfying sleep into the grinning face of Dusty.

"Come on," he whispered. "Want to show you something in the back of the bus." He'd already stripped off his shirt and he was almost as tattooed as Tex was. He was covered in swirled, some of which curved under the bulge of his pecs and made them stand out and emphasize how well-defined he was there.

I struggled up, knowing full well what he wanted to show me, but he was already reaching down and palming my belly under my T, and the touch was enough for me to want what he was going to give me.

He followed behind me to the back seat of the bus, a bench seat that stretched the width of the bus carriage, with the palm of his hand on my belly and his forefinger rubbing that rosebud tattoo. My knees were going to jelly, and I was whimpering, my dick hardening and forming precum, the rim of my hole already puckering.

When we reached the back of the bus, Dusty scooted into the seat all the way into the corner, pulled me down onto the center of the seat, a good two and a half feet from him, and unbuttoned the fly of his jeans and pulled a thick, stubby cock out. He reached for one of my wrists and pressed my palm to his chest so I could feel how hard his nipples were for me and he moved my other hand to the root of his cock. Then he wrapped a hand around my neck and brought my face down to his cock and I gave him head. I was good at it.

He didn't say anything. He just sat there and moaned and sighed softly, with his hand on the back of my head guiding me, and his hips slowly rolling up as I deepthroated him and his stubby cock slowly became not in the least stubby.

After I'd gotten him all hot and bothered, he turned me, full length on my belly on the backseat, one of my legs hanging down, the ball of my foot leveraging on the floor of the bus to keep me steady in the tossing and turning motion of the bus, which was pronounced at the back. Then he pulled my gym shorts off my legs; crowned his cock with a condom; and straddled my hips and fucked down in me to his ejaculation. He had both of my arms pinned behind my back, holding my wrists together with one strong hand, holding me quite immobile and giving me the feeling of being taken almost against my will in a dark, enclosed corner of the world, which gave me a little thrill.

We were both breathing hard when he was done, but I knew he wasn't finished. I knew these young, virile cowboys with their hard and hard-worked bodies. I'd had them by the hundreds, it seemed, in Abilene on their one night a month off and coming into town to get their rocks off. He'd shot off, I could tell, but he was still hard. I'd known of guys like him who could recharge and fountain off three times before they went soft. Just one night of relief a month that wasn't self-initiated for a young cowboy can build up a whole lot of cum.

And, sure enough, He was pulling me up. Not dislodging his cock, which had lengthened out to gigantic proportions. He struggled up into a sitting position, with me lapped, his lips and teeth working my shoulder blades and the hollow of my neck, his hands wrapped around my belly, a finger pressing into that rosebud tattoo. Almost in a frenzy myself again, not least at watching the muscle roll on those tattooed arms encase me, I started fucking myself on his impaling cock in long strokes. One of his hands snaked around and fisted my cock, and we came almost simultaneously, all the time softly moaning and groaning, careful not to project the sounds of sex toward the front of the bus.

I looked up as we climaxed—and into Tex's eyes and then down to his naked, tattooed chest. He'd come back to watch the second fucking and was leaning over the seat, knees in the seat bottom, and face almost touching mine. His pale blue eyes were alight with lust and he leaned in and took my lips with his as I spouted off onto the back of the bus seat in front of us.

Dusty pulled out from underneath me and, after a little whispering session with Tex, moved back up the aisle. When he got to my seat, he picked up the blanket and brought it back and draped it over the aisle between two seats a couple of rows up from the back. Now, in the darkness anyone from the front of the bus couldn't see what was happening in the aisle beyond that blanket, and the interior of the bus was so dark they couldn't even have told the aisle was blocked unless they were coming back to use the bathroom in the rear corner.

Tex pulled me over and planted my butt in the center of the backseat, lifted my ankles to the tops of the separated aisle seats in front of the backseat, crouched between my thighs, and fucked me long and deep. Dusty sat there, turned around in an aisle seat in front of the backseat, and watched the action. And when Tex was done, Dusty replaced him again, turning me and pressing my head and chest into the center seat of the backseat, my rump pointed up the aisle, and doggy fucked me.

They left me wondering if maybe they hadn't had any success in getting their rocks off while they were in Abilene. And leave me they did, to stumble back to my seat on my own, exhausted and stretched and sore—but well-fucked and happy. This wasn't anything I hadn't endured on any given night in Dave's clubs.

The next morning, after breakfast at a small way station where there was another change in drivers and the two elderly ladies got off—in the middle of nowhere, as far as I could tell—Tex followed me back to my seat and sat with me and jacked me off again while murmuring in my ear about how nice I was—and how really sweet I'd been the night before.

"We'll be in Durango this afternoon," he said when we were finished and I was laying back in the seat, mellow and satisfied.

"Will we?" I murmured.

"It's pretty expensive in Denver, you know," he said from out of the blue.

"Is it?" I asked.

"Sure you got enough to get started there?"

"There's never enough, I've found."

"Could you make good use of, say, two hundred more?" he asked.

"Who couldn't?" I responded. I was just making small talk. Tex gave great hand jobs.

But Tex wasn't just making small talk. "You know you can stop off in Durango and get on the bus later on the same ticket?"

"Can you?" I said.

"Yes you can. You know, I've been thinkin'. Dusty and I had promised to bring something back to the boys at the ranch from Abilene and we plumb forgot to do that."

"Did you?"

"Yep. We got a pole in the middle of our bunk house. You could stop over for a day or two and give them guys a pole dance. I'm sure I could collect at least $200 for you for that. What do ya say to that?"

What I was thinking was that no matter how far down the road this bus had taken me, I was still in Abilene. But what I said was, "Sure, why not?" As I said, Tex gave the best of hand jobs and there he was, hand on my belly, stroking my rosebud tattoo with his thumb while he was making his proposition.

The ranch was a good hundred miles out of Durango in the direction of nowhere, but the bunk house did, indeed, have a wooden pole holding up the center of it. There were six interested cowboys out there in nowhere in addition to Tex and Dusty. I danced for them to a scratchy record on an old-fashioned record player, wearing one of the sparkly gold G-strings I'd brought with me from the Rapier. I wowed them and then they fucked me—all eight of them in succession over a three-hour period. A few had seconds.

I heard Tex telling them how turned on I got when my rosebud tattoo was rubbed, and they all made sure to give it attention, and thus they all got enthusiastic fucks.

They may have gone another exhausting round, but the foreman broke up the party and extracted me and helped me hobble out of the bunkhouse and into his cabin—where he bent me over a chair and satisfied his own need.

I made $350 off that afternoon of work, and Tex suggested that I stay on for a while—that the cowboys worked harder with a daily fuck and that there was plenty of money from where the $350 had come from.

But I really, really wanted to get out of Abilene.

Tex was good for his promise; he drove me back to the bus station in time to catch the next bus rambling through from Abilene to Denver. We left early, though, because he stopped behind a rock formation before dropping down into Durango and fucked me again in the backseat of the ranch's station wagon. He gave me another fifty for that, though.

The bus between Durango and Denver was more crowded than it had been on its initial leg into Durango. We were getting closer to big towns. And there was much more of a variety of people getting on and off as we rumbled along.

In Colorado Springs, a middle-aged guy in a business suit got on. He caught my attention, because he looked like someone who should be driving a Mercedes rather than riding in a Greyhound bus. He was smartly dressed; was in good, and obviously pampered condition; and was flashing a big diamond ring. It struck me that this looked like just the sort of guy I was looking for in Denver.

He looked around the bus as he got on. It was half full, although most of the passengers were in the front half. His eyes caught mine, and thinking what I had been thinking about how he was the type that filled my Denver bill, I probably gave him a more welcome smile than was absolutely necessary. I thought I saw his eyes sparkle up and he returned my smile, and then he was moving toward me. I was surprised when he came all of the way back to where I was sitting and sat down in the aisle seat next to me. There were lots of vacant seats back here, but he was sitting next to me. He'd taken his suit coat off and slung it into the overhead bin before he sat down. His warm arm was rubbing up against mine, and his thigh was touching mine, and I felt like I was going to hyperventilate. I looked down and was somewhat distressed that if he looked in my lap too, he'd see that I was tenting up.

But he wasn't looking at my lap, or so I thought. He came on with a briefcase and had taken some papers out of it and was sifting through those, looking for something.

The bus was out on the highway now.

"Wouldn't you know it?" he was muttered.

"What?" I asked more out of politeness than curiosity.

"They gave me a receipt back there at the garage, and now I can't find it. It had their telephone number on it. I'll need that to find out when the car will be fixed."

"The car?" I asked. He was on a bus.

"Yeah. My Merc broke down back there in Colorado Springs. God, I haven't had to ride a bus in years. But I needed to get back to Denver by this evening and the bus station was right there by the garage. It would have been more complicated to get a rental car. You come from far away?"

"From Abilene," I answered.

"Working there, were you?"

"Yeah, a place called the Rapier." I have no idea why I told him that. Being disconcerted by him touching me put me off center, I guess. That and assuming he'd have no idea what the Rapier was.

"Ah, I see," he said.

And, for a moment, it seemed like he did, indeed, see. He had turned to me and was looking at me real hard.

To try to cover, I asked him about where he lived and what he did for a living.

"I'm a few miles out of Denver. Out toward the mountains. Run a specialty service of sorts."

I didn't pursue the question further.

But then he settled back in his seat and started talking to me about his family.

"Adolescent girls," he snorted as his monologue moved along. "Daughters are such a challenge. You have any girlfriends with tattoos?"

"No girlfriends," I answered. I was trying to keep my answers short. I was sure that he was able to hear my arousal in my voice if I said too much.

"Well then, boyfriends perhaps?" He'd let it come out straight, as if there was nothing behind it. But I saw him eyeing my tented lap now, and I was beginning to figure out he was building up to something. I said nothing, but I know he could feel the intake of my breath and how tense I'd gotten.

"Tattoos aren't so bad," I said after a pause.

"Oh, you got any?" he asked.

"One," I answered.

"Somewhere I can see it?"

"Just here, near my navel," I said, and I raised the hem of my T-shirt to show him my blue rosebud tattoo. And he touched it with his finger, and I fell apart and my gym shorts tented up even further—and noticeably. And he was looking now. No doubt.

He looked into my eyes for a moment and then said, "Go back to the restroom at the back of the bus, and enter, but don't latch it. If I'm wrong just stay here and I'll move to another seat."

Dumbly, knowing already what would happen, I stood up and walked by his legs as he swung them into the aisle and unsteadily—not only from the rolling gait of the moving bus—walked back to the compact bathroom at the back corner of the bus and entered it.

Shortly afterward, the door opened, and he was inside with me. He'd rolled a condom on before coming back and he merely unzipped himself again, reached down and pulled my gym shorts and briefs off my legs and pulled my T-shirt over my head. I was naked. He wasn't but he unbuttoned his shirt so that our chests would be my bare skin against his hairy chest, and then I climbed his hips with my legs and he was holding me there against the back paneling of the bus restroom, his legs straddling the toilet basin, and he fucked me hard and deep by pulling me up and down on his cock with a broad hands palming the small of my back.

I turned my face toward the mirror over the basin and watched his other thumb strumming my rosebud tattoo, and I ejaculated up his belly.

I returned to my seat first, leaving him to try to clean up the damage to his shirt. I looked around the bus as I moved up the aisle, but no one was showing any interest. No one had noticed.

Soon thereafter, he plopped back down into the seat next to me and reached into my gym shorts and pulled out my cock and slowly stroked me.

"That was nice," he said. "You know what you're doing. You mentioned the Rapier in Abilene. A professional are you?"

"A dancer. A professional dancer, yes," I answered between sighs brought about by what he was doing with my cock.

"And other things too?"

"Yes . . . OK . . . yes. I've done other things too."

"You're good. You're really good. I like that little thing you have going of turning on quickly when your tattoo is touched. Genuine is that, or an act?"

"It's what happens," I said.

As if he was rechecking, he reached over and pressed a finger from the hand not working my cock into the tattoo, and I shuddered and collapsed into myself and moaned for him.

"Sweet. How well can you give head?" He was unzipping himself and pulling my head down to his cock, and I showed him that I was an expert in that.

"Very nice," he said when I was done. "That special service I said I operated in the hills above Denver. It's a men's club. A special men's club. Would you be interested in working for me up there. At, let's say, $1,000 a week plus any tips you get, for starters?"

As far away from Abilene as I traveled, I still never could leave Abilene, it seemed.

Toys

Double Rings

"H Ring"

I was laying there in his arms, nearly exhausted from his fucking, and he leaned over me with a grin. He had a silicone rubber ring in his hand—much wider than required by any finger—holding it for me to see. He turned it over and showed me there was a silicone nub on the side—in the form of an H. He stroked my belly lightly with his fingers while he told me it was especially made using my initial—and that he wanted me to brand him as mine.

I was sighing as he stroked my belly, and my cock was rising—I wanted him to fuck me again. He leaned over and kissed me, and while he was doing so, he was pulling the ring down over my dick head. It went down over the bulb and lodged just under the rim of the glans. He held his hand there, over the cock ring, and encircling my hardening cock. He held me closely embraced to him with his arm. I trembled in his arms. My hips started to move, slowly churning, as he loosened his grip on my cock and began stroking me up and down in his hand, rubbing that H across his cream-slathered fingers. He lowered his lips to my nipple and closed his teeth over it, and I arched my back and groaned. And then he was kissing me on the lips again, deeply. I felt the weight of his body shifting and he was swinging his leg over my body, encasing my pelvis between his thighs. Positioning his channel on my cock bulb.

He had never given himself to me before; it had always been him mastering me. He had told me he loved me and I had laughed. But he had told me that he would show me that he was mine.

He was sliding down my pole, shuddering, the H of the cock ring rubbing his channel walls, branding him from the inside as mine—forever. He was riding me hard, arching his back, crying out "Oh Godddd!" Fucking himself on the H ring.

* * * *

"Ring on the Sly"

"I don't know, Becca, which do you think we should hit first? I heard there were a few new Vera Wangs at Clementine, but that bangly thing I told you about is at Pinks, I think. And you know how fast things go from their shelves. Do you—?"

"Don't know about Pinks; the last time we were in there, that sales girl was a little snotty, you know," Chrissy cut into the gushing of her old college roommate Rebecca, "I don't want to miss getting to Annette Dean's. Maybe—"

"And shoes—and a bag to go with them. Gotta get to Occasionally. And Lex's; I've been thinking about—"

"Ladies, ladies, the Carytown stores won't be open all night. You begged to meet here in Richmond so you could shop while you caught up on your college days. So, go off and shop. Get out there and buy." Barry Holden was smiling, but only on the surface.

Barry's wife, Rebecca, and her College roommate Chris Worthington insisted on these "catch up" outings twice a year, and they got more involved and more expensive each year. Not that Barry begrudged the money. His boat storage business in Norfolk was doing very well—very well indeed. The Worthingtons—Chris and her husband Stan—lived in Northern Virginia, where Chris was a realtor and Stan was undersecretary of somethingorother in Washington, D.C. The two couples had met this time on neutral ground, in Richmond, Virginia, where the girls wanted to shop in the artsy fartsy Carytown district, and both couples were booked at the swank Jefferson Hotel for the long holiday weekend.

A waiter drifted by one more time to see if they wanted anything else. Stan had already paid the bill. It had been his turn. Barry paid the previous night for dinner right before the girls trotted off to an opera performance both husbands had refused to subject themselves to. The two couples were sitting in the best restaurant in Richmond—or at least one of the most expensive ones—tj's, the dining room of the Jefferson hotel. Both husbands had been forced to suit up, which neither one was all that wild about.

"Have you heard about Heidi Story?" Chris picked up their conversation as if Barry hadn't commented at all. "Under new management, I've heard. I hope that means they've brought in more petites."

Rebecca was taken aback slightly. She didn't know whether or not that was a dig; Chrissy had been good with such smiling backstabs in college. Rebecca was painfully aware that she would never fit in a petite size again. "We need to check out that new store, Eurotrash," she countered. "Anything with a name like . . ."

Barry looked over at Stan for some sort of help in getting the women going. But Stan was just sitting there, looking inscrutable, smiling his secret little smile, and looking benignly and with more than a bit of derision on the field of chattering woman at the surrounding tables—and not least at the magpies at his own table.

But then Stan caught Barry's look of desperation and lifted his hand and started moving a ring on his finger around and around, smiling at Barry. It was a Stan mannerism Barry knew so well, and it always stopped him in his tracks and made his blood boil. Stan was frequently given to such cocksure mannerisms.

The ring itself was a rather strange one—made of some sort of stretchy gold mesh that would expand to accommodate any size digit, and it had a sizable golden bead as its ornament. Not for the first time Barry wondered where Stan had gotten it. But the Worthingtons traveled abroad extensively with Stan's work, so it could have come from any exotic market worldwide.

" . . . you know, the red-spangled jacket that women a few rows down from us at the Landmark Theater last night," Chris was babbling. "We may have to go over to Dillard's in the mall for that. Maybe on the way out of . . ."

"Did you enjoy the opera?" Barry cut in. His head would explode, he thought, if these ditzy women didn't stop talking about shopping and started doing something about it. He might just have a nervous breakdown if he couldn't get them out of the hotel soon. "Neither one of you have said anything about the Opera. What did you see? Was the music good?" Maybe if he changed the subject for a second, it would break the logjam and they'd start moving out.

Rebecca gave him a blank look. How stupid of me, Barry thought. They were together; they had no idea what opera was playing. They were caught up in each other. It's the same no matter when or where they meet. Anything else happening around them was lost to them.

But then Barry chuckled at that thought and gazed over at Stan again, who was still giving him that inscrutable smile and twisting that ring of his around on his finger.

Chris swept in to save the day. "It was OK, but the soprano was a little flat—of voice that is, she was so top heavy I have no idea why she didn't tip over into the audience. So, what did you two do while we were gone? Stan? You said you wanted to watch a game on the TV. What . . .?"

"Oh, I just screwed around," Stan said, smiling wanly at his wife. "Just screwed around for a while."

"And you?" Rebecca turned to Barry.

"Oh, me too," Barry said. "I . . . um . . . just screwed around too." He took the remainder of the water in his crystal glass in one gulp for whatever diversion he could manage. A waiter promptly stepped forward and refilled the goblet—the mark of a great restaurant, pristine service even after the tip had been paid.

If only you knew, if only you knew, Barry thought. And then he sighed and looked at Stan, sitting there, also smiling, twisting that ring, while the women resumed their shopping plans.

It was the first time Stan had used the ring, and the novelty of it had sent Barry over the edge, making the experience much more arousing and climatic than last Christmas at the Homestead while the women were horseback riding and Stan had brought out those beads on a string. He and Stan had been stretched out on the bed alongside each other, naked, in Stan's hotel room. Stan was always the one in control. Barry always had gone to Stan, and they never were finished until Stan was fully satisfied. And Stan was always inventive and full of surprises.

Barry had been laying inside Stan's embrace and Stan was stroking Barry's cock languidly. Stan already was ready, condom in place, and Barry's body was moving in waves of pleasure, in rhythm with the slow pumping of his cock under Stan's always-expert attention. Stan was using that ring of his—the golden bead nub—rubbing it around on pressure points of Barry's cock, running it down the length of him to the root and applying pressure, moving it under Barry's balls and across his perineum, rimming Barry's twitching, soon-to-be blissfully filled hole. It was driving Barry to distraction.

"Oh, god, Stan. That ring. That hard bead. Oh, god, oh, god," Barry moaned.

"Like that, do you, Barry?" Stan whispered, smiling his inscrutable smile. "Know a secret about this ring, Barry?"

"Oh god, no . . . yesssss, there, like that. No, tell me the secret, Stan. Ohhhhhhh . . ."

"Here. Take the ring off my finger, Barry. Just pull on it. The gold mesh will expand. There, wasn't that easy? Now, open it up and slide it down over my cock head. Go ahead, it will expand. Yes, yes, like that. You're trembling, Barry. Are you beginning to understand? Just down beyond the rim of the bulb. Now your leg. Here let me help you. lift it up my chest. Move like this. Open to me, baby."

"Oh, Stan . . ." Moan.

"See the golden bead? See where I've moved it. You know what it will be making love to when I enter you . . . like . . . this?"

"Ohhhhh. Ahhhh. Stannnnnn! . . . Oh GAWD!"

"Barry, my coat."

"Eh, what?" Barry asked, snapping out of his reverie and realizing that the women had risen, at last, and Chrissy already had her coat on. And the women weren't the only things that had risen. Stan had his hand under the table—and on Barry's engorging cock through the cloth of his suit trousers. The golden bead on the ring had been twisted to the underside of Stan's hand so that it rubbed up and down along the length of Barry's hardening cock. Stan was smiling that inscrutable smile of his.

"My coat, honey. You are sitting on the tail of my coat."

Barry moved his butt off his wife's coat—pushing his crotch closer into Stan's hand. He thought he might feint on the spot. Barry's mind was silently screaming. Could those damn hens just get out of here so he and Stan could get back up to the room before he creamed his shorts?

"So, what are you guys going to do while we're shopping?" Rebecca tossed over her shoulder as she and Chrissy, arm in arm, started out on their afternoon shopping spree in Carytown.

Stan looked up, graced them with his inscrutable smile, and murmured, "Oh, something will come up, I'm sure. It always does."

The Commander

"Ahhh, that were very nice," I said with a deep, satisfied sigh, as I spilled my seed down Des's chin. We were in the boathouse on the lower lake, here because Des had wanted me to fuck him. But now we'd have to sit and talk for a bit, listening to the racing shells grind against the dock outside in the bit of a squall that had come up over Sandhurst. It would take me a few to recharge.

"Cig?" I asked, reaching into my pocket and pulling out a pack while he scrubbed at his face with a dirty handkerchief.

"Thanks," he said, reaching out for the fag. He stood and turned, leaning back against the gunwale of the boat I was sitting on. "God, you are built hanging."

"That's what you came for, isn't it?" I asked with a laugh. I was unbuckling his belt with one hand and moving the other down the small of his back and under this waistband, moving into his crack. I'd need time to be in form again, but there was no reason not to prepare him.

"Yes, you are a legend over at New College . . . ugh!" I'd found his hole with my forefinger, and he was rising up on the balls of his feet in surprise. But with a shudder and a little moan, he settled back down on the finger. This is what he'd come here right after dark for. To check out the Sandhurst military academy legend for himself.

"And you're over at Old College?" I asked. He groaned an assent as I pushed the trousers down off his thighs and reached for his dong. Not much more than ordinary, but thickening well. "Valeting for the cadets, are you?"

"Yes . . . oh, shit, oh fuck." I had three fingers in him now. He'd need to be real open for me. "Yes. And you? Over at New College."

"The same."

"Valet for that new cadet, Sandy Coleridge I hear. Father's the big snot for the 6th D.C.O Lancers out in India on the North West Frontier."

"Yes, I do for him."

"And does he enjoy that big cock of yours in him? Particular nice piece of arse that."

"No," I said and then laughed. "I don't do for him that way—would like to, but no. The lad's stiff as a board proper. Really up tight. A bit of the old man, I hear. A virgin."

Des snorted. "Not a virgin, I hear. I hear he has a regular appointment with his tutor, Percy Hopewell."

"Percy Hopewell?" I asked, incredulous. "Hopewell is almost as stick up the arse as young Coleridge is and puny as a beanpole. I can't see them doing it."

"Well, check it out for yourself. Tuesday afternoons at two, or so I heard. In Coleridge's room. Faithful as clockwork."

"I still don't believe it. But here, you came to get a taste of this," I waved my ready wand at him, and his eyes went wide. "and I don't have all night. So, let's get to it. Here. Hop up on the ledge of the gunwale. Here where it's thickest."

He did as I asked. He was trembling a bit, and he looked scared, his eyes constantly going to my cock, which was hardening up nice, and then looking away. I stripped off his trousers.

"On the small of your back. Yes, like that, roll your arse up to me and hold your thighs out yourself." I let him watch me pull a rubber on, and then I went down on my knees between his legs and lifted his dick out of the way and squeezed it as my tongue went to his buttocks and the crevice between.

He was making little grunting and groaning sounds.

At length, when I thought he was open enough to take me just, I stood, rubbed my cock and his hole with cream, and, taking that big breath that all athletes take before making the big plunge, presented at the rim of his hole.

"Oh god, you're huge," he whined and went rigid as I got the rim of my bulb past his entrance. He had been gasping but now he was still and straining to take me, and his complexion was turning red.

"Here, now," I said. "You've got to breathe. Breathe. Relax. You act like a first-time school girl. You've had it before, haven't you?"

"Yess . . . oh god, oh god . . . but nothing as big as this. Oh fuckkkk."

He'd come for it because it was big; he wanted it. So I gave it all to him in one deep thrust.

"Oh, god! . . . . . Oh GODDDDD!"

* * * *

Turned out Des was right. The next time I was tidying up Sandy Coleridge's room, I flipped open his appointment book and there it was, the notation at two on each Tuesday for "tutorial with Percy."

The next Tuesday at two I made sure I was in the service back hall, with the valet's door into Coleridge's chambers open a crack. I heard voices and soft laughter down the service stairs behind where I was standing, and I went down to find the men in service Hugh and Cedrick crouched down on the turn of the stairs. Hugh was giving Cedrick a blow job, and I stood there and watched for a while, pleased by the good, straightforward sex of it. Then I remembered why I was in the back hall and went back to the door into Coleridge's room and pushed the door open to a wide crack.

They were already going at it, if you could call it that. I had to check myself from laughing out loud. They were side by side, close together, in overstuffed chairs, naked. Arms were extended over the chair arms, Percy's hand working slowly on Sandy's cock and Sandy's hand pumping Percy languidly. Percy was reading poetry from a book. Sandy was a real beauty, tanned and hardened from life on the Indian frontier. Handsome as a movie star. Sandy hair—obviously the derivation of the name that had stuck—from head down to the downy tuffs on his sternum leading down his belly and bushing up around a very nice cock. Percy was another matter—an indoor scholar—all angles and height, concave chest, hairy as a dog, dark, and with a poor excuse for a cock. I could hardly see it encased there in Sandy's hand. The only attraction that I could see must have involved seniority—but then, here at Sandhurst, seniority was everything.

Call this fucking? Reading poetry and calmly jacking each other off. Gorsh. I'd say Sandy was still a virgin in any way that mattered. But it wasn't all the fucking they did, and I decided that Sandy, technically, couldn't be called a virgin. Percy snapped the poetry book shut and stood up and pulled Sandy up as well. They moved over to the desk in front of the window. Percy gently pushed Sandy's chest down onto the chair that was inserted into the desk hole, and as he did so, Sandy widened his stance. A rolled on rubber and a few minutes of rubbing cream in and Percy was pushing his small cock into Sandy's arsehole. Sandy flinched a bit at the first breaching, but nothing significant or painful looking. Percy bottomed quickly and just held there, moaning softly, his head flung back in what passed for ecstasy for him, while, holding a wash cloth over his tip, Sandy slowly beat his own cock to ejaculation and stared out of the leaded diamond windows of his bay window onto the parade grounds below. Percy was reciting poetry again, and the pace of his voice picked up and he became breathy. There was a slight lurch and a tightening of his thin buttocks, and then the ritual was all over.

It seemed so sad. Sandy looked like he was just marking a "to do" activity off his life's experiences lists. His beautiful body and sensuous lips told me that he wanted so much more out of life.

They dressed in silence, there was one pecking kiss on the lips initiated by Percy, and then they settled down in the upholstered chairs and opened their books for the justifying tutorial session.

That was it? That was all? I thought. There hadn't even been enough for me to take my meat out and beat it. Although I was hard. That was from watching Sandy. As Des said, he really was a nice piece of tail. He deserved better than Percy.

But then I guess that was the way in the British colonial army life. Attend Sandhurst as your father did and his father did, become imbued with the gentleman soldier's training as your father did; become manned by a sensitive but consumptive upperclassman as your father did; find an appropriate bride from a suitable family to marry just before embarking for your colonial posting as your father had; produce sons as your father had—and pick out the best looking of your sepoys and fuck him for your only sense of self and rebellion as your father did.

I turned and crept back to the top of the stairs and did now take my meat out and beat it while watching Hugh splayed out on the stairs on his belly and Cedric crouched over him from behind and fucking him furiously, both of them grunting like pigs. Now *that* was fucking. A difference between upstairs and downstairs perhaps. I suddenly had a desire to find out.

* * * *

509

I spent the next night trying to forget Sandy Coleridge—the beauty of his young, supple, yet muscle-hardened tanned body—and not being able to do. I resolved to act and justified it by telling myself Sandy wanted more out of his male-male experience and ultimately would be grateful to me. It was a gamble, and it might lead to me being booted out of a pretty cush Sandhurst job—but it wasn't as if Sandy was repulsed by the idea of being fucked by another man. All of the rationalization came down to the simple fact that I wanted to fuck the cadet from colonial India just to get my cock in him for my own pleasure, however.

So, in the still of the night, I threw some necessities and a couple of toys in a bag, and just in my sleeping briefs, I padded down from my attic room in the New College service area and crept up to the service door into Coleridge's chambers.

All was dark inside, and I could hear him gently snoring. I crept through the door and silently shut it behind me and stood, still, for some minutes until my eyes had fully acclimated to the dark.

Sandy was stretched out on his bed, on his back, his legs tangled up in sheets. He was wearing long sleeping drawers, and nothing else, but his cock was hanging out of the fly and his hand was still on it. The front of his drawers were spotted where he had finished masturbating as he went to sleep. He was as beautiful and sexy in sleep as he was awake—maybe more so, as he looked so vulnerable and peaceful.

I was going to fix that—the peaceful part of that.

The handcuffs made a clicking noise when I took them out of the bag, and I froze, afraid it would wake him. It didn't, though. He just snuffled and turned a bit more on the side away from me and moved his arm over his head. His wrist went between brass railings in the headboard. Perfect. I had that wrist locked in the handcuffs and a good grip on the other wrist before he woke with a start and began the expected confused and indignant objecting to what was happening to him.

I rose off the bed from where I'd gone down on a knee to snap the hand restraints on and turned and clicked on his bedside lamp. I wanted him to see what was going to happen.

"Alec," he muttered in surprise. "What the hell? Release me this instant."

"Sorry, Mr. Coleridge, I've come to give you a proper fucking, sir."

"A proper . . . what is this? Are you joking? I'll have your job for this."

"No I'm not joking. And we'll see about my job. But you can't even say it. Fucking, fucking, fucking. You can't say it, can you?"

"What in the world are you talking . . . no don't do that. Put those back on this instant."

I had been stripping my leggings off, and then I reached over and did the same for him.

"No. Stop that . . . let me go. What *is* this about?"

"This is about you doing it with a man, sir, but not having any idea what that means. I'm going to give you a good idea, and then you can choose whether you want to do it with the likes of Percy Hopewell or with a real man. I think you deserve knowing the difference."

"Percy Hopewell . . . what?"

"I seen you and Percy, sir, and I don't call that fucking."

"Percy and I . . . we . . . we do too do it."

"Do what, sir? You can't say it. Fuck. Say it."

"We do too have sex. And that's enough for . . . free me this instant."

I had taken his dick in a fist, and he was writhing around, trying to get away from me. But I could feel him coming to life.

"Bet you can't say this either, sir. Cock. This isn't an 'it.' This is a cock. And this is a cock too, sir," I said, wagging my own proud member at him. "And this cock is going to be in your arse. Say it. Say cock."

Sandy was still writhing, trying to get out of the restraints and away. I climbed up on him and knelt over his chest, wagging my cock in his face. "Cock. A hard cock. Show me you know what real sex is with a man. Suck it. Suck my cock." I was beating him on the cheeks with my cock, but he was having none of it. His lips and eyelids were shut tight, and he was jerking his head back and forth, still trying to escape my onslaught.

"Aye, well you'll give me suck soon enough—and enjoy it, I'm betting," I said. And then I scurried over him and down behind him and between his legs, swallowed his cock whole, and began pumping my mouth on it. I moved my thumbs to his hole and pushed them in and spread him just a bit. His curses and demands filtered into moans and groans, and his writhings merged into waves of going with the rhythm of the suck as I relentlessly pumped his engorging cock until he ejaculated, which happened quite quickly, this all being a shock to him and him not having been expertly blown before.

Then I rolled his buttocks up and moved my lips and tongue to between his crack, and he was groaning right proper for me, although he occasionally was making an attempt to tell me I had to stop.

He pretty much was under control and his cock had gotten rock-hard solid again when I stopped, slapped him on the butt, and reached down and took a toy out of my bag.

He peered down to see what I has holding up above his belly, and I felt his whole body shudder. "Wha . . . what is that for?" The shudder told me what he knew what that was for.

"I think you know what this is for," I said. "I call this the Commander—because every moment it's in use you will know the Commander is in control."

"Ahh . . . no . . . you can't," he cried out. And he tightened his thighs together as much as possible and arched his back off the surface of the bed and was rolling back and forth and rattling the handcuffs holding his arms above his head so that they rang hollow, almost musical notes on the brass rails—all of this expense of energy as if that was going to get him out of the predicament.

I held the toy suspended over his belly, and he couldn't take his eyes off it. They were wide with fear. It was twelve inches of cascading rubber nodules, the one at the tip, the first of five, a pointed tear-drop shape about one inch at the upper rim, graduating up in connected tear drops of increasing size so that the fifth, uppermost was a good three inches across at the upper rim. At that point a four-inch rubber lead ended in a strong handle that all four fingers could wrap around for good leverage.

"Tell me. Does this look anything like Percy's cock?" I asked sweetly. "Is he twelve inches and three inches thick at the widest point?"

"Noooo . . ." Sandy moaned, and I didn't know whether he was belittling Percy's dimensions or objecting to the Commander. And it didn't matter.

511

Sandy groaned and whimpered and begged as I fished cream out of my bag and lavishly greased up the Commander while holding it suspended over his heaving belly.

"Here, I think I'm going to need that pillow," I said, pulling the pillow out from underneath his head and inserting it under the small of his back. "And I think you'll find you've going to want to widen the stance of your thighs just as much as possible."

He, rather, tightened his thighs and rolled his hips back and forth, trying to escape me, as, after I'd greased his hole with some finger work, I placed the tip of the Commander at his rim.

He gasped and cried out and spread his thighs wide, though, as I pressed the tear drop at his hole. The first one was the hardest to get accepted, but, although it was easier with the next two before being quite difficult with the last two, he was as noisy in the invasion of each successive tear drop over the next twenty minutes. As the wide edge of the third tear drop was swallowed by his entrance, he ejaculated again in a great spouting of semen. He was grunting and moaning profusely. No longer objecting. Voicing a little appreciation now for all of my efforts. When I asked him if Percy's cock made him feel this way, he was quick to acknowledge that Percy couldn't do anything like this.

After the fifth teardrop had disappeared, I moved back up beside him and held him in my arms and looked into his eyes, which were open wider and looking more wild and electric than ever before. He was panting hard and trembling all over, and his expression was flipping through pain and ecstasy and wonder.

"Good for you," I crooned to him. "You've taken it all. You know I'm nearly as long and almost as thick. And I can move it in ways that will send you to new heights of pleasure. What do you think now?"

"Oh, yes, yes," he whimpered. "I want it."

"What do you want?" I asked.

"It. I want it."

"And what's 'it'?" I persisted.

"Your cock."

"My what? I can't hear you."

"Your cock. Your COCK!"

"And where do you want it?"

"Inside me. Oh, please . . . now, oh please."

"What do you want me to do to you?" I was biting on his nipples and fisting his cock. His back was tense, arched, and his thighs spread wide, the Commander still fully encased in his channel.

"Fuck me. I want you to fuck me!"

I went up on all fours and straddled him in reverse and swallowed his hard cock again. I was pleased to note that his mouth went to my cock, instantaneously, without hesitation this time, and he was sucking me—not expertly, but giving me good suck and extraordinary pleasure nonetheless.

My hand went to the handle of the Commander, and I ever so slowly pulled it out of Sandy's arse. In response he went into a frenzy of passion, sucking hard on my cock and writhing under me. Before the Commander was fully extracted, he had ejaculated again, and I took it at the back of my throat, pleased and awed at the stamina of healthy youth.

I released his hands then and knelt between his legs and gave him a proper, expert, total, working-man's fucking. And he, in turn, gave me the proper lust-released responses for one being well fucked—and now knowing he was well fucked.

* * * *

The next Tuesday afternoon, still employed by Sandhurst, I was standing in the service hall outside Sandy Coleridge's door when I heard the knock on his main entrance. Sandy walked, gingerly, to the door and opened it.

"Oh, Percy, it's you," he said to the one standing at the door, but not given entrance. "You didn't get my message then."

"What message?" Percy said, almost in a huff.

"No session today, I'm afraid," Sandy said. "In fact, we might have to leave off altogether. I haven't been sleeping nights recently, and I feel all fagged out. Sorry. I'll see you at lecture tomorrow."

As he closed the door, I stopped shining Mr. Sandy's boots and gave him a turn of my head and a secret little smile. My chest was puffing up in pride, being as how the dark-hours fuckings he begged me for now were the reason young Mr. Sandy wasn't getting enough sleep at night.

Haitian Carvings

I decided that if I was going to add Haiti to my list of countries visited, disembarking for a day's frolic in the fenced and well-guarded Disneyesque pleasure enclave of Labadee was the way to go. I was trying to push my collection over the hundred-country list, and, thanks to Henry Goslan the Third's money and patronage, I was well on my way.

Henry was pushing seventy, but he still wanted a companion to help him get around, to take care of all of the little chores he couldn't be bothered with, and to keep him warm at night. He was an elegant old man—quite a looker when he was younger, I was sure—and was generous and not too demanding. But there were times when I craved younger flesh. In the city that wasn't a problem. Henry was somewhat sympathetic to my needs and didn't shorten my leash—too much. But we'd been on the seas for a week now, and I was getting a little antsy.

I suggested several times how nice it would be to get out in Labadee and enjoy the day in the full-amenities resort enclave there—but even the descriptions of how easy they made wheel-chair conveyance there didn't move Henry.

"I think a light lunch, a massage and perhaps a little fuck, and then you can certainly explore Labadee if you wish—for an hour or two. I can take a little nap."

An hour, two hours at the most, I thought. Just that long on my own. But I was grateful for that much time.

I picked up the phone and ordered Henry's lunch, and then half fed it to him, as he had little appetite but needed to keep his strength up. Then, after room service had cleared the lunch trays away I undressed Henry and laid him down gently in the middle of the bed we shared. I opened the cabinet and paused, wondering what he'd like me to be today. The cowboy costume won the day, because it was about the easiest to put on and I wouldn't have to make many adjustments along the way. Just low-rider jeans, a red bandana, and a cowboy hat. No boots. They would be too clunky in the bed.

Henry sighed as I gently rubbed his back and arms and legs with the special oil he liked. As I stood beside the bed, he reached over and slowly unbuttoned the fly of my jeans and pulled my cock out and leaned over and ran his tongue over it before closing his lips over the head and helping me be ready for him.

I climbed over him and straddled his hips, being careful not to put too much weight on him, and moved my dick up and down between his butt cheeks and across his rim while I gently ran my fingers through the oil on his back and shoulder blades and lubed up my dick and his ass well with the special oil.

When I gauged his sighing was at the pitch where he wanted it, I slowly worked my cock into his hole and fucked him in slow, shallow rhythm. When I felt him tense, I took a long stroke deep into him, pulled back slightly and then drove in all the way one, two, three times, and he gave a little snuffly cry and jerked, dribbling his cum on the sheet under him. And then he promptly went to sleep.

I stood and cleaned my dick, still hard and not satisfied, stuffed it back in my jeans, without bothering to take them off to put briefs on, grabbed a tight T-shirt and my sea pass, slipped on a pair of loafers without socks, stuffed my wallet in my jeans' back pocket, and was out the cabin door and headed down the stairs for the gangway as quickly as I could. I wanted as much alone time as I could manage.

I was sitting in the Dragon bar looking out to the El Tortue island, where they'd filmed part of the *Pirates of the Caribbean* movies, when the young Turk who was one of the ones who cleaned our suite on the ship stopped and asked me if he could join me.

I said OK, even though I suspected where this was heading, and I knew it couldn't go anywhere.

"I'm on furlough today—well for a few hours," Selchek said. He turned those dark, dreamy eyes he had on me and the big, all-teeth smile. "You been to Labadee before?"

"No, you?"

"Yes. And although it looks like every square inch is taken with recreational stuff and all landscaped and neat, I know of a trail or two that leads to small, private beaches—turned away from the tourist beaches. No one to see. No one to know what is happening."

He had the fingers of one hand playing in the hair on one of my forearms and the other on my knee under the table. His eyes told me everything he was offering. He cleaned our suite on the ship. He changed our sheets. He knew Henry and I were sleeping together—and it was pretty obvious what happened when we did.

"It's tempting, Selchek, but just not possible."

What I had with Henry was too good a thing. He didn't mind me going off in New York for an hour or two now and then. But he made quite clear he didn't want to know specifically what I was doing—and most certainly who I was doing it with. It was just too volatile for me to get anything on with someone from the ship.

The Turk looked glum and was about to say something else.

"It's not you, Selchek. It's the man I'm with. I can't. That's just the way it is. Besides there are rules about anything going on between crew and passengers. We could both get kicked off the ship."

"Ah, that is regrettable," was all he said, and he stood and slowly walked away.

But he left me with a hard on.

I walked the beach until I had my body under control and then I walked over to the artisan's village, which was a string—a long string—of open-air shanty stalls,

516

opening out onto a walking deck—all made to look primitive and haphazard, but of course it wasn't. There was little variety in the goods being offered. One shop was more or less like the next. Textiles or wood carving. Painted metal art and art on canvas that would look original and colorful when you got it back to the States, but here looking like there was maybe a dozen designs, painted over and over and over again.

And vendors all around, pulling at the tourists off the ship, wheedling them to look at their wares. "Just a look, sir, madam, no obligation. Special price just for you."

I did want to buy something, to help get some money in the economy of a superpoor country that recently had been hit by a devastating earthquake. But it all looked just too touristy.

It all became a jumble, everything looking the same—until my eyes were arrested for some reason by carvings in a stall that looked different from the others. The vendor there caught my hesitation—as no doubt they all quickly learned to do—and was up from his hammock and out onto the deck in a flash. He was a tasty little morsel. Short but slim and great muscle tone in his arms. He was wearing the pink shirt and tan trousers that they all wore in this overly planned false paradise. But his shirt was open down to one button at his waist. His chest muscles bulged despite his size and gleamed nearly black as the sunlight filtering through the exotic trees struck him. I sort of wondered if he'd oiled himself up and was offering more than wooden souvenirs.

He tapered down into a tiny waist, but I could tell by the way that his thighs worried the legs of the tan trousers that he probably was a soccer player. He wore a gold necklace with some sort of religious pendant resting at his clavicle, nestled between the swells of his pectorals.

A handsome face. Dark brown, the almost European features of the Caribbean mulatto and dark, flashing eyes.

"Special carvings. Just for you sir. You not find anything like them anywhere else here."

I almost believed him. What had arrested my attention was that the carvings were slightly erotic. It was subtle. I probably only caught on to the suggestive themes because I had an eye for erotic art. Henry collected it—he had masses of it in his New York penthouse.

This wasn't quite what Henry collected—what I could see was hetero, although there were enlarged penis images discernible in the curves of the carvings—in ebony and mahogany mostly, although some stone carvings too.

I had been trailing my eyes along the shelves, and the vendor had followed the focus of my gaze, all the time pointing this and that out and yammering on in repeated phrases of "This very nice. None like it anywhere here. You like? You buy? I wrap it for you."

He caught the dulling in my eyes as I didn't see anything that would be appropriate for Henry's collection. I wanted to please Henry, and I knew he'd like a nice piece of erotic art—if it was appropriate to his collection.

"I have more. More not right to show here. Come, come, sir, through curtain here. I have more behind."

517

I followed him into another shanty room immediately behind the first. There indeed were more wood carvings here—and more erotic. But still male on female (or female kneeling before male). A cacophony of fucking and huge penises. Nice and erotic. But not quite right.

"Yes, very nice," I said. "But not for me, thanks." I turned and started to pull the curtain aside to leave, but the young man grinned wide at me and winked.

"I understand. More. The same but different. You look, you see. I have more you will like. Beyond curtain there. You take look. you like. Good prices. Best in Labadee. No one else has these."

He shuffled me toward the back of the room and through a curtain into yet another room. And jackpot. He'd figured out exactly what I might be interested in. Carvings of men on men, in a huge variety of fucking poses. And carved penises. Huge dildos, their bulbous heads painted in bright red, or green, or yellow, or white.

I reached over and picked up one of the dildos with a red cock bulb on it. I ran my hand up and down it. Smooth ebony.

The vendor was watching me like a hawk. "Very nice. You take. Special price. Just today. Just for you."

I walked slowly around the small shanty room, taking in all that was on offer. I saw what I thought Henry would like almost immediately, but I was careful to pick up one or two others—never letting go of the ebony dildo with the red-painted head and a pair of plump balls at the base. We haggled and I slowly zeroed in on the piece I wanted.

"Oh, very, very, nice. Only $120 U.S."

"Maybe $40, I said—if you throw in this too." I raised the dildo. He, of course, knew I'd never let go of it.

He grimaced. "Oh no, no. Far too little. You can't get this art anywhere here. Anywhere in the world."

"Oh, maybe $60 for the two. Maybe more, but I don't think this really works." I held up the dildo again.

The vendor stood there, looking hard at me. "$100. Best price." He was sporting a beleaguered expression that I didn't believe for a moment.

I put the dildo back from where I had picked it up—which seemed to distress the vendor greatly—and turned to leave, giving him a smile and a shrug.

"$90 U.S. for both and I show you that red-headed penis work," he said in a strangled voice.

I smiled, seeing that there was yet another curtain at the back of this shanty room.

I played his asshole with the greased dildo in the small room at the back. A narrow table was set against the back wall, and he was perched on this, facing me, his trousers off, his hips rolled up, and his hands wrapped around his widely spread and elevated legs.

I worked him expertly, and when he started to enjoy it, I stood back, unbuttoned my jeans and let my hardening cock free. I dug into my pocket and extracted a condom and held it up for him to see.

His eyes were wide and buggy and his lips were trembling, but he wasn't making a break for it.

"$40," he squeaked with a whimper.

"20," I countered with, as I rolled the condom on my cock.

"$30," he croaked in a hoarse voice.

But now I was already at his entrance. "$20," I sternly said as I plunged my cock inside him, and he settled into concentrating on taking me all in without further haggling.

I took him long and hard—and with exuberance. I hadn't had young, fresh ass in so long that I fucked with abandon. Henry would have no cause for complaint. He'd get his titillating Haitian carved art for his collection. But for now, I needed this release.

And the young vendor was enjoying himself too. After he'd gotten me off well enough that I threw in another $10, he gave me a second toy, a string of graduated mahogany balls he took out from underneath the counter as I was leaving, helping him hobble along now on slightly bowed legs.

Back on the board that evening, I costumed as the gladiator, I delighted Henry so much with my purchases that I was afraid he might stroke out on me. He enjoyed the erotic carving I'd bought him immensely. And he enjoyed the work I did with the red-bulbed dildo within his channel just as much. He quickly went off in sleepabye land after he'd dribbled his cum in the sheets a second time for the day—an exhausted but very happy man.

I was still feeling my oats and devil-may-care—not carrying now if I was caught playing with the cruise staff or not—so Selchek was immensely surprised and pleased when I found him wandering down the corridor and I swung my free gift of the graduated string of beads in front of his face and asked him if there were any really private areas up on a deck with a beach lounger this time of night—and which was the largest ball he thought he could accommodate.

We discovered he could take the biggest in the wake of playing hide the red-painted ebony cock head. And then my cock afterward for nearly an hour as the waves of the Atlantic rolled on by beneath us.

Vehicles

On the Trunk of a Car

(Chapter One of *House on Park*)

I found I had a carefree weekend on my hands, so I had driven into the small town to answer an ad for a classic Triumph convertible that I might want to add to my collection. But I had been up and down the Park Street address given in the ad several times without finding the house I was looking for. So, I just parked my car and started hunting on foot. I did find the address, but no one seemed to be home. There wasn't any evidence of the Triumph, either.

I looked around, hoping to find a neighbor or someone I could ask about the car, when I saw them, there, across the street. They were both looking mighty fine. The car was a 1963 Pontiac Tempest convertible in pristine condition, and the guy working on the car seemed to be in pretty pristine condition as well. I was sure I was in luck. This guy must be a classic car buff as well and would be able to tell me about the Triumph. But my foot wasn't even off the curb before I forgot all about the Triumph I'd come to see.

As I crossed the street, I kept my eye on the young man. He was smiling very enticingly, and I saw him slowly move the wrench he was holding to his crotch and move it up and down against the taut material. The move provided an unmistakable message. When I reached him, I started to speak, but he turned and walked around to the trunk of the Tempest, in the shadows from the buildings on either side of the drive. I followed him around to the back of the car to where I faced him, very close, but not touching. My eyes were locked on his, and the lust in his eyes was almost electric. He sat back on the car's trunk and, winding his left hand around the back of my neck, he pulled my face to his. Our lips met in a lingering and tender kiss. I felt my dick coming alive, uncoiling in my pants, pushing against the fabric. And suddenly there was other pressure down there. The man's right hand had found me and his fingers were following my growing hard-on from the root down to the head. I felt his intake of breath, as he got a sense of my measure. But I knew he would be even more surprised when I was fully engorged.

Our lips parted and he pulled his face away, looking at me imploringly. I tugged at his net T-shirt, and he raised his muscled arms, as I pulled the shirt over his head. I grabbed his left wrist and brought his fingers to my mouth, where I, took the fingers, individually, into my mouth and sucked on them. With his right hand, he tugged my shirt out of my trousers on both sides and started unbuttoning my shirt. I worked my mouth down his finely muscled arm and buried my face in the curly black hair of his armpit. He was extremely hirsute. There was black curly hair everywhere on his body as far as I could see, but especially around his pecs, down across his abs, and trailing down into the front of his tight jeans. I had a fetish about men with fur.

His right hand had found my nipples and was gliding across my chest from one nipple to the other, rubbing, rolling, and gently pinching them until they stood erect under his attention. That wasn't the only thing that was standing erect on me now. My dick was growing, pressing out, wanting to be free. But even more pressing was that inviting well-muscled hairy chest that heaved below me.

I took both of my hands and pressed them to his chest. I hunted through his curly chest hair until I had ferreted out his nipples, and then I first rubbed and then flicked his nipples, which stood up at attention, and then I moved my fingers in swirls through his chest hair and then down to his washboard belly. I returned to working his nipples and chest hair with my left hand, while my right hand followed the trail of hair down beyond his belly, across his beltless jeans, and down to where I could feel his rod pushing at the tight jeans, getting very hard, but unable to stand up. I followed the line of his dick down along the side of his thigh, and began to stroke, in regular downward movements.

The man shuddered underneath me, and having finished unbuttoning my shirt, he took both hands and pulled the shirt up and off my body. He then dove his hands down to the front of my trousers and, struggling slightly, unbuckled my belt, unzipped my pants, pushed both my trousers and briefs down my legs as far as he could, and encircled my dick with both of his hands.

He gasped at the size of me and looked straight into my eyes, his awe and need expressed in that look. His left hand released my cock and his right hand traveled down the length of that rod and moved to exploring my balls. With his left hand, he grabbed my tie, which was still dangling around my neck, and pulled me back down to him, to his lips, which opened, as did mine, and our tongues expressed our mutual need.

My hands went down to his jeans. I unsnapped them and slowly unbuttoned his fly and peeled the jeans down to his knees. He wasn't wearing anything under the jeans, and his cock flew up and out of the jeans like a jack in the box. He pulled his lips away from mine so that he could laugh and grin. I grinned back at him, and we dove back into our lip lock. But only briefly, as I pulled away from him and reached down and unpeeled his tight jeans the rest of the way off his legs. His loafers came off as well, as I pulled the jeans free. He wasn't wearing any socks.

So, now he was completely naked there before me, in all his hairy glory. He was perfectly formed, rock solid muscle. Rock solid muscle covered with black curly hair that swirled around his nipples and down the front of his belly and around his hard cock and then down his muscled thighs and calves as well.

He was candy. I couldn't resist. Throwing his jeans to the side, I put my hands on either side of him as he leaned back on the car truck and brought my mouth down on his left nipple. I suck that ever so briefly and then moved my tongue across his chest and to his other nipple. After giving that a little suction, I started down his heaving chest, using my tongue to wetten and pattern his curly hair. I moved down his pulsating belly and then down and through the pubic hair and groin and along his shaft until I reached the tip, which I slowly took into my mouth. His entire body gave a shudder, and he gasped.

He gasped yet again and again as I took more of him in, until I had him entirely in me up to the root. Taking my hands from the trunk of the car, I moved the left one onto his belly and gently massaged him from belly to nipple to other nipple and back to belly. With my right hand, I encased his balls and began soft pulling and rolling, pulling and rolling. He began to moan, and I could hear him whispering, "Yes, yes, yes. Suck me. Take it all in. Suck me dry."

Then I started pulling away from his dick, bringing my mouth back up toward the head, stopping momentarily and giving the sides of his cock a little teeth and suck. I took my mouth away from his dick and licked around the helmet, where it met the shaft. I then put my mouth just over the helmet and flicked my tongue on his piss slit. His whole body tensed as if the ecstasy was just too much, and I took his entire dick into my mouth again. His moaning increased, and he started moving his dick on his own.

In, out. I allowed him to take over the movement, which got increasing stronger and insistent. He was fucking my face, and I was taking it all in. He started to tense and moved as if to take his cock out of my mouth, but I held him and began to move with him. He let out a little cry, and I felt his cum hit that back of my throat. I swallowed several times as he kept shooting off down my throat.

Then he went limp, and I slowly released his cock and worked my tongue around and down his right thigh. He lifted both of his legs onto my shoulders then. He brought his hands down to the back of my head and ran his fingers through my hair, as I worked my tongue back up his right thigh, briefly took the head of his cock into my mouth again, and gave it a little suck and a flick of the tongue on the piss slit. Then I slid my tongue down the length of his shaft, gave his balls a bit of a suck, and then continued tonguing down to his asshole, which was puckered and tightly closed. I gave that a gentle kiss and a flick of the tongue, which resulted in a spasm from my partner. Then I moved my tongue to his inner left thigh and worked down that and back up. While doing this, I moved my right hand to his asshole and started a gentle circular movement around that and a bit of flicking with the fingers. Eventually, there seemed to be a relaxing in that area, and I returned to it with my tongue.

All the time I was hearing gasps of pleasure from above, and he was winding his hands through my hair furiously and massaging my scalp.

I got to more serious work on his asshole with my tongue, running it around the edge, flicking at the hole, and making brief penetrations. To widen the area of attack, I lifted both of his legs off my shoulders and held them up and out. The hole widened and invited deeper tonguing. The man became helpful by taking control of holding his legs himself, which freed my hands. My left hand went back to cuddling his balls, and I put the fingers of my right hand to work on my current project. I tongued for a brief moment or two and then I started playing with the hole with my fingers, first with just my index finger, and then with a couple of fingers, alternating with a thumb. And then back to the tongue. When I went back to the fingers, I was probing deeper and opening the passage wider. At last he was well lubricated and completely open to me.

I stood up and away from him and pulled my trousers and briefs the rest of the way down my legs and threw them to the side. I took hold of his raised legs and started to move in toward him But at that moment, he lifted his head and spoke in a raspy voice. "No, first let me look at you."

I complied. I stepped back and raised my arms in a "this is me" gesture, and turned completely around.

"God, you're beautiful," he said. "And you're huge. Show it to me, please. Play with it."

So I stood there, back from him, cupped my cock in my hand, and slowly pulled at it and rubbed the head of it for him. My rod stood even straighter out and grew even larger.

The man gave an animal sound and came down in front of me. He covered my cock in kisses and took it in his mouth, working it up and down vigorously. He cupped my buttocks in his hands and kneaded them. His appetite was voracious, and I was afraid I was going to come then and there.

That wasn't in my plan, though, and I reached down and got my arms under his. I raised him up in one movement and slammed him back down onto the trunk of the car. In nearly the same movement, I grabbed his left leg and pushed it up to his shoulders, moving my left hand up until I had him by the calf muscle, holding his leg down nearly parallel to the left side of his head. I looked into his face, and he was laughing. He was enjoying this. With my right hand, I grabbed my cock and guided it to him. I put out a finger and moved along under his now reengorging rod until I could feel his asshole, and I brought the head of my cock to that pulsating orifice. I looked back into his eyes and he was no longer laughing. There was almost a look of fright on his face, but it was quickly replaced by acceptance and desire.

I slowly worked my cock into his anus, a bit at a time, giving him time to adjust . . . at least until I had a good purchase between his butt cheeks. I was in a good four inches now, so I took my right hand away from my cock and raised his right leg up and out. I simultaneously raised his left leg up and out. He was completely open to me, and I held myself in that position. The man fanned his hands across my chest and worked my nipples. His right hand left the nipple and worked its way down along my belly. His head was thrown back and he was reaching for the sky with his eyes.

When one lunge, I buried my cock, up to my root, into his ass. His body lurched, and he cried out to the heavens. Then he faced forward again, entwined a hand in my tie, pulled my lips down to his, and opened to my tongue, which searched his mouth. His other hand went down to the root of my cock, his hand flat against my belly and a finger at each side of my cock, while I worked my cock in and out, in and out. First slowly and then more rapidly, and then I lost all sense of what I was doing and shot off, long and hard, as we both arched our backs and threw our heads back and yelled for joy.

I collapsed on top of him, my dick still up his ass, he brought his legs to rest across my shoulders. I stretched my arms out across and on the trunk surface, and we entwined our fingers. I laid my head on his chest and listened to the beating of his heart.

From that position, I said, "I guess I should ask you your name before I leave."

"Eric," he answered in a low voice. "And yours?"

"I'm Peter."

"I should have guessed."

The Yellow Cadillac

I was feeling quite horny and knew it wouldn't be long before I was hungry too, and I didn't expect another check for two days, so I decided to saunter on over to that county park near the campus that had a lot of out-of-the way parking places and was known in my circles as a pickup spot. With luck, I'd pick me up a short-term sugar daddy with munch and lunch on his mind. I was sitting there on a picnic table near the entrance, contemplating the condition of my fingernails, when a big yellow blur whooshed past me and turned off into a wooded area, well away from the main picnic section.

I didn't think much of that for a couple of minutes, until I heard a somewhat irritated voice wafting a question from over that direction.

"Well, are you here for something special, or are you just wasting the day away? If the first, get your little ass over here."

I unfolded myself from the picnic table and strolled through the fringe of trees to the small parking area. When I got to the clearing, I saw a hippie-type guy leaning up against an old yellow Cadillac convertible. He had a craggy face that looked somewhat familiar, except the dark sunglasses hid quite a bit. He had a light beard and mustache and long silky dirty blond hair that reached below his shoulders. He was wearing a T-shirt with his own face and some writing on the front, and there was a guitar case in his backseat. And then it dawned on me. This was a guitarist from a local band that had gone national and still had tunes on the charts. At least that boded well for a free meal possibility.

I stood there and looked at him, and he sat up against his car and looked me up and down, and I didn't quite know what to say.

"Well, up close, I like what I see," he said in a twangy voice. "So, do you want to come around and get in, and I'll give you a ride?"

"A ride?" I asked lamely.

"Yes, a ride." And then he snickered, having become aware of the double entendre he'd created all on his own.

"Why do we need to ride anywhere? We can just do it here, can't we?" I asked.

"This park's too well known. I know where there's another one nearby that's safer."

"OK, why not," I answered. I bleakly walked around to the passenger side, we both got into his car, and he pulled out of the parking area.

"Drag?" he said, as he offered what obviously was more than a cigarette to me. I politely declined the offer.

"Don't worry, I won't keep you long. Gotta gig myself, but I like, you know, like to get off before I go on stage. And after too, for that matter," and he gave another little laugh. "And on stage whenever possible." This one gave him the giggles. I don't know how high he was already, but I kept very quiet so he could concentrate on his driving.

"Do this often?" he asked, as we drove out into the countryside?

"No. No, I don't," I answered.

"Sweet."

He pulled into another, larger county park and drove into the far end of a secluded parking lot, where he turned around the Cadillac around and backed it up to the edge of a little dell.

"Get on out, and come around to the trunk," he said, as he opened his door, got out. Without fanfare, he stripped his jeans and briefs off and threw them in the back seat beside the guitar case. We both walked around to the trunk of the car. He got me between him and the trunk and turned me so that I was facing him.

"Take off the shirt." I did as he asked, and he ran his hands around my torso.

"Nice," he said, as he took the joint out of his mouth and offered it to me again. I declined once again.

"Oh, well, your loss." Then he unbuckled my belt, unfastened my jeans, pulled down my zipper and took my jeans and briefs down and off my legs.

"Oh my, yes; nice, very nice indeed. Lean back on the trunk, please." I did so, and he asked me to hold his smoldering joint and started tonguing my chest and nipples, his silky hair swishing over my torso, producing a not-unpleasant sensation. He worked his way down to my cock and balls and then pushed my legs up into my chest with both hands and started tonguing my asshole. After a while, he stood, releasing my legs, and spit in his hand a couple of times. He worked this into his cock. He lifted my legs again and spread them wide; walked his pelvis into mine; plugged his hardened, but not particularly large; rod into my asshole; and started a slow pumping movement.

After a while, he asked for the joint back and puffed on that while he worked my ass with his dick. He had one of those cocks that started off unimpressive but lengthened and thickened nicely with the proper attention. He came inside me and then slurped his cock out of me and instructed me to put my clothes back on as he walked around to the driver's side. He asked me where I wanted to be driven, and he dropped me off right at my dorm. Before I got out of the car, though, he put his hand on my arm.

"Here's a twenty for the trick. Best fuck I've had in a week. Thanks a lot." And then he handed me a ticket, which had a red band on the side. "Here's a ticket to my concert here Saturday night. The red band on it will get you into the party afterward. Hope to see you there." And then he just drove off and left me there on the curb.

The twenty saved me from writing home for a quick bridge to my next regular check, and come Saturday, I ran across the ticket to that crazy guy's concert, so I thought why the hell not check out that scene.

The featured band really was quite good. They had a large crowd in the university's soccer stadium, and it was even being filmed for national sale as a video. The rocker who had fucked me had a great, raspy, character-laden voice, and he played a mean guitar. I was also impressed with his backup singer, a statuesque brunette in a halter top and flowing crinkly skirt. She played a hand harp as well as sang. The drummer was an evening's entertainment all himself. Stripped to the waist, and sweating from the exertion, he was a massive, muscle-bound Jamaican, with flowing dreadlocks that flew all around him as he made love to his drums. The spots were on him more than on anyone else that evening.

Caught up in the euphoria of the concert, I decided to see what my special red-banded ticket would get me. I really wanted to see that brunette up close. My wish about that was granted, because when I was ushered back to the rocker's dressing room, she and he were in a lip lock and fondle exercise over on one of a pair of couches that faced each other in an alcove. The room was thick with the smoke from various drugs, and a small crowd was freely handing around a foaming drink in big plastic cups. The rocker saw me and waved me over. I sat across from him and the striking brunette. They offered me a joint, but I turned it down, just as I had the other day. I did take a drink and down it, though, which likely was a mistake.

I think I had been slipped a Mickey of some sort, because it wasn't long before I got groggy and my connection with all that was going on around me kept going in and out. I started to disappear, while the brunette appeared wrapped up in whatever conversation I could muster to avoid telling her I was here because her colleague had had me for a snack a few days earlier. She must have fancied me herself, because after my first blackout, I found her on my sofa, sticking her tongue in my ear and playing with my chest and belly. My shirt had disappeared somewhere. I didn't stay aware long, and the next time I put in an appearance, the brunette was still there, toying with me, but my rocker friend was now on the other side of me.

My pants were down around my ankles, and the rocker and brunette were kissing each other across my body and each of them had a hand on my hardened cock. Surprisingly enough, the room still seemed to be full of boisterous people. Next I was aware; the brunette was sitting astride my lap with my cock up her cunt. Her skirt still flowed around us, but her big tits were flapping against my chest and her long hair was whipping my face. The music, which had a good beat, was louder than the crowd now, and, good musician that she was, she was keeping great time with the beat in her bucking in my lap. As far as I remembered, the rocker was puffing a weed and playing with both the brunette's tits and my nipples as they bounced against each other.

In the next scene that I was awake enough to witness, the brunette was still fucking herself with my hard cock, but now the rocker was under me. I was sitting in his lap, my butt nuzzled into his pelvis and his hard penis up my ass.

I don't know how all of that came to a climax, but it must have satisfied them, because they gave me a ride home in the rocker's yellow Cadillac convertible. For the brief time I was awake, I found that I sort of was sitting sideways on the back seat of the Caddie, at least the back part of my bare butt was in the brunette's

531

lap. She was sitting in regular fashion on the passenger side of the backseat and must have been sitting on a cushion, because we were sitting pretty high up out of the seat. I was leaning back against the side of the car, and she seemed to be playing my torso like her harp and spending a lot of time on my still-hard—or hard once again, as far as I knew—cock and my balls, while I weighed and squeezed her big jugs.

My left leg was hung on the back of the seat and my right leg was draped over into the front seat and my calf rested on the rocker's shoulder. He was driving while trying to suck my toes. What was most interesting, though, was that the Jamaican drummer was kneeling between my spread legs. He had a club of a dick disappearing in my asshole and reappearing from my asshole in a heavy rock rhythm, while he drummed a beat to set his pumping with his fingers on my belly. His beautiful, glistening chocolate chest was heaving and rocking back and forth, and his head was spinning, keeping his long dreadlocks twirling in the air in time with the thrusts of his pelvis into my ass. It was really a wonderful sight for the short time I was aware of it. I'm sort of sorry I missed most of the performance—and especially the climax.

They were nice enough to get me to safety on the front steps of my dorm, where my roommate found me I don't know how long thereafter. By the next morning, the memory of what all had happened was beginning to drain from me, so I sat right down and wrote out as much as I could dredge back up. I wasn't going to do anything with this as far as getting it published or anything, but it was one hell of an experience, and I didn't want to forget it altogether. I bet I would have always remembered that old yellow Cadillac, though.

GTO

"A cherry red convertible? 1965?"

"Yep, six coats of base under six coats of clear."

"And completely rebuilt"

"Yep, all genuine Pontiac GTO parts. A 389 V8 trimotor, four-speed manual, with 3.73 gears. I'm telling you you won't find a honey classic GTO like this anywhere else for much under a hundred grand."

"Can you hold it for three hours? No, two hours. I'm in Ashville. I can be in Knoxville in two hours. Can you just hold it that long? I'll bring cash."

"Well, OK—unless, of course, someone comes in offering more for it than I listed. I doubt that will happen . . . but no one ever can tell, can they?"

"$85,000. If it's what you say it is, I'll go $85,000, if you'll just hold off on any other offers until I get there."

"You'll be needing directions then, I guess. I live just south of the city on . . ."

That started Craig's long journey out of his hermit-like existence. It seems ironic that this is how it started, because developing a love for collecting classic muscle cars was what Craig had chosen to sustain himself in his life of isolation in the first place.

Craig hadn't always been a recluse. He had been an open and friendly guy, with few cares in the world; a good, if not great, job; and comfortable in having come out in his late teens and established that he was who he was and going to get his sexual enjoyment where his inclinations led him. And he had quite an appetite for what men could give him.

Then he'd been so lucky that it drove him into seclusion and a life of distrust. He'd won $20 million in the North Carolina lottery. From that point he'd become one of the most popular guys in Ashville. And suddenly he was everyone's friend and he was the most handsome and studliest guy at the local gay bars.

He now had his pick of men. And it wasn't more than two months until he'd met, Franco, the love of his life, the golf pro at the Grove Park Inn resort, and that Franco had moved into Craig's new mansion out near the Biltmore Estate. Franco was a classic car enthusiast, so Craig started buying classic cars and added a ten-car garage at the rear of his new mansion. Franco liked name-brand tailored suits, so

Craig bought him a closet full of those. Franco liked expensive wines. Craig didn't care much for wine, but he bought Franco a wine cellar full. Franco liked Rolex watches; Craig was happy with his own Timex, but he was happy to buy Franco a Rolex.

Then one afternoon Craig visited the Grove Park Inn golf club unexpectedly and found Franco liking one of the women members too closely and intimately on top of the desk in his pro shop office.

When Franco was gone, along with Craig's trust and self-respect, Craig was left with a collection of classic cars. They at least still pleased him and didn't laugh at him for his naiveté. So, he shut himself off from the world and concentrated his love on his cars.

* * * *

"I'll take it, Mr. Williams. It's exactly what I needed for my collection."

Craig had hightailed it over the Great Smoky Mountains from Ashville to Knoxville in record time and had fallen in love with the GTO convertible the moment he laid eyes on it. He'd been looking for exactly this car for a year; he'd just recently been to a car show in St. Louis where he heard one was for sale—but it never was brought forward there.

He'd had a little trouble finding the place south of Knoxville, although it was a nice enough place when he got there. No more classic cars about, which Craig had found surprising. But the house, a log cabin affair, but of a modern design, was sitting in a nice stand of forested land, and the owner was a young, clean-cut guy. Actually, he was quite good looking, and, from the looks of his muscled body, Craig would have believed he'd built the log cabin himself. He had a nice, friendly smile.

"You can call me Bob, please. Well, I'll sell my baby to you on one condition."

"What's that, Bob. I assure you that I'm offering top dollar."

"And don't I know it," Bob said. And then he laughed. "But I really wasn't lookin' to sell this honey, except for the economy bein' the way it is, ya know. I'll sell it to you, but I'd like to visit it occasionally."

"Well . . . that's not a problem, of course," Craig said. "But isn't it sort of far to come over the mountains just to visit a car?"

"It ain't just a car," Bob said, his voice dripping with shock. "It's a 1965 Pontiac GTO. It's *the* classic muscle car of all time. But it so happens I'm resettling near Ashville anyways—down near Hendersonville."

"Well, then, it's a deal," Craig said. "I have the cash here, and I'll arrange for delivery."

"Oh, that's OK. I'll drive it over to you myself. I can do that now, if you like. I already got folks and a car down in Hendersonville I can use for the return trip."

It was dinnertime when they got back to Ashville, and it would have been impolite for Craig not to invite Bob in for a bite to eat. They hit it off famously over a meal and a couple of beers, while sitting on the back screened porch and watching twilight set over the GTO on the parking apron. They talked a lot about classic cars and car rallies, and Bob mentioned there was one in Winston-Salem the next weekend that Craig should take the GTO to. And Craig noted he hadn't heard about that rally and that he didn't really go to the car rallies—that he didn't go out much at all, just to a car dealer's show every once in a while when he knew a car he wanted was being shown and sold.

"Well, you really should go, Craig," Bob said, turning his winning smile on his new acquaintance. "I had half promised to bring the GTO there myself. I probably would have if it hadn't sold before then. They're gonna be a mite disappointed when it doesn't show up."

"I don't really go—"

"Say, I could come over and drive you there in the GTO."

"Well—"

Bob had said the rally would probably run late and maybe they should spend the night in Winston-Salem. And then he said he'd make the arrangements himself.

But that day, when they got to the motel, there had been some mix-up and there was only one room reserved.

"I'll check the reservation," a concerned, frowning desk clerk said.

"Ah, no bother. We can make do in the one room, can't we, Craig?" prompted Bob. That winning smile again.

"Well, I—"

"And there isn't time to find another one anyway," Bob cut in. "We're pretty late gettin' to the rally as it is. We really—"

"It's not really a problem," the desk clerk said. "We do have—"

"No, no, it's just fine," Bob cut in. "Just let me have the key, and we'll drop our bags and be on our way to the rally."

Craig thoroughly enjoyed the rally. It was the most pleasure he'd had in some time, and he quickly lost the shyness he'd built up from months of seclusion. And he warmed even more to Bob, who was glad-handing everyone and looking good as he sauntered around the maze of cars in his tight, low-rise jeans, a cut-off T he said he wore to keep himself cool and that showed off his washboard abs and a very intriguing belly button, and his brown-leather cowboy boots. He was the star of the show—if you didn't count the cars.

They stopped for dinner and beers at a steak house and didn't make it back to the motel until late.

Bob declared he had to have a shower right there and then and, with a wink, told Craig to choose one of the double beds in the room for himself while Bob was gone.

When he came out of the bathroom, with just a towel around his waist, Bob asked Craig which bed he'd picked, and Craig, having spent the time fighting with the thoughts he was having rather than picking a bed, hazily pointed to one of them.

"That's the nicest one," Bob said, flashing that smile again. Then he dropped his towel and said. "Do you mind if we share it?"

It had been months since Craig had kicked Franco out of the house, and he had lived in isolation from that time, not even going to any of his old haunts down on the strip. He'd been pretty active before that, so he'd be the first one to admit that he was ripe for what Bob was offering.

Bob was built and strong and virile and long lasting. Craig had no idea that a man could be taken in as many positions—not to speak of so frequently in the span of a night—as Bob fucked him on the shared bed that night and over the desk chair in the morning and in the shower as they were getting ready for the hearty breakfast they then both needed.

Bob had talented hands and a sweet mouth on Craig's cock and an ability to bring Craig to the brink and then back and then up again and not nearly as far back as the first time, and then to clamp his lips and teeth down at the base of Craig's glans and to pull and roll Craig's balls at the point of ejaculation in a way that made Craig come in waves of intense pleasure. And then Bob stood between Craig's legs and spread them, and laughed as Craig arched his back and cried out when Bob slowly entered him with an upward curved cock that made love to Craig's channel walls and responded instantaneously to what the intensity of Craig's moans revealed he found most arousing.

Bob arranged to visit the GTO nearly monthly for the next half year, always about a week after Craig was in so much heat over the memory of what Bob could do to him that he rushed, flushed and aroused, to the door to greet Bob on arrival. It was almost like Bob was timing his visits for that rather than for a need to see the GTO.

Craig wasn't totally dumb about what possibly was going on here. It hadn't been just Franco. There'd been various other schemes afoot to part Craig from the portion of the lottery winnings the government hadn't taken in taxes, so that he was already down to something under a third of the original sum. There'd been a lot of people with their hands out, all with plausible stories of needs, and it had taken Craig some time to steel himself against them. The Franco fleecing had just been the most cutting, the most hurtful of all.

Still, Craig was besotted with Bob. On the sixth visit, he met Bob at the door, naked, and ran with him to the GTO, and they fucked in the car as it sat under the crepe myrtles out on the parking apron. Bob's beautiful, young, lithe body was slouched across the backseat, and Craig straddled his pelvis and rode his cock, yodeling his pleasure. Happily, there were no neighbors close enough to see or hear how wanton Craig had become.

"It's a long way from Hendersonville," Bob whispered in Craig's ear when Craig had collapsed across his body in the GTO's backseat.

"Uh, huh," Craig murmured back.

"I wouldn't mind seein' the GTO more often," Bob whispered.

"That would be nice," Craig responded, thinking of more than the car at the moment. More visits by Bob would mean more attention paid to Craig's channel.

"Perhaps it's time for us to start thinkin' of me movin' in here," Bob said. Craig lifted his head and looked into Bob's eyes. All he saw was the friendly, fetching smile he always saw there.

Still, Craig's antennae and defenses clanked into position. He didn't want Bob to sense the sudden chill in the air, so he moved off of him slowly. "That's certainly something we should talk about. Maybe the next time you come. But the reason we got right to it today is that I have someplace I need to go. So, maybe I'll just leave you out here, visiting the GTO this evening, and I'll go get ready for that— and we'll talk more about this the next time you visit."

If Bob noticed the sudden change in climate, he didn't say anything about it. Still, he had to call to try to arrange the next meeting several times before Craig set a date and time.

"I don't see the GTO out here," Bob said on that date when Craig answered the door. "You've always had it parked out here when I came."

"It's not here, Bob," Craig said, not opening the door all of the way, not giving room for Bob to feel like he was being welcomed into the house. "I sold it."

"You sold it?" Bob asked, in astonishment. "You can't just have sold it."

"But I did, Bob. So, you see there's no reason for you to stalk me now. I can't be worth your effort now."

"Stalking? Effort?"

"I've been hurt before, Bob. This lottery money has become a curse. You are too good. I could give up a piece of fluff like Franco. I knew—in my heart—what he was when I bought him. But it's getting to be something else with you, Bob—it is getting too close to my heart. It's best we just cut it off here. The car is gone. There's nothing here for you to visit anymore."

"You think I've been comin' here to visit a fuckin' car, Craig?" Bob burst out. "God, man, I'm here for you."

"No, please, Bob. Don't. I can't—"

But Bob had already pushed his way into the foyer, bringing Craig with him, stripping Craig down as he pushed him to the floor, and fucked him hard and deep on the circular carpet in front of the gracefully curved staircase rising to the second floor. Bob struggled and fought him, but only until Bob had mounted and skewered him, and then he moaned and groaned and slowly gave into the invasion of the curved cock of his channel, his channel walls beginning to undulate in waves of pleasure and his betraying hips taking up the rhythm of the fuck.

After he had come and Bob had ejaculated deep inside him, Bob stood and took Craig up in his arms and carried him up the staircase to the master bedroom and started the fuck all over again.

Hours later, when both were exhausted, Bob moved his lips to Craig's ear and whispered, "I lied about the stalking. I've stalked you from the beginning. I saw you at a car show in St. Louis and knew I wanted you. And I was told you were there lookin' for a 1965 GTO convertible. It took me three months to find one, and then I told dealers you were in contact with that I had one—but that I'd only sell it to you. I paid more for it than you paid me. It's not the GTO I want, or your money—I've got money aplenty—it's you, you dumbass."

They kissed, and Craig smiled at Bob through his tears. "I lied too. I didn't sell the GTO. It's in the last bay in the back of the garage."

Road Romeo

He was half on, half off the short bunk, with one foot leveraged high to one side on a grab handle in the top center of the back wall of the cab, his back arched on two hard pillows, his hands open wide over the driver's naked buttocks, fingers digging into flesh, moaning in long, building moans matching the long slides of the hard ramrod inside him. The driver, clad only in cowboy hat, red bandana neck scarf, tooled-leather boots, and a broad grin, was crouched over the bunk between the young man's legs, giving him what the young guy had been begging for all the way from Lusk, where the Wyoming landscape had gotten so monotonous that the young man could only think about why he'd bummed this ride and had started moaning for them to stop and get into the back.

The young man started to quiver and writhe, and the driver laughed and stepped up his thrusting, quicker, deeper, all the way out, and then the long slide back in and holding there, as the young man gasped and murmured his surrender. The driver only had to wrap his fist around the young man's cock and pump slowly three times and put his thumb over the piss slit of the angry red bulb before white, slick cum was flowing around his thumb and down the young man's engorged dick.

With a little cry and a long moan, all of the tension and cum flowed out of the young man. But the driver drove on. Still deep, rotating his hips, making the young man rise to him, encircling him with his arms, holding him close, burying his face into the driver's hard chest, asking him now for it never to end.

* * * *

"See, wha'd I tell you? Lookee over there."

"Where?" Dwayne asked, moving his eyes to where Stan was motioning, out beyond the dirty glass in the front wall of the truck stop café in the complex where all the guys stopped to gas and feed up when they were driving through Cheyenne, Wyoming, on a long haul.

"Him? He's the guy with that fancy rig out there?" Dwayne asked, his voice incredulous. And his judgment not all that suspect. Walking toward them from the big, shiny burgundy rig with the extra-deep sleeper behind the cab was a rangy-looking cowboy. And not a new one either—probably no younger than his early forties. He wasn't too tall and certainly wasn't too fat. In fact he looked a little gaunt, all angles, and leathery tan, and wrinkles. Much like most of the rig drivers up here in the badlands of the upper West—well-worn jeans, a faded plaid flannel shirt, tooled-leather boots, a weather-beaten black ten-gallon hat, and a red bandana around his neck. But he walked tall, and his step was jaunty.

"Yep, him," Stan answered.

"And you say you can always tell when he's goin' through?" Dwayne continued.

"Yep. It's them young guys over there, just as I told yer."

Dwayne and Stan swiveled to take in the three young guys sitting together at a table set down not far from the doorway, between the café and convenience store section. Definitely out of place here. Not truckers by any means. Too young and preppy and "from money" looking. College guys just pulling over for a cup of coffee, Dwayne had surmised. But then he'd agreed with Stan that this wasn't the place that three college guys would pull over to on this stretch of road. There were fast food joints nearby—not to mention a Starbucks nearly across the road.

"Them guys?" Dwayne repeated.

"Yep. I've noticed it before. This is the third time this year," Stan said, turning away from the boys and watching the rig driver approach the café. "He don't come in here that often—I see him maybe once a month, maybe not as often. But I do short hauls, so I'm in here more than I'm not. But I noticed the last three times. Two, three guys like that come in here and order coffee and watch the door, and not long after, his rig drives up and here he comes just a struttin' in the door, pretty as you please."

"Gotta be drugs," Dwayne said.

"Yep, that's what I figure too," Stan said, very pleased with himself—and with Dwayne too.

The rig driver had reached the door and entered the café and, after taking one long look at the young guys at the front table, turned and brushed past Stan and Dwayne's table on the way to one nearer the back.

"Afternoon, Stan," he muttered as he passed the table. He raised the tip of his hat, although he didn't actually look straight at either Stan or Dwayne, and he didn't slow down his walk. There was no hint he was going to ask if they wanted him to sit at their table.

"Same ta yer, Ralph," Stan answered.

Dwayne started to say something, but Stan shushed him, waiting for the rig driver to get to another table and settle. When he looked up, he was looking at the young men up front—and they were looking at him. Another young man, moving slowly and a little bowlegged, a sloppy grin on his face, entered the café, looked around, and moved to the table where the other three young guys were already sitting. They put their heads together and were whispering across their table.

"You know him?" Dwayne asked in a lowered voice. "You called him Ralph."

"Yep, we've met in passin'," Stan said. "I'd heard some other truckers snigger and refer to him as the Road Romeo once, and I didn't know what that meant. So I asked him. He said they must have been makin' a joke about his love for truckin', but then he told me his name was Ralph."

"Anything else? Did you find out anything else about him?"

"Not much. Just that he does the Cheyenne to Billings to Rapid City route, but only now and again, when he gets the hankering. He didn't say—others have—but he didn't say either way that it's more of a hobby with him. That he's got a spread of his own down near Denver and does right well out of it. I did ask him why he trucks, and he just said there were some nice perks involved. I don't know what to think."

"The Cheyenne to Billings to Rapid City route?" Dwayne asked. And then he snorted. "That's got to be the most monotonous route on God's brown earth."

"Yeah, but someone's gotta do it," Stan said. "Them folks need things trucked in too. God knows they don't have much of anything worthwhile just lying around to pick off a tree."

"Yeah, but look at the rig out there," Dwayne said. "That's the goddamnest nicest rig I've ever seen. What do you suppose that set him back?"

"More than a dozen roundtrips from Cheyenne to Billings and Rapid City a year, that's for sure," Stan said. "A man could drive that route for a lifetime and not pay for a nice rig like that. Look at the sleeper cab. You ever seen one that big?"

"Nope, I haven't."

Their discussion at that point was arrested by noticing not only that the last young guy to enter the café was now gone, but also that one of the other guys got up and left right after he did. And then one of the two guys who were left was moving toward the back of the café, like he was going to the men's room or something. But when he got to Ralph the trucker's table, he abruptly sat down and started whispering to the trucker. The trucker was smiling a tight little smile and nodding his head from time to time and answering in monosyllables.

"Drugs. Gotta be drugs," Dwayne turned to Stan and whispered.

"That's how I got it pegged," Stan whispered back.

The young man was standing up from Ralph the trucker's table now and as he moved back toward the front, the other young guy, smaller than the first, with sandy-blond hair, was walking to the trucker's table and sat down and started whispering, just like the first one had.

"But you say he maybe has a big spread down near Denver of his own? Like maybe he's rollin' in money and just does this as a hobby?" Dwayne sounded more than a little dubious when he was saying this. "Course you could make a lot of money sellin' drugs," he continued.

They both sat there, finishing up their coffee, each already projecting out to where they were going next—Stan to deliver a washer over on Elm and Dwayne to haul ass down to Denver with a load of hogs.

There was movement at Ralph's table again, and Dwayne and Stan looked up. Both Ralph the trucker and the sandy-blond young guy were standing now. Ralph had one hand on the arm of the young guy and he was pointing to him with the hand of the other. They were both looking to the front. The other young guy sitting up there, stood, looking disappointed, and turned and walked out of the café. Then Ralph and the young guy sat back down at the table.

"Drugs, gotta be drugs," Dwayne muttered.

"That's what I think," Stan agreed.

541

Having now finished their own coffee and big-gulp breakfasts, Stan stood up and moved to the cash register over in the convenience store area and Dwayne went back to the men's room.

When they returned, Ralph, the sandy-blond young man—and Ralph's fancy burgundy rig with the really big sleeper behind the cab—were gone.

* * * *

The big burgundy rig was parked at the back of the lot at the truck rest area off Interstate 80 near Rock Springs, Wyoming. The sleeper behind the cab was much too big and stable to be rocking back and forth, but if you walked up real close to the door to the sleeper, you would have heard the noise. The sandy-blond college kid, who had come all of the way from Fort Collins for this opportunity, was a real screamer.

The young man was kneeling on the side of the short bunk, thighs held out wide, fists bunching up folds of the spread on the bunk, and crying out his love for the long, thick cock churning inside his channel—at least he was very vocal until Ralph, the Road Romeo, who was crouched over his back from behind, pulled the young man's face around to the side with a hand under his chin and took full possession of the sandy-blond's lips with his own.

Ralph, the Road Romeo, wearing only a black, weather-beaten cowboy hat, a red bandana, and tooled-leather boots, was taking long, slow slides inside the youth's channel, making him feel every inch of the talented monster cock that young men gathered from all over the region to enjoy and schemed and networked to be in the right place at the right time to petition to get the fucks of their lives.

The young man jerked his face away from the Road Romeo and arched his back and yodeled to the low ceiling of the sleeper cab as he came on the bedspread in a prodigious ejaculation such as he had never experienced before.

And then he started whimpering and panting and groaning as the Road Romeo laughed and just continued his slow pumping deep inside the youth, knowing that the combination of the youth's recuperation powers and his own stamina meant the sandy-blond young man from Fort Collins wasn't yet even half way through the fuck he'd come so far to get.

* * * *

"How long did you say you've been driving this route?"

"Twelve years," answered Ralph. He blew into his coffee to stir up the steam to cool it down, but he was hunched over the table and palming the cup in both of his hands to try to stay warm.

"Twelve years," the other trucker said and then he whistled.

They both sat there for a few minutes, looking through the glass window of the truck stop café outside Billings, Montana, at the ground frost that wouldn't burn off for another hour or two, certainly not until after the sun had come up.

"Nice rig," the trucker said, nodding his chin toward Ralph's shiny, burgundy rig with the extra large sleeper behind the cab that was strung out on the other side of the concrete pad beyond the line of gas pumps.

542

"Thanks. I like it," Ralph answered.

"But, man, twelve years on the Cheyenne to Billings to Rapid City route," the other trucker said. "How can you take it? Some of the most monotonous miles on earth, and lonely. God, is it lonely out there on the road."

"Well, I have company sometimes on the road," Ralph answered. "And then there's the perks; they make it worthwhile. And I only get on the road when I get a hankering to get off the ranch. Looking for something different."

"Perks?" the other trucker said. He just shook his head when Ralph didn't answer.

Ralph was busy eying the door. A young man, his breath still misting in front of his face as he came in from the cold, had entered the truck stop café and stood there a minute, surveying the room. His eyes lit on Ralph and he smiled. And Ralph smiled back.

"Speaking of perks," the other trucker continued. "I heard you called the Road Romeo the other day. You know of some nice chickies around these parts? Always seemed so dry and dull around here to me."

Ralph just smiled. But he wasn't smiling at the other trucker; he was smiling at one of his perks.

Virgins

Virgins

"Ahhh, Professor Caldwell. That poetry. It's so moving. I had no idea—"

"Hush, Lawrence. Live the moment. How does this make you feel?"

"It's like nothing I've felt before. But should we . . . should you . . . ? I've never—"

"No words now, Lawrence. We let the Romantic writers speak our words for us. They do it so well. This poem from Keats. Did it not make you feel alive—fully alive?"

"Yes, but your hand . . ."

Actually, it was two hands. The young man didn't seem to notice the one under his shirt at his nipples. All of his senses were focused on the hand Hunter Caldwell had in his lap making slow motions over something inside the material of the young man's trousers that was certainly coming to life at the attention.

"Ahhhh, Professor Caldwell."

The silence—other than the crackling fire in the fireplace—was so deadening that the sound of a zipper being pulled clanged like a warning bell.

But the young man was too far gone for this already. Hunter Caldwell had prepared him well. He was one of three in Caldwell's Romantic Poet's course at the college that semester that he had identified as ripe for the plucking and still virginal.

Virginal was important to Caldwell. That's what got him off. That first ejaculation from the young men after Caldwell's penetration and plowing inside their virginal holes. That's all he wanted from them. After that they were of no use to him—they no longer aroused him.

Caldwell had chosen Lawrence first because he both seemed the neediest of the three and the least desirable conquest. He was on the pudgy side and still pimply, but he had what could be called a "pretty" face and nice brown cow eyes—eyes that had followed every move Caldwell made in front of the class. Worshipping eyes. Easy-make eyes.

And there was little doubt he was virginal. He wasn't all that bright, although the Romantic Poets seemed to have set off a whole new world for him. Caldwell intended to widen that world significantly this evening.

The young man had nearly melted at the invitation to dinner at the professor's house. The gourmet meal had set the stage, and the fireplace and the overstuffed leather love seat set directly in front of it and the book of Keats had been all Caldwell had needed.

The young man hadn't even noticed the hands starting to work on him, as engrossed as he was in Caldwell's rich reading from Keats and the port wine that was making him mellow and taking the edge off his already-susceptible and fully innocent response to the seduction.

"Oh, Professor Caldwell. Oh, oh, ohhhh."

Caldwell was on his knees between the youth's spread thighs and had his lips over the young man's throbbing cock, pushing the foreskin back and flicking at the piss slit with his tongue.

"Oh, oh, ahhhhhhh!"

Surprised, Caldwell jerked his lips back, although his hand was still wrapped around the base of the engorged cock and gently stroking it.

Cum burbled up from the piss slit and dribbled down to Caldwell's fist.

Caldwell turned his head to hide his disgust and disappointment. This sometimes happened. This was the downside of taking them for their first journey. They sometimes came almost immediately.

"I'm sorry, professor. It was just so, so . . ."

"Yes, that's quite all right Lawrence. Nothing to be ashamed of either. All of the Romance poets experienced life to the fullest like this. This will enhance your studies. I was glad to be able to enhance your appreciation for the subject."

Caldwell was standing now, and bustling around and picking up half-empty wine glasses and clattering off toward the kitchen. He was finished with this one. There had been a second of thrill—taking for the first time again—but only for a second with this one. He had greater hopes for the others this semester.

Lawrence was standing now and zipping himself up. "Sorry, professor, sorry. But this has been such an experience. I'd like to—"

"Yes, yes, we must do this again. I think you can find your own way out, can you?"

They both knew they would not be doing this again. But in his own way, Lawrence had gotten more out of this experience than Hunter Caldwell had—much to the chagrin of Caldwell, who always wanted the best and freshest of everything.

* * * *

Floating along green-leafed tunnel on the river of life
world opprobrium casting off in rivulets in our wake

Hunter Caldwell stopped reading and cast an eye on young Joshua at the back of the scull, pulling on the oars, guiding the boat into the eddy in the river beyond the dipping branches of a willow tree. Caldwell knew the cove very well. Completely deserted, its banks lined by a deep stand of closely spaced trees and an overabundance of ferns and other lush plantings undergirding the broad oak branches and hanging Spanish moss.

A very romantic spot.

"I love to hear your voice reading this poetry," professor, Joshua whispered reverently as they entered their own private grotto.

548

Joshua's shirt was off, as he'd solely taken on the job of paddling them down the small river, dark and lush under a canopy of trees, whose branches met across the top, creating very much a private, romantic tunnel effect. Caldwell had chosen the poetry just for this reason.

Caldwell was more pleased with Joshua than he had thought he would be. He was thin, yes, but his musculature was good. He was beautifully formed. Always the shy, thin, shortest one in the class. The one who would never raise his arm to answer, but always would have the answer if challenged. Perhaps what had taken away from the first impressions were the eyeglasses he wore in class. Practically bottle glass with big, heavy lenses, the beauty of Joshua's face was only apparent now when Joshua had taken his glasses off and put them away in the short sprinkling they had just gone through. Joshua's wet shorts clung to his legs, and Caldwell longed to reach out and trace the promising length of the youth.

The combination of the wine, and the atmosphere of the river, and Caldwell's reading of the poetry, with each poem he read studiously becoming more and more explicit, had put the young man into the mood Caldwell wanted him in. Caldwell saw that Joshua was hard through his clinging shorts. Nearly as hard as Caldwell himself was.

They had arrived in Caldwell's special place along the river. He liked to think of it as his grotto of deflowering. How many young men had lost their virginity to him here, in the soft-swirling water between banks of ferns and the weeping willow tree? He had lost count himself.

"You read the lines to me now, Joshua. Here, give me those paddles and lay back in the stern and rest. Yes, stretch your legs. Go ahead you can run your legs along each side of the gunwales. That will be fine. But you're soaked. Let's take these off and lay them over the bench at the bow to dry. Oh, no worry, it's just you and me. No one will see us here. We're in our own world. We'll just let the rivulets of opprobrium drift away, shall we? Just as the poem said."

The young student was weakened with wine and the effort to paddle them here—and the romantic mood of river and the soothing, rich voice of his professor, who had been reading him suggestive and arousing poetry as they paddled away from the college pier and into the world of the enchanting river.

And besides, he wanted this. He had been in love with Professor Caldwell since the beginning of the semester. And he was sure that the professor had shown interest in him. Of course, he'd never done it with another man—or with a woman either, truth be known—but the poetry of the Romantic poets that the professor had assigned to the class to read had opened a whole new world for him—as had the guided study of the pasts of the poets—guided by Professor Caldwell.

Thus, although he was trembling—and scandalized, in a titillating way—when the professor pulled his wet shorts off him and laid them over the bench he'd been sitting on in the bow, Joshua raised no objection, gave no alarm.

"Read the next lines to me Joshua," Caldwell said as he moved to the bench in the center of the boat, placing him between the legs Joshua now had stretched along the gunwales on either side of Caldwell's torso. Joshua's cock was standing nearly erect.

Neither man mentioned the compromising position, though—Joshua trying to pretend it didn't exist; Caldwell not about to upset the balance.

Joshua took the book from Caldwell and read:

Piercing rapier, boat's bow and lover's gift, slicing like a knife.
Being all, giving all for discovery's sake.

As he finished the line, he let out a gasp. No longer able to pretend. "Professor. I don't . . . I've never—"

"Shush, Joshua. It's all right. It's all as it should be. And it's very private here. Just lay back now and close your eyes and take in the moment. Experience it all, fully, like the Romantic poets did."

Caldwell had one hand cupping Joshua's balls and the other wrapped around his cock and rhythmically, but tentatively, gently, squeezing and releasing.

Joshua, now laying full back, legs spread along the gunwales, hands dipped in the water on either side of the boat, eyes closed, body trembling all over. A deep moan, with a catch of breath at the end. "Professor. We must stop. I'm not—"

"The Romantic poets didn't deny any sensation that would give wings to their poetry. You've told me you want to be a poet. To be so, you must be totally free. You must experience it all. Listen to those words again, Joshua: 'Piercing rapier, slicing like a knife'; 'gift of the lover'; 'giving all—experiencing all, being open to all—for discovery sake.' Food for the muses, Joshua. You know what the poet was speaking of. You can feel it. Tell me you can feel it."

"Yes, yes, I feel it," Joshua whispered through another moan. "But, oh, ohhh, not—"

"Tell me what the poet was describing, Joshua."

"I don't—"

"Yes you do, Joshua. You do know. I've taught you to interpret poetry—to open it up, reveal it."

And here Joshua gasped because Caldwell was pushing back his foreskin and lightly rubbing the young man's glans with lubed fingers.

"The poet was talking of love, Joshua. Of making love—to another man."

The hand cupping Joshua's balls had moved farther down and under. There were two fingers at the rim to his channel, and Joshua was shuddering and his hands had gone to the professor's shoulders, the professor being hunched over his torso now. At first trying weakly to push the shoulders away, but as Caldwell's lubed fingers, prepared while Joshua was laying back, eyes closed, entered the channel far enough for Caldwell to find the prostate, the hands on Caldwell's shoulder no longer were pushing; they were gripping hard with fingers pressed into skin and pulling Caldwell to him. Obligingly, Caldwell's face dipped down, and he took one of the Joshua's nipples in his mouth and rolled it between his teeth.

Joshua gasped then, trying to gather his resolve to resist and he pushed on Caldwell's shoulders with his hands.

Caldwell raised his mouth from Joshua's nipple but not his hands from Joshua's cock or his channel and smiled down into his young student's eyes. What he saw was victory. It was so achingly obvious that the young man had never experienced this before—that he was virgin—just as it was evident that Caldwell was going to win this battle of seduction.

"Do you know how the poem concludes, Joshua?"

"No, tell me," Joshua said with a breathy squeak.

Sunbursts, filling possession, completion with a sigh,
New worlds opened to my lover and I.

"New worlds. That's what I have to offer you, Joshua. On the other side is so much more understanding and creative thought—so many more possibilities and rhymes will open to you. Don't you feel the rhythm already? Don't you feel part of the rhythm?"

And in this, Caldwell wasn't exaggerating. He was rhythmically stroking Joshua's cock and finger fucking him, and Joshua was moving his hips in rhythm with Caldwell's attentions. And he was gasping each time the tip of Caldwell's middle finger rubbed across his prostate.

But then Caldwell stopped and withdrew his hands and ran them slowly up Joshua's torso and covered the young man's breasts and slowly began tweaking his nipples.

"It that all?" Joshua asked. "Should we go back now?" His voice sounded both hopeful and slightly disappointed.

"It's not all if you want to cross over into the possibility of being a real poet, Joshua. It's in the poem. 'New Worlds opened'; 'my lover's rapier'; 'full possession.' To live fully, to appreciate fully, to be able to create fully, you must experience it all."

"Full possession?" Joshua asked. It was almost a whimper. Almost a "say it isn't so" prayer.

"Yes. Lover's rapier. Full possession," Caldwell answered in a low voice, taking one of Joshua's hands and placing it on his own cock that he had released some time ago.

"Oh, God, oh god," Joshua whimpered.

"Your choice, Joshua. If you want to experience it all, I can help you. And I'll be gentle." He was stroking Joshua's lower belly with his free hand, the other one still holding Joshua's hand to his engorged cock. "If you don't, you'll never make it across that river of understanding and full experience."

Joshua was trembling and shuddering, undecided, tempted, scared, aroused.

Caldwell reached into the pocket of his shorts and took out a condom. "Your choice, Joshua. You can come of age and join the enlightened and fully understand the world of the Romance poets now. Or you can wait and wonder and pine. I won't force you. If you want to take that step, you will have to put this on me yourself."

Caldwell split open the packet and held the disk up to where the dappled sunlight caught it so that it glittered. Joshua's eyes were big. He reached out, but only half way. Caldwell had to guide the young man's hands to it and then help him roll it onto Caldwell's cock.

Caldwell then went down on his knees between Joshua's legs in the stern of the boat. His lips went to Joshua's nipples and Joshua was already breathing heavily and groaning. The bulb of Caldwell's cock just pressing into the rim, Joshua began to voice second thoughts, but Caldwell raised his mouth to the younger man's and fully possessed it, muffling the grunts and groans of the initial tight entry.

As Caldwell's cockhead breached Joshua's sphincter, the younger man tore his mouth away from Caldwell's and arched his back, his head bending back to where his long hair dipped into the slowly swirling water and let out a cry of first taking.

Caldwell thrilled at that moment. That was the very moment he lived for. His excitement aroused him to the heights, and he engorged further and relentlessly pushed in. Joshua started to fight him, writhing and arms flailing and cries of "too big," "too painful," "too much" pouring out of him.

To hold the youth still, Caldwell laced his stronger arms under the young man's pits and then bent his forearms back across Joshua's chest and locked his fists, effectively immobilizing the young man's hands from reaching Caldwell's body.

He just let the young man cry out at the taking. That's what Caldwell wanted to hear. He wanted that to go on forever. But it didn't. As Caldwell bottomed and started to create a rhythm of the fuck and Joshua's channel began to adjust to the taking, the cries slowly merged into grunts and groans and then moans and sighs and Joshua was finding the rhythm as well. It wasn't long before Joshua ejaculated up Caldwell's belly and went almost completely dormant except for the sighing.

Caldwell pulled out of him almost immediately. He had already ejaculated—back when Joshua was at the height of his crying out—when the youth had effectively lost his virginity. It was a secondary thrill to feel the young man come in his arms for the first time. But then Caldwell went numb.

It was over. He pulled away from Joshua and sat back on the bench at the bow, moving Joshua's only slightly dryer briefs and shorts to the middle bench. Then he looked down on the naked youth with something akin to disinterest.

Joshua cooled down by sighing and running his hands over his body and fondling a cock that was spent—but with his youth—could quickly come back to life.

"Read me some more, professor," he murmured. "Read me some more and then make love to me again." His eyes were glistening. He felt fully enlightened. Words were spinning in his head that he knew would float to the ground in the form of a memorable poem.

"I don't think so. It's getting late," Professor Caldwell said tightly. "And I think it might rain again. Paddle us back up to the college now, Joshua, if you please."

* * * *

Caldwell had saved Brandon for last. He was the real student. His poetry already excelled—and he knew it. Caldwell was sure that he'd only signed up for the class because he wanted Caldwell to be his first—to be the one who took his virginity.

Caldwell was sure that Brandon knew the worth of his virginity, where most of the other men he took it from didn't—that Brandon valued it highly and was choosing who would get it. This made Caldwell feel both grateful and privileged. Brandon was discriminating. He knew that Caldwell was the best one to take him beyond the beaded curtain.

Thus, Brandon was even more special than anyone else Caldwell had mentored—which is what he called fucking a young man's virginity away. He really had the potential to be a poet. A good first fucking would do him and the pantheon of poetry a world of good. And Caldwell would have been the moving force behind the unleashing of this talent. It made his mission in life—the collection of as many male cherries as possible—worthwhile.

Brandon even looked the part. He out Byroned Lord Byron. Curly golden locks like an angel's halo; dreamy, hooded eyes that were a vortex into his pure soul; thick, sensuous lips. His smile lit up the universe; his body was that of Apollo. His voice was rich and deep with emotion. The young man was perfection itself.

Caldwell chose a secluded spot along the banks of the river. A gourmet lunch, excellent wine, a sunny spot encouraging an al fresco swim in the river. A private embankment for seduction and fucking.

He was laying on his back on the blanket, the book of poetry open above him—placed between his eyes and the dazzling sun.

Brandon was sitting beside him, making a chain of daisies he had lazily selected and gathered from where he sat, cross-legged. His shirt was neatly folded on the grass beside him and he had removed his shoes and socks.

Caldwell hadn't thought of the sexiness of a man's foot, but as he read, he glanced down at Brandon's feet. They were beautiful. Tanned, like his magnificent torso. The toes long and plump at the end. The nails perfect, as if the young man had them manicured. The curve of his instep tantalized Caldwell, and he felt the urge to put his lips to it. He was feeling sensations he'd never felt before.

He wondered what it would be like to fuck a young man for the second time. Whether he could capture the thrill of the first taking. If it could be done with anyone, Caldwell thought it might be possible with young Brandon.

Floating along green-leafed tunnel on the river of life
World opprobrium casting off in rivulets in our wake
Piercing rapier, boat's bow and lover's gift, slicing like a knife.
Being all, giving all for discovery's sake.

"You make it sound beautiful, professor . . . and inviting."

"Is he flirting with me, giving me signals," Caldwell thought. And a chill of anticipation was running up his spine. The young god was ripe for the picking, Caldwell could see. Brandon's shorts were tented and his voice was thick from the wine and the ambiance.

It was about time to suggest a swim in the river.

Brandon gently took the book from Caldwell's hands and read the last line of the poem in a voice even more refined, and sensuous, and arousing than Caldwell was capable of doing.

Sunbursts, filling possession, completion with a sigh,
New worlds opened to my lover and I.

"'New worlds opened,' 'lover's rapier,'" Brandon intoned slowly, "'Full possession.' This could not have been written for a woman. I think it's true what you noted in class, Professor Caldwell. I think all of the great men Romantic poets must have had men lovers as well as women. Isn't that interesting?"

Before Caldwell could respond, though, Brandon had stood and was speaking again. "It's hot. I feel like a swim. Join me?"

Caldwell whispered an affirmative and than took in a hard breath as Brandon stripped down to nothing and strode toward the river and neatly dived in.

Caldwell was struck by the open innocence of it all. The beauty of the youth's body and the innocence with which he just tossed off his clothing and entered the water. Caldwell followed, and Brandon playfully scooped water at him and dove in and swam circles around the professor and pulled his feet out from under him.

And then he was out of the water and running, naked, and dripping and magnificent, up the bank and plopping down full length on the blanket on his back. Caldwell focused on the young man's half erection as he more slowly moved out of the water and up the river bank.

Caldwell sat down on the blanket next to Brandon. He picked up the daisy chain Brandon had made and tentatively ran it across Brandon's chest and belly and down, lassoing the young man's half erection with it—testing Brandon. But Brandon didn't react. All open innocence, an innocence Caldwell found disarming and totally arousing.

Brandon picked up the book of poetry and began to read.

With the kiss of the lover, the rosebud opens, petal upon petal.
The sword of the lover quivers, quickens, trembling to the scent of the chase.

Caldwell reached down and gently took Brandon's staff in his hand.
The young man barely seemed to notice.

Opening lips of ruby red o'er the marble obelisk, hard as metal.
My lover, the trembling Godhead encase.

The young man seemingly lost in the poetry, not fully aware of the merging of the fantasy with reality, merely moaned a deep moan as Caldwell's lips enclosed over his majestic tool and drank of his honeyed precum.

"Yes," murmured Caldwell, careful as he could be not to burst the magic moment. "All of the major Romantic poets knew men as well as women. It enriched everything they wrote after they had moved to this level, had gained this added experience. Are you willing to—"

"Yes, professor . . . but possibly not in quite the way you envision."

With lightning speed, Brandon encased Caldwell with his arms and brought him to ground on the blanket. He flipped the older professor over onto his belly. And before Caldwell could guess what was happening to him, the younger, stronger man had gotten his arms into an incapacitating full Nelson, and his cock was rubbing up and down across Caldwell's hole.

"No. This isn't the way it's supposed to . . . I've never . . . I don't," Caldwell cried out. But his cry was even louder and more belabored, as Brandon's cock thrust inside his channel.

Caldwell cried out his indignation and then his fury and then his pain at the taking of his channel—an experience he never before had had himself—and then his groaning and grunting as his innermost channel walls were breached and caressed and then his ecstasy as the rhythm of the deep fuck commenced and his begging for release and then for more and deeper and faster and harder—until exhausted and filled with Brandon's cum, he collapsed—only to be brought to his knees and the young, vigorous student beginning the rhythm of the deep fuck a second time—to Caldwell's consternation and then his melting as he realized that he couldn't get enough.

"You've never been fucked like that before, have you, professor?" Brandon murmured in Caldwell's ear as, still fully encased, and stretched out on the back of the older man on the blanket, he nibbled at his ear.

"No, never like that—never at all. This was my first."

"Well, sorry to disappoint you, professor. But you weren't my first. Not by a long shot. So I thought we'd best do it like this."

"Can you . . . can you . . . do it again?" Caldwell whimpered.

"Oh, no, I don't think so. The first time is always the best, don't you think? After that, it's just a tedious biological act."

Voyeur

Glass Canyon Connection

My boss, Sid Jamison, had told me that tonight was one of "those" nights and that I was to be in his office at precisely 8:15. Such a summons was not that unusual; Jamison had been fucking me regularly for a couple of months on the desk top in his office after hours. I didn't mind this, because he was really hot and not all that old and he was being really good to me professionally. But I thought it a little strange that he'd given a precise time I should be there.

We worked in one of those all-glass downtown high-rises, where land was at such a premium that the office buildings faced each other closely across narrow canyons bottomed by busy streets. Jamison's office was on the eighteenth floor, and he got off on topping me in front of floor-to-ceiling glass in the early evening hours while it was still light and while the traffic noise from below was still at a high level. But at 8:15 this time of year, it would be darker out than when we usually fucked in his office. Not a problem for me, because I hadn't planned anything that evening, but it meant I had to stay around in the office a little longer than usual.

I showed up to his office early and he kept me up against the wall, just inside the door, for several minutes, while he got us all hot and bothered with his roaming hands and lips. We undressed each other there and then rubbed chests, bellies, and cocks until we were both panting and hard for each other. He went down on me there, my back up against the wall and him kneeling between my thighs. He was really good with his tongue and teeth and the soft inner sides of his cheeks, not to mention his fingers at my balls and back door, and it wasn't long until I'd creamed his tonsils and nearly collapsed on top of him, with my knees buckling at the intensity of the cocksucking.

It was almost precisely 8:30 when Jamison stood and led me over to his desk. I couldn't have asked for a more studly guy bossing me around. I took my usual stance on the desk top: on my back; butt at the edge of the desk, legs open wide, held by my hands: my back to those floor-to-ceiling glass windows. I was waiting, all atremble, as usual, for those lips at my ass, followed by the cool feel of the KY, and then by the invigorating drive of that seven-inch, very thick cock that I'd come to love plowing my canal.

But tonight, to my surprise, Jamison told me to come down off the desk and turn around, stand on the floor, feet wide apart and lay my chest on the desk top. I did as he asked—he, after all, was the boss. And as he was pressing his face into my crack, successfully finding my puckered hole, and giving that attention with his lips and tongue, I rested my cheek on the desk blotter and sighed and moaned for him, assuring him that I was enjoying his attentions to me. His face came away and his teeth gave my butt cheeks a little nip here and there, causing me to writhe a bit, rubbing my rehardening dick on the leather surface of Jamison's executive desk. I gave a little lurch and yelp and instinctively grabbed for the corners of the desk with my hands and jerked my head up as I felt the first of his KY-slathered fingers enter me and begin to probe.

When my head came up, my eyes went to the window, and, instinctively, to the glass office tower immediately across the narrow street canyon from our own glass office tower. Few lights were on over there, so it wasn't hard for me to zero in on a brightly lit office in the mirroring building just about opposite from ours and two stories higher. That particular window was arresting, because there was a young, well-cut man leaning against that window, looking out, seemingly looking directly at me. The most arresting aspect of that young man was that he was stark naked, his hands spread out wide and supporting him against the window, his forehead plastered to the window, his legs out at a wide stance—and another naked, bulky and hirsute, but not exactly fat, man kneeling behind him, his face buried in the young man's butt, and his arms around the young man's legs, hands tightly holding the young man's thighs.

I could clearly see the young man's face, and his facial expression at having his ass eaten out was surely, I thought, no less pleasure driven than my own was at what Jamison was doing at my back door.

As I watched, the hairy man across the divide stood. I saw his hand glide back around the young man's hips, and I saw the young man lurch as the hairy man forced fingers into his asshole. I knew that was what he was doing, because at the same time, the second of Jamison's fingers forced its way into my ass, and I also lurched. The hairy man brought his body in close behind that of the young man, and his lips went to the hollow of the young man's neck. They both seemed to have their eyes glued on me. I felt Jamison lower his chest closely on my shoulder blades, his fingers still in my asshole, and he kissed and nuzzled the hollow of my neck. I licked my lips and moaned, not sure whether I was doing this on my own or suggestively, because the young man across the glass canyon was doing the same.

Jamison came up off my back; the hairy man pulled away from the young man's back. Jamison clutched my hips; the hairy many clutched the young man's hips. In one swift, painful movement, Jamison entered me with his seven thick inches and plowed up to the root. I howled to the ceiling in pain and surprise, and grabbed back at him with my hands, trying instinctively to pull him off me. But my eyes were glued to the window, where the hairy man had impaled the young man in one swift movement and the young man had lifted his head and howled to the ceiling and clutched back at the hands imprisoning his hips with his own hands.

The young man's eyes were linked to mine, beseeching me for help, trying to convey his pain and suffering at having been possessed so fully and brutally. But I couldn't help him; I was trying to seek the same solace from him. Mouths open in a screams that almost made the separating window glass between us reverberate, the young man and I shared our debauching and Jamison stroked my ass with his huge tool swiftly and deeply and the hairy man stroked the ass of his prisoner equally swiftly and deeply. All four of us were in a quartet of open mouths, cries of passion, and slitted eyes.

Jamison and the hairy man were keeping the same rhythm and tempo, almost as if they were doing so on purpose, and I knew exactly the point at which my pain was overridden by the pleasure of this wild fuck because my emotions were being exactly mirrored in the eyes of that young man across the glass canyon divide. Everything was all right now. No, more than all right—ecstasy. I was having the hot ride of my life, and it was only being enhanced because I saw that my young counterpart was also having the hot ride of his life. I writhed and moaned and slammed my hips back to meet each thrust of Jamison, just as the young man was doing to his hairy attacker.

And I knew exactly when Jamison would release and flood my insides with his rich cream because I could see the point of release in the eyes of the hairy man. And my mouth joined that of the young man in my cry of joy at being filled so fully and so deeply.

Jamison collapsed onto my back, and the hairy man collapsed against the young man onto the window across the canyon. The hairy man lifted a hand to the young man's cheek and turned his face fully to the window, making the young man's eyes latch onto mine for a last time. Jamison was doing the same to me, and I could see the hairy man whispering in his young lover's ear just as Jamison whispered in mine.

"See that man over there, the hairy one?" Jamison whispered. "That's my pal Ned Treadwell. He and I planned this little mirroring encounter for you and his young employee. I hope you liked it."

I'll never be able to fully tell Jamison just how hot this glass canyon connection was for me.

I Only Wanted to Watch

Brandon had told me that if I wasn't going to move to a new, all-the-way level with him, he was going to a gay bar and would bring someone back to the dorm with him. He said he couldn't take the frustration any longer. I thought he had been joking, that he was as scared about this as I was. But there they were, entering the door from the street and moving toward Brandon's room at the other end of the suite in the middle of the night, having awakened me from a light sleep when Brandon's friend knocked over a lamp and exclaimed a four-letter word.

I had only been dozing, because I had been aroused by Brandon's plan, even though I hadn't really believed he was going to go through with it, and I hadn't been able to keep my hands off my own cock and couldn't go to sleep when I was that hard. I wasn't any less frustrated at the nonmovement in our relationship than Brandon was. If he had been here, we would have just jacked off together, but I just couldn't bring myself to do certain things yet. I was more of a watcher than a doer still.

I thus was quickly out of my bed at the sound of their arrival, and when I'd opened my door a crack and peeked out, I could see that Brandon had brought back a four-letter-word kind of guy. He was decked out in black—black leather vest over a tight black muscle shirt and black jeans, shredded at the knees and also tight on well-muscled legs. He had a square-jawed face, covered in a couple of day's growth of black stubble. His hair was long and tied off in a ponytail, and I wouldn't have doubted a claim that he was a gangbanger straight off his motorcycle.

Brandon's friend had almost fallen when he'd run into the lamp, and when Brandon instinctively put out his arms to keep his friend from going down, the friend came up hugging Brandon tight. He was kissing Brandon on the lips and arching him over backward in a possessive stance.

When he broke away from this, I could hear Brandon whisper that they needed to wait until they got in his room, because he didn't want to wake any of his suite mates. And then they were out of my sight and down the hall toward where Brandon's room was.

My dick went hard and I thought I was going to hyperventilate. Brandon had done it. He had said he was so horny for a guy that he was going to go out and pick one up, and he'd done it. I'd thought that was all talk.

I scurried down the hall as quietly as I could and came up real close to Brandon's door. He hadn't gotten the door shut tight, and I pushed it open a smidgen, giving me a full view of the bed in the glaring light of the overhead bulb.

They were both sitting on the opposite side of the bed from me, next to and close to each other. Their shirts were already off, and Brandon's friend had Brandon's smooth, cut torso arched back, with one arm wrapped under Brandon's shoulder blades. The guy's lips were already on Brandon's nipples, and I could tell from the angle of the guy's other arm that he had a hand on Brandon's basket. The expression on Brandon's face told me a lot. I could see apprehension and a little fear, but an overwhelming helping of desire and excitement that were overpowering the other two emotions.

Brandon's friend came up for air from nibbling at Brandon's nipples and loosened the hold of the arm around Brandon's back, permitting Brandon to slowly lower himself on the bed. The friend's torso was turned toward me now, and I could see it clearly. Where Brandon was the blond, smooth-bodied college jock, his visitor was a dark, hirsute gypsy—lithe and sinewy, with a hairy chest and arms, and a look of danger about him. This impression was only enhanced by the two silver rings in his nipples, the stud in one ear, and the crown-of-thorns tattoos around both bulging biceps. Even the expression on his face contrasted perfectly with Brandon's hesitancy and indecision at this point. Full confidence; full control. He conveyed that he knew exactly what he wanted and that he was going to get it.

He placed his thumbs under Brandon's pecs and his fingers around his sides and pushed the blond's body up until it was fully on the bed. And then he came down, full length, on top of Brandon, pecs to pecs, belly to belly, and basket to basket. They were only in their jeans now. They had removed both their shoes and their socks. They kissed deeply, and then the gypsy put his arms on Brandon's upper arms, pinning him to the bed, and raised his chest up, putting the weight of his body on his hips and pelvis. He proceeded to grind his basket into Brandon's while he possessed Brandon's eyes with his own, focusing Brandon on what was happening, forcing Brandon to acknowledge what was going to happen, no matter what simpler, less dangerous ideas Brandon might have had when he brought the man back to the dorm with him. The gypsy reached around and undid his ponytail, and long, silky black hair cascaded down to his shoulders.

Uncertainty and a bit of fear were fighting the lust in Brandon's eyes—and slowly losing the battle. The gypsy had his knees between Brandon's legs, and Brandon slowly opened his stance and then, in resignation, brought his legs around and placed the backs of his calves over those of his new-found friend. The gypsy raised up on his knees then and unbuckled Brandon's jeans, pulled the zipper down, fanned out the two sides of the material, pushed the band on his briefs down to below his balls, and brought out Brandon's rod. Brandon had a very nice dick, rather thin, but of good length. I had admired it often when we were showering. I instinctively pushed my sleeping shorts down to below my own respectable cock, and lightly fingered what had already hardened nicely.

Then I almost audibly gasped when the gypsy proceeded to undo his own belt buckle, unzip himself, and fan out the waist of his jeans. He hadn't been wearing anything under the jeans, and his cock was mammoth—both long and thick, truly horse hung. The bulb of his dick was a dark red and bulbous, and a silver ring piercing it caught the light of the overhead fixture. I could feel my own cock beginning to form precum.

The gypsy came down onto Brandon again and mashed his pelvis into Brandon's, introducing the cocks to each other. Brandon's hands had gone to the slats of the headboard above him, and I could see the whiteness of his knuckles as he held onto the iron rods. The muscles of his arms were bulging under the strain, as the gypsy ground his hot cock into Brandon's pubes. The gypsy was holding Brandon firmly by the wrists with his hands, and he had his lips and teeth buried in the hollow of Brandon's neck. Brandon's back was slightly arched back, and his head was bent back at even a greater angle. His eyes were wildly searching the ceiling, as if he was on the brink of trying to bolt from the room.

But there was no bolting. The gypsy was firmly in control, both physically and psychologically. He was the older of the two by a good ten years, but there appeared to be limitless strength in his body, and he had the manner of a man who knew exactly how to get what he wanted. Brandon was a soft, spoiled college student in comparison, no matter how well built he was. He was probably thinking now that this obsessive lark of his hadn't been such a great idea, but the two were well beyond just calling it a night and going their separate ways.

The gypsy was so fast in stripping them both of the rest of their clothes, that I hardly noticed it had been done. My attention was arrested by that blunderbuss of a cock swinging between the gypsy's legs as he rose up over Brandon. I'd certainly never seen anything this formidable in the dorm shower room. The first I noticed, he was up with his knees on either side of Brandon's pecs, and, while still holding Brandon's wrists at the headboard slats, he was forcing his cock between Brandon's lips and pumping his face slowly. I was getting all of this in a side view, and I couldn't help but start stroking my own cock as the gypsy's seven or eight inches started working their way down Brandon's throat.

Brandon's knuckles were even whiter than before from the pressure on the iron rods of his headboard, and I saw his knees come up and his heels dig into the bedspread under the strain. The muscles of his calves and thighs were popping out, and I could hear him moaning and groaning and gagging under the assault. I tried to see his eyes, but he had them shut tight.

I could almost hear the audible sigh of relief from across the room, as the gypsy pulled out of Brandon's mouth and turned him around until he was laying across the width of the bed on his back, with his butt cheeks at the edge of the bed.

The gypsy was giving Brandon head now. Although I was watching from the angle of the top of Brandon's head, I was standing at the door and looking slightly down on the tableau on the bed, so I could look down Brandon's trembling torso and see the gypsy's head bobbing above his pelvis. The gypsy was running one hand up to Brandon's nipples and then down, fanning out over his flat, pulsating belly. And the other hand was between Brandon's thighs somewhere, probably doing something lustful with Brandon's balls.

Brandon had his head arched back between his arms, which were bent at the elbows close to each side of his head, with his hands bunching up the bedspread above and to the sides of his head. I could tell by the rhythmic bunching of Brandon's fists in the bedspread and the bouncing of his hips that the gypsy was stroking him deeply and fully with his mouth. He was probably an expert at this. I found myself matching the rhythm with the stroking of my own cock, and I was beginning to begrudge Brandon his adventure. He had such a look of pleasure and abandon in his eyes that I envied him that. We had talked about the pleasure of getting good head, and even had done some fumbling experimentation with each other, but I could tell from the expression on Brandon's face that we had never even come close to the real thing.

I realized then that Brandon could see me. His eyes were piercing mine. I could almost tell that he was trying to convey that this could be us—that it might very well be us on another night, if I could suspend my inhibitions as he now had. My cock gave a lurch, and I moved my free hand up and glided up my taut stomach and pecs and squeezed my nipples. I returned his look of expectation and desire as best I could, sealing the unspoken agreement. He seemed almost to be telling me that this whole episode had been constructed to bring me out fully, to make me acknowledge that I wanted him and was willing to go the distance. I lifted my cock and pointed it at him, and he gave me a kissing gesture with his mouth. The agreement was ratified.

I now could see Brandon's cock bouncing on his belly. The gypsy had moved on—and down—with his lips. Brandon sighed and then moaned and then gave little yipping sounds and beat his fists against the bed in ecstasy as the gypsy expertly worked his asshole with his lips and tongue. Brandon raised his legs and then pulled them down onto his chest with his hands under his knees, giving the gypsy the deepest, widest possible access to his ass. All the time, Brandon was holding my eyes in his, conveying the deepest sense of pleasure and desire that he could across the room to me.

With a little cry, Brandon unfolded his legs wide, dug his heels into the edge of the bed. He then wrapped both of his hands around his long, engorged cock and stroked himself to ejaculation. I found that I had been stroking myself along with him, and we shot off together. I had cried out myself upon release, but the gypsy showed no sign of having heard me.

This might have been because he was changing position now. I saw the look of elation on Brandon's face at the prodigious release of his cum up his belly change almost instantly to surprise, pain, and fear upon the realization that his new-found master had come up and had his bludgeon at Brandon's back door. There was little warning and no mercy as the gypsy pushed his humongous cock into Brandon's ass. Brandon first arched back, his heels scrabbling for purchase at the edge of the bed, and showed me a face of deeply wounded pain, his mouth open in a big "O" that somehow couldn't muster a sound, and his eyes rolling back into his head so that about all I could see were the whites. He was clawing at the air with his hands at first. Then he raised his shoulders, and reached for the gypsy, trying to put an end to the relentless plowing up his ass canal. But the gypsy just laughed and pushed Brandon down onto his back on the bed with strong hand in the sternum.

Brandon's hips were briefly rolled up and the gypsy came up onto the edge of the bed with his knees, and I now could see the impossible thickness of his cock buried under Brandon's balls. He was fucking down into Brandon now, with a good four inches of dark cock root still showing against the paleness of Brandon's thighs. I held my breath and pulled at my own, reawakening cock, as I watched those last four, thick inches bury themselves in my classmate. Then the gypsy emitted an evil laugh. The cock came out almost the whole way, and, as Brandon cried out, it slowly started to disappear inside him once more.

The gypsy came back off the bed and onto his feet between Brandon's legs, and the horse-hung cock continued its second, less hampered journey to the center of Brandon, during which Brandon writhed under the gypsy's hand and gulped and gasped for air. Then I could see from my vantage point black silky pubic hair meeting and mingling with the blond down on Brandon's balls again, and the world held still. Brandon's gulping turned to panting and then to just quiet moaning, as his body slowly decreased its trembling and twitching and he accommodated himself to having been so thickly and deeply skewered.

After a short while, the gypsy removed his hand from Brandon's chest and took Brandon's legs in his hands at the ankles and spread-eagled them up and out. I saw the gypsy's hips go into a slight in and out stroking motion. He looked down into Brandon's face and gave him a big, appreciative smile. I couldn't see that Brandon was smiling back, but I could see that the tension had gone out of his body, and his own hips were moving slightly now, in rhythm with the man who was fucking him, the stranger who he had brought back to the dorm, the mysterious gypsy who now had seven or eight inches of pulsating cock up Brandon's undulating ass canal.

I could feel the strain going out of my body now too. I had seen the unknown and it could be conquered. If Brandon could adjust to seven or eight thick, horse-hung inches, I surely could manage Brandon, and he me. Brandon had arched his head back and he was watching me again, his eyes glued to my face, telling me that it was all right; that the pain had been worth the pleasure.

And then his eyes took on a look of pure ecstasy, as the gypsy started pumping him fast and deep. He was rotating his hips as he pumped and his undulating torso was glistening with sweat in the overhead light. I found his hairiness, with the silver nipple rings and bicep tattoos mesmerizing in their exotic dance of lust. His head was moving, and his hair was flipping around in the air. Brandon's hips were meeting his gyrations, and the younger man's legs were now propped on the older man's shoulders and their arms were entwined with the firm grips of their fingers on each other's elbows. They were one now, one pulsating, pumping, fucking machine. One part blond, smooth and all-American; one part dark, hairy, and mysterious—but both united as one, at the pelvis, exchanging pleasure, moans, sighs, and body fluids.

I thought the dance had gone on longer than it actually had. They had stopped before I noticed it, with no sign of the gypsy's release. And they were both looking up, at the door, at me, suspended in time. Waiting for me to realize that there were three of us in this, not just two. Brandon wasn't the only one who had seen me in the shadows just beyond the door.

I have no idea when the gypsy had realized that I was there. But it had been long enough for him to decide what he wanted to do about that.

Through the fog of discovery, I heard him mutter, "Next." And before I knew what was happening, he had me over at the bed, bent over, my legs spread wide, and that big juicy cock of his was probing beyond my protesting sphincter and then, with a bursting of the dam inside me, being pulled in by my undulating ass muscles and making its journey up my ass canal from behind. He had his fingers

567

digging into my nipples, and his cold, nipple rings were sliding around on my shoulder blades. I was writhing and struggling, my fists buried in the bedspread and mounding that up just as I had seen Brandon do under the same circumstances. I had my mouth open to scream, but as with Brandon, my lungs were in shock and I couldn't form the sounds.

Brandon came to my rescue then. He had his knees under me, at my belly. He helped me stretch my arms around him and cup his butt cheeks in my hands for leverage and for some place to put them, and he was gently pushing his rehardened dick between my lips, giving me something pleasant to concentrate on while the gypsy stretched and plowed me deeply from behind, giving me that education I could use for the rest of the semester with Brandon.

The two of them found each other above me with their lips, and I heard Brandon whisper a thank you to the masterful stranger. It occurred to me then that this had all been Brandon's plan, all of it, from the start.

On the Docks

I was moving among the containers on the dock, looking for the one that had the goods I'd had shipped from Portugal in it, when I reached a pocket of isolated dock space between the stacks of truck containers and the waterfront. I was about to turn and move back along the row of containers to examine the numbers on the other side of the tight aisle, when I heard moaning.

Thinking that it might be someone who had fallen and hurt himself, I went to the end of the line of containers and was making a turn toward the sound I'd heard when I saw them and drew back into the shadows.

The bigger of the two figures, a muscle-bound dockworker, was on his back on some sort of thick matting. He was wearing a yellow safety hard hat, a denim shirt open to expose a darkly tanned barrel chest, a tool belt around his waist, and heavy workers' boots—and nothing else. The wiry young Hispanic sitting on his hips and fucking himself on the prone figure's thick cock in long strides was only wearing a yellow hard hat and work boots. The Hispanic youth was doing all of the work and most of the moaning. He was leveraging off his knees and calves and holding his ankles with his hands, while the big guy under him was lying steady and holding him on both sides at the waist.

The big guy was smiling and muttering something in Spanish that must have been arousing to the young guy fucking himself on the thick pole, because his eyes were glassy and his jaw slack in the transport of the fuck.

I watched, mesmerized, as I liked to watch and was already guiltily envying the smaller man, as the big guy dug his heels into the matting and slowly pitched the young Hispanic forward over his chest and began taking over the upward stroking, more vigorously, and the young Hispanic groaned and moved his hips in a rotating motion to make love to the cock inside him at all angles. My eyes went to the root of that thick cock and the few inches above that were disappearing and then reappearing again, rhythmically, as the big guy drove his cock. The young man's hole puckered closely around the plowing cylinder, his light brown a stark contrast to the hard-white marbling of the big guy's cock. I felt a gravelly moan building up from deep in my belly.

Although I had my hand on my own engorging cock through the denim of my jeans, I was afraid the fucking couple would hear me groaning my arousal at the sight of their raw coupling. So I drew back—only to find there was no place to go. Thick, hairy arms surrounded me from behind and I was being lifted off the ground by a monster of a man. My clipboard clattered to the ground, and the fucking couple glanced my way. Little surprise was being registered, though. They both gazed at me with hooded eyes that showed they were lost in their own lust—and no doubt that they recognized a comrade, the man holding me, as someone who could easily control the interloper.

An arm crossed up my chest, holding me to a mass of muscle and the other hand was pulling at my belt buckle and my zipper. I cried out, and the sound reverberated down the tiny aisle I had walked up between the containers. But I had little hope of rescue. As my trousers and briefs were being stripped off my legs, I turned my head up to see who was assaulting me, only to see in my confusion and consternation a blur of stubble on a square chin topped by yet another yellow safety helmet.

I struggled—fruitlessly—as the giant of a dockworker turned me and slammed my back against the ribbed steel side of the containers on one side of the aisle. His hips were roughly insinuating themselves between my thighs; he rolled my pelvis up toward his pelvis, and his cock cap was pushing insistently at my asshole. He was a swarthy guy with a profusion of black, curly hair and a sloppy grin that told me that he was going to get what he wanted.

And he did just that. His bulb popped into my entrance to the tune of heavy groans and cries from me. He somehow had gotten a condom on, which sent a flash of relief through me in counterpoise to the knowledge that I most certainly was going to be fucked. He held the bulb there, giving me a chance through groans and panting to open to him. And then with a throaty laugh and a profusion of Spanish mixed with the more understandable "fucks" and "nice," he was splitting me wide with his ravishing cock. Having been fucked thick before, I instinctively widened my stance as best as I could and dug my heels into the containers across the narrow aisle.

As he pumped, the pain slowly filtered into a flowing of a familiar, consuming pleasure deep inside me and a rising of my own fluids. Almost involuntarily but with animal instinct, I took up the rhythm of the fuck with him, leveraging my own thrusts off the wall opposite with the heels of my feet. The tones of my moaning and sighing changed, and the unwilling verbalizing of my "yes, yes, like that, oh yes" caused the man to grin down into my face, knowing I was fully under his control now and wouldn't have stopped what had become a mutual taking even if given the opportunity. My hands clutched his butt cheeks, fingernails digging into flesh and pulling him into me with each thrust. I felt him relax and his lips came down to mine, and I opened to his tongue. When he started to take his tongue out, I closed my mouth over it and sucked it, causing him to moan and shudder—and his cock to increase the rhythm of the fuck.

We were full partners in the fuck now, and knowing I was going with him, his fucking took on more finesse, as in long-time lovers giving and taking all of the mutual enjoyment they can. For a few moments he stopped the movement of his hips, and I took over the fuck, leveraging off the wall with the balls of my feet. I released his tongue and he grabbed mine with his lips and gave me the same suck I had been giving him.

With a shudder, he regained control and started a screwing motion with his dick, rotating his hips and moving his cock around in me as my walls stretched to accommodate him—no longer resisting him, making caressing love to his cock. He was hitting and rubbing against all walls inside me, driving me wild in the long strokes as his bulb rubbed across my prostate. I was as lost in the fuck as my assaulter was, and I threw my head back and, with the thought that I had reached the height of passion, ejaculated up my belly between us.

I would have been at least neutral about the forced taking if it had stopped then. But it didn't. The dockworker continued stroking me hard, increasingly roughly, ever faster and deeper, as he lost his own control. I raked his back under his shirt with my fingernails, and I cried out for him to split me asunder—my body telling him what I wanted to convey even if he didn't understand my words—and he lowered his head and ravaged my nipples with his teeth as my chin bounded off his yellow safety helmet. I had been fucked before, but it had not been as primevally animalistic about it as with this surprise, forced fucking. I was transported to new heights of sensation and passion and came again. I wanted him to come in great gushes and with a total loss of his control. I wanted him to be as amazed at and moved by this coupling as I was.

I no longer was neutral. Now I wanted it to go on, pushing me to an even higher level of passion. I wanted a third and a fourth creaming. But my body could only take so much pounding, and the dockworker, as young and virile and strong and lusty as he was, could hold his load for only so long. I was exhausted and was just flopping around on his pistoning cock when he finished with me—with the yelp of victory I was seeking from him at his climax.

He let me down to the ground then and I collapsed into a moaning heap, grateful that I had survived the size and power and endurance of him, sorry now that it was over. I nonsensically grabbed for his ankle as he stood over me, panting and muttering in Spanish. I didn't know how I was going to manage it, or how soon he would be capable of delivering it again, but I wanted to be transported back to the heights of that virile, primeval fucking.

His hand was on mine, prying my fingers away from my grip on his ankle.

"No, no," I was moaning softly. "You don't understand. I want it again. Fuck me again." All of my previous experiences with men had been too bland. I had no idea such passion and pleasure could be wrenched from me. I was a slut for him—for that long, thick cock swinging free above my head now. He could do anything with me now. Just as long as he fucked me again—when I'd had a chance to recover myself. Just a bit longer. I had to make him understand.

I have no idea if what I wanted conveyed. But after he'd pried my fingers away from his ankle, he was lifting me up and carrying me out onto the apron of concrete at the edge of the dock. The big dockworker I'd first seen on his back was still there, the younger Hispanic drawn off the side, crouched down on his haunches, pulling at his cock, watching the new activity. As we approached, me being carried under my erstwhile lover's arm at his side like a sack of potatoes, my lover said something in Spanish, and the young guy smiled and scrabbled around in the pocket of jeans lying nearby and fished out a condom packet.

The reclining hulky dockworker's cock was standing up straight and hard and thick, and he had a big grin on his face as the younger Hispanic rolled the condom down over his rod. The grin only broadened as my original assaulter hovered me over his midsecton and spread my thighs and butt cheeks . . . and lowered my channel onto this new, ready cock.

Stolen

I had the creepiest feeling I was being watched. I was sitting at the table in the small dining L of my high-rise apartment and diddling through my favorite Web sites. I liked all-male bondage fucking. It certainly wasn't something I admitted to in my day job down on the stock market trading floor, but that's how I unwound. In the evening, after a tough day among the bears and bulls, I retreated to my small seventy-second-story hole in the wall and entertained my sensations and my cock in a solo session with my male bondage sites on the Internet. I had them all booked so that I could quickly run through them, looking for what was new until I found something I wanted to masturbate to—to erase the tension of the day and to entertain a fantasy that I was too shy to bring to reality.

I was sitting, sprawled at my table, naked, and cock in hand. Just beyond the table was a full plate-glass window that would probably have a gorgeous view out over Central Park if there wasn't another, taller high-rise apartment building just across a narrow street between my building and the park. So, in essence, I had a full view of three floors of someone else's high rise.

I stood and moved over to the window and leaned into it to scrutinize the other building. I still had the creepiest feeling of being watched. It was only when I felt the head of my erect cock rub up against the cool pane of glass that I recalled that I was naked—exposed to several stories of the brooding building just across the narrow divide of Colombia Street. Had there been lights on across there earlier, I wondered. Now the windows were either dark or close-draped.

I must try to put the money aside to buy draperies for my own windows, I thought. And the time and effort in getting it done, which was an even greater nuisance for me.

Anyone could be watching me from inside those darkened windows in that other building, I thought. My dining L was brightly lit, and I couldn't see into any of those rooms. Wasn't that one just across lit up when I first padded naked into the dining room? That's where that hunk who was always working out, building muscles on his muscles, lived. Boy I'd like to meet him in the back room of one of those gay clubs down near Times Square I'd heard about but never been brave enough to go into. I frequently sat and watched him work out—in the nude—and fantasized having sex with him. He was arousingly hirsute, with black curly hair all over his body.

I moved away from the window and turned off the lights in my living area and settled in front of my computer again. I pulled up URLs with one hand and stroked my cock to the images I found arousing with my other hand. Than I reached for the dildo that was on the table top, lubed it liberally, and scrunched down in my seat, my eyes glued to the computer screen as I held the head of the dildo to my hole—and started to gently press in.

* * * *

I knew I'd been ripped off as soon as I got off the elevator after work. The door to my apartment was ajar. Someone had jimmied the lock, and they hadn't even bothered to shut the door after them.

Well, they were sure to have been disappointed, I thought bitterly, as I entered the apartment, because I lived quite sparsely. Virtually the only thing of value that I kept in my apartment beyond the TV system that was firmly bolted to the wall was my computer.

And, sure enough, my computer was the only thing that had been taken—although I was somewhat distressed to find that my bureau drawers had been opened and my underwear briefs were strewn on the floor. And then, when I entered the bathroom, I discovered that my dirty clothes hamper had been turned over—and all of my soiled briefs were missing.

How odd, I thought. But a little chill went up my spine that wasn't at all unpleasant, and I had the urge to go to my computer and run through my favorite Web sites. Only I didn't have my computer anymore.

What a bother. I'd have to file a police report—which I knew would go nowhere other than support an insurance claim that would also be almost more of a hassle cashing in on than it was worth. And I'd have to get a new computer. And, oh yes, the lock would need to be fixed on the apartment door. But it was late already. I'd stopped for a couple of beers down at O'Donnell's after work—trying to build up the courage, unsuccessfully, to move on to that gay leather bar across the street from the tavern, and it was already dark when I'd returned to my apartment. All of this hassle would have to wait for tomorrow.

So, I just shut the door with the broken lock, with the assurance that lightning didn't strike twice in quick succession and that it was unlikely anyone would be trying the doors on the seventy-second story of my building to see if any opened. And I showered, toweled off, and pulled on a pair of the red silk bikini briefs I liked to sleep in.

As I was sitting at the side of the bed, I had that creepy sensation once again of being watched. There was another full-length uncovered plate-glass window beside my bed, just on the other side of the wall from my dining L. I got up from the bed and padded over to the bedroom door and switched off the light. Then I went over to the window and let my eyes travel across the surface of the building across the narrow canyon of Columbus Street.

Nothing was amiss, but the feeling of being watched didn't go away.

* * * *

I was jolted from a deep sleep by a heavy body covering me as I lay on top of the covers on my belly. Swimming up from unconsciousness, I drunkenly tried to turn and push the weight off me, but the sharp crack of a backhand across my cheek snapped my head to the side and brought bright orange stars to my eyes. Before I could recover, my wrists were being bound together and tethered to the rails of the headboard.

I started to cry out in shock and indignation, but my bikini briefs were being stripped off my legs and stuffed in my mouth.

I gagged for breath as I was being forced up to my knees on the bed and I felt the wetness of a tongue at my asshole. I moaned deeply. This had never happened to me before. I had dreamed of it happening to me, but I'd never been brave enough to bring reality to fantasy.

This was no fantasy, though. My cock was being pulled through my legs and was being swallowed and worked and my balls were being licked and fingers were invading my asshole. I squirmed and tried to pull away, but big hands roughly pulled my hips back into position, and my buttocks were slapped hard.

"Stay still," a low growl commanded.

And then I felt him crouching over my hips, his thighs encasing me and a fist between my shoulder blades forcing my chest into the surface of the mattress. And I knew it was a "him," because I felt the cock head at my hole. Moving insistently inside me. Spreading my virginal hole, making me gasp and groan at the thick invasion of him. Until suddenly his bulb was past my sphincter muscle, and I felt my channel drawing him in—different from any of the dildo work I had done on myself: warmer, throbbing, more pliable and filling. And moving with a purpose of its own.

I panted hard and moaned deeply as his cock moved deeper into me. And then he began to pump inside me and I writhed under him in agony mixed with ecstasy. I never knew it would be this way. Fully possessed; fully under his control. Whimpering for release but now not wanting him to stop either. A fist on my cock, stroking me. For the first time being stroked by someone else—being worked at someone else's whim and rhythm other than my own. I couldn't help myself. I quickly creamed the sheets beneath my pelvis.

But my tormentor fucked on and on. My knees got weak with the exertion and I collapsed onto the bed, but he just followed me down, straddling my pelvis between his knees, and continued stroking into me in long, deep thrusts. At last I felt him stop abruptly, nails dug into my hips, and then a jerk and a little cry and he was finished.

I felt the weight of him leave me, and then he turned me onto my back on the bed. Even though it was dark, the lights of the city coming through my uncurtained window let me clearly see my attacker. He was a big brute of a fellow, all muscle and dark curly hair. His head was covered with a ski mask, but I had little trouble identifying the rest of his body as the bodybuilder from one of the apartments in the high rise across Columbus Street from me.

No more mystery. He had been watching me just as I had been watching him. And I had little doubt who had burgled my apartment and taken my computer—no doubt wanting to verify in a search of my favorite sites that I was drawn to what he was doing to me.

And I was, in fact, drawn to it. And perhaps he could see that in my eyes, because, as I watched him, he stripped the condom he'd been wearing to fuck me off his cock, which was still half hard, and scrambled back up onto the bed and straddled my chest. He pulled the sleeping briefs out of my mouth and pressed his cock head at my lips. I opened my mouth to him, not knowing what to do but, having now been taken over the edge, more than willing to learn. I gagged as he possessed my mouth with a cock that was coming to life again. But he held my head in place with a palm on my cheek and a thumb under my chin and face-fucked me in shallow strokes that weren't too taxing, as I sucked on his cock head. Meanwhile, he raised the other hand, holding my sleeping bikini to his nose and sniffed the essence of me.

Then he was untying my wrists but rebinding me as I laid on my back, trussing up a wrist to an ankle on either side in a form of hogtying that had me helpless, bent over, and spread wide.

He disappeared for a while, and I heard him rummaging in my refrigerator. He returned, drinking a beer from a bottle—just sauntering into the room as if he possessed it—and me—and at least for now he did possess me. I should have been scared and angry. But I was beyond anger now. He was doing to me just what I had fantasized for months and had been too much of a coward to initiate myself.

He set the beer bottle down on my bureau, and I watched in fascination as he rolled another condom onto his rehardened cock. Then he walked over to the bed and pulled me down to the foot so that my rump was on the edge of the bed. He leaned over and took the beer bottle from the bureau top, tipped me over so that my hole was pointed to the ceiling, and let a stream of the cold liquid tipple into my hole.

Then he was fucking down into me again, lubricated by the cool beer. On and on he stroked inside me—until I was exhausted and had passed out.

When I awoke, he was gone and my wrists and ankles were free of bonds. My bikini sleeping briefs were missing and the fingers of dawn were creeping down the canyon that was Columbus Street.

I rose, sore, but exhilarated and padded into the living area. He wasn't there either, and the door to the apartment was shut. My computer had been returned and was turned on. I keystroked it to life and there on the screen was an e-mail address and the words, "If you liked it."

I sat down at the computer and, with tremulous fingers, opened my e-mail and keyed in the e-mail address. "Yes, yes, yes. Again tonight, please. Door unlocked."

And then I made myself a cup of coffee and sat back in the chair and luxuriated in the hassles that had been removed from me today—no missing computer, no need to file a police report, no need to replace the lock on my door, and no reason to sit for hours in O'Donnell's and try to build up the courage to walk across the street and enter the world of the gay leather bar. And above all else, no need to buy drapes for my windows.

The only thing that had been stolen—other than a few soiled briefs—was my virginity—spectacularly stolen—and I certainly wouldn't miss that now.

Triangulation

"I know you'll leave me. You're just waiting for us to get back to Manila, and you'll leave me."

Stanley was curled up in the fetal position on his berth in the compact cabin of the Bayliner 2855 yacht. He and Lance had been anchored off the Hilton Cebu Resort twin towers in the Philippines for two days, and Stanley had been drinking himself beyond pout and into a blue funk for three.

"Please, baby, please don't be like this. You know I wouldn't leave you; you know I couldn't leave you," Lance murmured.

He sat on the berth beside Stanley and laid his hand on his lover's belly. This had always worked before. It wasn't unusual for Stanley to sink into this mood, if not often this deeply, and the drink always made it worse. Ever since Stanley had passed his fiftieth birthday, he had become convinced that Lance, now half his age, would leave him—that his money wouldn't be enough to hold Lance. Even Lance's suggestion that they take this around-the-world trip, just the two of them, alone, most of the time on Stanley's streamlined yacht, hadn't reassured Stanley.

"I've grown so old," Stanley moaned. "Old and dumpy. I saw the looks you were getting the other night at that club in Manila. I knew they were thinking 'How can such a well-built hunk like that be with such an old man when he could be with me?'"

"No you're not too old, Stan," Lance said, the exasperation in his voice clear. "You still have the looks of a model. And here. I grab you here and you are hard as a rock." He had placed his hand over one of Stanley's nipples and squeezed on Stanley's well-worked chest muscles. "And you're still flat as a board here." Lance put his palm on Stanley's belly again. "And you still can get it up here." He grabbed Stanley's cock through his Speedo. "And you still have the sweetest one of these I've never known." Lance was sliding his hand under the rim of the Speedo at the small of his back.

"No, no, no," Stanley cried out. He jackknifed out of the fetal position, pushed off of the bed and away from Lance. "You wanted this sort of vacation because you are embarrassed to be seen with an old man like me. We could have gone to New York or Vegas and been with people. No, I know you'll leave me in Manila. I might as well throw myself off the boat now." Then, grabbing up an

577

oversized beach towel, he flounced out of the cabin and to the bow of the boat, where he laid the towel on the sharply raked windscreen of the cigarette boat and laid down on his back, wanting the sun to bake the liquor out of him while he watched the twin towers of the Cebu Hilton and the activity on its beach.

Only a moment later, Lance popped out of the cabin, a panicked look in his eyes. His eyes wildly scanned the water, looking for a sinking suicidal Stanley, until he saw that Stanley was sunbathing instead on the bow of the boat.

Mad now, having had enough of this, Lance slipped off his Speedo and came around to the bow and stood, legs spread, between the sunbathing Stanley and the vista of the Cebu Hilton's busy beach and two tall hotel towers. He took his long and thick cock in his hand and wagged it at Stanley.

"Suck this!" he demanded. "Can't you see that it's hard for you?"

"What?" Stanley opened his eyes. And then he opened them even farther, focused on the midsection of his naked horse-hung young lover. "Lance," he cried out, "What are you doing? People will see you."

"People will see us, Stanley. Not just me. You said I would be too embarrassed to be seen with you. I'm going to fuck you right here, in full view of everyone in that resort. That's how embarrassed I am to be seen with you. And if you won't suck me, I'll blow you." With that, he knelt between Stanley's legs, stripped off his Speedo and inhaled Stanley's cock.

"Oh, god, Lance, oh god," Stanley cried out. His hands went to the back of Lance's curly head and held him close. "Oh, god. All of it . . . yes . . . yes. Oh, god."

Changing to fisting Stanley's cock, Lance started moving his lips up across Stanley's belly and up onto his nipples and to his lips. He was writhing around on top of Stanley, getting as close into him as he could.

"Lance! Not here. In the cabin. We must go below. Oh . . . ahhhh." Whatever else Stanley was going to say was muffled as Lance brutally attacked his mouth with his own.

After working his mouth until Stanley was almost out of breath, Lance broke away. "No. Here, Right here, Stanley. I'm going to fuck you for anyone to see who wants to see. I want you now, here. I love you. I'm never going to leave you. You couldn't get rid of me if you wanted to."

Lance quickly worked his mouth back down Stanley's torso, and after giving his cock a little more loving, Lance put his hands under Stanley thighs, rolled them up, and was diving into Stanley's hole with his tongue.

As Lance stood back up, his hands still lifting Stanley's thighs up and spreading them wide, Stanley looked down at him. "God, Lance. You're so hard. You're huge. I never know how I can take all of you."

"You always take all of me, Stanley. You've got the sweetest ass. I'm hard for you. You make me hard. Can't you accept that?"

"Yes, yes. I . . . Arghhhh!"

His ass had accepted all that Lance had for him again, and Lance was fucking him hard, power driving up between his spread thighs, pushing his back up and down on the raked windscreen of the yacht.

* * * *

Will Thruston worked hard on the key mechanism of his tenth-floor Hilton Cebu hotel room door. He was in such a state that he was doing more cussing at the unresponsive lock than effective key turning. Once in, he tore off his shirt and threw it on the bed; headed straight for the minibar; grabbed a beer, despite his intent never to take anything from an exorbitantly expensive hotel minibar; flipped off the cap; stumbled out onto the balcony; and stood at the railing, trying to gain control of his anguished trembling. He stared hard out onto the yacht basin, trying to calm down, trying to tell himself these things happened, that it didn't mean anything.

But this was the third time this week. He had to face that maybe he was growing unable to get it up. Maybe he was losing it altogether.

Business hadn't been all that good this week. This afternoon's trick, who he had cultivated for nearly an hour in the hotel bar before landing him, had been ugly and pudgy. And he had to have been at least in his mid forties. But Will couldn't let that turn him off. Most of the marks at this hotel were ugly and fat and old. The younger guys here didn't have to pay for it. And Will only did it for the money.

Everything had worked OK at the start. The guy was half drunk when Will helped him to his hotel room. And he paid up front—what Will asked for without haggling.

Will had planned to fuck him in the shower and then again after the full body massage he had agreed to as part of the price. Lucky, he hadn't told the trick of these plans, though.

The man had been more than ready for Will. He was half hard before they got into the shower, and Will had gone down on his knees in front of the man while water was cascading over them and gotten him to jack off with a minimum of mouth work on his dick. And the guy had gone hard and come again when Will had turned him belly to the tiles and given him a full-tongue rim job. Then Will had planned to fuck him from the rear, but he hadn't been able to get it up. It hadn't helped that the pudgy guy had already hardened and come twice. Will felt emasculated by that. Twenty years older than him and able to spout out twice in an hour when he himself couldn't even get it up. And the worry about it probably didn't help either. As a substitute, he'd finger fucked the man while covering him close from behind for a while, which seemed to satisfy him.

The full body massage on the hotel bed went OK, too. And the trick hardened and came again while Will was giving him a hand job. Still, Will himself hadn't hardened up. Maybe part of that was that the guy gave Will's cock no attention at all. He seemed happy for Will to be making all of the moves. This was both good and bad. Good because the guy didn't seem to notice that Will wasn't aroused; bad because Will had promised to fuck him.

Will's flexible dildo came to the rescue. The mark was so mellow when Will had jacked him off and then turned him on his belly and rubbed down his back and legs, that when Will at last mounted him, the guy didn't seem to notice—or care—that it was a dildo working inside him rather than Will's cock. The man went to sleep, and, having already been paid, Will quickly dressed and left him there.

And he'd come straight back to his own room. Worried and mad, but mostly scared. Was he finished? Would he ever be able to perform again. This was his "career"; he was a hotel stud for pay. A good-looking hunk hanging around the pool, waiting for an old rich lady or a middle-aged businessman wanting to be taken for a ride and willing to pay big bucks for the fuck. If the hotel got any inkling he was having trouble stepping up to the plate, they'd toss him out on his ear. They didn't keep around any duds to fail to service their rich patrons on demand.

Three more swigs from his beer bottle and Will was able to actually focus on the magnificent vista of the Hilton Cebu seascape laid out before him.

Oh, my god, what was that? Surely not. Will reached for his binoculars and trained it on a gleaming white, sleek cigarette boat yacht anchored off the beach.

What were they doing? God, they were fucking. An older, but very trim guy—much more appealing that any of the marks he'd been stuck with this week—was lying against the sharply raked windscreen of the yacht, and a younger hunk—hunkier than Will himself, he had to admit—was hunched between the older man's spread thighs, pounding away in his ass. Both naked, fucking, right there, not far off shore, for all on the beach and in the hotel towers to see.

Will couldn't take his eyes off them. He felt the binoculars waiver, and he had to fight to maintain focus on the vigorous fuck the young hunk was giving the older man. The binoculars were heavy in his hand, which was trembling. He'd return the other hand to the binoculars to hold them steadier, but his other hand was busy. Without realizing it, he'd unzipped himself, let his trousers fall to the floor, and he was pulling on his cock. And his cock was big and hard. His breath was getting ragged, and he masturbated vigorously. Gloriously alive again.

Maybe all he needed to do was imagine arousing bodies fucking when he was with a mark. Maybe that would keep him in business for a while. It wasn't because he *couldn't* get it up—because, by god, it certainly was up now! And it wanted lots of attention.

* * * *

Edward Frampton got up from the bed, finding himself unable to sleep in the afternoon despite his exhaustion, and deciding he didn't really need anything more on than his sleeping shorts in the middle of a hot Philippines day, went out onto the balcony of his thirteenth-floor Hilton Cebu hotel tower room.

He collapsed more than sat onto the patio chair. God he was tired. But then he smiled, in remembrance of why he was tired, why he hadn't gotten any sleep last night.

He'd never done anything like this before. He had heard that it was this easy in the Philippines and in some of the other resort hotels throughout Southeast Asia. But he was shocked at himself—and amused and, yes, proud of his audacity and boldness—to have tried it here. And it worked a charm.

The room boy who had brought his luggage up to the room was slight and brown as a berry and achingly beautiful in an androgynous way. Clearly male, but as beautiful and lithe and graceful in his movements as a courtesan. In the elevator, they had chatted a bit, and Edward had been surprised to find that the room boy was in his early twenties. He looked no older than a teenager. It was a trait of the Filipinos, Edward had noticed during his various business trips here from Hong Kong. Perpetual youth. He wished he could latch into that. He was feeling his thirty-six years. Nearly forty and nothing exciting had happened to him yet. He'd fucked around in gay bars in his twenties, but when he'd been sent out to Hong Kong, he'd become respectable—and closely watched. He couldn't get away with much of anything in Hong Kong. And, although he'd traveled to the Philippines twice before, and each time had become aroused by the small, well-formed berry-brown young men of the country, he had been too timid to act on his impulses.

Until this, the third trip. He'd been told that all you had to do in a hotel like this was to ask. So, when they'd gotten to the room and the room boy had asked if there was anything else he could do for Mr. Frampton, Mr. Frampton told him what he could do for him and held out two 1,000-peso banknotes. The room boy's eyes had bugged out and he'd smiled broadly.

The room boy had proved to be very willing, very able, flexible, resilient, and inventive. He also, once naked, proved to be very desirable. The years of an adult, the body of a lithe but well-muscled, perfectly formed youth. And a well-worked hole that not only opened immediately to Edward's thickness but also was trained to make undulating love to Edward's throbbing cock.

Edward fucked him under the cascading water in the shower, the room boy's feet leveraging off the frame of the shower door while his shoulder blades were sliding up and down on the wet tiled walls opposite, propelled by the strength of Edward's driving cock. Edward recharged quickly while the room boy toweled him off and then fucked the room boy from behind as he was bent on his belly over the back of the room's upholstered tub chair.

Exhausted then, Edward bedded the room boy, who, still resilient, massaged Edward's screaming muscles, including eventually, the reawakened muscle between his legs. In the darkness of the early night, Edward drifted off, but the room boy awakened him again within a couple of hours. Edward was stretched on his back and the room boy was riding his loins hard, drawing yet another ejaculation out of him. Yet another fucking only a couple of hours after Edward had drifted off nearly paralyzed him. He was groaning hard and the room boy could get no more than a dribble of semen out of him. Mercifully that marked the end, and when he woke next—to the light—and to entirely too little sleep and too much vigorous exercise, he opened his eyes to the thought that maybe 2,000 pesos was entirely too much to have offered.

It was afternoon before he could struggle out of bed. But he hadn't slept. Besides being exhausted, he was incredibly satisfied and pleased with himself. He would have to make more business trips to the Philippines.

When he felt a bit recovered, he picked up the binoculars from the table beside him and started to check out the sights around the busy hotel complex. He decided to take a sweep of the hotel tower next to his for beginners, moving up from the base. When his view reached the tenth floor of the other tower, he let out a gasp and a "Holy shit!" and had to lift a second hand to the binoculars to steady his trembling hand.

The man, a Caucasian, like him, was stunningly handsome. Edward instantly recognized him as a beefy, suntanned hunk he'd seen at the pool as he was taking a walk around of the facilities before checking in. The man had been a large dose of eye candy, and Edward had remembered thinking "trophy stud" when a beet-red European with a distinct pouch and puffy face had spoken to the young man and they'd walked off toward the hotel together.

Now he was standing at the rail of the balcony of his tenth-floor room in the other tower, shirtless and his trousers down around his ankles. He was holding binoculars in one hand, trained out to sea, and he was stroking the loveliest, hardest cock Edward had ever seen. Edward couldn't take his eyes off him, and he felt his own cock begin to renew its interest in spite of the Herculean workout it had gotten the previous night.

Edward was so engrossed in watching the young man masturbate at the balcony rail that he didn't hear the door to his hotel room click open and the room boy reappear to make up the room.

Suddenly, a hand was taking the binoculars out of Edward's hands. The room boy was pulling his sleeping shorts off him, and he has holding Edward's erect cock in his fist as he moved his thighs around Edward's, positioned his hole on Edward's rosy-red bulb, and started to descend into his lap. Edward threw his head back, took a pert hard brown cock in both hands, driving it like a stick shift on a sports convertible, his eyes closed but still seeing that hunk on the other balcony slowly jacking his gigantic meat off, and he sighed in appreciation of how far 2,000 pesos would stretch.

* * * *

Stanley had already come, in three jerks and heavy spoutings, as he was spread out on the window screen of his Bayliner 2855, the palm of his hands on Lance's tight butt cheeks, enjoying how they contracted with each thrusting of his young lover's rock hard cock up into him. How could he have ever doubted his Lance? It was the liquor. He'd swear off liquor for good if it kept Lance with him, in his bed, churning his cock inside him.

After ejaculating, Stanley lay back against the windscreen, letting Lance pound away inside him, knowing it would be several more minutes before he came.

Stanley loved this, but having reached his own climax, reason flooded in to struggle with emotion, and he started to worry again at the spectacle they were making of themselves. Binoculars were within reach, so he retrieved them and put them to his eyes and started scanning the beach and the Hilton Cebu twin towers, checking on who might be watching.

Lance wouldn't notice. When he was deep in a fuck like this, he became a wild, focused man, all of his attention locked on the working of his cock inside Stanley. Stanley knew this was only further evidence that he was still desirable to Lance. Lance couldn't have even gotten it up, let alone become lost in the fuck, if he didn't still want Stanley. Stanley knew he'd been such a fool to raise doubts.

As he scanned the towers, Stanley's attention focused on the thirteenth floor of one of the towers. Two men fucking. A very well presented young man, maybe early thirties, slumped in a chair, his head thrown back, a look of ecstasy painted all over it. And a small, lithe brown-bodied man crouched over his pelvis and fucking himself on a thick, long cock in long, plunging rhythm.

Stanley began to melt and to quicken all at the same time. His cock gave a lurch and came alive. He reached a hand for it, but Lance slapped the hand away and took charge of the cock himself, stroking it in fast rhythm with his vigorous fucking.

A triangulated cry of simultaneous release shot out over the Hilton Cebu complex, sending a flock of disturbed sea gulls screaming and fluttering up into the air. Five long sighs of satisfaction followed, drifting down in the lapping of the surf onto the resort beach.

Glorious Banishment

Clifton liked to watch. In a way that's what led to his banishment, I guess. I didn't know at the time that it could have been called a glorious banishment, but my more recent one certainly qualified for that.

I was in my second season as a dancer aboard cruise ships. I worked as one of ten dancers—five women and five men—and two women and two men singers who also did a little dancing. We worked up two programs a year and went from cruise to cruise. When we could get full booking, we'd do two performances each of two shows on a ten-to-twelve day's cruise in exchange for a cabin bed and pretty good board, some world sightseeing, and income that was more steady than trying to land musicals of any length on Broadway or the road.

The biggest downside of this was rather strange—it was the pitch and roll of the cruise ships. They have this down to a science enough that most passengers can manage it without giving it much of a thought—but get up on stage and try and do some fancy footwork while you're also fighting for balance and see how long before you've gotten a sprained ankle. That's why we have five of each gender for dancers. The routines are designed for four of each, which can be scaled down to two in a pinch. We have to maintain the extras to guard against being banged up.

I guess a dancer being banged up also figures in Clifton's glorious banishment story—but my own experience leads into an update on his.

I'd felt quite pleased about this eleven-day Eastern Caribbean cruise gig we'd landed. I'd done the landing of the job myself. The cruise ship was sailing out of Bayonne, New Jersey, and, at a time that the troupe didn't have a cruise and I was nursing a sprained ankle, I met a guy several months before this sailing in a bar in New York City. He was looking for what I was in the mood to give and we clicked pretty good. It was a Friday night, and he took me back to his hotel room and fucked me into Sunday evening.

He was interested in more than just a straight fuck. After what were pretty short preliminaries of him establishing control by going down on me and then forcing me to my knees to suck him, instead of leading me to the bed, he took me right there on the carpet. He pushed me down on the floor and grabbed my hips in strong hands and pulled me up onto my shoulders and stood over me and fucked down into my channel with my legs spread wide. While he was fucking me, he kept

585

corkscrewing around my torso in a 360-degree rotation that had his slightly upward curved, long and rather thin, cock moving the full circle around my channel, with his cock head caressing my channel on all sides. It was a pretty nifty feel—and I've got to admit that I have been felt in my day.

I'd told him I was a stage dancer, so I guess he wanted to try my flexibility out—and it was quite an interesting testing. And it was easy on my ankle too.

It turns out we were both in the cruise industry. He was the cruise director on a company sailing out of Bayonne, and I was a dancer in a troupe looking for work on such cruises.

After that first, frenzied "get-acquainted" fucking and having found he liked me enough to do it again, Keith showed me that he liked to give massages that turned more and more intimate as his pre-sex play. And, as a dancer, I knew how to give and liked taking massages almost as much as I enjoyed the sex that followed.

He wanted more of what I could give him and so he offered my troupe this spot on an Eastern Caribbean cruise. I was well aware of the very strict rule of no sex between the crew and the passengers—and it often got boring just to get off with the other guys in the dance troupe—but the cruise director pointed out to me that there was no rule against sex between the members of the crew as long as they kept it on the hush-hush and didn't let it interfere with their jobs, which required their full attention during the many hours they were on duty.

His offer seemed like a win-win situation, and the cruise was a pretty plush one, so I didn't have any trouble getting the rest of the dancers and singers to sign on.

Everything would have gone OK—I spent more time in the cruise director's cabin giving and getting massage, head, and fucking than I was spending anywhere else on the cruise. But Keith was good at it, so it was easy to think that everything was fitting together real well.

But Keith was the jealous type—and also vindictive.

It was actually the mid-thirties blond hunk who sat in the first row of the ship's theater during the night's first performance while we were still sailing out to sea and steaming past Bermuda on our way to San Juan who was my undoing.

He came to both shows—and managed to sit at the front both times. And the way he stared me down and looked me up and down while we were performing told me in no uncertain terms that he was interested. He'd applaud and cheer and cat call when I was doing my featured spots, and when he wasn't doing that I could see that he was sitting there with his hand on his crotch. That night he was waiting for me in the side corridor when we'd changed and came out of the stage door.

Keith was already waiting for me in his cabin. After the first show, he told me that I'd put him in heat and he wanted to fuck—he said he'd arranged for his assistant to cover the rest of what he had to do in the way of passenger programming that evening and that he wanted me to come straight back to his cabin for some "special" sex. Although Keith was bigger and older than I was, he'd been a Broadway dancer himself, and he was still flexible enough to take me in some really interesting positions, like the one he'd used our first time, after we'd done our massage preps.

But here the muscle guy was—older than Keith, but still in tip top shape, a lot more muscular and better looking in the face than Keith was—standing at the stage door, tongue hanging.

"Hey," he said, putting his hand on my arm to make sure I knew he was talking to me and not to one of the other dancers who was coming off the backstage with me.

"Hey yourself."

"I enjoyed your dancing . . . a lot."

"Thanks. I guess that's why you made both shows."

"You saw me?"

"Yeah. We can make out faces pretty well about three rows back. You were a little hard to miss."

"Being that obnoxious was I?"

"No, being that good looking." If there was any doubt in his mind which way I swung, I could tell that I'd just dispelled that. He moved closer and put his hand on my butt. I knew I was going to have to cut that off, but I didn't really want to—certainly not until I'd enjoyed his touch for a few moments.

"Ummm, I thought maybe you'd let me buy you a drink."

"Sorry, I can't," I answered, trying to be polite, which is rule number one for cruise control in the care and feeding of paying passengers. But I wasn't really having trouble keeping a smile on my face either. He was a real looker, and if we didn't have this stringent, drop-dead rule about fraternizing with the passengers, I'd be happy to jump in bed with him in an instant.

He looked glum, and then even more glum when I put my hand on the one he had been squeezing my butt cheek with and gently moved it away.

"Listen, sorry. I have an appointment, someplace I have to be now. But also I'm afraid there's a solid rule around here about getting cozy with the passengers. Both you and I could be kicked off the ship."

"You don't find me attractive enough, do you?" he asked. He had such a wounded puppy dog look—and looked so good doing it—that I could have knelt right there in the corridor and given him a blow job that clearly showed what I really felt about him. God knows I'd done it on impulse enough when I felt like it and there was no impediment.

And I'm not particularly shy either.

"You look plenty good to me," I said. "I'd sit on your cock right here in the hall if it wouldn't get us kicked off the ship. Hold it until we're back in Bayonne, and I'll march right off the ship and into a motel room if you want. Hell, I'll let you do me in the backseat of your car in the cruise line's parking lot, if you can't wait for it."

For some reason this seemed to heat him up rather than cool him down. I guess I'm not all that great at cruise control.

"I know a place up on deck topside nobody'll be at this time of night. We could—"

"Sorry. As I said, I have a meeting with my boss I'm already late for—and we can't on the cruise. That's a rock solid no-no."

"I'll pay," he said with a whimper. "I'll pay off anyone who has to look the other way."

"It's not a question of money. I need this job. If you still want to do it when we get back to Bayonne, just whistle."

I physically disengaged his grip on my arm, but also gave him a smile, and started moving down the corridor. I ached to go topside with him to see if he was as well equipped and as proficient as his looks suggested. But . . .

"My name is Seth," he said to my back as I moved away from him. "Here, write down where I can find you once we get back to Bayonne."

"I'd be willing to meet you on the gangway in Bayonne," I answered. But then I sighed and turned and saw that he was holding out a business card and a pen. I looked at the business card before I jotted a telephone number and address where I could be reached when I was in New York—a two-bedroom apartment I rented with nine other guys who operated out of the city like I did but who, like me, weren't there all that often. According to his card, he was a stock broker in the big city—or at least claimed to be. The clothes he was wearing and the flashy Rolex watch on his wrist bore out the claim.

"I'm Dale," I said as I handed his card back to him and turned to continue on to my tryst with the cruise director, Keith, who indeed had a very inventive approach that evening. He turned me on my side and strapped my thighs and calves together and fucked me sideways, which gave us a really tight fuck.

I put Seth out of my mind after our brief encounter—or tried to—because his failure to offer to take me back to his cabin—which would have been very tempting regardless of the rules—or to take me right from the ship when it docked back in New Jersey screamed of commitments he had. He probably wasn't alone on the cruise and wouldn't be leaving the ship alone.

I'd already had enough in my life of married guys cruising for that little extra exotic experience with variety tail.

So, I forgot Seth, which was pretty easy to do considering some of the other offers I was getting from bored cruise passengers on the high seas—both male and female—and the new ways Keith was showing me he could mine my channel. At least I forgot about Seth until three nights later, after we had left after a day in St. Thomas and were headed for Samana in the Dominican Republic.

We did the second of the two sets of shows for the cruise that night while we were sailing, and there was Seth, tongue hanging out, hand on crotch, in the front row during the first show.

He wasn't there for the second show, though, which made me feel a little deflated. It had been flattering that he had wanted me so bad. I thought that he certainly could cool off fast.

In the middle of the second show, Keith told me to come to his cabin when we were finished.

He was on the bed, on his stomach, just in a pair of athletic shorts, when I entered the room. By routine, I stripped down to the altogether and straddled his thighs and began to massage his back and shoulders—and then down to work his glutes and his thighs, calves, and feet. He was hard when he turned over and I only briefly massaged his chest and hips until I was massaging his cock with my mouth.

He slowly face fucked me until he murmured he was about ready to come, and then I finished him with my hand. He pulled my face down to his and we kissed. While we were doing so, he turned me onto my back and began running his hands over my body, pushing and pulling, and kneading—but only with one hand, because the other one was busy stroking my cock.

He knew how to bring me to the edge but not take me over, so that I began to writhe under him and beg him for his cock.

At that point, he laughed and turned me onto my belly. With a hand on my lower belly, he raised me onto my knees and I felt his knees pressing into my hips on either side and the long slide of him into my channel, and he rode me slowly and deeply. He slid back out after several minutes of long-stroking and left me briefly. He'd pressed me flat again on my stomach as I felt his weight lift off me, and then my thighs were being straddled and forced together by knees, and while my back and arms were being massaged, a hard cock was sliding up and down across my hole between my butt cheeks.

I begged him for it again and moved with the rhythm of the stroking—and then jerked and gave a little cry as the head of the cock broached my rim and was slowly sliding into me.

I thought that Keith must have had his Wheaties that morning because he seemed thicker and seemed to be mining me deeper than ever before.

But then I looked over at the sofa beside the bed and saw that Keith was sitting there and stroking his cock and watching me being doggy fucked by . . . I discovered Seth, when I cranked my head back to see who was doing this to me.

Rules or no rules, I was being covered by a blond hunk who already had his thick, hard cock a good nine inches up into my channel. So, I gave in and went wild with the fuck—he was entertaining and tantalizing me, with a tattoo of three short digs from rim to prostate and then to long, deep plunges, a twist of the hips and then all of the way out and then a kiss of my rim with a rotation of his cock head before the next shallow penetration. I lifted my hips to his pelvis and started thrusting back hard with his first plunging stroke—and then he lost control of his artistry and just started pistoning me hard and deep in long strokes while I went wild and cried out for him and twisted and turned my hips and thrust back to capture the full length and girth of a cock that seemed to grow with each plunge.

We went on for what seemed to be an eternity. From time to time, I looked over at Keith who was beating his cock furiously, but who had a little frown on his face. The blond and I exploded together in a harmonious cry of release and ecstasy and we both fell to the surface of the bed, he stretched beside me, legs akimbo, and arms in an entwining embrace.

We stayed that way until I heard his breath regularizing. He may have thought he was done, but I wanted more. I reached between his legs and wrapped my hand around his cock. He was in good shape and virile, so it didn't take much to arouse him into action again. I turned onto my back and opened my legs and made him take me again—with kissing and nipple chewing and heavy sighing this time.

He paid Keith at the cabin door, with a big wad of greenbacks. Keith tossed a fifty on the bed beside me and told me I needed to leave—that he had another event to announce within a half hour. He'd always let me shower in his cabin afterward, but this time he tossed my clothes at me and I quickly pulled them on and slipped out of the cabin.

The next afternoon, I and my luggage were standing on a pier in Samana, Dominican Republic—with a voucher for a plane ticket home, but a banishment from the cruise line's sailings into perpetuity.

589

That's how I found out Keith was both the jealous and vindictive type. He'd taken Seth's money to set me up for a fuck in his cabin—but obviously I had enjoyed the fuck too much and had given Seth what Keith perceived I wasn't giving him. So, I was put off the ship. There was no hint that Seth would be put off the ship too, though.

But, no matter, really, as it worked out. Seth hooked up with me again in New York later, and he was as great a fuck on land as he'd been on the sea. So I'd call my experience with Keith's cruise line a glorious banishment.

* * * *

As luck would have it, I knew that my old dance master, Clifton Ware, himself had been banished to the Dominican Republic—and to a villa in the mountains above Samana, as a matter of fact. So, I thought it would be nice to check in with him as long as I was here.

Clifton was a funny guy. He was a master dance teacher—as sure a ticket to a Broadway audition as a dancer can get. Any guy would have been happy to let him fuck them for what he could teach them—or to fuck him, if that was what he preferred. But Clifton preferred to watch. He was a voyeur. And he didn't apologize for it. He didn't crave the physical contact himself. He wanted to watch it while he masturbated.

That's what had gotten him banished at the dancing school I attended in New York in preparation for getting in Broadway shows. The other master teacher at the school, Jacques, did like to fuck his protégés. He called it the ultimate control, necessary for discipline, and he wouldn't teach anyone, male or female, who would not totally surrender to his will.

I had done so gladly. I'd known what I was and had fucked my way into the attention of drama coaches and dance masters in my home city, state, and region before moving on to New York.

Jacques liked to fuck, but he didn't like to be watched doing it. Clifton, conversely, got his rocks off solely by watching. One day on the upper landing of a set of stairs on a stage set, Jacques had been instructing one of his students to pirouette with Jacques's rod up his ass, when he noticed that Clifton was watching them from the side of the stage and doing himself with his hand. Jacques had flown into a fury of "being spied on by that pervert" and in the process had fallen down the stairs and broken himself up so badly that he never was able to dance again. He continued to teach the dance, but he no longer could demonstrate positions and he felt only half the master from that point forward.

He naturally blamed Clifton and threatened lawsuit—and jail time, if he could—not to mention a blade between the ribs some night when Clifton least expected it. Jacques was of the Latin temperament.

Clifton's ancestry was steeped in cooler climates and emotions. In response to Jacques's threats, Clifton just disappeared. Only years later did I learn that he had escaped to the Dominican Republic and was living there in well-enough style.

Well enough was somewhat of an understatement I was to discover. When I contacted Clifton, he was delighted to have me come visit him—and to stay as long as I wanted.

I took a taxi from the Samana harbor up winding roads into a mountaintop area called El Vista Cayo, where Clifton had a rambling villa with magnificent views down into the Bay of Samana and the harbor city of the same name.

"Ah, Mr. Ware," the young cab driver said when I gave him the address. "Yes, yes we all know where he lives—all of the young men know where Mr. Ware lives." And then he gave a little laugh and smacked his lips together and leered over his shoulder at me.

Luis, Clifton's "do everything" man, met me at the door. He was tall and well-built and big white smiled and bulging in the crotch and a deep chocolate brown.

Within the hour of my arrival I was on my back on a lounge chair on a deck off the back of the villa looking down toward the sea, Luis's plump cock up my channel, and the happy native was doing a plunging dance between my legs that was having me moaning and squealing with ecstasy. Clifton was sitting close to us in a deck chair and stroking his cock and still declaring how happy he was to see me. I didn't need much convincing to see how happy he was.

I hadn't really been asked if I wanted it—although I might have been sending signals I couldn't control as I watched Luis pad around the house in just shorts. But I wasn't a stranger to Clifton. He knew I liked being taken by surprise and manhandled. And he liked watching that happen to me. One minute Clifton and I were hanging on the rail of his deck, looking on my departing cruise ship in the harbor, and the next Luis was kneeling behind me, beefy hands on my thighs and my trousers and briefs down around my knees and his big lips sucking on my rim. I squirmed and moaned as Clifton turned to watch and slid down the rail far enough to get a good view of what was going on. In short order, Luis was covering my back with his heaving chest, holding my wrists far out at the sides on the rails and his dick moving deep inside me. At Clifton's direction when the cruise ship had rounded the rocks at the promontory at one end of Samana Bay, Luis turned me and lowered me to a lounge chair and began pumping me in earnest.

Clifton was happy and Luis was happy. I was happy too. Although I didn't think I'd be able to take a steady diet of this for very long.

That evening after a delicious dinner under the gathering stars on the deck, Clifton proposed an outing.

"I feel like young Dominicans tonight. Shall we go down into the town?"

We did so. Clifton obviously knew just where to go—and had done so frequently before. We had a couple of drinks in a bar, but after only the second one, we also had a couple of very young, slender, but supple and pretty-of-face Dominican men willing to come back up the mountain with us in Clifton's old Mercedes sedan.

A good part of the night, we, Clifton and I, watched the two young men fuck each other—in poses Clifton would set, making full use of his master training in the dance. The two sixty-nine sucked and then they took turns fucking each other—happy to move at Clifton's bidding, obviously making more at this than whatever the alternatives were. The pay obviously was good, and they knew that Clifton himself would never lay a hand on them. If they'd gone with one of the Dominican thugs, they might not have ever come back after the experience. Clifton, though, would just sit there and watch, with slitted eyes and a hand working his own cock.

In the early hours of the morning, while Luis was driving the two, exhausted, but happy young men back down into Samana, Clifton and I sat on the deck, bottles of Presidente beer in hand, and watching the dawn struggle to subdue the night. In the afterglow of an arousing and fulfilled evening, I broached what I thought would be a welcome revelation to Clifton.

"You know you are still a legend on Broadway, don't you?" I said.

"That is very pleasant to hear," Clifton answered, although he sounded more like he knew that was a basic truth and his due rather than that he was flattered that he was remembered after all these years in such a volatile profession.

"I haven't the slightest doubt you could snap up an excellent job or two if you were back in New York."

"I certainly would hope so."

"And you could come back now, you know."

This arrested his interest. "How so? How so could I come back to New York now?"

"Jacques is dead. Perhaps you hadn't heard. He had a heart attack early last year—rather a messy deal it was. He was fucking a young college student during a session he was supposed to be teaching and just keeled over dead, with his dick hanging out and all. In any event, he's gone. There's no one to sue you or make trouble for you otherwise in New York now. You could come back. I'm sure they would like to have you back."

"Humph. Of course they would," he said. But I could sense the wheels of assessment starting to roll in his brain.

At that point Luis returned from his driver duties and popped his head out of the door onto the deck.

"Ah, there you are, Luis. I feel a bit of arousal. Could you fuck our young guest, Dale, for me again now please." Spoken so matter-of-factly. Like he was some sort of all-powerful potentate—which in his DR setup perhaps he was.

"I think I'm too tired for that," I said with a laugh. I also stood and put my nearly finished bottle of Presidente on the table and started to move toward the door into the house. "I think I should get some sleep now. As nice as the invitation sounds, though."

"It's not an invitation, Dale. It's the price of the room and board here."

"Mr. Ware?" Luis asked, blocking my way into the house with his bulk.

"Yes, please, a good fuck, Luis. I feel like watching a good fuck."

"No, really, I—"

That's as far as I got, though.

"On the dining room table, if you please, Luis," Clifton said, as he rose from his chair and unzipped his trousers.

Still trying to be polite and struggling only slightly in disbelief, I wasn't that hard for Luis to control. He literally picked me up and carried me into the dining room, where he laid me down on my back. He pulled my shorts and briefs off my legs in one swift move and pulled my T-shirt over my head in the next. His knees were pushing my thighs apart and the heel of one hand in my sternum was pinning me firmly to the table at my chest, while soon—much sooner than I was really prepared for it—his dick was pinning my pelvis to the table as well—driven straight through me and into the wood of the table top, it felt like.

Clifton settled in a dining room chair and sighed and moaned. I initially objected and grunted and groaned, but Luis's cocking was just too good—and there were many fetishes that moved me. Being taken like this, roughly and forcefully was a primary one of mine—and Clifton's fortune, and mine too, I suppose, was knowing this was so. It wasn't long before I didn't care a bit that my vote hadn't been taken, and I was crying out for Luis to dig deeper and to stroke longer—and then faster, faster, faster. And when I shuddered and came, I just laid back, my eyes on Clifton taking his pleasure, as Luis grunted and fucked on . . . and on.

Clifton knew me and my weaknesses too well from earlier days.

I slept almost until noon, but was awakened by Luis having his breakfast—me—in my bed, while Clifton sat nearby and masturbated and watched with slitted eyes.

While we were lunching on the deck, Clifton pointed out that another cruise ship was in.

"After lunch we go down into Samana, yes. I think I know a Lithuanian and a couple of Russians on the crew of that boat who have very nice cocks and who would be happy to let me watch."

I didn't quite know what to say about that, and so I said nothing. Within an hour Clifton and I were in his Mercedes and skidding down the mountain.

"They should have had time to get to the bar by now," he was muttering to himself as he shifted gears. "Yes, we have a very nice bar in Samana—behind another building and a walk up. Only those who like such places even know it's there."

I could very well see how a tourist couldn't have found the place. It was four blocks off the waterfront, when most anything that looked like a half-way prosperous joint was set no more than two blocks in. The bar was approached through a driveway abutted by one building being built but appearing not to have had any work done on it for a couple of years and another building in the process of falling down. There was a concrete building behind them, though, and a wooden staircase going up to a precarious balcony, and I could hear loud music with a heavy calypso beat coming out of the upper story of the building.

I could see what kind of bar it was as soon as we entered. All men, a cloud of blue smoke, beer bottles, both empty and full littering a scattering of small tables, with captains' chairs, sprinkled around the room. A wooden bar running along the long wall facing the entrance.

And rough. Those providing the local service were all young and slender Dominicans—quite like the ones we had picked up in less obvious bars in Samana the night before. As far as clientele, it was obvious a ship was in—but it would have seemed more logical that it was a naval vessel than a cruise ship. The men in here off the cruise ship obviously worked more in the boiler room than the dining room. They were all bulky and big and muscle bound.

It was also obviously a no-holds-barred sort of place. One of the small Dominicans was being fucked by a big black guy on top of a table over in the corner. Three other equally big guys were standing around, watching. A lighter-skinned black guy had his dick out and was working it up, no doubt planning to be next in the Dominican's channel.

"Ah, yes, they're here," Clifton said, as he steamed right into the room and up to the bar. There were three huge Slavic looking guys there just receiving their beers.

"Hello, you three," Clifton said. "I saw the ship was in. You arrived a half hour early."

"Jah, but we were an extra hour getting the platform in place and the tenders down," said one in a broad, jovial voice. "The passengers were pissy about it. We enjoyed it big."

"Speaking of enjoying it big, I'd like you to meet a friend of mine. Dale. He's off yesterday's ship. He'll do you for a beer."

"Ahh. Really. Nice to meet you guys, but—" I said, with a deep gulp, as suddenly three beer bottles were thrust at me. "Clifton and I—" I began again, turning toward Clifton. But he was already gone. He'd drifted over to the table in the corner to watch the Dominican being fucked.

The three burly crew members from the cruise ship gathered close around me and tried out small talk in their various Slavic dialects as their beefy hands patted and prodded me.

Clifton was back at my side then.

"You can fuck him, if you want. As long as I can watch. You Russian guys do doubles don't you? I think I'm in the mood."

They wanted, and although I turned to flee to the door, they were too fast for me. The Lithuanian took me right there and then. He was perched on a barstool, and, between the three of them, they had me stripped and settling down on his beefy cock, facing away from him, in no time. One of the Russians had his face in my crotch and was giving me a blow job.

Clifton sat at a nearby table, cock in hand, and switched his attention between what was going on in the corner, the second black guy now getting his strokes, and what the Lithuanian was doing to me on the bar stool.

I would have objected—if I hadn't been enjoying it.

When the Lithuanian was finished, Clifton gestured to the two Russians, and I suddenly wasn't too sure how much I was going to be enjoying this. One Russian perched on the stool next to the Lithuanian who had me lapped, and pulled out a hard, long, not overly fat cock. While I huffed and puffed and whimpered ineffectually, I was pulled off the Lithuanian's cock and transferred to the Russian's. As I was sliding down his pole, he leaned back, holding me firmly in place by the waist with his giant paws and rotating my hips up. While I was hyperventilating and complaining between gulps, the Lithuanian held one of my legs up and out while the second Russian pushed my other leg wide with his forearm on my inner thigh. His hands cupped and squeezed and spread my butt cheeks, as his cock—thicker than the first Russian's—struggled to push into my channel on top of his mate's.

Clifton was having a great time watching and stroking himself, and I was grunting and groaning and sure I'd be split asunder. But I wasn't. I somehow managed, as Russian one kept his cock rock hard and stiff inside me and Russian two did the stroking with his fatter cock. They were busy exchanging kisses over my shoulder, and I might as well not have been there for anything but providing a tight channel for them to make love to each other in.

594

Before they were done, Clifton made a request and the two Russians changed our positions to give Clifton a closer look at the action. I was laid on my back on the table next to him and one Russian stood over my head, feeding his cock into my mouth while the other was standing between my legs and holding them spread as he fed his cock into my channel. This was certainly less strain on me.

The black guys from the corner table gangbang started to drift our way later, and I serviced them too. I have no idea how many.

* * * *

Clifton was in seventh heaven as we drove up the mountain. "I'm so glad you came," he said. "I haven't had this much entertainment in months."

"I'm happy for you, Clifton, but I don't think I could survive another day in your paradise here. I think I'll book out on the first flight I can get tomorrow. And will you be coming back to New York now too? Now that it's safe. You can have a great life there."

"Oh, no, dear boy. I have a great life right here. You've seen it. You know I have this fetish. Where else do you think I could be served as well as here? This was a banishment, yes. But it was an ideal retreat for me. A banishment. But a glorious one. Can't you see that?"

Yes, I had to admit. I could see that. But this particular one was more glorious for Clifton and his fetish than it could be for me and my fetishes for any length of time—being well fucked—rough—and manhandled, but only periodically, not constantly.

Clifton didn't prevent me from—almost reluctantly—sucking myself out of his tempting world to return to what commonly was thought as civilization.

But it didn't prevent him, either, from having Luis have me for desert that evening, while he sat there attentively watching, and stroking his cock.

Workplace

Gotta Keep This Job

I had been summoned to the medical suite at my office at the end of the Friday dayshift of my second week on the job, and I showed up with a great sense of trepidation. It had been hard finding this job, and I just had to keep it. But I'd scored drugs for a short time when I'd been in college, and I knew this company had a strict drug policy. I hoped that they hadn't found out about that—or that they wouldn't find out about it in this surprise appointment, because, come to think of it, I hadn't actually stopped in college.

"Come in here, take off all your clothes, and sit up on that table," a perky young nurse told me. "The doctor will be in to see you in a minute."

"Take off all my clothes?" I asked dubiously.

"Yes. Don't worry. I go off shift now. It will be just you and the doctor."

"Great," I thought, as I followed her direction. I didn't know why I felt self-conscious. I was in great shape and wouldn't have minded the cute little nurse knowing just how great shape I was in and how well hung I was.

But I was in shock when the doctor walked in. It was Larry, my boss, the owner of the company.

"Mr. Sturgis," I stammered. "What . . .?"

"Oh, didn't you know?" the handsome young redhead said, "I'm the company doctor too. It saves a lot on the medical bills. Now, let's see what we have here. Everything seems to be in order and in good shape. Yes, in very good shape, I'd say. Here, put this in your mouth and cough for me."

He stuck a wooden tongue depressor in my mouth, and I coughed for him. He ran long, elegant fingers up and down the sides of my neck and prodded around the top of my breast bone. Then, in turn, he lifted my arms, pushed a finger up into my arm pits, and gave my arm muscles a good feel.

"OK, very good there," he said. He whipped out a stethoscope and listened to my chest.

"Take deep breaths and hold them," he said. His stethoscope went to one nipple, and he laid his hand over the other one.

"Cough," he commanded. I obliged.

Then after a long time, he reversed the stethoscope and the hand over the other nipple and commanded me to cough again. I obliged again, hoping he hadn't noticed that my nipples were hardening up from the attention.

"Good, full chest," he said. "Lungs seem fine. Not a smoker, are you?"

"No," I answered too quickly. That had been another one of my vices in college. But I'd also been on the swim team and had developed a deep chest and lungs.

His hands glided down the sides of my torso, and he put one palm over my belly and left it there for a minute. I had no idea what sort of new examination technique this was, but I was mortified that it was causing me to have a half-hard on.

He had a hand on my balls, and I flinched as he rolled them.

"Cough," he commanded, and I did so.

"Everything seems in fine shape here," he said. "In fine shape."

He had his hand on my dick and was flopping it around gently. "Get it off regularly?" he asked.

"Uh, yes, regularly enough," I answered. "Uh, Mr. Sturgis. I mean Dr. Sturgis . . ."

"Would have liked to stick it to that cute little nurse who was just in here, would you?" he continued.

"Well, yes. Wouldn't anyone?" I responded, embarrassed. I was doubly embarrassed, because my cock had thickened and lengthened significantly at this suggestion.

"Sorry about that," he said with a laugh. "I was just checking to see if everything was in working order down here. It sure seems to be. That's good news. Now, I want you to lay back on the table and draw your knees up to your chest. I need to check your prostate."

He was putting a glove on his hand and dipping his fingers into a jar of lubricant.

"But, shouldn't I stand and lean over for . . .?"

"Naw," he answered. "I have my own procedure for this. It's less painful this way."

So, I lay back on the table and drew my knees up to my chest. It seemed like quite a while before I felt anything else, but then there was his cold and wet gloved finger working its way into my asshole. I knew when it had reached my prostate, because he was rubbing me there, sending strokes of pleasure through my balls and dick, and I felt precum forming on my cock helmet. A moan escaped my lips.

He withdrew his finger, but I heard him mutter something about thinking he'd felt something odd in there and needing to probe farther.

And then he was probing farther, but it seemed like he was probing with a bigger finger, and then I realized that he had both hands on my knees, squeezing them.

I lurched up in pain and surprise, but he already had his dick far enough inside me to maintain leverage, and he just kept unwinding his hose up my ass chute. My legs shot down and my torso came up, and I flailed around as his strong hands grabbed my shoulder blades. His long, slender hands wrapped around the sides of my chest to my pecs, and his thumbs landed on my nipples. His white doctor's coat was open and he otherwise was naked. He had a good build, and there was fluffy red hair covering his pecs and working its way down to and beyond his belly.

I cried out in pain and frustration as his cock continued its journey up my ass canal until I felt his pubic hair tickling the insides of my thighs.

"Oh, God. Sturgis. Don't . . ."

"I already did, Mark. You're already split and filled. Can't go back now. Just calm down and enjoy it."

"Enjoy it?" I screamed. "Get off me, you—"

"Get off you, or what?" Sturgis asked with a heavy laugh. "I'm already in you, and I'm going to fuck you regardless. You can either enjoy it or fight it, but you are already fucked. I've had my eye on you since we interviewed you for the job. Why do you think you got the job over all those others?"

I was fighting him now, but he was too strong, and every time I tried to move, his dick went a little deeper into my ass.

"Stop fighting for a minute and listen to me," he commanded. I stopped moving. He moved his torso into mine, and his chest hair felt silky against my bare skin. My cock was throbbing against his belly. "Do you think you were picked because you were the most qualified? No, you were picked because you were the most desirable. And do you think you were picked only because you are a stud?"

"I don't understand. Why . . .?"

"You were also picked because you had a drug history. You were picked because if you want to keep this job, you are going to let me fuck you now. And you are going to let me fuck you again and again, if I want to. Do you understand?"

"But, but . . ." I whimpered.

"How badly do you want this job, Mark?"

A long moment of silence and then I whispered, "Badly."

"I didn't hear you, Mark. How badly do you want this job?"

"Badly," I almost screamed back at him. "I gotta keep this job."

"And what do you want me to do to you so you can keep this job, Mark?"

"Whatever you want," I whimpered after a moment of contemplation.

"Tell me you want me to make love to you, Mark."

"I want you to make love to me, Larry."

"Like this?" Sturgis asked, and his lips went to my nipples, which he started to ravish with his tongue and teeth.

"Yes, like that," I moaned.

"And like this?" he asked as he set his cock in action. Stroking me, first shallow and deep and then in longer strokes that brought his cock helmet almost to the rim of my asshole and then glided in again down to the hilt.

My cries of "Oh, god, no, you're splitting me," turned to moans of pleasure and "Yes, yes," as my ass passage calibrated to the size of his rocket and ripples of pleasure ran around my ass walls.

"I asked you if you wanted it like that," he said in a hoarse voice.

"Yes, yes, like that."

"Deeper and harder?" he asked.

"Yes, yes, deeper and harder. Plow me. Fuck me."

I no longer was thinking just of the job. I was thinking of having a piston alive inside me, filling me and stroking me in waves of pleasure.

His lips went to mine, and I opened to his tongue. I was gasping for breath and groaning and moaning. He was completely turned on by my compliance. He turned me on the table and pumped me in a side split while he stroked my cock with his hand. In my excitement and nervousness at the newness of all this, I came quickly, which set off his ejaculation as well.

He pulled out of me, buttoned up his coat, swept his pants off of the floor, and turned toward the door.

"Let's see how well you can do with a blow job tomorrow. Say ten in the morning in my office? We'll see how permanent we can make your job from there. If you can learn to suck as well as you take a fuck, I see a quick promotion in your future."

And then he was gone. I lay there and collected myself and tried to pull the shreds of my pride back together again.

But what was I to do. I gotta keep this job. And truth be known, I was looking forward to my next session with Larry.

Master of the Boardroom

The reports of the week were winding down, and I looked around the table, only half conscious of what was being reported. The three older guys at the table would take care of all that for me. I was sizing up all of the young and beautiful people I'd stocked the board with. The power to do this was the joy of heading a robust family business; I could stock the board with the pick of the crop, and as long as I paid them top dollar, they'd all lay down for me. They'd stay with me through thick and thin—actually, thick and long in my case. Now who would it be this morning?

I had faced my seat at the boardroom table toward the big picture window looking out on the other big skyscrapers of Manhattan. This view gave me a sense of comfort and of power. I could feel the sense of power coursing through my veins now as I contemplated who it would be; hard and young and ambitious, cynical, and compliant. That seemed to suit me this morning.

"Chas," I said, as everyone was rising from their seats and shuffling their papers at the end of the meeting. "Could you stay for a few minutes, please?" A command rather than a request, which he very well understood.

"Yes, of course, JR," Chas responded. And the look he gave me of pleasure and anticipation made my cock stand at attention. I'd made the right choice.

I glanced around at the others I had been considering. Candice looked disappointed. Good. There was always this afternoon. Joe, however, looked relieved. I filed that in the back of my mind; maybe something really special for Joe when his next time came.

I walked around to the side of the table and pushed Chas's chair back as I heard the solid click sound of the door being shut behind the last departing board member. Chas was standing there, facing the table. I came up close behind him, a young, solid, blond hunk. I could smell his after shave, a musky, inviting smell.

I brought my arms around him, under his arms, and started unbuttoning his shirt, leaving his tie in place. He brought one hand around to the small of my back and the other went to the back of my head and buried itself in my hair, a signal of acceptance and compliance.

I had my hands on his pecs now—a hard bodybuilder. His pecs jutted out and his nipples were already hard. I loved big, firm tits—on both a woman and a man. He had little rings pierced into the aureoles of his nipples, and I played with those briefly as I buried my mouth and nose in the side of his neck and enjoyed the musk of his body.

I stripped both him and myself of our shirts and threw them to the side. I pulled him close to me and enjoyed the feel of skin on skin as I returned to playing with his nipples and pecs and then slowly worked my way down his belly and to the bulge at his crotch. After tracing his rising cock there, I started working at his belt and the buttons and zipper of his pants. He arched his back to me and turned his head so that we could go into a long, lingering kiss.

He had his hands at my belt and zipper as I found his half-engorged cock and pulled it out and started stroking it. He was sighing and moaning for me now, knowing that I liked that.

He had my cock out. I heard him gasp and felt him tremble, as he discovered once again how thick and long I was. He fondled it lovingly with both of his hands, holding the shaft at the bottom with one hand and running the fingers of the other hand around on the cock helmet, moistening every part of the helmet with my precum.

He arched his back to me as his cock hardened under my stroking. We kissed again, tongues searching tongues, before I pushed him down onto his belly among the papers on the top of the boardroom table.

I pulled his pants down and off and then started stroking his big, firm butt cheeks and his heavily muscled thighs, working my way to playing with his balls and dick from the rear, which he let me know he was enjoying immensely. My fingers went to his butt crack and I stroked him there to his audible sighs. His arms are flung out from his body on the tabletop, and his fists scrunched up sheets of paper in rhythm to my strokes, which became ever more penetrating at his asshole.

I positioned my hardened cock so that it lay up his butt crack and I stroked up and down there. I could tell I was sending chills of pleasure through his body. I took my cock in my hand and slapped it around his butt cheeks until he began revolving his hips, anxious for my entry. And then I teased him by moving my hips in and out, poking at his hole with the head of my dick, pushing against his hole with him trembling with the expectation that at any moment I was going to penetrate him and thrust deeply up his passage.

I reached into the pocket of my pants, which were still hugging my hips and buttocks, and fished out a tube of lubricant and a condom. I lubed up his ass real well and then opened the condom packet with my teeth and rolled the condom onto my throbbing nine-incher.

Pulling apart his butt checks with my hands, I moved the head of my cock to position at his hole. He shuddered when he felt the head of my cock at the door to his ass once more, knowing that this was going to be the moment of penetration. I took the cock in one of my hands and moved it around his hole, rimming him and seeking the best angle of entry. When I felt I had found it, I gently pushed the cock head into him. He grunted in pain, and I heard the crackling of paper as he bunched up his fists ever tighter. But he didn't tell me to stop. I pushed in farther, beyond the sphincter, and I could tell I was rubbing against his prostate because his body twitched and lurched and he let out a breathy groan. I held at that level, rocking back and forth gently, rubbing my cock head on his prostate, waiting for him to open fully to me, waiting for him to beg me to fuck him.

"Oh, God; Oh, God," he was moaning softly to himself. But I felt his ass walls loosening, and I slid in a good six inches.

"Oh, oh, awwww," he responded, and he arched his back up to me, raising his head to mine again, and we kissed. My hands went to those taut ringed nipples and thrusting pecs again and dug in.

I stroked him at that depth for a few minutes. In, out. In, out; at first slowly and than a little faster, and finally pushing in those last two inches and a third that I'd gained since entering him until I could feel the skin of his butt cheeks being tickled by my pubic hair.

"Awwww, Shit! Awwww, Shit!" Chas screamed, as his chest fell hard on the table top and his fists beat against the crumpled stack of paper.

"Too much?" I asked in a voice of concern. "Should I pull out some?" I had no intention of pulling back on this marvelous fuck, of course. But then I knew that Chas was too much of an ambitious prick to show any sign of weakness or unwillingness.

"Hell, no, boss. Fuck me. Fuck me hard and deep. God, it feels so good. You're so good. You're the best."

Just as I had thought, and so I did as he asked—with extra zest because of his vaunting ambition and my own undaunted cynicism. I fucked him hard and deep, with short, slow strokes, gradually moving to longer deeper strokes, pulling out to where my cock head rubbed across his prostate and then a deep thrust into the center of him. He was telling me how much he loved it and to ride him harder and harder. I grabbed his tie and pulled it around to the back and held his body arched half up toward me with those reins, as I slapped his butt cheeks with the other hand, riding his ass hard.

When my legs got tired, I pulled him back toward me and collapsed into his chair, my cock still buried nine inches in him.

"Now fuck yourself for a while," I said, as I grabbed his torso to me with my hands buried in his pecs and my mouth buried in his neck. He grabbed the arms of his chair with his hands and used his strong leg muscles to fuck himself, both shallow and deep, on my shaft and to rotate his twitching ass around my cock. One of my hands traveled down his abs and into his curly blond pubic hair and grasped his cock and stroked hard.

At length, with a spasm and scream of pleasure, Chas's arm and leg muscles gave out and he collapsed back on me in a fountain of his cum squirting up and onto the very carefully crafted monthly company report on the table in front of us. His mouth found mine, and he offered his thanks, feigned or not—I didn't really care which—in the form of a bruising kiss.

With renewed strength, I lifted Chas and myself up out of the chair, turned him, laid him down on his back on the top of the table, and side-splitted him until I had cum myself in a scream of power and release. Even while I was spasming inside the luscious, compliant blond hunk, I was thinking of what I would be doing to the lithe, dark and hairy, but apparently not fully willing Joe after the next meeting of the board.

Pecker Order

Some clients thought the "Bull" in the Bull Thorne Financial Services name related to Wall Street symbols, but those who had known Jim "Bull" Thorne the longest knew he had that nickname because he had the longest, thickest dick in Texas. Of course, it could just as well have been an acknowledgment that he also had the biggest pair of balls in Houston, based on the dictatorial and ruthless way he ran his highly successful corporation. Jim Thorne was still ruggedly handsome at fifty, and he surrounded himself with those who were equally ruthless, handsome, and on the make for financial success—at any cost or personal sacrifice. It was all about control, and who controlled who, Thorne always told his subordinates. So the gasp that went around the twenty-sixth floor boardroom when the newest vice president, Keith Turner, challenged Thorne's decision on the Mason account was audible down in the ground-floor lobby. It meant nothing that everyone in the room knew Turner had a good point.

Thorne had closed down the meeting immediately and told Turner he wanted to see him in his office—now.

When Turner arrived at the large, corner office of the corporation president, with its floor-to-ceiling windows on two sides, providing an eagle's view of Texas, Thorne made him stand in front of the mile-wide mahogany desk, while the angry president prowled around him, working himself into a frenzy. Thorne locked the door, came around in front of his desk, and addressed his subordinate through clinched teeth.

"When I made you a vice president, you said you clearly understood who made the decisions around here—who was in control. Right?"

"Right, Bull. But the Mason account—"

"And do you remember what, exactly, I said at the time that you were to do in terms of loyalty?"

"Umm, no, not exactly. But the Mason—"

"Let me refresh your memory, then. I said, in these exact words, 'Don't fuck with me or I'll fuck you.' Now do you remember?"

"Yes, sir," Turner answered weakly.

"And I've made no secret that I fuck men, have I?"

"No, sir." Turner was turning pale now. He knew what the original of "Bull" in Jim Thorne's name meant.

"And I also said at the time that my statement was a literal one. Do you remember that part too?"

"Yes, sir, but, I thought—" Turner was speaking in almost a whisper now.

"You didn't think too clearly. Well, you have two choices, Turner. I have to have control and total submission in this office. I've made no secret of that. You can either turn and leave—walk out of your job and this office without so much as a letter of recommendation—or you can give me total control and submission. Which is it?"

A slight pause, and then Turner whispered, "Submission. I will totally submit."

"And you will do so in a way you'll never forget," Thorne said with a sneer.

The Bull was suddenly on the move. "Strip," he commanded.

"But, sir—"

"Strip all the way down, move to the center of the room, and throw your clothes over there." While Turner was complying with a sigh of resignation, Thorne was searching around in his drawer for that tube of lubricant he always kept there. Then, with Turner watching him, his lips trembling and letting out a low moan at the sight of what was between the Bull's thighs, Thorne stripped down as well. He walked over to the pile of Turner's clothes and pulled out the younger man's expensive silk tie, and then he walked back to Turner, tie and lubricant in hand.

"Down on your knees and open your mouth to me," Thorne said.

With a sigh, Turner did so, and reached for that gigantic cock, already mesmerized by it.

"No," Thorne said. "I just said to open to me, not to show any signs of control. Hold perfectly still. And raise your wrists to me."

Thorne used that expensive tie to bind the younger man's wrists behind his back. Thorne then pushed his cock into Turner's mouth with one hand and took his subordinate's head with both of hands.

"A lesson of control," the company president said. "I control everything. You control nothing. All you are is a warm, wet chamber for my cock. Just be warm and wet and open to me. Leave the rest of the control to me."

And although Turner couldn't help gagging a bit, he tried to comply fully with his boss.

"Now go tighter. Touch me closely on all sides." That wasn't at all hard to do, because Thorne was so thick and long, even though he hadn't hardened out yet. Thorne pumped Turner's head back and forth on his cock for a few minutes, trying to demonstrate his obedience, which was total, and getting Thorne's cock real hard.

Then, pulling out of Turner's mouth, the Bull said, "Go down on your back right here." Turner rolled back onto his butt and then on his back without comment or objection. The athletic Thorne went down on his knees between Turner's thighs and pulled the younger man's butt up on his thighs. He also brought Turner's hands over his head and back to his front.

"Now, I'm going to fuck you—unless you've decided you don't want to work for me anymore."

Silence, filled only by the sound of lubricant slapping against tender asshole.

"Good. Now, as I work my way in, I want you to jerk yourself off. And I want you to come when I'm in to the hilt—and not before. Understand?"

Turner nodded, a serious look on his face. Thorne slathered his dick with lube, guided it to Turner's asshole, and rotated it around, working it in, while Turner began to stroke himself and pulling at his balls with his bound hands. Turner was concentrating hard on how he was going to ejaculate on cue. Thorne was pleased. Turner hadn't questioned the instruction. Turner had been a prime pick for vice president—and, truth be known, Thorne had been planning to pork his young associated for some time—so it was good that Turner was going to submit and be staying with the firm.

Thorne slowly worked his monster cock into his subordinate's ass, as the younger man obediently pulled on his cock. The Bull closely watched the tension build in the man he was fucking and managed to be at eight inches inside him when he yelled "Now" in a raspy voice, and Turner shot his load up Thorne's flat belly. As Turner ejaculated on cue, Thorne pushed his dick in the last half inch. He looked down at the white globs of semen running down his black belly hair and perched on top of Turner's golden-red pubic hairs. He liked what he saw, but this hadn't been enough of a turn-on for the Bull. The display of his control was turning Thorne on, but he needed the closeness the merging of bodies, his fully dominant over the other, before he himself could reach an orgasm.

"You realize this was just for instruction, don't you?" Thorne spoke to Turner as he squeezed his balls and pulled on his spent cock, his own cock still hard and buried to the root in his subordinate's ass. "I was the one who controlled when you had fulfilled this task, not you. Even though you thought this was your responsibility. It wasn't. You realize that now, don't you? You realize that I held off filling you until you had come."

"Yes, sir." Turner answered meekly.

"And you know now that this isn't all that I want, don't you? How quickly can you learn? Quick enough to save that vice president's salary of yours?"

"I can learn quickly, sir," Turner answered quietly. "I want you inside me. And I know that you want closeness, tightness as well as submission and control. Is that right?"

"Yes, that's right. I'm going to unbind you now, and I'm going to fuck your lights out right here and in this position, and I want you to show that you can handle the tightness and closeness without the bonds. You will know if and when you succeed because your insides will be bathed in my cum. Do you want that?"

"Oh yes, please, sir. Flood me with your cum."

Thorne untied Turner then and enfolded him in his arms, belly to belly and nipples to nipples. Turner's curly red chest hair tickled Thorne's hulking pecs. The Bull wrapped his arms around the younger tightly, holding his back down on the floor. Turner returned the hug, wrapping his arms around his boss as well and holding him tightly, almost taking the breath out of the older man with his strong arms. Turner's strong, swimmers legs wrapped around Thorne below his buttocks, pulling him in close, holding him tight and tightening his ass canal as much as he could around Thorne's already-buried cock. The two executives kissed deeply, and then Turner buried his face in Thorne's neck, trying to pull himself into Thorne at every point as much as he could. Turner was surrendering to Thorne entirely, and the older man felt the sexual urge flood into him. He pumped and pumped and pumped at various levels, sometimes pulling out to give Turner's prostate attention. The younger man moaned and trembled at this but continued to hang on to his boss as tightly as he could.

When the Bull came, flooding the very center of the younger man in spasms of semen, Turner ejaculated again himself and collapsed back on the rug, arms and legs askew.

"Sorry," he murmured. "It was just too much. I couldn't hang on any longer. I've been royally fucked. This is the greatest."

"Do you want me to pull out of you now?" Thorne asked.

"Whatever you want," Turner answered quietly. "You are in total control. Do what you want with me."

"Good choice," the Bull answered gruffly. "Remember, if you fuck with me again, I'll fuck you again. And maybe I will even if you don't fuck with me."

* * * *

Keith Turner wasn't all that displeased when he was released from the Bull's office. His ass was sore from the gigantic tool the Bull had, but this had answered a question he'd had since he'd come on board and heard rumors that the boss was horse hung. Yes, he could take almost nine inches of thick cock. He'd had that extension toy in his own desk for weeks, wondering if he could get one of his fuck buddies to try out that length, but now he wouldn't have to experiment with that.

He felt slightly humiliated at having had to give up control like that, though, so he was loaded for bear when he saw the memo on his desk from his own accounting section disallowing that bar tab he'd run up at the convention in Las Vegas the previous month.

Who did this Craig Wilson think he was disallowing whatever tab he, a vice president, chose to charge to the office? Sure, they'd played on the same office football team and had playfully snapped each other with towels in the locker room shower—and Keith had obviously been attracted to the young, studly blond—but, as the Bull said, this office was built on the concept of control and rank, and Craig Wilson would just have to be taught where he ranked in the pecking order.

He made Wilson stand in front of his desk at attention while he dressed him down for questioning his authority and then he came right up behind the trembling accountant and yelled in his ear, Marine sergeant style, "I was just talking with Bull Thorne today, and you know what he said about insubordination like yours?"

"No, sir," Wilson squeaked. "What did he say, sir?"

"He said that anyone who fucked with authority around here would be fucked—literally. Now what do you think about that, Craig?"

"Well, I don't know what to—" Wilson stammered. And then he squeaked again as Turner grabbed a butt cheek and squeezed.

"Do you like your job and your generous paycheck, Craig?"

"Yes, sir," Wilson answered.

"And would you do anything to keep them, Craig?"

"Uhh . . . Yes, sir," Wilson answered again.

"Well, you have two choices then. You can walk out of that door and clean out your desk, or you can take a lesson in control and a good fuck. Which is it?"

Wilson smiled broadly and answered. "I thought you'd never ask, Keith."

This didn't please Turner all that much. This wasn't asserting control over his subordinate.

"Come here," Turner said gruffly, and he literally pulled Wilson around the desk to where he stood between the desk and Turner's chair.

"Assume the position and strip," Turner commanded, as his eyes darted around the room. They lit on the window blind cords. Turner went over and jerked a couple of them down, causing the blinds to accordion down to the floor with a crash. As soon as Wilson had stripped, Turner tied his wrists with one end of the cord, a cord for each wrist, pulled the cords through the kneehole of the desk, crossed them, and then tied the other end tight above Wilson's knee, pulling the cords taunt so that Wilson was spread-eagled with his belly flat on the top of the desk and securely held in place. Turner ripped Wilson's belt out of his pant loops then and fashioned it around Wilson's neck like a dog leash.

Wilson was totally trussed up now. Turner had physical control. Total control. Wilson wasn't laughing now. Wilson needed to be taught the same lesson Turner had endured under the attention of the Bull's big cock earlier today. But Turner didn't have the length and thickness of Thorne. Or didn't he? Turner reached down and opened the bottom drawer of his desk and buried his hand under a pile of papers. He came up with a leather, studded penis sheath with a three-inch extension capped with an extra large stud-covered bulb he'd bought and had been building up the courage to use.

Turner did some lip and spit and finger work on Wilson's ass as the accountant moaned softly for him. After he was satisfied that he'd opened Wilson up sufficiently, Turner sheathed his cock with the oversized studded harness and positioned himself behind the fully trussed figure. Turner palmed the rounded butt cheeks and pushed his sheathed cock up to the opening of the puckered, lubricant-slathered hole with its circle of curly blond hair. Wilson moaned and groaned.

"Oh, shit. Oh, god, no, nooooo!" he muttered, as Turner rotated the studded sheath head around his ass shunt, relentlessly working it farther into the hole.

"The only way you are going to continue working here under me is by submitting totally to me," Turner said. "Do you submit?"

No answer. Perhaps Craig still seemed to think that since they were buddies on the football field, they somehow were on equal footing.

With a push, Turner had worked the sheath extension and two inches of his own cock into the asshole. Thorne's nearly nine incher had little length on Turner under these circumstances, and the extension made Turner's tool, if anything, thicker than Thorne's natural girth.

Wilson cried out. "Yes, OK, I submit!"

"That sounds good, but I don't believe for a minute that you believe it yet." Turner had no idea if this was true; he was just having too much fun skewering the young blond to end this yet.

Turner was in a good five, very thick inches now. The accountant was trembling under his boss and moaning for him to stop, that he was being split. Several more inches in and he was beginning to really feel those studs. Turner took the unburied part of his dick in his hand and rotated it around in Wilson's canal, coaxing him to open more. Wilson was crying and moaning now. The laughter was behind far behind him.

He kept screaming that he submitted, that Turner had won, and Turner kept creeping up his canal, trying to wipe out his own humiliation earlier in the day, until only about two inches of Turner's cock root were outside the young blond. With the extension, Turner's rod was in a good eight inches now.

"How? How can I convince you I submit?" he whimpered.

"I'll feel it in your body," Turner answered. "When you've totally submitted, all of the tension will go out of your body, and you'll stop yelling at me. You'll take it silently. You'll be totally mine. And then I'll encase your body with mine, and we'll be one. The submissive you and the dominant me. Only then can you work here with me and be my accountant and an acceptable bottom to my top."

"OK, OK, I'll try," he whimpered. "I want to be here. I want your cock inside me. I submit. Totally."

And Turner did, indeed, feel the tension slowly leaving Wilson's body, and he went silent, except for a few grunts and groans he couldn't suppress, while Turner pushed the last two inches of leather- and stud-augmented penis into the accountant's tightened asshole. He left it in there, all the way in, for several minutes, as he felt the tension and fight draining out of the young accountant—and then Turner rode his ass hard and long.

"Oh, god, yessss," Wilson was whimpering. "Fuck me. Fuck me deep. Like that. Yessss. Don't stop." And Turner didn't stop, at least for several minutes. A few minutes after Wilson had spilled his seed on the carpet behind his boss's desk, Turner shot his load into him.

* * * *

Craig Wilson had enjoyed the session in Keith Turner's office, but he hadn't much cared to have been shown so graphically where he stood in the pecking order in this office. It was just the misfortune of the file clerk, Alphonse Pointer, a saucy young black man of pretty Jamaican features, that he chose to give a flippant reply to one of Craig's instructions later that afternoon. Wilson had just stood up from his desk, taken Alphonse by the scruff of his collar, and pushed him out a door onto the twelfth-floor landing of a disused stairwell shaft. Alphonse had been swinging his hips and tossing suggestive glances at Craig for weeks, so Craig had little question of what Alphonse would take from him. But he doubted Alphonse expected the mating dance to be ended so abruptly as this.

Listen you little queen, Wilson exploded once the two were out on the landing. You work for me, see. So, you don't talk back to me.

"Uh, what's—?" Alphonse spouted, trying to wriggle out of Wilson's powerful grip.

"Listen, you've worked here long enough to know the office motto, haven't you?" Wilson continued.

"Uhh, I'm not—"

"It's fuck with me and you get fucked—literally." Wilson blustered through gritted teeth. He was going to assert some of his own control in this corporation now. He had a certain amount of rank too. Wilson pushed the file clerk down two more flights of stairs, to the level of a floor that was waiting to be refitted and thus where no one worked now.

"Stop and face the banister," Wilson barked.

Alphonse did so without question, fully cowed by this crazed—but delicious—blond stud from accounting.

Wilson came up close behind him, unzipped his fly, and pulled out a respectably sized cock. The accountant then doubled the young file clerk over at the waist on the banister with one hand, so that he was facing down the well from the tenth floor, and worked up his unsheathed cock with the other hand, spitting a few times on his hand to lubricate his tool. When Wilson was satisfied he was at least half hard and able to penetrate the younger man, he pulled Alphonse's pants and briefs down off his buttocks, pushed his legs out to open him up as much as possible under these circumstances, and pushed his dick into Alphonse's gaping, well-used hole.

Alphonse grunted and gritted his teeth as the angry accountant entered him, but he grabbed down for the banister slats with white-knuckled fists and took the blond stud without squeal or objection.

Once in, Wilson tightened the young man up by getting his legs between his own. He draped his chest over the smaller man's back so that they were both folded at the waist over the banister and facing down ten flights of the stairwell. Wilson latched onto one of Alphonse's ear lobes with his teeth and held on gently.

Wilson could feel the file clerk grunting and groaning, and then sighing and moaning in ecstasy as the accountant's cock lengthened and thickened inside him and filled him to capacity.

"Who's the boss?" Wilson breathed into the younger man's ear.

"You're the boss," Alphonse answered.

"Who backtalks me?"

"Not me, boss."

As Wilson filled Alphonse to the end and started to pump, the accountant took one of his fists and pushed down the front of the file clerk's pants and the two stroked Alphonse off together, the file clerk's hand under the accountant's, encasing his cock, while Wilson controlled the stroking. As Wilson sensed he was coming, he let loose of Alphonse's earlobe with his teeth and started tongue-fucking his ear. Alphonse held his head closer to Wilson's tongue, loving the sensation. Once more the two managed to come almost simultaneously, the accountant deep inside the file clerk and the file clerk down those ten floors of stairwell.

"Wow," was all the clerk said when it was over.

"Yes, wow," Wilson responded. "Now, how do you feel about needing control?"

"I love being controlled by you, boss. Yes, I certainly do, and you can control me anytime you want. But who can I control in this big corporation? Does the cum stop here?"

Wilson gave a low laugh. "There's always someone you can control in the pecker order, Alphonse. You might try that Cuban body builder in the mail room. You outrank him here. But if you try him, you might need to make an appointment. If I hear correctly, he's fucking Bull Thorne these days."

Index to Fetishes Found in Stories (By Story)

17. <u>Doubling Bets</u> (bareback, double penetration, ethnic, public sex)

18. <u>Double Rings</u> (toys)

19. <u>Dreamworld</u> (cybersex, ethnic, interracial)

20. <u>Elevator Man</u> (ethnic, servicemen, size difference)

21. <u>Ethiopian Cabin Boy</u> (big cocks, interracial, boats, voyeur)

22. <u>Family Day on the Pool Table</u> (daddies, gangbang, incest, pool tables, toys)

23. <u>Fetish Galore</u> (age difference, bad boys, bareback, BDSM, big cocks, bondage, breath control play, cigars, clothes, condoms, cops, cybersex, daddies, docking, dom/sub, double penetration, edging, exhibitionism, firemen, fisting, foot fetish, fur, gangbang, gynemimetophilia, incest, interracial, massage, medical, phone sex, piercings, pool tables, public sex, rimming, servicemen, shaving, size difference, sounding, tattoos, toys, uncut, vehicles, virgins, voyeur, water play, workplace)

24. <u>Fireplugged</u> (bareback, big cocks, condoms, dom/sub, firemen, uncut)

25. <u>Glass Canyon Connection</u> (age difference, big cocks, exhibitionism, fur, voyeur, workplace)

26. <u>Glorious Banishment</u> (age difference, big cocks, boats, dom/sub, double penetration, gangbang, interracial, massage, public sex, voyeur, workplace)

27. <u>Gotta Keep This Job</u> (dom/sub, medical, workplace)

28. <u>GTO</u> (vehicles)

29. <u>Hair's the Thing</u> (arm pits, boats, fur, public sex, voyeur)

30. <u>Heartbreak</u> (age difference, ethnic, fisting)

31. <u>Haitian Carving</u> (age difference, daddies, gynemimetophilia, interracial, toys)

32. <u>Hook or Crook</u> (age difference, bondage, medical, voyeur)

33. <u>I Only Wanted to Watch</u> (bad boys, big cocks, dom/sub, fur, piercings, tattoos, virgins, voyeur)

34. <u>Konan to the Rescue</u> (big cocks, cybersex, virgins)

35. <u>Licorice-Centered Milk Chocolate</u> (big cocks, dom/sub, interracial)

36. **Long John Silverman** (age difference, bareback, big cocks)

37. **Looking for It** (breath control play, edging, foot fetish. toys)

38. **Loosening Therapy** (age differences, big cocks, bondage, daddies, dom/sub, fur, piercings, rimming, size difference, tattoos, virgins)

39. **Malta Intervention** (daddies, edging, gynemimetophilia, pool tables)

40. **Marine's Choice** (age difference, Dom/Sub, toys, virgins, voyeur)

41. **Mascot** (clothes, ethnic, fireman, gangbang, size difference, vehicles, virgins)

42. **Master of the Boardroom** (age difference, dom/sub, piercings, workplace)

43. **Men in Tuxedos** (cigars, clothes, double penetration, gangbang, voyeur)

44. **No Pole Big Enough** (big cocks, bondage, dom/sub, double penetration, exhibitionism, fur, size difference, toys, voyeur)

45. **On the Docks** (clothes, dom/sub, ethnic, fur, servicemen, size difference, voyeur)

46. **On the Trunk of a Car** (big cock, fur, vehicles)

47. **P.A. Club Night** (gangbang, gynemimetophilia, medical, piercing)

48. **Painted Laddie for Mr. R** (big cocks, gynemimetophilia, piercings, toys, uncut, vehicles)

49. **Pecker Order** (age difference, big cocks, bondage, dom/sub, edging, interracial, toys, workplace)

50. **Pen Pal** (bad boys, big cocks, dom/sub, interracial, tattoos, toys, virgins)

51. **Phoned** (bondage, interracial, phone sex)

52. **Picky, Picky** (age differences, bondage, cigars, dom/sub, ethnic)

53. **Pierced** (bad boys, dom/sub, phone sex, piercings, public sex, tattoos, toys)

54. **Please Daddy, Please** (age difference, daddies, incest)

55. **Prepped** (big cocks, bondage, medical, shaving)

56. **Prisoner's Prisoner** (age difference, bad boys, big cocks, dom/sub)

57. **Prodigal Father** (age difference, bareback, clothes, daddies, ethnic, incest, voyeur)

58. **Ready4Daddy** (age difference, cock sucking, cybersex, daddies, public sex, uncut)

59. **Restrained Freedom** (BDSM, bondage, cops, piercings, toys)

60. **Road Romeo** (age difference, big cocks, vehicles)

61. **Rough Riding to BARUF** (BDSM, bondage, cops, ethnic, toys, vehicle)

62. **Scratching the Service Worker Itch** (bondage, gangbang, servicemen)

63. **Snowball Effect** (bad boys, double penetration, exhibitionism, interracial, massage, vehicles)

64. **Stolen** (bondage, clothes, cybersex, fur, toys, virgins, voyeur)

65. **Suits** (BDSM, bondage, clothes, dom/sub, piercings, toys, vehicles)

66. **Ten Slash Two** (big cocks, bondage, interracial)

67. **The Caregiver** (big cocks, massage, rimming)

68. **The Commander** (age difference, big cocks, bondage, toys, virgins, voyeur)

69. **The Cure** (bareback, BDSM, bondage, toys)

70. **The GED** (age difference, body paint, bondage, ethnic, gynemimetophilia, incest, toys, vehicle, voyeur)

71. **The Yellow Cadillac** (bareback, interracial, vehicles)

72. **To Die in Madeira** (age difference, big cocks, massage, rimming)

73. **Topsy-Turvy** (BDSM, bondage, daddies, size difference, toys, vehicles, voyeur)

74. **Trail "Doctor"** (daddies, medical)

75. **Triangulation** (age difference, big cocks, boats, daddies, ethnic, massage, public sex, size difference, toys, voyeur

76. **Triple Magnum Nabilum** (bareback, cigars, fur, voyeur)

77. **TRTrade.com** (age difference, clothes, cops, cybersex, daddies, double penetration, foot fetish, gangbang, public sex, voyeur)

Index to Fetishes Found in Stories (By Story Number and Fetish)

Age Difference (3, 4, 8, 12, 15, 23, 25, 26, 30, 31, 32, 36, 38, 40, 42, 49, 52, 54, 56, 57, 58, 60, 68, 70, 72, 75, 77, 78, 79, 80, 81)

Arm Pits (29)

Bad Boys (15, 23, 33, 46, 50, 53, 56, 63)

Bareback (8, 15, 17, 23, 24, 36, 57, 69, 71, 76)

BDSM (2, 8, 9, 11, 15, 23, 59, 61, 65, 69, 73)

Big Cocks (2, 5, 9, 15, 23, 24, 25, 26, 33, 34, 35, 36, 38, 44, 48, 49, 50, 55, 56, 60, 67, 68, 72, 75)

Blonds (10)

Boats (3, 11, 26, 29, 75, 78)

Body Paint (10, 70)

Bondage (2, 6, 8, 9, 10. 11. 12, 15, 23, 32, 38, 44, 49, 51, 52, 55, 59, 61, 62, 64, 65, 66, 68, 69, 70, 73)

Breath Control Play (23, 37)

Cigars (23, 43, 52, 76)

Clothes (5, 9, 10, 11, 23, 41, 43, 45, 57, 64, 65, 77, 79)

Cock Sucking (58)

Condoms (2, 23, 24)

Cops (23, 59, 61, 77)

Cybersex (9, 13, 19, 23, 34, 58, 64, 77, 80)

Daddies (3, 8, 11, 12, 14, 15, 22, 23, 31, 38, 39, 54, 57, 58, 73, 74, 75, 77, 80)

Docking (16, 23)

Sounding (12, 15, 23)

Tattoos (1, 9, 13, 23, 33, 38 50, 53)

Toys (2, 8, 9, 11, 15, 18, 22, 23, 31, 37, 40, 44, 48, 49, 50, 53, 59, 61, 64, 65, 68, 69, 70, 73, 75)

Uncut (16, 23, 24, 48, 58)

Vehicles (1, 2, 9, 23, 28, 41, 46, 48, 60, 61, 63, 65, 71, 73)

Virgins (7, 8, 10, 23, 33, 34, 38, 40, 41, 50, 64, 68, 70, 78, 79, 81)

Voyeur (1, 3, 5, 7, 11, 15, 23, 25, 26, 29, 32, 33, 40, 43, 44, 45, 57, 64, 68, 70, 73, 75, 76, 77)

Water Play (23)

Workplace (2, 23, 25, 26, 27, 42, 49)

About the Author

Habu is one of the pen names of a former supersonic spy jet pilot, intelligence agent, male model, movie actor, and diplomat. A wild youth in South East Asia was spent enjoying whatever sexual opportunities came his way, and much of his gay male writing is about recalling incidents from those days and inventing ones he'd perhaps have liked to experience. He now leads a very quiet and ordinary happily married family life.

An American, he is a published mainstream novelist and short story writer under another name and in another dimension of his life. He has written or cowritten (with Sabb) over 500 published short stories and nearly 100 published erotica e-books, primarily of gay fiction but also memoir, straight fiction and ménage fiction. His hand and creative writing can be seen in stories and books by habu, sr71plt, Dirk Hessian, Shabbu, and Stephen Kessel—among unrevealed others that might surprise readers. The fictionalized GM memoir *Flying High, Diving Deep* is loosely based on his life experiences. He can be found at the adults only gay male site BarbarianSpy, which he shares with Sabb and Dirk Hessian.

You can send feedback about this book directly to habu by going to www.BarbarianSpy.com the website he shares with Sabb, Shabbu, and Dirk Hessian.

Our authors always like to receive feedback, and appreciate it when readers post reviews at Goodreads, and other sites.

BarbarianSpy

FOR LITERARY HEAT

Not all books listed below may currently be on release.
BOOKS BY DIRK HESSIAN
Xtreme Erotica
The King's Men
Shores of Tripoli
Prophecy of Noto
Pretender's Fate
General Erotica/Romance
Constantinople
The Beautiful Way
Blue and Gray
Colonel's Treasure
Beginning of Time
Labyrinth
BOOKS BY HABU
Gay Erotica
Memoir Faction
Flying High, Diving Deep*
Xtreme Erotica
Second Coming
Vortex: Sacrificed by Curiosity*
Dark Angel Sounding
Sounding: Ultimate Control (Print Only)*
Sounding Five (E-book only)
General Erotica
Romance
Lower Than the Heart
Brambleton
Gotta Keep Trying
Finding Amnad
Platres Conclave
Other
House on Park
Dance of the Ravishers
Beyond the Beaded Curtain*
Hard Knocks U*
Habu's Christmas Balls
My Neighbor's Spa
Man's Man*
Trip Money

Clint Folsom Mysteries Compendium Volume 1*
Death to Blonds - Stolen Judgment (Clint Folsom Mystery)
Clint Folsom Mysteries Compendium Volume 2*
Grab Bag 1*
Grab Bag 2*
Grab Bag 3*
The Indian Doctor
Sailorboy
Home to Fire Island
The Sporting Life*
Fetish Galore!*
Choke Hold
Literary Gay Erotica
Cairo Surrender*
The Handyman*
Homeward Bound
Journey to Mirage*
Menage Erotica
13 Ways for Halloween
Luther*
The Indian Prince
BOOKS BY SHABBU
Finding Jason
Dirty Pool
Operation Black Jade
Cigars!*
Angel in the Barn
Gayly Complicated
Despoiling David
The Tree of Idleness
I Met a Man
The Interview
Rough Road to Happiness
BOOKS BY SABB
Hiring in Hollywood
The Legend of Holleystone Grange
Surprise Encounters
She is He
Wrong Man
Loyal to his King
Barbarian Tales - Book One - Traveler's Tales*
Barbarian Tales - Book Two - Journeys Begin*
Barbarian Tales - Book Three - The Inheritance*
Barbarian Tales - Book Four - Road to Persepolis*

~

* indicates the book is available in paperback and e-book.

www.ingramcontent.com/pod-product-compliance
Lightning Source LLC
Chambersburg PA
CBHW081138020726
47504CB00009B/1906